Swords from The West

Harold Lamb

Edited by Howard Andrew Jones
Introduction by Robert Weinberg

UNIVERSITY OF NEBRASKA PRESS
LINCOLN AND LONDON

Library of Congress Cataloging-in-Publication Data

Lamb, Harold, 1892–1962.
Swords from the west / Harold Lamb ; edited by Howard Andrew Jones ;
introduction by Robert Weinberg.
p. cm.
ISBN 978-0-8032-2035-5 (pbk. : alk. paper)
I. Crusades—Fiction. I. Jones, Howard A. II. Title.
PS3523.A4235S95 2009
813'.52—dc22
2009008546

Set in Trump Medieval by Kim Essman.
Designed by R. W. Boeche.

Contents

Foreword

Those familiar with Harold Lamb's work today likely remember the numerous histories and biographies he wrote from 1927 onward. They might know of his justly-famed Khlit the Cossack stories, but unless they themselves are pulp collectors they are unlikely to be familiar with the fiction printed here, most of which appeared originally in *Adventure* magazine in the 1920s and 1930s. Almost none of these tales have been reprinted since, and those that were turned up in fairly obscure publications.

Lamb was always fascinated by borderlands and the clash of East and West. Asian cultures were a special interest for him throughout most of his life, especially those of Mongolia. Thus it should be no surprise that a Harold Lamb crusader story is far more likely to feature a foray into the steppes of Asia than to the walls of Acre.

What may be surprising is Lamb's unprejudiced eye when portraying non-Western peoples. Lamb's Mongolians and Arabs are painted with the same insight into motivation as his Western protagonists. He takes no shortcuts via stereotype: foreign does not necessarily equate with evil, and villains can be found on either side of the cultural divide. Lamb went so far as to feature Moslems and Mongols as protagonists, though none of those adventures are printed in this particular volume (look instead to Lamb's Bison Books collections titled *Swords from the Desert* [2009] and *Swords from the East* [forthcoming, 2010]).

There are other surprises here besides. Older adventure fiction has a reputation for predictable plotting and melodrama, yet you will seldom find Lamb guilty of either charge. Neither will you find his prose laden with excess verbiage or talking heads, nor will you see any sign of that deadliest sin for adventure fiction, slow pacing. The action flows swiftly from scene to scene, and the images are sharply etched—always against thrilling, exotic, painstakingly researched backdrops.

Robert Weinberg's excellent essay introduces you to both *Adventure* magazine, Lamb's main fiction outlet, and "The Making of the Morning Star." As much as I enjoy "The Making of the Morning Star," which may yet be deservedly hailed as an adventure classic, I love the two Nial O'Gordon novellas contained within these pages even more. "The Golden Horde" and "Keeper of the Gate" are fabulous works penned at the height of Lamb's descriptive power. The triumphant final notes of these pieces ring in the air long after the reader has set them down, echoing with somber majesty. They were the very last stories he ever wrote for *Adventure* magazine. See if you, too, upon reading the last paragraph of "Keeper of the Gate," wish that Lamb had taken us with Nial O'Gordon on to Cathay. Surely if there had been more tales of Nial it would be the adventures of this character, even more so than those of the wily Cossack Khlit, with whom Harold Lamb would be most associated.

The other stories within this book are shorter tales from *Adventure*, *Collier's*, and *Cassell's*. *Collier's* preferred stories of briefer length than those Lamb usually wrote for *Adventure*, and seemed also to prefer work from Lamb where the conclusion turned upon the hero winning the hand of a heroine. As a body of work the *Collier's* tales are more repetitive than Lamb's earlier fiction. Despite these constraints, Lamb managed to inject variety into many of them, and most of those dealing with crusaders are printed here (the rest are printed in other Bison Lamb collections).

In the 1950s Lamb wrote a series of stories for the *Saturday Evening Post* where famous historical events were re-dressed—usually to include some romance à la the *Collier's* pieces—and given a contemporary framing story. To my eyes these framing stories are forced, and the stories themselves pale in comparison to Lamb's earlier work. One, though, Lamb's last published historical story, has the old fire. Thematically it doesn't belong in this volume, but it fits even less well in the other books in this book series—the protagonists, at least, come from the West. Step around the awkward frame opening to "Secret of Victory," and you'll be swept into an adventure about the fabled sword of Attila and a last desperate battle to keep the Hun from Roman lands.

The intent of this new series of collections is to reprint all of Harold Lamb's magazine historicals not already collected in Bison Books editions. Lamb's crusader stories don't end with this volume: crusaders make an appearance in *Swords from the Desert,* and the appendix in the same volume has dozens of pages of historical information Lamb wrote on the subject. There are yet more crusader stories, for crusaders seem to have been Lamb's favorite historical subject after Cossacks. I was forced to exclude three short crusader novels from these collections, due both to space limitations and because another publisher is already caring for them in fine editions. For some years the first two books of the Durandal trilogy, *Durandal* and *The Sea of Ravens,* have been available in marvelous illustrated volumes from the publisher Donald M. Grant, and the third book, *Rusudan,* should follow soon. I urge you to seek them out if you have not already done so.

Should these tales fire your interest in researching the historical period, look no further than Harold Lamb's own two-volume set on the Crusades. Later collected in one large book, both volumes, *Iron Men and Saints* and *The Flame of Islam,* can still be found on many library shelves. Lamb earned a medal from the Persian government for these books in recognition of the accuracy of his research, and the acclaim helped launch the rest of Lamb's career. The crusade books were well received in America and led to movie mogul Cecil B. DeMille hiring Lamb to cowrite his motion picture *The Crusades,* the first of many projects they worked on together. One interesting anecdote of Lamb's work on the film survives, reprinted here from Charles Higham's book *Cecil B. DeMille* (Scribner's, 1973):

> Harold Lamb was constantly present during the shooting of the siege [of Acre], dodging arrows and narrowly avoiding being crushed by the siege tower. "Is that realistic enough, Mr. Lamb?" the director asked him at the end of the first exhausting rehearsal of the conflict.
>
> "Not nearly," Lamb replied, wiping his spectacles. "Those soldiers seemed almost fond of each other. Medieval warriors were infinitely more sanguinary, let me assure you. What you need is a thousand battle axes red with blood."
>
> "That would make it a shambles," DeMille said.
>
> "Exactly. And also history," Lamb primly replied. (242)

Lamb thereafter cowrote a multitude of screenplays for DeMille and spent the rest of his working life either drafting for the cinema or producing biographies and histories for Doubleday—putting aside his service for the OSS during World War II, when he was posted to Persia. I discuss that period of his life in more detail in *Swords From the Desert.*

Now it is time to settle back and read of crafty Sir John and his brave and loyal Arab friend Khalil. Herein learn what befell the daughter of

Rusudan, from Lamb's *Durandal* trilogy. Read of the winged knights of Poland, the deadly horde of Tamerlane, and Richard the Lionheart's last stand. Ease back and let a master storyteller speak of fabled lands and far-off places and heroes who rode to doom or glory against all odds.

Enjoy!

Acknowledgments

Dedicated to the memory of heroic-fiction scholar
Steven Tompkins (1960–2009).

I would like to thank Bill Prather of Thacher School for his continued support. This volume would not have been possible without the aid of Bruce Nordstrom, who long ago provided Lamb's *Collier's* texts as well as his *Saturday Evening Post* and other research notes; Mike Ashley, who provided the text of "Doom Rides In"; and Alfred Lybeck, Kevin Cook, David Scroggs, and James Pfundstein, who provided "Camp-Fire" letters. I also would like to express my appreciation for the aid of Victor Dreger and Jan van Heinegen, gentlemen and scholars. Lastly I wish again to thank my father, the late Victor Jones, who helped me locate various *Adventure* magazines, and Dr. John Drury Clark, whose lovingly preserved collection of Lamb stories is the chief source of seventy-five percent of my *Adventure* manuscripts.

Introduction

The Long Journey of the Morning Star

ROBERT WEINBERG

Updating an old ethnic joke, what do you get when you put ten pulp collectors in a locked room and ask them to name the best pulp ever published? The answer, of course, is eleven different answers. Everyone who collects has their favorite, and with over a thousand different pulp titles published, it's hard to settle on just one, or ten, or even twenty favorite magazines. Still, if most of the collectors were forced to agree upon one title (or otherwise face the infamous Copper Bowl as so horrifically described by Major George Fielding Elliot in the pages of *Weird Tales*), there's a very good chance that the magazine they'd pick would be *Adventure*.

As a pulp (it turned into a rather mundane slick magazine late in its life), *Adventure* ran for an amazing 753 issues from 1910 to 1953. Many of those years it appeared twice a month (the first and the fifteenth) on the newsstand, and there were periods it appeared three times a month (the tenth, twentieth, and thirtieth, except for February, when it was published on the twenty-eighth). Issues from the early 1920s, a favorite period of many collectors, were 192 pages of eye-straining print and usually included a complete novel, two or three complete novelettes (in reality short novels), and a goodly chunk of a serial. There would also be five or six short stories and a bunch of departments like "Old Songs That Men Have Sung," "Ask Adventure," and "Lost Trails." The letter column, known as "The Camp-Fire," was perhaps the best letter column published in any magazine, ever. Usually, authors of stories in the issues wrote long essays where they detailed the historical background of their work. Letters from readers argued over facts in previous stories. In an America just emerging from the Wild West and the First World War, the readers of *Adventure* weren't just armchair adventurers spouting theories. A typical letter began, "I enjoyed Hugh Pendexter's story about the gunfight at the O.K. Corral, but he got some of the details wrong. I was there and remember quite distinctly—" and continue on for three pages about the famous gun battle. There's a spectacular oral history of the American West in the letter columns of *Adventure*, and hopefully someday it will see print.

Still, it was the stories that made the pulp memorable, and *Adventure* featured the greatest lineup of adventure writers ever assembled. There was Talbot Mundy, Arthur D. Howden Smith, Arthur O. Friel, Georges Surdez, Hugh Pendexter, J. Allen Dunn, and many hundreds of others, penning some of the finest, most accurate historical and modern adventure stories ever written. These were the top men in their field, men who knew how to tell a good story with plenty of action and a dash of romance, and who understood that their audience wouldn't accept inaccuracies in their fiction, so they kept their history straight. *Adventure* was considered the most prestigious pulp magazine in America. It was the very best the pulps had to offer. And the very best author in *Adventure* was Harold Lamb.

Lamb wrote seventy-five stories for *Adventure* from 1917 through 1933, many of them long novelettes and short novels. He was most famous for his series of stories about Khlit, an old and wily Cossack warrior. However, Lamb's finest fiction wasn't about Khlit but consisted of a thematic series of novellas featuring unjustly accused crusaders who joined the Mongol hordes of the great khans. The most popular of these adventures were three short novels featuring Sir Hugh of Taranto, which were later published in hardcover in 1931 as *Durandal, A Crusader with the Horde*. In the rambling adventure, Hugh fights treacherous Greeks and Moslems; finds Roland's lost blade, Durandal; and finally achieves a measure of revenge while riding with the hordes of Genghis Khan. Donald M. Grant Publications reprinted the first two short novels in this series, *Durandal* and *The Sea of the Ravens*, but has yet to publish the third and concluding volume, *Rusudan*. While the Durandal series is Lamb at the top of his form, it is not his best crusader-meets-the-Mongols story. That honor is reserved for the longest story in this volume, "The Making of the Morning Star."

This action-packed short novel was written in 1924, before the Sir Hugh series, and features a similar plot. A crusader, Sir Robert, is betrayed by his comrades and later is taken captive by the Saracens. Unwittingly, he helps one of the leaders of the advancing Mongol horde and wins his freedom, but not before he goes into battle wielding a gigantic iron ball and chain, a weapon known as a morning star. If set on Barsoom or in Aquilonia, "The Making of the Morning Star," would have been hailed as a fantasy masterpiece, but because it takes place in historical times without any magical elements, it has remained forgotten in the pulps for eighty years, until this welcome reprinting.

This short novel is just one of a number of superb stories contained in this long-overdue collection of Harold Lamb's crusader fiction. As a Lamb collector and fan for forty years, I envy all those who are reading his work for the first time. This book is a collection to be treasured, a book I guarantee you will read more than once.

As a brief historical footnote, in 1974 Ted Dikty, the co-owner of FAX Collectors Editions, asked me to edit two series of trade paperbound books reprinting the best adventure fiction from the pulps. One series was titled *Famous Fantastic Classics* and featured only science fiction stories, while the other was titled *Famous Pulp Classics* and was going to reprint only high adventure fiction. When I assembled the first issue of *Famous Pulp Classics*, there was no question in my mind what to use as the lead story—"The Making of the Morning Star." Rights to the story did not seem to be a problem, so Ted commissioned up-and-coming artist Michael Kaluta to paint a cover illustration based on the story. It was only when the book was ready to print that we learned that Donald Grant had licensed some of Lamb's work and was strongly opposed to us reprinting "The Morning Star" story. Don felt that our reprint would cut into sales of his planned Lamb reprints, even though they were years away. To keep the peace, we dropped the story, and instead substituted a Malcolm Wheeler-Nicholson adventure in its place. For those who might be interested, the Kaluta painting for "The Making of the Morning Star" still appeared on the cover of *Famous Pulp Classics #1*, though it didn't illustrate any story in the book. It's still great art for a great story!

Swords from the West

The Red Cock Crows

Piculph, the sergeant at arms, always made his rounds in the city of Tana at dusk. In that hour, after vesper bells and the muezzin's call, wine flowed in the taverns and blood in the alleys. A watchful fellow like Piculph could always pick up something good.

Tana was a slave port—the last post of Europeans in Asia—at the far end of the Charnomar, that is now called the Black Sea. Over this sea the galleys from Constantinople brought Christian slaves, boys and young women, Greeks and all sorts, to be sold to rich Moslems. And from the East, along the caravan road, came the turbaned folk bringing red leather and hemp and musk and opium and sword blades. And Tana had never been noisier at dusk than this evening of the year of grace 1402.

Piculph went warily, turning the corners wide, with his ear cocked to the bickering and brawling that went on, only half seen. It was the hour, he had said more than once, when the Horned One held open market. Piculph himself was a Lombard redbeard with a knack of stabbing and a nice touch for stealing. He served Messer Andrea, the master of the slave brokers, and he held himself to be better than the masterless rogues, the ribalds of the alleys—such rogues as he now paused to watch.

In the deep shadow under the stone arch of an open gate in the city wall some half dozen ragged figures were clustered, looking out at the road. Piculph, being mounted, could see over their heads. Beyond this gate, out on the plain, the glow of sunset lingered. And Piculph's curiosity grew as he watched.

Often he had watched stout Turks driving laden asses through that gate and sallow Armenians moving through the dust raised by their sheep and grim Tatars whirling lariats as they trotted beside the herds of their shaggy ponies. But he had never seen a man leading a horse.

And now a tall man was approaching with the long stride of one who had come far on foot. He wore boots of soft leather laced to his knees, a faded mantle gray with dust, and a tarnished steel cap set a little upon one side of his yellow head. Great of bone he was, and though alone, he did not seem to fear the darkness under the gate. The sword slung upon his hip in its leather scabbard was too heavy and too long to be handy in a brawl. So thought Piculph.

And so thought the ribalds under the arch who had seen that the stranger led a lame horse, a gray Arab racer whose saddlecloth was gleaming cloth of gold. Since the stranger was alone and the horse one of price, the thieves made ready to slay the man—there in the darkness under the arch that smelled of charcoal and sheepskins.

Piculph grinned in his beard, for he saw what they were about, and he meant to ride in upon them after their work was done and seize the horse himself.

The stranger entered the arch, and the masterless men thronged about him.

"*Yah huk—yah huk!*" they yelled in unison, the beggar's cry of Asia's streets. And at their call a pockmarked devil in a tattered cloak came running up with a lantern as if to light the way before the tall man. Instead he thrust the lantern close to the stranger's eyes—clear gray eyes that looked at them out of a lean, sun-darkened face.

"Give, in God's name!" whined a beggar, pushing through his mates until his groping hands closed upon the right arm of the stranger. The beggar was blind, his pupils white-filmed, his lids eaten by flies.

His comrades pressed in closer then, and Piculph saw that for which he had been looking. Behind the blind beggar appeared a stout Levantine boatman grasping a short ax, watching his chance to strike. The thieves clamored louder, and the boatman shifted his weight to his left foot, and the corners of his lips twitched in a snarl. Suddenly he struck, full at his victim's eyes.

But the tall man had caught the flicker of steel in the light of the lantern. His right arm shot forward, thrusting the blind beggar back, and he himself bent back from the hips. The boatman's ax swung harmlessly through the air.

At the same instant the stranger pulled clear his sword. The point of the long blade swept out and down, and the boatman shrieked. The sword's edge had caught his wrist and cut through it. The ax, still gripped in hairy fingers, dropped to the earth.

The boatman staggered against the stones of the arch and fell. At the flash of the long sword his companions vanished, as dogs flee the rush of the wolf—the blind beggar scrambling after them. The stranger picked up the lantern quickly and hooked it to his belt, a broad leather belt, Piculph noticed, set with silver plates and a miniature shield.

"Poor Bacco!" exclaimed the big Lombard, drawing closer, "what a cut that was!"

He had spoken in Italian, and the stranger neither answered nor sheathed his sword. Piculph saw now that he was younger than he had thought, but with the narrowed eyes and the lines about the mouth that came from hardship and long service.

"Whence are you, Messer Swordsman?" he asked, in the lingua franca that was the common speech of the Levant.

"From the road," the stranger answered calmly, and Piculph was no wiser than before.

The Lombard glanced at the bloodstained ax and shrugged a plump shoulder.

"Well, you had an ill welcome. They will use their teeth, and a good sword is worth a hundred ducats in Tana tonight. Aye, many souls are fleeing the gates, and few are coming in. A bit of trouble always cheapens women and raises the price of horses. Yesterday a Greek virgin, skilled at dancing and the guitar, sold for thirty-five pieces of gold. I saw it—I, captain of Messer Andrea's men, and I swear by ——"

"Enough!" said the tall man. "Lead me to your master."

"And may the foul fiend sit upon me, Your Grace, but I know not what he serves or seeks. He is no Frank or Lombard or man of Genoa like your illustrious lordship, and he keeps his tongue in his mouth. He wears the belt of a lord, but he came in alone from the Jerusalem road, and if he were a ghost and not a living wight, I would name him a mad crusader. 'Twas a sweet slice he dealt that clapper-claw—Zut!—and the dog's paw was off. But he says he was sent to Your Illustrious Grace."

Thus Piculph delivered himself to his master, Andrea the Genoese, sometimes called the Counter by reason of his great wealth in slaves and ships.

They were talking in the open gallery of the citadel, overlooking the flat roofs of the town and the bare masts of the galleys beyond. The last of the sunset glow had left the sky, and above the sputtering torch in its socket behind Messer Andrea, the points of the Pleiades shimmered. Against the stars rose the dark bulk of the donjon and corner towers, upon which moved slowly the vague figures of watchers.

Outside the glare of the torch Prince Theodore lay at ease upon a divan, a handsome young Greek, mindful of the dressing of his dark beard and the hang of the miniver cloak upon his shoulders, but at this moment sulky and out of patience.

Erect, clad in severe black velvet, Messer Andrea sat at a narrow ebony table inlaid with ivory, a roll of parchment between his bony fingers. His sallow face was dry and aged, his eyes expressionless. Men in debt to the Counter feared that shrill voice more than the slither of drawn steel, and Prince Theodore—who tried to drown in his cups the memory that Tana had once been his and was now in the hands of the Counter—would say when he was very drunk that the Genoese knew the art of making silver out of copper and gold out of human souls.

Messer Andrea glanced up fleetingly at the tall stranger, who had not understood what Piculph said.

"A belted knight in Tana," he observed dryly. "Young sir, I do not know your name?"

"Bruce," responded the swordsman, looking about him calmly.

"Bruce—of Famagosta? Vassal of the Sieur de Rohan? Rohan is dead!"

Three times the man called Bruce of Famagosta nodded assent, and Messer Andrea reflected. He knew of John of Rohan, a Count of Flanders, who had come to the East to wield his sword in the holy war against the Moslems. Adventurers served John of Rohan, among them this youth out of Scotland who was named Bruce and who had no property. Rohan and his men had been drawn into the crosscurrents of wars that swirled around Venice and Constantinople. Messer Andrea heard of them fighting at Smyrna, and in the long galleys of the Doge; they had besieged Famagosta and had in turn been besieged, and there John of Rohan had been slain not by a Moslem scimitar but by a Greek crossbow bolt—John of Rohan, who had been Messer Andrea's friend. Who had borrowed from him a large sum of money and had died still owing it.

"Faith," remarked the Scot, "'Twas Rohan sent me hither."

"And why?" Messer Andrea wondered how this man had found his way to Tana, through the danger that now beset the road.

"For his daughter."

On the divan in the shadows the Greek prince stirred and would have spoken had not Messer Andrea signed to him to be silent.

"And where is she, Sir Bruce?"

"Here."

For a moment Messer Andrea was silent, his thin lips pinched. True, the daughter of Sieur de Rohan was in Tana, under his protection. Rohan had requested him to safeguard her.

"What token bring ye as warranty of your mission?" he asked. "A writing, Sir Bruce?"

The Scottish swordsman looked calmly at the merchant. "Ye wit well, Messer Andrea, that my lord of Rohan could not write a paternoster. I am saying that he spoke with me after he had been cut down, and he bade me go to you and take in my charge his daughter, to shield and guard her to her home."

Messer Andrea lowered his eyes and stroked his long chin. The daughter of the dead seigneur, Marie de Rohan was still a child—but a child who was beginning to be beautiful. She was thin and white, and grieving had darkened the shadows under her eyes. Still, there was the hue of fire in her hair, with a glint of gold running through it. Such hair was the fashion in Venice, and Messer Andrea knew certain noblemen who would pay two hundred ducats of full weight for Marie de Rohan.

Her father had never paid his debt to the Counter, and Marie had no kinsmen to protect her. Messer Andrea was not minded to yield her to a wandering swordsman.

"How will you find a way," he asked, sharply, "back to Christian lands?"

"By the caravan route."

Prince Theodore propped himself up on an elbow and exclaimed shrilly: "By the hide and hair of the Evil One, this is madness! With forty lances I would not set foot upon that road."

"Betimes, my lord," responded Sir Bruce, "a maid is safer upon the road than behind walls."

The smooth brow of the Greek darkened, and his hand caught at the hilt of the long dagger in his girdle.

"Your Mightiness!" The Counter's dry voice was like the flicker of a whip. "Allow me to warn our guest of the peril outside the walls. Piculph—see thou to the watch. Send in cupbearers with Cyprian wine."

The Greek sank back upon the divan deeper into the shadow, stifling his anger with whispered oaths. At first he would not touch the silver goblet of cool white wine offered him by the two Circassian women who came unveiled, silent and graceful as animals upon the soft carpet. Then he clutched his cup, gulped it down and signed for more.

Sir Bruce waited to see him drink first, and in the pause the keen ears of the Scot caught the movement of armed men all about him—the clank of the iron butts of crossbows against stone parapets, the crackle and flare of the cresset newly lighted that showed him the steel caps of a score of bowmen, the dark arms of mangonels and the bronze tubes of flame throwers on the outer wall. Even in the alleys below, the night was full of sounds—a man's sudden oath, the clatter of hoofs, and the ceaseless wail of beggars.

"You have noticed, young man, that Tana is strongly held. I have been warned." Messer Andrea tapped the parchment in his fingers. "There is one near at hand who fears not the wrath of God nor the weapons of man.

"And here is the message he sends me." Messer Andrea unrolled the parchment and held it so the Scot could see the strange writing—tiny scrolls and curlicues—that covered it. Some of the marks were inscribed in red upon a gilt circle.

"'Tis Arabic, with a royal name emblazoned," commented Sir Bruce. "I ken—" he was silent for a moment. "Read it, I cannot."

"That name," assented the Genoese, "is Tamerlane."

Sir Bruce looked up reflectively. In bazaar and caravansary he had heard men speak of Tamerlane, a lame Tatar king who had emerged with his horde from the unknown steppes of the east.

Messer Andrea read slowly:

"By command of TAMERLANE, King of all Kings, the Victorious, Lord of Fortunate Happenings—to the master of Tana, these words are sent. With sharp sword edges and swift horses we are passing thy city. Send out to us therefore a suitable gift, and no harm will befall thee at our hand."

Messer Andrea was silent a moment, studying the parchment. He resumed:

"If the tribute is not sufficient, we will turn aside and make war upon ye. We will set the red cock crowing. We will build a pyramid of the heads of the slain. Do as thou wilt. It is all one to me. I send this writing—I, SUBAI GHAZI, lord of the lords of Tamerlane's host."

He loosed the parchment from his fingers, and it coiled itself like a snake upon the table.

"I have heard it said," he mused, "that Tamerlane's Tatars make towers out of the skulls of their foes."

"Aye," asserted Sir Bruce, "when they are angered."

"But the meaning of the red cock—"

"Fire."

The merchant glanced fleetingly at the soldier. "You know something of these accursed Tatars?"

"I have seen them in battle."

"Then you know the peril in which we stand. Out yonder"—Messer Andrea motioned toward the dark line of hills behind the citadel—"they are riding to the south, God knows why, but"—he smiled bleakly—"I am no lover of ill chance. I shall send out tribute enough to satisfy them."

"By the souls of the saints," Theodore muttered, "it will need a mighty ransom."

"My agents have visited the horde," responded the Counter, "and they say that Subai Ghazi rides in haste. He does not wish to linger here. 'Tis said of him that he is a man of his word, for good or ill."

He turned to the Scot and spread out his hands. "Will you venture beyond the walls with a woman?"

"Aye, so," said Sir Bruce slowly. "Peril there may be, but the Seigneur Christ will guard a maid among pagan swords."

The Greek prince threw himself back on his cushions. "Fool!"

But the faded eyes of the Counter—eyes quick and shrewd to weigh men and their moods—gleamed approvingly. "Swear," he whispered. "Swear that you will safeguard the girl with your life."

Sir Bruce smiled. "Faith, I passed my word to her father."

Messer Andrea nodded swiftly as if closing a bargain. "Good! And now hear me, young sir. There is a path from Tana to the northern caravan road that should be clear of the pagan horsemen. It follows the coast. I am sending thither some men of mine, and they shall guide you. They will be horsed and armed after matins on the morrow."

"Then, by your leave, missire, I will sleep." The Scot rose, stretching his long arms and turned on his heel.

"A good night to you," Messer Andrea called softly, motioning one of his link-men to attend the knight. He listened until the firm tread of the mailed feet dwindled down the corridor; then he sent a slave for candles, a luxury he seldom allowed himself.

"Nay," he observed to Theodore, "that is no fool, but a simple soul that will hold to his given word—like Subai Ghazi." Suddenly he laughed, stroking his cheek with thin fingers.

"Body of Judas!" the Greek prince cried. "You have given the maid to him!"

"Content thee—content thee! By this hour on the morrow night he will lie in his own blood. A cup, Theodore—the white spirits in the stone jar."

The Greek drank deep, frowning as he watched the Counter clean a sheet of parchment and sharpen the pen of a quill. The candles were placed on the table, and the pen began to move over the parchment; but Theodore, peering across his companion's shoulder, beheld only meaningless curlicues—Arabic.

"'Tis a missive to the Tatar!" Prince Theodore exclaimed.

"True—the matter of the tribute."

Theodore bent over the table. "Will you send gold?"

"Gold! A mule's load would only whet the Tatars' greed. Subai Ghazi would give it to his bathmen."

"Jewels?"

Messer Andrea shrugged. "Will your Illustriousness contribute the precious stones?"

"I have not—" Theodore's dark eyes widened. "Ah, you are sending forth Marie de Rohan to the Tatar."

"A little wine sharpens wit," Messer Andrea muttered. "Drink, your Illustriousness."

"Are there no other women in the market?"

Messer Andrea finished writing, yet did not sign the missive. "Ehu—I am not so foolish as to send a slave to one who has had his choice of the women of the Circassians and the Golden Horde. And you forget the honest soldier who is surety of our—gift. This is his authority. Another cup, my lord?"

Theodore seized his silver goblet feverishly. His head rolled on his shoulders, and Messer Andrea rose, pushing forward the chair to him. "Life is sweet, my lord. It is needful to write thy name on this paper." He placed the quill in the Greek's quivering fingers.

"What evil is this?" Theodore peered at it drowsily.

"Has your Illustriousness forgotten? It is the death of the swordsman." Again Theodore found his cup filled and from habit he drank. With the Counter guiding his hand, he scrawled his name. And Messer Andrea, tucking back his long sleeves, bestirred himself to melt red wax upon the parchment and press into it the signet ring of the almost unconscious prince. Then Theodore laid his head upon the table and slept.

Messer Andrea blew out the candles and slipped away into the darkness to attend to other matters.

It was late in the afternoon of the next day before Sir Bruce's guides came to fresh water—four leagues from Tana. Here the trail wound upward, among gray clay buttes overhanging the sea's edge. The servitors, resplendent in the crimson and white livery of Prince Theodore, placed the pavilion pole in a sheltered spot, and hung upon it the striped silk covering under which Marie, the maid of Rohan, was to sleep that night.

"Glad am I," cried the girl, "to be again in the sun."

Sir Bruce, staring through narrowed eyes at the glitter upon the sea below them, was troubled by her beauty.

It was a miracle to Sir Bruce that he, who had not seen a woman of his race for years, now had in his charge this maid. Because he had given a promise to John of Rohan, he had wandered and searched and fought his way by land along the course the Counter's galleys had taken by water. And when he had first seen Marie the blood had throbbed in his veins. Now he was proud and exultant. Yet the grim purpose in him ever kept him silent, and she looked sidewise at him curiously.

"Oh, this is a barren land," she said, "but Messer Andrea has given me a great store of comfort. At first I did not like him, but he was generous."

Sir Bruce drew his hand across his chin. He wore this day his mail, a linked habergeon, with coif and thigh pieces. He stood beside the gray Arab that he had not yet unsaddled.

"Nay," he responded bluntly, "he is no man of faith."

"He sent his knaves to serve us."

"Aye so." Sir Bruce knew that these men, though they wore livery, were masterless fellows, and he expected no good of them. Yet Messer Andrea had given the girl a swift-paced mare and caparisons of cloth of gold.

"He took thought for me. See, he instructed to me a safe conduct to Constantinople."

"To you? I must see it."

Obediently she sought in her saddle bags until she drew forth a roll of parchment, tied and sealed with red wax. Sir Bruce took it silently and broke the string at once. He frowned over the missive, written in Arabic,

and Prince Theodore's signature. After a moment's thought he went to the
fire the guides were kindling and thrust the parchment into the flames.

"That was mine!" Marie cried. "Why did you burn it?"

"It had a name upon it, a royal name emblazoned." Sir Bruce swept
his long arm around the encampment. "Here no seal of wax will avail
you, my lady."

The girl lifted her head proudly. "I have no fear. You are a harsh man,
Sir Bruce, and my father said of you long since that you would turn aside
neither for weapon of man nor spite of the devil."

In the flaming tamarisk the parchment crumbled, and from it ran a
thin stream of crimson, so like blood that Marie was startled and caught
at the warrior's arm. "Look—"

"Be quiet!" he bade her sternly.

His head bent forward, the lines in his dark face deepened. Then all at
once she heard the thrumming of hoofs, and from the ravine at the upper
end of the valley trotted a dark mass of riders—men in dull chain mail
with long cloaks and sheepskin kaftans. At sight of the pavilion they
shouted and lashed their horses to a gallop.

"Mount!" Sir Bruce's voice sounded in her ear.

She turned, and when she fumbled with the stirrup he caught her by the
waist and lifted her into the saddle of her mare. For an instant he glanced
at the approaching horsemen. Then he reached up and pulled the hood
over her head, drawing it close to hide her face.

"Tatars!" shouted one of the guides.

Some of the servitors began to run away, casting down the spears that
they had caught up at first; others cried out in fright, and when Sir Bruce
mounted his gray Arab and took Marie's rein, leading her mare toward
the pavilion slowly, they clustered around him in fear.

The tide of riders swept toward the pavilion and divided into groups
that galloped around the camp. Here and there a curved steel blade was
drawn and flourished, flashing in the level sunlight. Lances were tossed
up and caught again, and the drumming of hoofs grew to a roar, while
dust eddied about the pavilion and the Christians in the center of the
wild horsemen. The Greeks who had fled were headed off and herded back
again like stray cattle.

Sir Bruce had drawn his sword, but made no other move. "'Tis part of
Tamerlane's horde," he said to the girl. "Faith, they greet us well, after
their manner."

The Tatars had not fallen upon the pavilion to plunder, nor had they snatched the weapons from the trembling Greeks.

"They are on the march," Marie whispered, with a sigh of relief; "they will do us no harm."

But Sir Bruce knew by the actions of the first riders that the Tatars had expected to find people at this spot, and that command had been given them not to seize what they found. Still the dark tide, brightened by crimson shields, moved past. A burst of plaintive music came from it—the shrilling of pipes and clash of brass plates and the roar of kettledrums.

Nodding heads of laden camels came into view about the horses, but before the camel train moved a standard, a pole bearing a gold crescent and swinging horsetails. And with the standard came a cavalcade of Tatar princes helmed or turbaned, with gilded armor and reins and saddles gleaming with silver. One who carried in his hand an ivory staff galloped forward, and thrust down his baton.

"Choupek gasaur!" he growled. "Down, infidel dogs."

The Greeks flung themselves on their faces, but Sir Bruce and Marie sat as they were, erect in the saddle. The mirza of the baton reined close to them and snarled, "Bend the forehead to Subai Ghazi, Emir of emirs."

A deeper voice resounded harshly, and the mirza drew aside. A white horse paced forward slowly. From thigh to chin its rider was wrapped in pliant Persian mail, a *khalat* of red satin thrown over his shoulders, massive as a bear's. He rode with short stirrup leathers, so that he seemed to crouch in the saddle. One hand, veined and scarred, rested on the worn hilt of a heavy, curved saber—a hand that could move as swiftly as a leopard's paw, that had earned for Subai Ghazi the surname of Sword Slayer.

"*Ahai!*" he exclaimed, seeing the slight form of the girl. His green eyes gleamed under a jutting brow and shifted to the tall figure of the knight. He waited for Sir Bruce to dismount or to salaam before him, and the Scot did neither. "Eh," grunted Subai Ghazi, "there is a stubborn devil in this one. Bid him uncover the face of the *khanim*."

Khanim meant "princess" in the Turco-Tatar dialect, and Sir Bruce, who had heard this speech for years, understood the words. He raised his left hand weaponless, and shook his head slowly. "Yok! Nay, it is not permitted."

Subai Ghazi's broad shoulders lifted in sheer astonishment—that he should have been answered and answered thus. The Tatars attending him reined their horses close about the warrior and the girl. The officer with the baton was the first to speak:

"Subai Ghazi, the Emir of emirs gave the command. Is his word smoke, O dog of a Nazarene?"

Again Sir Bruce shook his head, while his thoughts raced. Surely the Tatars had expected to find a woman here—Subai Ghazi had expected it. No one had touched them or questioned them until his coming. He had called Marie a princess and himself a Nazarene—Christian. The riders of the advance had moved on, but the main body was preparing to camp by the well. The camels of the baggage train were kneeling.

To refuse Subai Ghazi would be to anger him, and to allow him to look once upon the face of the girl would make him eager to possess her. Swiftly—there was need of swift thought—Sir Bruce fashioned in his mind a frail defense of words.

"Koudsarma," he responded gravely—"Lord, thy power is great indeed. There is a command about thine, unutterably great. It is written that the face of a woman must be veiled. Are ye kin to her, to lift the veil?"

The Tatar struck his fist upon his mailed thigh. "What words are these words? By Allah, will thou say she is thine—thy woman?"

Sir Bruce, striving for time in which to think and to divert the attention of the Tatars, had invoked one of the oldest laws in Islam. He looked at the slender figure, so bravely erect, that had drawn close to his side.

"Aye so," he said, and his voice rang true and certain. He knew, in that instant when death was so close, that he loved Marie of Rohan.

He stretched out his hand and placed it upon her shoulder, and when he did this the thing that he most dreaded happened. At his touch Marie turned quickly to meet his eyes, and her hands—that had clasped the edges of the hood about her throat—slipped down to his fingers and gripped them. The velvet hood fell back.

Subai Ghazi leaned forward with an exclamation of triumph.

"What is it?" she whispered, for she had understood no word of their talk.

The flicker of a smile passed over his set face. "Cover your eyes, my lady. I would not have you look upon weapon play."

The deep voice of the Tatar chieftain broke in upon his words:

"Thou hast lied, dog of a Nazarene. Allah, thou hast lied! Of the Nazarenes in Tana I asked this—that they bring forth to me a gift. This day, at the hour when the shadows turn, a warrior with a red beard came to my tent from Tana, saying that the Prince of Tana would send forth to me a maiden, his sister, to this well."

He looked about him calmly and nodded. "Surely here is the well and the tent with the banner, as the Nazarene prince promised. Besides, the maiden was to be protected by a man of valor until she came under my hand. What other art thou? And where is the letter?"

Sir Bruce glanced at the embers of the fire, where the red wax had long since disappeared. So Messer Andrea had sent Piculph out to the Tatars at midnight! And Messer Andrea had yielded Marie to him, knowing that the Tatars would never believe that a fair woman could make even the journey of a day without an armed guardian. Indeed, the Counter had bought his own safety cheaply—at the price of a girl and a few ribalds, some horses and a pavilion.

"I have not lied," he cried—aware now that the issue was at hand. "Be ye witnesses that she is mine." His left hand dropped from Marie's shoulder and gathered up his reins.

Subai Ghazi made a gesture as if casting something from him. "Strike!" he commanded.

The officers nearest him freed their swords and pulled up their horses' heads. But Sir Bruce did not let them rush in upon him. He drove in his spurs and the gray Arab leaped toward Subai Ghazi.

Sir Bruce had no chance to escape or defend himself. The ring of warriors broke and closed in, as wolves leap at a stag. An arrow crashed against his helmet and sent it spinning underfoot. He heard the whistle of steel at his ear and flung up his left arm—and felt the edge of a saber bite into the mesh of his mail.

He rose in his stirrups and lashed down with his sword. The long blade caught the Tatar in front of him and cut through the man's up-tossed shield and arm and shoulder, crushing the bones of his chest. Sir Bruce freed his sword with a wrench as a second rider shouldered aside the rearing pony of the dying man. He had not time to strike again, but he leaned forward, dashing the iron pommel of his heavy sword into the scowling face of the Tatar.

No one was between him and Subai Ghazi.

The Tatar chieftain might have pulled back among his men; instead, he reined forward, his broad face alight with eagerness. His scimitar flashed down at the knight's uncovered head. But the long blade parried his cut, and Subai Ghazi half wheeled his rearing horse, to take Sir Bruce upon the left hand.

And then he flung himself back, only warding with a desperate twist of his wrist the point of the long blade that leaped at his throat.

Before Subai Ghazi could recover his seat in the saddle—before anyone could come between them—Sir Bruce caught the Tatar's right forearm in the mailed fingers of his left hand and thrust back. Subai Ghazi's knees bent, and his shoulders were forced down to the rump of his horse. Under the red coat his massive body tensed and strained against the arm that held him helpless on his back. He slipped his feet from the stirrups and would have slid to the ground, but in that instant the point of Sir Bruce's long sword darted down through his beard, through the skin under his chin—and stopped, with half an inch of steel in his throat muscles.

Subai Ghazai's big body lay passive. The Tatars who had been about to cut down the solitary swordsman checked their horses. Blunt fingers released taut bow cords slowly. A warrior on foot stepped forward and grasped the reins of the white horse, holding him quiet, lest he swerve or rear.

"Two lives for thine, Subai Ghazi!" Sir Bruce said deep in his throat. "Mine and the *khanim*'s!"

"*Ahai!*" the Tatar grunted. Blood was trickling from his beard.

A flashing thought had stayed the knight's hand. He held the life of Subai Ghazi in his fingers. If he freed the savage chieftain, there was a chance that Subai Ghazi might release the girl and himself—without him she would be lost. Somewhere he had heard that Subai Ghazi's word would stand.

The green eyes glared up at him malevolently, and the muscles in the Tatar's throat worked. Suddenly he gave his answer in his own way. He spat weakly toward the tense face above him, and growled a single word "Strike!"

A clamor of amazement, rage, and sorrow burst from his followers. Then there was utter silence. Sir Bruce had lifted his sword and sheathed it in its scabbard.

"Subai Ghazi *bahator,*" he smiled. "A brave man, thou."

The Tatar, who had once sworn that he would never yield to a foe sat up in the saddle, found his stirrups—took up his reins and lifted the scimitar that he still grasped. Curiously he gazed at his foe, indifferent to the blood dripping down his beard.

"Thou hast sheathed thy sword!" he exclaimed. "Thy head is bare—and," he added grimly, "I did not pledge thee life!"

"Nay," Sir Bruce assented gravely, "but now thou art witness that my word is true. This woman is mine. Would I stand between thee and—a gift?"

Sir Bruce smiled, because he had played his last stake and the game was out of his hands.

"*Kai!*" the Tatar growled. "The dog-born dog in Tana sent out to me another man's wife. Veil thy wife and go!"

At the end of that night sitting on a height by the pavilion where Marie slept, Sir Bruce kept watch over a camp deserted by all but the horses. He looked back into the darkness along the way they had come. Leagues distant, against the faint glimmer of the sea, a point of flame rose and sank. Smoke drifted against the stars.

Subai Ghazi had galloped far that night. And now at dawn, in Tana, the red cock crowed.

Sir Bruce needed no guide to follow the edge of the sea, over the dry steppe. With Marie at his side, he rode through the barren land where only the eagles of the sky and the wild marmots watched them—until the girl saw a long dust line moving across their path, and in the dust the nodding heads of beasts. "The caravans!" she cried.

"Aye, the caravans." The eyes of Sir Bruce kindled and he smiled. "And now ye'll be after coming home—wi' me."

The Golden Horde

The winter's blanket of snow lay deep on the land. It stretched from the frozen tundras down to the southern sea—down to the shallow, tideless gray water of the Sea Gate.

Here clear skies and a warm sun melted the snow. Reed-bordered lakes overflowed into the alleys of the Gate itself. And lines of galleys jostled like feeding dogs along the embankment of the caravan road. Out of these galleys swarmed men of all kinds—warriors striding under their gear and slaves bent under hemp sacks—to the bank where sable-clad merchants argued in many tongues and riders in wolfskins spattered them with mud, unheeded. The jangling bells of mules echoed the grunting of lines of camels kneeling for their loads.

For this Sea Gate, as the newcomers called it, was the port of Tana. To the north and east of it stretched a new and limitless empire, an empire ruled by horsemen and filled with unknown treasures. The caravan road that began at Tana went by thousand-mile stages into the heart of Cathay.

To Cathay where, in this year of the Leopard in the second cycle of his reign, the great Khan Kublai ruled all the Hordes.

Mardi Dobro sniffed the morning air with relish and went down to the waterfront to begin his day's work. Being a shaman, he lived by his wits. He knew the tricks of conjuring and telling omens; he was an old hand at making or unmaking spells and writing prayers for the sick to swallow.

In his soiled red robe, with a white bearskin pulled over his high shoulders, Mardi Dobro pushed through the tumult to a dry spot by a fire. His green eyes, framed in the tangle of his long black hair, seemed to take no notice of the men around him as he knelt and picked a glowing ember from the fire.

"Ai-ha!" The watchers breathed expectantly.

Without haste the shaman placed the ember on a bone, the cleaned shoulder bone of a sheep. As the ember scorched the bone, tiny cracks appeared around it.

"O lord of omens," someone asked, "what do the signs foretell?"

From the tangle of his hair, Mardi Dobro had been watching the crowd that gathered as usual to the omen-telling.

"Great powers are arising, unseen," he muttered, and waited.

"Against whom?" asked the questioner.

Mardi Dobro glanced at him and saw only a fat Tatar.

"The powers," he explained, "are like snakes in the dark. They are moving against the feet of the Lord of the West and the East."

"That is Barka Khan." The Tatar nodded.

"They have poison in them, and they will strike him unless he slay them first."

Behind the shaman a rider reined in for a moment. Mardi Dobro did not turn his head; but he watched the horseman move away and, without waiting to hold out his bowl for payment, he got to his feet and followed.

The horseman passed slowly through the crowd, staring about him. He had the beak and eyes of a hawk, and his close-clipped beard flamed red. Mardi Dobro laid a hand upon his stirrup.

"*Ai, tura,*" exclaimed the shaman, "O master, I have tidings for your nobility."

He spoke in Arabic, seeing that this stranger was a Christian from the lands of the Franks, and a merchant. Most merchants knew something of Arabic.

"*Y'allah,*" cried the horseman. "Go on. I have naught for thee!"

"But a woman! O master, I have seen such a girl—"

"I have naught for girls."

Mardi Dobro kept his grip upon the stirrup, shaking his great head reproachfully.

"Yet the woman is of the race of your nobility. She is in the caravan of Yashim the Bokharian. She is beautiful as a white, swift camel. Look!"

The stranger looked. He was, as Mardi Dobro had guessed, a merchant. He was also a rich man, owning four cargo ships and warehouses upon the Dark Sea,* being one of the astute Genoese who were gleaning fortunes out of the new Eastern trade. Although he traveled about alone and apparently without weapons, he had agents in every port and could summon an armed following with a word. The name of Messer Paolo Tron was known from Constantinople to Baghdad.

He did not need to ask what girl Mardi Dobro meant. Yashim's caravan occupied a courtyard behind a wall, which served to screen it from the eyes of common men on foot, while horsemen could look over it. In the shade of the far wall a rug had been spread and groups of unveiled girls sat in noisy talk under guard of a giant swordsman.

Tron uttered an exclamation of surprise and urged his horse through the open gate. He ran no risk in doing so, because these girls were certainly slaves, and as certainly placed here for sale, unveiled. One sat apart from the rest, and the sun struck upon the mass of her red-gold hair. Her drowsy eyes looked up at him curiously.

When he asked a brief question, she answered in a low, clear voice. For a moment he weighed the worth of her beauty in his mind, and then, as the swordsman came up, turned away.

"Eh," cried Mardi Dobro at the gate, "will your nobility not buy her away from that black dog, Yashim?"

"Nay," said Tron impatiently, "she is only a mountain girl, a barbarian. Why did you lie, saying that she was of my people?"

"Her hair is like yours. Such as she—these fair mountain women—are strong and faithful. She is worth a high price, and you may find a great profit in her."

"I buy no slaves." The Genoese rubbed his saddlehorn with a gloved hand thoughtfully. "Why did you say, at the fire, that enemies were rising against Barka Khan?"

Mardi Dobro held out his bowl, pointing to the sheep bone.

"Eh, the fire itself spoke. By this sign—"

With a grunt of impatience Tron brushed the bowl aside with his foot and rode off.

---

*Called the Charnomar by the Turks, and now known as the Black Sea. Tana, in the thirteenth century, the time of this story, was the chief port east of the Crimea. Its site was near present-day Azof. Sarai was the great city of the Tatar Golden Horde, and it was still impressive in the time of Tamerlane. Little trace of it remains today, but it stood on the bank of the Volga north of the Caspian. The best caravan route—although hazardous in winter—ran through it to the Far East.

"A man," the shaman muttered to himself, "who trusts his ears and not his eyes will come to a bad end."

But as he stood in the alley, bowl in hand, he used his own ears which were keen as a hound's. He was following a scent where a hunting dog could not follow it, through a multitude of men. Listening, he heard a babble of voices on the embankment—a babble of many tongues—and he made his way toward it.

His path was blocked by two men. One, with turban awry, stumbling at every other step, knelt at a command from the other, a Tatar soldier carrying a drawn saber. Before Mardi Dobro could pass, the Tatar placed himself behind the kneeling man and reached his free hand over the turban, catching two fingers in the other's nostrils. Then the soldier bent back the head without haste and thrust the curved edge of the saber across his victim's throat.

"Agh-a-a—"

A wild scream was choked off, and the Tatar executioner drew his sword free with a jerk, severing the backbone as he did so. He let the head fall, wiped his bloodied blade on the garments of the body and hastened toward the tumult. An execution mattered little; but brawling was forbidden by Barka Khan.

Together, the soldier and Mardi Dobro came out on the embankment. At a table by a stairhead a Chinese secretary sat with his seals and record rolls. Around him had gathered a throng of interpreters and beggars. The Chinese officer, Mardi Dobro knew, was supposed to write down the names of all who came from the ships to the port, to list their occupations and destinations, whether they were Russian princes or negro slaves.

But the man who stood before the *bakshi*—the officer—was a strange figure. Half a head he rose above the crowd, with a brown camel's-hair cloak hanging from his wide shoulders. He wore neither hat nor turban, and his sun-lightened hair fell to his shoulders. He leaned quietly on the top of a kite-shaped shield, upon which was the battered semblance of a lion.

"He has no voice," cried the *bakshi* of the rolls. "He knows not Armenian or the speech of the U-luss."*

And Mardi Dobro, who knew all the types of the caravan road, had never beheld one like this man without a voice. His darkened skin showed that

---

*Russians.

he came from a hot country, yet his eyes were a clear blue. He bore himself like a man grown; but he was young, almost a boy.

"*Yah rafik*," asked the shaman at a venture—for the cloak was of Arab work—"O man of the roads, art thou of the Arabs?"

"Nay," the youth answered at once.

"Was there ever," demanded the *bakshi*, irritated because the voiceless one had responded to another, "an Arab with hair like ripe wheat and a lion upon his shield? What is his name?"

"What name bearest thou?" the shaman asked in Arabic.

"Nial."

"Ni-al." The secretary wrote it down. "From what place is he? What lord follows he? Whither goeth he? And why?"

"Patience," muttered Mardi Dobro as he put the questions to the stranger. "Eh, *bakshi*, he says that he is from beyond the sea. He has no master and he goes to no place."

"*Cha!*" The Chinese flourished his reed pen angrily. "How can I write that in the book?" He turned to the Tatar soldier, who was eyeing the lion on the shield with curiosity. "Take thou the weapons from this wanderer from nowhere who serves no one."

Stretching out his arm, the burly Tatar caught the hilt of the stranger's sword and half drew it. Instantly the man named Nial swung up his clenched fist, striking the warrior where the throat meets the jawbone. The guard whirled and fell, his long-skirted coat flapping about his boots.

The crowd stared in amazement. Few had seen the blow, and fewer still dreamed that a man's hand without a weapon could knock another down. The Tatar lay without moving, although he breathed heavily.

Clang! The *bakshi* struck hard upon a bronze basin hanging beside him, and other soldiers appeared, hastening toward him. Death was the punishment for attacking a Tatar with a weapon.

The crowd fell away from the man named Nial, who, feeling the menace in the air, raised the lion shield on his arm and drew his sword, a long straight blade of gray steel. But Mardi Dobro sprang in front of him.

"Move thou not," he commanded, "and say naught."

And as the guards ran up, the shaman thrust them back with his hands, shouting—

"O fools, would you cut down one who brings a gift to Barka Khan?"

The Chinese who had demanded the stranger's life cried angrily—

"Where is the gift?"

"Look at it," retorted Mardi Dobro, his green eyes glowing. "It is the sword in his hand. But touch it not."

Pressing nearer, they gazed at the long blade, observing that an inscription in gold was set in the gray steel. This was no common sword, and the man who held it faced them without fear or excitement.

"This," explained the shaman, who knew well how to work upon the feelings of a throng, "is indeed no ordinary sword. You all saw how when this man laid his hand upon it he fell senseless. It is a sword of power."

"*Kai!*" exclaimed the listeners. They all feared the power of magic, and who should know more of it than this sorcerer? Only the shrewd Chinese suspected that Mardi Dobro was trying to protect the wanderer.

"Why, then," objected the official, "does he wear it at his side, if it be truly a gift for the illustrious khan, our master?"

"Fool! If he did not keep it sheathed at his side, others might come to harm by it, as thou hast seen. Wilt thou stand in the way of one bearing a gift to Barka Khan?"

Slowly the official shook his head. He wrote down on his record that on the fourth day of the third moon of the Leopard one named Nial had come out of the Western Sea bringing with him a sword of power to be given to Barka Khan—all this upon the testimony of the Mongol sorcerer named Mardi Dobro.

"And see," he added grimly, "that the sword is given."

And he motioned to the guards to let the stranger pass into Tana. Promptly Mardi Dobro led his companion away from the crowd into the shadow of an alley. Here he thrust out his bowl, grimacing.

"Pay me, lordling Ni-al. I saved thy head for thee. Pay now the worth of thy head."

Nial took from his leather girdle a small wallet and tossed it to the shaman, who untied it and examined the single gold *byzant* and the few silver coins within it.

"Is this all?"

"All." The stranger smiled. "I have no more."

"But thou hast friends who will lend to thee?"

"Not in this place."

Tying up the wallet and stowing it within his girdle, Mardi Dobro stared at the youth with insolent green eyes.

"Then why art thou here?"

"I heard that in the lands of the great khan a man may find service for his sword."

"*Ohai!*" Mardi Dobro grinned like a cat. "Thou—a Christian without even a horse, without gold or servants—seeketh service with the Lord of the World! Thou art a prince of fools. Go back to thy people. Find a ship sailing into the west and go!"

Again Nial smiled.

"My people are dead. I have set my foot upon this road. I will go on."

"The child rides a calf and cries for a horse." Mardi Dobro snapped lean fingers contemptuously. This boy had stood up to the Tatars foolishly, yet his sword was a good one. Perhaps it might please Barka Khan. And then there was the lion on the shield, the same rearing lion of the seal of Barka Khan. This might be an omen. "Thou canst not abide in Tana and live," he muttered. "There is a way for thee to go to Sarai, the city of Barka Khan. I will set thy foot on the way, if thou wilt."

"Aye," said Nial.

Shaking his head, and motioning Nial to follow, the shaman made off through the crowded alleys, dodging horses and mules, until he came to the face of a stone building into which a string of laden camels was passing. He led Nial through the gate into a courtyard open to the sky. Here he pointed to the open gallery of the floor above them.

"At the head of the stair, in the fourth sleeping chamber, thou wilt find a Christian merchant who is as wise as thou art foolish. He goes to Sarai. Look to thyself!"

When Nial turned to thank the shaman, he had disappeared among the kneeling camels. Climbing the stairs, the young swordsman counted the open compartments along the gallery and stopped. In these stalls slept the travelers who owned the beasts in the yard below. But at the fourth place loitered two bearded and shaggy men who glanced at him furtively and waited for him to pass. He had seen their like before, even to the long, curved knives they fingered restlessly.

"Go," he said to them quietly. "Go and rob in the alleys below."

They looked at his sword and the spread of his shoulders, then slipped away. Nial glanced into the compartment.

"Ha! What art thou?" a sharp voice challenged him.

Messer Paolo Tron sat at a small table before a steaming dish of rice and mutton, apparently heedless of the knifemen who had slunk off. A good carpet was spread on the floor, and the merchant's bed of quilts had been laid over several chests and bags at the rear.

"Nial O'Gordon am I," responded the wanderer, "without gear or gold in this land of paynims. Faith, it was a magician who got me through the port and told me I would find a Christian merchant here."

"What seek ye, Messer Nial?"

Tron spoke in the Norman French that was common to most of Europe. Secretly—although he carried a short falchion under his mantle and wore a shirt of linked mail under his jerkin—he was glad to have the loiterers driven away, but he did not show it. Instead his lips tightened at mention of gold.

"A bite to eat, a place to sleep, and a way to Sarai, which is the city of the great khan."

Tron clapped his hands. A frightened Greek servant came to fetch another plate and glass for Nial. The two men helped themselves with their fingers and washed the food down with wine, in silence. The merchant was not given to idle talk, and Nial was hungry after weeks of being pent up in the galley.

"Now," Tron asked suddenly, "how is it that you speak like an Arab?"

"Easy to say." The boy smiled. "I was born among them. Aye, in a castle over the Jordan. My father and his father lived there, in the wars, but now they are dead."

A crusader's son, Tron thought. A luckless lad, raised in Palestine and driven out into the sea by victorious Moslems. He had met crusaders returning through all the ports of the Mediterranean in the ships of the Templars. They were all poor, seeking hire for their swords in a Christendom that cared not at all for them. Strange that this one should come to the road to the Far East.

"Better for you to abide in England. Have you no kin there?"

"Aye, so," Nial nodded. "One would have fed me, if I had tended his cattle. Another wanted me to carry cloth to the dyeing vat. I sold my horse and took ship."

Tron frowned. So it was with these younglings who had grown up in the wars. They would have naught of honest service at a trade, nor would they abide content within the four walls of a room. Probably this Nial would never forget that he had once ridden with his hawks along the heights of the Promised Land, or had watched for foemen to darken the sheen of a river at night.

"Here," he pointed out, "a man can do naught with a sword. The Tatars rule with a heavy hand, and they watch every shadow. Aye! The very horses are spies, carrying tales to them."

Nial bethought him of the quarrel at the customs.

"Still," he said, "a good blade serves well at times."

Slowly Tron shook his head. He was thinking that he had need of a man he could trust, a man whose courage would be like unbending steel. He would need such a man in Sarai. And here was this homeless Nial without other friends. Bold enough to meet the test, and young enough, Tron suspected, to be loyal to the man who gave him aid. At least, the merchant could make trial of him.

"I can give you service," he observed, "as far as Sarai, which is a caravan journey of three weeks. It will be your part to yield me armed protection at need and to go with me upon my ventures."

"That is fair," Nial assented, "and I will do it."

Tron pointed to the chests beside them.

"They have double locks of good Milanese work. But they hold only wine and gear and claptrap for gifts. If thieves get them, 'twill be small loss. Make a show of guarding them, but watch this other thing."

Rising, he looked up and down the gallery, then went back to thrust his hand among the quilts. He drew out a small sack of plain leather and untied the thong that bound it. After listening a moment he poured out into his hand a small stream of barley. Nial saw that in the barley lay loose jewels—tawny opals, blue turquoises inlaid with gold, and some small rubies.

"I am a jewel merchant," Tron explained, watching him, "and I mean to sell these at Sarai. They are worth a year's tithe of a great city."

Nial said nothing. He did not know what else the sack held, but the stones he had seen were not valuable in the Eastern market. Of course, Tron might have better stones hidden elsewhere.

"This sack," the merchant explained, tying it up again, "is your charge. Carry or keep it where you will."

"Aye, so," Nial assented.

In Christendom a merchant could keep his trove in locked chests. Here, upon the caravan road, a good pair of eyes and a ready sword were the only safeguard. If they were to travel together, Tron must needs trust him.

"Now," the merchant added, "abide here. I must look for horses to hire and a road follower to tend them. The Greek is too frightened to steal from me, but he is of no more value than a hare among wolves."

When he had gone, Nial replaced the sack in the quilts and lay down, wrapping himself in his cloak. As the light grew dim he dozed, half hearing the pad of passing feet and the voices in the courtyard below. The Greek came with a brazier to heat the chamber, and the smell of charcoal mingled with the stench of mud and wet sheepskins.

But Nial did not hear—because he came crouching, silent as a creeping cat—the man whose head was hidden under a white bearskin. Mardi Dobro squatted at the entrance of the stall, only his green eyes moving as he scanned every object, lingering upon the chests with their locks in full view.

Deep in thought, Mardi Dobro left the house of the caravans. Although he peered into open doors and scanned the faces of passersby from habit, he paused at times to stare into the trodden snow and shake his shaggy head.

"*Kun bolkhu bagasan,*" he muttered once. "Does the foal show what the horse will be?"

Then—for the sorcerer had as great an appetite for meat as for silver, and the air had grown bitter cold—he felt the ache of hunger, and went swinging through the dusk toward the shop of Ku Yuan, who, being a man of Cathay, would have meat in the pot about that hour, and perhaps part of a tea brick boiled.

Ku Yuan's shop would have given pause to one who did not know it. A narrow door opened into dimness and smells unmentionable. A snarl and then a bird's scream greeted Mardi Dobro, and a long chain clashed as a black panther leaped from one end of it to the other. Livid eyes fastened upon him and blinked as he made his way familiarly through the caged beasts and the roped hawks sitting their wall perches. Ku Yuan kept a fine selection of hunting stock, leopards, cheetahs, and falcons. The shaman smelled broiling mutton among the other odors, and pushed past a screen to find an old Chinese squatting beside the hearth, dipping into a steaming pot.

In silence the shaman knelt beside his host and pulled part of a fat tail from the grease, seasoned with tea. He stuffed himself expertly, pausing only to belch, until he sat back and wiped his hands on a sleeping dog.

"It is true." Mardi Dobro nodded, while he filled his cheeks with lumps of mastic. "More and more Moslems come from the boats with arms."

Ku Yuan dipped a cup into the pot.

"They are like wolves gathering together. And they are taking the road to Sarai."

"What seek they?"

"What seek the wolves? I have warned thee."

The sorcerer thought for a moment in silence. He was a Mongol from the Gobi, and he served Barka Khan faithfully after his fashion. He knew that Barka Khan, the lord of the Golden Horde, was far to the south with his army. So there would be only a small garrison in Sarai, the khan's city. These Moslems were going there for no good. He had observed that Yashim, the slave merchant, had landed a few days ago with a boatload of White Sheep Turkomans—excellent fighters but no kind of guards for women slaves.

"What hath Shedda to say of Yashim?" he asked finally.

"I sold her to the Bokharian only four days ago. Am I able to change my shape like thee and go among the swords of Turkomans to ask what her ears have heard? Go thou! She may not find it easy to escape again to me."

Mardi Dobro grunted.

"Have I not listened with the ears of a ferret? The men of Islam know not that I understand their talk. Certain ones came from Sarai to sit down with Yashim and Ahmed the Persian, who hath an escort of cavalry. The ones from Sarai bade them make haste before the ice breaks up in the rivers. Others await them in Sarai."

Sipping his greasy tea, Ku Yuan closed his eyes indifferently.

"The camel men in the *serais* know as much," he said.

"Look upon this." The shaman drew from his girdle sack the white sheep's bone and laid it on his knee. "Today I took the omen of the fire and the bone. This sign is a strange sign. First appeared the mark of water, so large it must be the sea. Then—look upon it—the sign of a sword coming from out the sea. Then here is traced the sign of war."

"Aye," muttered the Chinese, "a sure omen, when thou knowest the armed men are coming in from the sea."

But when Mardi Dobro thrust the bone into his hand, he stared curiously at the network of cracks. No human hand could have traced them.

"But at the end," he whispered, "there is good."

"True." The shaman nodded. "Ignorant ones, knowing naught of the powers of high and unseen places, questioned me. I led them astray. But I went to search out the one who might be the bearer of a sword. For the sword is one, not many." He shook his head moodily. "First I beheld a merchant of the West, a man of authority. I followed him and led him to Shedda, so that she might see him. But then I beheld a young warrior with a sword drawn in his hand."

He replaced the bone in his pouch and crouched over the fire.

"A foal, a colt untried. Still, I watched over him. He hath a lion's head on his shield and he turns his feet toward Sarai. What if he be the one of the omen?"

Ku Yuan only smiled.

"I led him to the merchant so that he should be cared for. This merchant hath many great chests with locks." The shaman's brow furrowed as he pondered. Without another word he departed, and the snarls of the beasts rose from the darkness as he passed.

Within a half hour he was down on all fours upon the ground, a bearskin pulled over his shoulders. Patiently, moving a little at a time, he made his way across the wide enclosure in which Yashim had pitched camp.

Avoiding the tents of the Turkomans, he sought out the great round yurt with sides of white felt bound upon wicker work. After a glance over his shoulder, he scratched gently on the felt.

After a moment slender fingers pried up the edge of the felt, and Mardi Dobro thrust through his hand, touching and recognizing a silver armlet that could only be upon the wrist of Shedda the Circassian, the spy of Barka Khan.

Even after that he whispered cautiously.

"What hath the peregrine falcon seen in the tents of Islam?"

"The Turkomans say there will be steel drawn in Sarai . . . Yashim keeps a rein upon his tongue . . . One boasted that more than twelve thousand Moslems are ready to arm themselves. The talk is of Barka Khan and the day when the ice will go out of the rivers. They will do nothing in Tana . . . I have need of gold."

"As ever!" Mardi Dobro checked a snarl. "Nay, thou—"

"Be still. Yashim pays little heed to us women, his head being full of other matters. His guards will look the other way for a gold piece, but they spit upon silver. Wilt thou say nay to the bearer of a falcon tablet of the khan?"

The shaman ceased to argue and felt cautiously in his girdle. He selected some coins and passed them under the felt to Shedda, who fingered them and gave them back swiftly.

"I said gold, not dog-dinars."

Pensively Mardi Dobro brought out three coins, smooth and heavy, and this time Shedda accepted them.

"Patience!" he muttered. "Nay, I have no more. Thy fingers would lift the horns from a bull. Now give heed. Thou hast seen the *farangi* merchant with the red beard. He rides to Sarai, as doth Yashim, with the next caravan. He hath with him only one swordsman, yet he bears heavy chests. He hath talked with Yashim, yet he buys no slaves. Do thou pry out what is in those chests, O nimble of fingers and wit!"

"*Akh!* Is that work for me?"

"On the book of the *bakshi* it is written that this Tron is a jewel merchant. Still he swears that he hath upon him only precious stones to the worth of a single horse. The chests are locked."

Crawling away from the yurt, Mardi Dobro gained the gate and stood up, chuckling to himself. After a glance at the stars to learn the hour, he retraced his way to Ku Yuan's house and found the Cathayan reading by an oil lamp.

"There is a letter," the shaman said, "to be written to the khan."

He himself could write prayers to sell to the ignorant. But a message to his master was another matter, calling for deft brushwork in the Mongol characters.

"By courier or pigeon?"

"By pigeon. It must go swiftly to the camp."

Ku Yuan brought out a small square of rice paper, a slender brush, and a tablet of ink.

"To the Lord of the West and the East," the shaman dictated, "from the humble reader of omens at the sea gate of Tana, these tidings. The wolves of Islam are gathering in packs about his city of Sarai, and they will hunt before the breaking of the ice. Let the khan turn his eyes to the golden domes of his city. His men there are few, the wolves many. Now, Master Ku, let me see thee make thy mark below."

Mardi Dobro could not read the lines of Mongol characters, but he knew the Cathayan's mark. Satisfied on this point, the shaman snatched up the rice paper, folded it, and rolled it into a tiny silver cylinder. He did not let the cylinder out of his hand until he had fastened it over the claw of a pigeon that he took from a cage bearing a special mark.

Going out into the darkness, he tossed the pigeon up and stood to watch it circle up against the sky. His keen eyes saw it rise and head to the south and west. Then he yawned and bethought him of sleep.

Four days later the great caravan from Tana to Sarai was on the road. They had halted for the night in the *serai* at the beginning of the desert that stretched as far as the rivers of Sarai.

Tron, Nial, and the two followers had quartered their ponies in a corner of the enclosure. They bought hay for the beasts and brush and dried dung for a fire. The merchant, who knew the cold of the snow plain, had secured for Nial and himself two *chabans*—long sheepskin coats, with hoods that could be drawn over their heads and sleeves that hung down to their knees. Wolfskin caps and boots of soft greased leather kept them warm.

The walls sheltered them from the north wind. A score of fires like their own illumined the dark masses of camels kneeling by their loads, the lines of ponies crowded together, and the throngs of men: helmeted Tatar guards who watched, like the indifferent sentinels of purgatory, over the mingled cattle drivers, merchants, and princely envoys seeking the road to Cathay; blue-cloaked Iranis with towering turbans, shivering in the northern air; sallow Armenians gabbling in a tongue of their own; and the strutting bulk of pockmarked Yashim, the Bokharian slave dealer, who wore three coats and gave commands to a hundred wild Turkoman weapon men who served as guards for his women freight, and who had elbowed a Khotenese jade dealer out of the best place in the *serai*. Through this encampment moved Mardi Dobro in his red robe, alert as a dog.

After supper, while the Turkomans were noisily making the night prayer and the fires had died down to embers, Tron went over to talk with the Armenians, leaving Nial to watch the packs.

A half moon lighted the *serai*, and the swordsman retired to the angle of the wall, taking a sheepskin and the jewel sack with him. Here he could stretch out in the darkness and see all who passed in the haze of moonlight.

The Greek servant was snoring among the packs, wrapped up in a rug, and the guide had gone to gossip with friends. For a time Nial watched the bearded faces gathered about the dying fires. A figure would rise, now and then, and cough and come to the well near Nial to drink. Drawing the sheepskin over his legs, he turned over on his back, picking out among the stars the Flying Geese, with the Bear.

How long the figure had been bending over the packs he did not know. Raising himself on an elbow, he watched the prowler examining Tron's chests, and he heard the clink of metal thrust into a lock. The figure wore a hooded *chaban* like his own.

Taking his sheathed sword in one hand, Nial got to his knees and leaped forward silently. The figure in the white *chaban* started back, but Nial's free hand closed on the visitor's arm.

"*Hai*, thief!" he grunted.

A knife flickered under his eyes, and he bent his body aside swiftly as the blade ripped into the folds of his heavy coat. He did not loose his hold of the intruder and, before the knife could strike again, he swept the heavy hilt of his sword down on the other's wrist. With a sharp moan of pain his antagonist let the dagger fall.

Taking the other's wrists in his right hand—for the slender strength of the thief was no match for his own—Nial thrust the hood of the *chaban* back. He looked down upon a woman's heavy hair, bound by a silver band, and a young face, tensed in pain. Tears trickled from the closed eyes.

"*Yah bint*," he cried softly. "O girl, what is this?"

From half-closed lids her eyes searched his face. Nial was aware of the scent of jessamine oil. He had not seen her before, upon the road or in the *serai*, and certainly he had seen none so fair as she.

Instinctively he relaxed his grasp, knowing that he must be hurting her, although her heavy sleeve had broken the force of his blow. He wondered what she might be and whether she understood Arabic.

"Who art thou," he asked again, "to steal in a corner?"

This time she answered swiftly—

"Hush, thou!" And then, imploringly, "O my lord, master of swordsmen, I did not steal. Nay, I was looking only at the strange boxes."

"And their locks," said Nial, who had met other thieves upon other roads.

He set his foot upon the dagger, but he wondered again what girl of the steppes could have hair like that, and how she came to be loose, unveiled.

Most of the travelers in the *serai* were Moslems, and even Yashim, the slave dealer, carried his women in camel hampers.

"Nothing is harmed, my lord," she whispered, "and it would shame me to be dragged before the guards."

"What is thy name?"

She glanced from right to left.

"Shedda it is, and my lord hath hurt my arm."

Bending down, Nial pushed the sleeve back from her slender wrist, finding upon it a heavy band of silver. There was writing upon the silver of a kind unknown to him. As he peered at it the girl Shedda suddenly wrenched her arm free. Before he could seize her again she had darted among the piled-up bales between the fires. He heard a low laugh in the shadows.

Nial knew better than to try to follow; for a woman like Shedda would have men within call, and the men would have arms. And he had a mind to let her go. He picked up the dagger, and then remembered the jewel sack he had left in the corner.

Hastily he went and felt in the sheepskin. The sack with its barley and precious stones was gone.

Nial drew a long breath and silently cursed himself as he listened and heard only the steady snoring of the Greek. So the girl had tricked him, drawing him out of his covert while another, who must have known what to look for, had carried off the sack. But then, why had she struck at him with a knife? For he who drew steel in a *serai* must be ready for steel in return. Nial turned away and sought Tron among the blanketed traders.

"I have lost the sack, your sack," he said bluntly.

With a cry the Genoese sprang up and hastened back to their corner.

"Now tell me—" he whispered. "Ah, what in Satan's name?"

Upon the topmost pack of their baggage lay the leather sack, tied as usual. Tron snatched it up and thrust his hand within it. Then he shrugged his shoulders. The barley was there but every jewel had been taken out. He listened intently to Nial's account of the theft.

"Shedda!" he muttered. "Who moves like a panther and hath fire-red hair?"

"Red or gold."

"Yashim's slave." Tron remembered the courtyard in Tana. "A Circassian wench who will serve one man faithfully and draw blood or gold from all others. Eh, she led you about like a sheep. And this is your skill, to be plucked by caravan thieves."

"The fault is mine," Nial agreed quietly. "And if I can, I will make it good."

"A lordly pledge from a beggar."

"Yet," Nial added, "will I listen to no abuse."

The Genoese snarled, but put a rein upon his tongue and sought his sleeping furs. Both of them knew it would be useless to complain to the Tatar guards of the *serai* without witnesses to back their tale. A dagger gave no proof, and Shedda had not carried off the sack. To go to Yashim would be worse than useless. Only Tron knew the amount of his loss.

But within the week he discovered that the young swordsman, who had been tricked by a girl, could hold his own against men.

They were passing over a bare hollow, where a stagnant salt lake was bordered by white crustations, and the wind and the sun had swept the sand clear of snow. Red sandstone buttes towered over the hollow.

That day Tron's cavalcade was in company with the Armenians and the envoy from Persia. As all of them rode horses, they had drawn a little ahead of Yashim's *kafila* and the other laden camels, the horses making better going in the snow. A squad of ten Tatar warriors accompanied the envoy, who had besides a score of his own followers, nobles and servants. From the rock pinnacles on their flank a cloud of horsemen swept down upon them without warning of any kind.

Yelling like demons of the wastes, the raiders raced toward the caravan track. They numbered several score, perhaps a hundred, and they carried lances with tufts of horsehair beneath the points. They bestrode shaggy ponies and were so wrapped in dark skins and leather that they seemed to be animated beasts, tearing in for the kill.

In the caravan the Armenians huddled together like sheep, while the servants shrieked in terror. Only the Tatars, who had been half asleep until then, acted in silence. Their squad came together at a single command. The riders drew bows from their hip cases, strung them and sent shaft after shaft whirring into the raiders.

Separating to escape the deadly arrows, the nomads drove at the ends of the caravan. Some Armenians, kneeling in helpless terror, were ridden down, lanced or clubbed, to writhe on the ground.

Tron, pale but calm enough, had urged his horse toward the Persian prince, while the envoy's escort snatched out their weapons, crying upon Allah. Nial had got his great shield on his arm and had drawn his sword, wishing heartily for a good charger between his knees instead of the hired pony.

"What devils are these?" he asked the Genoese.

"Tribesmen. Nogais raiding after the winter—ha!"

The raiders plunged in among the Persian horsemen, stabbing with their light lances and hacking with their short, curved swords. Horses wheeled and reared, as iron crashed upon leather shields and a man screamed.

Nial drove his pony into the mass of them. His shield was proof against the lance points, and his long sword slashed over the shorter sabers of the nomads. He turned slowly in a half circle, upon his shield side, checking the jumps of his startled pony and beating off the tribesmen who rushed him. They drew back before the steady lashing of his sword, and the Persian swordsmen formed around him.

"*Ghar—ghar—ghar!*"

The Nogais clamored like gulls, swooping about their prey. But their round leather shields broke under the weapons of the warriors of the caravan, and they had no heart for a hand-to-hand fight. When saddles began to empty they hung back, and the Tatar guards, who had cleared their end of the skirmish, sent a volley of arrows among them that tore through furs and leather like paper. The Nogais turned away, snarling.

Nial had watched them with steady eyes. He had marked a tall bay horse with a fine head. As they drew away he urged his pony forward, parried the slash of a saber, and came knee to knee with the rider of the bay horse. The man tried to shorten his lance, then reached instead for a knife.

They were too close together for a sword thrust, but Nial smashed the tribesman between the eyes with the pommel of his sword before the knife could touch him. The man reeled from the saddle. Nial caught the reins he let fall and turned swiftly to rejoin his friends of the caravan.

"*Kai!*" cried a Tatar who had watched him. "The boy hath taken a horse from his enemy. That was done like a man."

By the time Nial had mounted his new charger, the raiders had withdrawn beyond reach of the Tatar arrows. They hovered before the rocks, shouting and whipping up their courage for a fresh charge, when Yashim's *kafila* hastened up, attracted by the sound of fighting.

The Turkoman warriors raced their ponies forward to snatch spoil from whichever side might have had the worst of it. They turned upon the Nogais, who fled like wild dogs before a wolf pack. The men of the caravan sheathed their weapons and went to examine the wounded and claim the spoil upon the ground. Many came to look at Nial's prize, saying that it was a Kabarda, a racing breed.

"Eh," said Paolo Tron, "you have skill with a sword, Messer Nial. We can get forty *byzants* for the horse in Sarai."

"Here—" Nial laughed—"'tis better to have a horse than forty *byzants*."

Flushed with excitement, he examined the saddle, which had worn silver work upon the horn and the short shovel-stirrups. He did not heed Yashim's camels that paced past him with creaking loads, until a soft voice called to him:

"O lord of swordsmen, what need hast thou of a little dagger? Give it back, I pray. In the garden of Mahmoud the Blind, the horsedealer—" the camel had passed with its screened hamper—"in Sarai."

Nial recognized Shedda's voice. He had kept the dagger, a slender thing of pliant steel inlaid with a gold inscription, in his wallet. And she dared ask for it!

"Nay," he called after the voice, "even an ass will not drink twice of bitter water."

Paolo Tron had faced *serai* thieves and tribesmen with cool courage; but now, with only the open road ahead of him, he became ill at ease.

"In two days," he told Nial, "we shall be over the rivers, if the ice holds."

They were coming out of the barren land to a rolling plain where villages nestled in the hollows, and Tron decided to push ahead of the others. The road itself became crowded. Trains of fur-laden sledges came in from the North, and immense herds of horses and cattle appeared out of the plain.

Once Tron's band had to draw aside when a high-pitched shout echoed down the line of caravans. Nial saw a rider go past on a white horse, dark with sweat and mud. The man was plying his short whip as a racer does to keep up a horse's pace at the finish. He wore no furs or armor and carried no weapons.

His stooped body was bound tight in oiled leather, and bands covered his forehead and mouth, while silver bells chimed on his girdle. With a cry, "Make way," and a thudding of hoofs, he was gone.

"A courier of the khan," Tron explained, as they turned back into the road. "He can take the road from a prince."

"He comes from the great khan?"

"Messer Nial, little know you of what lies before you. The great khan, Kublai, hath his city at Kambalu in the far land of Cathay, which is a year's journey to the edge of the world. Ha, so! 'Tis under the very rising of the sun, and no man of Christendom hath seen it, or hath lived to tell of it again."

"Yet Sarai—"

"Is the city of Barka Khan. He rules the Golden Horde, which is here upon the threshold of the East. Aye, he is master from Christendom to the Roof of the World, where even the valleys lie above the cloud level. But content you, young warrior. For if your king of England were here in this land, he might serve Barka Khan as Master of the Herds, no more. For the Tatars who came out of Cathay have overthrown all that lay in their path. They have divided into different Hordes. But in Sarai Barka Khan hath stored the treasures stripped from a hundred palaces."

"What manner of man is he?"

Tron glanced about him and shook his head.

"Guard your words! Even in Sarai there will be men who know our speech. They are the spies of the Golden Horde. As for the khan, he is a man of great courage, who is ever with the army. For the present he is away, at war with the Il-khan in the south. Yet men say that Barka Khan often rides through his lands with his face hidden. He listens to the talk in *serais* and taverns, and marks down here a man to be slain, and there one to be tortured for information. So it is well to see much, and say little."

At the bank of the first river the merchant reined in and pointed. The dark road led across a two-mile-wide sweep of glistening white. Ships drawn up for the winter on the far shore looked like specks. A line of men and beasts threaded over the frozen breast of the great river, all going east.

"The first," Tron muttered. "Already, perhaps, the ice hath gone out of its mouth, down in the heart of the sands."

And Nial knew that when the ice broke there would be no crossing the mighty stream for weeks.

"Nay, lords," quoth a high voice behind them, "this is the second gate, where the wise turn back."

On a shaggy riding camel, Mardi Dobro grinned at them, perched sidewise on a roped quilt. And he leaned down to hold out an empty begging bowl to them.

"Away!" Tron snarled. "I will pay nothing."

"Look beyond the gate, O lord of nothing. The wolves are sitting on their haunches, the vultures are hovering in the air. I have eyes to see!"

In spite of himself Tron glanced around, and Mardi Dobro struck his camel, urging it past them.

"Ye may see nothing," he cried over his shoulder, "but they are there."

"A mad mountebank," the Genoese muttered.

The next day they crossed a second, smaller river. Climbing the eastern bank, Nial halted with an exclamation. The dark line of the road stretched straight to the east, between twin lakes. Far in the distance he made out a gray wall, dwarfed by the immense white wall of mountains behind it.

"The city of Sarai," Tron said, "and the palace of the Golden Horde."

Sarai had grown up around the *ordu*, or camp, of the Tatars fifty years before when Juchi, the son of Genghis Khan, first conquered and then settled in the vast steppes between the Caspian Sea and the northern forests. The Tatars had made their headquarters in this spot between the lakes and within reach of the rivers; and the first huddle of sheds had spread out into wide streets, where Moslems and Kipchak desert men had their quarters beside the shops of traders from Cathay and barbarians from the mountains. Upon the height overlooking the lake, the Tatar khans had built a walled-in palace, with gilded domes rising where the yurt summits had stood. These domes, and the wealth they contained, had given their name to the Golden Horde.

Tron did not wish to stay in the Moslem quarter; he selected a room in a small house kept by a Greek near the cemetery under the palace height. They stabled their horses in the courtyard shed, and when the chests had been carried into their chamber the Genoese shut the door and looked to see if the horn window was fast. Then he went to warm his hands over the smoking brazier.

"Messer Nial," he said slowly, "you have lost me my stock of jewels; and so you have sworn to make good the loss, and also to aid me in my venture."

"Aye, so."

"There is danger to be faced, and a great reward."

Nial looked up inquiringly from the handful of nuts he was cracking. And Tron made up his mind to speak openly. The young swordsman trusted him and could not betray him in any event.

"I have come to Sarai," he explained, "not to sell jewels but to get one. A single one that hath no equal, not even in the markets of Constantinople."

"Who has such a thing to sell?"

"I could not buy it." Tron's beard twitched in a smile. "Nor could anyone. 'Tis an emerald, cut in the shape of a lion's head. I have seen it, and it would fill your open hand. Surely its weight must be over a hundred *piccoli*."

"An emerald?" Nial knew little of precious stones.

"Aye. Flawed perhaps, but still a stone unlike any other. It came from Ind, where it was cut for an emperor. Then, in the wars, it was carried off to Baghdad, where it was kept in the treasury of the caliphs. Barka Khan brought it away from the sack of Baghdad twenty years ago. They call it the Green Lion. That is why it may not be bought; and so I mean to take it."

As Nial was silent, he added:

"I know not what the Green Lion would fetch in the West. Only the emperor in Constantinople or the treasury of Rome could buy it. But meseems your profit would be not less than five thousand *byzants* of Venetian weight."

"A great sum," said Nial quietly. He understood now why Tron had not turned back after the theft of the jewel sack. Such stones were as kernels of corn beside this one.

"With it you could live as a man of gentle blood, with horses and followers and a palazzo, in Genoa. Eh, you could buy yourself a delicate young woman slave with sound teeth and sweet breath."

Nial smiled at the merchant's idea of luxury. And Tron, excited by his scheme, misinterpreted the smile.

"I know well what I say, Messer Nial. Two years ago I saw the Green Lion where it is kept in the Altyn-dar, the Gold House, or treasury of the Horde. At that time I judged its worth. A simple, swift venture, and the great jewel is in our hands, with no one to hold suspicion or make a hue and cry against us. 'Tis a sure game we will play. What say you, young sir?"

Cracking the nuts between his fingers, Nial answered without hesitation:

"It likes me not. Your ventures are your own, Messer Paolo, but I have not put my hand to theft yet."

Nial's grandsire had come out of Scotland upon the crusade and, although neither he nor his father had set eyes upon the land of their kin, the boy had been taught the strict code of clean knighthood. Raised as a lord's son in the castle among the Arab peasantry, Nial had never been allowed to forget this code. A crusader's word must stand, and he must back, at need, his word with his weapons. He must take the toll of hazard, and might keep what he could wrest openly from others, his enemies. But to steal would be to cheat his own inner sense of honor.

Tron eyed him warily.

"You have slain a man unknown to you to take his horse, aye, the bay charger which you cherish—yet you will not lift hand to carry off a treasure!"

"The one was fairly done." Nial frowned, stubbornly. He was not skilled in argument. "We were e'en beset by those pagan horsemen who outnumbered us."

"And here we be, two against two hundred thousand! Bethink you, my stripling. 'Tis no placid monastery here, where brother smiles on brother. Nor is it a garden of paradise, as many ignorant ones in the West have dreamed. Here the law is only one—the strong take, and the weak yield. This very Green Lion was reft from Ind by the caliphs, and torn from them by the bloody hands of the khans. Would you say that was fairly done?"

"As to that," Nial responded gravely, "I know not. But to snatch a jewel is foul work, fit for a purse cutter."

"Is it indeed?" The Genoese rose to pace the chamber, with a quizzical smile. He was more certain than ever that Nial was the man he needed. "Think you a mump or scrag nipper could get even a sight of this Green Lion? Think you so? By all the bones upon every altar, I swear that only a warrior dare attempt it. And only a man with courage of steel can do the trick. Now hear how the thing lies."

Stooping, he peered into Nial's face.

"I trust you with this tiding. The Altyn-dar is a place of strong stone, without embrasures within reach of the ground, and with only one entrance. This gate and the walls and corridors are all guarded by picked Tatar soldiers, commanded by an *orkhon* of Barka Khan. The only others allowed within, upon a signed order of this *orkhon* or the khan, are rare souls who, like myself, may be called in to judge the worth of jewels, or to repair broken gold work. And they have always two guards within sight, one beside them, and one within the chamber. Moreover, they are searched to the very toenails when they go out."

Thoughtfully the merchant nodded.

"Perhaps a skilled thiever could find his way over the wall of the Altyn-dar—except that it is in the center of the Sarai itself, the palace enclosure where the Tatars are quartered and few others admitted. The Tatars cannot be bribed, and I tell you truly that no thief could force a way in. Nothing has been stolen from the Altyn-dar. Nay, the only way in is the open entrance, without concealment."

"How?" asked Nial gravely.

"By a Tatar warrior, complete in every detail of his armor, and faultless in his bearing."

"But you have said they could not be bribed."

"True. And so my Tatar must needs be another, whom I can trust."
Nial laughed.

"I? Why, I know not a word of their talk."

"Words would not be needed, if this man bears a talisman."

"A *talsmin*?" Nial used the Arabic word. "A charm? Faith, have you got a cloak of invisibility?"

"Better than that." Eagerness shone in the close-set eyes of the Genoese. "I have made ready something that will admit a Tatar without question. And once within, he would not be watched. He could go where he wished, and could pass out without being searched, carrying the great emerald under his coat. And who would know where to look for him after?"

Nial shook his head slowly.

"Granting that, it is still thieves' work. You must find another for your mask and your token."

"*Par Dex!* Can I find one to trust twice—first not to betray me, and then not to make off with the Green Lion? I trust you, Messer Nial, and you will do this thing."

He stood over the younger man, tense with anxiety.

"I have aided you—aye, sheltered and brought you hither."

"And have I not done my part?"

"Nay, by God's head, you have not! For you swore to aid me in my venture."

Nial shook his head wearily.

"Not in such a venture."

"Will you deny that, when by your folly with that girl you lost my stock of jewels, you did swear to make good the loss if you could?"

Nial was silent, staring at the brazier. Tron's eyes fastened upon his troubled face.

"Will you recant your word? Then must I seek out another, and risk my life in doing so. For I will not draw back."

"What was the worth of the lost jewels?"

"What?" Tron shrugged indifferently. "Perhaps five thousand *byzants*, perhaps more."

"Then," Nial responded suddenly, his eyes blazing, "will I set my hand to this thing and do it. Upon one condition."

"How, then?"

"That my share in the theft will go to repay you for the loss of that cursed sack. Five thousand will pay you, and we will then be quitted of each other."

Tron nodded, closing his eyes to hide the triumph in them. The Green Lion would be his. For if Nial should fail, he knew of a way to get into the House of Gold himself. And, whether Nial brought the emerald to him, or he himself laid hand upon it, he need pay the boy nothing. The jewels he had lost in the *serai* had been almost worthless, merely carried for display, at need.

"Agreed!" he cried.

The Genoese had made his preparations shrewdly and had bought, piece by piece, a Tatar's attire at Tana. From one of his packs he produced a pile of garments that he made Nial try on at once. Skillfully he aided the young swordsman to fit on tunic and breeches and horsehide boots, tying the girdle himself and hanging upon it a metal seal-box and horn paper case. Over Nial's wide shoulders he flung a long blue coat with wide sleeves and embroidered collar. Then over this he placed something like a kaftan—a stiff black covering that projected beyond the arms, with twin letterings in cloth of gold over both sides of the chest. Finally he added a *kalpak* of white felt, a hat with a leather drop behind that covered Nial's hair, and a long eagle feather. So attired, Nial looked inches taller, and Tron surveyed him complacently.

"Eh, he who wore it formerly was larger in the waist. The shoulders are right—aye, it will do."

Nial's dark skin and high cheekbones needed no artificial touch. And Tron knew that many of the Horde had gray or blue eyes. He was more concerned with the details of the uniform, explaining that it was the dress of a *gur-khan*, or commander of a thousand. He showed Nial a baton, or short staff of white bone.

"Is that your talisman?"

"Nay." Tron grinned until his beard bristled. "More than this is needed. But this is the baton of your rank. Wear it in the girdle, so."

"What is the talisman?"

Paolo Tron shrugged.

"When the time comes, you shall have it. With it, you could ride from here to Kambalu, with the best horses led forward for you, and every wish granted."

"Where is the sword?"

"You need none. A *gur-khan*—"

"Messer Paolo, say what you will. I will not set foot in this treasure house without a good blade at my side."

Tron's thin lips curled in a sneer.

"'Twill serve you less than that baton. But I can get one in the bazaar. Then, too, you will need a new horse. It should be white, bearing a Tatar saddle. You have seen them. Good! I will give you thirty *byzants*, and five for the saddle."

And Nial reflected that the merchant had taken care not to have his own hand seen in this undertaking.

Making his way through the Moslem quarter the next day in search of a horse, Nial came face to face with the unexpected. Entering an arched street, he found himself in semidarkness amid familiar smells of frying mutton and onions, of leather and musk. Except for the cold, he might have been in the bazaar of Aleppo. Everywhere he saw the beards and turbans of Islam, occasionally the fur cap of an Alan or Russian.

If Tron had penetrated this city-within-a-city, he would have been stared at and mocked—for Islam is arrogant to its foes—but Nial, reared among Asiatics, sauntered by unnoticed in his *chaban*, pausing to handle rolls of felt or damask while he listened to the talk. He passed the open gate, with a loose chain hanging over it, of a mosque courtyard, and a glance showed him that scores of desert men were squatting where the sun warmed the stones.

Turning a corner beyond the mosque, Nial found himself in an alley, between lines of horses, where some tribesmen were arguing fiercely with a dealer. He noticed one of the horses, a powerful gray with saddle sores and marks of hard riding. But when a boy came up to accost him and beg him to look at leisure upon the splendid steed, he turned to stare at a shaggy steppe pony.

The boy, however, had seen him sizing up the gray and, after trying two or three languages, being clearly puzzled by the stranger, harangued him in broken Arabic.

"Nay, this one is not suited to your nobility. That one is tall and swift."

"He hath the look of the mule which sired him." Nial bargained with the ease of habit. "Moreover, he hath been ridden by a devil with sharp stirrups. Behold the marks. Nay, I go to see the beasts of—" he searched for a dealer's name—"Mahmoud the Blind."

"By Allah, is not Mahmoud here?"

The dealer, who had been listening with one ear, forsook the tribesmen and hastened over. He used a long staff, and the pupils of his eyes showed white in his pockmarked face. But he moved alertly as one who could see all before him. The boy whispered something that Nial could not catch.

"*Ai-a*," Mahmoud nodded complacently. "That gray steed is a Kabarda. It will run down a wolf."

"And leap a tent," put in Nial. "And turn in its tracks at a gallop. Verily this is the breeding place of all lies, and I go."

Loiterers on the balconies that overhung the alley—the whole quarter seemed teeming with men that day—grinned and coughed, nudging each other to listen to the chaffer. Mahmoud cast down his staff and lifted sightless eyes to the sky.

"May dogs litter on my grave! May the Ram come out of the skies, if there is one lie in all my words." He lowered his voice to a whisper. "A hundred *byzants* would not buy him, if his coat were sleek and fat. Yet will I sell him to Your Honor for less. For how much?"

"A fool would pay twenty."

"May Allah teach you wisdom, young lord. Verily, I know this horse, and he is from the stable of Barka Khan. Still, I will forego all profit and give him up for five-and-seventy."

"So do I know of him, and it was the command of the khan to have him slaughtered, and thou didst buy him from the skinner's market."

A cackle of laughter greeted this exchange. All the listeners were well aware that both men were drawing on their imaginations. While Nial examined the eyes of the gray, and forced open his jaws, and—remembering a certain Tatar trader—even lifted his tail, the boy brought forth saddles until he found one to Nial's liking. Meanwhile Mahmoud had come down to forty-six, in whispers, and felt for Nial's hand to strike palms on the bargain.

"Nay," quoth the swordsman, "first will I try his paces and see how lame he is. And I will pay no more than thirty, with five for the saddle."

It was a high peaked saddle, and he had to sit forward in the Tatar fashion to keep his knees down. As he tightened the rein Mahmoud hissed warningly, and the boy trotted after him. At the entrance of the alley a voice called softly, almost in his ear:

"Well done, Lord Ni-al. Come in by the door around the corner."

In the shadow of the balcony opposite him he saw a veiled girl and he recognized Shedda's voice. When he was clear of the corner he threw the rein to the boy and strode to the door.

"Will it please your nobility," cried the boy hastily, "to make payment now before entering there?"

"Why?"

"Because it happens often that young masters go in there with gold, but never has one come out with anything at all."

Nial smiled as he knocked on the door and then pushed it open. He had a certain matter to settle with Shedda, and he had always found the boldest course the safest. The courtyard proved to be empty, but several pairs of slippers lay outside the house door. Instead of entering here, Nial, who did not wish to take off his boots, climbed the narrow stone stairs leading up to the balcony.

This had lattice work around it, and was littered with worn rugs and garments—women's gear. Shedda stepped from the window, holding a great cat on her arm.

"Was not the door of hospitality open, that the noble lord should climb by the women's stair?" she asked impatiently.

And then, sinking down on the best cushions, she smiled. She had discarded her veil, and her splendid hair lay uncovered upon slim shoulders. But Nial could only stare into eyes that matched his own.

"So you have come," she added, "to the house of Mahmoud the Blind to give me back my dagger."

She motioned to the rug beside her, but Nial, looking away with an effort—the magicians have less power in their eyes than a girl of Shedda's training—kept his feet.

"Thou shalt have thy dagger back," he said quietly, wondering why she esteemed the thing so much, "in return for the jewels that were stolen in the *serai*."

Chin propped on her hand, she gazed at him curiously.

"What jewels were they?"

"In my bed, the evening thou didst come to—" somehow Nial could not utter the word steal—"to make pretense of looking at our chests."

Shedda looked amused.

"Did one rob the young lord while he talked with me? I did not know it."

If she had sworn an oath, he would not have believed. As it was, he thought she spoke the truth. He drew the little blade from his wallet and balanced it in his hand.

"Who was the thief, then?"

"I saw him not, and I know him not. Were there many jewels?"

"Many, and not mine."

"The *farangi* merchant's?" Shedda pondered, watching him beneath lowered eyelids. "Did he send thee here to me? Knowest thou the work he has in hand?"

Nial's fingers tightened upon the knife, until the sharp edge cut into his skin. Shedda was stroking the cat, but she missed not the least of his movements.

"Did the rich *farangi* bid thee give back my dagger and say aught?"

"Not a word. I came to buy a horse."

He wondered again how a girl with Shedda's face could be a slave in the open market, and what she wished of Tron, and how she managed to leave Yashim's caravan. And Shedda seemed to follow his thoughts. Putting the cat aside, she rose to her feet without effort, brushing her hair back from her cheeks.

"Not even a word for the men of Islam?"

"Islam? The Moslems?"

"Hush!" She laid a hand lightly on his arm, and the scent of jessamine crept into his nostrils. "O my lord, hast thou not heard of the Night of Judgment that is coming, when the men of Islam shall have power in their hands and shall cast down the Tatar?"

"Nay, Shedda, I have heard many prophecies, but not this."

Nial thought he heard something move in the room beside him. And he remembered the throngs in the Moslem quarter. Something, no doubt, was brewing among them. Such men were restless as a broken thorn bush under the wind.

"Did the *farangi*, Tron, not tell thee, my lord, that he is one of us, preparing for the night?"

"He has naught but jewels in his mind," said Nial grimly, "especially those he lost on that other night. Art thou an owlet, Shedda, to whisper in darkness, and to flit from Yashim's house to this?"

"Nay." She laughed gaily. "A parrot am I, to say only what pleases my masters. Now I have escaped from Yashim's guards—they looked too long on the bribe I held out—and I hide in this nest. Do not betray me to Yashim, Lord Ni-al!"

By some magical change she seemed to have become a different woman, full of mirth. The hot blood throbbed in Nial's throat, and he longed to snatch her up and bear her off with him upon the gray charger. Instantly Shedda became silent.

"Here is thy dagger." He laid it in her hand. "But why dost thou cherish it?"

She looked as pleased as a child when a toy is given back.

"It hath a sigil, a charm, written upon it." Her slender finger rested briefly on the gold inlaid inscription. "To others it would be naught. To me it is much. Thou art generous." Swiftly as before she seemed to change, to become older, a troubled light in her eyes. "Allah knows I have no worthy gift to give thee in return, Lord Ni-al."

She came closer, her head touching his shoulder, and whispered so low that even a cat could not have heard in the room near them.

"Promise me one thing. If there is war—sudden and fierce as the black windstorm—thou wilt ride hither, at once, turning aside for nothing at all."

Her eyes pleaded silently.

"To aid me," she breathed softly, "for I will need it."

"If there be war, aye."

Nial turned away abruptly, made his way down into the courtyard past the empty slippers. He did not trust himself longer with Shedda. He mounted the gray charger swiftly and trotted back to thrust the money into Mahmoud's hand.

"A noble steed and a princely buyer," cried the blind man. "Come again to look at Mahmoud's horses."

But Nial was already beyond hearing, riding heedlessly, a strange fever in his veins.

From the screened balcony Shedda watched him go, and settled back listlessly on the cushions as a man in a red robe, covered by a dervish's camelhair surcoat, crawled through the window and reproached her.

"Eh, has the tall warrior robbed you of wisdom? What said you to him at the end?"

Shedda sat up suddenly.

"What concerns thee not at all, who art a snake, to crawl and steal from these strangers."

It was a chance shot, but it made Mardi Dobro chuckle.

"Eh, the jewels from the sack! While thou and yonder swordsman were exchanging blows and endearments in the *serai*, I ferreted it out, with the skill of a swooping hawk. But the jewels were shining and worthless. They would not buy one sick camel."

The sorcerer rocked thoughtfully on his heels, his lined face puckered.

"This youth knows naught of the game that is to be played," he murmured.

"Nothing," she assented. "He hath honor in him, and his thoughts can be seen in his face."

"Already he loves thee, O most splendid of women. But as to Tron we know no more than before." Mardi Dobro glanced about him cautiously. "What brought thee to this place? Eh, even the mules shy at this gate of Mahmoud's where the girls he calls his wives wear no veils."

"Yet the girls come and go, and Mahmoud is blind. Much can be seen through this lattice. I have seen hundreds go forth on fresh horses." Shedda shrugged her shoulders and fell to playing with the dagger, flashing the bright steel in the flecks of sunlight, while Mardi Dobro waited patiently for her brooding to end.

"Ahmed and Yashim," she whispered at last, "feed their men with suspense. It is true they number more than twelve thousand. Mahmoud has furnished the horses, while Tron, who knows their plans, hath ships waiting for them at Tana."

"Ships? What have they to do upon the sea?"

"Perhaps they will flee when this thing is done. They will rise and strike and flee."

The shaman considered this.

"Today," he muttered, "a writing came by the courier from Tana. Ku Yuan says that—" he barely breathed the words—"the khan hath left the army. Alone, he rides the northern road, very swiftly, changing horses by day and night."

"Alone!"

"To Sarai he draws his reins. He could not loose the army from the war, nor could a single regiment of the Horde keep pace with him. He comes to strike down these heads that are rising up against him here."

"But alone." Shedda tossed her head proudly, even while sudden fear darkened her eyes. "What if the Moslems know of his coming? They will wait at the gates like panthers hunting in the dark."

The shaman's thin fingers caught at his hair.

"If they take him—"

"Alive, they could not. But if they slay him and fling his head into the palace!"

Mardi Dobro cringed. Barka Khan ruled with an iron hand, yet without him the alleys of Sarai and all the steppes would be drenched with blood. If the Moslems had spies with the army, word of the khan's coming might reach Sarai ahead of him. A messenger pigeon would outstrip the fastest post horses. And now there was no way to reach Barka Khan with a fresh warning. He might enter Sarai the next day. He might even now be dismounting at some tavern.

"The omens," Mardi Dobro cried.

"Oh, I am weary of portents." Shedda sheathed her dagger angrily. "Go off to thy white bones and smoke!" But as the sorcerer shuffled to his feet, she motioned him back, to whisper, "What say the omens concerning the—this Lord Ni-al of thine."

"Of thine, rather," grumbled Mardi Dobro. "It is as I told thee before at Tana. Then I beheld the ring of misfortune around a silver moon, and a reading of the bone foretold this: that one would come out of the sea marked by a great fortune, yet unaware. Aye, he would give aid to the khan with his sword, unknowing. As the signs foretell, it must be."

At his own courtyard Nial reined in, to look to right and left. There were perhaps a hundred gray chargers like this one in Sarai, but he did not want to be seen leading it into his quarters. The alley was deserted.

Nial led in his horse and, after rubbing it down with hay, gave it some water and barley. He hung up the saddle and cast a blanket over it, then made his way up to Tron's room.

The merchant lifted his pallid face as he bent over the glowing brazier.

"At last! I see you have the nag. Now must we work apace." His red beard twitched as he spoke. "You must go tonight to the Altyn-dar."

Nial's pulse quickened and he drew a long breath.

"Faith," he said, "I'll eat supper first." He ate heartily of the food the Greek brought up, but Tron only drank goblet after goblet of wine.

"In the bazaar," he explained, "the rumor runs, Messer Nial, that Barka Khan will ride into Sarai at any hour. I had not looked for that. When the khan is here, the place swarms like a hive, and the Altyn-dar will be full of Tatars. We must try it tonight, after the guard is changed at the fourth hour."

Nial nodded. That would be in about three hours, since the first hour of the night began at sunset.

From his wallet the merchant drew a folded slip of white silk upon which a plan had been sketched.

"Know ye how to read a map, Messer Nial? Good. This is the upper floor of the treasury, where the rarer things are kept. I worked therein, judging precious stones, for hours once. See where the corridors run from the stairhead. This central chamber is called the heart, and it holds the Green Lion with some other jewels of the khan."

Taking the silk in his hand, Nial studied it between mouthfuls.

"You will have this small iron saddle-lantern that burns oil. The Tatars hook them to their belts. I was told the Green Lion stands alone on a marble block."

"And if it doth not—if it is not to be found?"

"Nay, it will be there. I know the khan hath not taken it into the field, and it is always kept in its place." Tron hesitated. "There is a tale that it hath some unseen guard about it, mayhap a spell laid upon it by some ranting pagan sorcerer like the one who carried a bone about in Tana."

He explained that the Altyn-dar was a huge structure, and that once past the guards at the entrance, Nial might see no one until he came out. Nial had watched the Tatars in the street, and had seen them salute each other; and Tron had taught him a word or two of greeting. Unlike the Moslems, the Tatars rarely talked.

"All this I know," put in the swordsman quietly, "but where is the *talsmin*?"

Reluctantly, as if surrendering his own blood, Tron drew from the breast of his tunic a silk-wrapped package. Unrolling it, he held out a strange object, a flat oblong of bronze as long as his hand and more than an inch in width.

"Here," he said slowly, "is the key that will unlock all gates and yield to you all that you ask."

Nial took it and examined it. A hole had been pierced in one end and the other bore, in raised gold, a lion's head. Between the two ran an inscription. The characters of the writing were not Arabic or anything known to him, but they seemed familiar. The inscription on Shedda's dagger had been in these characters, but—Nial had an eye for details—not just the same.

"What says it?" he asked.

"'By command of Barka Khan, the Lion Lord, obedience shall be given to him who holds this.' It is the Mongol speech, written in Uighur characters. 'Tis called a *paizah*, or tablet. But the tiger and falcon tablets are held by couriers or generals of the Horde. This lion *paizah* grants to its possessor the veritable authority of the khan himself. I think there are not ten of them in all the lands of the Horde."

Nial wondered what had been written on Shedda's dagger.

"Are not these ten possessors known to all men—to all the officers of the khan?" he mused.

"Nay, some are envoys in far lands, and some are secret agents. I had a man who got one into his hands long enough to make, unseen, a fair impression in wax. From the wax I had this imitation made in Genoa, exact in every item."

Then Tron showed Nial how to hang the *paizah* upon a cord of twisted silk and wear it about his throat under his outer garment.

"In an hour," he muttered, "you will have the great emerald, and this talisman, which could open a way to Tana as fast as the swiftest post horses could gallop."

"Or," added Nial thoughtfully, "I may be hung up for torture like a plucked raven. Have you a sword for me?"

The Genoese looked blank.

"Nay, by God's head, I forgot."

"Then," Nial said, "will I take mine own, for better or for worse."

After the fourth hour of the night he rode out upon the gray horse. From boots to eagle feather he was a Tatar *gur-khan*. Even his skin had been oiled and the lines about his eyes touched up by the careful Tron. At the first corner he passed a hurrying Moslem, who drew back with a mutter of fear. Nial smiled and rode on leisurely toward the palace. Off to his right he could hear the wail of a muezzin calling a summons:

"Come to prayer—come to prayer . . . Come to the house of praise . . . No God but God . . ."

This would be the night prayer after the fourth hour, and the punctual Tatars would have changed their guard at the palace. Nial headed through the empty streets toward the height, dim against the stars. Skirting the wall of the Moslem cemetery, he began to ascend a long slope, guiding himself by a fire at the top.

Presently he could make out the helmets of soldiers squatting by the fire, and then their faces. His horse shied suddenly. Looking down, he made out a heap of dark objects that smelled of rotting bone. They were human heads, some shrunk to the bone and others picked bare by the kites. Tightening his rein, he rode past this place of execution, and was saluted by a solitary horseman who glanced at him, lifting his right hand and carrying it to his mouth.

"*Ahatou!*" Nial muttered acknowledgment.

He was by the outer guard, and the loom of rock walls fell behind him. His horse neighed as he trotted along the stone fence of a remount corral—the Horde kept its horses close at hand—and a mounted guard turned to watch him casually. Tron had told him how to go; by the well beyond the corral, past the barrack and the dark palace of Barka Khan, to the dome of the Altyn-dar.

When he reined in, with the mass of the dome over his head and a high, blank wall confronting him, he delayed an instant before dismounting. He could still turn back and ride down into Sarai, and every instinct in him cried out to do so. Narrow embrasures peered at him, like veiled eyes, and he knew that human eyes were watching him.

He had proof of this at once because the arched gate, looming black in the gray wall, creaked, and by the glimmer of his small lantern he saw one half of it swing toward him. It opened enough for a horse to pass through, and a Tatar with a shield came out and stood aside casually.

He could not hesitate, because uncertainty would bring questions that he could not answer. Swiftly he reflected that the men of the Horde went everywhere in the saddle, even from one end of a street to the other. And surely there would be other guards with lights somewhere within. This man could only be a gatekeeper. Nial urged his horse forward, bending his head under the arched portal.

He was in a square chamber with blank stone walls except on the right where an inclined way led gradually up.

Glancing over his shoulder, he saw the guard close the half of the gate and bar it. Lights gleamed at the head of the ramp a stone's throw away, and Nial started to ascend it, his ears strained for a challenge.

The darkness behind him remained soundless as a tomb. Nial noticed that narrow embrasures pierced the inner wall upon his left. And holes appeared in the arched ceiling. Arrows and fire could be showered upon any invaders of the ramp. His horse plodded up, switching his tail and pricking his ears forward. Torches flared and smoked above them at the head of the inclined way.

Here he was halted. A guard stepped forward and caught his rein. Nial swung down from his stirrup, rubbing his hands against his hips to dry them. Under his long blue coat hung his sheathed sword.

One of the Tatars called out, and the darkness of the ramp echoed in answer. Nial saw that in front of him a similar inclined way led down, and he wondered briefly what lay below. Then an officer confronted him with a guttural question.

Without hurrying, Nial drew the *paizah* from the breast of his coat. At once the Tatars, even the torch bearers, fell to their knees, lowering their heads to the floor. Nial forced himself to wait until the officer had risen; then he replaced the tablet, unhooked the lantern from his belt and turned to ascend the stairs on his left.

He moved stiffly as if he had been long in the saddle, and he did not look behind him.

"They may send an arrow or a man after me," he thought, "but at least they can't talk to me now."

At the turning of the stair he glanced down. The Tatars were tying the horse to a ring in the wall. Only the officer stared after him, as if puzzled. Nial drew a long breath of relief as he climbed the last steps. And then he stopped in his tracks.

Red eyes glared at him, and he lifted his lantern hastily. From a black basalt stand a green beast glimmered, and it was a moment before he saw that it was a grotesque lion of jade with rubies for eyes. And behind the lion appeared shapes out of a magician's dream.

The djinn himself might have brought his treasures to this House of Gold. Upon a table of clear crystal stood a horse so exquisitely wrought in gold, it must have been the work of Greek artists a thousand years before. Beyond the table were piled in haphazard fashion ivory images that must have come from an emperor's tomb. Against the wall stood great plaques of gold, set with lapis-lazuli.

Involuntarily he stopped to stare at a throne upon a dais of polished jasper. It was ebony inlaid with pearl, and its arms glowed with the violet-purple of amethysts. On the seat an empty skull gaped at him, and Nial was wondering if the skull was that of the monarch who had once sat upon the throne, when the shadows swayed and danced before him, although he had not moved his lantern.

He caught the pad-pad of felt boots behind him and saw a guard with drawn sword making toward him. When the Tatar came up, Nial was studying the white silk Tron had given him, as if verifying some list. When the guard would have come closer to stare at him, Nial turned, letting the man see the *paizah* hanging in plain sight on his chest.

"*Kai!*"

The man shrank back, falling to his knees. For awhile he waited, as if expecting a command, and then, as Nial took no notice of him, he hurried off toward distant voices.

As soon as he was out of sight, Nial sought for the jewel chamber beyond which the great emerald was kept. Tron's map had been carefully drawn, and he found himself at the entrance of the center room.

No need to search for the emerald. In the faint lantern light it gleamed at him from its dark marble base, which looked as if it had once been an altar. So fierce was the fire within it that the lantern seemed the dimmer of the two, and it was a moment before Nial could make out the crude lion's head into which the great jewel had been cut.

As he stepped forward he was aware of two things—the air felt fresher here and, except for some chests about the dark marble pedestal, the chamber was empty, quiet. Yet something stirred and something else creaked, as he stood before the marble. He stretched out his hand to pick up the emerald—but it was gone.

"The devil!" he cried involuntarily.

A black hole appeared in the marble where the emerald had been, and as Nial bent forward to peer into the hole the silence of the chamber was broken by a hissing chuckle.

He leaped back his own full length, for the sound had come from above. And then he threw down his lantern. For he had seen an opening in the ceiling above the marble stand. As his lantern went out an arrow crashed down, striking sparks from the floor where he had stood two seconds before.

Nial turned, plunging into the darkness among the piled-up treasures beyond. He stumbled against what seemed to be a pile of armor and stopped to listen.

High over his head something wailed up skyward and dwindled to a faint, clear whistle. And he heard a pounding of feet and shouting below him.

Even while he drew his sword from beneath his coat he frowned thoughtfully. The Tatars were not wont to make such a tumult, and it seemed to him he could hear weapons clashing far off.

"'Tis a very breeding place of spells," he muttered, seeking through the darkness for an embrasure.

Presently he came to one, a narrow slit for archers. And he stared out, amazed. Below him torches flamed and turbaned heads tossed. Steel flashed, and a great shout went up.

"*Yah Allah—il allah!*"

Down at the gate of the Altyn-dar massive iron thundered against wood. A ram, that would be. Nial saw one of the torchbearers below drop back with an arrow through his throat.

"Now this," he told himself, "is neither spell nor hocus. Faith, I had no hand in it."

Several Tatars with lights ran past without heeding him and disappeared down the stairs toward the entrance. Nial felt his way after them until he could look down upon the landing below.

Here the officer and a score of guards were working their bows at the embrasures, while his gray horse jerked restlessly at its tether. Nial realized that the Moslems were attacking the Altyn-dar in force.

"And so," he considered, "the fire burns hot and the pot boils apace."

If the Moslems had invaded the palace height, his life would be worth little outside these walls. While within, the Tatars would not be long in discovering his disguise and making him prisoner. The Green Lion lay beyond his reach. He could have filled his belt with jewels from a chest, unheeded, for by now all the guards must be in the fight below him. But he had no mind to loot like a bazaar thief, and to be caught like one.

Yet he did snatch up a shield, a heavy round shield embossed with silver, from a pile of armor on the landing. As he did so the gate of the House of Gold came down with a crash, and the Moslems outside roared in exultation.

Thrusting his arm into the shield, Nial ran down to the lower landing. He need hide behind a mask no longer. Now he would have to fight his way out.

The ramp was an inferno. Three deep the Tatars stood, shield to shield, across the inclined way, beating back the flood of Moslems that surged into the gate. Arrows hissed above them. Nial stopped short, seeing more Tatars trotting up out of the darkness on his left. They passed him on the landing and ran down into the fight. Nial had not seen them before among the guards and he thought they must have made their way into the Altyn-dar through another door. Loosing his horse and gripping the rein, Nial started down the other ramp, away from the tumult. If men were coming in, he might get out.

He had his hands full with the shield and the rearing horse, and he had to thrust his way blindly among the warriors. Then, around a turning, he saw a gray half light and came to an open postern. It was a moment before he could drag his horse into the narrow opening, and another moment before he could get a foot into the stirrup of the restless beast outside. He saw that they were in a walled garden, through which the Tatars were passing from their barracks. The postern was hidden by trees, and the Moslems did not seem to be aware of it.

Nial circled the garden, and the gray horse headed of its own accord out of a half-seen gate.

When houses closed in around him, Nial found himself in a quarter of the city he did not know. He turned to the right, seeking Mahmoud's horse market. Rounding a corner, he came suddenly upon torchlight and din. The gray charger swerved violently and brought up against another horse.

It was a Moslem's mount. Five other horsemen of Islam jostled each other and circled, to get at a solitary rider who had backed into an angle of the alley wall—a Tatar officer in a white camelhair *chaban*. Nial caught a glimpse of his lean, tense face, and the flash of precious stones upon the handguard of his long scimitar.

The Tatar, who had no shield, wielded his sword with desperate skill. As Nial rode into the fight he tossed the scimitar from his right to his left hand, as the Moslems drew back for an instant, and slashed open the face of one of his foes. But his horse was bleeding, staggering with weariness, and he could not hold off five men for long.

The Moslem beside Nial gave tongue.

"Yah hai!"

He swung up his curved blade, and Nial thrust up his shield to meet a blow that numbed his arm.

Before the Moslem could strike again, Nial had drawn his long sword.

Flushed, with glaring eyes, the Moslem pressed upon him, whirling high the short scimitar. Instead of guarding himself, Nial thrust with all his strength, the point of his straight blade passing through the other's thick beard and grating against bone. The man reared in his stirrups and came down against the wall when Nial jerked out his sword.

For the moment he was free and could have drawn out of the fight. But if he did so, the lone Tatar was doomed. Already the Moslems were baying like hounds before a kill.

"O dog—taste thou of death!"

And Nial went into the fight again. A Moslem wheeled to meet him, on his shield side. Nial was slashed on the hip and felt the frame of his shield snap. As the Moslem drove against him, knee to knee, Nial smashed his broken shield into the panting face. Drawing back his sword, he thrust through the man's ribs, and the rider of the black horse laughed beside him.

Then Nial's horse, flicked by a saber, reared frantically, trying to turn against the wall. He grasped at his reins, slippery with blood, expecting to be slashed with steel. But only two men remained to face the gallant Tatar and, as Nial reined his horse forward again, they turned and fled. Through the sweat that dripped into his eyes he saw that both were wounded.

The Tatar of the white *chaban* looked at him curiously and smiled. *"Ahatou!"*

He said something else, pointing to the alley behind them. A Tatar mounted patrol had halted to peer in at the fighting. The rider of the black horse wheeled to meet them.

But Nial had no wish to be questioned by the Tatars. He galloped into the darkness after the two wounded men.

Behind the lattice of the house of Mahmoud the Blind, Shedda crouched in fear. The night was full of new sounds and perils, and she listened as heedfully as any animal in a cage.

Men were looting the horse market, while Tatar houses burned. A distant wailing of women told of other plundering. A boy rode by on a soldier's horse with a sable cloak over his knee, shouting with all his lungs:

"Allah hath opened the gates of plunder. O brothers, come forth!"

A beggar hurried beneath the balcony, clutching a silk dress. There were dark stains upon the silk. At the corner he ran into another thief. There was an oath and a blow, and one of the shadows screeched. The alley men were out with knives to snatch what they could.

Anxiously the girl looked toward the palace height. The torches thronging into the House of Gold looked like fireflies at that distance. She knew the Moslems must have forced their way in; and if they took the House of Gold they would have in their hands the treasure of the khan. Such a victory would bring new allies out of the rabble, and all Sarai would be looted.

"Yield thyself, O red she-tiger," a mocking voice cried up at her. "We know thou art the slave of the pagan khan. Verily, Yashim longs for thee. He will prepare needles to take sight from thine eyes that were the eyes of the khan who now lies slain in the mud."

Stifling an exclamation, Shedda drew back from the lattice. Two men had stopped beneath the balcony. She heard them pass around the corner and enter the courtyard, and she wondered if they had been taunting her idly, or if they had come in search of her. To flee out of the house into the streets would be madness. She burrowed among the cushions and held her breath to listen.

Hoofs clattered on loose stones below, and someone shouted. Steel clashed once, and footsteps hastened away. Then the courtyard became silent.

"O Shedda," a deep voice called, "I have come hither for thee."

The girl wrapped her *khalat* about her and hastened down the stair. Here was a shield for her, and a strong arm to strike for her. She greeted him softly.

"O lordling Ni-al, I was in sore need of thee." Then she caught her breath, peering up at him. "What is this? Hast thou changed thy shape?"

"Aye," said Nial.

Shedda saw no sign of the Moslems. Nor was any one else with the tall Christian. And the girl felt that, by changing his shape, this man with the long sword in his hand had become grim and purposeful.

"Why hast thou come for me?"

"I gave thee a promise." Nial threw the rein over the head of a horse he had seized on the way. "I saw the talisman, the dagger that bears the sign of the khan. Knowing that thou didst serve the khan, I feared for thee, alone among the Moslems."

"Death is near us." The girl caught his hand in hers, as a frightened child might have done. "What can we do?" A moment before she had known terror, and the chill of it was still about her heart.

"We can go from here."

He lifted her into the saddle of the other horse, and while she pulled a heavy veil over her head and long hair, he mounted the tired gray charger. Through the dark alleys he led the way to Tron's quarters. But the chamber was empty, without a sign of the merchant.

Nial did not want to take refuge behind a door. If the Moslems became masters of Sarai, nothing was more certain than that they would hunt down all unbelievers, and he knew what the sack of a city meant. Better to try his luck with Shedda in the open.

In the courtyard the girl greeted him excitedly.

"Listen! An arrow has called."

That part of Sarai was nearly quiet, and presently Nial heard very faintly the long drawn whistle that had startled him in the Altyn-dar. It rose into the air, dwindled, then sounded clearly again.

"A Tatar arrow, a whistling arrow," she explained eagerly. "A summons to rally, to come together."

She urged her horse out into an open space, where frightened Armenians huddled like sheep around a bearded priest, waiting for misfortune. Shedda peered over the housetops and cried out. High on the palace height a white ball of light shone.

"The great lantern is lighted. And Barka Khan has come. *Akh!* He is here now." She clapped her hands eagerly, and the shaggy heads of the Armenians turned toward her fearfully. "O ye People of the Book," she cried at them, "now there will truly be fighting."

They looked at her, voiceless with new fear, but Nial made up his mind.

"Take me to this khan of thine," he said.

"Aye, what else?" Shedda was aglow with hope, and he wondered a little at that. "Now thou art a Tatar, Ni-al, and the khan loves a good swordsman. Come!" And they put their horses to a gallop, for speed was the best safeguard. She explained, "The light is over the dome of the House of Gold, and there the *noyons* of the Horde will gather at the signal. I know a way into the dome that leads not through any gate. This way!"

No one tried to halt them because the girl chose narrow streets where only men on foot were seen, and these gave way readily to two galloping horses. When they passed the cemetery, the girl reined in her horse and entered a garden.

They tied the tired animals in a clump of cypress, and Shedda slipped through the cypresses to the hillside beyond, where white marble appeared in the dark earth.

"This is a door known to few, only to those who bear the Lion or the Falcon. But that is a thing beyond thy knowing, my lordling." She laughed and pressed against one side of the marble with her hands. "Why, it is open. One has gone in before us. Come, thou."

Impatiently she caught his hand and led him into darkness, until she paused to feel about the wall on one side.

"Here should be a lantern. What art thou doing?"

Nial was cutting the cord that secured the *paizah* about his neck. He cast the bronze tablet into the mouth of the passage behind him.

"I threw away a cord that might have strangled me."

The girl's soft fingers touched his face and felt for his arm.

"We must be quick. Here is dry flax and steel and flint. Canst thou make it light?"

Sheathing his sword, Nial took the implements and began to strike sparks. He was rid of the *paizah*, and his Tatar dress could cause no harm now if he were brought into the House of Gold by this girl who knew the secret of the hill passage. When the flax broke into flame, she held out a hand lamp, shaking it to make sure there was oil in it, and lighted the wick.

"Now we will find the khan," she promised, smiling.

And when Shedda smiled, with her veil thrown back over the red-gold mass of her hair, she was lovely beyond belief. Excitement brightened her clear eyes and brought the color into her cheeks.

"Aye, lead the way."

But Shedda laughed, running ahead, the scent of flowers hanging in the air behind her. Nial had to quicken his pace to keep up with her.

The passage ascended steadily, turning often. Its stone walls rumbled faintly with echoes of trampling feet outside. Nial noticed that wet tracks of a man's riding boots went before them. A Tatar wearing high heels had passed that way within the hour.

"Now are we in the House of Gold," Shedda called to him, "but none can see us. Those who are trusted by the khan come in this way, and only the watchers under the dome know of its inner door. *They* do not speak."

Lifting the lamp, she nodded at the massive foundation walls of a square chamber into which the tunnel had led them. From one corner a spiral stair led up, winding into a passage so narrow that Nial had to turn his shoulders to enter. Shedda tripped ahead of him, around turn after turn, until she stopped at a door of heavy wood.

"We are under the dome," she whispered. "I can hear the *noyons* talking, so we are safe, O my lord of battles."

Setting down the lamp, she turned to Nial, so close that her fragrant hair brushed his cheek, and her eyes caressed his. Swiftly her parted lips brushed his cheek, and she smiled as if rewarding a child. Then she lifted her hand and struck the bronze knocker upon the door four times, then thrice slowly.

Steps approached the door, a lock clicked faintly, and the passage was flooded with white light. Nial and Shedda entered the very heart of the treasure house. And the girl drew from her breast a bronze tablet smaller than the one Nial had discarded, bearing on it a falcon's head. At sight of it two tall Chinese guards bowed and stepped back.

"*Ai!*" Shedda cried. "The khan is not here."

There were officers standing at embrasures, and boxes of messenger pigeons by the walls. Couriers came and went by other doors, and the place was tense with the suspense of battle dimly heard in the night. Sharp exclamations echoed under the immense dome that formed the walls and roof of this lofty post of command. The white light came from a ball of malachite or painted glass hung under the summit of the dome, and Nial saw that this summit was an opening to the sky. Perhaps astrologers used the dome, or messenger pigeons came in through the aperture, he conjectured; but Shedda was too occupied in listening to the rapid talk of the Tatars to explain. No one heeded him for the moment, and he went to an embrasure to look out.

Far down the palace height, beyond the wall, a line of torches flared and shifted. Masses of Tatar cavalry moved downward against the light, and volleys of arrows flickered from them. They were outnumbered by the mobs below them, but they were gaining ground. Fighting was going on in the cemetery. The Moslems had been driven out of the House of Gold, out of the palace height.

Nial watched, until the torches broke up into little groups in the alleys of Sarai below him, or died out, and the roar of conflict dwindled to a murmur.

"Barka Khan did that." Shedda, at his elbow, had guessed his thoughts. "In the moment when Yashim and his friends were in the very treasure house, he came and took command and led an attack. Even the watchers of the Green Lion took up arms to follow him. Look!"

She led Nial to the center of the floor and pointed down through a square aperture. Then she cried out, bending down to see more clearly what lay below. Nial peered over her shoulder.

The white light above him penetrated through the aperture to the floor below. Directly under Nial stood a black marble shaped like an altar, and sprawled out before it lay the body of Paolo Tron the Genoese, the tufted end of a great arrow projecting from his chest. One hand clutched the base of the marble, and his teeth gleamed through the tangle of his red beard.

"Thy companion!" The girl shivered and turned to speak to one of the Chinese archers. "He says that Tron ran into the chamber of the khan's jewels when the Moslems broke into the upper floor. An emerald called the Green Lion was kept upon that marble, twice guarded. If a thief approached it, by stepping upon the stone before it, he released a spring that let the emerald fall into a cavity below the marble stand. And these Cathayan bowmen keep watch over the khan's jewels. They are ordered to shoot down anyone unknown to them who enters that room. They say Tron searched about the marble as if mad—"

One of the Chinese caught her arm and drew her back, while Nial stared down at the dead merchant. So Tron had come himself for the great emerald, and since he had come with the Moslems, he had known of the attack to be launched upon the House of Gold. But he had not warned Nial. He had feared that the Tatars would make off with the khan's jewels, or that the Moslem onset would fail, and he had sent Nial ahead to carry off the emerald.

Nial's brain was weary, and his wounds in forearm and thigh ached. He saw that Shedda was staring at him strangely, while the Tatar officers were crowding around him. Some of them spoke to him, but the girl thrust her way to his side.

"O Ni-al," she cried, "these watchers of Cathay say that thou didst come earlier in the night and try to take the emerald. Others say thou didst show a *shir-paizah* at the gate. How—"

One of the officers brushed her aside and growled a question at the Christian. When Nial did not answer, he reached out and tore open the throat of his coat. Finding no trace of the *paizah*, he snarled and reached for the Christian's sword. But Nial was not minded to give up his weapon. He sprang back and set his shoulders against the door of the passage by which he had entered. He felt behind him and pushed against the door, but found that it had been locked.

Instead of closing in on him, the Tatars stood rigid in their tracks. Even the Chinese bowmen turned and bent their heads before a man who had entered alone, muddy to the waist, with a white camelskin *chaban* flung over his wide shoulders. His cheeks were gaunt, and a stain of dried blood ran from his thin lips to his wide chin. But his eyes, restive as a hawk's, fastened instantly upon Nial.

"Throw down thy weapon!" Shedda besought Nial. "The khan—it is death to hold a drawn weapon near him." And as Nial, with set face, clasped his sword grimly, she began to wail. "*Ai-a!* Fool—bringer of misfortune!"

Nial recognized the khan as the Tatar who had been at bay before six foemen in the alley.

But Shedda flung herself on her knees before the tall master of the Horde, fearing for her life. She had brought the Christian hither, vouching for him at the door, and now he stood armed against the most dreaded soul of the steppes.

"O lord of the West and the East," she cried, "O Victorious Lion—"

A gesture from Barka Khan, who understood Arabic, brushed away her praise of him. The girl, however, had thought of a way to clear herself of blame, and her voice shrilled on:

"My Khan, this man is a foe. I drew his secret from him, and kept watch upon him, until I brought him hither to thee. He is a Nazarene from the West like that other, his comrade who lies dead below us, but skilled in swordplay. He changed his shape and came to open the gate to thy foes the Moslems. He carried a *shir-paizah*—" her quick wit seized upon a faint memory—"which he threw away at the mouth of the dome passage. Now behold him, at thy mercy."

Barka Khan drew the soggy gloves from his hands and let them fall in silence.

"Hast thou a witness?" he asked the girl after a moment.

"Aye, my Khan." Shedda looked up at him reverently. "Mardi Dobro, the reader of omens."

"He is at the gate. Bring him."

When a warrior ran from the chamber to seek Mardi Dobro, the khan took a cup from the hand of a servant and drank a little. Holding the cup, he walked quietly to Nial, even coming within arm's reach although his scimitar was in its sheath at his side.

"Thou hast heard—understood? What word hast thou to say?"

Nial smiled wearily. What could he say? Shedda's betrayal would stand against any denial.

"I came," he said bluntly, "knowing naught of the Moslems. I came to steal the great emerald called the Green Lion for this other man, who was my friend."

For a moment the dark eyes of the Tatar lord met the blue eyes of the crusader's son. Then he turned on his heel to go and stare down the opening at Tron's body.

The color came again into Shedda's cheeks. Even the dead Genoese served to prove her tale, and she relied upon Mardi Dobro's cunning. When the shaman entered, the khan turned upon him instantly.

"What is this man, O interpreter of omens, who hath changed his shape and now stands before me with a drawn sword?"

A single glance told Mardi Dobro the story of Nial's set face and the anger of the Tatars. Running forward, he threw himself down before the khan, beating his shaggy head against the floor. His wrinkled face tensed with anxiety, for Barka Khan was the only human being the shaman feared.

"At the Sea Gate," he croaked, "I beheld this youth land from the sea, bearing this sword. In that hour I read the omen of the fire upon bone. Clearly I saw the sign, that this sword was bound up with thy life, as an arrow with its feather."

The listeners edged closer, for this was a strange sign that had proved true. Even Barka Khan was deeply attentive.

"For good or evil?" he asked.

Mardi Dobro's green eyes gleamed shrewdly.

"For evil," he lied. "Behold, I warned thee of perils gathering, rising against thee, and now is this sword come against thee, as the sign foretold."

Nial tightened his muscles, to await the speeding of an arrow from the long bows of the Chinese guards who had drawn near him, weapons in hand. Barka Khan struck his hands together in anger.

"This night," the khan said grimly, "there has been too much changing of shapes. I have listened to words that hide like foxes in tall grass. Thy words—" he turned to Shedda—"were lies. This bearer of a sword was not among the Moslems; he was beside me. And thy sign," he added to the startled shaman, "was false. The sword struck down two of my foemen, giving me life."

He strode to Nial and touched his arm.

"The khan does not turn his face from one who has shed blood for him. I know naught of what is behind thee. It is like a mist over the water. Now sheath thy sword and fear not. Thou hast taken the shape of a *gur-khan* of my guard. Be one. But—" he smiled slightly—"do not change thy shape again."

Shedda tried to touch the edge of his *chaban*, and Mardi Dobro muttered frantically, but Barka Khan heeded them no more than the stones of the floor. He had been six days and almost as many nights in the saddle; he had cut his way through the streets of Sarai to get here. He had been wounded more than once, and had hours of fighting ahead before he could rest.

"Come to me," he said over his shoulder to Nial, "after the time water takes to boil."

One of the officers brought a cup of spiced wine to Nial, and another asked if he would accept a horse, a Kabarda.

Nial sheathed his sword, emptied the cup and drew a long breath.

"Aye," he said.

With the *noyons* of the khan, he went from the chamber under the dome. Gray light filtered through the embrasures, and sunlight flashed upon a distant snowy peak. The giant Chinese resumed their vigil, and quiet settled down upon the House of Gold. Shedda clutched her cloak about her, shivering. She lived, but she had been scorned by Barka Khan, who had not even troubled to slay her; and Nial no longer had eyes for her beauty.

"Fool, and son of a witless dog," she whispered at the shaman, "to lie to thy lord. He spoke the truth."

But Mardi Dobro did not hear her. In stricken silence he was turning over between his fingers the shoulder bone of a sheep that had prevailed against the power of armed men and his own cunning.

The Long Sword

It was a time of hunger in the dry lands. When the Yamanite rode in with a bit of news, he bargained for it shrewdly, being hungry himself.

"Six riding camels they have, and twenty good horses," he said. And he watched the gray eyes of the man sitting above him in a chair. But the eyes told him nothing. "Aye, tents in the baggage, and women slaves," he added, for good measure.

"It is more likely," put in Khalil from across the table, "that thou art lying."

"Nay, I saw them. I counted them." The lean Arab from Yaman bent closer to the chair of the lord of the castle and whispered, "*Yah khawand*, it is truly an escort. It is not a raiding party. Perhaps they are escorting the family of an emir of the Hauran. That would be good plunder for thee, O my master."

"Where," asked Khalil again, "is this notable caravan?"

"In the valley—" began the Arab, and remembered to guard his secret. He thrust thin arms from his rags. "Is it not enough that I have sworn upon the Koran? Now—listen, ye Christian folk—I swear by the oath of the divorce. If this thing that I say be not true, may my wives be divorced."

Khalil laughed, but the man in the chair stirred his long length.

"How many men?" he asked briefly.

Swiftly the Arab counted upon his fingers.

"More than thirty, O my lord, and less than forty, good and bad. But the horses are worth a risk."

Sir John drew patterns in the spilled wine on the table. The hall in which the three were sitting—he, Khalil, his friend, and the strange Arab—had nothing to cover its bare stones, stained with smoke. The carpets under his feet were loot taken from Moslem caravans. The big chest behind him

held nothing within it, more than a few sword blades and silver cups.
Money he had not, that was certain.

"And what is to be the payment," he observed to the desert man, "for
thy news?"

"I will guide thee to the halting place of the caravan, and a fifth of
everything taken is my just due."

"*Y'allah!*" cried Khalil. "O God!"

"However," said the Arab, "I will leave the small matter of payment
to the measure of my lord. Men say that the Long Sword hath a generous hand."

Sir John, whose name among the Arabs was the Long Sword, glanced
out of the narrow arrow slit into the midday glare of the courtyard. Gray
lizards scurried about the cracks in the stones, and black goats nosed in
the shadows for the grass that had been plentiful enough after the last
rains, but which was now an idle dream. He had been obliged to send his
cattle to a distant valley, trusting to Providence that his Moslem neighbors would not discover the herd. His sheep were scattered all through
the *wadis,* keeping alive somehow or other.

No rain had fallen that season in the desert beyond the river Jordan,
and his wheat had dried in the earth. A month ago he had gone to Jerusalem to try to sell his sheep, without avail. He had gone to the abbot of
Mount Sion to borrow a sum of money until the next rains, but the abbot would not lend to any one who held a castle on the border, beyond
Jordan. The risk was too great. And Sir John of the Mount knew himself
poverty-ridden at last.

True, he had the Mount, a tawny mass of stones upon the limestone
butte above the sycamore grove. A fair, strong castle, it was—the stones
cracked by siege and by sun, yet still intact. His father, coming overseas
in the crusade, had built it and now lay buried beside his mother under
the stone flags of the chapel.

The Mount was manor of a thousand acres. Without rain, the land yielded
nothing, and the granary held only dust. The Moslems had cut down his
orchards in the last raid at harvest time, and the olive groves belonged to
his Arab villagers whose domed huts clustered by the sycamores and the
well below the Mount. The young Lord of the Mount lived alone—so lonely
that no priest cared to keep up the service of his little chapel.

Sir John, being noted for his skill with the sword, might have gained
gear and gold and men to follow him, if he sold his sword to one of the
great princes of Antioch or Acre.

But this was his manor and his birthplace. He had learned to cling to the back of his pony here not so many years ago; he had led his dogs in the hunt through the shrub pines by the high road from Damascus. And John of the Mount came from a breed of men who do not leave their land.

He needed sorely those twenty horses and anything else the caravan might have. But it puzzled him. Good horses, pavilions, slaves, a strong escort—that might mean a woman. Yet why had the escort halted within his lands, even for the noon rest?

Silently he summed up the chances. He thought the Yamanite was speaking the truth. If the Arab had offered to lead them to the caravan without reward he would have suspected a trick. The trouble was, he had not men enough—even to garrison the Mount properly. If he left old Renald and five archers to watch the castle, he would have Khalil and six men-at-arms, mounted, with the usual volunteers among the Arab swordsmen of the village, who would pillage with a will but would not stand to fight. Not enough to overpower the caravan escort. And yet, Sir John had no mind to let a chance slip by.

"We will go and see if thou art lying," he said to the strange Arab. "Khalil, let him eat first."

"And my reward, O Master of the Long Sword?"

"Thou wilt come with us," said Sir John. "And thy reward will be as God wills."

For leagues around the Mount the surface of the earth was gashed by rocky ravines known as *wadis*, through which ran streams in a time of rains. But now the *wadis* were dry and empty. On the plateau above them the intolerable midafternoon sun glowed against the white limestone and yellow clay. Sir John wore the native *khoufie* over his light steel helm, and over his shoulders a heavy black cloak to shield his mail from the sun's touch.

Under the drapery, his face was lined and somber, his harsh lips unsmiling. He watched for his sheep and saw nothing of them, and knew that they had been driven off by raiders, or by his own shepherds. When he came to the deep ravine the Arab pointed out he rode slowly and drew rein at its edge. For a moment the men from the Mount stared down into the shimmering glare and the dense shadows.

"What is thy name?" Khalil asked the ragged tribesman.

The Yamanite responded absently:

"Malik ibn malik, Ibrahim ibn Sulaiman al Akabi."

"Son of Solomon thou mayest be, O Ibrahim," murmured Khalil, "but thou art a very father of lies. The caravan is not here."

"It was here—yonder in the shadow by the well that is the Well of Moses."

"Then it must have grown wings like the angels and flown elsewhere. Thou hast brought us to the wrong *wadi*—"

"Am I a fat sheep, not to know one place from another? Go and look at the dung of the beasts—"

"And am I a blind she-dog, to put my nose into a trap—"

"Peace, ye addleheads!" said Sir John, who had satisfied himself that the valley was empty. "We will go over and look at the road."

He was thinking of his sheep as he led the way along a cattle path that kept clear of the heights without descending into the gullies where they might have been set upon by the unseen Moslems. The path ended upon the shoulder of a hill and the young knight uttered an exclamation.

"Yonder is the caravan."

Under their feet wound the narrow high road and, beyond it, in the shadow of a cliff, stood two silk pavilions. Horses—a score of them—were tethered beneath some olive trees. Men walked about idly, or stretched out in the sand. But the men wore cloaks and hose, and crossbows and spears were stacked by the baggage. Ibrahim squinted at them and shook his gray head.

"Nay, my lord, this is another caravan. Certainly these are Franks."*

"Merchants," added Khalil, eagerly. "By the Lord, those are princely tents. Let us cross the road at another place and drop down upon them from the height."

Nothing would have suited him better, for Khalil was a Kurd of the north, with all the courtesy and the predatory instinct of his people. He had lingered at the Mount as a guest and he knew that the Christian barons of Jerusalem were not reluctant to glean plunder from passing merchants. But Sir John cantered down to the road.

The men in the camp took notice, running out and snatching up shield and bow, while a slender figure in black emerged from one of the pavilions beneath a parasol held by a slave.

"Who comes?" the man in black hailed the horsemen in Arabic.

---

*Christians from Europe.

"John of the Mount of Moab, vassal of the King of Jerusalem."

"Then throw back your pagan hood," the voice responded in Norman French. "And bid your children yonder keep their distance."

But the Arabs who had followed Sir John lingered down the road of their own accord. He did not dismount, although he pulled his horse into a walk, and the men from the castle did likewise. For the youth in black seemed half minded to greet them with crossbow bolts. He stood his ground, staring at them coolly, clad in immaculate velvet, a heavy silver chain at his bare throat. An older man, even more richly dressed, had come out and seated himself in an armchair. Sir John knew them to be Venetians from the coast cities.

"The Lord of Mocenigo," said the youth of the chain briefly, "Comptore of Acre, and my father. What is your wish, Sir John?"

He spoke with the harsh accent of an Italian, and the careless arrogance of a Venetian who knew himself superior in wealth and culture to the rude crusaders.

The elder Mocenigo leaned on his staff, without words. But Sir John's eyes were upon the other pavilion.

The girl who stood there under the entrance canopy might have come from paradise itself. Not in all his years had the knight of Moab land seen such red-gold hair, shimmering against the blue of her robe. The young Mocenigo glanced over his shoulder and smiled—

"It is evident, good sir, you are not blind."

But the girl spoke impatiently.

"Is this the escort? Now by my faith, they are infidels and I like them not."

"Infidels they may be, my lady—" the younger Mocenigo bowed—"but escort of yours they are not. You will not find us so lacking in courtesy or care of you."

John of the Mount felt his cheeks grow warm. He had no skill in such polite phrases of cultured folk. He kneed his horse forward—he had not been invited to join the strangers, even to have a cup of wine. And still he stared down at the girl of the red-gold hair. Surely, so clear was her skin, she must be a newcomer in Palestine. He had not heard such a voice in all Jerusalem. And, with her eyes upon him, he felt himself grimy and ill at ease, and he did not wonder that his men seemed to her no better than a Moslem crew.

"Where i' God's name are you going?" he asked bluntly.

"To my uncle at Kerak," she said, "if it please you."

And he thought that she had no liking for his words. So he turned to the younger Italian.

"Then have you come upon the wrong road. Kerak castle lieth behind you." And when they were silent, he added, "It were best to take shelter at the Mount for the night."

"We give you thanks," said the young Mocenigo, "but we are camped here; and as for the road, we follow our own."

"Under whose safeguard?"

The Italian shrugged impatiently.

"This lady hath need of no safeguard where Christians hold the land, and my father is known from Aleppo to the desert. We need not Michael the archangel, nor his flaming sword."

And it seemed to the knight that he was being mocked. Again he dared question the fair girl who stood before the two older women—servants by the look of them.

"This uncle of yours, demoiselle—how is he named?"

"You should know well his name," she replied instantly with a toss of her small head, "for he is the Lord of Kerak, and I have come from Chatillon to take shelter in his great hall."

The Venetian had spoken truly. Reginald of Chatillon was the most powerful of the barons who held the frontier, and more than once John of the Mount had gone with him on foray or battle quest.

"Is it your way, messire," she went on, "to ask such questions of those who fare past your hold?"

When she spoke to him, John of the Mount felt disturbed and irresolute in mind. Now he could not think of any words at all, and the younger Mocenigo smiled. Seeing this, the knight turned to him and dismounted.

"A word with you, messire."

Into the other pavilion he strode, flinging himself down upon an ebony bench. The air of the darkened tent was fragrant with the scent of sandal, the walls were hung with silk saddlebags, and serviceable chests stood against the two sleeping pallets. Upon one of these the old Mocenigo seated himself, caressing the ivory head of his staff, his eyes moving restlessly from his son to Khalil, who had chosen to sit unbidden in the shade of the entrance, and then to the giant Italian crossbowman who came to stand behind Khalil. The Mocenigo sire understood no Norman speech.

"Have you come hither, in truth," Sir John broke the constrained silence, "without the protection of the Moslems—of the Emir of Damascus?"

The youth looked at him curiously.

"Why should we pay for a safeguard we need not? And what, pray, is this word of yours we fain must hear? I have little joy i' this talk."

"Be that as it may, you are now upon my lands."

"The Well of Moses is yours?"

"The well here, at this spot, is dry. The Well of Moses lies a half league distant. Now this must be said between us: your men are not at home in this country, and you stand in peril of your lives. For yourselves I care not. But for the woman who is the niece of Kerak, I do care. Even now a Moslem caravan is within sight—know ye that?"

"By Saint Bacchus, I did not."

Many things were clear to the knight. These merchants had left the proper road; they had camped at a dry well. Strong as their following might be—they had nearly forty men-at-arms—they did not seem fit for desert travel. But the cold faces of the Italians were set against his warning. In this day and place no man might trust a stranger. Along the frontier few could be found who would not sell their kin for a good price.

"It is clear to me—" Sir John looked from one to the other—"that I must guard the demoiselle across the desert to Kerak."

"What would be our surety, if we yielded her to you?"

"My word."

"Undoubtedly, your word is good." The younger Mocenigo smiled. "But we have pledged the patriarch of Jerusalem to deliver the maid, unharmed, to the Lord of Kerak—since we are journeying thither."

Sir John was silent a moment.

"Then," he said reluctantly, "I must join your company with my men."

The two Italians spoke together swiftly, and the elder fumbled in his cloak. He took out a small leather wallet, loosening the cord and letting a stream of coins run into his other hand. Replacing the gold, he tied the wallet and thrust it across the table to the knight. Sir John looked up inquiringly.

"Messire," said the younger merchant, "this is payment for intrusion upon your lands and for your trouble, otherwise. We have no need of your escort to Kerak."

The gray eyes of the swordsman gleamed, and again his cheeks flushed dark. He picked up the wallet, weighed it in his hand and tossed it across the table. Then he left the tent, summoning Khalil from an interested inspection of the Italian crossbow. The Kurd, after a glance at his companion's face, strode after him silently.

"Where is Ibrahim?" the knight asked.

Khalil nodded toward the horses. Ibrahim had taken possession of the rein of Sir John's charger and was squatting in the nearest shade, thus establishing in the eyes of the distant Arabs his right to serve the Lord of the Mount. He rose when the knight approached and held the stirrup.

"Ibrahim," said Sir John, "knowest thou this sword?" And he touched the steel pommel of the weapon at his side.

The sword, a long, curved saber of Damascus make, was an old blade, inlaid with gold, although hilt and pommel were plain. It had a broad head, sweeping to the point, and men said they had seen its owner take it within his fingers and bend point to pommel.

"Aye, verily," said Ibrahim.

"Then wilt thou feel it within thy ribs if thou liest to me, now." Sir John spoke under his breath, but the old Arab shivered. "These Franks of the caravan say that no Moslems have been seen near here. If thou hast lied in the first place, it is forgiven. Confess, and I shall not lay hand upon thee. But if now thou liest, it shall be as I said. So bethink thee and say truly whether the Moslem horsemen were by the Well of Moses."

The tribesman breathed deep, and his bent fingers twisted in the strands of his gray beard.

"All things are appointed by Allah," he replied wearily. "And it may be that this is the hour and place appointed for my death." He looked up into the crusader's eyes. "I know not what these others say, but I saw the camels and the men as I told thee."

Sir John gripped the pommel of his sword, then his hand dropped and he called to his men to mount and ride off.

"Nay, not to the road—to the gully yonder."

"What is upon thee?" Khalil asked; and added, "Why didst thou throw back the gold? It was a good sum."

"It would have made me no better than a dog," the crusader responded through set teeth. "And now there is trouble upon my head. Tell me, canst thou manage thy horse at all times?"

"Can I breathe?" Khalil wondered. "Can—"

"Then mount thy saddle and keep close behind me, and be ready to ride off at any instant. But go into the ravine after the others. Is this clear to thee?"

"Aye, certainly," muttered the Kurd, his lean face alight with curiosity.

For a moment Sir John surveyed the bare stretch of the road, the deepening shadow of the cliff, where the Italian men-at-arms loitered, having put down their weapons at the departure of the strangers. He even looked up at the summit of the cliff, and at the young Mocenigo who stood talking to the girl at the pavilion. Leading his charger, he went toward them slowly, Khalil pacing behind him.

"Demoiselle," he said, "it is time to bid farewell."

Her brow puckered a little, as if she were trying to see the face under the shadow of the white silk.

"And yet—" she smiled—"I would not have thee leave, messire, without a cup of wine."

Although Mocenigo seemed ill pleased, she took a silver goblet from the serving woman and held it out toward him.

"Nay—" he laughed—"'tis time for thee to bid farewell to these others." And he tossed the goblet to the ground, slipping the rein over his arm. Bending forward swiftly, he caught her about the knees and the waist—turned and thrust her up, into Khalil's arms. "Now, ride," he said.

He moved aside as Mocenigo, snatching out a poniard, struck at him. Khalil, astonished, gripped his prize in a sinewy arm and wheeled his plunging horse. The crusader's charger snorted and started forward as the rein was slipped over his head. Sir John got a foot in the stirrup and was in the saddle when the Italian threw the long knife. It slapped into the crusader's cloak, the point catching in the links of his mail. Another moment, and the two horsemen were galloping clear of the tents.

"Bows!" screamed Mocenigo. "A thousand pieces to the knave who brings down a horse!"

But it took time to wind the crossbows and when the first quarrels whined in the air the riders were passing out of range. And it took longer to saddle the horses, so that the two had joined their men in the ravine before the Italians were able to go after them through the turns of the gully.

"I will take the maid," Sir John said then, "and do thou look to it that they do not press us too close."

"By the Lord," grumbled Khalil, "thou art a fool not to have taken the gold instead."

Marguerite de Chatillon brushed some of the dust from the solitary bench with the edge of her skirt and sat down. She was quite sore in her slender waist and knees, because it is no light matter to be carried at a gallop over rough country. Moreover, she was very hot. The cool air in the dark tower chamber felt pleasant after the sun, but it did not quench her anger.

Everything in the cell, from the hard pallet to the crucifix on the wall, was coated with dust; and Marguerite had searched in vain for a mirror. The single narrow embrasure overlooked a courtyard full of noisy infidels and clattering men-at-arms—quite different from the quiet garden and the cloisters of Mount Sion. Marguerite sat very still and thought. When she heard a knock at the door, she shook her tawny hair back from her shoulders, and said quietly—

"Come in."

She was more than ready to speak her mind to the lord of this tower.

But a native woman appeared, her bare feet moving noiselessly over the stones. She carried clean linen and a mattress stuffed with straw and, after staring without any evidence of pleasure at the girl, she proceeded to make up the bed. A second woman entered with a silver tray bearing wine and grapes and a bowl of water. This Marguerite did not touch. Presently they came back hurriedly with a towel and a parchment book.

When they had gone, the girl picked up the book and opened the stiff pages. It was a book of psalms, and music. She replaced it on the stand and, since she did not cease to be thirsty, she had reached for the wine when Sir John came in.

She knew his height and his stride and the long sword in the curved leather sheath, although he was now fully clad in mail and he had discarded his headdress for a battle casque. Because this was a solid cylinder of steel with only a narrow slit before the eyes, she could see nothing of his face. So, she thought, he had the manner of a brigand, to enter a woman's chamber wearing his helm. But she said nothing at all.

"Will you not take some wine?" he muttered, standing rigid before her.

"I thank you—I will not," and she took up the psalter, turning the leaves indifferently. And when Sir John continued to watch her in silence, she went on, as if to make conversation, "Know ye, Sir Rogue, that the

Lord of Kerak will come with his spears and break through this tower of yours, pulling stone from stone. He will hang your men and take your life for this hour's work."

The man in armor seemed to ponder this.

"He could do all of that," he said, "but I do not think he will." And he went over to inspect the bed. "Is this comfortable?"

Receiving no answer, he explained.

"This place is the priest's hole. We have had no woman at the Mount for years, and so we lack woman's gear of all kind. The Arab wenches say they have no sugared fruits or tidbits of such nature. But if you will tell me, demoiselle, what other articles you may need—"

"Where are the chains?" she asked hotly.

"Chains—chains? Why, you may walk where you will!"

"Even from the gate?"

"Aye so, but not this day. The Venetians will be coming hither. But when we are rid of them, I will find you a fair horse, and the Mount lacks not falcons or hunting dogs for your sport."

"It is a most hospitable place," she assented. "But I find these same merchants more chivalrous than the Lord of the Mount, since they will adventure their lives for my sake."

If she could have seen Sir John's face then she would have known that he was sorely troubled and ill at ease. He had come to reassure the girl, but her talk of chains and chivalry set him aback. He knew so little of the language of romance.

"They must *needs* do it," he corrected. "If I have judged them aright. Did not they ask the patriarch to allow you to travel with them?"

Taking her silence for consent, he went on thoughtfully:

"This must be said. The Venetians were leagues from their proper road, and they told you they awaited an escort. Well, that is true. The Yamanite swore to me that he had seen such an escort waiting at the Well of Moses—a Moslem caravan, equipped for a woman's travel. Now the Venetians came to a dry well, which they took to be the Well of Moses. They would not come to the Mount for protection, nor accept aid from me. I could no longer linger in the plain with the Moslem riders within smell. So I carried you hither, demoiselle."

The demoiselle sat up very straight and opened her lips twice before she uttered a word.

"That is a clown's tale—a most stupid mummer's gibe. Why did you bring me hither?"

"So that you would not be sold to a Moslem emir. The Venetians could have gained eight thousand gold *byzants* by selling you."

"For me—eight thousand pieces of gold?" She shook her head slowly. "Nay, that is surely false. No slave would bring such a price."

"You are fairer than any woman who ever set foot beyond the sea. God knows the truth of that. And yet it is true that the emirs would pay less for you than for some Persian singing girl who has been taught the ways of pleasure. But for the niece of the Lord of Kerak they would pay all of that, because the Lord of Kerak would have to ransom you, even at the cost of his castle. And he is the foe most feared by the Emir of Damascus."

"Messer Mocenigo did not take me to Damascus."

"Nay, to the Well of Moses, upon my land. If the Moslems came for you—a secret payment, a mock attack, and you would have been in their hands. And no accusation could then be laid upon the Mocenigos. The dogs offered me a purse, which would have tied my tongue."

"They said an escort from Kerak would be waiting here."

"And they told me they themselves were journeying with you to Kerak."

Marguerite wished she could see the face behind the cylinder of steel. The Venetians had been most courteous to her.

"And where, Master Rogue," she asked, "is the proof of this thy tale?"

John of the Mount wished that she could understand Arabic, for the Norman words shaped awkwardly here upon the border. What proof lay in a wolf's track, or the shadow of a hand uplifted? Yet by such things men lived or died here.

And then like a ragged prophet of Israel, the old Ibrahim swept into the room without apology of any kind. Where he came from, Sir John could not guess, because he had last seen the Yamanite scurrying into the brush of the ravine.

"*Wallahi!*" he cried eagerly. "Behold, my lord, the caravan is here."

The knight strode to the embrasure, and for a moment the two men looked forth with evident interest. Then Sir John swung out of the chamber, calling to her over his shoulder to keep away from the arrow slot.

Before his tread had died down the stair, Marguerite was at the embrasure, and it seemed to her that pandemonium reigned outside the tower.

Women were screaming and pulling cows through the courtyard gate. Dogs barked, and children tumbled over sheep. The whole Arab village was cramming itself within the walls of the castle.

Through the open gate the girl saw the familiar Italian horsemen riding into the village And with them came strange Moslem riders carrying a green banner and followed by a string of camels. Even while she watched, the gates of the Mount swung shut, and men-at-arms took their stand along the parapet.

Sir John thrust his way through the bedlam of the courtyard and climbed to one of the small gate towers with Khalil. For awhile she could see the Venetians and their companions ascending toward the rock. Then the wall shut them from sight, and presently silence fell like a curtain upon the courtyard.

She heard Sir John speak to men beyond the wall, but could not catch the words. Then he lifted his shield. Something bright flashed in the sun above his head. The men near him crouched down behind the stone parapet, some of them stringing their bows, others busying themselves about clumsy-looking wooden engines. She heard the thud-thud of missiles striking against the tower.

One of the Arab women came and pulled her back to the bed, and she sat there, listening. At home she had seen no more of war than the tournaments of Chatillon, but her kinsmen had borne arms, and she knew the sounds of a siege.

For awhile she watched the slit of blue sky deepening with the purple of sunset and wondered what was passing at the wall. The tumult, that had quieted, now grew apace, and the Arab girl went to the embrasure. Marguerite followed at once. The sun was setting behind the tower and crimson light flooded the rear of the wall and the gate. The villagers had withdrawn from it and four men stood close behind it—Sir John and Khalil and two men-at-arms with axes. Bewildered, she saw that they were taking down the massive iron bars that held the portals shut.

When the last bar was free, they swung back the gates, clear of the entrance. And then all four of them took their stand shoulder to shoulder athwart the threshold, Sir John and Khalil in the middle, a pace before the others.

Above their heads Marguerite beheld a thing that made her clasp her hands, and the girl beside her breathed heavily. A score of men in mail,

Moslem and Italian, rushed at the open gate, sword in hand. They shouted as they ran, and the wailing cry of Islam echoed against the tower.

"*Allah-il-allahi!*"

And with a spring and crash the wooden engines on the wall shot their stones and iron bolts. Some of the running men were dashed from their feet and others flinched aside. The rest flung themselves on Sir John and the Kurd.

The two swordsmen planted their feet, bracing their shields. Above their heads the long, curved blades swung, and slashed down. First one, then the other stepped back, and leaped forward again. At times the ax-men behind them would strike over their shoulders.

The men on the wall were hurling down heavy stones, and the engines crashed again, over the tumult of shouting and grinding steel. More of the Venetians flung themselves against Sir John, and the long sword whirled and slashed—parried and cut while Khalil yelped in exultation and the archers above plied their bows.

Then the pressure of the attack ceased, and Marguerite saw men running down the slope. The glow of sunset faded along the wall and the gates were shut. But soon another glow sprang up in the village, where the mounds of hay and thorn bush were burning, and the Damascus men were plundering the huts. The village Arabs thronged the wall to stare down moodily at this destruction of their property. But Ibrahim the Yamanite slipped through the postern door in the rear, and when things quieted down toward morning he managed to steal two good horses from the besiegers' camp. With these he departed on an errand for Sir John.

Marguerite climbed the winding stair and seated herself upon the sunny parapet of the tower the next noon, to the delight of the solitary archer who stood sentry and who now found something more agreeable to look at than the bare countryside and the purple cleft of the Jordan gorge. And Marguerite beheld, in the camp of the besiegers, her own pavilion and the tiny figures that were her serving women. In that pavilion were all her clothes and brushes and chests. And yet even in the pitiless light of midday the girl seemed cool and fresh.

For awhile she did not move, and perhaps she pondered the strange, hard land, the gnarled olive trees and the distant patches of grazing cattle—the heights of Moab, beyond the Promised Land. Only when a mailed tread grated on the stair she turned quickly.

A tall and grizzled man in a stained native cloak emerged from the stair and bade her a gruff good morning. This was old Renald—she knew him to be captain of the men-at-arms—and when he had scrutinized the camp under the sycamores she decided to make him talk.

"It was ill done," she observed, "to open the gate at vespers yesterday."

Renald grunted.

"'Twas Sir John's doing."

"But why?"

The old Norman turned upon her, scowling.

"Why, my lady? We ha' fourteen men, and they ha' near a hundred. If they had scattered around the wall we could not hold them off. So Sir John says, 'We will invite them in at the door,' and they had many a woundy knock from our bolts and bows. Fourteen men!" He shook his head gloomily.

"It was a sore and bloody onset," the girl sighed. "But it was Sir John's doing. Is he friend to Sir Reginald of Kerak?"

"Aye," Renald muttered.

"Then you have sent a rider to Kerak, for aid?"

"Belike. An Arab went off that way last night."

It seemed to the girl that the Norman captain had not answered frankly.

"Of course," she said, "you are safe now, within this wall, until aid comes."

"Wi' fourteen men? Nay, Kerak lieth distant three days' ride, and the castle lacks food for two days."

"Then you must make terms with the Mocenigos."

"Terms? Not Sir John. Not wi' yonder parings of the devil's hoofs. The Mount will make no composition wi' blethering slave sellers."

"But they are honorable merchants and men of property in the cities."

"I doubt it not. There's a-many cattle thieves and slave traders who are men of property, my lady." He nodded sagely. "If they were true men, would ye be here, my lady?"

Marguerite told herself that this man had not seen her carried off from the tent the day before. But she could not help understanding that Renald and the men of the Mount felt that this siege was her fault, and she thought for a moment, twisting within her fingers the strands of her heavy hair.

"Will you tell your lord that I would like to—to speak with him?"

She waited in her cell, until Khalil appeared in the door and made signs to indicate that Sir John slept. She did not know that both men had been afoot during the night, and she sat in the dark chamber until sunset, when the impassive Arab girl came with her tray. Marguerite did not try to talk to her. She was weary of the silence and doubt, and she wondered if the Lord of the Mount had been hurt in the fighting. The thought frightened her. At least the knight was master here and would let no other hand harm her. If he were dead . . .

Straightaway she slipped out into the stair and felt her way down through the darkness. At the first turning she stopped, hearing men in talk within the hall below, and the familiar ringing voice of the knight. But they were speaking Arabic and the strange sound of it held no reassurance for her. Nor would she go down to be stared at by the men-at-arms.

Instead, she went back to her room. She had sent for the knight, and no doubt he would come after the meeting in the hall. Or at least send her a candle to light the room. But he did not come, and the tired girl felt hot tears upon her eyes. She threw herself down on the bed and cried herself to sleep.

And in utter darkness, late in the night, she was roused by a distant tumult. She ran to the embrasure, listening. Somewhere swords clashed and brush crackled. Torches flickered through the olive trees, and the darkness was astir with moving figures. Above the tumult rang out a battle shout that she knew well.

"Chatillon! Chatillon!" And again, "Kerak to the rescue!"

With a cry of delight she drew the hood of her robe over her head and ran down the stair.

Before evening of that day Khalil had forgotten all about the girl in the tower—even that Renald had asked him to tell Sir John that she wished to speak with him. While the crusader ate a hasty supper, the two talked earnestly, and at the end the Kurd threw up his hands.

"Art thou weary of life?" he wondered.

"Aye, weary of sitting here until we are beset," Sir John said grimly. "Hast thou any love for the Italian crossbows?"

"Nay, certainly." Khalil shook his dark head emphatically.

These powerful weapons, that drove their bolts through shield and armor, were heartily disliked by the Moslem warriors.

"Well, at night such bows avail not at all, and a sword is the best weapon. And thou knowest the Damascus men will flee if the Italians give way."

"That is true. But cattle and torches and these Arab sons of sloth are no fit weapons."

The crusader laughed, for he meant to press everything into service if only Khalil would agree to act with him.

"Thy people say," he suggested "'At night a dog may be a lion.' And our cattle may become something else. Khalil, the Franks outside offered me, before the fight at the gate, two thousand pieces of gold to give up the woman. Has it never befallen thee to know a girl more precious than two thousand *byzants?*"

"No," responded the Kurd, "never."

"It has befallen me." Sir John's eyes softened. "No hand but mine will be laid upon the girl I have brought hither, and the sons she will bear will be my sons."

Khalil nodded, intent on a calculation of his own.

"If the Franks offered two thousand pieces, they must have that and more in their chests, and the escort from Damascus will have much more. The spoil would be a good spoil. As thou sayest, it is better to go out than to sit here."

"Much better," agreed the knight. "Now I will go first, for the cattle and the herders wait. Ibrahim warned them, and Renald saw them at sunset from the tower."

Again the Kurd nodded.

"My part is easier than thine. But fail not to come, or we will be taken like sheep." He stood up and stretched lean arms with a smile. "It is written, and we may not read what is written."

So they went out together into the courtyard. And when Sir John's horse was led up, he glanced at the dark tower, thinking that he would like to have a word with his captive before setting out. But the women told him that she was asleep, and already he had delayed to argue with Khalil. He mounted to the saddle, spoke briefly with Renald, who was to hold the castle gate with one man and the village folk, and then rode from the narrow postern through which Ibrahim had slipped the night before.

For awhile the courtyard was astir. Khalil counted off the ten men-at-arms who remained to accompany him, and he selected as many of the Arab youths, making certain that each one had arms and a horse. Then he waited patiently until Renald called to him that the tally candle showed an hour elapsed.

With his twenty following in file, Khalil left the postern and turned in the direction opposite that taken by the knight. Although the castle was between him and the camp, he led his horse carefully into the darkness, into a gully where the starlight did not penetrate.

The gully turned away from the castle, but Khalil and his men knew every rock of the path, and presently they assembled on rising ground that overlooked the distant embers of the besiegers' fires and the gloom of the sycamore grove.

Khalil peered down uneasily. He did not know how many men might be awake down there in the gloom under the trees, and besides, he could see almost nothing at all because he had Sir John's heavy battle casque on his head. And his left arm was already weary with the weight of Sir John's long kite shield. From side to side he turned his head like an uneasy wolf, seeing only the red glimmer of campfires and the yellow points of stars overhead.

"May Allah confound this steel pot!" he swore.

"What sayest thou, Lord Khalil?" a man-at-arms asked anxiously. "Yonder come the torches."

It had taken Sir John a good hour's persuasion to induce the wary Kurd to put the great helm on his head, but having given his promise to lead the attack, Khalil would not hold back. With a shout he spurred his horse and dashed down the slope.

"The Mount!" cried his men-at-arms. "The Mount!"

And they followed with a clatter of hoofs and jangle of mail, while the Arabs behind them gave tongue. A wailing cry greeted them from the darkness, and arrows whipped by them. They were entering the camp of the Damascus men, and the sentries were wide awake. Cymbals clashed by the tents and an Italian horn echoed the clash.

Khalil swerved past patches of brush and pulled his horse out of a long stumble. He rode down a dark figure that seemed to spring out of the ground, and he careened into a tent. The pole of the tent swayed and came down upon other figures that struggled beneath the cloth, while Khalil's horse reared frantically and its master cursed anew.

Something crashed against the steel at his ear, and he beheld clearly enough the red flames that sprang before his eyes. An arrow ripped the mail links from his shoulder, and he lifted his shield in time to ward the smashing blow of a war club. Then his horse jumped clear of the tangle and, because the cressets hanging about the camp had been lighted, he saw that the warriors of Damascus were swarming out like bees, sword in hand.

Sir John's men had followed his example, and a half dozen tents had been overturned, while horses and running men leaped about the confusion like minions of purgatory welcoming a new host of the damned. Khalil cut the turban from the head of a passerby, and peered about, sawing at the rein of his maddened charger. A scimitar blade smote the mail upon his shoulders and he wheeled and slashed behind him, his sword sweeping vainly through the air.

Then the clatter of steel dwindled, and he saw the Moslems peering behind them. A greater sound filled the night, a stamping of reckless hoofs, a tearing of brush and a roar as of a freshet coming down a mountain. A black mass swayed and bore down upon the far side of the camp and on a knoll above it a strange trumpet resounded.

"Kerak!" A clear voice shouted. "Chatillon! Kerak to the rescue!"

Torches flickered on the knoll, disclosing a horseman in full armor, a light steel cap on his dark head, a drawn sword in his hand. For an instant he halted there, and then repeated his battle shout and galloped down to the mass that was moving on the camp.

And Khalil laughed.

All this the Mocenigos had seen, when they were roused from sleep, and ran out to stare and listen. They were men of nimble mind, and when they heard the cry of Kerak both thought of the same thing—of a rope dangling from the bough of a tree and their own bodies dangling from the rope. For Reginald of Chatillon would do no less than that to any merchants who made shift to sell his niece as a slave.

Although not accustomed to war, they were equally swift to act. They hastened to their horses and, finding them saddled, called to the nearest Venetians. And with some dozen riders they galloped from the camp as if the foul fiend had been at their heels.

Khalil saw them and spurred toward them.

"The Mount!" he cried, and men-at-arms hurried toward him.

The Mocenigos veered off, and Khalil went after them, wresting vainly with the lashes that bound the intolerable casque upon him.

But other Venetians and Moslems had beheld the flight of their leaders. While the Damascus men hesitated, the black wave smote the camp and resolved into a bellowing and trampling herd of cattle that bore down the remaining tents and sent the frightened horses plunging into the brush. The men of Damascus had come hither to escort a lady and not to fight. When a strange knight charged at them with a strange war shout, and torches waved triumphantly upon the wall of the Mount, they took thought for themselves and vanished.

Only here and there did men stand against the lances of the riders from the Mount and the young Arabs, who were delirious now with the prospect of slaughter and loot together. And the gates of the Mount burst open. A stream of old Arabs and women and boys emerged and bore down upon the fallen tents, to pillage in their turn. The remaining Venetians threw down their arms.

Marguerite of Chatillon hastened through the uproar, looking about her in vain for a familiar face. Stumbling over ropes and dodging frightened cattle, she made her way to where Renald had taken his stand by the Mocenigos' pavilion and her own, warding off with the help of some spearmen from the Mount the attempts of the Arabs to snatch away the spoils of the pavilions. But before she could reach him, a horse came up behind her, and she turned as Sir John leaped from the saddle to the ground. She drew a quick breath of relief and looked up into his brown face.

Strangely, he was flushed, and his shoulders shook and tears dripped from his eyes. And he spoke no word to her.

"Thou art hurt!" she cried, reaching out her hands to him.

He caught them and kissed them and found his voice.

"I am near perishing—"

"You are not!" she pulled away indignantly. "You are laughing, and there is no mark on your sword. Now, take me to my uncle."

"Demoiselle," he sighed and wiped his eyes with a scarred hand. "I am Reginald of Chatillon, and Khalil is John of the Mount, and—oh, if you could have seen the Mocenigos flee in their shirts—while the cattle butted—"

He gazed around at the confusion and, seeing that the fighting was at an end, wiped his eyes again.

"But I heard my uncle's shout!"

"And have I not gone on raid and foray with Chatillon, not to know his shout? Oh, it was a notable and mighty charge we made, I and the cattle. We have captured your pavilion."

Marguerite looked at him curiously, beholding for the first time the youth and the laughter of the man who had seemed unbending as iron.

"Then you did not send the messenger to Kerak!"

"Nay, I sent off Ibrahim with a letter, to fetch a gray priest from Jerusalem."

"Sir John," she said slowly, "I have mistaken you, and now I think that you have risked yourself and this castle to aid me, and—and I will thank you, if I may. And now you will take me to Kerak."

The dark face of the knight fell serious.

"I shall not give up Marguerite of Chatillon to any man. And if Sir Reginald will have you, he must even take the castle, for you will be my wife, and he will need be a bold man to lift hand or eye to my wife."

Now Marguerite glanced up at him, incredulous, and the dark blood surged into her throat and brow.

"You dare? You would dare!"

And her eyes wavered, and then turning swiftly, she fled—ran like a shadow through the torchlight, up to the open gate of the Mount. Without heeding the din around him, the knight strode after her, into the courtyard and the hall.

Sir John was in time to see the flicker of a candle vanish up the winding stair, and with his foot on the first step, he hesitated. The exultation of the fighting throbbed in him, but now fear came upon him. Up there Marguerite had fled, and he was afraid of the darkness in her eyes and the blood that stained her throat. Surely he had frightened her, at whose feet he had laid his love—and surely now she lay stricken, fearing him. He dared not go up, to feel her eyes upon him and hear her weep, or scorn him.

But then he heard her clap her hands three times, and the Arab woman, thus summoned, brushed past him. So he paced the length of the hall, wondering how Marguerite would try to speak to the girl. And when the Arab came down and would have left the hall, he stopped her.

"Speak thou! Is my lady weeping, and what doth she seek of thee?"

"Thus, O my lord, she doeth." And the girl held up her open hands together, first against one side of her face, then against the other, staring at them. "She must have—" the girl smiled—"a mirror."

Lionheart

That cold April afternoon Brother Clement felt an ache in his heart. He expected to see Satan running over the roofs of the hamlet of Limoges, vanishing with the chimney smoke and the damp mist. Brother Clement even glanced at the ground near his sandals to see if the mark of the cloven hoof did not show in the gray snow.

"There is so much of evil afoot," he said to himself.

And he counted the evils on his fingers as if they had been the beads of a rosary. "War." Limoges lay within the frontier zone, in France. "Avarice." (Yes, Achard, lord of Châlus, *bos sous*.) "Rapine."

That very morning after matins some of the shepherds had lingered at the church door to tell Brother Clement that Cadoc's men had been along the road. These men, *routiers*—fighters for whoever paid them and spoilers on their own account—were more dangerous than a wolf pack. Cadoc himself, a noble by birth and a mercenary by trade, boasted that no man could stand up to him and live.

"And sickness." Moodily the young friar ended his check of the evils around him. He was thinking of the girl Marie, the serf girl who embroidered in Limoges castle because she was too thin and weak to do outdoor labor. The mark of the white death was on her, though she was no more than sixteen years of age. Still, she could laugh, and her eyes had a way of slanting up at him.

Because he was thinking of her, the friar strode through the stubble of wheat to the field gate of the castle where she was apt to appear at this hour of the afternoon.

Almost at once he saw her, running toward the gate. She barely paused to glance at the geese in their pen—the geese for which Brother Clement knew she was responsible. With the mist sparkling in her loose hair and her cheeks flushed, the little Marie looked lovely as an elf. "My stint of work on the loom is finished," she cried when she saw the friar waiting. "The chatelaine bade me go—"

To feed the geese, Brother Clement thought, and she had not fed them. The girl drew her wide wool mantle closer about her throat uneasily, pulling it over the chunk of bread under her arm. But not before he had seen the slice of cheese thrust into the bread. The castle folk at Limoges allowed the serfs to take bread at will. The cheese she must have stolen. And she must have stolen it for Peter, to whom she was hurrying now.

"Take warning—" he began, and changed his words. "Cadoc's *routiers* are on the roads. You should not go forth, Marie."

At such a time it was dangerous for any woman to venture alone beyond call of the castle guard. Marie pulled the hood of the mantle over her hair.

"I will be a mouse. Besides, I am not going by the Châlus road."

She smiled up at him appealingly, and before he could speak she closed her eyes and breathed a prayer: "O Mary, full of grace, protect Peter wherever he goes; watch over my aunt and all her children; aid me by thy mercy to get more than thirty-one sous. And make me well—amen!" she added quickly.

Even more quickly she ran on to the gate waving to him. Brother Clement she knew to be very wise—he read pages of the written words of saints when other folks slept, by candlelight—she did not want him to read her thoughts. When the mud dragged at her feet she slowed to a walk, coughing and wiping a trace of blood from her lips.

Looking after her, the young friar murmured, "Amen." If by some means the girl Marie could leave the damp plain of France and venture south to the sun-warmed mountains—he had heard wayfarers tell of the Pyrenees—she might escape the white death. Yet how could a serf woman make such a journey, like a noblewoman? He thought: *If even a sparrow falls—*

Past the haystacks, in the dimness of the wood, Marie searched for the arms of the windmill, her landmark. The windmill was abandoned; people avoided it because the torn sails on the creaking arms made the spot seem eerie. Although it stood on a knoll above the Châlus road no one had come prying about the windmill when she was there with Peter Basil, dreaming that the mill was actually a ship borne by its sails over all the seas of the earth.

Lying on the chaff in the cold mill chamber, she peered through a hole in the broken boards. She could see the road, and—when the mist eddied away—the distant tower of Châlus castle. She did not see Peter Basil coming, because he ran through the trees, keeping out of view of the road.

"A wolf pack holds the road," he said, throwing himself down by her. Although he had run a league with that long stride, he did not breathe heavily.

Thin and smiling and dark with the sun he was. Taking her in his arms he bent her head back. When he did that she felt warmth in her body. The dark walls around them became friendly and safe. Marie wanted to tell him about that, but instead she held out the bread with the cheese in it.

"Wait!" Peter was excited. The shock of his dark hair hung over his eyes. Older than she in years, he was younger in mind, with his wild Gascon temper. Not touching the fresh bread, he held out a scarred fist, closed. "Little Marie, a miracle has happened here in Châlus wood." He opened his hand. "Look at it."

She smiled because he was joyful. Then she gasped. The thing he showed her was a round coin of heavy gold bearing a king's head. Marie had seen such gold in the armbands of the ladies of Limoges. "You found it," she cried, fearful that Peter had stolen it.

"An ox found it," Peter laughed, caressing it. A peasant starting his spring plowing had turned up some of the coins by a standing stone at the edge of Châlus wood. Digging down for more, the peasant had unearthed an iron pot. "Old as old." Peter nodded. "Who knows who buried it, or when?"

Gold. She touched it and shivered. Never before had she been within reach of it, and here Peter held it carelessly in his hand.

"With this you are free, Little Marie—to go. Tell me, do we need more? Three—six? Nay, six gold pieces must be worth three marks of silver."

Three marks of silver was her price. A huge sum, to pay for the labor of a serf for thirty years. Paid into the hand of the chatelaine of Limoges, it would free Marie from her service, so she could go to the southland with Peter.

"Take it back," she begged, "quickly."

Amazed, he stared at her. In a year she had been able to save only thirty-one sous—not nearly a single mark of silver. Peter never had a sou in his belt. "No," he said.

"Listen to me, Peter." Frightened, she told him carefully about finding buried coins. She had learned such matters of law by listening carefully to the talk of the Limoges ladies. True, three pieces of gold might buy her release, but how could a serf possess gold? This coin came from a treasure-trove, dug out of the land, and as the land belonged to its overlord so did such a trove. If they took even this one piece—and the peasant knew Peter had it—they would be guilty of thieving, and thieves were hanged from the trees along the high road where crows flocked to the dead flesh.

"Then I will pay them," cried the Gascon, "and they will fare but ill if they lay hand on me."

She had to be ware and yare with Peter, who knew or cared little about the seigneurs. A starveling, up from the south, he had sworn himself into five years' service as villein to Achard, lord of Châlus. Although he still had two years to serve as crossbowman, he wanted her to run away with him to the Gascon land where the wine grapes grew. When Marie thought of going with him, the two of them walking at will with their packs, she felt faint with joy. Peter was carefree as an animal; he could crawl into a cave after a bear and come out unscathed. But she could not run from Limoges because the debt of three marks would then be put upon her aunt and the children as they grew up to working age.

"It's a sin to talk of what you cannot do," cried Marie, angry because she wanted so to do it, and the gold coin made her afraid.

"What? A sin? And doesn't my Seigneur Achard sin? He'd drain the Tardoire if he dropped a sou in it. He gives us bread would make hogs vomit"—seizing the fresh bread from her he munched it angrily with his white teeth—"and it would be the greatest sin to let him have our gold! Yeux—Dieu. I will take only three pieces."

For the moment they forgot to lie quiet in their hiding, or to watch out.

"Nay, not one. Surely," she ventured, "if you and the peasant yield up the trove, there will be a reward."

"If Gabriel sounds his horn, Achard may part with a gold florin"— Peter laughed—"but not otherwise."

Abruptly he stopped chewing and slipped the gold coin into his belt where a pair of crossbow bolts were thrust. Marie had not heard the armed man come to the door of the mill. The soldier glanced quickly around and jerked his head at them. "Come out, lovebirds," he said without feeling. He carried a pack and a light hand ax.

The Gascon obeyed warily, tensing as he saw the road below filling with horsemen, dismounting and unsaddling their beasts. Already they were gathering wood for a fire, while bowmen threaded the forest on either bank, searching the coverts. At a glance Peter knew them for veterans making a halt in their march. Cadoc's men, he surmised, or—

"Keep walking, youngling," the scout advised him, "the captain wants to chat with all skulkers."

"The English," Peter exclaimed, relieved. Marie held to his arm helplessly. Until now she had only seen the war bands passing through the streets of Limoges. Sometimes they had been followers of the English king, Richard; sometimes they had borne the banners with the fleur-de-lis of the French king, Philip; but always they had snatched up loot or driven off cattle. She had heard it said that they fought about the frontier line from Abbeville to the Pyrenees.

She dreaded that Peter might provoke these emotionless men, so boldly did the Gascon answer the questions of the English captain. The officer hardly looked at her; his gray face seemed lifeless.

"Dieu!" cried Peter "If you think I am not of the Châlus guard, take me to the Sieur Achard—or give me a weapon and I will best you with it, at any distance."

Instead of answering, the English officer pulled one of the crossbow bolts from the Gascon's belt, and examined its barbed steel head and oiled wooden shaft curiously—as if the missile were more important than his two prisoners.

Then a deep voice called "Mercadier, if you will not take his challenge, I will."

"Sire," the gray captain, Mercadier, answered instantly, "these villeins are of no account, but this bolt has a rare good balance." His expressionless eyes shifted to Peter. "Kneel, thou. Richard the king speaks."

As they knelt in the mud of the road, Marie saw a man rise with an effort from a saddle by the fire. He moved heavily, like a bear. His mail shirt and steel cap bore no signia.

"A mark—a mark, some of you!" he called impatiently and held out the crossbow in his hand for Peter to see. "Can you hit a mark with this, youngling?"

It was a fine new weapon of tempered steel, the shaft inlaid with ivory.

"Aye," said Peter.

When his men had stripped a band of bark from around a slender tree fifty paces off, and had marked a black cross on the white band with charcoal, Richard wound up his bow himself. Raising it to his shoulder he sighted carefully, and pulled the trigger free. The bolt tore through the side of the tree—a good shot at that distance.

"Have you skill to better that?" the English king asked.

"Aye."

Rising easily, the Gascon balanced the fine weapon in his hand and quickly slipped one of his own bolts into the slot. As he did so Mercadier stepped between him and the king. Sudden excitement seized the girl Marie as she realized that Peter had a chance to show his skill before such great soldiers as these. With his own weapon, Peter could bring down a hawk in flight—

His shot cracked full into the edge of the cross.

Yet Richard said no word of praise. Grasping the bow impatiently the king took more time for a second try. His bolt struck fair beside the Gascon's near the cross, and for the first time merriment gleamed in his tired eyes.

Peter however, took the bow again. He had the feel of it now, and he lifted it and loosed it in a single motion. His shot cut the center of the black cross, and the onlooking men-at-arms shouted involuntarily.

Marie felt a stab of exultation. Even Mercadier grunted, and bent his head to Richard's. Marie heard him say, "This marksman's worth having in our force. Achard will yield him for a florin. You'll take him?"

Holding her breath, Marie waited for the answer that might mean honor for Peter. Richard, flushed with anger, turned to the young Gascon. "You proved your skill," he choked. "For this minute, keep out of my sight." And he strode back to the fire and snatched and emptied a goblet of wine.

Defeat at this boyish test of skill stirred him more than a sudden wound. Mercadier looked at him and shooed Peter away. The Gascon walked through the silent men-at-arms as if he cared nothing for Richard's anger.

Marie did not move. Down the road, the English were questioning a slender friar astride a donkey; it was Brother Clement. At sight of him the girl felt her fear diminish. She thought he might have come to look for her out of the goodness of his heart when he heard a war band had camped by the mill.

Mercadier, confronting the friar, laughed suddenly, contemptuously. Drinking, Richard glanced over that way and motioned them over to him, bidding them say their say in plain words before him.

"The little shaveling lies greatly," protested one of the English knights with Mercadier. "He says and he maintains that he hath come this hour from the mark of the king of France."

"Let him say it to me," snarled Richard, in his restless mood. Brother Clement dismounted before the king, his diminutive figure dwarfed by Richard.

"You know my face?" Richard demanded.

No more than Marie did Clement recognize the mailed figures around him. He shook his head. "You are not Cadoc—"

"Cadoc!" Richard stared, amazed. "Have you never seen Ricard of England?"

Marie longed to cry out to Brother Clement. In the hard watchfulness of these *routiers* she felt a danger she did not understand. Brother Clement lived with his books, and his mind otherwise was simple. "Why, yes," he said at once. "In years agone I saw the Lionheart. He was riding to the great crusade. He was gay."

Richard stepped closer. "Then who am I?" he asked.

Troubled, Brother Clement gazed up at the bloodshot blue eyes and the broad head encircled by steel mesh. "I know not," he said honestly, "except that you are sick."

"Sick?" Richard's ungovernable temper rang in the words. "By the Horned One—how am I sick?"

Uncertainly, the young friar tried to explain. "Not in the body. In the spirit."

Richard emptied the cup in his hands without tasting the wine. The gray mist clinging to the treetops weighted on him. Within an hour he had seen his own likeness in the carefree Gascon, as he had been when he first mounted the saddle to ride to war. And the friar had seen him ride to the great crusade, to the battles beyond the sea, to the heights of Torun, where he had turned away so that he would not see in the distance the summit of Jerusalem that he had failed to take with his sword.

"Will you heal that with prayer?" he asked the friar.

The friar did not answer.

The moment at Torun was gone, and the bright day he had been greeted back on England's shore after his imprisonment in Germany. The scarlet coronation robe they had brought him, the hue of blood, to be crowned again, with the good Archbishop Walter speaking the words about the spirit of a king—he had that coronation robe somewhere in the packs, still.

Richard did not reason about this. His wine-soaked memory searched for what angered and hurt him. In England, he had not been able to endure the arguments of the assembly of barons. He had taken ship in a storm to cross to the frontier in France—to march with his men-at-arms, as in the Holy Land, seeking relief in action—to lead *routiers*, veterans of many wars, like Mercadier's crew, gleaning their pay from spoil while they raided Philip's border castles. . . .

Philip lay safe at Orleans with the French court, scheming, taxing, bribing, getting his clutches on new lands. Philip was wiser than he, Richard, who could endure only the camps of his veterans. Because he was so painfully aware of this, it seemed somehow important that he should make this wandering servant of God understand that he was the king.

Perhaps if he showed the friar the coronation robe—but he had never put that on his shoulders again. Instead of calling for it, Richard went to the fire and brought back in his own hands a weather-stained mantle embroidered with the crouching lions of England. "If you do not recognize me," he said mildly, "you may know what this means."

Brother Clement nodded. "It is the royal signia of England." Suddenly he smiled. "Strange it seems to me, that I passed a rider an hour agone with the royal sign of France upon him."

"What!" Richard stared.

Mercadier almost smiled. "For a little friar that is a great lie."

Every man within hearing knew that no one except Philip Augustus, king of the French and Richard's most dangerous enemy, could wear such royal marking, and Philip had never been known to risk himself within a day's ride of the adventurous Richard.

"I have told," said Brother Clement, "the truth of what I saw."

He repeated it to Richard—how, riding hither through Châlus forest, he had passed a band of armed riders. They were going away by the river road, toward the ford, and their chief, who kept his face hidden, had worn a cloak ornamented with the fleur-de-lis of France.

"At dawn," Richard reflected aloud, "the shepherds sighted a war band on this road."

Still, he could not believe that Philip was so near. The clever Frenchman would never venture so far from a safe fortress. "Why did you come here?" he asked the friar abruptly.

"To find this woman," Brother Clement explained simply, pointing to Marie.

"Sire"—Mercadier touched his arm—"this riddle smells of treachery. Aye, it smells of bait for an ambush. Beware of it."

"The roan horse!" Richard called suddenly. "Saddle the roan, I say. I'll see for myself if it be Philip, or a trap."

A craving for action gripped him though the sober part of his mind admitted that Mercadier must be right. Philip would be more apt to pay another to set a trap than to lay one himself.

Richard ran to his horse, feeling the ache of old wounds in his legs. His sight, too, was not so sharp as it had been; he had not seen the black cross clearly in the white band of the tree. Taking a shield from an esquire, he swung himself into the saddle and turned the great war horse into a forest path without waiting for his companions, who were saddling in desperate haste.

Left to himself, Brother Clement persuaded Marie to climb to the donkey's back. While he led her home she told him wearily of her fear that harm would come to Peter Basil for taking the gold.

The mist was darkening with the end of day. It seemed to Brother Clement that no human power could check the evil gathering about the girl Marie . . .

Riding headlong through Châlus forest, Richard felt himself again. As he beat to clear the branches and searched for a pathway to the river, he felt free and joyous. The roan charger was fresh and, even carrying Richard's weight, it had the pace of the other road-weary chargers.

When he glimpsed the castle tower through the trees he turned away toward the river. Often he had hunted this forest with its lord, Achard, and he knew the way. He did not think of riding to the castle for aid, now. He pressed the roan hard, not looking back for his followers.

The trees fell away on either hand and he galloped out into a meadow. He heard the rush of the river beside him and at the same instant sighted the other horseman.

On the path before him this rider had his back turned, and from his shoulders hung a mantle of blue velvet, splendid as Richard's coronation robe. With a glance over his shoulder the other put his white horse to a run. The light was failing fast.

The white horse flitted through the mist, and up over a rise. Following at a gallop Richard topped the rise to find a pavilion where a score of horses grazed, and as many armed men waited quietly.

And here the rider of the white horse turned in his tracks. Richard did not slacken his pace as he thought: *They do not call out, so they wait for this; they do not move, so they have their orders given them.*

The other's face was half hidden under a light helm. As Richard came up, he held the path. This is never Philip, Richard thought. Without warning, the man's sword lunged toward Richard's eyes, then swerved down to his groin. Richard's shield followed the swerve, brushing the point clear as he rode past.

As he thundered by, he drew his own sword, and instead of reining in, he bent in the saddle, circling fast to the right. Quick as he had been, the unknown rider was behind him and upon him. Richard's sword lashed back at him, and sparks flared as the other's shield deflected the long blade.

The nameless man was fighting silently, viciously, and to kill. His horse shouldered the flank of Richard's charger, and the point of his shield ripped across the king's face. Richard struck back, covering himself with his shield. The other's sword point went under the shield, and broke the links of the king's chainmail.

Feeling the bite of the steel, Richard twisted his body. The blade slipped across the leather covering his body and Richard, with his shield arm, tried to hold the other's sword against his body with all the strength of his great shoulders into the grip as he struggled for life.

The white horse was reined back, his sword was wrenched away. But in the seconds before the other got clear of him, Richard smashed the pommel of his long sword at the man's head. And deftly, the other's shield came up. This time it was beaten down against swordsman's head.

Hurt, the other lashed out blindly at Richard's head. Richard bent under the blow, his legs clamping the saddle, gripping the roan horse. As the horse leaped forward he swung his sword in low, beneath the shield. He felt the steel snap as the blade cut over the man's hipbone deep into his body.

The other shouted a curse, and lifted his sword weakly. Knocking it to the ground, Richard reined forward and pulled the helmet from the head of the dying man.

Peering into the face draining of blood, he knew it and said, "Cadoc, you have earned your death."

The captain of mercenaries clung to his saddle, the blood rushing out of his body as his horse backed up in fright. Richard heard the beat of hoofs behind and turned to meet the onset of Cadoc's followers.

They rode at him warily, trying to circle him. He backed the roan to the river edge, jeering at them, bidding them watch Cadoc die. They knew they faced Richard, and they pressed against him slowly.

Then over the rise came one of Richard's knights. At sight of them, the king flung himself at the pack of mercenaries, followed by Mercadier on a wearied black horse, and others behind him.

Richard reined his horse into the fray as his followers came fast to the ford. They drove the mercenaries headlong into the water and across the river.

When the English turned back in the twilight they counted eight men dead and eleven horses captured. They had taken no human prisoners. They found Richard inspecting the pavilion, fitted up in royal style, with wine jars waiting on the carpet. He filled a silver goblet and drank, saying that Cadoc had never paid for all this finery. "Look about, my lieges," he urged, "and see if any French gold be hid away here."

Tasting the good cool wine, he felt pleased and excited—almost as if he stood again on the field of Arsuf or at the broken wall of Acre in Palestine, where thousands had waited his command—

Torches flared in the mist. From the ford, Achard of Châlus approached warily with a strong following of men-at-arms. In the castle they had heard the clatter of steel down the road. "He smells gold," muttered Mercadier, "as a hound scents out a hare." Although the English had ransacked all the trappings of the pavilion, they had found no money.

Recognizing Richard, Achard reined back and dismounted hastily. "Majesty!" Coming upon Cadoc's body covered with the blue cloak, he paled visibly.

"My lord of Châlus," Richard laughed, "you sent me no warning of this ambuscade on your land."

"Sire," Achard stuttered, "I did not know—I was busied with another matter."

Richard silenced his mouthings with a contemptuous motion of his hand. The exultation of the fight left Richard. What had it availed him to risk his life? A soiled pavilion and a baker's dozen of horses—the death of a soldier who had merely tried to earn a payment. Richard had craved more than that. "Did this hireling leave aught of valuables with you, for safekeeping?" he asked Achard.

The man's thin face puckered as if in pain. "I swear by the Holy Three," he protested, "that Cadoc left no gold coins with me."

Richard studied him, the blue eyes curious.

"I swear no other gave me gold," cried Achard.

Filling two goblets with wine, Richard said, "Did I speak of gold? Faith, Achard, we'll drink together till you resolve me the riddle of what gold you have, and for what."

And out of that drinking by torchlight came the doom of Châlus.

Peter Basil felt it coming like the wind in the treetops before a storm. He whispered it to Marie the next afternoon at the haystacks in the field where he stopped her on her way to the mill. "The gold, little Marie. Achard smelled it out. The churl who found it told of it. Achard e'en took the coin from me. Then worse befell. Richard the King looked around for hidden gold, and my lord Achard lied to him, swearing he had not a florin—aye, while he had the trove locked in his coffer, the skulking fox!" And the Gascon swore at his liege lord.

He told her, too, that the English king demanded the treasure-trove be yielded up to him, as Achard's overlord, or he would tear down the walls of Châlus to get at it himself.

"Come away," he begged. "Fetch your gear and goods here on the morrow—we'll go while we can."

How could she go? The next day she waited at the hayfield to tell Peter she couldn't, but although she waited until dark, he did not come.

Frightened, she went around to the street gate to hear the talk of men coming in, and she learned the fate of Châlus.

The English were attacking it. Achard had refused to part with his gold and had fled, after ordering his captains to defend the tower castle. She made bold to ask of the gossipers, "Did no other souls escape?"

The men laughed at her. One said, "Wench, I cannot tell thee of souls. Yet four men-at-arms tried to steal out and were noosed and hanged by the English."

Then she waited by the door of the great hall until Brother Clement came by. He listened to her, and said quietly, "Only the king can grant mercy to those who have taken arms against him. Pray for them, little Marie."

Still she did not understand the doom that had befallen those in Châlus. The next morning she performed none of her duties. Instead she did up bread and cheese, putting them with her good leather shoes and rosary in a kerchief to carry.

Escaping out the field gate with her bundle, she stopped only briefly to say her accustomed prayer. "O Mary, full of grace, protect Peter Basil wherever he may be." It did not seem necessary today to repeat the rest of the prayer. If she could reach Peter she would go where he wished, now, never leaving the touch of his hand.

When she was out of sight of the castle guards, she began to run, not to the windmill but toward the forest of Châlus.

The edge of that forest had changed, the far edge where huts and tents rose unexpectedly before Marie. Horses grazed and carts leaned drunkenly on the fresh grass. Above them two huge machines of beams and twisted ropes flung their long arms skyward, casting stones against the outer wall of Châlus. Behind the wooden palisade that sheltered them, men tended these machines calmly, or bound ladders together. They are harvesting, Marie thought.

But they wore mail. Above them the sunlight glinted as crossbow bolts and arrows flew. On the ground before her three men lay huddled together, seemingly asleep. In one an arrow was bedded deep. The body did not stir. Marie went around it, unafraid.

The machines thudded like giant hearts beating, and dust rolled down the outer castle wall, hiding for a moment the tower behind it. Then from slots in the wall, arrows flickered again. Marie was hardly aware of this as she searched patiently for the king, who alone could give commands.

She saw Mercadier at the palisade talking to a man leading a roan horse, and the man was Richard, clad in plain mail like his captain, swinging the fine crossbow in his free hand.

Edging behind the horse, she drew closer to Richard, wondering if he would hear her. She cried out above the uproar, and Mercadier caught her roughly by the arm. "Let be," she cried. "Let me go on, into the castle, where he is."

Richard, unheeding, was giving orders for an assault to take the curtain wall, and smoke out the tower with fire. Desperately she tried to touch him, "Let me go in!"

He turned on her with surprise. "In there, every one of them will die." Then he said to Mercadier, "The Gascon's wench—send her beyond bowshot."

Impatiently Mercadier thrust her toward an archer, who pulled her away by the arm, grinning. Drawing her past the tents he gripped her waist,

making a hissing sound as if to a horse. She tore herself away from him
and ran toward the trees of the forest.

From the first tree hung long strings of flesh, clothed—the carcasses
of four men. None of the dark faces was Peter's.

Like an injured animal, helpless, the girl felt her way into the forest . . .

Before sunset that day the curtain wall of Châlus toppled to the
ground.

The machines ceased their groaning and thudding. Voices were hushed
as the English veterans thronged out, ready for commands.

When the dust cleared, Richard mounted and rode forward to examine the breach himself, taking his light shield and crossbow. He moved
through a break in the palisade, with Mercadier and a few men to guard
him. Behind him, hundreds awaited his order. But only Mercadier saw
clearly what happened.

Richard's gaze traversed the silent battlements. He thought how ladders could be run up on either side of the breach, to attack at three points.
Only one man moved on the broken stones of the breach, a slender crossbowman.

Richard recognized the Gascon marksman. Raising his weapon, he
loosed the bolt at the man, who moved to one side.

Evidently the other had used up all his bolts, because he bent without
haste to pull the king's shaft from the stones. Watching, Richard muttered, "Well done . . ."

So quickly did the man on the stones raise his weapon that Mercadier
heard the crack of the steel bow and impact of the bolt close to him. He
started to raise his shield, then lowered it.

The bolt had struck above Richard's mail, at the base of his neck. His
hand went to it, straining at it without moving it.

"Eyes of God!" Mercadier sobbed, covering the king with his shield.

"Give the assault now!" Richard ordered.

Sitting motionless in the saddle, gripping it with his hand, he waited
while the soldiery advanced past him, carrying the two ladders with them.
Then he turned the roan horse back toward his pavilion.

There he lay motionless while attendants cut the lashings of his mail
and someone worked with a knife to draw the bolt from his body, but
failed. It was stuck fast. The shock of it numbed him and he could not

make out the faces around him clearly. It bewildered him that he could
no longer move an arm.

His eyes watched the shadow of time climb the tent wall as the sun
sank. He had a feeling there was something he must do but what that was
he did not know. The voice of a kneeling man questioned him. Should
they send for the Archbishop Walter?

By sunset it was quiet around the tent. Richard did not try to move his
arm, or to ask questions himself. He thought he was aware of men crowding into the tent. He had to force himself to look up at them, and to pick
out Mercadier's white face bending over him.

Behind the captain was a prisoner, bleeding from the head, but strong
on his feet.

Richard looked into the face of Peter Basil, the crossbowman who had
wounded him. Then he asked in a voice thin as a whisper: "What will
you do with him?"

Mercadier did not say that the English had stormed Châlus like fiends
when they heard Richard had been struck down, or that they had searched
the tower, careful not to injure this man who would be tortured to death
in pain beyond imagining.

"Why," Mercadier said, "we'll cut him out of his skin and let him live
raw—if he can."

Peter nodded. He had expected just that.

Richard, watching, saw no fear in him. He saw in this lank youth the
likeness of himself twenty years before, when he had carried a weapon
carelessly to war. And in that moment, Richard felt that he himself was
challenged. Closing his eyes, he thought about that for a moment. "No,"
he said after a moment, "let this man go."

Before Mercadier could speak he raised his voice: "I command it. Give
him his freedom and some coins now."

Mercadier hesitated briefly, then reached down into the iron pot they
had brought to Richard's bed; he drew out some gold coins, and gave them
to the crossbowman, who stood like a man transfixed.

Richard tried to think of something else he had to do. "Yes," he said,
"I forgive you my death." And he motioned for Peter to leave.

There was nothing more to be done.

The next day Brother Clement helped Peter Basil to buy Marie's release, and when the girl had made up her pack, he walked with them as

far as the windmill on the road south. There they waited a little, to say farewell to him.

And, as they waited, they saw the English pass toward Limoges. The roan horse was led past, saddled. After it came Mercadier and the knights bearing a hurdle on their shoulders, and on the hurdle a body. They had wrapped the body in the crimson coronation robe.

"See," the friar said to Peter, "it is the king who is dead."

Protection

Black Odo's road was stopped. And he grunted with satisfaction, because this meant a fight, and nothing warmed the blood in his veins like a fight.

Big he was and bold—he could swing his four-foot sword with either hand and with cunning, being Norman born. Besides, he was Duke of Bari with the rents of a countryside to squander and eight hundred good spears to follow him. Black Odo his men called him, because he would draw back neither from peril nor sin. They said of him that he feared not the powers of darkness. Some said more—that for every horse in his stables, he had a woman to his will. They whispered that the tale of his sins was blacker than a pit in the hours of night. But now, in the Year of Our Lord one thousand and ninety-nine, he was Jerusalem bound, a cross upon his shoulder.

"God's life!" breathed Duke Odo, "'Tis no land flowing with milk and honey as the shave-pates swore."

He could see nothing around him but the barren, dry lands covered with tangles of thorn and nests of boulders. The driving dust was worse than the sun, in this long valley between low hills where it was a torment to wear the chain mail that they dared not take off. It was midafternoon, and the fleshy Norman sat under his pavilion flap nursing his long chin in his hand and gulping warm wine. On his jutting shoulder gleamed a scarlet cross, the edges sewn with rubies, for Odo did nothing in niggardwise, and he had seen to it that the crusaders' cross was an emblem of price.

His eye roved over the camp, on the boulder-strewn ridge. His banner with its rearing lion swelled and drooped in the wind gusts. Wherever the rocks gave any shade, his men-at-arms were clustered. The faded tents of his knights topped the horse lines, and between them a few women

moved wearily, toward the uplifted arms of a barefoot friar who prayed
for water.

Odo wondered why these daughters and sisters of his liegemen had
taken the road to Palestine. They hungered for Jerusalem, and the salvation of their souls, and they would not turn back, although they were dying by the way. Odo had not seen a shapely throat or a sparkling eye among
them. He himself looked forward to his fill of fighting and the despoiling
of the pagan castles. The prospect was fair enough.

Ahead of him, only half a league away, some three thousand Arabs were
encamped. And his Armenian guides told him that the Moslems were in
possession of the only well in this stretch of the Stone Desert. The Normans were out of water—they had a little wine still—and unless they
turned back at once to the coast, they must reach the well. Odo meant to
reach the well, after dawn before the heat should weaken his men. And
he counted the black tents of the Arabs grimly, for they were the first foemen to come into his way.

"Think ye, Sir Guy," he asked, looking up suddenly, "they will stand?"

A sallow Norman, his eyes dark with the fever that lurked in his veins,
came forward. Unlike the giant duke, he wore faded blue linen, the cross
sewn upon the back of his surcoat. He had been with the host that had captured Jerusalem the summer before, and the desert had left its mark upon
him. Moreover, to Odo's thinking, he kept too much to himself, with his
half dozen scarred followers and a girl who wore a veil like a Moslem—Sir
Guy of the Mount they called him. He had joined Odo's company, with
some Genoese merchants, for protection during the short journey from
the sea to the city.

"They will do more than that, my lord," he answered.

"What, then?"

"They are a fighting clan. Having seen the bright armor and shining
gear of thy men, and the merchants' caravan, they know thee for a newcomer in this land, and they will loot thy camp, if so be they may."

"By my faith," swore Odo, "they will not do that, for I shall break them,
and gladden the foul Fiend by their death."

"Then guard thee, my lord, against one peril," the knight of the Mount
advised. "These Moslems will come against thee, where thy standard is
lifted. At first they will give way, then come in from all sides, assailing
thy horse with arrows, and putting thee afoot. Long is thy sword's reach,
but they will venture their lives fearlessly to ride thee down, and slay

thee. 'Tis their way thus to make an end of the leader of a Christian host, knowing that his men will lose heart if he dies."

"Out upon thee, for a faint heart!" Odo grinned at the crusader. "Put some wine in thy belly."

A flush tinged the gray cheeks of the man from Jerusalem, and he turned on his heel with only a silent salutation. It was not good to bandy words with Black Odo.

But the Norman pondered what Sir Guy had said. He glanced over his shoulder at the couch where his helm stood—the polished steel crest of which was a rearing lion, nicely gilded. Few men of his day had such crests, but Odo liked to be known wherever he went. He liked to see foemen shrink away from him. As for arrows, he made mock of them—fit weapons for Genoese churls and Arab pagans who could not strike a good blow with steel. Still, he was too shrewd to make light of Sir Guy's warning. The man from Jerusalem had faced the Moslems too often not to know their ways.

And that morning, Odo had had a sign. A raven, a grave bird, had croaked at his ear. He rubbed his chin reflectively. It would take more than the croaking of a grave bird and the maundering of a sick man to make the Duke of Bari discard his crested helm and gilt mail and wear the plain steel casque and mail that his weapon man, Arnulf, carried in his sack—

Odo sat up abruptly, his hands gripping the arms of the chair. Down below his pavilion Sir Guy was walking away, slowly. And, hastening through the idle men-at-arms, that veiled girl came to meet him. She moved gracefully, and Odo thought that she must be strong, and not old. But others had noticed her, and a bearded Norman swordsman reached out an arm and tore the veil from her head. The girl was thrown to her knees and cried out involuntarily.

The Norman stood over her, roaring out something about the veil being Moslem and accursed. Another man stepped to her side, a man great of bone who overtopped the Norman by half a head. Long hair fell from the edge of his steel cap to his shoulders, covered with a bright crimson cloak. Heavy bands of gold shone against the brown skin of his arms, and Odo saw that his only armor was a corselet of square steel plates rudely fastened together.

The stranger stepped forward and thrust out his left arm, the heel of his open hand thudding against the Norman's forehead. To Odo's muttered surprise, the bearded swordsman fell with limp limbs, and did not rise. There were shouts and other men hastened up, surrounding the tall stranger. Steel rasped against leather, and more than one weapon flashed in the sun. Wine, in that heat, was not soothing to the blood.

Above the head of the stranger an ax was upflung—a broadax, as long as a man's forearm, with a curving, blue blade, the weight of the blade balanced by a heavy spike at the back. And at sight of this weapon in the warrior's hand, the Normans fell back.

"'Ware ye, the Viking!"

Meanwhile Sir Guy had made his way into the group, and at sight of him the Norman men-at-arms turned their backs. For a moment Odo had a clear view of the girl's face, as she caught the knight's arm and smiled up at him. An elfin face, with its pointed chin and fresh young lips. The girl had the fair skin of a child, and her dark eyes were more angry than afraid—the eyes of one who had never known harm. And a glimpse of her stirred Odo like hot wine. Then Sir Guy drew her away with him, leaning on her shoulder.

Odo had encountered no woman of her like for many weary months, and he followed the sick man and the girl with his eyes until they disappeared in Sir Guy's tent.

"In God's name—ho, Arnulf, what brat is that?" he exclaimed.

A slender man in a black tunic hastened forward and knelt by the duke's side. He had been polishing the silver plates of his master's sword belt in the back of the pavilion, but Odo often said that Arnulf, his armiger—weapon-bearer—could see out of the back of his skull, and could hear all the better for his ears being cropped.

"Eh-ch! That one was the daughter of the Sieur Guy."

Odo grunted. "Her name?"

"Ilga." Arnulf considered. "He keeps her veiled, like a jewel in his tent. I have heard her singing." And, with a swift upward glance at his master, "Yet the Jerusalem knight is sick."

"The Fiend will not want a gossip, when thou diest. Nay, this sunrise I heard a grave bird call."

The henchman crossed himself hastily, and Odo frowned at a new thought. "Who is the churl in velvet and gold? My men gave back at his ax, as if a mad bull fronted them."

The stranger, after knocking down the Norman, had seated himself on a stone, his weapon between his knees. He said nothing, but the men-at-arms took care to keep out of his way.

Arnulf shook his head. "May it please my lord, he is not a liegeman of Bari. And I know not—"

"Go, and learn, and return apace."

It puzzled Odo that his men should have taken a blow from the stranger, who was clearly no fellow of Sir Guy's. Within an hour Arnulf enlightened him.

"Eh—that one is a Viking, a sea king of the north. Body of an angel, he has no land to his name—only a galley that they call a dragon ship. Eric the Landless they called him at Constantinople, where he served the great emperor as captain."

Why the Viking had left his mist-filled fiords in the north, Arnulf did not know. There were many northern warriors in the emperor's guard. They followed the wars, and served faithfully the men who paid them— otherwise they were dull of wit and drowsy, fit only to wield their weapons and fall in their own blood. So said Arnulf. But with those heavy weapons they were deadly as mad giants, when aroused. Arnulf himself had seen this same Eric the Landless hew a man through the body, from shoulder to hip, in a brawl at sea.

That Eric meant to go to Jerusalem was evident. He had joined the Normans at the coast. He had offered to stand shield to shield with them if they were attacked, provided they guided him to the city.

"He wears no cross," Arnulf shrugged. "He eats his own bread, serves himself—aye, he carries a bundle wrapped in fur on his shoulder when we march."

"A Viking," Odo mused. "Stands he to my height?"

"Aye, that doth he my lord."

The duke smashed down his hand upon his mailed thigh. "Then, by God's life, is he my man!" He lowered his voice.

"Hearken—thy chopped ears heard Sir Guy's warning? *Who leads the Christians doth court death,*" said he.

"Aye, lord, and true it is. The Moslems will seek thee with their swords."

"On the morrow," Odo said thoughtfully, "one in my armor, wearing the crested helm and mounted on my charger, will lead the men of Bari. But I shall remain here."

"Eh—" the armiger laughed silently—"A mock duke!"

It was often done, he knew. Another man would wear the garments and carry the shield of Duke Odo; the heavy helm, being of the basket type, would hide his face. And the Norman leader, from the safety of the pavilion, could watch the battle unharmed—could join his men in case of need. And the trick would succeed. Moslems would naturally mark the man in the crested helm, beneath the standard, riding the duke's caparisoned charger. They would assail the mock duke. But who would take Odo's place?

"The Viking," said Odo. "Fetch me him, after candle lighting."

That evening the Normans ate dry bread and shivered in the chill air that stirred out of the gullies. The breath of the desert, it seemed, was not always hot, and they had no wood for fires. When candles were lighted in the tents, Eric the Landless strode through the camp at Arnulf's heels. He thrust up the entrance flap of the duke's pavilion and looked within before he entered, to find the Norman leader seated alone by a flagon on the table.

"Who gives the welcome?" the deep voice of the Viking boomed.

"I, Odo, lord of Bari, greet thee, Eric the Landless. Sit, and sup." He signed to Arnulf to fill a goblet for the stranger, by the leather platter of broken bread.

Eric flung himself into a chair that creaked under the weight of his long body. Limb for limb, the two were a match, but the dark, lined face of the Norman resembled in nothing the fair head of the Viking, whose soft mustache hid his lips, whose blue eyes above the high cheekbones were as quiet as still water. Odo thought he might be twenty years in age. And he held the shaft of the great ax, dark with oil and usage, in one broad hand. Sipping his wine, the duke considered his guest.

"Men say thou art a mighty giver of blows," he observed.

Eric emptied his goblet with a ringing "Skoal!" Then after a moment's thought he responded, "That is not to be denied."

"'Tis said thou wert a captain of the emperor's Varangian guard, and hast faced the paynim before now."

The Viking nodded.

"On the morrow," explained the Norman, "my men go against the Moslems who hold the well." And when Eric made no response except another nod, he added, "Thine armor is not proof against arrows. I have a mind to offer thee this chain haburgeon, and the shield and the helm. Look!"

Eric's eyes gleamed when Arnulf held the heavy mail up to the light—a mesh of fine steel chain-work that would cover a man from chin to toe.

The armiger pointed to the helm, surmounted by the rearing lion, and the long shield bearing the same lion painted upon it in gilt. His own iron plates fastened together by leather thongs and girdled by his broad leather belt were poor stuff beside this armor of a prince.

"The gear is good," he said frankly, "and I like it well."

"I will lend thee likewise a good horse for the battle."

"That may not be," Eric shook his head. "I will stay at the camp on the morrow."

"God's life! With the merchants and churls?"

"Aye, so."

Black Odo threw himself back in his chair frowning.

Here was the stout fellow he wanted to take his place, a man whose life was spent in handling his weapons, and as accustomed to take blows as the iron-thewed Spartans or the trained gladiators of Rome. And he did not intend to fight. The duke knew of no one else, his very twin in size and bearing, fit to wear his armor. If he ordered one of his own men to take his place, the rogue would talk. Behind his chair, Arnulf whispered, "Offer him gold."

"Hark ye, Eric the Landless," said Odo grimly. "I seek one to lead the charge to draw the onset of the Moslems—for they will come against the leader. If I should be unhorsed, the battle would go badly, for my men are new to this land and the Saracen. The peril is great, yet this armor is good, and I will give thee a score of stout lads to shield thy back—and a score of gold *byzants* to fill thy purse."

The mild blue eyes of the Viking dwelt on the Norman curiously.

"The risk is yours," he responded. "And I have a duty at the camp. I am thinking that the Arabs may reach to the camp seeking loot, for that is their way."

The thin lips of the Norman curled. Only a victor in battle, he thought, could gain and plunder a hostile encampment. "Thirty pieces—of Venetian weight," he offered.

Something troubled the Viking. For a moment he brooded.

"I am thinking all this is not good. Perhaps there is a sign between us. But to wear the garments of another man is not good. Hark ye, Duke Odo! Do you hear a whetting of sword edges, and a rushing of ravens' wings? There will be a breaking of shields and a snarling of wolves and sorrow after the next sunset."

Arnulf crossed himself, but Odo smote his hand upon the table. "'Tis someone without!" Steps sounded on the ground and a woman's voice cried out. The Norman commanded, "Enter!"

The entrance flap was lifted by a man-at-arms and Ilga stepped into the candlelight. Throwing back the hood of her robe, she hastened to the table and held out a slender arm to the Viking.

"Messire, thy pardon," she whispered, curtseying to the duke. "O come back to the tent, Eric. My father cannot rise from his bed, and he cries for water, the fever being upon him."

Her eyes were bright with anxiety. A child, Arnulf thought, frightened at the sign of death. He had watched her on the road, listening to Eric's droning talk of northern trolls and elves. Surely she loved the yellow-haired giant, as she loved the great horse that carried her and the hound that ran by her. And because she was frightened, she had come to find him here.

Duke Odo spoke before the Viking. "Nay, little Ilga, water we have not, yet here is Cyprian wine, and cool." Motioning Arnulf aside, he handed her the flagon on the table.

"I thank thee, my lord," she cried softly. "My father said thou wert an ill man to meet with, but surely thou art of heart, to give this to him."

A ghost of a smile touched the Norman's lips. "I give to the daughter, not the father."

Silent, she looked at the two men. Eric, hands clasped on his ax shaft, did nothing, and she bowed again, slipping from the pavilion while Odo watched, still smiling.

And Arnulf—who knew his master's whims—said to himself that the lord of Bari desired this brat of the Jerusalemite; and what Odo desired, he took. Ilga being gentle born, and Sir Guy still living, Arnulf felt that Odo might venture too far, unless the disorder of the march and fighting should place Ilga in his hands.

"Now I see Eric the Landless," murmured Duke Odo, "that thou art no man of thy word."

As at the sight of the fine mail, the Viking's eyes quickened. "That is ill said. Nay, it has not been said before," he responded in his deep voice. "And how is it true?"

"Upon joining my company, thou madest pledge to stand shield to shield with my men, at need. Now when the battle is near, thou art a coward and foresworn—bound to the tents by a woman's girdle."

Swiftly Arnulf moved behind the Viking, his fingers on the dagger at his hip. Eric's blue eyes had clouded, and his face was bleak. Odo's thrust had touched him.

What Arnulf did not know was that Eric all his life had been a leader of men—in the voyages over the gray waters of the north, and in the great palaces of Constantinople where he had ruled the warriors who fought the wars of an emperor for pay. A Viking must hold to his service, and his sword.

"That will not be said of me," Eric answered grimly. "I will wear your gear—" with his ax head he pointed at the gleaming helm—"on the morrow, and sit in your saddle. And 'twill say nothing of that to any man. But there is this to be done. Before darkness, there will be weapons drawn between us, and the death of one of us."

"Granted," Black Odo nodded.

"But when I take your place," Eric went on, "by your own hand safeguard the girl Ilga from danger. For I pledged her father I would ward and shield her from harm, while he lies sick."

"I swear," assented the Norman quietly, "that no Moslem living shall lay hand upon Ilga of the Mount while I live."

"Swear upon the Cross."

Odo picked up his sheathed sword, holding the hilt high, and laying his hand upon the crosspiece. And suddenly Arnulf laughed.

When the curtain had fallen behind the Viking, the henchman stared curiously at his master. Odo rubbed his chin reflectively. He had got the Viking to serve him, but if Eric lived Odo would have a duel on his hands. Ordinarily the Norman would not shun that—he trusted his arm and his sword edge. Yet Eric was Ilga's watchdog, and Odo lacked not cunning.

"By the mother that bore thee, if so be thou knowest her," he observed pleasantly to Arnulf, "mark well what I say. Choose thee some ten bold rogues, and follow this landless wight in his onset. Follow and keep his back, until he is hard pressed—then draw away and let him go down. But if he is not slain, put thy knife behind his ear. If he lives, thou wilt not. Am I clear?"

Arnulf grinned, and touched the dagger hilt at his hip. He knew well where to find the ear hole in his masters' helm.

"And then," Odo mused, "stand thou guard over his body, saying that Duke Odo is stunned. Bear back the carcass—unhelm it not—to this pavilion, after sunset. I will await thee here in other guise, and speak with thee then."

And Arnulf's bow was deep with respect. What a brain! Odo had arranged everything to his will. He would be in his pavilion, watching the battle, yet no man would know this. He might even play with the daughter of the sick Jerusalemite while everyone thought him in the saddle pursuing the Moslems, and afterward, in the pavilion—Arnulf's ready mind played with still finer fancies—Odo might change places with the dead Viking—might say, if he chose, that Eric had been slain for an affront to the girl Ilga. He, Arnulf would be witness.

Still amused at the baiting of the Viking, Arnulf went in the half-light before sunrise, to call Eric to be armed. He found the warrior in Sir Guy's tent—the sick knight awake upon his cloak, haggard and breathing swiftly. A guttered candle flared and smoked upon the ground and beside it the girl curled up on her pallet asleep. In both hands she held the Viking's fist. He nodded to Arnulf, drawing free his cramped arm slowly, so that Ilga only stirred and sighed and slept on.

But Sir Guy propped himself on an elbow and whispered:

"Remember thy pledge, Eric—my daughter will be shielded?"

"On the honor of Duke Odo," said the Viking, "she will be."

When the glare of sunrise struck into the valley, the hills took shape, the mists thinned away, and the Normans moved forward as Duke Odo had commanded, before the morning heat should be upon them.

They kept no order, being only to come to grips with the bands of Moslem horse already in motion toward them from the rocks of the distant well. The men watched in silence, being sore with hunger and wracked with thirst. Only when their leader trotted up to them did they shout hoarsely.

They had no slightest reason to suspect that this leader was not Odo—some of them indeed noticed that he carried upon his saddle horn a heavy ax instead of his sword, and that he did not speak to his knights as usual. Instead he sent Arnulf to bid them halt and form in a half circle, with the archers in front.

It surprised Arnulf that Eric should sit the gray charger almost as easily as his lord the duke. From foot to head he was now encased in loose chain mail, and over his head had been thrust the steel helm with only an opening as large as his finger for him to see through. On his left arm—looped by a leather band over his shoulder—was braced the long painted shield of Duke Odo.

When Arnulf urged him to form the mailed horsemen for a charge, he laughed inside his steel dome:

"Arrow fight before sword stroke. Watch ye, little man."

Amid drifting dust clouds three thousand desert men swarmed about the seven hundred Normans. They dashed forward in groups, round shields upraised, cloaks flying about them. And the long arrows of the Normans dropped them from the saddle.

The back-curving ends of the Christian arc were still too close to the ridge and Odo's camp for the Moslems to cut in behind them, and the darting charges of the excited Arabs failed to break the Christian line. The short Moslem bow was not effective at that distance, and the Norman archers began to enjoy good sport. As the Arabs rode over their dead, their fury grew, and their shouting became a pulsing roar—

"Allah 'l allah!"

The Norman horsemen, standing beside their stirrups, chafed and grumbled. They dared not ride to their leader to protest, although they were ill content to be out of the affray. "'Tis not our lord's way, to hang upon the leash."

It was not, indeed, Odo's way, and a rider galloped down from the closed pavilion—a man of Arnulf's who sought the armiger beneath the upraised standard. And Arnulf shouted against Eric's helm, holding up a gleaming signet ring. "The token of my lord the duke. He bids thee cease this play and go forward before the heat comes."

Again Eric laughed in his dark dome. "Truly said I there was a sign between us. Let us try the sword strokes. Sound thy horns."

At the blare of the horns the Normans mounted, and walked their horses between the archers, who moved after them. Before the standard bearer rode Eric, holding back until the mailed riders had closed in and formed a double rank. Suddenly his eyes swept from flank to flank and he urged on the gray charger. Behind him massive hoofs drummed the hard clay and roared into a gallop.

The uplifted spears came down, the long shields were raised, and a war shout went up.

"Forward, with God!"

The Arabs had launched a counter charge, to strike the leading rank before it gained full headway. A thousand or more of the wild horsemen came on, their scimitars swinging by their knees, their horses maddened by blood.

But the first wave broke against the long Norman spears, and the lighter horses of the Moslems swerved or went down at the impact. A swirl and check—a brief clanging of steel—and the gray Norman line went on gathering pace. Again the spears were lowered as the Arabs closed in from all sides.

Eric, his ax-head resting on his shield arm, drove between two cloaked riders, took the lash of a scimitar on his shield and struck to the right. The curving edge of the ax sliced upward, beneath an Arab's jaw, and Eric freed the weapon by a jerk of his wrist that laid open one side of the rider's head.

A scimitar bruised the muscles of Eric's right shoulder, and again the ax slashed out, catching the new assailant beneath the arm. And part of the arm and shoulder flew off.

The Viking was little excited. The clash of weapons left him calm, and he struck out instinctively, knowing what the result would be, and always freeing his weapon swiftly. While the Normans lashed about them, shouting their exultation, he rode silently—a fighter plying his trade, a weapon man, killing where he willed.

Never before had he been so protected by steel. He felt an arrow jar in his left thigh, and reached down his left hand to break off the shaft. Twice something crashed against his solid helm, and he shook his head and went on.

So the hard-riding Normans broke the Arabs and followed up, until dark faces whirled past Eric again, and his ax rose and fell, scattering blood from its edge. And then his horse went down with a stagger and lurch—the length of a sword blade in its belly.

The Viking freed his feet from his stirrups and fell clear. He raised the shield over his head and shortened his grip on the ax. Dodging, hitting out as he ran, he fought for a way out of the press of rearing and circling horses.

Hands caught at his ax arm, but the Viking heaved back, and an Arab tumbled to earth before him, and lay motionless a second later with his skull crushed in and his brains scattered over the ground. Eric strode over him, ran for a moment beside his horse—glimpsed a rocky knoll through his eye-slit—and swung himself to the top of a four-foot boulder.

Arrows flicked past him and he swung his shield against the gleam of javelins. Arabs scrambled from their saddles to climb to the ground beside him, and shield and ax he battered them down.

They reached up to catch his legs, but that giant body in its chain mail was firmly rooted. Never, thought the Norman men-at-arms, straining to reach his side, had Odo fought with the sword as he now fought with the ax.

"Aid for good Duke Odo!"

He heard their shout, saw their long blades sweeping nearer.

"Good blows, ye men of the Cross! Good blows!" his deep voice boomed.

And then he saw no Moslems before him. Norman men-at-arms were sitting in the saddle beneath him, panting, resting their bloodied sword arms. They were looking at him silently. Many of them had hated, and almost all had feared Duke Odo. But this leader of theirs in the dull and dented helm, the chain mesh hanging in shreds from his right arm, and blood bubbling through the links on his chest and thigh—this man had led them through four onsets of the Moslem masses, and they were ready to follow him hereafter to Jerusalem or to purgatory. The valley was theirs.

Eric blinked at his men through sweat-tormented eyes, steam rising from his body, the lust of conflict like hot wine within him. The steel helm, heated by the sun's glare, irked him and he pulled with unfamiliar fingers, to tear it off. But it had been laced to his shoulder links by an expert hand, and he croaked for Arnulf to rid him of it.

A tall swordsman, black with dust, gripped his arm and pointed: "My lord, yonder is thy weapon bearer, and he is sped this life."

Eric looked down, seeing the carcass of his own horse and, a space in back of it, Arnulf's body outstretched. The Italian's head lay to the rear, face down, an arrow fairly through his throat. So Arnulf must have turned back, when Moslems surrounded the Viking, a moment before the charger was slain.

But Eric was not thinking of that. His eye had been caught by smoke and dust on the summit of the ridge where the duke's camp stood. Through the haze moved cloaked horsemen and gaunt yellow camels. At times steel dashed in the sunlight. He could hear no uproar but it seemed to him that the large pavilions of the knights were down and burning—and surely Odo's pavilion had vanished from its stone summit.

The fleeing Arabs had turned aside to storm the camp. And Eric, who cared little for that, remembered the sleeping child who had held fast to his hand through the night's watching. He thought of her shot through by arrows, falling under the galloping horses, or bound to an Arab's saddle, and he leaped from his high ground.

He pulled the swordsman who had spoken to him out of the saddle, and he swung upon the Norman's charger, and lashed the horse to a gallop toward the ridge. The others made haste to follow.

But Eric was the first to climb the ridge. The Arabs had fled. Upon the knoll, the duke's pavilion lay in flames.

The Viking urged his horse toward Sir Guy's tent, and reined in.

"Here was fighting," he muttered.

The tent was down, and atop the wreckage lay the figure of a Norman man-at-arms, his chain mesh broken, his body slashed open below the ribs. His head, encased in a basket helm, was turned to the sky, and upon him and about him sprawled the bodies of eight Moslems, all cut and crushed by gigantic blows.

Others of the duke's men came up to stare and to say—what Eric's eyes had told him—that they knew naught of Sir Guy and his daughter, save that no captives had been carried off by the Arabs. But when they said that, the folds of the linen tent stirred upon the wreckage, and a faint voice cried, "God for Bari."

The Normans started back and exclaimed, but Eric bade them cut through the tangle of cloth with their knives and this they did after making the sign of the cross—for it seemed to them that the dead had spoken.

They found the tent pole and table piled against the pallet, and upon the bed the girl Ilga, shielding the head of her sick father with her body. When Eric bent over them she stared back and looked around fearfully. The knight of the Mount raised himself upon his elbow.

"Forgive her, my lord," he whispered. "She hath been sorely tried and all this day she looked for the tall Viking, who came not."

"What befell here?" Eric's voice was hoarse within the steel dome.

"Christ be my aid, a strange thing befell. Anon we watched thy charge and the main battle. Then there came to the tent a tall fellow, wearing a nobleman's helm such as thine, but without device of any kind. He spoke not, but took Ilga up in his arms. She cried aloud for Eric, the Viking, but this man laughed and heeded me not. He bore her to the entrance, then we heard the shouting of the Arabs."

Sir Guy brushed the sweat from his white face "The man of the helm said nothing. He turned back and again he laughed, when he tossed Ilga down beside me. He laid the table—so—and heaved up the center pole, letting it down upon us, with all the canopy about us. Then he pushed his way clear of the cloth and took his stand near us, for we heard his battle shout. Aye, he struck heavy blows, and it seemed to me that a score of swordsmen came against him. Yet he held his ground, and shielded us. He had great strength, being a madman, touched with the sun, or God's anger."

"Not so." The Viking thrust his fingers through the openings in his helm beneath his ears, and wrenched off the steel casque when the links and laces broke.

A hundred eyes stared at him mutely, until the maid Ilga left her father and caught the Viking's arm against her heart. "Thou—thou didst leave me!"

Eric's blue eyes clouded, and he nodded slowly. "True—it must be said that I have that weakness. When steel is bared, I have nothing else in my head." And when she pressed her face against his torn shoulder he bent down, brushing his lips against the tangle of her hair.

A Norman strode up to him. "What then of my lord, the duke? Eric the Landless, it does appear to me thou hast stolen his gear, and helm."

But Sir Guy lifted his hand. "Ill said! This smells to me of Odo's trickery, and I doubt not that he will presently come out of his hole, like the fox he is."

Before anyone could answer, the Viking's deep voice checked them. "Not so!"

He stepped to the body upon the wreckage, and with the edge of his ax cut the thongs of the helm. He drew it off and cast it away, and in the silence that followed his action, leaned on his ax to look down into the pallid features and the open eyes of the dead duke, Odo.

"I am thinking," his voice rumbled on, "that this was a man of hard deeds, but he met his death well. And it must be said, that is a great thing in any man."

Keeper of the Gate

Chapter I
Master of the Hawks

The road ran straight as an arrow's flight over the red clay plain. But the plain itself rose and fell, in swell after swell, as if it were a motionless sea on which floated black rocks and a scum of gray tamarisk. A haze of dust shut it in on all sides, veiling the skyline. Through this veil burned the midafternoon sun.

Broad wooden wheel tracks and round camel pads, cut by the sharper hoofs of horses and laden donkeys, marked the line of the road. The dung had been picked up and carried off to be dried for fuel. Only down in a gully, under a grove of wind-stripped poplars, were men to be seen.

They had been watering their animals at the well, in a nest of limestone rock. And, being Afghans, they lingered to dispute among themselves, idly hopeful that plunder might come their way along the caravan road. Like heavy-headed birds of prey they squatted in the shade, wrapped in their striped *abtu*, with long knives in their girdles.

So far, they had seen nothing promising pass by—herds of sheep and black goats, a well-guarded caravan with rice up from Ghazna, hastening into the orchards of Samarkand a few hours' travel to the west. At about this point the road left the fertile land by the Samarkand River and entered the Kizil Kum, the Red Sands. Beyond the Kizil Kum the road ascended through the foothills to the high plateaus known as the Roof of the World. And beyond this barrier, far to the east, lay Cathay, the dominion of Kublai Khan.

At the sound of hoofs the Afghans turned on their haunches to stare at a single rider coming from Samarkand. After a glance they settled back again, seeing no hope of loot in him.

For one thing, he had light saddlebags. The white felt coat rolled and
tied to the saddle behind him was that of a Tatar officer. These Afghans
had found it unwise to meddle with the Tatars, who ruled all the world
they knew with an iron hand. Yet this rider was not a Tatar. He did not
crouch in the saddle with shortened stirrups, but held erect his long straight
body clad in a loose tunic of chamois leather. The sun-bleached hair that
fell to his shoulders was the color of ripe wheat. His eyes were casual and
blue, although his face with its high cheekbones was almost as dark as
their own.

Every one of them glanced enviously at the clean-limbed bay mare he
rode and looked curiously at the long sword with plain hilt and leather
sheath slung to his hip. Unlike the Tatars, he carried no bow or shield.

"*Awafikh!*" One of them rose to greet him. "Thy health! Dismount
and sit. Let thy horse drink."

The stranger smiled.

"There is no need, O brothers of the road. May Allah not turn his face
from ye!"

And he trotted on without a backward glance, which in itself was a
matter for surprise. They grunted and talked him over.

"He speaks Arabic like a hadji—nay, like one born among the people
of the tents. Surely he hath come from afar. The horse is worth more than
silver, it is worth gold. But he rides alone. Then, verily, in a little while
will we see the others of his band coming after."

The stranger, however, was alone. He was traveling faster than the caravans, and he disliked the delay and confusion of the mixed bands that
filled the great road to the East. And, as the Afghans had suspected, he
came from a far place.

Nial he was, Nial O'Gordon, with no land to claim for his own. Born
in a crusader's frontier castle overlooking the gorge of the Jordan, a Scot
by blood, he had been driven out of Palestine by the victorious Moslems.
Weaned and trained in the East, he had found no tie to hold him to England, and no kin who would do aught for a wandering son of a crusader.
He was no more than twenty years old, and he had a longing to make his
way through the barriers to Cathay where the great khan reigned.

From Constantinople Nial had sailed to the sea gate of the Golden Horde,
where his swordsmanship had kept life in him and brought him reward
from Barka Khan, of the Horde. In that year he had learned to speak with
the Tatars, and he carried sewn to the inner side of his belt a bronze tablet

certifying that he had served faithfully as *gur-khan* of the Golden Horde. He had, besides, enough gold to take him far on his road.

After riding half a mile beyond the well, he halted on a rise and let his horse nose the ground while he watched the track behind him. The Afghans looked as if they were on the prowl, and he wanted to see whether any of them had decided to come after him. He did make out one horseman surmounting a ridge with red dust spurting behind him.

But the man was alone, going at a steady gallop. Soon Nial heard a distant jingle of bells, and made out that the oncoming rider was unarmed, with nothing carried on the saddle—a Tatar courier, going at racing speed to the next post station. Those Afghans would never molest the messenger.

The courier swept down into the last hollow and disappeared. With an abrupt jangle the sound of the bells ceased. Nial waited, listening. He heard a confused clatter, as if horses were stamping over loose stones. Then nothing at all.

Nial picked up his rein after a moment and turned back along the trail. Odd that such a rider should have been thrown on an open road. The man would have halted for nothing else. He might have been hurt, and Nial would need to catch the horse and bring him along to the station.

As he had expected, Nial saw the courier lying motionless in the bottom of the hollow near a grove of dense tamarisk. The horse had vanished. He dismounted beside the Tatar and bent over him quickly. The courier's body had been slashed through to the backbone beneath the ribs, and he was dead, although his blood was still draining into the sand.

Turning him over, Nial saw that the long leather case fastened to his belt had been ripped open. Whatever he had carried had been stolen, and the man himself slain out of hand. In the patches of sand around the body Nial traced the tracks of two horses that had come out to the road, barring the way. The slayers had gone off at once, down the gully, to keep clear of the skyline.

Then Nial sprang up, catching at his sword. Something moved behind the screen of tamarisk. Two horses trotted out, and their riders drove at him before he had a chance to mount. As he braced himself, swinging his blade back of his shoulder, he saw that the scimitar of the nearer man was stained with blood. And it flashed through his mind that they had surely seen him coming over the ridge and had turned back to put him out of the way as he knelt over the body.

Even as he thought, he leaped his own length to one side—from the left hand to the right of the horseman who was already bringing down his scimitar in a slash. The sudden move caught the man unaware, and he tried to turn his blade as he shifted in the saddle and jerked at his horse.

But Nial, with both feet planted firmly on the ground, swung his long sword savagely. The horse could not be checked in time, and the steel blade swept down over its head, brushing back the scimitar and biting deep over the hips of the rider.

"*Y'allah!*" The man screamed, straightening convulsively in his stirrups and falling heavily as Nial pulled the sword clear, turning in time to parry a slash from the second rider.

The man galloped by and pulled in for a moment to stare malevolently at the tall wanderer. Then, clapping his stirrups against the ribs of his horse, he galloped back toward the well, keeping to the road.

Nial listened until he was sure that the surviving slayer had gone off in earnest. Then he went to inspect the man he had cut from the saddle, who had lived only a few moments after striking down the unarmed courier—a tall man in a wolfskin *chaban*, smelling like a wolf. A black lambskin hat lay beside him, and from under his arm the end of a silver tube projected. Nial drew it out and looked at it curiously.

The tube, little more than a foot in length, was of heavy silver inlaid with gold tracery and polished by constant use. The open end had been sealed with red wax and stamped with the impress of a lion's head.

"Faith," the Scot muttered, "there will be more to do about this."

For the lion's head was the *tamgha*—the mark—of Barka Khan, lord of the Golden Horde. The tube, then, had come from Sarai, and it might contain a letter, an urgent command, a summons to war, or precious stones. The courier who had carried it hither in the leather case had been no ordinary post rider; he had been an express rider of the khan, traveling at the utmost speed to his home toward the East.

To hold up a carrier of the post was a crime calling for death; to slay a courier of the khan was a thing unheard of in the dominion of the Tatars. Yet the two wearers of the black lambskin *kalpaks* had waited here in the gully to do just that. Had they known that this one rider would carry something of value from the khan? But how could any tidings have come from Sarai ahead of an express? Nial examined the seal again to make sure that it was intact.

Then he went to his horse, drew a silk cloth from one of the saddle-bags, wrapped the silver tube carefully and stowed it in the bag. When he handed it in at the next post station and explained the attack upon the courier, he wanted to be certain that the seal had not been broken.

"Fool!" he exclaimed suddenly, and swung himself into the saddle.

He urged his horse up the slope and glanced over his shoulder.

A quarter mile behind him the tribesman of the black hat was coming up with a half dozen Afghans. Faintly he heard their shout when they sighted him. He tightened his knees, driving the bay mare into a long gallop.

He had to get away from them, and quickly. It would be safer to argue with wild dogs than to try to explain matters to them. The black hat had told his tribesmen his version of the murder. Now the tribesmen were launched on a manhunt, eager for reward if they brought Nial's head in to the Tatars. To throw away the tube would not mend matters; nor could he stand his ground against seven men.

At the next rise he looked back without reining in the mare. The pursuers had not gained on him, and they had scattered a little. Another mile, and he knew that his mare had the speed of them; but he knew as well the endurance of the Afghans' lean ponies, and he forced the mare on while he pondered his chances.

To turn off would be useless in that open plain. They would be watching his tracks; and the ground was becoming more sandy. But by now the post station ought not to be far off. He wondered about that station until he swept around a turn into a camel caravan, making camp by a well, thronged with noisy Tadjiks who ceased their clamor to stare at him when he reined to a halt among them, pointing his finger at the most dignified white beard he could see.

"The *yamkhanah*—how far is it?" he shouted.

The white beard wagged plaintively.

"Ai, *tura*, oh Lord Protector of the unfortunate ones—"

"How far?"

"Eh, a laden camel goes there in one watch of the day. A lowly fellow such as thy servant walks there in a watch and a half, and—"

But Nial was off down the road. The post station, he guessed, would be less than an hour's gallop, and he dared not waste another moment. To do what he planned he must gain a mile or so on his pursuers, and he must sacrifice the mare. It would be useless to seek the Tatar officers at the station, hand over the khan's missive and tell his story. By now the

Afghans would be ready to swear that they had all seen him slay the courier. There was blood on his sword, and he was fleeing from them.

"Nay, lass," he whispered, "there is no other road. So hie thee on."

The mare bore him well and kept her feet among the stones. When he sighted the haystacks of the station the tribesmen were not in sight. At the gate of the guardhouse he reined in, shouting impatiently:

"A messenger from Barka Khan, Lord of the West and the East! Bring out a fast horse, a good horse."

He had put on his white felt *chaban* and had slung his saddlebags over one shoulder. As he dismounted, several men in long blue coats rose from their seats and ran with a curious, bowlegged waddle toward the line of horses waiting ready saddled outside the pen. The ring of command in Nial's voice was unmistakable, and the Tatars had learned obedience from infancy.

"Nay," Nial cried impatiently. He had cast his eye over the half dozen remounts and made his own choice. "Not the gray pony. Am I a boy in weight? The piebald horse with the mane!"

The grooms hastened to lead out the long-limbed, Turkoman-bred horse and, as he flung his bags over the saddlehorn, Nial prayed inwardly that he had made a good choice. The piebald looked like a famished brute, but it must have speed in those long legs.

A tall Mongol* in horsehide boots—the *darogha*, or officer, of the station—came up. Nial greeted him courteously but briefly as he mounted

---

*Two generations before this Genghis Khan had led his Mongols to the conquest of the greater part of Asia and the borderland of Europe. But the Mongols themselves, the warriors of the clan of the Yakka, or Great Mongols, formed only a small proportion of his armies. Tatars, Uighurs, Turks, Kipchaks, and Kitans (Cathayans) made up the mass of the armies. Like the Romans of Trajan's time, the Mongols dominated the nomad empire, in which other peoples made up the bulk of the fighting forces. Europeans, unable to distinguish between the different clans, christened them all Tatars. In this story the word is used for the warriors of Kublai Khan.

Although at this time the vast empire was nominally under the dominion of Kublai Khan, who resided in China, the two western segments, the Ilkhan Empire and the Golden Horde, were actually independent under the rule of their own khans. Barka Khan, master of the Golden Horde, had his headquarters at Sarai on the lower Volga. His dominion stretched from the steppes of mid-Asia, between Lake Balkash and the Aral Sea, westward more than forty-five degrees beyond the border of Poland and Hungary.

and would have spurred off. The officer caught his rein and stared curiously at his light bags.

"*Kiap seme kene*," he ventured. "Swiftly thou ridest."

"Aye, swiftly." Nial nodded, forcing himself to show not the least impatience. "For I carry that which is sealed by the seal of Barka Khan."

The Mongol grunted understanding, but pointed down the road to several black specks drawing nearer in the drifting dust.

"And they also, they come as if the ghost wind follows after. What are they?"

"Have I the eyes of an eagle, to see what is hidden and afar?" Nial lifted his rein. "Nay, I may not sit here like a woman with a burden, to see what comes upon the road."

Reluctantly the Mongol officer stepped back. The Scot puzzled him and the approaching riders stirred his curiosity, but it was impossible to delay a messenger of the khan of the Golden Horde. Nial lashed the piebald with the end of the rein and thrilled with satisfaction. The horse was away with a bird-like swoop, head up and muzzle tossing restlessly—a steppe-bred racer, accustomed to keeping to a gallop for hours and expecting no mercy from its rider.

Until sunset he pushed on steadily, noticing that he was climbing out of the loose sand into bare foothills covered with dwarf oak. With the last of the light he paused to breathe his horse and think.

Thanks to his choice of the piebald Turkoman the pursuit was far behind and below him. But he had caught glimpses of a score of horsemen, and he knew that some of the Tatars of the station, led perhaps by the tall *darogha*, had joined the pursuit. Those men were capable of following the track of a horse over the dry grass of a prairie, and it would be useless to try to throw them off in this brush and sandy clay.

Nor did he dare push on to the next station. He had watched the sky constantly and had seen no pigeons flying high overhead; but messenger pigeons chose their own course and one might have passed him too far off to be seen. Already the clear afterglow of sunset was fading. In a few moments the sky would be dark. It was only a question of hours before word of the murder of the post rider and the loss of the silver tube would go far ahead of him along the road, born on the wing of the pigeon post. And with these tidings would go his own description—even to his height and way of talking. No, the road was closed to him, and his life at hazard wherever Tatar officers, or Moslem spies who served them, might be met.

If he dared face them—if he circled back to Samarkand, surrendered the silver tube and told his story—he could prove nothing. He had no witness; the slain tribesman found lying by the courier's body would be a silent witness against him.

There was nothing for him to do but turn from the road and trust to luck to throw off his pursuers in the hours of darkness. He looked to right and left, seeing only the darkening line of distant hills, purple against the faint glow at the edge of the sky. On the right hand the stony bed of a dry stream ran into a gully.

"'Tis no true road," he observed gravely, "but it will lead somewhere."

When the Daughters of the Tomb had swung nine lights of their constellation nearly overhead, and the night was half gone, Nial found himself threading a path on the brow of a hill. On either side thornbush clustered, whispering under a dry wind. But he caught another sound ahead of him, and the piebald horse went forward with new willingness, lifting its head and whinnying.

Nial fancied that wild horses were moving along the trail, but he was careful to bend forward over the saddlehorn, keeping his head down by the neck of the horse, a trick he had learned in night riding with the Tatars. Then he listened, surprised.

A girl's voice sang in the darkness. A fitful, drowsy song, about a wizard who leaped on the wind from mountain summit to peak. The song ceased and saddle leather creaked.

"Ho, thou wandering devil, art thou here? I waited long for thee."

Nial was aware of a shape beside him and the faint scent of dried flowers.

Other dark forms appeared, moving slowly along the white clay of the trail—loose ponies, he thought, herded together by the girl. At a word from him she would be off into the night. And he had need of a fresh horse.

He groped forward to catch her rein.

Instead his hand fell upon a slender knee that started under his touch.

"Ai!" A frightened gasp, and the heavy thongs of a whip stung his wrist as the girl's pony bounded forward.

He heard her cry at the other horses and, before he could make shift to follow, they were all speeding away like startled deer.

The big piebald plunged after them and presently, rounding a bend in the trail, Nial saw a glimmer of light ahead.

Warily he approached it, watching it spread to an open doorway with the vague shapes of upended carts and a stone wellhead on either hand. The people of the house were still astir. He caught quick voices and rapid footfalls, and guessed that the girl had come in with her ponies. Out of the doorway came a grizzled Tatar in a loose horsehide coat, carrying a newly lighted torch.

Without a word he held the torch close to Nial's head and peered with expressionless eyes into the darkness beyond.

Behind him, as if at a signal, appeared a taller figure—a man of authority in a blue-padded *khalat*, reaching from throat to slippers, with a majestic black beard flowing down to his girdle. His shaven head was covered by a velvet skullcap and his brown eyes dwelt upon Nial quietly.

"Neshavan of the Khosh-khanah I am," he said. "You ride late, O stranger, and alone."

It was more of a question than a statement, and Nial dismounted as courtesy required.

"Alone I come, Neshavan. I wish to change my saddle to another mount. This road is not known to me, and I have far to go before the first light."

The master of the house nodded understandingly.

"Then, my guest, you will honor me by sitting and eating a little of my poor food before taking the road again. Few come along this hill trail."

Nial took his saddlebags over his arm and surrendered the sweating Turkoman to the Tatar servant, noticing as he did so that the man had a powerful bow ready strung and a case of arrows under his loose coat. The Scot felt the irk of hunger, and he needed information even more than food. If Neshavan invited him to eat he had nothing to fear from this house, and he was hours ahead of the pursuit.

When he followed his host into a long room, dimly lighted, he saw why it was called Khosh-khanah—the Hawk House. The other half of the place was given over to dozens of hawks, drowsing on their perches, ranging from small, shapely gyrfalcons to great brown golden eagles. By the assortment of hoods, jesses, and thongs lying about, he suspected that Neshavan trained the falcons himself.

"Aye"—his host followed his glance as they knelt on a clean rug to wash their hands—"my goshawks will take hares. My *bouragut* will bring down a great crane, or attack antelope. Karabek and I have taught them since

we were milk brothers together. Now the nobles of Samarkand pay high
for Neshavan's falcons, a just price. Will the road of my honored guest
take him beyond Talas?"

In the shadowed alcove behind Neshavan a slender shape appeared silently and settled down on the cushions of the rug to watch them. Nial
could distinguish a girl's white kerchief and dark eyes. He did not stare,
nor did he mention the woman and the horses upon the trail. This was a
Moslem household, and therefore the women did not exist—for the eyes
of visiting men. Neshavan had not even asked his name, although he was
curious enough about the solitary young rider and about the saddlebags
under Nial's elbow.

"Who knows?" The Scot guessed that Talas would be the next town
on the trail he was following. "*Illah a'lam*—God alone knoweth. Is there
not a Tatar *yamkhanah* in Talas?"

"Nay." Neshavan shook his head. "They keep to the great road behind
you, that runs through Khodjent to the East. They do not come into these
hills except to hunt. Besides, what caravans would go beyond Talas?"

"Is there not a road?" Nial wondered aloud, dipping his fingers into the
bowl of rice stew that a servant set between them.

"Once there was a way, from Talas up the river that is called the Gold
Bringer. I have heard that in former times many caravans came and went
by the river, and the Gate."

"To the East," Nial suggested, because he wished to know.

"To the Far East, through the heights. But now—" Neshavan hesitated—"the Gate is closed."

"Yet there is no snow now, even on the peaks."

"On those peaks the snow lies always—aye, and ancient ice. But the
pass that we call the Gate is free of snow now in the hot season. Still, it
is not open."

"Allah forbid," Nial ventured lightly, because he wished to find out
more, "what harm could come of it? I have a tablet from Barka Khan, and
I go where I will."

"Where the Gold Bringer rises from the ground, the command of the
khans is not obeyed. A Tatar army could not go through."

A whisper no louder than the rustle of silk came from the alcove, and
Neshavan checked his words. His tone changed; he smiled.

"Such are the tales that come down from the hills. Men who have gone
up the river say that it is safer to ride with the ghost wind, or to steal a horse
from the great herd that Satan drives of nights over the barren lands."

"What did they see to frighten them?"

Neshavan still smiled.

"Nothing. But they heard much and turned back."

Again he fell silent. Karabek, the Tatar bowman, came to the rug hastily, without apology.

"*Tura,*" he grunted, "two Kara Kalpaks ride to thy threshold."

The effect upon the master of the house was instantaneous. His eyes opened wide and he drew a long breath. Then he made a sign with his hand toward the alcove, glanced moodily about the chamber and strode to the door. Nial, hearing horses' hoofs on the hard clay, was at his side—wondering whether a pair of the Tatars, knowing this trail and the Hawk House, had come up.

Instead he saw in the light of a torch held by a servant, two tribesmen who looked like gaunt wolves on weary horses. They wore ragged black lambskin headgear, like that of the two slayers of the courier, and Nial understood how they came to be named Kara Kalpaks—Black Hats. The taller of the pair reined forward impatiently, his pony wincing from a prod of the sharp stirrup edge.

"In the name of Allah," he cried, "give us water."

His slant eyes flickered restlessly as Neshavan turned and gravely ordered the man with the torch to fetch a jar. Karabek lingered by the door, bow in hand, tense as a hound scenting game.

"Water," said Neshavan, "thou shalt have, in peace."

He took the filled jar from the servant and stepped forward. The tribesman leaned down and, as Neshavan held out the clay jar, whipped a curved knife from his waistband. Swift as a panther's paw the Black Hat's hand shot out, plunging the knife into Neshavan's throat.

The master of the Hawk House staggered aside, clutching at the ivory hilt projecting from his beard. Then with a queer whine he collapsed on the ground, blood rushing from his mouth. His slayer had drawn scimitar and, with no more excitement than if dealing with a jackal, slashed the forearm of the dazed servant holding the torch.

"Strike down the dogs!" he shouted.

A girl's scream rang through the room, and Karabek turned instinctively to catch in his arms the slender figure that darted from the alcove toward the dying Neshavan. And out of the darkness emerged a dozen Black Hats who must have been waiting beyond the torchlight for just this moment. They flung themselves from the saddles, and their leader lifted his head to laugh.

"*Yartak bish yabir*—the young woman awaits ye, O my brothers!"

Nial had drawn his sword instinctively. Seeing bows in the hands of the men who remained in their saddles, he stepped back into the room, caught a glimpse of Karabek carrying the struggling girl into the alcove and picked up his roped saddlebags. The quarrel was not his affair, and it would be sheer folly to stand his ground against these raiders.

But they were on his heels with a rush and, in a hot wave of anger, he whirled at the curtain of the alcove, striking down the sword of the foremost and laying the face of another open with a side-long slash.

They snarled and hung back, peering into the gloom of the alcove. Then Nial felt a hand on his shoulder and heard Karabek's quiet voice.

"Come."

He stepped back between the curtains, saw Karabek hastening down a passage and ran out into darkness that reeked of cattle and manure. A lantern on the ground guided him to the stable shed, where the Tatar and the girl loosed a horse swiftly.

"Take thine!" Karabek grunted at him, and Nial made out his Turkoman still saddled beside him.

He untied the rein and swung himself into the saddle as the girl ran off, tugging at the halter of a pony. He followed her past the shed, down a path that brought them under heavy trees. Here he heard his companion stop and busy herself with the pony's head, putting on a headstall as he judged by the click of the iron bit against rebellious teeth. She was sobbing quietly, while the shouts of the Black Hats echoed in the house behind them, above the screaming of the excited hawks.

Then she must have climbed to the pony's back, for he heard them moving off. He followed.

"Where is your servant, Karabek?" he asked.

He repeated the question before she answered, in a whisper:

"Nay, he was Neshavan's servant and foster-brother. He would not go. *Ai-a*, may God grant that he slays that dog-born dog!"

She would say nothing more, even when they came out upon the road beyond her home and looked back to see a red glare rising among the trees. The Hawk House was burning, and around it the raiders were carrying spoil to their horses. Nial waited, but she was not weeping now.

"Karabek has not come," he ventured. "Will you go on to Talas?"

She lifted her head, brushing back the thick tresses from her eyes, and in the starlight he could see only her small white face.

"Why not," she responded calmly. "All places are alike to me now."

Chapter II
The Seal of the Khan

After the noon prayer the next day, when the streets of Talas were deserted except for black goats, a gaunt Kara Kalpak rode at a footpace across the one bridge, paying no heed to the beggars who sprawled in the shadow of the creaking waterwheel.

Guiding his horse through alleys where the sun beat remorselessly upon clay walls, drawing a stench from the trodden ground, the tribesman glanced from side to side until he came to a rickety wooden door marked with two red stains. They might have been uplifted crimson arms, or rude towers, but they satisfied the Kara Kalpak and he dismounted. He yawned, spat, muttered an invocation, "*Hazz-shaitan*—Satan in his abode," fidgeted with his waistband, and finally knocked on the door.

It was opened by a lame boy who did not trouble to brush the flies from his sore eyes.

"Hast thou no key?" he exclaimed with the insolence of a child who knows he is protected from harm.

"Nay, little one," the tribesman muttered pacifically, "no key was given me; yet have I gone beyond the Gate."

"So have many," the child sneered. "By what token?"

"I have heard the voice that is not seen."

"What brought thee hither?"

"A message—tidings for him who sits behind the red towers."

"Of silence." The boy laughed, pointing to the marks on the door. "Nay, these are but gateposts and thou art a braying ass without wit. Come and bray."

Without taking offense, the Kara Kalpak led his horse into the courtyard, turned him loose in the shade, and followed the limping boy up an outer stair to a room on the second floor that overlooked the roofs of Talas. He went slowly, as if coming with empty pockets to a moneylender who held long-overdue interest against him. Leaving his peaked riding slippers on the mat, he advanced slowly into the shadow toward a young Persian who knelt by a low table that bore a silver cup of mastic and sugared fruits. He touched the carpet, then his forehead with his right hand, clumsily as a performing bear.

"Ai, tura," he vouchsafed, "I have tidings from the caravan road for him who sits behind the outer gateposts of silence."

The Persian did not smile. He had blue eyes, bloodshot from too many opiates or too little sleep, and soft, protruding lips. His turban cloth was immaculate white silk.

"I am Mir Farash," he said idly, "a poor interpreter of dreams, but I will hear thy tale."

Squatting on the carpet, the tribesman fingered his beard uneasily.

"As the command came, so it was done," he began. "Two of us waited beyond the first well of the great road. We watched in turn, six—eight days. Then when the sun was high we beheld the light flash twice and twice again from the tower of the ruined mosque above Samarkand. We went down to wait in a gully for the rider of the *yam*. We came out before him, and Yussuf slew him with one stroke when he would have swerved past us."

He paused to glance restlessly behind him at the window.

"The boy watches," Mir Farash observed. "And then?"

"Lord, it was Yussuf who took the silver tube. It bore a Tatar seal."

"Thou hast it not?"

"Yussuf had it. But, Honored One, before we could ride off a strange horseman came to the dying Tatar."

"And ye twain, being greedy of more than payment, lingered to loot him!"

"Nay, by the ninety and nine holy names! We feared that he had seen. He knelt there, unaware—"

The youth's dark eyes flashed.

"He had seen, and yet knelt unsuspecting! What poor lies are these?"

The big tribesman rocked on his haunches. Although he was girdled with weapons and the slender interpreter of dreams looked harmless as a girl, his voice thickened with fear.

"Kulluck! I am thy slave! My words are dull, but it is all true. Am I not here in the dust at thy feet? Do not let anger come. Hearken, we thought to ride down this horseman. He turned like a panther. He struck Yussuf such a blow it slit him open.

"Who was I to ride in where Yussuf had fallen? Nay, a thought came to me, and I hastened along the road to the well, calling upon some dog-born Afghans to aid me. I swore that this nameless one had slain the courier and Yussuf also. We gave chase, swift as the black storm wind. At the next station we should have caught him, but he tricked the Tatar guards and went off on a good horse. The officer of the station joined us with ten and two men, after I had sworn to the murder of the courier."

"This nameless one—he had taken the silver tube?" Mir Farash murmured. "And thou, O sharp of wit, thou didst tell the Tatar officer of this also?"

"Nay," exclaimed the tribesman with pride. "I was like a fox in guile. I said only that the *yam* rider had been robbed and his wallet torn open. Those Afghans had seen that. The Tatars could follow the man's trail. After the last light he turned off into the hills, toward Talas. The Tatars were like a dog pack, with their noses to the ground. They made torches and followed slowly. I decided to cast ahead, along the upper trail to Talas. I did not see the thief, but the Hawk House was burning."

Mir Farash nodded reflectively.

"What was he like, this nameless one?"

"A *batyr*—a matchless swordsman—like to no other I have seen." The tribesman gave a shrewd description of Nial, while visibly he pondered something else. "Surely he must come out of the hills upon this river. The Tatars are behind him, and they will not turn back. Give command to hunt for him here."

Again the Persian nodded, impassively.

"I understand. Thou hast failed."

"*Kulluck!* But I alone know his face."

The Kara Kalpak tugged at his beard anxiously.

"Then wait below until I summon thee."

When the tribesman had gone off, grateful to escape punishment for the present, at least, Mir Farash nibbled at one of the sugared fruits. Then without enthusiasm he rose and went up to the roof of his house, where he leaned against the parapet in the full glare of sunlight. Idly he scanned the vistas of alleys below him. Talas sprawled from the river halfway up a stony hill, and his house was one of the highest.

It was a dangerous thing to do; for that was the siesta hour and groups of women were lying under canopies on the flat roofs, where layers of fragrant grapes had been spread to dry. A good Moslem dislikes to be stared at, and will resent violently having his women watched from a roof, no matter how distant. Although Mir Farash's white turban reflected the sunlight, drawing instant attention to him, neither taunts nor arrows came his way. Instead, some of the younger women near him began to chatter in the hope that he would notice them.

But he continued to inspect the narrow valley, the twin slopes of gray stone cut up into terraces heavy with grapevines, the turgid Zarafshan* River, and the empty bridge. The great waterwheel groaned and wheezed. A breath of cooler air from distant heights passed down the valley, mingling with the warm odor of tamarisk, of mulberries ripening in the sun, and the dung and offal of the alleys. Mir Farash called a boy to him and gave command to send watchers to the gates and others to search along the river for a solitary rider—a tall infidel with blue eyes and a lion's mane, who spoke both Arabic and the speech of the Tatars.

By midafternoon he had another visitor, a Kara Kalpak who was as voiceless as the first had been voluble.

"Neshavan hath found his grave," he reported.

"And where," Mir Farash asked, "is the proof?"

Reaching into a wicker basket beside him, the tribesman lifted out a human head and placed it before the Persian. It had a long black beard, clotted with dried blood.

"The keeper of the hawks," grunted the Kara Kalpak, and took a second head from the basket. "Karabek, the archer."

Drawing a sharp knife from his waistband, he slit an ear from each and pouched these two pieces of evidence of the success of his mission before rising silently to depart. Mir Farash smiled fleetingly.

"But what of the girl, Alai?" he questioned.

The Kara Kalpak swept his arm outward.

"Gone into the night, like an arrow lost among reeds."

"She will cause trouble. Watch for her and bring her to me. Hast thou seen a tall infidel with blue eyes and a lion's mane? He hath only one straight sword and two saddlebags."

"*Allah tzei!* Yes, we have seen him and his sword. He also escaped because Karabek stood upon their trail with his bow."

"Go thou and search for him. Let no one plunder him, but bring him hither with all he carries."

The creaking of a far-off waterwheel roused Nial late that afternoon. His first thought was for the saddlebags under his head, and when he had sat-

---

*The Gold Bringer. In Tamerlane's time gold was washed from its bed.

isfied himself that the silver tube was safe, he looked around for the Tatar girl. She was not in sight, although her pony stood by the piebald horse.

Nial pushed through the poplar grove in which they had taken refuge early that morning, for both were tired and neither wished to ride into Talas in daylight. The girl was sleeping in a hollow, curled up on saddle-cloths, her white linen headgear drawn over her face. She did not stir when he stood beside her nor when he knelt and lifted the white cloth gently.

Her eyes were closed—long eyes that slanted upward a little under heavy lashes darkened with kohl. Her full lips were blood-red against her white face, the face of a weary child. Around her throat curled the mass of her unbound hair, black as night itself. But, seemingly asleep, she was watching him under the veil of her lashes. And when the tall Scot would have gone away, she looked him full in the face, curiously, without a word.

"How do men call thee?" he asked awkwardly.

"Alai."

The girl rose to her knees, brushing back her hair and winding the white coif around it deftly, but without veiling her face. Nial knew that the Tatar girls often went about freely without the heavy veil of the stricter Moslems.

"I have a little food," he ventured. "No water."

From a bag he produced barley cakes and dried curds, arranging them in two equal piles. Alai took up her share and knelt with her back to him, reaching behind her to break the cakes upon the heel of her boot.

"Was Neshavan thy father?" he asked.

"Nay," she murmured, "he nourished me and protected me. He was like a father."

Alai had been left at the Hawk House by her own father, a Tatar *noyon* of the great Horde, who had been fleeing through the hills, closely pursued. He had been slain, and no one had claimed the girl, who had been raised by the kindly Neshavan.

"Why did the Black Hats seek him out last night? They meant to kill him."

"The dogs!" She lifted her head and spat. "May Allah turn from them. May their days be bitter and fiends trouble their dreams. They are Gutchluk's men."

"Who is he?"

Alai swept her hand toward the hills.

"All this is his. Our falcons brought down some of his messenger pigeons, and Neshavan read the messages, unknowing. We meant no harm."

She pondered a moment and felt in the broad pocket of her *khalat*, offering Nial a handful of sugared ginger. She glanced at him shyly when he took some, then turned her back to nibble at hers. When Neshavan was slain she had stormed and wept, but now it was all over except the hoped-for vengeance; the women of mid-Asia were accustomed to the turns of fate. Alai must have been thirsty, but she did not complain as she curled up by the horses, watching Nial's movements curiously.

Going to the edge of the grove, he looked out over the valley of the Zarafshan and the distant roofs of Talas. Several horsemen were passing below him, but no Tatars were visible.

"Soon it will be dark," he said, "and then where will you go—in the town?"

"With you, Lord Nial."

Laughing, he shook his head.

"Nay, Alai, that cannot be. I ride far—alone."

"I have kept the saddle for months with Neshavan. I can point out the way to you."

"You must go to your friends."

"I have not one—" She shook her head vigorously. "Did you not lift the veil from me? By Allah, have we not shared bread?"

Nial did not try to argue; instead he asked if she knew a house outside the wall where they would be safe for a night. He could leave her where she would be protected.

"We can find Abu Harb," she said after thinking it over. "He hunts antelope and at times steals horses. He owed Neshavan a debt, and so he will give me a saddle. Why do you flee, Lord Nial?"

The Scot had fewer words than this girl, and he could not keep pace with her thoughts.

"How did you know?" he asked

"*Wallahi*—have you not watched the back track? And where are your goods and servants? You are not a merchant, not a Tatar."

"Nay—" he smiled, the harsh lines softening 'round his lips—"I am a devil from over the dark water, the sea."

"Then where will you turn your reins?"

"To Cathay."

This silenced Alai only for a moment.

"*Bilmaida—good!* If Allah wills, I may find my own people."

When he saddled the piebald, she had the headstall on the pony and was watching him with amusement as he finished. The sunset glow was fading down the valley when they rode from the grove, Alai leading him along a path beyond sight of the bridge. In the gloom by the river's edge she found a ford, passing through fishermen's huts, up the side of the hill. Casting about in the darkness, she drew near what seemed to be a cleft in a solid cliff.

"*Ai*, Abu Harb," she called softly. "The eagle waits at the hunter's door."

A voice rumbled in the bowels of the hill and presently a torch flared within the cleft. Without waiting for an invitation, the girl dismounted and led in her pony, while Nial followed more slowly, the piebald objecting savagely to crowding through the rock passages.

Rounding a turn, he found himself in a small cavern with smoke-blackened roof. A one-eyed Arab stared at him suspiciously beneath the tomb.

"He is the very one!"

Nial turned as if scenting unseen danger.

"Nay, Abu Harb! He is the Lord Nial who struck a blow for Neshavan, and he hath shared our salt."

At once the Arab lifted his head. His long hair, gray at the temples, was braided close to his skull under the flapping headgear, and his gaunt frame looked like a skeleton draped in rough brown cloth. But he moved swiftly; and Nial, who had been raised among such men, knew that there was strength in the lean arms.

"*Hadd!*" cried the master of the cave. "Be welcome." His eyes opened wide when Nial made answer in sonorous Arabic. "What man art thou, to know the speech of the Nejd! Behold," he added to the girl, "this is the one they seek along the river."

"True, he hath many enemies."

Alai nodded complacently and in the same instant was rocking on her knees, her hair drawn over her face, without a sound. The calamity of last night had struck her afresh.

Abu Harb, who seemed to know how to deal with the grief of women, led her to the rear of the cavern to a rug spread upon a quilt and talked to her, low voiced. Nial noticed that several passages led out of the place and he wandered over to the nearest one, finding it a storage space heaped with hay, antelope horns, odds and ends of saddlery and irons. Before he could look at it more closely, the torch brightened and Abu Harb's lean head was at his shoulder.

"Come, thou," the Arab whispered. "But first, cover thyself with this."

While Nial was putting on the long, light kaffiyeh, winding it across his arms and drawing the edge of it over his head, Abu Harb tied the two horses to rings in the far wall and kindled a fire upon the hearth beside the girl.

"We cannot talk near her," he explained when they were in the darkness outside. "She understands my speech, and the Iranis—everything. *Ai-a*, she was a piece of Neshavan's liver, and I would lay my one eye at her feet. But now by Allah, Mir Farash is looking for her. How can she hide from him? He will pay gold for her; and the lice of Talas would sell their mothers, if they knew them, for silver. Nay. She must go hence with thee before the next day."

"Nay," the Scot objected. "I go alone."

"How canst thou? She said she belonged to thee. They will search my house."

"She is not mine."

Stopping in his tracks, the Arab shook his head slowly.

"Khawand Nial, I do not understand. Of what use are words? She is a breath from Peristan, and all men look after her. If she wishes to go with thee, she will go. By Allah, I will go also. Come, we will need many things."

With long strides the hunter was off toward the distant lights of the town. But when Nial caught up with him he stopped to whisper fiercely.

"What good comes from sitting in one place? These dogs in stinking sheepskins offend my nostrils. *Wallahi*, they slew Neshavan, my companion of the road. Am I to sit in peace with them? I will show thee a new road to Samarkand where the horse herds and the antelope run. But we will need barley, dried meat, garlic, a soft blanket for Alai, a packhorse."

Muttering to himself, Abu Harb checked off necessities on his long fingers as he steered Nial toward an open gate in the wall. He had no hesitation and seemed to expect Nial to take care of himself. Dogs rushed out to snarl at them, and drew off before the sweep of the Arab's long stick. Then both men halted to stare ahead of them.

There were lights in the open square at the head of the alley, and a group of the Kara Kalpaks stood their ground like jackals facing wolves. Three horsemen rode toward them, three Tatars with an officer in the lead. Nial recognized the *darogha* of the post station who had questioned him.

As the Tatars came on, the tribesmen fingered their weapons and one spat noisily. The *darogha* glanced at him and loosened the coil of rope that hung at his saddlehorn. The Black Hat knew the meaning of this, because he drew back reluctantly when the horse's muzzle was almost touching him. The tribesmen went off, as if at a signal, and at a word from the officer the two Tatar warriors followed them.

Abu Harb chuckled silently, but Nial watched the officer who remained at the alley mouth, rubbing his arms as if they were stiffened by long riding. Presently, hearing the drip of water from a dark court off the alley, the *darogha* let his horse wander toward it, and Nial heard him dismount.

"A knife—swiftly," he whispered to the Arab.

Abu Harb asked no questions. He thrust the bone hilt of a curved knife into the Scot's hand and nodded eagerly when Nial bade him follow but not interfere in anything that happened. Only when Nial turned toward the court did the Arab pluck his sleeve.

"Nay," Abu Harb breathed. "That is one of the khan's men. A panther is easier to stalk."

"Hold thy tongue."

Thrusting back the Arab, Nial went on, making no effort to walk quietly. He stepped into the yard, paused to stare in the faint starlight at the horse, and moved to the well. The Mongol, who had finished drinking, looked toward him casually and jerked the horse's head back from the water. As he did so, Nial's left hand closed upon his right wrist, and when he turned angrily he felt the tip of a sharp steel blade press through the coat beneath his ribs.

"Be silent!" Nial whispered. "It is for me to speak, for thee to listen."

"*Kai*," the man grunted softly, "thou art the slayer of the *yam*."

"True. But I am here to tell thee more that is true. The man I slew was the robber, the Kara Kalpak."

And in brief words Nial related how he had come upon the dead courier. The Mongol listened intently, showing no excitement except that he breathed swifter than usual. His quick eyes had sighted Abu Harb standing within hearing, and the iron grasp on his right wrist did not relax. Nial knew that the officer would have his sword slung upon his back with the hilt over his left shoulder where it could not be reached with the left hand.

"I hear," the *darogha* responded calmly. "Perhaps it is true. What would you have me do?"

"Go back to Samarkand. Report what I have said and question the one who lied again."

"He hath gone, like a stone dropped into deep water. Hast thou the message tube?"

Nial thought for a space, conscious of Abu Harb breathing heavily behind him.

"Aye so. If thou wilt cease pursuit I will bring it untouched to a station."

"Nay, an order was given to pursue thee, and caught thou wilt be. If I fail, others will come, unerring as the birds that see in the night."

This Nial knew to be true. If a general order had gone out to find him, the Tatar cavalry would be loosed from the nearest camps to bring him in.

"What was in the tube?" he asked.

"We have not been told. But it is from the hand of Barka Khan to the feet of the great Kublai Khan, Lord of the East."

Nial silently cursed the silver tube, for other hands than the Tatars would be stretched out for a missive of the great khan. Suddenly he dropped the officer's wrist and reached up, drawing the other's short saber from its sheath. This he tossed into the well, and backed up a step to feel for the horse's rein.

"Do not take the horse," whispered the officer quickly. "*Kai*, I am no speaker of vain words. I will not move from this place nor follow thee for the time milk takes to boil."

A hoarse cluck of warning sounded behind Nial, who pondered. He could not keep the beast. It would be recognized by these Tatars as far as they could see.

"What is thy name, thy rank?" he asked.

"Chagan, *ung-khan* of the Almalyk regiment."

"Then keep to thy word, Chagan!"

Turning and calling to Abu Harb, Nial ran from the courtyard and across the alley into the mouth of another lane. Before they could turn a corner, they heard the snap and hiss of arrows shot after them. The shafts crashed against unseen walls, and Nial laughed under his breath. Chagan had carried out his pledge after his own fashion. He made no attempt to follow them, and the Arab doubled back to the gate, racing ahead until Nial could make out the loom of the cliff.

"Surely Allah hath afflicted thee with madness," panted Abu Harb. "Even the birds and wolves flee before those Tarim riders. And thou hast stolen from their great khan. What is in the tube?" When he received no answer, he sucked in his breath admiringly. "Eh, eh, thou art a very father of strife. By Allah, I will surely go with thee."

He held out his hand eagerly.

"Hast thou gold? I must buy what is needed in the bazaar. Soon we may be in our shrouds, thou and I, but first we must eat."

He took the gold Nial held out to him as a matter of course and strode off with the air of a man of affairs who has much to do in little time. With difficulty—for the rock was honeycombed with fissures—Nial found the entrance to the cave, guiding himself by the smell of smoke and the drowsy stamping of the horses.

Alai greeted him with silent satisfaction, showing no trace of the grief of an hour before. Moving over to the edge of the carpet, she made place for him by the fire and curled herself up comfortably.

Half hidden in shadow, her eyes were dark as the night itself. Within them danced two pinpoints of light, reflected in the glowing embers of the fire. It was Nial who first looked away, into the fire, wondering if she had a power of witchery in her. A woman of Christendom would have plied him with questions or complained of hunger. But this Tatar girl was as untamed and as unknowable as a young animal. And he did not want to bid her farewell.

"Abu Harb says," he ventured, "that there is danger here for you. I also must ride hence without stopping for thorns or stones. So Abu Harb will take you to Samarkand, toward the setting sun, while I go on to the rising sun."

He thought she would exclaim or protest. Instead she seemed to ponder his words gravely.

"Once," she observed, "I went to Samarkand and the men there followed me about. Now that I am alone they would take me and sell me as a slave. I will not be a slave."

"But where I go the Tatar horsemen will follow."

"Allah sends evil with good. This is my country. In the hills are many safe places good for hiding. Abu Harb knows them. And I will not leave my hills."

When Abu Harb returned, leading a packhorse laden with purchases, he spoke briefly with Alai and confided to Nial that he was quite willing to set out to the east, up the Zarafshan. It appeared that certain owners of herds in Samarkand had set a price on his head. He was full of zeal to depart without a moment's delay, explaining that Chagan had ridden off toward Samarkand and that the night in general was full of calamity.

Nothing, however, hindered them as they left Talas behind and rode along a deserted trail by the river until the rising sun gleamed in their faces.

Abu Harb was in the lead, tugging the pack animal after him, until he halted to let Nial come up. Something seemed to amuse him, and he pointed behind them.

"Look!"

All Nial saw was the girl, who had slipped back behind the saddle, and was leaning on a blanket pack tied to the horn, her head on her arms, sleeping quietly.

"Didst thou not swear, Lord Nial, to ride hither alone? The Arab smiled reminiscently. "She will go where she will. Is she not rightly named The Eagle? She seeks the high and distant places, taking no thought of danger. By Allah, thou canst train the young hawk and the leopard to hand, but not the eagle."

Chapter III
Road to Cathay

Late that afternoon they halted in a cross gully where some grass clung to the edge of a dry stream and creeping mimosa offered fuel for a fire. The gray Zarafshan had grown more noisy as they ascended, and the ravine had narrowed to a gorge where the rubble of the steep slopes lay almost at the river's bank. Abu Harb was careful to build the fire where it could not be seen from the trail below.

"At all times," he explained, "riders come down from the Gate. They would not draw rein for me, but they would dismount to plunder thee and this girl."

The fire had died away and they had finished eating the chicken and rice that Alai boiled for them, when the beat of a horse's hoofs echoed down the gorge, drawing nearer. Loose stones began to clatter and roll, and the rider swept past unseeing and unseen, as if reckless of anything but time. The Arab, who had hastened to the horses' heads, went down to stare after him.

"There is smoke far below," he announced, returning to crouch on his blanket by the Scot. "God alone knows what has happened. It is well that we are here and not down there. What is that?"

Nial had taken the message tube from the saddlebag and was inspecting it again in the last of the daylight—knowing that Abu Harb would be eaten with curiosity concerning it, and would probably pilfer it to examine the thing unless his curiosity were satisfied.

"The post to Kublai Khan," he said. "Do not touch the seal."

The Arab had stolen more than horses in his time, but he held it gingerly in his scarred fingers, shaking his head in amazement. Carefully he shook it close to his ear, sniffed at it, and weighed it thoughtfully.

"*Ma'uzbillah!*" he exclaimed. "May God protect us! What a thing to have. Wilt thou not open it?"

"Nay, I shall give it back as it is."

"But it is too heavy for a writing. It does not smell of musk or sweet scent. It may have emeralds within, or the precious stones from the throne seat of a shah. Or perhaps some rare carved jade which the Tatars cherish. We could not keep such things, but I could sell them."

"Give it back!" cried the girl suddenly.

All the Arab's instincts rebelled at this.

"Only a fool casts away treasure," he growled. "With this Lord Nial can bargain for his life."

"Thou art a blind mole, feeling only the earth under thee!" she scolded him. "*Kai*, why did the Black Hats slay a courier to get this one thing? Why do the khan's horsemen keep the saddle without sleeping to find it again? Death awaits the holder. And thy greed would take it into a bazaar."

"Eh, eh, I did but think of its value. Is it not Lord Nial's?" He handed the tube back to the Scot, who did not smile at his sudden zeal to be rid of it.

"Thou art leading us, Abu Harb," he observed, "to a safe place of hiding. But here I see only the bare gorge. Where is thy place?"

Tracing in the sand between his knees, the Arab explained. For seven days' ride the Zarafshan wound up toward the heights, ending finally in what he called a wall of ice. It was old ice that never melted, although at times it moved.* Not quite halfway up the valley there was a trail leading

---

*The same glacier is still at the head of the Zarafshan.

to a nest of small valleys, where good grass, cold water, and game could be found. Abu Harb had spent more than one summer there hunting.

"Perhaps in three days, perhaps in four we will set our feet on the trail," he calculated. "I think that Tatars will follow us up the river, but first that emir, Chagan, will muster fresh riders from Samarkand. By Allah, the Tatars will never come up this valley with less than a regiment. They will not overtake us."

Nial wondered why the men of the Horde, who seemed to have no fear of anything, should wait for a thousand sabers before entering this deserted gorge; and he remembered Neshavan's warning at the Hawk House.

"Aye, so. Yet, Abu Harb, this road comes not to an end at the ice. Surely it goes on to the East, for caravans once passed over it."

"Who knows where it goes? By the blood of Ali, I have not seen the man who knows."

Neshavan had said that wanderers had turned back from fear. Nial knew that both Tatars and Moslems dreaded the high passes, saying that the spirits of the upper air were encountered there, meaning that cold and storms made such passes hazardous.

"If there is a road," he pointed out, "we could follow it."

This time Abu Harb shook his head and laughed good-naturedly.

"Besides the ice stands the Gate," he vouchsafed. "Within it is the breeding ground of the Kara Kalpaks, their city. They are vultures, feeding on the dead, but they are watched ever by Gutchluk Khan."

"The Wizard King," Nial translated the name into Arabic. "What is he?"

"What is the voice of the wind? What is the sound of the storm? I have heard his call, but of him I know only that he is an *ifrit*. He is a devil, biding himself on the height."

"*Yah ahmak*," cried Alai impatiently. "O witless! Would a devil send written missives upon a pigeon, or send his men to slay Neshavan? Gutchluk Khan is a man who hides from sight. Because he is hidden and feared, the cities pay him a tribute, also the caravan merchants. They lie who say otherwise."

"*Shway, shway*," murmured the hunter. "Softly, softly, little Alai. I have seen Gutchluk in the shape of a white vulture who settled down beside me and spoke."

During his summer in the upper valleys near the Gate, Abu Harb had tried to cut out horses from the Kara Kalpak herd until the day when, watching from a rocky ravine, he had seen a white vulture circling over him, and descending upon the bones of a *markhor* not a lance toss away. Instead of plucking at the bones, the great bird had sat motionless, its red eyes upon him, and a voice had come from it cursing him by the blood of Kerbala; and Abu Harb had fled without looking behind him to his horse. No other man had been in the ravine.

Alai mocked him, chin on hand. "Other fools tell other tales of how Gutchluk spoke to them from the face of a cliff where nothing could be. Aye, and how he hath a trumpet that resounds down the valley a day's ride. I tell thee the truth, that he hath gained power over the Kara Kalpaks, until they serve him like slaves and spread the fear of his name with their swords."

Considering this, Abu Harb grunted.

"A man, perhaps, he may be. But then he hath devils to serve him. And I would be worse than the fool thou hast named me if I drew my reins within the Gate."

Still muttering, he went off to seek his blankets. Alai chuckled to herself as she settled down to sleep near Nial, but presently she raised herself on her elbow.

"Lord Nial," she whispered, "wilt thou go with Abu Harb or try to follow the road through the Gate?"

"Only God knows," the Scot answered frankly.

"In your land, the place you come from, do the women wear veils and chew mastic?"

"Nay, *kuchik khanim*."

"Lord Nial, I am not a little woman, I am a strong girl. *Wallahi*, have I braided up my hair as the women of any man? Do the girls of your land take off their boots when they go into the tents at night?"

"They take off everything when they sleep at night, and they keep very quiet, like young antelope."

For awhile Alai considered this, her eyes dim in the twilight.

"Still," she ventured, "when the *buran* blows cold, as it does here from the snow, they would not take off everything?"

"Certainly not," he assured her. "But they would keep quiet."

He was half asleep, after the hard riding of the last three days, while the Tatar girl had managed to doze in the saddle. He heard her whisper to herself, and was conscious of the faint scent of dried roses. Abu Harb had volunteered to keep guard down by the trail, and Nial dropped off to sleep without misgivings.

When he roused and glanced about before sunrise, he saw the Arab sitting up in his ragged blanket and scratching his head, where Alai had been.

"Only God knows," exclaimed Abu Harb, "what is in the mind of a woman. She came down in anger a little after starlight and took my place. But I was glad to sleep."

It was Alai who discovered the riders on the trail behind them, early in the afternoon of the fourth day. The two men had noticed nothing; even the Scot's keen sight could not penetrate the sun's glare reflected from the bed of the valley. But after long scrutiny Abu Harb admitted that the girl was right.

"The vultures," he explained. "They rise and follow after something. Nay, it is not cattle going at such a pace."

And he searched the ground ahead of them with an anxious frown.

They had penetrated to the upper reaches of the Zarafshan, where the valley walls stood back from the river and the trail ran along the gravel bed, circling round buttresses of red clay cut by centuries of erosion into the shape of gigantic lions' paws. The scent of juniper and stunted sage clung to the hollows, but when they topped a rise they were buffeted by the icy wind from the heights. Above the bare red walls of the valley loomed peak upon peak, carpeted with fresh green that gave way to bare black basalt, which in turn was covered by white snow caps. "The White Ones," Abu Harb had said when the summits first came into sight.

Here was silence, except for the swift rush of water over the stones. The songbirds had left the air to the vultures, and black eagles began to appear. The valley had grown vast, but now it was dwarfed by the huge ranges above it. Nial felt that he was approaching the ramparts of space itself.

Only once had he caught a glimpse of the gut in this barrier. Before the last sunset Abu Harb had shown him a distant break in the mountain barrier. At either side of the gut rose two stone pinnacles, blood-colored against the black rock behind them. They looked tiny at that distance, but Nial knew they were high. They might have been the sacrifice stones of vanished giants.

"The Pillars of Silence," the Arab had said simply.

Now he quested along the river like a dog on a scent until he found a brush-filled ravine up which the horses could force their way. Nial and the girl dismounted, scrambling over loose rocks until they halted in a small clearing hidden from the trail beneath.

"Now," Abu Harb explained, "we will see who comes after. *Ma'uz-billah!*"

Open mouthed, he stared beyond them, his face suddenly gray with fear. Glancing over his shoulder, Nial saw a brush-covered slope and what looked like a rude hut. Stones had been piled together and roofed over with poplar poles, with horns of antelope and mountain sheep fastened on the ends. Weather-gray poles leaned about it crazily, and rags moved drowsily in the wind. On the highest pair of antelope horns perched a great white vulture.

"Like to that one was Gutchluk!" Abu Harb whispered. "Look, it awaits us upon a shrine, a grave."

He listened anxiously but the vulture did not speak, and when Nial tossed a stone toward the shrine it flapped away clumsily.

"Evil power is here," the Arab insisted, "and now it is too late to go back to the trail. Go thou and watch from those rocks."

With a nod the Scot climbed past the shrine up a chute of broken rock to a pinnacle where, lying down and edging forward between two boulders, he could see the trail, but could see nothing of the clearing where Abu Harb and the girl were tethering the horses. It was some time before he made out horsemen coming around a bend in the river trail, and longer before he recognized them as Kara Kalpaks, fully armed.

Alai came up to the lookout and crouched beside him, without excitement.

"Many of those dogs come and go," she whispered. "Why should they follow us?" Then she added thoughtfully, "Soon we will be where the roads cross. Promise me now that you will come with the hunter to his hiding place in the valley."

Still intent on the groups of riders below, Nial answered absently:

"How can I promise, little Alai? Have I not said that I mean to follow the road to the East?"

"Fool! Have you a token from Gutchluk to open the way?"

Her eyes were angry, her white teeth showing between her parted lips, her small hands clenched on her knees. Her white, intent face had lost its boyish playfulness; she turned to him wistfully, confidingly.

"Have you not said," he responded, "this Gutchluk Khan is a man, not a magician? Why should I fear him more than the Tatars?"

"Because he is truly a khan, who rules men. I have spoken with one who saw him, sitting alone upon a black stone with an unchained eagle beside him and a panther asleep at his feet. He seemed to be asleep, but suddenly he whispered and the panther rose and snarled, and this man fled away for his life. You are like a lion cub, being stubborn and stupid, and Gutchluk will be amused when you stand bound before him. When I watched the herds for Neshavan, I often thought that I would go and sit at the feet of this man whose power is a thunderbolt, who is feared by the Tatar Horde. Perhaps I shall go."

Chin on hand, she glanced at him from the corners of her eyes, half smiling. She was lovely as an elf maid, and quite conscious of it. Nial turned abruptly and kissed her lips.

"What is that for?" she asked, surprised. No one had ever caressed her in that fashion.

"Thou art beautiful, little Alai, and I—" He bit his lip fiercely. "Go thou with Abu Harb, to safety."

The girl's hand was on his shoulder when she thrust him away and sprang to her feet, her eyes flashing.

"Thou! Thou art an ox with grass between thy teeth! A blind ox, with head hanging. And I thought thee a lion among men, since the night thou sought me in the dark. Nay, I go to seek Gutchluk in his aerie."

She ran down the pinnacle, springing from rock to rock, turning once to laugh at him.

"And if thou wilt see me, I shall be sitting at his feet, telling him the tale of thy folly to beguile him."

With that she was gone, and when Nial stirred to follow her he remembered the men on the trail below. A group of the Kara Kalpaks was outlined against the yellow gravel, their heads lifted curiously. Several of them pointed to the sky above him. Turning cautiously, Nial saw the white vulture moving in lazy circles over the pinnacle.

But the riders did not dismount. In spite of their wounds—many had bandaged faces and bound arms—they whipped on their stumbling ponies. Others came by, hurrying on foot, their horses burdened with heavy bales that might have been loot or possessions—it was all the same in these hills. Presently Abu Harb crept up beside him and grunted with interest.

"Allah hath caused fighting down the valley, yet these do not bear themselves like victors. They go too fast."

More of them appeared with mules and even a burdened Bactrian camel, led by women who plodded listlessly along. It was an hour before the trail was emptied of its human tide.

"Where is Alai?" Nial whispered.

"With the horses—praying at the shrine. She bade me come hither, saying thou wert useless as a child unweaned. Truly that vulture was an omen of evil, for now these dogs are ahead of us."

Restlessly the old Arab slid back and retraced his steps to the shrine, followed by Nial, who wondered what Alai might be up to. She was not in the clearing, and they dared not call to her. Abu Harb prowled about uneasily and came to a stop before the horses.

"*Wallahi*, her pony is gone, Lord Nial." He hastened to inspect the pile of packs by the brush. "Yet she hath taken nothing else that was hers. What more is to come upon our heads?"

"Look at the ground," Nial whispered. "Nay, over there by the sand under the rocks!"

Alai and he wore softened horsehide boots with heels that left a clear imprint, while the sand revealed the tracks of bare feet moving about haphazardly. He was certain those footprints had not been there when he left the clearing. Abu Harb clucked gloomily and muttered the name of Gutchluk.

"Salaam, O my companions of the road!" a strange voice saluted them. "I have looked for ye very patiently."

It was a courteous, amused voice, and it belonged to a slender young Persian with an immaculate white turban, who was making his way up through the brush. Abu Harb eyed him as a dog eyes an innocent-appearing leopard.

"Mir Farash," he ejaculated.

"Verily thou knowest the interpreter of dreams of Talas." The Persian stared curiously at Nial. "My ears have heard much talk of this noble *farangi*, and my heart rejoices at this unlooked-for meeting. That wild girl, Alai, sought me upon the road below and said that he was waiting here in the brush."

"By Allah, that is a lie!" stormed the Arab. "Thou art Gutchluk's man, and he sent thee."

The good nature did not fade from Mir Farash's opium-shadowed eyes, although he glanced once over his shoulder at the dozen tribesmen who made their way after Mir up the slope, fingering their weapons. Nial moved over to the packs, standing between them and the steep bank.

"Now—" Mir Farash smiled upon him—"we are all friends together, and surely thy troubles are past, since I have come to lead thee out of the abyss of peril to the height of safety."

The Persian's lilting cadence was barely intelligible to the Scot, but Abu Harb accepted him as the messenger of inevitable disaster. He looked once at the bows of the Kara Kalpaks carried ready strung, and squatted down indifferently to listen to what might be said.

"What seekest thou, O servant of Gutchluk?"

"No more than a gift, a useless little thing from this *farangi*. He carries a missive to Kublai Khan, and now thy servant will relieve him of its care."

There was no chance of flight. Even if Nial could have caught up his saddlebags and escaped the arrows of the tribesmen, he would not have been able to outrun mounted men. So, without moving, he nodded at the Persian.

"I have no gift for thee. Take what thou wilt."

Smiling, Mir Farash shook his head.

"By the beard and the breath of Ali, am I a thief? Are we not friends?" But he crouched like a hungry jackal over the packs, loosening the thongs swiftly from Nial's saddlebags and dumping the contents on the ground.

"Nay," muttered Abu Harb, "thou art the father of all thieves. If thou wert minded to give even a bone to a dog, thou wouldst first break out the marrow."

Astonished, he fell silent. In all Nial's scattered kit there was no sign of the worn silver tube with the red seal. Intently he watched while Mir Farash ran his fingers through the Scot's garments without result except to uncover a sack of gold coins. Then the Persian searched Abu Harb himself thoroughly, despite the old hunter's comments upon the ways of human insects.

But Mir Farash still smiled.

"Hearken, Lord Nial, to thy peril. After ye three rode from Talas, that uncircumcised Tatar, Chagan, summoned other riders of the Horde from the Samarkand road. They cut their way through the Kara Kalpaks who stood against them, and when I set the foot of discretion in the saddle of preservation, they were within sight of Talas. Long since they have discovered the path of thy flight, for watchers on the river saw thee pass. A

man of mine, who rode up without sleep or rest, said that they were pushing up the river.

"If thou art taken, they will not wait a minute before lifting the skin
from thee slowly, beginning at the feet, until thou art minded to give up
to them what they seek. We are making haste toward the Gate. Even those
infidel Tatars cannot force the Gate, and safety awaits thee, if thou wilt
yield me the missive to the great khan. Is it not a fair payment? Within
the Gate thou art free to go where thou wilt."

He waited a moment to let Nial ponder.

"Where hast thou hidden that which was in the silver tube?"

"I have hidden naught and the tube is gone."

Suspiciously Mir Farash savored his words.

"What was within it?"

"I know not."

"Now verily am I a blind ox to be led by the nose?" He spat out red be-
tel pulp and turned to his men. "Search this place and bring hither their
saddles."

He was careful to leave warriors with bows to watch his prisoners
while he searched all the packs anew. At the end of an hour he had found
nothing except some carefully hidden trinkets which Abu Harb had not
seen fit to reveal to his companions. His brow black with fury, Mir Farash
struck his hands together to summon his men.

"To the Gate!" And to Nial he cried, "Better for thee to have spoken
here than to go to the one who awaits thee."

For two days Mir Farash and his cavalcade pushed along a trail that was a
path through a nightmare. Ascending from the river, it climbed the slope
of yellow conglomerate until it crawled upon the face of solid basalt. The
wind gusts swept the weary beasts from their footing.

More men and camels pressed up from behind, and a rumor ran through
the tide of fugitives that the Tatars were cutting down the hindmost. At
night—for even the hillmen could not travel that trail in the dark—the
red eyes of fires and the tossing specks of torches outlined the way behind
them. High-pitched shouts, tossed from fire to fire, echoed back from unseen cliffs. A half moon stared down from the rim of the valley upon restless, loaded camels tied to outcropping rocks, and knots of men sleeping
where they could find shelter from the wind's blast.

It was after the third sunrise that Nial heard a reverberation in the air,
faintly at first. Then it swelled to a metallic roar which beat back from the

opposite cliff and dwindled away down the valley, as if mounted trumpeters had galloped at lightning speed over their heads.

"Gutchluk's horns," Abu Harb whispered.

Although Nial peered ahead, he could see no habitation of any kind,
or any human above them on the mountain. A veil of mist hung about
the peaks, forcing the eagles to fly low. Thousands of feet below them
the gray Zarafshan twisted through its bare bed between the red lion's
paws that looked diminutive from the heights. Abu Harb contemplated
it listlessly.

"Before the sun is high, we will see the Gate," he observed, and added
moodily that it was easier to pass through it once than twice.

The old Arab had sworn every day by all the ninety and nine holy names
of Allah that he had not taken the silver tube from Nial's bag and he did
not cease speculating as to what had happened to it. Nial only knew that
it had been safe that morning when they had broken camp, and he wondered what Alai would say when she knew of its loss. Although he watched
for her—and Mir Farash's stout horses and quick-tempered escort forced a
way with knees and feet through the fugitives on the trail—he saw nothing of the Tatar girl.

When the mist cleared ahead of them, Abu Harb nudged him and pointed.
The Zarafshan ended in a deep pool, and beyond the pool rose the ghost of
a river, gray and motionless between the shoulders of two mountains. Over
the summit of the gray ice gleamed the pure white of distant snow.

"Not that," said the Arab, "it is here, the Jissn al-Hadid."

Beside them stood the mighty pedestals of the twin rock towers, rising from the lower valley, looking from the trail like pyramids. Between
these pillars in steep traverses, more than once crossing a rude bridge of
tree trunks and stones, the trail ascended to the gut of the pass.

The Kara Kalpaks who escorted them paid no more attention to the
mighty gateway than to the rubbish lying beside the road. But even they
dismounted to pass over some of the bridges that led across narrow chasms.
And once, looking down, Nial saw the bare bones of a horse and man
stretched on the rocks.

They climbed steadily, for Mir Farash had gone on ahead, and the tribesmen had orders to make haste. Above them the gate itself began to take
shape—roughly cut limestone blocks fitted together into a wall. Above
the wall shaggy heads peered down at them; and once a tribesman near

Nial howled up at them like a wolf until the alert echoes yelped back like fleeing jackals. More heads appeared; and when they stood at last, breathing heavily, a mocking clamor greeted them.

"Ai, the antelope have been driven from the plain! They come panting with ropes on their necks."

"*Wallahi,* O brothers, open to the emir of the infidels!"

"Nay, his woman was more of a man."

But the Kara Kalpak shouted impatiently, and the dark gate swung back. It was of massive teak, cracked with age and bound by bronze wrought into the shape of flying birds. Nial was thrust through by the tribesmen, who beat back the guardians of the wall until a fight seemed in the making. Abu Harb, who had used his tongue to return abuse for insult, was borne along.

"May dogs litter on your graves," he yelped. "May God preserve me from the contamination of your touch, and assuage my nostrils from this stench that is worse than the stench of camels rolling in dry mud. What hath befallen your noses, that they are slit? Now I know why the women of this place of abomination have no noses."

Stones flew at him, and the hillmen rushed with drawn knives, while the Kara Kalpaks held them off with sword and shield and Abu Harb's shout rose to a crescendo.

"Spawn of a dunghill! Is this the city of goat tenders—the abode of those who have left shame behind them?"

But presently even Abu Harb drew a breath of silent amazement, and the Kara Kalpaks looked ahead with interest. They had come to the far end of the gut, where they could see out upon the eastern side of the range. Accustomed to the desolation of the upper Zarafshan, they beheld now the very opposite. A circular valley lay some three thousand feet below them, surrounded by the familiar red mountain slopes, rising terrace upon terrace, darkened by pine growth.

But the valley itself gleamed pure green except where the water of a lake reflected the blue sky. Wind ripples passed over the tall grass and wheat fields, divided by tiny streams and clusters of fruit trees. But the round domes of tents and the square roofs of tiny stone huts marked a city of some size.

"Eh," breathed Abu Harb, with a desert man's appreciation of flowing water, "an oasis on the veritable top of the world!"

"Nay," grunted one of the Kara Kalpaks, "Paldorak, our city, where thou wilt dwell for perhaps one dawn and darkness again before thy grave is dug yonder."

He curved a scarred finger toward the center of the valley, above the lake and the roofs of Paldorak. Here rose a single height of red rock, so serrated by erosion on the summit that it might have been a ruined citadel built by men of another age.

"The house," the tribesman vouchsafed, "of Gutchluk Khan. It is empty."

"And where is he?" Abu Harb glanced up involuntarily.

The only answer was the wave of a long-sleeved arm across the valley and the sky.

As he descended the road Nial noticed that two other passes cut the circle of mountains about the flat basin of Paldorak. The one to the north seemed to be a gorge that might lead anywhere or nowhere. But to the east a narrow valley opened up, and beyond it showed the white summits of distant mountains. He wondered if this were the caravan road to Cathay that had been closed by Gutchluk's will.

He wondered more when they rode through the alleys of Paldorak. The place was a labyrinth of dwellings built of stone so old and worn that it was black and smooth to the touch. From the open doorways came a stench that made him choke. Even the dogs that nosed the offal in the alley dirt knew him for a stranger and snarled at his passing. Bald vultures squatted on projecting roof beams. Men sprawled in sleep underfoot, with their arms thrown over rag bundles. Felt tents covered every vacant space, and ponies that bore signs of desperate riding were tethered wherever the streams of human beings gave them space.

Paldorak had become a rendezvous for the lawless. Gaunt Turkomans sat with their heads together, turning to curse in unison at sheepskin-clad hillmen; a man with a shaven head and a robe of cloth of gold over his rags sold swallows from a skin of reeking arak to a mullah who carried a sheathed sword in his hand. Behind other men walked veiled women, staggering under bundles, heedless of the taunts of the bare-faced painted women who loitered by the gate of the bazaar.

They all stared with avid curiosity at the tall youth with the yellow mane of hair who rode unarmed, for the Kara Kalpaks had taken their weapons from the two captives.

Abu Harb listened in vain for any chant of prayer, and shook his head virtuously.

"'Tis without faith, this place," he announced. "By Allah, it is a veritable breeding place of evil."

Nial did not smile. The old Arab was no strict servant of Islam, but he made shift to mutter the five prayers between sunrise and full dark.

But when they stopped in the near darkness of the covered bazaar, and Abu Harb dismounted, placing his ragged prayer rug on the least filthy part of the alley, four of the Kara Kalpaks fell upon him without warning. While one held his feet and two others forced his arms behind his back, the fourth lashed tight his wrists and elbows.

Nial was down from the saddle without an instant's delay to go to his aid, but one of the tribesmen spurred forward and checked him with a drawn sword—his own blade which had been taken from him in the valley of the Zarafshan.

"Thy time is not yet," the swordsman assured him.

The four led Abu Harb away on foot, holding to the end of the rope that bound him. Over his shoulder the old Arab called back to his friend:

"Seek for Alai. By Mir Farash she will be. Think not that she betrayed us to these sons of jackals. May Allah watch over her!"

The throng in the bazaar only glanced casually at the struggle and resumed their haggling. A boy snatched up Abu Harb's carpet and darted off with it as the Kara Kalpak led Nial through an archway to a door that was opened grudgingly to their pounding.

"Here is thy house," said their leader, yawning, "where Mir Farash will look to thee."

Chapter IV
The Taste of Steel

The dwelling of Mir Farash, like most of those in Paldorak, had one fortified gate and several secret runways; it had cellars that opened upon the bazaar, and a square tower from which the height of red rock could be seen. It had curtained alcoves for opium smokers, and a space barred by iron grilles through which veiled women peered indolently.

But Alai had been placed in a silent and embrasureless cell, and left to her own devices. The hag who came to summon her after moonrise found her apparently asleep on the carpet, but in reality keenly awake to every sound in this house which had become her prison.

"One hath sent for you, *kuchik khanim*," the hag explained indifferently. "Rise and follow."

She led the Tatar girl down a vacant stair to the street, where Alai veiled herself with her white headcloth, noticing as she did so that two armed men fell in behind them. The few tribesmen who met them seemed to know the hag, for they kept their distance from the girl. The way led up steadily, until the last roofs fell behind them and a clear moon shone down upon a bare rock slope.

Following what looked like a goat path, the hag climbed steadily until they entered the shadow of a wall, above which the jagged line of ruined towers stood against the sky. Alai had satisfied herself that the two guards waited at the edge of the houses below, and thus flight down the slope would be useless. In any case she could not escape from Paldorak or the valley.

"Go in," said the hag without emotion.

"Why?" Alai objected. "To what?"

"To listen to the voice of Gutchluk Khan."

The hag sat down on rubble of a ruined gateway with the air of one who may have the night to wait. Alai hesitated only a minute before climbing into the ruins, outwardly confident enough in her slender *khalat* and small boots, but inwardly much afraid. Even Paldorak was less ominous than this deserted domain of a wizard.

Some distance ahead a lantern rested on the ground. When she was about to take it up, the shrunken figure of a man appeared beside her and picked up the light. He moved with a curious shuffling step, and in a moment she discovered that he was blind. He must have known every foot of the height, to lead the way as he did, down one lane between broken rock walls into another.

The Tatar girl had a keen sense of direction and she was aware that the blind lantern bearer doubled on his path, making circles through the labyrinth, until he came to a square pool coated with green scum. Tamarisk and creepers grew out of the crevices above the stagnant water, and, as the guide made his way slowly along the edge, a sluggish snake slid from beneath his feet into the water.

To comfort herself, Alai sang under her breath a song of the sheepherders, to ward off evil spirits:

> *Ai-a-a, come away brothers,*
> *With me. Ai-a-a...*

Turning his wrinkled head, the man snarled at her voicelessly and beck-oned her under an archway. Descending some steps that had been cleared of debris, he came out into what looked like an open court. Grass grew in the cracks of the flagging, and some effort had been made to repair the walls, which were too high to climb.

Taking his lantern, the blind guide retraced his steps, and Alai heard a wooden door rasp shut. For a moment she thought she was alone in the court; then in the far end, flooded by moonlight, she saw a man stand-ing with outstretched arms. Except for his head, which turned restlessly, he made no movement. Alai made out that he was bound on a stake, his arms fastened to the crosspiece.

And he was Abu Harb, except for his head which resembled a black pan-ther's. Slowly the girl advanced into the moonlight, and the head turned toward her without a sound. Black hair hung about it, and white fangs gleamed in the mouth aperture.

And out of the mouth came an unknown voice.

"Thou art the daughter of Neshavan."

It was an expressionless voice, dull and inhuman. Alai shivered sud-denly and clenched her hands at her sides. The garments and figure were undoubtedly Abu Harb's, the muzzle was a black panther's and the hair might have been anything. But the voice! Then slowly the head turned to one side and, following its glance, she saw a white vulture perched on the edge of the wall.

"I slew Neshavan," the voice went on tonelessly. "Because he betrayed to the Tatars the messages carried by my pigeons. Now it hath been said to me that thou hast taken the message sent by one khan to the other. I had possessed myself of that missive, and now I seek it. Where is it hidden?"

Alai was not too startled to think clearly. This must be the voice of Gutchluk Khan, yet it asked a very human question. Wisely she waited for more, while she steadied her thoughts.

"Already the Arab Abu Harb hath been questioned, telling only lies in answer. This that you see is his body. It is well not to lie within these walls. Where is the silver tube sealed with the seal of Barka Khan?"

Now that her head was clear the Tatar girl fell to her knees, pretend-ing fright she did not feel.

"Truly thou sayest—" the quiver in her voice was not all assumed—"O voice from the dead. My hand took the silver tube from the pack of the *farangi*, who is a fool besides being accursed."

"And within it there was a writing. Where hast thou hidden it?"

"*Ai*, hast thou the eyes of a grave bird, to see through darkness and distance? I meant no harm. I heard talk of emeralds sealed within the tube. So I opened it secretly, breaking the seal of the khan. As thou sayest, it held a long roll of writing, stamped with a seal."

"And the place of this writing?"

Alai, who had been watching the panther's head intently, was nearly certain now that the voice came from the wall behind it.

"I cast it into the swift waters of the Zarafshan, and now it is gone like a stray leaf in the wind."

"Why?"

"Be not angry, O voice of the night. I was grieved that the tube held no precious things. I thought harm would come of breaking the khan's seal, so I cast it beyond sight."

Silence fell upon the courtyard and, as if emboldened by it, Alai rose and edged toward the outstretched figure. Suddenly she reached out and touched the panther's head, feeling the hard surface of a lacquer mask. Gripping this in both hands she lifted it, disclosing the very much alive head of Abu Harb. A gag had been thrust into his mouth, and his jaw bound tight.

Glancing behind him swiftly, she made out a large crevice in the stone wall, a yard away, and thought that the voice must have come from there. She tugged loose the cloth, and Abu Harb spat out the gag.

"Where is Lord Nial?" she whispered, so that he barely heard.

"In the house of Mir Farash. Nay, do not touch me. This is a place of many devils."

A hissing as of a dozen snakes rose from the empty pavement beneath them, and when Alai started back the scream of a panther rose from the wall. She waited, breathless, expecting to see a living beast spring over. But the lantern appeared behind her, and the blind custodian of the gate beckoned toward her angrily.

"Go," Abu Harb moaned. "Obey them. There is no hope for me."

There was menace in the silence of the court, and she was powerless to loose the Arab's bonds. Quietly she followed the blind man out.

When the old slave woman had escorted her back to the house beside the bazaar and the door had been barred behind them, Alai lifted her head with sudden decision.

"Take me to thy lord, Mir Farash."

Uneasily the hag peered up at her.

"Nay, at this hour he is taking opium, and women may not come into his presence."

"I come at the bidding of Gutchluk Khan."

As though against her intuition, the hag led the Tatar girl up the tower stair to a drawn curtain, and motioned toward it. Alai pointed down the stair impatiently.

"Shall such as thou linger to hear the words the voice sends to thy lord? Go and wait below."

When she was sure that the woman was really frightened and out of hearing, Alai lowered her veil, ran swift fingers through her dark tresses and repressed a shiver as she parted the curtains. The chamber within was close sealed, lighted only by a colored lamp upon the floor. She caught a glimpse of a shrine behind it, bearing a gilded statue of many-armed Siva in the pose of the dance of death. The hangings were embroidered with rose-colored figures of dancing *yakshas*, while the air reeked of scent.

Mir Farash sat back indolently upon the cushions of the divan, staring at her through half-closed eyes.

"What devil brought thee hither?" he wondered audibly.

In a single glance Alai decided how much he had drunk and how far he was master of his own mind. With a half smile, and unmistakable delight in her dark eyes, she knelt by the divan.

"*Ai sarkar-i-'aziz*—O cherished master, I come at Gutchluk's bidding, for I have been to the court by the pool. Verily also I would thank thee for taking me from the hand of that infidel."

"And verily by the gods—" Mir Farash forgot to play the devout Moslem—"thou hast changed thy heart, for in the valley when I found thee under the circling vulture thou didst fight like a she-leopard against being carried to the trail. But I had seen the horses of the two men and I was not to be led astray by thy tongue."

His words came slowly, although his memory played nimbly down the space of years. To his eyes, Alai appeared a youthful and lovely goddess, clad in strange garments, surrounded by an elusive crimson light. In that glow the trail to Paldorak took shape dimly. Alai weighed his words instantly, pondered what lay behind them, while she held his eyes locked in hers.

"Have I not come hither to serve your exalted presence?" She whispered long praise of him in Persian. "Look, O Earth Shaker, I make ready a new drink for the pleasure of your Nobility."

She let him run his fingers through the smooth tangle of her hair while she inspected the enamel jars of liquids and powders on the table beside her. Selecting raw arak, she mixed the spirits with bhang and offered him the cup with a melting smile. Warily he sniffed at it and drank a little. And Alai appeared to become lost in contemplation.

"In the court," she murmured idly, "Gutchluk Khan said that the accursed Tatars had lifted their standards to attack Paldorak. May they become lost and stray!"

"All is at the feet of the gods, little Alai. Siva the Destroyer strikes unseen. Nay, would the Tatars have come if they had not seen the missives written by Gutchluk to his men in Samarkand? Before then they feared him, as a wizard dwelling upon the heights. They knew how he took plunder from the caravan trails, but they would not go against him. Neshavan sent the missives taken by his hawks from our pigeons to the Tatar *hazara* khan at Samarkand."

This, although interesting, was not what Alai had hoped to hear. She seemed to pay little heed.

"Still, they did not move against the power of Gutchluk, who is not to be seen."

"Our spies told us of preparations made, and of a report to be sent to the great Kublai Khan, who dwells by the garden of Xandu where all magic is made." Mir Farash followed the drift of his thoughts, until Alai prompted him again, this time holding his eyes, her dark head swaying a little.

"Surely that was the letter your men stole, and that I stole from the *farangi* with the head of a lion and the heart of a stupid boy. Now he lies within the chains of your power here in this tower."

"Nay, below. In a chamber beneath the quarters of the dogs my servants."

"By the stair?"

"The first chamber by the door into the bazaar." Mir Farash blinked uneasily as he emptied the cup. "We will give him up to the Tatars for gold, perhaps. Who knows what his portion in life is to be? There was a prophecy told in the *serai* of Samarkand that this Lord Nial would carry his sword to Kublai Khan despite all that lies in his way. Our kismet will be known before the moon is full."

"How?" Alai whispered.

But Mir Farash was lost in his thoughts. She watched him for a moment, then sang under her breath the song of a wizard who leaped from height to height on a winged horse, and of a horde of warriors who sought to shoot him down with their arrows.

"Aye, the Horde," he breathed, his hands quivering. "The Horde that finds its way over the mountain barrier. It goes where the wind goes, and how can it be turned aside?"

"Then it is coming?"

"It is drawing near the gates. It is coming with power to crush and to slay."

"By what road?"

Alai's voice no longer caressed. She cried out the words, penetrating the drug stupor that enveloped the Persian's brain. Already she had discovered where Nial was confined, and something more. Mir Farash fought against fear of peril and dread that the Tatar warriors might raid the city of Gutchluk. The letter that Gutchluk sought might have tidings of an attack to be launched upon Paldorak. Gutchluk had known that the stolen tube contained a letter. But Alai knew that Paldorak had nothing to dread from the Tatar regiment coming up the Zarafshan valley. The gate at the summit of the pass surely could never be forced. And Mir Farash had spoken of gates.

"By the other road, from Khodjent, from the north." The Persian's voice was only half conscious.

And Alai drew a long breath of satisfaction. So a second division of Tatars was on the march toward Paldorak through the northern valley. She remembered the break in the barrier hills there.

"Where lies the gate upon this road?" she demanded.

Mir Farash shook his head slowly.

"The path of the valley is open—open, if Gutchluk cannot close it."

He seemed to be asleep, although his hands moved restlessly at his throat. No longer heeding him, the Tatar girl investigated the room swiftly, taking up a rose-colored *khalat* she had noticed in one corner, and searching until she found one of the Persian's long turban cloths. Then without a sound she picked up his girdle cloth and long scimitar. Slipping out of the lamplight, she drew on the pink *khalat*, which covered her own long-sleeved coat, the two making her appear almost the size of the slender Persian.

More carefully she coiled her dark tresses close upon her head and wound the white silk turban cloth fold upon fold, glancing at the motionless figure on the divan for guidance, until the heavy turban became the image of Mir Farash's, except for the long end which she drew across her lower face. Winding the waist cloth above her hips, she thrust the scimitar sheath through it and slipped through the curtain.

"*Ohai*," she called with the Persian's intonation. "By Siva, who waits below?"

A rustle answered her, and she stepped into the shadows beyond the stair. The hag appeared, muttering, with a candle. When the woman had vanished into a room, Alai descended the stair quietly, passing her own room, and searching through the dark corridors until she found another flight of steps leading down. It was then the early hours of the morning and the only souls awake seemed to be a half dozen Kara Kalpaks who yawned over dice by the main gate.

Alai dared not risk calling for a light. In half darkness or moonlight her figure might pass for the Persian's. She made her way down to the lowest corridors, seeking for a door that might lead to the bazaar. Instead, she found a tribesman squatting against the wall by a smoking lantern; he scrambled to his feet at her approach. The door behind him was bolted.

"I will take the *farangi* with me," Alai murmured, keeping her distance from the light. "Do thou go and saddle two horses swiftly. Bring them into the alley of the bazaar."

Evidently Mir Farash was feared, for the man almost stumbled as he hastened to unbar the door at the corridor end and vanish into the darkness. Alai possessed herself of the lantern and entered the room he had been watching. And Nial, waking at the sound, looked up indifferently, then in amazement, as the girl tossed the loose turban end from her face.

"Be silent," she whispered. "Come!"

Leaving the light in the corridor, she passed out into the alley. When he followed she took him by the hand, leading him into the gloom of an archway opposite.

"Wait for a little," she cautioned him. "Do not speak. There are ears awake in this place."

"You have a sword."

Impatiently she thrust the sheathed scimitar into his hand and placed her own hand upon his lips. Then she watched while slouching figures emerged from nowhere and hawk-like faces peered in at the half open, lighted door. The prowling tribesmen passed on, and presently the Kara Kalpak appeared, leading two restive saddled horses. He seemed startled when Alai and Nial came up from the darkness, but the girl put a stop to his questions by mounting with a leap and trotting off, raising echoes in the alley courtyards.

Not until she reached an open square, where only hungry dogs moved, did she draw rein and wait for Nial.

"*Wallahi.*" She bubbled over with pent-up laughter. "Where have I not been! Oh, it is good to breathe clean air again. Did they take your great sword away, valiant Lord Nial?" A glance at his grim face silenced her amusement. "But you have another sword, and now must it clear a way for our escape. I know the way. There is a path to the north, to the great caravan road at Khodjent. Aye, the Tatars are in that valley, moving upon Paldorak. They will take vengeance for the blood of Neshavan. They will greet me as a friend. Come, before Mir Farash rouses to search for us, or Gutchluk makes new magic!"

"What befell Abu Harb?"

"Up yonder he is—" Alai inclined her head toward the ruin upon the height—"bound, in Gutchluk's hands. Perhaps he is dead by now."

At Nial's exclamation, she told him of her visit to the court beyond the pool and her words with the old Arab.

"He bade me go, and what he hath seen I know not. As for Gutchluk, I think he is no more than a man skilled in trickery who throws his voice from place to place, like the conjurers of Ind. Aye, he makes his voice fly back from cliffs. I lied to him about the letter of the khan."

"You stole the silver tube!"

"Nay, I hid it. You would not cast it away, so when anger came upon me, when we watched the Kara Kalpaks, I went down to the horses, sending Abu Harb away. I took the tube wrapped in its silk and hid it where no thieves pillage, under the stones of the shrine, the grave. But first I looked to see what was within it."

"The devil!"

"A writing, bordered with crimson and heavy with gold, with gilt lettering. Aye, how could I read it? It was the Mongol writing, from one great khan to another."

"So the seal is broken," Nial said gravely.

"What harm? Gutchluk hath it not and the Tatars will not find it upon you, O slow of wit. Come! Soon the moon will be low."

But Nial shook his head slowly, his hands gripped on the saddlehorn.

"Go, little Alai, seek the men of the Horde. I may not take the road while Abu Harb is a captive. We have shared his salt."

"His salt! And hast thou not shared mine, that day near Talas? Have I not made smooth thy path, putting aside the thorns and spying out the peril that was hidden?" She urged her horse closer to his side, her eyes dark with sudden anxiety. "Think, Lord Nial, how the path of safety lies there below us. Among the Tatar warriors thou wilt have honor, and I also—for the name of the *noyon*, my father, is not forgotten among them. In the camp of war thou art like to a raging torrent; none can stand against thee."

Nial smiled reminiscently.

"I thought it was thy wish, little Alai, to serve this wizard khan."

"O fool, to believe that!" Impulsively the girl lifted her head. "*Kai*, I can reveal to thee the wisdom of unknown things. Thou canst take command in the Horde, crush these snakes of Paldorak and make a kingdom out of these hills. Together we can ride where the eagles play."

Timidly her fingers brushed his throat and lips, while the moonlight painted in elfin colors the loveliness of her face, eager as a child's.

"Only come away, now. Up there is an evil power that will break thy sword and destroy thee. Come with me!"

"Nay, Gutchluk is a man." Nial laughed under his breath. "And if he hath slain Abu Harb, he shall know the taste of steel."

The girl's arms fell to her sides. She knew beyond doubt that he could not be turned from his purpose—that he would always make his own path and follow it.

"Then will I show thee the door of Gutchluk," she whispered, "and I will wait until thy coming."

When she gathered up her rein she was singing, so softly that he barely caught a word or two, something about a lion among men that would never be chained. Behind them the alleys of Paldorak resounded with shouts that were like the snarling of dogs.

Chapter V
The God of Darkness

A faint haze hung about the moon, and the chill of the air told Nial that dawn was not many hours off. Even the shadows were blurred, as if a veil had been drawn across the height and the great ruin upon it. To the Scot, making his way cautiously along the dark side of the broken walls, this stone citadel appeared to be the work of an ancient civilization before the time of Cathay. Certainly neither Arabs nor Iranis would have known how to shape these massive limestone blocks.

Such ruins were held in superstitious awe by the tribes, and it occurred to him that Gutchluk had taken up his quarters here to be safe from intrusion. All the valley lay open to his watch, but he could not be seen from below, and it would be a simple matter to come and go as he wished at night. Abu Harb had insisted that not even the chieftains of the Kara Kalpaks knew the face of the magician khan; and Gutchluk might sit in the bazaar below or ride down the Zarafshan trail unnoticed. He sent commands by the blind guardian of the door, or in written messages. Perhaps Mir Farash knew his secret.

"Faith," the Scot murmured, "where will he be sleeping?"

Over rubble heaps and upended columns Nial climbed as quietly as possible, ducking under pale wraiths of fig trees, and more than once standing motionless when the hiss of a snake rose from the ground. Although he listened intently, he could hear no other sounds; the night wind carried away the fretting of Paldorak. And he saw nothing moving. Steadily he made his way toward the point where Alai had found the stagnant pool.

He did not come upon the pool, but when he crawled over the breast of a wall he looked down directly into the grassgrown courtyard. A triangular cross of wood stood at the far end, but nothing was to be seen of Abu Harb.

Investigating the roofless passage at the rear of the court, he came upon several small crates of pigeons, having been guided thereto by the faint rustling of wings. The crates bore different silver labels, and he knew these must be messenger pigeons.

That passage, too, seemed clear of debris, and he followed it to the gaping door of a half-fallen tower. It was free of creepers, and he found the steps within solid enough. Climbing without hesitation, he came out on the fragment of the upper flooring and risked thrusting his head over the parapet.

All that end of the ruin lay exposed to the dull glimmer of the scumcoated tank. But what caught his eye was a faint light coming from the ground a stone's throw away. Studying it, Nial satisfied himself that it rose through a square opening. Evidently the source of the light was below the level of the tower and court.

The opening would be a light or smoke hole, and he would have to search elsewhere for a stair leading down. Doggedly he descended the tower, and bethought him to search its lower chamber for other steps. He almost fell down them, for the tower had stairs leading below as well as up. They were also clear of rubbish, kept smooth by use.

"Now," Nial thought, "here is a runway, but whither?"

At the bottom of the steps he could feel both sides of a smooth, walled passage, and he wished heartily for the light he dared not use. In a moment he discovered twin gleams of green light that moved uneasily, keeping always together. It did not need a swift snarl to tell him this was a leopard or panther in the passage.

Drawing his long scimitar, Nial advanced slowly, watching for the animal's eyes to lower for a spring. Breathing heavily—to face a great cat in darkness is no light task—he swung the sword before him, and the beast whirled away. Nial went on, trying the stones before him with the sword tip.

Presently he was aware that the passage had opened into a larger chamber with rows of squat columns on either hand. Once his outstretched hand touched a face of cold stone. He felt it curiously, discovering that it was a statue with many arms. But behind it a line of reddish light stretched along the floor.

Nial made his way toward it, felt the heavy folds of a curtain and parted it cautiously.

He looked into a red chamber. At one end upon a polished dark stone sat a resplendent figure in a crimson robe with a face as black and impassive as the stone. Its arms were resting on its knees, and through its fingers were wound strings of precious stones that sparkled in the glow of the single lamp. The shade of the lamp was thin horn, colored red, filling the chamber with its hue, except for the face of the sitter directly above it.

Before the impassive figure stood a taboret bearing food, beside which knelt a figure in the plain *khalat* of a servant—an emaciated man with a shaven head that turned uneasily from side to side.

"A temple," Nial thought, "with a strange god therein."

He stepped through the curtain, sniffing the heavy, musk-tainted air. The servant faced him like a startled snake.

"What seek ye?"

Advancing to the lamp, Nial looked curiously at the motionless figure.

"I come to Gutchluk Khan. Where is he?"

"He hath gone from this place."

"Whither?"

The servant was not the blind man. His green eyes had the uneasy stare of a beast's.

"Who am I to know? He changes his shape and goes whither he will. As a vulture he circles the valley, untiring; as a snake he spies out the secrets of the earth."

"Nay." Nial laughed. "I think he is a man. But what is this?"

"Do not touch it! Hast thou no fear? That is his body, to which he returns when he would take human shape."

More than ever the servant's eyes reminded Nial of a leopard's; and as he stared into them he felt a physical weariness. A band seemed to be drawn about his forehead, and he shook his head instinctively. Then he was aware of the servant rising slowly from the floor, coming closer to him. Twin points of light glowed in the green eyes, growing larger as he looked.

With an effort Nial turned his head away and strode toward the seated figure on the pedestal, breaking the hypnotic spell that had drawn him close to stupor. Sharply he struck the black head with the flat of his sword. As he had expected, he heard a hollow impact with lacquered wood.

The figure in the crimson robe was lifeless, but so cleverly prepared that even the eyes of painted porcelain seemed human. He would have examined the amazing jewels in its hands, but the servant, drawing back, moved silently toward the curtain.

"Stay, thou!" The Scot faced him abruptly, the scimitar raised. "Thy name?"

"Toghrul."

"Tell me no more lies. Where is Gutchluk Khan?"

The man stared at him sullenly.

"Who can know? He leaves no tracks, and not even I have seen his face. But there is one sure sign by which he is known: Even the birds and wolves flee before him, for whatever he touches is blighted."

"What is he—a Kara Kalpak?"

"Would they obey one of their own clan? Nor is he a Tatar, nor a Cathayan.

"What, then?"

Toghrul blinked at the scimitar, his thin lips drawing back from his teeth. Yet he showed more hate than fear.

"Some say he was once a priest of Siva, who learned how to draw power from the dead. Perhaps he himself is a *yaksho*—one of the dead souls, dreaded by beasts."

Picking up the lamp, Nial cast a glance around the temple chamber. Toghrul was its only living inmate, and he could see no other door.

"Take me to thy prisoner," he ordered, "the Arab, Abu Harb."

"Come, then." The shaven man grinned evilly. "I will show you his tomb, his living tomb."

Warily Nial kept close to him as they entered the outer chamber, only noticing swiftly that a great deal of wealth lay piled haphazardly here. Bales of white camel skins were stacked beside blocks of jasper and clear rock crystal. A peacock fashioned of plated gold and lapis lazuli, sparkling with amethysts, stood by a jade urn. Valuable weapons lay rusting on the floor, while in one corner rested two gigantic horns tapering gradually to trumpet mouths. He wondered if such horns, turned down the valley, could send a blast that would be caught and carried on by the echoes. Gutchluk seemed to know the vagaries of the echoes.

"Here is what thou seekest!"

Toghrul lifted the bar from a gate of marble fretwork and drew it toward him so that he stood between the wall and the gate. Within the opening was darkness.

"Go in! Thou wilt see where he is buried."

But Nial heard a movement within the cell, and quickly set down the lamp upon the pavement. The next instant he was fighting for his life, wielding the scimitar with a desperation he had never felt in conflict with human foes. Without a sound, except the scraping of claws upon the marble, three large dogs had rushed at him.

They were part mastiff and part wolf, the breed that in some mountain regions of Asia is kept to devour human bodies. They whirled to spring at him from the side, while Nial stepped back, slashing the first across the head and leaping clear of the others. He struck one upon the ribs without effect, but a second blow cut a foreleg from the brute.

The third mastiff hung back, snarling. Nial had an instant's respite, to see that Toghrul had vanished. Then, struck by something unseen, the lamp shattered and the light went out.

Nial turned and ran to where he had seen the outer passage. Against beasts and a man like Toghrul he was helpless in the dark. His shoulder struck the side of the passage, and in a moment he stumbled upon the steps.

"Oho!" A strident voice laughed behind. "Gutchluk Khan comes! Who will await him, at his feet? Oho-ho!"

A sound of rushing wings drowned the snarling of the dogs, and Nial took the stair in long bounds, running out of the tower into the cooler air of the night. The moon had vanished, but a half-light filled the sky, and he made his way grimly through the ruins, forcing himself to remember familiar turnings until he came within sight of the entrance gate. No one followed him.

But the whole height was astir around him. A white vulture flapped drowsily away, and scaly feet scurried into deeper darkness. A man in rags hastened down an intersecting lane, a long staff tapping the ground before him, and blind eyes fixed on nothing.

Nial shivered, feeling his body cold with sweat that did not come from fear, but from loathing—the ageless loathing of creeping, shapeless things that chills the blood of men. He knew now why Alai had said a sword could not prevail against Gutchluk's power.

Then he came out into the open space by the entrance and drew a deep breath of relief. He leaped over the tumbled stones and saw Alai.

She was lying in front of the gate, her head on her outstretched arm. The turban had fallen off and the dark mass of her hair spread over the ground. It was strange that she should fall asleep on the cold earth in the pathway.

"Alai!" He knelt beside her, his hand on her shoulder. "We will go now, to your people."

Swiftly he drew her other arm from her breast. She had pressed the turban cloth against her side, and the whole cloth was dark with blood. Nial caught his breath, and his fingers quivered. He felt for some movement of her heart or lungs. Alai no longer breathed, and her eyes, half closed, did not seek his.

Silently he pressed the eyelids shut, setting his teeth as the girl's long lashes brushed his fingertips.

A low laugh, mocking and maudlin, came from the murk of the wall.

It was the voice of Mir Farash, and it stirred cold fury in the Scot. He was on his feet when two Kara Kalpaks rushed out at him. His scimitar slashed down the first blade to strike at him, and he leaped among the struggling figures of the tribesmen as a wolf leaps into a dog pack, or as an Arab rushes, to strike and whirl away.

Because he reeked not at all of caution, because the long curved blade driven by the force of a steel-like body slashed through shields and sheepskin coats, because their own number hampered them in that dim light, the Kara Kalpaks were struck by fear.

"*Shaitan!*" one cried. "A devil."

At the cry they fled—some of them staggering—leaving two of their band moaning on the ground. And Nial saw before him, shrinking back from him, the white turban and broad face of Mir Farash. The Persian, still somnolent from his opium, had not realized that the *farangi* could scatter the half-dozen swordsmen of his bodyguard. Before he could turn to flee, the scimitar whipped around his *yataghan* and drove into his vitals beneath the heart.

Screaming, Mir Farash bent forward, falling as the scimitar was drawn clear.

"A dog's blood is on it!"

Nial threw the scimitar down upon the body of its owner. Then, because he must have a weapon, he searched the ground with his eyes, stooped to pick up a familiar sword.

It was his own, dropped from the hand of one of the Kara Kalpaks. Nial gripped its hilt and thrust it through a fold of his waistcloth.

"Faith," he muttered, "I'll not be needing a sheath for awhile."

Wiping the sweat from his eyes, he looked around, seeing nothing moving in the heavy murk of the getting moon. Gently he picked up the dead girl and sought the wall where she had tethered the horses. Why had she not slipped away from Mir Farash and his men? Surely she must have seen them coming. Had she tried to enter the citadel to warn him—had she sought to save the horses? He could not know.

The horses were where he had left them, and he chose the better beast. Carefully he mounted the restive horse and, bearing Alai on his arm, rode into the darkness at a footpace.

Circling the mass of Paldorak, and avoiding the huddled camps in the fields, he made his way to the shore of the lake. He searched patiently until he came upon a poplar grove with an outcropping of sandstone within it. Then he dismounted to wait for daylight when he could see to dig a grave.

Behind him, at the dark entrance of the citadel, a lean form prowled over the ground, examining the three corpses. Toghrul made no sound as he went about his investigation, his eyes seeming to penetrate the night like an animal's.

When he came to Mir Farash he turned the dead Persian over contemptuously with his foot. As he did so the scimitar clattered on the stones, and Toghrul picked it up. He felt it curiously and knew it to be the one the tall *farangi* had carried earlier. Puzzled, he weighed it in his hand—his bent head ever turning from side to side, for he felt danger near him.

In the second watch of the following night Mara Nor, in command of the advance of the Tatar column from Khodjent, made his rounds with his usual care. He was a veteran of many campaigns, whose pride was his clothes. But pride in his personal appearance did not prevent him from covering his body mail with dark grease to prevent its reflecting the moonlight.

On short, calloused fingers Mara Nor checked off the points of his inspection. His first pickets were awake, in pairs, on either side of the stream that bisected the narrow valley. They had whistling arrows to give warning and bronze basins to beat in case of an attack. He himself had colored lanterns ready at hand which, if lighted, would signal his needs back to the commander of the regiment, camped a short ride behind him.

That afternoon he had investigated the pine growth on both slopes of the valley, finding traces of many haphazard encampments, but no lurking tribesmen. Now he had sentries in pairs within the screen of the pines. His fires were out of sight, in a gully. The horses of the detachment were saddled and amply guarded. Everything was as it should be, in case a *gurkhan* came down to inspect his command.

But Mara Nor did not feel contented. Within bowshot of where he sat, the ravine with its trail debouched into the grass of the wide, sunken valley, and that afternoon he had scrutinized with keen eyes the distant red stone height of Paldorak.

On that height a *koldrun*—or wizard—dwelt. Unfortunately the Tatar column had been sent to destroy this wizard with all his warriors, coming in from the northern valley, while a smaller detachment of the Samarkand region diverted the attention of the defenders by attacking the western pass. A good plan when dealing with ordinary men, but useless, to Mara Nor's thinking, when facing a wizard, who would know just where they were advancing and who could easily read their thoughts.

Had not vultures circled over them that afternoon, and had not unseen trumpets challenged them at sunset?

Were not the conditions—a mountain height, by running water—most favorable to a wizard?

"*Ay-a tak.*" The stocky Tatar nodded.

Reflectively he chewed a strip of fat that had once been a sheep's tail. As he did so he touched the demoniac figures embroidered on either shoulder of his *khalat*, the angels of good and evil. Mara Nor believed in obeying both.

A silvery wail rose from the darkness ahead of him, then dwindled to sound clearly again as the warning arrow descended to earth near the watcher who had shot it. Stuffing the remainders of food into his mouth, Mara Nor mounted the pony grazing near him and rode forward.

Out in the moonlight he saw his men confronting a tall horseman in a ragged felt *chaban*, whose eyes smoldered from a gaunt face.

"A *gur-khan* am I," the stranger said, "of the Sarai *ordu*. Lead me to thy lord commander."

Mara Nor scrutinized him with interest. Touching his hand to his shoulder he muttered—

"*Khuru, khuru!*"

"Be silent!" The stranger slapped his saddlehorn. "I am no spirit, but I will send a thunder devil to follow beneath your horse's tail if you do not take me to the *orkhon*."

"At once!"

Mara Nor could not leave his post, but he sent two men from the herd guard to escort this man, who was like no other, to the tent of the Tatar commander.

"It is one named Nial, from the West," they explained to the servant at the entrance.

Basankor, the *gur-khan* in command, was a red-haired Mongol of the Gobi region, powerful as a bear and as obstinate. He had wrapped himself in a purple silk gown for the night. Two Chagatai Turks, his lieutenants, were with him—craggy, bearded men, much cleverer than Basankor, but less able to lead men through a tight place. The three stared at Nial curiously.

In response he detached the *gur-khan* tablet from the inner side of his belt and offered it to the Mongol.

"I see. What words have you to say, Nial Khan?"

"First give me kumiss."

At a sign from Basankor, the servant brought forward a bowl of fermented milk from the leather sack at the entrance. This Nial drained thirstily—he had had little drink and less food for a day and a night—and tossed aside.

"I come from Paldorak," he said bluntly, "and I want nothing but to see Gutchluk Khan trampled to death and his power ended. I can show you the way to accomplish it."

Basankor grunted. A man of few words, he found the brevity of the stranger admirable. Yet, he sniffed a trap.

"What is the way?"

"How many are your warriors? How many *hazaras*?"

"Two regiments—Chagatais of Issyk Kul, and Mongols of the Kerulon. A few scouts, worthless."

Nial shook his head. Two thousand riders of the Horde, to be matched against the teeming clans of Paldorak. The Kara Kalpaks were formidable in their own hills, and the odds would be almost five to one.

"Another division of eight hundred approaches from the Zarafshan valley," put in one of the Turks cautiously, "to close the pass called the Gate."

"They cannot enter the Gate. You alone will enter the valley. What is your plan?"

The two Chagatais fell silent, but Basankor was no quibbler over trifles. If the stranger came in good faith, his information would be vital; if he should prove to be a spy, he was in their hands. The Mongol explained that he meant to move in column toward the lake and feint at the town, in reality to draw off to the west, occupy the road up the inner side of the Gate and open the pass to the Tatars in the Zarafshan ravine.

Again Nial shook his head.

"If you turn your backs upon them, the clans of Paldorak will come out boldly and gnaw your flanks. They are jackals, but they will follow and strike and pull down the wounded. The Gate is too strong to take from either side. I have seen. There is only one sure way."

The three officers waited expectantly, wary of a trick.

"Attack without pause," Nial said quietly. "Divide the regiments and enter Paldorak from two points. Do not try to capture house after house, but press forward to the clear ground by the citadel. Thus you will seize the *kurgan*, the castle of Gutchluk."

"Verily, it will be defended against us," one of the Chagatais objected. "Thus we will have foes behind us and others facing us within the walls."

"The walls will not be defended. No man of Paldorak dares enter them."

"*Ahai!* Because of the wizard's magic?"

"Nay, because of their own fear. Gutchluk Khan is alone in that *kur-gan* that can hold all your men, all your horses."

The three were veteran soldiers, knowing the power of a disciplined attack, but they all had some dread of magic workers who brought about storms and plagues and sent thunder down from the sky. Moreover, they knew the Tatar ranks might be shaken by fear of such magic.

"How great is his power?" Basankor asked.

Nial did not make the mistake of trying to convince them that Gutchluk might be an ordinary man.

"Gutchluk," he explained grimly, "can throw his voice from one place to another. He can change his face and work death by poison. That is true, as I have seen. Yet he has no power to bring down thunder, nor is his skin proof against arrows. He is evil. His men have slain the daughter of a *noyon* of the Horde. When you have captured him, and when you hold his citadel, his people will be like a snake without a head. You can attack them from the *kurgan*. And the garrison of the Gate will not be able to come to the aid of Paldorak."

Nial knew that the unruly clans would be dismayed at sight of the Tatars in the citadel. But given time, Gutchluk could work mischief even against the disciplined cavalry.

"*Kai,*" Basankor assented curiously, "you look thin and weak—as if you had been struggling with a wizard, Nial Khan."

"Three of his attendants I slew, yet the debt of blood I hold against him is not paid."

"What does he look like in his human shape?"

Nial meditated while the three waited respectfully to hear his views. Men who have fought hand to hand with wizards were not common.

"He might have been a treacherous Persian, but that one is in his shroud by now. He might be a blind old man who carries a lantern, but perhaps is not blind. But I think he is a priest out of Ind, with green eyes and a turtle head, dressed like a servant of a god."

The three breathed heavily in unison. This was verily a magician, a worker of magic. Nial made haste to turn their thoughts another way.

"Basankor Khan," he said crisply, "order the attack for the beginning of the last watch of the night. Then by the first light your columns will be near to Paldorak; and when you reach the height the sun will be up and you can see all things clearly. I will guide the regiment through the center of the city, for the way is known to me. The other regiment will find only a few camps in its path up the slope. Is it good, my plan?"

For a moment Basankor considered, stirring the red crust of the dung fire.

"It is a good plan," he assented. "Go thou with the men of the guard. We wish to talk together unheard."

Before an hour had passed the Scot was summoned by a Tatar archer who said that the commander had ordered all men to saddle at once.

Chapter VI
"Give Me a Knife!"

At sunrise Paldorak resounded with the din of pandemonium. Courtyards and caravansaries spewed forth half-clad hillmen and riderless horses to add to the tumult. Scrambling out of sleep, men and women snatched up weapons and rushed to the housetops, while belated drums thumped and renegade mullahs screamed curses at Allah.

Up the steep streets came the grinding roar of trampling hoofs, the smashing of arrows upon shields and the hoarse yelling of struggling men.

The dawn attack of the Tatars had succeeded as only the advance of disciplined cavalry can succeed against irregular fighters. Paldorak had sent scouts out to watch the valley entrance, and these had galloped in with word of the Tatars' approach. But so swiftly did the regiments of the Horde move that they were not a quarter hour behind the tidings, and the bands of horsemen mounting hastily by the lake had been swept away by a charge following a flight of hard-sped arrows.

In the semidarkness the clans could not guess the number of their assailants, and the Tatars were well into the streets before the Kara Kalpaks could form above them to offer real resistance. Yelling throngs began to appear on the roofs, to hurl stones and javelins. But the regiments had seen street fighting before. Heavy leather shields and helmets with horsehair crests protected the riders, and powerful bows kept the men on the roofs back from the parapets.

Nial, riding by Basankor Khan with the Mongol regiment, behind the standard, saw groups of Kara Kalpaks charge at the head of the column, to be cut to pieces by long lances and short, curved sabers. Clans assailing the rear fared no better, and the thousands of Paldorak hung back to see what the Tatars would do. Heads turned up to the height, outlined against the sunrise, watching for a sign from Gutchluk.

But the Tatars did not break ranks, or enter the square. Nial guided them up to the open ground above the highest roofs, where the rearmost ranks wheeled and began to search the streets with their arrows.

Hot from the fighting, the foremost squadrons did not hesitate to enter the deserted gate of the citadel, although murmurs of *"Khuru, khuru"* were heard as they made their way between the ruined walls.

They pointed to the vultures that flapped away, wondering aloud whether the magician khan had taken the shape of one of those. The blind man was found, running helplessly about the pool; and before Nial could reach him the Tatar troopers had cast him in, to see if he would turn into a fish and save himself in that way. But the blind man sank in the scum, and whatever he might have told died with him.

Basankor made his way to the outlook tower to watch the progress of the second column, which was having more difficult work with the swarms of mounted Kara Kalpaks from the camps on the east slope.

"Stay at my side," he ordered Nial. "Now that we have this *kurgan*, I care not where Gutchluk Khan hides himself."

But he sent a squad of dismounted men to search the chambers below at the Scot's urging. They lighted torches and disappeared with grim faces. One of them reported presently at the tower top.

"Ahatou," the warrior grunted. "We have come upon treasure, fine white camel skins and jade—many things taken from the caravans that were robbed in former years by these dogs."

It was some time before a second messenger appeared.

"Only one man was below, although we saw the white bones of others. But he does not look like a magician."

Nial and the Tatar khan turned to see Abu Harb brought up, held fast by the arms, with a sword against his throat.

"Ai, Nial Khawand," the Arab shouted, "What is this battle? Am I a dog to be led about like this? Give me a knife and I will make them sick."

"This is not Gutchluk," Nial explained to Basankor. "It is a hunter, my companion of the road who was taken captive."

"Wallahi—" Abu Harb stretched his long arms and yawned at the rising sun—"I see you have won a victory. That is good, but have you brought food fit to eat? I have set nothing between my teeth for a night and a day and a night."

Mara Nor offered him some dried meat, but Abu Harb would have none of meat not slain by Moslem ritual, so they gave him fermented camel's milk until he was content. To Nial's questions he would only answer that he had seen no living man in the citadel but Toghrul, the servant, who had taken him from the Kara Kalpaks and had bound him upon the crucifix, hiding him away in a distant cell thereafter.

He laughed when the Tatar soldiers announced triumphantly that they had found the figure of a seated god playing with precious stones. A god with a black face and eyes that peered with the glare of the dead.

Nial, however, suggested to Basankor that the resplendent figure be brought up and hung by a rope from the wall, so that the men of Paldorak might see how the power of Gutchluk had been broken.

This had a greater effect than he had expected. Masses of people gathered on the rooftops to stare up at the hanging image. Perhaps some had seen it before, or had heard of it. By then the sun was high, and the second column of Tatars had gained the height.

When the horsemen moved out upon the slope, the throngs thinned away below them, and soon strings of camels and horse herds were seen hastening from the city. When the Tatar officers wanted to ride in pursuit of them, the redheaded Mongol refused.

"Let them go, and others after them. When the people below are scattered we will take possession of the town. Later we will follow the caravans. *Kai*, they have no way to go but east."

To Nial he remarked:

"Gutchluk dug his own grave. If he had not kept his people from this *kurgan* it would not have fallen into our hands. If he had not kept his true shape hidden from their eyes, they would not believe him to be that image we have overthrown."

"True," the Scot assented, "yet the real Gutchluk has escaped our hands. And so long as he lives his evil power will endure. Give me a hundred men and permission to seek for him."

"It is a little thing." Basankor was in a genial mood, after the rapid success of the attack. "Take whom you will, and search with the eyes of a ferret. But who could find a wizard in this swarm of ants?"

Basankor told off Mara Nor with a picked hundred from the Mongol regiment to go with Nial, and the riders from the Gobi stared with the curiosity of children at the gaunt man with fever in his eyes. Before long they were too occupied to wonder about him. The Scot led them like a pack of hounds through the alleys of Paldorak, heedless of the wailing of women who thought their last hour had come. He dismounted to run through the house of Mir Farash, and then swept the bazaar, overturning stalls and slashing down curtains, until even the ponies became frantic.

"With him it is always '*Nent-en*,'" Mara Nor grumbled to Abu Harb, who rode with them, grimly silent after hearing of Alai's death. "Knoweth he no other command than 'Forward'?"

"Disobey him, O slayer of flies," the Arab muttered, "and thou wilt learn how much more he knoweth."

Never in a generation of service had the gnome-like *ung-khan* disobeyed an order; yet that afternoon he grew rebellious. Noon had filled the valley with unholy heat, without a breath of the cooler air from above. In this ominous stillness black clouds gathered round the peaks, the sky darkened and a sudden icy blast swept away all memory of heat. The sweat-drenched ponies shivered, and at the first reverberation of thunder the men of the Gobi crouched unhappily in their saddles.

Nial was leading them at a relentless gallop across the plain toward the road to the Gate, paying no attention to the scattered groups of Kara Kalpaks who took pains to leave them the road. It had struck him suddenly that Gutchluk would not have hidden himself in the corners of Paldorak, now emptied of warriors. The magician would have sought shelter in the hills, most likely with the still-unmolested caravan of the Gate. And as he rode the Scot scanned every face within sight.

His body Gutchluk could disguise, but not the down-thrust head or the glare of his green eyes.

Then, with a gust of wind that sent billows of dust racing ahead of the riders, rain smote the valley floor with the force of a thousand giant hammers. It beat upon the shoulders of the men and drenched the laboring ponies. In a moment the temperature dropped unbelievably. Under the lash of the wind the poplar groves creaked, and in another moment the red clay of the road softened to mire.

Steam rose from men and beasts to be whirled away into the gray flood that veiled everything a stone's throw from them. The cold increased, until the rain became hail and glistening pellets danced under the hoofs of the horses.

"Now thou seest," Mara Nor remarked to the Arab, "how this magician sends down his weapons from above to wound us. He covers himself with mist to blind our eyes."

Wiping the blood from his brows where a hailstone had cut the skin, he groaned aloud at a peal of thunder, tossed back from slope to slope until it vanished, grumbling in the upper air.

Then the hail and the wind ceased, and Nial sighted a group of fugitives climbing the road ahead of them. It was a mixed party, well mounted, pressing on rapidly after the drenched figure of a Hindu priest who did not look behind him. A fresh downpour hid them from sight until the summit of the pass was reached.

As if a veil had been lifted, the mist and the rain cleared and a fresh wind whistled through the gorge, over the wall and the closed gate. Some hundreds of tribesmen clung to the wall uneasily, threatened now by the Tatar detachment down in the Zarafshan ravine, and now by the victors of Paldorak. Caught men will either run in a panic or fight desperately, and the defenders of the wall seemed undecided which to do.

They shouted no defiance at Nial's small band and no arrows flew; for every hillman knew that a single wounded Tatar would be avenged with sword and fire. And these Tatars, led by the bareheaded *farangi*, were at the heels of the weary band of fugitives following the solitary priest. The priest, whom some of them recognized as one who appeared at times to listen to the talk in the bazaar of Paldorak, now seemed silently intent upon reaching the wall at all costs.

But the *farangi* lashed his horse into a stumbling gallop, circled the priest's companions and caught his rein. Nial had recognized the thrust of the shaven head, and now he looked into the restless eyes of Toghrul.

"Nay, Gutchluk Khan," he cried, "thy road ends here."

Many heard, and Toghrul's companions halted in uncertainty, while the tribesmen on the wall crowded closer to hear the better. The Tatars, coming up on weary horses, were assembled by the matter-of-fact Mara Nor into ranks against one side of the pass, while the wind buffeted and tore at them. All this Toghrul saw as he answered in high pitched protest:

"What words are these, unbeliever? I am no more than a poor follower of Siva—"

"Thou wert but a servant in the *kurgan*. Aye, and a slayer of girls, a feeder of flesh-eating mastiffs, Mir Farash's master—through him thou hast preyed upon the caravans, taking spoil which lay hoarded in the vaults of the *kurgan*. How much better, O one who calls himself Gutchluk, if thou hadst given that spoil to these men of the hills who were kept in the bonds of fear unrewarded."

The words carried to the wall and caused a stir there. Mara Nor, his men being drawn up to his satisfaction, edged closer to witness this encounter with something he had never seen before, a living wizard.

But Abu Harb's shout rang in the pass.

"Dog, who set upon Neshavan treacherously, who learned deviltry from thy devil god!"

Toghrul's lips drew back from his teeth, and his eyes glowed. His strange intelligence could force obedience from crowds by trickery in which he was not seen; yet he could not, as could this *farangi*, sway men face to face by his will.

"Yea," he screamed suddenly, "I am Gutchluk. No weapons can harm me. Hark to what follows after me!"

His lips tightened, moving only a little. Above his head a clamor broke out—the harsh screaming of eagles. All heads except Nial's turned up in amazement, for the storm-swept sky had not a bird in it. Nial, however, was not swift enough to intercept Toghrul, who in this moment of respite slipped from his saddle and ran with fluttering robe toward the wall.

Abu Harb shouted and leaped down to follow, too late to overtake him. But something did overtake him, flashing over the Arab's head and tearing through the small of Toghrul's back. The flying figure leaped convulsively and crumpled against the wall, shrieking with pain.

Mara Nor lowered his bow and stared.

"*Kai,*" he exclaimed. "He lied. My silver shaft went through him. I brought it forth when I heard that this was indeed a wizard."

In the moment of silence that followed Nial laughed, and the echoes answered glibly.

"Throw down your weapons, O misguided ones. The voice of your master is silenced. Open the Gate now, at once, if you would live."

Hearing this, the tribesmen on the wall muttered uneasily. They had heard the dying man proclaim himself Gutchluk, and now quite clearly he could give them no aid. They knew the futility of trying to hold out against the disciplined Tatars, and slowly—a scimitar or two at first—they cast down their arms at Nial's feet. It was best to yield to one in authority.

The great gate was unbarred and pushed back by the Tatars, who shouted down to their detachment on the far side.

"The way is open. The arrow stitches of vengeance have been taken. Come!"

Nial was setting a guard over the captured weapons when the cavalry from the Zarafshan camp filed past. Among the officers he recognized the long body and impassive face of Chagan, who had been at his heels since their meeting on the post road.

"*Ai*, Chagan," he called, "thou wilt find the silver tube that bore the *tamgha* of Barka Khan hidden in safety beneath the stones of the shrine beside the trail three days' ride down the Zarafshan."

"I will send for it. Yet now I no longer follow thy track, Nial. The order was given me to join this command to advance to Paldorak." He glanced curiously at the throngs of prisoners and the piled-up weapons behind the Scot. "Eh, it is well that I need not take thee and bind thee as a prisoner now."

In a week the aspect of the valley had changed. The Kara Kalpaks had scattered to distant haunts in the hills, herded off by patrols of the cavalry. Paldorak, divested of its unruly clans, had settled down to its village routine of cattle tending; many of the hillmen were busied under Basankor's orders in repairing the ruined citadel that would be the station henceforth of a Tatar garrison.

Already a caravan was being assembled, in readiness to make the first trip in years from Paldorak to the Far East, through the passes to Kashgar. This caravan was to take with it, as an offering to the great khan, Kublai, the spoil found in Gutchluk's chambers.

And Nial asked Basankor for permission to travel with it.

"Yes, certainly," the *gur-khan* assented readily. "It is a small thing as reward. Thou didst show us the path to enter Paldorak."

"Nay," Nial responded moodily, "it was a girl who opened the path."

Basankor clucked politely, inwardly wondering; he had seen no such woman. But then he considered the *farangi* a little mad.

Abu Harb had been absent from the city, rounding up sundry stray ponies that he had roped and hidden in a ravine, and not until the day of the caravan's departure did he hurry in to say farewell to the Scot. He searched down the line of kneeling camels without finding him. Nor was he with the Tatar officers. The Arab traced him to the lake and found him pacing through a poplar grove where a heap of broken sandstone lay against an outcropping of rock.

"*Wallahi*," he exclaimed, "what is this? It is the hour of departure. Where is thy horse?"

"Waiting."

Puzzled, the old Arab seated himself on the stones, and presently bethought him of the shrine and the khan's missive that had been found in it.

"Eh, Lord Nial, then it is true that the girl Alai hid it away. I knew naught of it. *Ai-a*, she was a piece of my liver, the delight of my one eye. May Allah watch over her."

Nial, on the point of telling the Arab that he sat beside her grave, realized that he wished to tell no one where the grave lay.

"After all," Abu Harb ruminated, scratching his ribs, "she was a woman. She loved thee. Thou wert blind in both eyes. Once she wept, saying that after she had lain once in thine arms, thou wouldst hold her fast in thy heart. But it did not happen."

"Yet it did happen," Nial said under his breath.

"Eh, what?"

"It is time to mount my horse."

He glanced around the grove, then strode away so swiftly that Abu Harb barely kept pace with him.

"Well," the Arab muttered, "that is the way. An hour for a girl, but a man must follow the path of war. May Allah shield thee—thou wert as a son to me, a piece of my liver. Before setting out, it would be well to buy more ponies, good ones, accustomed to the mountains. I have such. The very ones to delight thy heart."

The Tower of the Ravens

Renald weighed three hundred and fourteen pounds, and the horse that carried him must be a horse indeed. He could eat at a sitting more than any two of his men—which was a great feat—and he had a tankard in his hand more often than a sword. His flesh was the color of crushed grapes. They said of him that he had a tight fist and a nimble mind, but he loved a jest well.

When he took the Cross and vowed to go to Jerusalem he got as far as the Taurus Mountains in Asia Minor. There, in the year of Grace one thousand and one hundred and six, he stormed and gained the castle of Montevirbo, which had been the stronghold of a Turkish sultan. It overlooked vineyards and cattle country, and my lord Renald stayed there with his knights and men-at-arms. Wine, women, and beef—he had them there, and was well content, at Montevirbo. In time, of course, he would go on to Jerusalem; meanwhile he pillaged the neighboring hills of anything that struck his fancy—droves of horses, silver and carved ivory, silks from Cathay, and jewels of all sorts. Here every man was his own master, if he had swords enough to follow him. And here Renald lived as he had lived in Normandy, where they called him a robber baron.

But he did not go near one castle, although Syrian merchants who wanted to buy from him the plunder of the Tower of the Ravens told him it was rich indeed. My lord Renald said little to his men about that. He meditated upon it frequently—the Tower the Ravens.

It was not a Christian dwelling, nor a Moslem *khalat*, and he thought it was without a master at this time. But it had upon it a power of protection that even Renald respected. No, he would not go near it, himself. He could not send one of his vassals.

Because the tower belonged to the emperor of Byzantium, or to one of his immortals, as they called themselves. Byzantium* lay off there to the north, and Renald had never seen it. The last remnant of Rome in Asia it was, and the emperor served strange gods. He defended himself with a mysterious fire that could not be quenched, even upon the sea. And he had his slaves throughout all Asia. Besides, he was allied with the crusaders.

That would not have troubled Renald much, but the Syrians had told him long tales of the fire that burned on the sea and daggers that flew in the darkness, and he wracked his brains about the Tower of the Ravens. Until that midday at table, when the thought came to him that he could send another man—a stranger—to sack the Tower of the Ravens. And surely, if he lent his swordsmen to the stranger, he could claim anything that was found there.

And he had this thought because Hugh of Dol sat at the table. He pushed away his goblet, belched comfortably, wiped his chin and spoke.

"By the Horned One," he rumbled, "they tell me there is no chant you cannot sing and no horse you cannot back. Have you heart for a venture, Hugh?"

"If it likes me." Thus said the minstrel, who called himself Hugh of Dol.

The bearded knights around him stretched their legs under the table and stared at him mockingly, as a wolf pack eyes a newcomer. They were northerners—Normans—and the minstrel was of the south, of Provence.

He had a dark and thin face and a quick smile, and eyes that were steady and bold. He carried a long, light sword in a worn leather sheath. His cloak, worn with a flourish over one shoulder, was embroidered with gold, yet stained and faded by weather. That afternoon he had come to the gate of Montevirbo and thrown his rein to Bellame, the sergeant-at-arms. And Bellame had said in the hall that the minstrel's horse was Arab bred, fit for a lord. He added that the Provençal knew horses, because he had saddled and backed the spotted Turkish charger in the loose corral—having seen the men of Montevirbo trying to break in the horse when he went to the stables with the Arab.

"'Tis an enterprise," Renald explained, "will win you gear and gold. I have set my mind upon the sacking of a small tower, yet I dare not leave Montevirbo or these circumcised dogs, the Turks, will be after raiding it."

---

*Constantinople, which alone had survived the ruin of the Roman Empire.

"What is your quarrel with the lord of this tower?" the minstrel asked carelessly.

"God's faith—I have not set eyes upon him. Yet is he a pagan, and so it will be a good deed to lighten him of his goods. Nay more, the Syrians say he is from home, and you will find no more than a small guard at the tower. Ride to the village of Baalbek, then east through the burned fields and look for the gray tower on the line of hills to the north. I'll give you twenty horsemen, full armed."

When the Normans at the table would have spoken, Renald checked them by a gesture. He knew his man. These Provençals were hotheaded and poor as plucked crows. Hugh of Dol had not the manner of a proper minstrel; he was some lordling's son with an empty purse faring from one castle to another and making shift to sing a ballad to pay for his board and bed—aye, working his way to the Holy City.

"A third of all you find will be for your keeping," Renald urged. "What, lad, you have fed in my hall. Does a man of Provence need to be bid twice to a venture?"

"I'll go."

The minstrel smiled, looking around at the five dour knights, Renald's vassals who sat by him, at the long-limbed esquires of arms who waited upon the table; but he kept his thoughts to himself.

"And, faith," he said softly, "it will not be the first time a Provençal rode where six Normans would not go."

Before anyone could cry out at that, Renald roared with laughter.

"A fair jest and a good gibe, Hugh of Dol," he acknowledged. "Now I promise to keep my retrievers in check and leave the field of the tower to you on the morrow. Mark ye, lad, they say in Provence, 'A swift horse and a swift sword'—but gold and gear is not to be passed by. The hour is late. I'll bid them light you to your bed. By nightfall on the morrow you'll be the richer by me."

And when the stranger was gone, he turned upon his liegemen who had chaffed at the minstrel's words.

"Will you bay like dogs when I have a matter to be done? This man from Dol knows not that the Tower of the Ravens is under the emperor's protection. He will go and gut it—I'll send Bellame to lend a hand—and the emperor's anger will fall on him, as the leader of the raiders. By then this man of Dol will be off on his way."

And my lord Renald, well content, loosened his belt to make room for yet another tankard of wine.

Hugh, the minstrel of Dol, turned in his saddle and looked at his men. They were climbing the mountain path in single file. Bellame, the sergeant-at-arms, rode behind Hugh, and the glow of sunset flamed on the man's broad, sweating face and red beard. The Norman horsemen—long-limbed, powerful fellows, well clad in mail—made little noise. This was not their first raid and they knew that the ridge of the mountain was near.

"Faith," laughed Hugh, "'tis well named."

Through the thick growth of cypress and lofty pine he had a glimpse of the tower's summit. It was round and gray, dark against the ruddy clouds, and black crows rose from it with a clamor and flew off. Bellame glanced up appraisingly.

"The lord of the *mesnie* is not there. They have no banner displayed."

The minstrel looked down at the tilled land below the forest—deserted orange groves and vineyards. The long handle of a well sweep stuck up into the air. It was good land, and fine pasture for cattle, but he had seen no slaves at work, and not so much as a sheep grazing.

"This is not a good road," he said over his shoulder. "There must be another."

"Aye," nodded the gray-haired sergeant, "on the far side of the ridge, for I have seen it. This, I ween, is the cattle path."

Hugh noticed that many horses had been that way not long since. The dry clay was hard, and the light bad under the trees, and he could not make out more than that. A stone, loosened by a horse's hoof, clattered down into the brush and the minstrel thought he heard voices above him in the twilight.

But no one appeared on the path, and it was almost dark when they crossed a fallow field and plunged into gloom again. Hugh reined in suddenly, and Bellame came to his side. Within a spear's length of them a stone wall was visible. The gates stood open between the gate towers, so that the raiders had almost passed the wall without seeing it.

Hearing only the snuffling and clamping of the horses behind him, Hugh rode forward after a moment. He expected to find huts and stables within the wall; instead he made out lines of poplars and dim shrubbery that seemed to be a garden. Under the starlight, water glinted in a pool, and he sniffed the fragrance of acacias.

Clear against the afterglow of sunset, the round tower loomed with a cluster of flat roofed buildings at its base. Light shone from several embrasures of the tower, but the houses beneath were dark.

"Look'ee, Messer Hugh!" Bellame's breath, heavy with ale, struck against his ear.

The sergeant pointed to the right, where a white figure stood motionless upon a square stone. Hugh peered at it and smiled. It was a slender warrior leaning on his spear, a strange round helmet covering his head.

"A statue," the minstrel explained, but Bellame went over to examine it.

"'Tis a stone pikeman," he admitted, "with a king's casque on his skull, and not even a shirt to his body. God send that I never need to stand watch unbreeched like that." He stooped to listen and shook his head. "Not a dog to bark at us. 'Tis no proper watch they keep, wi' the gates swung wide and yonder tower lighted like a beacon."

"A true word!" A hoarse whisper came from the cluster of Normans. "The powers of evil have been here afore us."

"Still thy gabble, Giles o' the Sheds!" growled Bellame.

"Nay, 'tis a true thing," spoke up another voice, "and where are the horses that climbed the path ahead of us, by token of the fresh dung that lay there?"

"By the body of Lazarus, I'll clip the tongue of him that speaks next!" It was Hugh of Dol who spoke then in his deep voice.

"Dismount," he said, "and wait for me here. I will go forward and look at the tower. If I shout, come after me. If you hear weapon play, do as you will."

He knew that the Normans were uneasy, not because of possible danger but because the garden and the castle were silent—apparently deserted and yet occupied. Bellame offered to go with him, and he told the sergeant to remain and keep the men in charge. Then he gave the rein of his horse to the sergeant, swung down from the stirrup and paused to wrap his cloak around his left arm. He carried no shield.

He took his time going forward, keeping near the hedges and the lines of statues. The light from the stars and a quarter moon was enough for him to make out a long line of outbuildings beyond the garden that he took to be the stables. He went around a wellhead and climbed to a tiled terrace cluttered with bales and carts. Here he stopped to listen by the black square of an open door.

Although he heard nothing, he took for granted that the guards of the castle were above in the tower. He was used to making his way about the forest in the dark, and this was not his first night ride. The wars of that age had taken toll of him, for the household of Dol had been stormed and sacked and left to the flames when he was a child, and in the years since then he had fared alone, gaining a living in the hospitable halls of the nobles of Provence.

He knew well that Renald of Montevirbo had sent him on a pawn's errand to this place, but he was free to act as he chose, and he saw no reason yet to draw back. This was a pagan household and he had need of gold. The minstrel drew his sword and strode into the door—a narrow postern—probing the darkness with the point of his weapon.

The chamber proved to be small and led to a passage that brought him out into the open air again. Now he saw the plan of the castle. The outer building was shaped like a rough circle. He had passed through it and had come forth upon a balcony that overlooked the inner court. But this hollow was a moat—the water gleamed dark many feet below him. In the center rose the mass of the tower, sheer from the water. The tower was the keep of the castle, and it could be defended even if the outbuilding was carried. After a long scrutiny Hugh saw that a narrow wooden bridge crossed the moat to the tower. And from his balcony steps ran down to the end of this bridge.

"Faith," he thought. "They've left the draw down and lighted the keep as if for guests."

The place was unreasonably quiet. Either its warders had set a clumsy kind of trap for him, or the tower was deserted. Hugh could see into one of the lighted embrasures, although only a bit of the room within was visible through the slot in the stone. He could make out the corner of a disordered bed and a bench lying on its side. It looked empty enough, this round tower in the water within the castle.

The minstrel felt his way down the damp steps and crossed the wooden bridge. The ironbound door was not latched, and he thrust it open with his foot. It swung back slowly and clanked against the stone wall within. A lighted lantern hung from a bracket in the hall, and after a moment's scrutiny the minstrel entered without hesitation and took down the lantern.

Swiftly he went through the hall and up the steps. A few moments later he seated himself on the edge of a bed and laughed. The Tower of the Ravens had been pillaged—looted from hall to roof.

"Plucked like a capon," he thought.

Even the bed had been pulled apart, the silk sheets tossed on the tile floor. The chests had been shaken out, leaving piles of woman's gear all about him. A scent of rose water and incense hung in the air. Something had been wrenched out of the wall above the bed; broken plaster littered the lace pillows. Only the gilt crowns remained upon the bed posts. Whoever had owned this room was a nobleman, or noblewoman.

The looters must have been well rewarded. This tower was really a palace, built in the days of old Rome—the marble columns in the corners gleamed with the polish of ages. All the lamps and candleholders had vanished, and the guttering candles were stuck haphazardly upon ebony tables. Hugh eyed them thoughtfully.

The raiders had lighted those candles. So they had been in the tower when he and his men climbed the path in the rear. The light up here on the summit had been good enough to see by, until then. Had the raiders left by the main road, on the other side of the ridge? Laden men travel slowly in the dark. Their torches might be visible from the tower. He rose to investigate and stopped abruptly.

In the outer darkness a dog howled, as if it had come upon the carcass of a man. And Hugh, straining his ears, heard a faint stamping of hoofs.

Running from the bed chamber, he turned into a corridor that led to the front of the tower, and thrust his lantern under his cloak when he came to the first embrasure. It looked out over the moat and a heavy wooden bridge to the main courtyard. And this was full of men.

They were still coming in through the front gate, carrying smoking torches. The red light gleamed on their gilt armor and the silver trappings of their horses. Negroes on foot, covered with dust, helped them to dismount. Barefoot slaves tugged at the halters of mules—white mules, heavily laden. A stout man in a robe of checkered black and purple leaned panting on a long gilt staff and yelled shrilly at the confusion. He had a face round as a moon and a hat like a sugar loaf with tassels over his ears.

"Faith, the fairies have come in." Hugh smiled. "Nay, yonder's the god of war i' the flesh."

A helmeted rider had come into the courtyard—a man as young as himself, magnificent in purple leggings and a crimson cloak of embroidered velvet. His open helmet was plated with gold and his fine face was as colorless and emotionless as a statue. Behind him several women appeared in traveling robes, and then a litter slung by ivory poles between four horses. Slaves lowered the litter to the ground and opened the lattice shutters. The horsemen dismounted, the slaves and negroes prostrated themselves, and the women bowed.

"So," Hugh thought, "the lord of the Tower of the Ravens hath come home."

It was time he went back to his Normans, for there were sixty or seventy of the newcomers, and whether he decided to attack them or to draw off, he must warn his men. But he stood rooted at the window.

The girl who slid out of the litter and stood up, yawning, was more elf than human, it seemed to him. And a tired and drowsy elf-woman. From chin to the toes of her sandals her slim body was encased in stiff gold tissue, sadly mussed. One cheek was flushed dark, as if she had slept upon it. But she held her small head straight under its coronet of silver peacocks with arching plumes.

"That boar of a Renald sent me to strike at a woman!" the minstrel said under his breath.

Above the clatter of tongues in the courtyard, he heard her speak for the first time. The clear voice was distinct and angry, and she spoke in Latin—so like his own tongue of the south that he understood well. And he knew that this girl of the purple girdle came from Byzantium—by her dress he fancied that she was the daughter of a princely house. A Norman would have left the tower while the way was still open, but the Provençal wanted to speak with this lady of Byzantium and give her a word of warning. He ran down the stair to the main entry and so appeared, lantern in hand, upon the bridge over the moat.

Some of the slaves saw him and shouted, and silence fell in the courtyard. Hugh took his helmet upon his arm and bowed to the girl by the litter.

"Well come art thou to the Tower of the Ravens!"

In utter astonishment the men from Byzantium stared at this long and lean stranger in the worn cloak and weathered mail, until the youth of the gold helmet strode forward, hand upon sword hilt.

"O barbarian," he demanded, "what is this? And where are the servants of the tower?"

"Only God knows," Hugh responded, his eyes on the silent girl—he could see now that her eyes were gray, and her hair the color of ripe straw—"and surely I do not."

A murmur went up at this, and the stout wearer of the sugar loaf waddled forward, making signs with his wand that Hugh should kneel to the
young noble, and shouting excitedly. Hugh caught the words *strategos* and
"province of Asia" and guessed that the youth held high command in the
empire. But he kept his feet, though the *strategos* frowned.

"What is thy name?" the Byzantine asked sternly. "And whom servest
thou?"

"I am Hugh of Dol, and no overlord have I, save the Seigneur Christ."

"*Eheu!* If thou wilt jest—"

"In a merry hour I will match jests with thee, but not now. The tower
is sacked and there is a smell of evil i' the air, and of that am I here to
warn ye."

The young warrior's frown deepened. He was short and swarthy and
proud as the Roman senators who had been his ancestors. At a word from
him several swordsmen ranged themselves around Hugh, who surveyed
them quizzically while the sugar loaf and his slaves ran into the tower.
Presently they reappeared, throwing up their arms and lamenting. Then
they fell silent as the girl of the peacocks came forward.

"O stranger," she asked of him, "how did this happen?"

Hugh bethought him there was no need to mention his errand, or the
men that came with him. He explained that he had been riding up the
other side of the ridge in the rear of the castle, when he passed through
the open gate of a wall and saw the tower lighted. Finding no one within,
he had wandered through it until he heard them enter the courtyard.

While he spoke the girl's eyes never left him, and it seemed to him that
they glowed green in the flickering torchlight, as if she were something
untamed—or a fair and slender statue with clear opals set within it for
eyes, gleaming in the candlelight of a church.

"That is not all the truth," she said softly. "What befell the *castellan*,
aye, and the men-at-arms who had this place in charge?"

"I have come upon no sign of them."

"We have heard enough of lies, barbarian," exclaimed the young noble.
"By thy tale, thou wert upon the path while we climbed the road. Thou
hast seen naught of the dogs who ravaged the castle, and surely we have
not. But there is no other road to this summit and the thieves were here
at the hour of candle lighting."

Hugh smiled at both of them.

"And so, I warn ye, there is peril in this tower. If the raiders did not leave, they are still here—"

"Not so. Mavrozomes—" the fat wand bearer waddled toward them at the word—"and his fellows looked into the vaults, and the outcastle around the moat. By all the gods, will you say that the looters took wing i' the air, leaving the candles burning, and that thou hast lingered to tell me of it?"

"Nay—" Hugh laughed—"to tell the lady."

"Dog!" The *strategos* thrust his chin forward. "Thou art in need of a lesson. Thou art one of the band of accursed crusaders who have plundered the Tower of the Ravens. Thou didst linger too long, and came forth upon us. Now thou thinkest to open a way of escape, by a smooth tongue."

The minstrel's brown eyes grew bleak.

"Even a dog will warn a woman of peril—but as for thee, thou art baying like a cur with a pack at thy heels."

The face of the *strategos* darkened and his teeth gleamed between his thin lips.

"This maid in my charge is Irene, daughter of the Comneni. I will teach thee to kneel to her."

He spoke a word to his men that Hugh did not understand. The one nearest pulled out his short sword suddenly and slashed at the minstrel's leg below the knee. The Provençal turned at the flash of steel. His hand was on his sword hilt and in a single motion he snatched the long blade clear and parried the soldier's cut.

Another man struck at his left leg and he leaped back until his shoulders met the courtyard wall. The Byzantine soldiers followed him up, and one thrust a long spear at his knee. Hugh lifted his arm and slashed down, and the steel head flew from the shaft. So they meant to bring him down on his bleeding legs!

But the shining body of the girl Irene pushed between two of the swordsmen and she stepped before the Provençal.

"Away from me, ye sons of slaves!"

The soldiers hesitated, and looked to their lord, who held out his hand to the young woman.

"*Eheu*, daughter of the Comneni, I wished to cut down this vagabond before thee, but if the sight of blood likes thee not, allow me to bear thee into the castle."

"The Tower of the Ravens is mine still!" Irene clenched her hands at her sides and her gray eyes blazed. "And I will give the orders, despot."

The noble raised his brows and glanced at the assemblage, and Irene became more angry at his silence.

"O, I see well that not a man of mine is here, my lord, captain of the Immortals. Nay, even my waiting woman lies sick at Nicea upon the way. These are thy men and they will obey thee, I suppose. But I am not pleased to have this wanderer mauled like a penned wolf within my wall, and so thou wilt command thy weapon men to stand aside and open a way for him."

"Whither?" The *strategos* smiled.

"Into the castle. I will speak with him, alone."

The *strategos* bowed, sweeping both hands to his helmet—but he was still smiling.

"I hear, and by the gods I would obey. Yet this—wanderer—holds a sword and, being a caged wolf—"

"Nonsense!" said Irene calmly.

The *strategos* started, and muttered under his breath something about a mad vixen. But he turned away, speaking to the Byzantines over his shoulder. Hugh waited until they had drawn well apart from the wall before he followed Irene across the moat bridge and into the entry hall of the castle. Nor did he sheathe his sword.

And after a moment he noticed that the stout eunuch, Mavrozomes, came with his wand to stand by the gate, while other men appeared within the shadows of the other door. Only one candle was still burning, at the rim of the fountain in the center of the hall, and here Irene seated herself. She glanced around at the mutilated walls and brushed back the hair from her temples.

"O that I had the power to do something! Now, thou must tell me the truth. Who sacked the castle?"

Hugh met her eyes fairly, though the blood pounded through him. So straight and slim and lovely she was, to be looked upon.

"Lady Irene," he answered, "I have told what is true. Yet this will I add—I came hither to raid the tower, not knowing it was a woman's hold."

"Alone?"

"Nay."

Hugh bethought him swiftly of his men. The Byzantines outnumbered them three to one, and he had no mind to let the *strategos* learn where his

Normans waited. There might be peace between the crusaders and Byzantium, but it was a wolf's truce.

"As to my men, they matter not. I found the tower as I have said."

For a moment her eyes were intent upon him, as if she could probe the soul within him.

"What is thy name?"

"Hugh of Dol."

"Then I thank thee, Messer Hugh, for the service thou were minded to do me. Meseems there is nothing now to be done. Ivan Michael and twenty and four good men, the warders of the castle, my followers, are wiped out and—" she bit her lip that trembled a little—"here am I. And I cannot even save thee thy life. John the *strategos* has seen to it that thou wilt leave this place only with a knife in thy back to pay thee for thy words in the courtyard."

"Then will I even stay here."

"To do what? Thy time is short."

Going down upon one knee, the Provençal took the girl's hand in his and raised it to his lips.

"To thank thee, fair and brave as thou art, to have shielded me in the courtyard. Without that, I would have been shorter by half my legs."

Withdrawing her hand, Irene gazed down at him curiously.

"'Tis a strange custom, that—to take a woman's hand. Nay, I wished only to question thee and now I have found thy words true. And so thy death will grieve me."

She spoke as simply as a child, and by that same token the Provençal knew that she expected him to fall in his blood that night. But Hugh had seen his father and mother die under the swords of raiders when the castle of Dol was burned, and he had been in straits as bad as this before. The danger did not seem past remedy to him, but the girl's plight weighed upon him, for his nature was quick to feel a woman's need. So the girl and the youth mused while the candle flared and burned lower.

"Thou art not wed to this *strategos*," he observed presently. "Tell me if thou art here with him of thine own accord."

"*Eheu!*" Irene Comnena started. "I have never gone anywhere except by my own will—and never before now save with my own attendants. The *strategos* was kind. He brought me safely from Byzantium over the desert. Not many would have done that."

"I will do more than that."

A veil dropped from her eyes and she smiled down at him.

"And what, pray?"

"I will bear thee from this castle with me."

For an instant she shook her head, amazed.

"The ravens could not do that. I did not think thee mad, barbarian."

"I do not relish this *strategos*—" Hugh followed the trend of his thought—"for his way with thee. Thou art too youthful to have him for a warder."

"Nay, I am wiser than thee." She smiled. "Always I have been old. I have lived at the court of the emperor, and every day I went in this dress to kiss his knee with the other maidens of the palaces."

"And now, where is thy guardian—a safe place of refuge?"

Irene flung out her arms at the shadows of the hall. She had come hither for refuge. No other had she. A year ago her father had been poisoned—it was said by the emperor's will. No one talked to her about it and she did not know. But the daughters of other patrician families no longer came to visit her, and her kindred avoided her. Her brother had died in the wars of Asia and they had buried him with scant honor, because of the shadow of suspicion that lay on the house of Comnenus, because her father had been an enemy of the emperor, so people said. For months she had kept herself in the great rooms of their Byzantium palace until the servants began to leave and the halls filled with dust. Only the *strategos* of all her suitors came to visit her, and he had suggested that she go to the summer house of the Comneni, in the hills of the Asian province . . .

"So I put on this court dress and did my hair up," she said, "and ordered the horse litter made ready. But the palace slaves would not bear it away, and the *strategos* had to call his negroes. Now I will stay in the Tower of the Ravens."

It was a grim tale, this, of the girl in the dress of gold—preyed upon by an emperor's suspicion. Hugh did not think she had ever wept, and yet he could see no hope for her in this place. In the dim light of the candle she glittered against the spray of the fountain like a statue in an aged temple. Around her, shadows and watchful eyes. Like himself, she was solitary.

"And the *strategos*," he mused aloud "is he a favorite of thine emperor?"

"Aye, so, commander of the Immortals, the imperial guard."

"Then meseems he will be the master of the Tower of the Ravens."

"Nay," she whispered, and caught her breath angrily. "I see well that thou art a barbarian—"

"Like this *strategos*, who has thee in his power."

Her lips quivered, although her eyes were scornful.

"And thou, Messer Hugh, by token of the cross upon thy shoulder, art a very righteous pilgrim faring to Jerusalem."

"Not so," he said gravely. "I am a man who loves thee and who will lose his life if he may not gain thee. Like the *strategos*," he added.

"Then go, for I will not hear thy words—nay, they will set upon thee in the dark." She pressed her hands against her eyes and shivered. "Do not go."

Hugh, who had taken up his sword, returned to the fountain, and she looked up at him with quiet dignity.

"I have taken thee under my protection and—I may not send a man to the hazard of a knife."

"Mavrozomes hath left his listening post," the Provençal said under his breath, "and for no good; hark to that."

She sprang up, catching at his arm. A man's scream echoed through the corridors. Then a swift uproar of voices. Hoofs clashed on flagstone and steel rasped and clanged.

"What is it?" she cried.

A figure rushed across the hall and out the entrance. The tumult came from the courtyard, increasing every instant, and above it swelled an exultant cry.

"*Allah-hai! Allah-hai!*"

Drawing her with him to the entrance, Hugh stared at the courtyard in silence. Moslems were swarming into the outer gate that had been left unguarded. They were dropping from the wall, their scimitars in their teeth. And from the gloom-shrouded summit of the wall bows snapped and arrows flew.

"*Ahai! Allah il 'allahu!*"

Their ululation was the battle shout of Turkish warriors. Into the outer gate swept a group of horsemen crouching behind round shields, tattered cloaks swirling above the bare brown arms and the shining arcs of steel.

The Byzantines had been caught by surprise. They had been unloading the mules and taking the saddles from the horses. Already they were dropping with arrows in them. The negroes ran along the moat, groaning with terror, while the women servants shrieked. Mavrozomes turned this way and that like a bewildered cow and started running toward the bridge that led to the tower. He was fairly on the bridge when an arrow thudded into him and he stumbled. His heavy body crashed down on the boards and lay there clawing with his fat fingers at the planks. Two Byzantine soldiers who had followed him turned back uncertainly, but a fear-maddened slave, torch in hand, leaped the body of the eunuch and rushed at the gate where Hugh and Irene stood.

The Provençal stepped forward and jerked the torch from the negro's hand, thrusting him away from the girl. The man vanished into the darkness, his bare feet slapping through the corridors.

"May the Seigneur Christ aid us!" Irene cried.

The first tumult had subsided, and the men-at-arms of the *strategos* were fighting stubbornly. Many of them had discarded their armor, and others had not been able to get to their shields. They gathered in small groups, those with shields on the outside, their heavy swords beating down the lighter weapons of the Moslems—but the arrows from the wall thinned them. Before the uproar began again, Hugh shouted from the bridge.

"To the tower! Rally here, at the bridge!"

Some of the men heard and moved toward him. The Turks had come through the far gate and few were near the moat. The *strategos* heard, because he rose in his stirrups and looked directly at Irene. He had got to his horse near the courtyard wall, with a score of his men, and these few had held their own so far. The rearing horses and long swords held back the desert men, and Hugh saw that the *strategos* could gain the bridge.

And the young captain of the Immortals shouted to his men, putting spurs to his horse. The other riders closed in about him and, with flailing swords and upraised shields, they crashed through the Moslem horsemen and swerved suddenly, to gallop through the outer gate. Some of the mounted Turks made after them, like wolves on the flanks of stag. Then the hoofbeats dwindled down the mountainside and Irene cried out—

"He hath forsaken us."

Hugh wasted no words on that. His eyes swept the courtyard and he groaned silently. A dozen bold men could have held this bridge while others went for the Normans and secured the rear of the tower—and sent a man to Montevirbo. But only two or three had gained the bridge and the Turks were upon their heels. He and the girl would be beaten down in the rout in another moment. He dropped the torch into the moat and caught her hand.

Pulling her with him, he turned and ran through the dim hall into a corridor that led to the rear. She hung heavily upon his arm, stumbling again and again. He cried at her in the darkness—

"I' God's name, can you not run?"

"My robe is too narrow," she said calmly. "And why should we flee? 'Tis better to face them with light—"

She gasped when the Provençal whipped out his dagger and slashed open the stiff tissue of her dress from thigh to ankle.

"Hold to my belt behind," he whispered, "and do not cry out."

He felt her grip his sword sling, and he went forward with his sword and dagger crossed before him. At the turnings he ran into the wall, but no man met him, although he heard the rush of feet and shouting nearby. Groping through the darkness, he found the rear door and flung it open.

Before him lay the same narrow bridge he had crossed early in the night. He could see it clearly because three Turks were standing in the middle of it and one carried a lantern.

"Keep thou back," he said over his shoulder to the girl. "Nay, loose my belt."

He had only a few moments before the Moslems would range through the tower and come out behind him. The three on the bridge seemed to be a patrol, posted there to cut off fugitives. They waited for him expectantly, one dropping back to hold the lantern high, throwing its light in his eyes. There was scant room for the other two to stand abreast—and this gave the Provençal his one advantage, for he could move a little from side to side. But a long straight sword was no match for two sabers in that evil light.

One of the Moslems was broad and short, and his teeth gleamed in the tangle of his beard when he laughed at the solitary Christian. Like Hugh, he gripped a dagger in his free hand. The taller warrior on Hugh's right held his scimitar high above his shoulder and his shield against his chest.

As the Provençal walked to meet them he unrolled the cloak from his left arm until it hung loosely from his dagger. When he came within spear's length of them, he bent forward and flung the cloak up into the face of the bearded warrior. With his sword he parried the other's scimitar slash and struck with the full sweep of his arm. His heavy blade smashed through the leather shield and he heard steel links break and bones snap.

At the same instant the short Turk—who had freed himself of the cloak—cut him heavily on his left shoulder, so that his dagger dropped from numbed fingers.

"Yah Allah!"

Hugh leaped back to avoid the thrust of the curved knife that would have disemboweled him. But the tall warrior, enraged, sprang after him and slashed twice at his head. With an effort the Provençal shortened his arm and parried the curved blade. His sword hand was within a yard of the other's dark face, and swiftly the Provençal struck, straight into the man's forehead, with the iron pommel of his hilt.

The tall Moslem groaned and reeled back, and Hugh slashed off one of his legs at the knee.

Before the maimed man fell to the water, Hugh was engaged with the bearded swordsman, who struck the steel cap from his head. The blood roared in his ears from the blow and trickled from his nose into his throat. The other stabbed upward with the knife, but the point caught in the Provençal 's chain mail and snapped upon his hip bone. It flashed through Hugh's brain that his left arm and leg were lamed, and he must deal with this man before the third came up. Already the lantern was waving near his eyes. Yet he could not free his sword for a thrust.

He caught a blow of the scimitar upon his hand guard and struck down with his full strength. His blade crunched into steel chains and flesh, and the man panted like an animal in pain. The scimitar struck Hugh again on his injured thigh, and he swung his sword down, feeling it bite into the soft turban cloth and break the solid bone of the man's skull.

It needed a wrench to free his blade, but he knew that the bearded Moslem was done. Again the lantern flashed in his eyes, and he smote at it. Darkness covered the bridge like a veil, and for a moment neither the Christian nor the surviving Moslem could see anything. Hugh knew that the other man could hear him panting, so he ventured a lunge forward and a blind slash in the air.

The Moslem was nearer than he thought. His arm struck the other's shoulder, and they both staggered. Hugh thrust at him swiftly, but his blade met nothing—and he heard a heavy splash below him.

"He has fallen from the bridge," the girl cried softly.

Hugh felt for the edge with his sword. He was standing on it.

"Come, then," he said hoarsely.

And she groped her way to him, taking hold of his belt again without a word. He limped up the slippery steps to the balcony, turning into the corridor of the outbuilding. Almost at once he stopped. Feet were padding through the passage toward him, heedless of the darkness—slippered feet.

Hugh braced himself against the wall and held his sword straight out from his shoulder. The feet came up to him, and he felt his point tear into something heavy. Grimly he thrust forward, and a gasping scream echoed in the passage

"Ai-ai!"

Freeing his blade, Hugh bent down and caught Irene about the knees. Holding her in the crook of his arm, he lifted her and limped forward again.

"'Twould soil thy feet here," he muttered.

Before him appeared the gray square of the postern he had entered, and he stepped through it, out upon the terrace, beneath the stars. At the edge of the terrace he peered into the garden below.

It was full of moving figures—men and horses—and a deep buzz of voices. Hugh held his breath to listen, and the girl upon his arm stirred, and bent to whisper in his ear.

"Nay, my crusader, this is the end of our way. But I would give thee thanks, for brave thou art."

"Body of Lazarus!" rumbled a voice below them. "'Tis no fiend, but a living Wight—"

"Bellame," cried Hugh. "Bring my horse to me."

"And mark ye good, my lord," said Bellame, the sergeant-at-arms, in the courtyard of Montevirbo castle after matins the next sunrise, "he is a man who knoweth his own will. Forby, he carried the strange maid before him on his horse from the mountain to the crossroad of Baalbek, nor would he suffer one of us to carry her—though his arm was hacked. And upon the way he made clear all that befell at the tower.

"'Twas the Moslems sacked the tower afore us. By Lazarus, his body—there was a sweet hewing and smiting at the courtyard, my lord! But Messer Hugh would not stay for a blow at the Moslems since they were a power too great for us. Aye, they set torch to the tower, and it fair lighted our way.

"And at sunup—" so Bellame explained the events of the night to my lord Renald—"we had a sight of the maid, a strange piece and outlandish, but fair to look upon. And she had been weeping, but Messer Hugh said to her, 'Did I not swear I would take thee with me?' And he bade me hand over a horse to her. 'Where will ye be going, Messer Hugh?' said I to him. 'Why, to Jerusalem,' quoth 'a. ''Tis a long road, that,' said I. ''Twould be longer, if I went to Montevirbo,' said he. And—''

"By God's life and thy cup-shot addlehead, didst thou let him go with that maid? She is the lady of the Tower of the Ravens," my lord Renald roared, "and would fetch a ransom."

"Well—" Bellame scratched his head thoughtfully—"the tower is burnt, see you, and the Turkish sultan is bearing away its gear and gold. I mind now that Messer Hugh said you could ride with all your men and overtake the Turks—"

Renald glanced up at the sun and at the liegemen who clustered around him. He hesitated a moment, as a man will when he chooses between two roads.

"Saddle up, lads," he said then. "We'll follow the Turks. And the minstrel will get nothing out of this but a maid, when he might have had gold."

The Grand Cham

Chapter I
The Gate of Shadows

It was evening on the plain of Angora in the Year of Our Lord 1394. The sun was a glimmering ball of red, peering through a haze of dust at the caravan of Bayezid the Great, surnamed the Thunderbolt, Sultan of the Osmanli and Seljuk Turks, master of the Caliphate and overlord of the mamelukes of Egypt.

Bayezid reined in his white Arab.

"We will sleep the night here," he announced, "for this is an auspicious spot."

At Angora a decade ago, as leader of the hard-fighting Osmanlis, Bayezid had won his first pitched battle. He had been acclaimed sultan and straightaway had slain his brother with his own hand. From that moment Fate had been kind to the man called the Thunderbolt.

"To hear is to obey," cried his followers. "Hail to the Mighty, the Merciful, the All-Dispensing One!"

Bayezid glanced around through the dust haze and saw the quivering shapes of silk pavilions rising from the baked clay floor of the plateau as his camp-followers scurried about. A line of grunting baggage-camels stalked into the nest of tents that marked the quarters of his grandees. Attended by Negro slaves, the several litters of his women halted beside the khanates that separated his household from the small army that attended him.

A slow smile crossed his broad, swart face.

A powerful hand caressed the pearls at the throat of his tunic. Fate had indeed exalted him. He had been called the spiritual effigy of the formerly great *khalifs* of Damascus and Baghdad. He knew himself to be the supreme monarch of Asia, and in that age the courts of Asia were the rendezvous of the world.

True, on the outskirts of the sultan's empire, to the east, was Tamerlane the Tatar and his horde. But had not Tamerlane said that Bayezid, given the men to follow him, was the wisest of living generals?

As for Europe, Bayezid had advanced the border of his empire into Hungary; Constantinople, glittering with the last splendor of the Byzantines, was tottering; Venice and Genoa paid tribute for permission to use the trade routes into the Orient.

Bayezid glanced curiously at the group of Frankish* slaves whose duty it was to run beside his horse. They were panting, and sweat streaked the sand that coated their blackened faces. Fragments of cloth were wrapped about their bleeding feet.

Five of the six captives bent their heads in the salaam that had been taught them. The sixth remained erect, meeting the sultan's eye.

Bayezid half frowned at this boldness which broke the thread of his thoughts. His hand rested on the gold trappings of his splendid horse. To the side of this horse slaves were dragging a cloth of silver carpet that stretched to the opening of the imperial khanates.

This done, the hawk-faced Sheik of Rum, through whose territory midway in Asia Minor the sultan's caravan had been journeying from Constantinople to Aleppo—the lord of Rum approached his master respectfully.

"O Light of the Faith," the old man observed gravely, "it is the hour of the *namaz gar*, the evening prayer."

"True." Bayezid started and his glance went once more to the white man who stared at him. "I will dismount. Bid yonder Frank kneel by my horse that I may step upon his back."

All around Bayezid the grandees were kneeling in their heavy robes upon clean prayer carpets, washing their hands and faces in fresh water brought by slaves from the springs that marked the site of the camp. The sheik bowed and gave a curt command to the master of the slaves, El-Arjuk, a stalwart, white-capped janissary, whip in hand.

"The body of the Frank will be honored by the foot of the Great, the Merciful."

At this the captive stepped forward before the janissary could touch him. Bayezid reflected that the white man understood Turki, which was the case.

*European.

And then to the surprise of the onlookers, the captive folded his arms and shook his head.

"Kneel," hissed the sheik. "Dog of a *caphar*—unbeliever—"

"I hear," said the captive. "I will not obey."

The janissary reached for his whip and the old Moslem for his scimitar. The sultan checked them, springing easily from his peaked saddle to the cloth of silver carpet. From his six feet of muscular height he looked down at the white man. His beaked nose seemed to curl into his bearded mouth and his black eyes snapped.

Then the sultan knelt, facing toward the southern skyline beyond which was Mecca, and repeated the *Allah akbar* in his clear, deep voice. When the last of his followers had completed the evening worship Bayezid arose, his smile cold as the glitter of steel, his nervous fingers playing with the jeweled sword hilt at his girdle. He noted the wide brown eyes of the captive who still stood quietly at his side, and with the interest of a born leader of men he scrutinized the square high shoulders, the long chin and the wide, delicate mouth upturned in a half-smile.

The man's face was burned by the sun to the hue of leather; his ragged tunic fell away from a heavily thewed pair of arms. His body had the lines of youth, but his eyes and mouth were hard with fatigue.

"You know my speech," observed the deep voice of the Thunderbolt. "And your eyes tell me that you are not mad. What is your name and rank?"

"Michael Bearn," responded the Christian.

"Mishael Bi-orn. Your rank?"

"None, my lord." The man's smile broadened slowly.

"In what army did you serve?"

"None, my lord."

The patrician sheik, whose fathers had been warriors, spat upon the ground and assured his master the sultan that this dog and the other Franks had been taken when a Christian galley was shipwrecked on the Anatolian shore a year ago. The Turks who took them had said that this dog was khan of the galley, that he was a *caphar* magician who steered his craft by a bedeviled needle that pointed always to the north.

"What is your country?" demanded Bayezid.

"I have no country. The sea is my home."

Michael Bearn had been born on the cliffs of Brittany. His mother, an Irish gentlewoman, had landed from his father's ship for the birth of the boy. When his father, a taciturn Breton, had died, Michael had left his mother in a tower on the Brittany coast and had taken to the sea.

There had been talk of a crusade against the Turk who was master of the Holy Land. Michael's mother had pleaded with the boy to wait and join one of the bands of warrior-pilgrims to Rome. But Michael had no yearning for the cassocked priests. The sea called him and his father's blood urged him to strange coasts.

It was the way of women, he had told the Irish mother, in his young intolerance of belief, to seek comfort of priests and to covet the insignia of the Cross. His mother had hid her tears and Michael did not know how he had hurt her.

Following the bent of that time, a few years had brought him to the Levant and the glamour of trade with the Orient. He had been master mariner of the galley wrecked on the Anatolian coast while it was being pursued by Turkish pirates.

"And so," mused Bayezid, "a slave without rank, without race, and an unbeliever dares to disobey a command of mine? So be it. You have strength in your arms and pride. It pleases me to put both to the test."

It was part of the secret of the Thunderbolt's achievement that he enforced cruel discipline among his followers. Michael Bearn's eye lighted and he lifted his head.

"Set a scimitar in my hand," he said quickly. "My lord, choose one of your skilled swordsmen and let him wear his mail. With a scimitar—his weapon, not mine—I will stand against him in my shirt."

The stubborn pride of the Breton that had not let him prostrate himself under the foot of a Turk flared at the chance to strike a blow with a weapon. He had endured captivity doggedly, seeking for a chance to escape to the hills to the east where were tribesmen who did not owe allegiance to the sultan.

But he had not been willing to demean himself, to gain time for a further chance at liberty with his five comrades. Like all seamen of the age, he was experienced in the use of sword and mace.

A swift death was better than months of running beside the horse or litter of a Turkish master.

"Shall a dog be given a sword?" growled the aged sheik, quenching Michael's new hope. This time Bayezid glanced at his follower approvingly.

"Bring this man," he ordered, "with the five *caphars*, his comrades, before my tent. Bring a sword, and"—he nodded thoughtfully—"the iron sleeve."

At mention of this instrument of torture which broke the bones of a man's arm as easily as glass, the slaves who understood Bayezid's words shivered and stared at Michael. They followed, however, after the white cap of the swaggering janissary, to see the torment inflicted.

The dark face of the Thunderbolt softened in pleasant expectancy as he knelt on a priceless carpet under the open portico of his tent and scanned the six Christians. He was accustomed to play with his victims. Disdaining further to address the captives openly he whispered to the Sheik of Rum, who stood in the half-circle of courtiers behind the sultan.

"Know, O ill-omened ones," translated the old Moslem in bastard Greek, "that your leader has offended against the Majesty, the Splendor. Torture will be the lot of your khan unless—"

With an eye to dramatic effect he paused, nodding to the master of the slaves, who advanced from the group of watching janissaries, a spear's cast away. The warrior carried a misshapen thing of iron resting on a wooden table. The rusty metal was formed in the semblance of a lion with an enormous mouth, lying prone on the table. Twin bars projected on either side from the ribs of the beast.

"—unless," resumed the sheik, "one of you five *caphars* will offer to fight in defense of the body of your friend."

Michael Bearn looked up quickly, intending to warn his mates not to accept the offer of the Moslems. But they did not meet his eye. They were Portuguese and Italians, wasted by sickness and misery.

"It is not fitting, verily," the spokesman went on, interpreting the low words of Bayezid, "that a good weapon should be given to the hand of one who is accursed. Yet a lion may slay a dog, and the sight of an infidel's blood is a blessing to a true believer. So, one of you may take up the quarrel of your comrade and fight with swords against one of the champions of the janissaries. Whether your champion conquers or not, the man named Bearn will be spared the torture."

Whereupon the sheik drew his own scimitar and held out its hilt.

Michael Bearn would have taken it, but the wily Moslem shook his head.

"Not you," he explained in Arabic. "The Most Wise will presently make a test of your strength. Now he tries out the Christian hearts of your comrades."

As none of the others volunteered for the duel, the sultan made a further concession. The man who offered to fight would be set free—if he lived—with Bearn.

But the five men would not hazard their lives on a chance of liberty. They cast sidelong glances at the glittering scimitar and at a stalwart warrior who stood forth from the guards, his shield dressed ready for the conflict.

It gave keen pleasure to Bayezid to see these men refuse the issue. He smiled to think that they clung to the ignoble life of slavery. His own men were trained to value their lives lightly in battle and to die for their faith.

It pleased Bayezid, also, to deny Bearn the chance of the fight, for he knew that the young seaman would have welcomed it.

"So be it," he nodded. "The torture."

The expectant master of the slaves summoned the waiting warrior and set the table before Michael Bearn.

"Hold forth your arm," he commanded.

Michael paled and set his lips as he extended his left hand.

"The right one," objected Bayezid, following all that passed with the eye of a connoisseur.

A moment later Michael's right arm had been thrust up to the elbow into the iron gullet of the lion and strapped into place.

The Breton stiffened as he felt the cold touch of the vise, concealed within the form of the lion, grip his bare forearm. Bayezid nodded, leaning back on his pillows, under the sweep of a peacock fan in the hands of a slave.

The two janissaries threw their weight on the projecting levers and there came to the ears of the spectators a dull *crack* as if an arrow had been snapped in half.

But Michael did not cry out. Sweat started on his face and blood dripped from his lip where his teeth had set upon it. This did not suit Bayezid, who had expected screams and a prayer for mercy.

"Again," he snarled.

The two torturers altered the position of Michael's broken arm slightly and clamped the levers into place a second time.

This time Michael groaned softly and swayed on his feet, sinking to his knees.

"Now the *caphar*'s pride is broken because his strength has passed from him," thought Bayezid, watching keenly. To the attentive sheik he whispered:

"The broken ends of the bone of the arm have been ground together and he will whine for mercy—like the other dogs who have no stomach for pain."

The janissaries released Michael's arm from the instrument of torture at a glance, from the sultan. On the back of the forearm the skin had been broken by a bloodied fragment of bone.

Supporting himself by his left hand on the table, Michael rose slowly to his feet, wincing and setting his lips as he did so.

His eyes were dark with agony as they sought Bayezid's face.

The youthful pride and humor had vanished from Michael's countenance, leaving a grim mask of purpose. The abundant vitality of his powerful body had been sapped by the ordeal. But there was a new vigor in his poise, the strength of an unalterable determination.

So the captive faced his tormentor.

"I shall not forget this, my lord sultan." He indicated his maimed limb. "I shall be avenged—" His voice choked.

The Sheik of Rum, who had been studying the eyes of the injured man, now drew his weapon again and salaamed before Bayezid.

"O Most Wise, it would be best to slay this one. An injured snake is quick to strike."

The Thunderbolt shook his head coldly. He had not yet tasted the delight of the torture to the fullest.

"Nay. I would watch the *caphar* run beside my litter on the morrow, and see how he bears his pain."

The Sheik of Rum was very wise.

It was a week later that the six captives made their attempt to escape from the caravan of the Osmanli. During the week they had been ascending to the cooler plateau of Lake Van, where the summits of the Caucasus were visible far to the north.

Yet it was to the east that the six had decided to flee. They had seen that the outriders of the Turks who pillaged supplies in the villages of lesser Armenia had kept a vigilant outlook in that direction.

To the east lay a pass called the Gate of Shadows, leading into the lands of Tatary. Michael and his mates did not then know why the Turks shunned this pass. But they believed that once in the Gate of Shadows they would be safe from pursuit owing to this superstition of the Turks.

The night on which they made their venture was clear. The stars shone brilliantly through the colder air of the height by the lake. Men and beasts of the caravan were weary after a long march. Bayezid was never sparing of his followers.

Two things had decided the Christians upon this night. They were at the point of the march from Constantinople to Aleppo which was nearest the Gate of Shadows. And the Moslems had fasted for three days. That night was the feast of Miriam, when the long fast was broken and warriors and courtiers alike satiated themselves with meat and wine.

Bayezid, although calling himself head of the faith, always allowed his men their fill of debauchery, knowing that it drew soldiers to his ranks.

Consequently the janissaries who watched the *aul* where the Christian captives were kept apart from the slaves of other races were a little drunk and more than a little sleepy.

Michael, by tacit consent, had been chosen the leader of the six. Memory of the torture to which he had been subjected had made the Portuguese and Italians eager to flee. Cowards at heart, the nearer peril of the "iron sleeve" made them willing to risk the death that was penalty for an attempt to flee their bondage.

And Michael, who yearned for the freedom that would afford him a chance to strike back at Bayezid, had formed a plan readily.

The *aul* was a rough square shelter of rocks resembling very much a large hut without a roof. The stone walls were as high as a man. The two yawning spearmen who acted as guards had built a fire just within the entrance.

As usual the prisoners gobbled down the evil-tasting *pilau*—broth of rotting sheep's flesh—that was set before them in a kettle. The evening prayers of the Moslems had been completed long since and soft radiance coming from the silk pavilions of the nobles indicated that the feast was well along.

A heavy guard of wakeful mamelukes stood about the enclosure where Bayezid was quartered, and other mounted sentries paced about the circuit of the fires around which warriors and slaves alike drank, sang, and slept.

It was the first watch of the night when one of the Portuguese rose and tossed a double armful of dried tamarisk branches on the fire that had sunk to embers. A crackling blaze climbed skyward barely three paces inside the *aul* entrance.

For a moment the interior of the walled space would be concealed from the glance of passersby. One of the janissaries growled and spat, motioning the Portuguese back to his place. The other sentry leaned on his battle-ax half-asleep.

Making signs that he wished to communicate something, the captive moved nearer the first sentry, while one of the Italians arose stealthily and, keeping within the large shadow cast by the three men near the fire, slipped to the rear of the janissary.

Michael appeared to be asleep. In spite of his crippled arm—the bones had been rudely set by a *hakim* of the sheik who, in obedience to the pleasure of his master, intended Michael to live—in spite of his weakness and the fever that had set upon him for several days, the guards always kept vigilant watch upon him, knowing that the Breton was more dangerous than his mates.

Through his half-closed eyes Michael could see the Italian detach a stone from the top of the wall behind the three men silently. The arms of the captives had been left free although their ankles were secured at night by heavy leather thongs that would not yield to their fingers. Naturally none of them had a weapon of any kind.

The sentries had no reason to expect an attempt to escape. Even if the two janissaries could be disposed of, the captives would have to pass through the camp and pierce the cordon of riders in the outer darkness in order to gain the plain.

Even clear of the camp they would be pursued by well-mounted warriors and the odds against them in a hostile country were very great.

The first sentry was staring mockingly at the Portuguese who cringed beside him, gesturing futilely. And then the Italian cast his heavy stone with both arms.

It struck the janissary at the base of the skull and pitched him forward a dozen feet. He fell, stunned, with his face within the edge of the fire.

The second warrior started out of his doze and his lips parted for a cry. But the Portuguese, frenzied by peril and hope of escape, clutched his throat. The Italian had leaped after the stone and caught up the spear of the man he had slain.

This spear he thrust into the clothing over the stomach of the choking sentry.

"Hearken." Michael had run to them and addressed the struggling Moslem. "Be silent and do as I bid ye or your body will lie in the fire."

A stringent odor of burning flesh and cloth came to the nostrils of the sentry and he ceased struggling, waiting for the blow that would slay him. But Michael with his left arm dragged the smoking corpse from the flames and swiftly directed two of his men to conceal it under some of their robes in a corner. Before doing so, he saw that they took a dagger and scimitar from the dead janissary and stowed the weapons under their own clothing.

"Now," Michael commanded the watching sentry, "your life will be spared if you do this; call twice for El-Arjuk, master of the slaves who is in command of the *aul* this night. He gorges himself at a nearby fire. Do not cry for aid, but call his name."

The man winced as the spear in the hands of the Italian pricked his belly. He did not believe that he would be permitted to live, yet he had smelled the burning flesh of his comrade.

"El-Arjuk!" He lifted a long, wailing cry while Michael listened closely. "*Ohai*—El-Arjuk!"

"Again," whispered the Breton and the call for the master of the slaves was repeated.

This time a harsh voice made answer. Michael's eyes narrowed and he ordered the fidgeting captives back to their sleeping robes with the exception of one man who stood against the wall, drawing the sentry back with him and pressing a dagger's point from behind into his flesh.

Michael caught up the long battle-ax that had supported the janissary in his ill-timed doze. He hefted it in his left hand, found its length unwieldy, and broke the wooden shaft in two under his foot.

Taking up the shortened weapon, he held it close to his side, away from the fire.

"Keep back," he hissed at the others, "for this is my fight."

They mumbled and straightaway fell to staring in fear as a burly form strode through the entrance of the *aul* and came around the diminishing blaze of the fire.

"Who called?" growled El-Arjuk, glancing at Michael and the one sentry swiftly.

He was flushed from drinking, although his step was steady. In feasting he had laid aside his armor, but held a small target of bull's hide and a scimitar. Noticing the absence of the other janissary and the strange quietude of the one sentry, he started.

"Blood of Shaitan—"

"I summoned you," said Michael grimly. "To your reckoning. Guard yourself!"

With that he leaped, swinging his haft of the battle-ax. With one motion El-Arjuk flung up his shield and slashed forward under it with his sword.

The blade met nothing but air. Michael's jump had carried him over the low sweep of the Turk's scimitar, while the hastily raised target momentarily obstructed the vision of his adversary.

The Breton's broad chest struck the shield, bearing it down, and his shortened ax fell once, the full weight of his powerful body behind it. El-Arjuk had started to cry for aid when the blade of the ax crashed into his forehead and the cry ended in a quavering groan. Michael fell to the sand with his enemy, but he rose alone, listening intently.

From somewhere outside the *aul* a question was shouted idly, for the thud of the two bodies and the moan of the master of the slaves had been heard.

"Reply," snarled Michael at the staring janissary who was going through the motions of ablution, kneeling in the sand. The Moslem wished to die with this rite performed. "Reply with the words I put into your mouth or we will fill your throat with the unclean flesh of the dead."

The warrior hesitated, then bowed his head.

"It is naught," he called back over the stone wall as Michael prompted him, "but the death of a dog, upon whom be the curse of Allah for his sins."

A satisfied laugh from the listeners without, who believed that a Christian slave had been killed, came to the ears of the captives. Wasting no time, Michael had green tamarisk branches cast on the fire causing smoke to fill the *aul* entrance.

Behind this makeshift curtain he ordered El-Arjuk stripped of his brilliant yellow coat and insignia and instructed the nervous captives how to rewind the white turban so as to conceal the blotches of blood.

This done, the Portuguese who was like the master of the slaves in build was clad in the garments and given the shield and scimitar. Meanwhile the excited men would have slain the stolid sentry had not Michael intervened.

"I made a pledge," he said coldly. "You want blood, methinks, and you will find plenty before long."

So the surprised sentry was bound and wrapped around with the clothing of the Portuguese until he was helpless either to move or cry out. Then, with the two bodies, he was laid in a corner of the enclosure and covered with sheepskin robes.

"Say to Bayezid," smiled Michael, "that I bid him not farewell—for I shall seek him again."

When the fire died down presently and passing soldiers glanced idly into the *aul*, a group of men issued forth without torches. At their head was the familiar uniform of the master of the slaves, and their feet were bound with leather thongs, permitting them to walk only slowly.

It was entirely natural that El-Arjuk should have work for the *caphar* slaves to do that night, so the revelers paid scant heed to the group. It was whispered, moreover, that one of the infidels had been slain, so it was entirely to be expected that the others would be used to dig a grave.

At the outskirts of the tents where darkness concealed them Michael called a halt. Passing near the fires, the garments of El-Arjuk had been their safeguard; in the dark they would be challenged at once by the mounted riders who patrolled the camp.

So Michael waited, kneeling on the ground in order to raise passing figures on the sky-line. He ordered his comrades to cut off with the weapons they had concealed under their clothes their bonds and to carry the cords until they could be concealed at a distance from the camp. Not until he was satisfied that a patrol of horsemen had passed the ridge in front of him did he give the word to advance.

An hour later they were beyond the outer guards and running due east, under the stars that guided them, toward the Gate of Shadows.

On the second night they took their ease. Michael had gone among the hill villages at twilight. He had worn the dress of El-Arjuk and when he returned to the men waiting in the thicket up the mountain-slope he said:

"The Darband-i-Ghil, the Spirit Gate, lies six hours' march above us. Come."

The six had run before now—too swiftly at first for long endurance—by the north shore of Van. Michael had steadied them to a slow trot and had taken pains to pass through such rocky ravines as offered, in order to wipe out traces of their passage. They had seen no pursuers, even after leaving the lake.

"Nay," growled a Genoese. "*Par Dex*, our bones ache and our feet bleed. We must sleep."

"Sleep!" cried Michael. "With mamelukes riding in our tracks who have orders not to return alive without us. I'm thinking that Bayezid made short work of the janissary guard whose life we spared. Will his horsemen yearn for a like fate?"

He himself was near the point of exhaustion, for his arm was scarcely knit and fever had weakened him. But the men would not move from the spot where they had been watching the lights of the Kurd village and talking among themselves.

Realizing that they must rest, Michael sat down against a tree for a brief sleep. The half-light of dawn was flooding the thicket and the sky over the black hills to the east was crimson when he woke at the sound of approaching footsteps.

It was his own band and they were coming up from the village. Some of them were reeling, though not from fatigue, and their breath was heavy with olives and wine. They looked back over their shoulders and grinned uneasily when they met his eye.

"We've taken the Moors' food," boasted one fellow. "It's their own law, methinks. An eye for an eye. They'll remember us."

Michael glared. These were common men, very different from the belted knights who had sometimes visited his mother's home in Brittany. She had hoped that he would be a knight. Instead, he had led a rough life and had toiled against hardships until—this.

"——, what fools! That was a Kurdish village, and the men have good eyes and horseflesh. Well, I must bide with you, for you have named me leader. Come."

They ran sturdily through the dawn. Months of trotting beside the nobles of the Osmanli had schooled them to this. By midday they were above the fields in a place of gray rocks and red clay. In front of them a half-dozen bowshots away a great gully between mountain-shoulders showed the blue of the sky.

"The Gate of Shadows," they cried.

And with the words riders came out of the woods behind them.

Michael measured the distance to the gully, glanced back at the shouting mamelukes, and shook his head. He pointed to a mound of rocks nearby and led his five men there.

"'Tis the gate of heaven you will see," he grunted. "No other, and not that, if you cannot die like Christians."

And the five, to give them their due, fought desperately, using the few weapons they had carried from the Turkish camp, and eking these out with stones.

The mamelukes, reinforced by Kurds from the hill village, tried at first to make them yield themselves prisoners. But the captives knew what

manner of death awaited them at Bayezid's tent and hurled their stones.
The big Portuguese went down with an arrow in his throat. The Genoese
leaped among the horses, knife in hand, and struggled weakly even when
his skull was split with a mace.

The rearing horses stirred up a cloud of dust that covered the mound.
Into this cloud Michael strode, swinging his half-ax. The first rider that
met him was dragged from the saddle and slain. Michael went down with
a mameluke on top of him and neither rose, for Michael's left hand had
sought and found the other's dagger in his girdle.

When the last Christian had been shot down with arrows, the Turks
dismounted and proceeded to pound the skulls and vital parts of the bodies of their victims with rocks. If any of the men of El-Arjuk had been in
the party Michael would have suffered the fate of his comrades.

But the mamelukes had neglected to give him the *coup de grâce* owing to the body of their warrior that lay upon his. When they lifted up
their dead they saw only a prostrate Frank besmeared with blood—not
his own—and with a swollen, bruised right arm that looked as if it had
been crushed with a stone.

The senses had been battered out of Michael by the mace of the dead
mameluke and it was a fortunate thing for him. Because by the time he
crawled to his feet there were no Turks within view.

Instead, black-winged birds casting a foul scent in the air hovered over
his head. The vultures had been descending on the bodies of the five men
when Michael Bearn stood up.

Now they circled slowly in the air or perched on the rocks nearby patiently.
Michael looked at them long, and then at the bodies of his comrades.

The five had not been brave men, but they had died bravely.

Michael walked slowly away from the knoll toward a rivulet issuing
between rocks in the mountainside that rose mightily above him. He
knelt and drank deeply. Then he dipped his head in the stream, wiping
away the dried blood. The flapping wings of the vultures impelled him
to look up.

His glance penetrated straight down the ravine that was called the Gate
of Shadows, and he studied thoughtfully the vista of brown plain that lay
beyond. Once within the pass he knew that he would see no more of the
Turks. The evening before he had been told when he visited the Kurd village that the rock plateau in front of the pass had been the scene of a massacre by the Turks.

The skeletons of the dead were in the pass, and a superstition had arisen that the souls of the slain had not left the place. The voices of *ghils* had been heard in the darkness. So the Moslems considered the place not only unclean but accursed.

"'Fore God," he sighed, "we were at the Gate, the very Gate. Well, here must they wait for me—my five mates that were."

So saying, he went back to the knoll, driving away the birds, and dug with his battle-ax a broad shallow grave in the loose sand. Dragging the bodies into this with his one useful arm, he covered them up first with sand, then with large rocks that he rolled down with his bare feet from the knoll.

From a wisp-like tamarisk thicket clinging between the boulders of the plateau, he cut two stout staffs with his ax. These he bound roughly together at the middle with a strip of leather cut from his jerkin. The longer staff of the two he imbedded in the sand at the head of the grave.

He had fashioned a cross.

"Rest ye," he said gravely and extended his left arm over his head. "*Vindica eos, Domine.*"

Now as he said this he glanced again at the ravine and the plain beyond, where he could find food and a tent among the Tatar villages. Then he turned to the northwest where beyond the hills lay the Mormaior, or Black Sea, and beyond there the great cities of Europe.

To the northwest, if he could penetrate thither, were his countrymen, and theirs, he thought, was the power that might some day strike at the Thunderbolt.

It was to the northwest that he began to walk, away from the grave and the Gate of Shadows. Greater than the will to live was the will to seek again the man who had crippled him.

When darkness came and covered his movements he pressed forward more rapidly, swinging his short ax in his left hand. As he went he munched dates and olives that he had plucked from trees near the mountain villages. He found no men to accost him in these orchards, for the fields were scarred by hoofs of many horses and the huts were charred walls of clay.

Bayezid's riders had been pillaging the villages of Lesser Armenia.

Once, walking barefoot, he came upon a young wild sheep and killed it with his thrown ax. By now the villages had been left behind and below and the moon stared at him steadily from above the pillars of huge pines as he entered the forest belt.

Another thought came to Michael. He remembered that, in the tower of ill-fitting stones on the sea cliffs of Brittany where the grass was short because of the ceaseless winds, a black-haired woman waited, sitting by her weaving. He had vowed that he would come back to sit at his mother's table and tell of the voyages to the East. And this, she would know, he would do. A lawless boy, with his father's hot blood in him, he always kept his word.

From time to time he was forced to beat off the attacks of wild dogs with his ax as he worked through the passes of the Caucasian foothills. His bloodshot eyes closed to slits under the lash of the cold wind, and he swayed as his heavily thewed limbs carried him down toward the place where he had seen a glimmer of water in the distance.

It was bodily weakness that drew his thoughts home to the tower and the coast where he had played as a child. For a space he forgot Bayezid and the torture. He had been hale and strong as a boy. Was he to go through life a cripple? Was that the will of God of which his mother had spoken, saying—

"The ways of God are beyond our knowing."

Thirst had been his invisible companion, and the watercourses that he crossed were dry. They led him down to a plain of gray rocks and white salt, where the salt particles in the air dried up the moisture in his throat and brought blood to his lips.

The smell of water coming toward him from the wide shore fired him with longing. He went forward in a staggering run and knelt to dash up some of the water in his hand.

It was thick with salt and dull green in color.

"The Sarai Sea," he reflected, "the sea of salt. Eh, a rare jest to a thirsty man."

He knew then that he had come out on the border of the sea now called the Caspian and not the Mormaior (Black) Sea. But, rising, he saw some dull-faced Karabagh fishermen staring at him from a skiff in an adjoining inlet and he laughed exultantly, lifting his hand to the sunset in the west.

The skiff would fetch him to a Muscovite trading galley, and in time Astrakhan, then Constantinople. He had heard at the court of Bayezid that the Franks were mustering a crusade, to assemble at that city. The chivalry of Europe was taking up arms against the Turk.

"There will be a battle," he whispered to himself, "and I shall have a share in it, God willing."

Chapter II
The River of Death

Another sunset, and a war galleass was feeling its way with a double bank
of oars against the sluggish current of a broad river. There was no wind
and the heavy red pennon emblazoned with a winged lion hung nearly to
the water between the steering oars of the high stern castle.

The dark figures of men-at-arms pressed close to the rail of the benches
that ran along each side of the waist of the vessel, above the moving gray
shapes that were the rowers' backs.

"Give way, to the shore," called a voice from the stern platform.

As the heavy-timbered galleass drew in, fully manned for action, toward the rushes of the bank, the speaker cupped his left hand to his eyes
and stared at the ruddy light of countless fires. His right arm hung stiffly
at his side.

A year had not availed to restore the use of his injured arm to the man
who had been a Turk's slave. Now by infinite pains he could manage with
his left. Unlike the men-at-arms and the mailed Venetian archers clustered upon the stern, he wore no weapon.

Michael Bearn had reached the Venetian fleet in the Black Sea at an
opportune moment. Experienced ship-masters were needed to take command of the new galleys that were to cooperate under the Venetian flag
with the Christian army on the mainland.

The body of the Venetian fleet lay off the mouth of the Danube, waiting to convey the victorious army of the Christian allies to Asia Minor
and Jerusalem.

It was a great array that had come against the Ottoman. Besides the
Venetian war-craft, Sigismund of Hungary was up the river, and the co-
horts of Slavs, Magyars, and the Serbs. With these were the pick of the
chivalry of France, the forces of the Elector Palatine and the Knights of
Saint John.

They had struck down through the mountains of the Serbs and besieged Nicopolis, on the river. Warnings of the approach of the conqueror
Bayezid had reached them, and the French knights who had brought ship-
loads of women and wine down the Danube had laughed, saying that if
the sky were to fall, they would hold it up with their spears.

Verily it was a goodly array of Christendom before Nicopolis—an army
blessed by the Pope and dispatched against the Ottoman, who had swept

over Arabia, Egypt, Asia Minor—far into Greece, now impotent, and the rugged mainland behind Constantinople.

The Moslems held Gallipoli and a *khadi* held court beside the marble and gold palace of Paleologus. Bayezid the Conqueror, surnamed the Thunderbolt, had never met defeat.

Bayezid had advanced to the relief of the Moslem governor of Nicopolis, and Emperor Sigismund and Count Nevers, commander of the French, had given battle.

For days, hearing of the coming struggle, Michael Bearn had chafed upon the narrow afterdeck of his galleass. He had urged the Venetian commander to make his way up the river, to assist in the struggle if possible.

Bearn had been told by the *proveditore* that the fleet of the Signory of Venice had promised to convey the army only to Asia Minor. It was not the policy of the Maritime Council to risk the loss of good ships—but Bearn was allowed to go, to bring news.

It had been a dangerous path up the Danube, for small Turkish craft thronged the shore and bodies of janissaries were to be seen from time to time in openings in the dense forests.

Now, conning the darkened galleass close to the bank, Michael Bearn strained his ears to read the meaning of the tumult on shore. He could see horsemen riding past the glow of burning huts, and the clash of weapons drifted out over the quiet waters.

"Sigismund pursues the Saracen!" exulted a man among the archers on deck.

Wild hope leaped into the heart of Michael Bearn. Was the issue of the battle so soon decided? Had the armed chivalry of France outmatched the power and skill of Bayezid? He yearned for the first glimpse of victorious French standards. Yet, knowing the discipline and power of the veteran Moslem army, he doubted the evidence of his eyes that the emperor and the French could have pursued their foe so far.

"What ship is that?" cried a high voice, and the splash of hoofs sounded in the rushes as a man rode out toward the galleass.

"Venetian," answered Michael promptly. "Is the battle won?"

The men on the vessel held their breath as the rider, before answering, swam his horse out to them and, grasping at ropes lowered over the stern where the oar-banks permitted him to gain the side of the galleass, climbed heavily upon the deck.

"If you are a Venetian—fly!" he cried, staggering against Michael. "Never have the eyes of God seen such a defeat. Bayezid has sworn he will stable his horse in Saint Peter's. I am alone, of a company of knights who followed the Constable of France."

Michael Bearn gripped the knight by the shoulder fiercely.

"The Constable of France—defeated—"

"Slain."

The wounded man was too weary to be surprised at the fire in the eyes that burned into his. Michael drew a long breath. He was too late. And his countrymen had fallen before Bayezid.

The knight was removing his mail hood with shaking hands.

"We thought the Saracen was shattered," he said hopelessly. "Our camp was surprised, yet the French mounted and rode to the attack, through the skirmishers and the cavalry with white woolen hats—"

"The janissaries," nodded Michael.

"—and past them, into the ranks of the horse-guards that are called *sipahis*, of Bayezid. Our lances, forsooth, had broken them asunder. We had lost many and our ranks were ill-formed when we gained the summit of the hill where we found not a rabble of defeated soldiery, but a forest of forty thousand lances. Ali, Saint Denis!"

"Bayezid ever keeps his best troops till the last."

"He has ordered slain ten thousand Christian captives, sparing only the Count of Nevers and twenty knights. I escaped."

"And the emperor?"

"Floats down the river in a boat. He made a brave stand, 'tis said, until the Serbs joined the Moslems and struck his flank—"

"'Tis done. Rest you and sleep." Michael spoke curtly, what with the hurt of the news. "There are wounded to be brought off from shore."

Urging his vessel almost upon the shore, he formed his men-at-arms into lines to pass up what of the injured they could find, while he made his way inland to turn aside the fugitives he met into the galleass.

He saw only haggard and dusty men, weaponless and exhausted. On mules and purloined horses camp followers dashed past along the highway, striking aside those who got in their path. Semblance of order or discipline there was none.

Wounded foot soldiers who had cast aside their heavier armor limped into the light of the burning houses nearby, silent and grim-lipped. Michael was mustering a group of these at the water's edge when a mailed horseman spurred up and grasped at his shoulder.

"For the love of ——! Is't true there is a ship at hand?"

Michael looked up under drawn brows and saw a handsome Italian cavalier, his velvet finery besmirched and his jeweled cap awry.

"A hundred ducats, sailor, if you will take me on your ship at once," the horseman cried, fingering at a heavy purse with a quivering hand.

"Spare your purse-strings and wait your turn," responded Michael shortly.

But the cavalier, befuddled by fear, was pushing aside the watchful foot soldiers, to leap at the ropes that had been lowered from the vessel, when Michael's left arm, thrust across his chest, stayed him.

"You are a captain, signor," he observed quietly. "Help me to get these wounded to safety."

The Italian glanced back and saw that a fresh route of fugitives had come into the light at the shore. A tall bazaar trader with his servants was striking down those who sought to climb into a muddy cart drawn by nearly exhausted horses. Michael could read the fear in the red-bearded face of the trader. A woman, her skirt dragging about her knees, ran screaming into the path of the cart, holding out imploring arms.

The servants, under the oaths of their bearded master, lashed the horses on and the woman, in all her sad finery, was cast to earth under the hoofs of the beasts. The cart disappeared into the darkness but she lay where she had fallen.

"You see!" cried the Italian. "Death is upon us unless we fly. Out of my way, dogs—"

Drawing back his arm, Michael struck the man, sending him headlong into the water. Heedless of the blow, the other rose and fought his way to the ropes that offered a way to safety.

"Wo!" His cry came back to Michael. "Death is upon us. Fly!"

"Fly!" echoed the wounded, struggling toward the ropes. "The Turks are at our heels."

Those who could not stand unsupported were thrust down into the water. Men, striking at one another's heads and tearing at the surcoats which bore a crimson cross—the stronger among the fugitives, up to their necks in water, fought for the ropes.

When Michael at last—seeing that the galleass was crowded to capacity—clambered up the gilded woodwork of the stern and gave the signal to get under weigh, the tumult on shore took on a fiercer note.

Looking back, he could see the flash of scimitars among the huddle of the fleeing. Lean, turbaned horsemen wheeled and charged through the burning houses. A shrill shout pierced the wails of the injured.

"Yah, Allah! Hai—Allah—hai!"

Michael Bearn, hearing this familiar cry of triumph of the Moslems, saw again in his mind's eye the ruined villages of Armenia, the tortured slaves, and—most clearly of all—the grave in the sand before the Gate of Shadows.

He looked at the two men beside him, the sleeping French knight whose valor had been fruitless, and the sullen Italian officer who regarded him askance, fingering his bruised face.

The army of crusaders that he had journeyed for a year to join was no more. And Bayezid, angered by the loss of so many of his men, had doomed ten thousand captives to death. Was there no power on earth that could match the Thunderbolt?

"I wonder," thought Michael. He knew that of one place Bayezid was afraid, or at least that the Thunderbolt shunned that place.

It was the Gate of Shadows.

Chapter III
The Blow in the Dark

It was an hour after vespers and the lights of Saint Mark's were glowing softly against the vault of the sky over the great city of Venice. Along the narrow streets, however, and the winding canals, the square houses with their grilled doors and carved stonework showed only slits of light from barred windows.

At that hour worthy citizens of the City of the Lagoons went abroad attended only by linkmen and with armed retainers to guard their backs. Those who were more cautious, or who had more powerful enemies, paid *bravi* to watch the retainers.

A stranger wandering from the lagoons and the main canals would soon have lost his way. In the poorer quarters where the high buildings seemed to lean together against the sky, men looked closely into the faces of those they met and turned the corners wide.

Near the Piazza where the walled palaces of the nobles lined the canals the alleys were filled with refuse and ended more often than not in a blind wall. Servants stood whispering in the shadows of the postern doors and often a soft laugh came from an invisible balcony overhead.

"A pox on these castles," said Michael Bearn heartily. "Is there never a place where a body can see before and behind him at the same time?"

He glanced up, trying fruitlessly to guess his direction by the few stars visible between the buildings. All that he could make out was that he seemed to be standing in a space where two alleys crossed. Listening, he could hear the music of fiddles and flutes somewhere near at hand.

A fête, he knew, was going on in a nearby palace and he had promised himself a sight of it. It was exasperating to hear the sound of the festivity and still be unable to reach it. Michael laughed, realizing that he had lost his way completely.

There had been no lack of offers of a guide. For only that day Michael had received a gold chain and a key of the same precious metal from the Consoli di Mercanti—the Maritime Council—as reward for his services in bringing back a galley with the survivors of the army of the Count of Nevers from the ill-fated field of Nicopolis.

It had been a stormy passage, beset by Turkish pirates in the Levant, and Bearn, thanks to his skill as mariner and his knack of handling men, had been one of the few captains to return without loss.

But in spite of this honor Michael's purse was light and he could not afford to pay a retainer, or even to take up his quarters at a good inn.

"Faith," he thought, "'twould have availed more if the worthy council had given gold ducats instead of this chain, and as for the freedom of the city that they said went with the key—I cannot find my way to yonder music."

He had heard mention of the fête at the council, and also of a renowned voyager who was to be present. Two things had drawn Michael to the festivity: the hope of good meat and wine—he had not wanted to confess to the ceremonious members of the great council that he was penniless—and curiosity. Voyagers from the East were few in that age and Michael wondered whether he would find at the palace Fra Odoric, the priest who had built a church in Tatary, or Carlo Zeno, the sea captain.

Either one would have information that would serve Michael in his plans.

His reflections were interrupted by a light rounding the corner of a building and gliding toward him under his feet. He was surprised to see that he was standing on a wooden bridge. The light was in a gondola passing beneath him.

"Ho, my friends," he called cheerfully, "in what quarter lies the palazzo or whatever it is called of my lord Contarini? I can find it not."

If Michael had dwelt longer in Venice he would not have hailed an occupied gondola in the dark. His shout only caused the rower at the stern to glance up warily and thrust the long craft forward at greater speed. A shutter in the hooded seat was lowered briefly and a face looked out of the aperture.

Then the gondola passed under the bridge.

Michael grimaced, bowed, and was passing on when he hesitated. The light on the gondola had been put out.

This was not altogether strange, if the people on the vessel had believed that footpads, as personified by Michael, were on the bridge. But the keen eyes of the seaman caught a white swirl in the water. He fancied that the gondolier had checked his craft sharply and that it had halted a short distance beyond the bridge.

If the occupants of the gondola had been alarmed by his hail, they would not have chosen to remain in the vicinity. So Michael thought and was ready to smile at his own suspicion, when he heard a footfall and the clink of steel upon stones. From the direction in which he imagined the gondola had halted a man was coming toward him, feeling his way with drawn sword.

Michael planted his feet wide, with his back against a blank wall. Presently he could discern the grayish blur of a face moving toward him over the bridge. There was no sound and Michael knew that the newcomer was taking pains to be silent.

This quietude and the rapidity of the other's approach from the canal were ominous.

Then Michael stepped aside. He had heard rather than seen a swift movement toward him in the gloom.

Steel clashed against the wall beside him and sparks flew. An oath came to his ears as he snatched out his own sword, hung by its baldric on his right side. Long practice had accustomed Michael to the use of his left arm—had given to that limb the unusual strength possessed by one-armed men.

In the darkness he sought the other's blade, found it, thrust and when the thrust was parried, lunged again.

"By the Pope's head!" snarled the stranger.

"Amen," said Michael, drawing back alertly.

His weapon had bent against mail on the other's chest and Michael, who wore no such protection, was fain to risk a leap and come to hand-grips.

But even as he tensed his muscles for the spring he heard footsteps and the darkness was dissipated by the light of a lanthorn which rounded a corner behind him.

For the first time he saw his antagonist, a tall man, very fashionable in the short mantle and wide velvet sleeves and cloth-of-gold cap that were the fashion of the day in Venice. The man's olive face was handsome and composed, his eyes restless, his beard smartly curled.

His right hand held the broken half of a sword, his left a long poniard. Michael was rather glad that, after all, he had not made that leap.

Whereupon Michael frowned, for the other's face, although not his bearing, had a familiar aspect. Sheathing his own sword, the Breton smiled and took his dagger in his left hand.

"Good morrow, signor," he said from hard lips. "The light is better now than when you traitorously set upon me. Shall we resume with our poniards?"

The other hesitated, measuring Michael, noting the width of shoulder and length of arm of the Breton, whose featherless cap was thrust well back, disclosing black curls a little gray about the brows. Under the curls gray eyes, alight and whimsical, met the stranger's stare.

"You ponder, signor," prompted Michael politely. "Perhaps it surprises you that I who bore no weapon on shipboard have now mastered the use of blade and poniard with my one hand. Or perchance your sense of honor and the high courage you display in a crisis prompt you to refrain from matching daggers with a man in a leathern shirt when you wear a mail jerkin."

At this an exclamation sounded behind him. Michael had not failed to glance over his shoulder at the first appearance of the light and had seen only a fox-faced merchant in a long ermine cloak and attended by a brace of servitors who looked as if they would have liked to flee at sight of bare steel.

Now he perceived that the merchant was staring at him round-eyed as if Michael had uttered blasphemy or madness.

"By the rood!" swore the tall stranger.

"By whatever you wish," assented Michael, "so long as you fight like a man. Come, the sight of a coward spoils my appetite for dinner."

He waited for the other's rush. Michael had recognized in his assailant the Italian captain of mercenaries who had struck down his wounded countrymen in the effort to force himself aboard Michael's galley at Nicopolis. The other must have recognized him from the gondola and had sought the revenge he had sworn for Michael's blow.

Instead of resuming the duel, the Italian smiled coldly and stepped back, pointing to his chest where the doublet was slashed over the mail.

"I do not fight with cutthroats, Messer Soranzi," the Italian said to the merchant, who was staring at them, excusing his action. "This sailor beset me on the bridge after hailing my gondola under pretext of asking his way. You can see where he struck me."

The shrewd eyes of the merchant went from one to the other and he fingered his own stout belly tenderly.

"A lie," remarked the Breton promptly, "and a base one, forsooth. This fellow's blade is snapped and you can see on the stones behind me where it broke off."

Soranzi stared at him curiously and uneasily.

"You must be mad, good sir," he observed, "to wish to encounter further Pietro Rudolfo, the famous swordsman and *condottiere*."

"Faith," grinned Michael. "Is it madness to face the famous Rudolfo, instead of waiting to receive his knife in your back?"

He marked in his memory the name of his enemy. Rudolfo in spite of the open insult did not renew the fight. Instead he muttered that he had no time for night prowlers when he had already been delayed too long on his way to the house of a friend.

The merchant was sidling past Michael, holding up his long skirts, and shot a sharp question at the Breton, once he had gained the Italian's side, accompanied by his men.

"Your name and state, signor?"

Michael nodded at Rudolfo to indicate that the *condottiere* knew both, but Rudolfo was silent.

"You have an excellent memory, Ser Pietro," the Breton commented, "for it impelled you to let out my blood. Yet must I salve it myself."

To Soranzi he said—

"I am called Michael Bearn, the master mariner."

At this the merchant glanced at Rudolfo in some surprise for it was known from the Rialto to Saint Mark's that the young Breton had been honored that day by the all-powerful council. The interests of Venice and its merchants lay upon the sea, and the dictates of the Maritime Council were law.

Moreover Michael's bearing was hardly that of a cutthroat. Soranzi murmured diplomatically:

"Now that you two worthy captains have reached an understanding it behooves me to press upon my way. I am in haste to hear a most wonderful tale of a voyager who has found a new road to the riches of the East, more vast than those narrated by Ser Marco Polo himself."

Michael bowed, realizing that Rudolfo would not fight now.

"Will you direct me," he asked, "to the fête of my lord Contarini, the leader of the great council? I have lost my way."

Soranzi's lips parted to respond, but Rudolfo nudged him.

"Follow this alley," the *condottiere* directed curtly, "in the direction Messer Soranzi came for some distance."

With that he turned on his heel, took the arm of Soranzi, and with a backward glance walked away across the bridge. The lanthorn was soon lost to sight around a bend in the street where Michael had been wandering.

Sheathing his dagger, the Breton listened to the retreating footsteps, and laughed heartily but silently in the darkness.

"'Tis a rare jest," he thought. "Soranzi perchance would have directed me aright, but the excellent Rudolfo saw fit to send me mum-chance in the wrong course. Aye, make no doubt they are bound to the Palazzo Contarini themselves."

The reflection that Rudolfo had been at pains to keep him away from the fête caused Michael to wonder whether the *condottiere* had not had a stronger motive than the desire for revenge in attacking him.

Rudolfo had known from Michael's own words that he was bound for the Contarini Palace.

Of course it would not be particularly pleasing to Rudolfo to have Michael appear at the palace where they would, perhaps, meet. But surely if the captain of mercenaries had merely wished the killing of Michael, his wish could better have been fulfilled by sending *bravi* after the Breton when the latter left the palace.

Michael felt sure that Rudolfo had good reason for wanting at some cost to keep him from the palace.

By now Michael was conscious again that he was very hungry. Opposition served to whet his desire to go to the fête. Following the retreating footsteps by ear, he passed over the bridge again, into a dark passage he had not noticed before that led him presently out upon a wide terrace overlooking a brightly lighted court.

Chapter IV
Michael Is Admitted

Soranzi and Rudolfo were just disappearing within the gate of the Contarini house. A throng of gondoliers and servitors grouped on the steps that led from the tiles of the court to the door gave back with low bows. Just as ceremoniously a chamberlain, standing within the entrance, greeted them—as Michael observed.

He cast a swift glance around the court. It fronted a canal by which the guests were coming to the fête. In one corner some fiddlers and flute-players assisted by a bedraggled dancing bear were amusing the waiting servants and helping to empty a huge table of its meat and wine.

It was this music he had heard from the alleys in the rear of the establishment.

Near at hand a fat Turkish gymnast in a soiled silk *khalat* was making the commoners gape by balancing two swords, one above the other, on his forehead and squealing shrilly as if to call attention to his prowess.

From a window of the palace the low sound of a woman's laugh floated out over the court. It was not a pleasant laugh, holding as it did a veiled note of discontent.

"That would be the new *donna*, my lord Contarini's choice of a mistress," observed one lackey in the throng about the sword-juggler to another.

"A redheaded she-fox," mumbled a second who had had his share of red wine.

"Grant I stumble not over her train—"

"Or spill aught on her finery. 'Tis said she craves jewels as ye thirst for the flagon. She it was that coaxed my lord—who is made o' drier stuff,—wot—to have the voyager tell his tale."

"Nay." The lackey nodded solemnly over a tankard. "All Venice repeats that the riches of Cathay are found at last. Hide o' the ——, 'twill do us no good, but Messer Rat-Face Soranzi has come running holding up his skirts like a woman—"

Both laughed and Michael smiled at the description of the stout merchant with the thin face. He was ascending the steps confidently when the chamberlain stopped him at the door.

"I know not your face, signor. Were you bidden to the palace this evening?"

Michael halted, his foot on the top step.

Looking down the long hall within, he could see groups of the guests, young men in short cloaks of every hue, wearing under these tight tunics of crimson velvet and gold cloth, elderly men in long fur mantles, women in the jeweled exuberance of dress and with the red-dyed hair that was a fad of the time.

The splendor of it caused him to gasp. Meanwhile the chamberlain was insolently eyeing Michael's boots of soft leather and his ragged mantle.

"I have the freedom of the city," murmured Michael, still intent on the spectacle within.

It was the turn of the worthy chamberlain to gape and seize his long staff in righteous wrath. A commoner sought entrance to the fête at the Palazzo Contarini!

In another moment the guardian of the gate would have shouted for the servitors to fling Michael into the canal. It was well, perhaps, for all concerned that a diversion occurred at this point.

A group of lackeys approached the door from within, hauling along a shrinking, stumbling figure in grotesquely striped attire. It was the figure of a hunchback wearing a jester's cap.

Behind the lackeys and their captive strolled several courtiers, smiling expectantly.

"Give him to the bear to play with!" cried a servitor.

"Nay, set the dogs on him."

"Aye—the dogs, the dogs!" cried the courtiers. "'Twill be better sport than bear-baiting itself."

Michael saw that the craggy face of the jester was pale and that he winced at mention of the dogs. The anxious glance of the hunchback met his and then circled away as if vainly seeking some avenue of escape.

"Hold," spoke up the chamberlain irresolutely, addressing the courtiers and ignoring Michael in the more pressing matter at hand. "This is good Bembo, my lord's fool and favorite. Would you slay him, signori?"

"Verily is he a fool," answered one of the young nobles carelessly, "and so must pay for his folly."

"Not so. He is no man's fool," corrected another, "and so the dogs will have his limbs for their sport. 'Tis an ill-shapen thing, by the archangel!"

"Bembo," whispered a lackey, "had the cursed luck to spill a dish of syrup of figs on the train of the Donna, who is in a rage thereby. To appease her my lord has cast off the ill-begotten fool and my lady has bidden us make sport of him. The dogs—ho, the dogs!"

While one varlet ran eagerly out of the hall, evidently to fetch the dogs of the household, the courtiers dragged Bembo to the door and called the crowd below in the court to witness the coming spectacle.

A joyful shout went up and the servitors deserted both table and Turk to enjoy the more attractive spectacle of a human being worried by the teeth of animals. Michael had a swift recollection of his own torture at the hands of Bayezid's men and the way in which the slaves thronged to watch his suffering.

His back stiffened and he swung his right arm gently at his side—the only movement of which it was capable. And he stood his ground at the head of the stairs, although the courtiers were pushing against him.

"Strip him," counseled a rough voice from below—the same lackey who had commented upon the fiery temper of his mistress a moment ago. "The dogs will bite the fool more toothsomely if he be naked."

"Aye, aye, strip him!" the cry went up.

"Stay," said Michael gravely to the courtiers. "The man is a cripple, wherefore would it be small honor to you, messires, to make game of him."

"Blood of the saints!" A young fellow with a face like a woman made response. "By the splendor of heaven, what have we here?"

The chamberlain saw an opportunity to please the nobles.

"A man, my lord of Mocenigo," he informed loudly, "who claims the freedom of the city and so the liberty to attend the fête of my lord Contarini."

The jester's lined face had brightened at Michael's words, but now he appeared hopeless once more. Not so Mocenigo, who scented a finer jest, even, than the tormenting of Bembo.

"He does not look like a lack-wit, this burgher-sailor," he vouchsafed, wrinkling his nose, "but—phah—methinks he is foul of the sea."

They stared at Michael, the crowd below pushing and elbowing to gain a better view. A gentleman laughed and the lackeys guffawed. That a common sailor, or so they thought, should have construed the freedom of the city as an invitation to the fête!

A distant snarling and barking sounded from within the palace, plainly to be heard now that the fiddlers had ceased playing in order to watch the spectacle.

"Throw them both to the dogs; strip them both," called a lackey from the rear of the throng.

But Michael's glance had sought out the courtier who had laughed, and his gray eyes were very hard. Seeing his set face, those nearest him, with the exception of the slightly intoxicated Mocenigo, gave back slightly.

"No need to fetch the dogs, my good cur," Michael smiled at the man who had laughed. "The pack is here and—till now—in full cry."

There was an exclamation at this and a rustling of feet. The servitors sensed a quarrel and realized from the way Michael spoke that he was a Frenchman of good blood. Whereupon they discreetly waited for the quarrel to be taken up by their betters.

"'Od's death!" swore the courtier who had laughed, making however no move forward. "Seize him, ye varlets, and hale him into the lagoon."

The lackeys nearest Michael advanced obediently, but without enthusiasm. Baiting a victim lost its savor when the prey showed fight. Then one of them cried out shrilly:

"Ho, this is Master Bearn who conquered the Turks in the Orient. Not an hour since he overcame Pietro Rudolfo in the street with his sword."

A silence fell on the group at the head of the stairs. The servants remembered that they were unarmed and retreated promptly. Bembo looked up again with hope in his wavering eyes.

Michael, standing his ground with his left hand at his belt, reflected that Rudolfo must have a reputation here.

Muttering something about looking to the dogs, the man who had laughed slipped away, accompanied by his fellows. Mocenigo swore roundly after them and clutched uncertainly at his sword.

At once Michael stepped forward, gripping the other's wrist and wrenching downward as the young noble started to free his blade from its scabbard. The weapon clattered to the tiled floor and Mocenigo's right hand was helpless in Michael's left.

Now the courtier was no younger than the seaman, but his smooth face made a strong contrast with Michael's brown countenance wherein the skin was drawn taut over jutting bones and deep lines ran from nose to mouth.

Mocenigo, flushed, made no struggle, knowing that his strength was overmatched; instead he waited with a dangerous quiet for Michael to strike or taunt or reach for a weapon. He did not know that the Breton had but one useful arm.

"You are no coward," grunted Michael, "but you carry your wine badly, my lord. The cups make a man quarrelsome."

With that he released Mocenigo, picked up the latter's weapon, handed it to him and turned his back. The courtier handled his blade irresolutely, staring at the seaman's back.

"Close the door," Michael was instructing the chamberlain, who—seeing that Mocenigo made no move—obeyed, thus shutting out the curious throng in the court.

"You were best away from here, Bembo," said Michael quickly to the jester. "Some side postern; this is your chance."

When Bembo had vanished from the hall he wheeled on the gazing Mocenigo. "This mocking of a fool ill beseems your chivalry my lord."

At this the young courtier flushed more deeply than before, and sheathed his sword covertly. "'Od's blood, signor, you are a strange man and a ready one. I was in the wrong and I apologize." He bowed gracefully. "Surely you are of gentle blood in France?"

"Nay, signor—my mother was of gentlefolk, but I am a commoner, without land or till."

Michael nodded affably to the perplexed chamberlain.

"Now that I am here, announce me to your master. In the haste of the moment I forgot to say that he bade me come to the fête."

But when the three sought Contarini they found him and the circle of his friends seated, listening to the tale of the voyager. Only one of the listeners noticed Michael's entry into the audience chamber in the rear of the assemblage, and that one was Pietro Rudolfo.

Chapter V
Cathay

"Great lords, counts, knights, burgesses, and ladies! Attend ye, dispose yourselves to listen. Never have your ears been greeted by such a tale as this. Never have soldiers, priests, sailors, or astrologers breathed such a romance as this true recital.

"Signori, ladies; no man hath so much knowledge and experience of the divers parts of the world—and especially that of Cathay—as hath Messer Ruy de Gonzales Clavijo!"

The speaker, broad as he was tall, black-bearded and mellow of voice, bowed very low, sweeping the heron plume of his cap across the floor of the library of the Contarini Palace. His enormous cloak of Armenian velvet vied in color with his scarlet doublet of Persian silk.

"I am Messer Ruy de Gonzales Clavijo," he concluded.

In the library were gathered the leading spirits among the guests. Contarini with his mistress beside him sat directly before the speaker. Close behind him the pale face of Soranzi, the merchant, gleamed in the candlelight.

A hundred years ago Marco Polo had completed his book. Discredited at first, it had been confirmed to great extent by wandering Franciscan monks. It was known in Europe that Cathay existed somewhere at the eastern end of the world—this side of the Sea of Darkness.

Venetian galleys were engaged in trade with Persia and Arabia, at Ormuz. Continued tidings of the vast resources of silk, spices, and gems in China and India came in. The door of the farther East had been half-opened. Venice was agog with rumors of the riches of the Indies, and the Pope had more than once sent emissaries to find the land of Prester John.

"Consider, my lord—" Clavijo bowed to Contarini—"the marvel that I have seen. It is no less than a city of brazen walls, in the desert where a hundred caravan routes meet. It lies behind the lofty mountains which are a natural wall beyond the last of the three seas—Aegean, Mormaior, and the Dead Sea that is of salt, as you know."

The listeners nodded. Venetians to the heart, they knew the geography of the Black Sea and something of the Caspian. Clavijo, the Spaniard, went on.

"Seven years ago, my lord, did Ser Clavijo set out humbly from Constantinople over the perilous waters of Mormaior where no ships may have iron in them, lest the devil's loadstone that is at the bottom of the sea should draw out nails and braces and every soul perish."

Contarini shrugged. He did not set much store by the superstitions of the sea. Clavijo pointed to the map on the silver globe beside him.

"It was not the least of the marvels, my lord, that Ser Clavijo attained to the farther shore of this sea where the spirits of the waste are said to lie in wait for travelers. Aye, he heard their mutterings at night, on the desert floor, and in the morning his servant was dead. The natives say that this muttering comes from the sands—the *reg ruwan*, talking sands. Yet Clavijo makes no doubt that demons are to be met in the waste places.

"But beyond here exists a rich and fertile valley. My lord, it may well be that this is no less than the Eden of the Bible. Forasmuch as the Bible relates that the three strange kings came to the birth of Christ, bearing rich gifts of incense and myrrh, it is reasonable to suppose that this legend relates to Cathay, which may well be the kingdom of Prester John."

He glanced mildly at his intent audience. A dozen times within the last fortnight had the Spaniard been called upon to tell his story, and by now he well knew the phrases that best appealed to the religiously inclined. As for the ladies—

"The way to this valley is most difficult to encompass; forty bands of Moorish horsemen do swoop upon the unwary. It was one of these bands that came on Clavijo, alone in the desert, and guided him, a prisoner, through the storms of sand that are more fearful than the tempest of the sea. In this way he was taken to the gate in the brazen wall.

"Inside that gate he perceived the trees of gold and silver, of which you have heard, and the fountains that run with wine more delicious than the famous Chian.

"Great jewels are the fruit in these gardens of the brazen city. The inhabitants are fair of face and speak a Moorish tongue. Alas, your servant Clavijo has not the gift of words to describe all that he saw. Moreover, he was a prisoner, kept for the pleasure of the Grand Cham who is the king of this place."

Clavijo's broad face turned toward the stately red-haired woman who was the mistress of his host.

"My lady, it came to his ears in the city of the Grand Cham that all who entered the valley never got any older. There is no time in this city of Cathay, and people do as they please. It is a most pleasant spot. Many marvels Clavijo heard there—of the cameleopard and the taurelephus that gives most rare milk. But concerning this, Clavijo cannot know the truth. The gardens and the Cathayans he saw with his own eyes. Some of the silk of the place he had made into a doublet and this you yourselves may see—"

Clavijo tapped his broad chest with a smile.

"This is but a poor specimen. The robes of the slaves of the Grand Cham are of the sheerest gossamer, my ladies. The emeralds on his fingers are large as hens' eggs. The perfumes of the palace are finer than the dried roses of Persia."

The women who had been listening sleepily until now looked up with interest.

"Living unto themselves as they do, the Cathayans have no knowledge of the value of gold in the other world. It comes, Clavijo heard, from the mines of Ectag, sometimes called the Golden Mountains. Here there be slaves who labor in the mines, and but for the grace of God Clavijo would be such a slave."

The small eyes of Guistani Soranzi widened and he plucked at the edge of his fur robe.

"Did you bring back some of the gold, Messer Clavijo?" he asked.

"Alas, some I took with me when I fled from the city, but necessity compelled me to cast it away when I crossed the desert." Clavijo stepped back and bowed. "My escape was due to one of the servants of the Cham who was a Christian at heart. Otherwise, it would not have been possible to surmount the brazen walls."

"And the Grand Cham?" put in Rudolfo curiously. "What was he?"

"Some called him Cham, some Khan. Perchance the two words be the same. He is like to the Emperor of the Chin, because Persian and Turk and other pagan sultans render him tribute. Also, of all the caravans that pass by the valley he takes tribute. Some say he has the powers of a potent magician, yet this must be because he has the wisdom of a hundred years."

Clavijo ceased his tale with a low bow. Contarini studied him with green, fathomless eyes, but the mistress of Contarini was aquiver with eagerness and whispered to him of the gems of Cathay that might adorn her beauty.

Rudolfo's elegant figure advanced to exchange greetings with the voyager, as did the other guests, with the exception of Michael, who remained leaning against the wall, rubbing his chin reflectively as if something puzzled him greatly.

He saw that Clavijo presently left the throng. Straightaway Michael followed him down the narrow hall that led to an alcove where a table loaded with fruits, wines, and sweetmeats awaited the guests who had not yet arrived.

Somewhat to Michael's surprise the portly Spaniard dug his fingers into a fine dish—peacock pie. From the pie his hands went to his mouth. His bearded chin worked voraciously and the pie diminished apace.

Michael's hunger came upon him anew and he joined the man on the other side of the table.

"By your leave, Messer Voyager."

His left hand began to make havoc with the remnant of the pastry.

Clavijo glanced at him from small black eyes, as if disturbed by the interruption.

"It irks me to eat alone," smiled Michael invitingly. "Come, good sir, I see you looked at yonder Sicilian grapes desirefully. Proceed. Consume. Your long suffering in the Orient must have given you a rare stomach for such fare. See, I join you."

The Spaniard wiped his beard with the back of his hand and with the other covertly fastened upon some brandied figs. He seemed to have an unlimited appetite.

"Verily, I see that you are a man of parts," said Michael again. "Let me call to your notice this excellent Chian wine. A toast, Messer Clavijo—a toast."

"Ah."

The Spaniard nodded approvingly and poured out two cups of the fine wine. Michael, who had had enough of the food, lifted his politely.

"To Cathay," he announced, bowing.

"To Cathay," responded the other heartily.

"Sir, I know you not, but you are good company and a man of rare discernment—"

Clavijo fell silent and his mouth opened wide, while he did not raise his cup. Michael, glancing quickly over his shoulder, saw that two men in uniform had entered the alcove.

They wore dark cloaks and carried only stilettos at their belts. Both wore black masks that concealed the whole of their faces with the exception of the eyes.

"*Madre de dios!*" swore Clavijo.

The two masked servitors or officials—Michael could not decide which—advanced to the table.

"Signori," said one, "which of you is the renowned voyager from the Orient?"

It was politely said and Michael set down his cup reflectively, seeing that Clavijo's eyes had widened at the words. Under the circumstances the newcomers might be seeking either the Spaniard or the Breton. Evidently, if they desired Clavijo, they had not been in the audience-chamber when the latter was telling his tale.

This inclined Michael to the belief that he was the man wanted. He wondered briefly if these were agents of Rudolfo, but remembered that the *condottiere* would hardly resume his quarrel in the home of Contarini, unless imperatively urged.

It was hardly likely, furthermore, that Mocenigo would choose this way of punishing Michael for the scene at the door. Michael, unfamiliar with the customs of Venice, hazarded a guess that these were servants of Contarini sent to summon either him or Clavijo in this curious fashion.

"I am from the East," he responded, as the Spaniard was silent. "I am called Michael Bearn, of Brittany."

"Aye," put in Clavijo promptly, glancing involuntarily toward the hall down which the two had come; "this is the gentleman you seek."

Plainly he did not desire to go with the masked men. They, however, looked at each other questioningly and asked Clavijo's name, which was reluctantly given.

"Signori," decided the one who had first spoken, "we were sent for the voyager from the Orient by one whom you both know. Since we cannot be certain of your identity, will you both have the great kindness to come with us?"

Clavijo looked as if he would have liked to refuse, but the masked men ushered them down another hall and flight of steps. They passed out of the house into the darkness of an alley. The loom of the buildings against the stars, the smells, and the distant echo of a flute assured Michael that they were now near the bridge where he had met Rudolfo.

It was his turn to be reluctant, yet Michael strode ahead, whistling between his teeth. He felt morally certain that the two attendants had come for Clavijo and that Clavijo did not want to go with them. And Michael wanted very much to see where Clavijo was being taken—where the Spaniard did not want to go.

A second stairway took them to a gondola, a torch at its bow. Michael recognized the Contarini crest on the gondola hood as he scrambled inside, followed by his companion, breathing heavily.

The two masked attendants took their stand fore and aft by the rowers. In the darkness of the small cabin Michael sat down on what he first thought to be a cushion and then made out to be the form of a man.

He said nothing, wondering if the man were dead, until a whisper came up to him:

"Signor Michael, a service for a service given. Pietro Rudolfo plots against you. I heard it whispered as I fled the palace."

It was Bembo. A moment's reflection showed that he must have hidden himself away in one of the Contarini gondolas, expecting to leave the palace unseen in this way. Michael eased his weight off the other.

"Do not yield me up, signor," went on the whisper. "Soon we shall be far off from the redheaded donna and the dogs and servants."

"Faith, I will not, Bembo. Are these masks Rudolfo's doing?"

"Nay, generous sir. They are servants of Contarini."

A slight hesitation before the name did not escape the Breton's notice. "Whither are we bound? Have they business with me or Clavijo?"

"Clavijo." Bembo chose to answer the last question. "We—you and I—will be released at the Con—at the gate we are coming to—"

"Who in the fiend's name are you talking to?" demanded the Spaniard, who had been unable to understand the low whispers.

"A fiend—if it likes you, Messer Voyager," murmured Michael. "He says the devil and all the hellish brood have seized upon you."

"Madre de dios!"

Clavijo, it appeared, was superstitious and more than a little credulous. Then the boat stopped and the three—for Bembo joined them—stood before an iron-studded door in which a small square slid back, to cast a stream of light on their faces.

Michael saw a masked face staring at them through the aperture. Meanwhile the gondola and its men drew away from the landing and disappeared in the darkness.

Clavijo's olive countenance went a shade paler when he made out the stunted form of the hunchback. He had not seen Bembo at the fête and Michael's careless words had aroused his apprehensions.

Before he could speak the door opened wide and the figure within reached forth to pluck the Spaniard inside. The door was slammed in the faces of Bembo and his friend.

Through the square peephole Michael could make out the two men inside withdrawing down a hall. A second glance showed him that they stood on a narrow stone landing with the black surface of the canal at their feet. The door presented the only means of leaving the steps.

"Bembo," whispered Michael, "unravel me this coil. Where are we, and why are we left like varlets on the threshold of this hospitable place?"

"Because, signor comrade," the jester grinned up at him in the dim light from the opening, "we are varlets—or at least the gatekeeper believes we look like such attendants of the great Spaniard. Your cloak is—"

Bembo hesitated, fearing to offend, but Michael answered readily.

"Zounds, 'tis shabby enow!"

"This is the entrance to the Consoli di Mercanti. So many masks mean that the council is in secret session. We had best content ourselves with hailing a passing gondola and making off with a whole hide, for we are both here by mistake."

Michael wondered why Bembo's presence had been taken for granted until the hunchback explained that he had often come here in attendance on Contarini and the guardians of the place could not know that he was no longer the servant of the great Contarini.

"Good," he said thoughtfully and pressed against the door, thrusting his left arm within the opening. Bembo plucked his sleeve in sudden anxiety.

"What would you, signor?"

"Why, entrance, before yonder masked fellow returns to his post. I must hear what the council has to say to the voyager."

In spite of Bembo's protest that the night session was secret and that they both might end the evening in the damp cells of San Giorgio Maggiore prison, Michael worked away at the door until he had drawn back the bolts and pushed it open.

This done, he pulled the shivering hunchback into the stone passageway, closed the heavy portal and whispered:

"Now, good Bembo, you are verily a lost fool if you lead us not into a safe hiding place where we may hear what is said in the council. You say that you know the intestines of this place of masks—"

Michael's words received sudden point by the sound of footsteps returning toward the passage. Bembo fled with a crab-like motion down the narrow hall and slipped aside into the shadows of another passage opening into it, and Michael ran after him silently.

Taking the Breton's hand in his, the jester led his new friend through the darkness down a winding flight of steps until the dampness indicated to Michael that they were under the canal.

Here they were in a confined space where the air, however, was not stale and two gleams of light pierced the gloom from one wall. Michael was somewhat taken aback to hear voices echoing clearly in the stone chamber, although they were plainly the only occupants.

"'Tis the whispering gallery," explained Bembo so softly that the words were barely discernible, "that gives upon the council chamber. My lord

Contarini was wont at times to spy here upon the testimony of prisoners before the judges. Speak not, for the gallery runs overhead to an opening behind the councilors."

As the Council of Ten ruled political Venice, stamping out conspiracies and punishing any man it listed mercilessly and secretly, the Consoli di Mercanti ruled commercial Venice with an iron hand.

The prosperity of the Signory was linked indissolubly with the expansion of its trade, the crushing of its rivals, and the mastery of new routes into the East, such as gave to Venice the monopoly of the great salt industry. The methods of the council were secretive and cruel, but Venetian judges winked at this, so long as the trade routes were held, concessions secured, and enemies weakened.

Of these enemies Genoa was then the most pressing. A few years before, the army and fleet of Genoa had almost crushed the city of the lagoons—Venice being freed only by the dogged courage of Pisani and the intrepidity of Carlo Zeno. Since then Genoa had used every means to extend its trade to the eastward, away from the immediate power of the Venetian galleys.

Both cities had vied in making agreements with the on-sweeping Osmanli Empire which was even then extending from Anatolia into the mainland of Europe. But behind the armies of Bayezid were the spices, silks, and jewels of India, Persia, and China—veritable Golcondas to the trading cities which paid fat tribute for the privilege of plying the Black Sea and tapping the Damascus and Aleppo caravan routes.

So much Michael Bearn knew.

Standing close to the wall of the whispering chamber, he found that the two holes fitted his eyes and that he could see a long table covered with papers and globe-maps behind which sat a dozen masked men and before which stood the carefully groomed form of Ruy de Gonzales Clavijo.

The council was in secret session. A masked attendant clad in the manner of those who had ushered Bembo and Michael to the place stood by the closed door. Michael, studying the forms of the men behind the long table, singled out one in the center as Contarini and at the first words knew that he was right.

The voices rang clearly in his ear, conducted by a cleverly contrived gallery that ran from the shadows over the table to the wall above Michael's head.

"Signor," began the man in the center of the councilors. "You were summoned to speak the truth. Do not fail."

Clavijo glanced at the speaker swiftly, and measured the ring of masked faces. His brow was moist and his plump cheeks were flushed.

"This evening—" he responded.

"This evening," Contarini took him up, "you babbled much nonsense and some news. Signor, we are concerned now with the trade of Venice. Frequently we have heard of a Tatar or Cathayan potentate beyond the Sarai Sea. We wish to learn if it was his court you visited."

At this Clavijo nodded understandingly. He looked serious, now that he had weighed the mood of these men.

"Aye, signor. Last night, I was about to remark, I spoke mainly of fabulous gems and garments and such like, for the pleasuring of the ladies. But now I place the poor fruits of my journey at your service. Question me, therefore, at your will."

"Exactly where lies this city?"

"As you have said, beyond the Sarai Sea, a journey of a week by horse, until you come to the foot of the Ectag* Mountains, called by the natives the Golden Mountains. The way lies over the desert floor and is perilous indeed."

"So, one may go by sea to Trebizond, where we have a *bailio* and thence—" Contarini consulted a map—"by caravan across the land of the tribes. Karabak, it is written here?"

"Aye, my lord. Marvelous it is to know that in that land there is a pillar of everlasting fire, rising from the ground with a blue flame—"

"Naphtha!" broke in a councilor. "Near to Batum. No miracle about that."

Michael studied the eyes of the questioners, greatly interested, much to Bembo's surprise.

"Not in the least," assented Clavijo gravely. "Yet there also I beheld the holy mountain of Ararat where first the blessed ark came to land after the Flood. And beyond there, my lords—beyond there lie the fields of solid salt, at the foot of the Sarai Sea, which signifies in Cathayan—Sea of Salt."

The councilors looked up at this, for the monopoly of the salt trade was one of the greatest avenues of profit to Venice.

---

*The Akh-tagh.

"That is good!" Contarini made a note and Clavijo smiled. "Now, what of your statement that this Cham of Cathay is aged beyond human years and a magician?"

"My lord, does he not dwell in this paradise of Cathay, and was not the holy garden of Eden also a paradise? Have we not the testimony of the Bible itself that therein is no such thing as human age? Was not the holy garden itself in the paradise of Asia?"

"How do you know the Grand Cham is a magician?"

Clavijo smiled, shrugged and hesitated, but one of the councilors spoke up.

"The good Fra Odoric of Pordenone himself visited these regions *con pelegrino*—as a pilgrim. Did he not see great piles of human skulls raised to the sky and the horns of beasts stuck upright upon mountaintops? Also divers wonders such as a city upon the sand which vanished as he walked toward it? Aye, and he mentioned that the sand spoke with a human voice."

Hereupon Clavijo drew a long breath of satisfaction and twiddled his curled beard.

"As I myself have said," he reminded Contarini, who alone among the councilors seemed to weigh his testimony doubtfully. The punishment by the Maritime Council of one who gave false testimony before it was no light thing.

"These miracles have my eyes beheld. Lo, I sat upon such a pile of human skulls, reaching a thousand lance-lengths toward the sky—the bones of those who aforetime sought the earthly paradise and failed."

"The Grand Cham must be a potent monarch," mused Contarini. "Aye, I mind me Fra Odoric spoke of a great khan of Tatary who was the most merciless warrior upon the face of the earth—"

Michael strained his ears to catch the rest of the sentence, but Contarini had bent over a globe-map and was silent.

"'Khan' signifies 'Cham' in the pagan tongue," put in Clavijo, who seemed to be better pleased with the way things were going now.

Maps were produced and it was found that Ptolemy had outlined a kingdom beyond the Sarai Sea, under the star Taurus, and named it Chin, or Chinae.

"Which is verily the Chitae of Fra Odoric and my Cathay," pointed out the Spaniard. Sweeping his hand across the table in an eloquent gesture, he raised his voice.

"Here lies the power and magic of the East, signori. Alone, my comrades dead, I crawled from the brazen walls to bear this message to you. Others, like the good fra, have heard of the Grand Cham—or seen the city at a distance. But I—I have walked under the gold trees and heard the song of the slaves of a hundred races laboring in the mines in the bowels of the earth. I have looked upon the riches of pearls, emeralds, topazes set into the walls of houses. Beside the city of the Grand Cham Constantinople is a rook's nest and Venice—pardon, but Venice is no more than a village."

Perceiving that his voice fell into ready ears, he folded his arms, his uneasiness vanished.

"I have spoken of jewels. My lords, upon the person of the Grand Cham and his radiant women there are solid plaques of emeralds and rubies, greater than those that you have brought in your galleys from Persia. And these jewels the Cathayans value not, save as handsome ornaments."

"What do the Cathayan folk value—in trade?"

"Perchance weapons, rare steel, cunning inventions such as the sand clock and musical organs."

Bembo, who was still shivering from apprehension, now noticed that Michael's shoulders were quivering as if the Breton were stricken with the ague and that his hand was pressed against his mouth.

Within the council hall Contarini rose as if satisfied.

"Messer Clavijo," he said gravely, "if your tale had proved a lie you would have had a taste of the iron beds of San Giorgio Maggiore. But we are well content with the news you bring, and it is now fitting that we announce to you the result of our deliberations before your examination. This morning I had speech with a French mariner of the name of Bearn who warned me that the Turkish power threatens the safety of the great city of Constantinople and Venice. That is idle talk and the council is concerned only with trade, not politics. Yet this foe of the Turks confessed that somewhere beyond the Sarai Sea is a khan of Tatary who must be a potent monarch."

He paused and Bembo saw again that Michael grimaced strangely.

"The council has planned an expedition into the terra incognita," went on Contarini. "A jealous merchant will be sent with proper escort. By fair means or foul—mark me—he must win us wealth from the Cham. Our galleys will bear the voyagers safely through the Turkish pirates. You will be the leader of the expedition."

Clavijo was a graven figure of amazement.

"I?"

"Verily. Venice will honor fittingly the discoverer of the new trade route—when you return. But return successful, for we have no clemency for one who fails."

A flush mounted to the Spaniard's brow which had become moist again.

"I? My lord, the way is perilous. Scarce I es—"

"By your own words you would fain visit again this city that is an earthly paradise. You know the way. Have no fear that you will not be rewarded."

Clavijo started to speak again, hesitated, and bowed low. Then he jumped and swore roundly. A roaring, mighty laugh broke the silence of the council chamber. Yet none of the councilors had uttered a sound and certainly Clavijo and the attendant had not presumed to laugh.

Contarini it was who broke the spell of stupefaction by starting up and looking angrily at the wall behind which, in the whispering gallery, Michael Bearn was doubled up with mirth, laughing until he coughed.

The sound, magnified by the hidden gallery, had burst upon the councilors like a thunderclap and not a few crossed themselves in awe.

"By the blessed Saint Lawrence and his gridiron!" Bembo pulled at his companion in a frenzy of alarm. "Are you mad? They will be here in a minute with drawn swords. Come, or you will end your laugh in a dungeon—"

Fairly skipping with anxiety, he guided the still chuckling Michael up the steps, and listened a moment alertly. Michael seemed indifferent to the peril that was real enough to Bembo.

Hearing the sound of pikes striking the floor in the direction of the council chamber, Bembo turned the other way at the head of the stairs. He knew that there was a warder at the postern door by which they had entered.

So, instead of retracing his steps, he ran up another flight of stairs, slowing down as he emerged with Michael into a tapestried hall where several attendants without masks lounged.

"The council has broken up," Bembo announced when the servants glanced at him inquiringly. At the foot of the stair behind them Michael could see Contarini pass hastily toward the listening chamber with a group of halberdiers.

Following Bembo's lead he walked quietly toward the entrance at the end of the hall that was the main gate of the council house. The hunchback had reasoned quickly that the guards at the door, not having seen him enter, would take him and the Breton for Contarini's followers. Likewise, he knew that the aroused councilors would not be aware of the identity of the men who had been in the listening chamber.

So, playing both ends against the middle, he went to the gate, nodded to the pikeman on guard, and emerged under the stars. As they did so they heard a distant shout from below and saw the servitors run to the head of the stairs up which they had come.

"They will bar the gate," whispered Bembo. "But, praise be to Saint Mark, we are outside the bars."

Michael noted with disgust that they were again on a landing with the canal in front of them. While they waited anxiously for a gondola to pass, a flurried councilor rushed through the door, glanced hastily at Bembo, and, recognizing him, glared at the dark canal.

"Did you see a man flee here hence, Bembo?" he questioned.

"Not yet, my lord," replied the hunchback truthfully. "But, if it please you, I will watch to observe when a man leaves the building."

When the councilor had re-entered the hall, the great door was closed and barred. The two could hear the sounds of a hurried search within. They hailed the first empty craft that came abreast of the landing, and when they were fairly out of sight along the canal Bembo, who was curious by nature, turned to his new friend.

"What made you laugh, signor?"

Michael smiled reminiscently. "A splendid jest, my Bembo."

As he had listened to Clavijo's tale at the fête he had been struck by grave doubts as to its truth. The flowery descriptions of the Spaniard did not conform to Michael's knowledge of the Salt Sea and its tribes.

Furthermore, the man's face was vaguely familiar. Michael had a keen memory, but he could not place the man at first. Not until the testimony had been given before the council and Clavijo had been plainly disturbed did Michael remember him.

Then he recalled another frightened man. The scene on the shore at Nicopolis flashed before him, and he visioned a tall, stalwart camp-follower of the Christian army driving a loaded cart headlong through the fugitives.

Clavijo had been that man. And the year of the battle of Nicopolis had been the year that Clavijo claimed to have been at the court of the Grand

Cham of Tatary. Michael knew then what he suspected before, that the Spaniard had not been in the East. His tale had been a lie.

It was the decision of the council in taking Clavijo at his word that had struck Michael's grim sense of humor. It was, as he told Bembo, a rare jest.

Chapter VI
The Venture

Safe, for the nonce, in an odorous tavern hight the Sign of the Sturgeon, on the docks of Rialto, Michael reflected the next day on what he had learned and fell to questioning Bembo, for there was much that puzzled him.

Bembo wondered somewhat, as he squatted on the table where their breakfast platter still lay, how Michael could obtain the money to pay for their quarters because it was becoming apparent to him that they did not have a silver *soldi* between them. When he mentioned respectfully that the landlord was chalking up their score behind the door and was growling for payment on account, Michael assured him that something would turn up to yield them gold.

Skeptical, but willing to believe in the good fortune of his new master—Bembo had attached himself to the Breton—the hunchback answered the questions.

"My lord Contarini must have money," he asserted, following the trend of his own thoughts. "His large establishments have impoverished him sorely and he is deep in debt to Rudolfo, the leader of his soldiers, who has waged Contarini's battles on the mainland. Methinks my lord cannot pay—"

"And so has caught at the chance of riches wrung from Cathay," mused Michael. Egged on by his spendthrift mistress and his creditors, Contarini was planning to use his post as head of the Maritime Council to his own advantage.

This was more than probable because, while Contarini had aided Clavijo in spreading the tidings of a mythical kingdom beyond the Sarai Sea, he had been careful to have the council hear in secret the Spaniard's testimony as to the possible spoil to be gleaned from the Cathayans. So Contarini must believe the tale of Clavijo.

The Spaniard himself was merely posing as a voyager—an honorable figure in that age—and thriving on the gifts and hospitality of the Venetians. What of Rudolfo?

The *condottiere* had sought at all costs to keep Michael from hearing the tale of Clavijo. Why? Rudolfo must know of the coming venture into the East if he was in Contarini's confidence. He knew, too, that Michael had been on the border of the terra incognita.

What did Rudolfo fear that the Breton would disclose? Rudolfo's cowardice at the field of Nicopolis?

Michael shrugged, and dismissed the problem. It did not matter, he thought—and wrongly.

What interested him was Clavijo's magnificent lie. Michael knew that there was truth in the well from which the self-styled voyager had drawn his tales. Fra Odoric had spoken truly of a powerful khan of Tatary.

But would the khan of Tatary, of whom Michael had heard in the camp of Bayezid, prove to be actually the Cham of Cathay? Michael would have given much to know. For this khan was the one man Bayezid respected on the face of the earth.

"If I could know," he began, and looked at Bembo. "Fool o' mine, and withal, wise man, we must have more news. Go you to the plaza of the city and learn what you may of preparations being made for a ship to the East.

"Look you, wise fool," the Breton continued thoughtfully. "Is it not true that the natures of men will seek their proper end? Give a thief rope and he will halter himself; a miser will bleed others till there remains no blood in his own veins; a boaster will trip o'er his own tongue. I, being a wayfarer voyaging on behalf of five dead men, will see—the day of judgment, Bembo."

"And a fool, master?"

"Will be happy, God knows."

Now in saying this, Michael Bearn voiced the destiny that was to shape his own life and the fate of several others in one of the strangest adventures that was ever recorded in the annals of Venice.

Bembo found his master a queer mixture of moodiness and cheer. Michael had astonished the jester by forcing him to share their meals in common. Bembo had always fared, before this, with the hunting dogs of Contarini.

"'Tis said," he ventured, thinking of the gold they must have to pay for their food, "that you have seen the battles of the pagans in the East. Could not you gain a place and honor as *condottiere* with one of the noble lords of Venice?"

"Would one of the noble lords employ a slave, Bembo?" Michael smiled at his companion's surprise. "Nay, there is no man's work in these mock wars of Italy where the *condottieri* bleed—their masters."

He looked out moodily at the forests of galley masts and emptied his flagon of wine.

"Being idlers, good Bembo, an enterprise must come to us. Go you into the city and learn if this venture is to be had—one wherein we may sharpen our wits and laugh mightily."

Bembo went. It was evening when he returned.

"So you have come back to me?" remarked Michael. "Are you not afraid of poverty and the dagger of Rudolfo? Bembo, if you had favor with a magician, what would you wish to be?"

The hunchback looked seriously at his torn finery.

"Saving my present service to you, my master, I would like to be the Grand Cham who wears a ruby on every toe and scatters gold as the monks scatter indulgences."

"So, has the Spaniard's gossip stirred your blood?"

"Master, it is truth. The council has commissioned Rudolfo to command the soldiery of the expedition to the land of the Grand Cham."

So suddenly did Michael Bearn spring up from his chair that wine and table were upset on Bembo, who fell back in alarm.

"No!" the Breton cried.

"Aye. They only await the selection of a proper mariner to go with Clavijo and those already chosen. Fifteen thousand ducats have been granted Messer Clavijo for funds. 'Tis said, despite his zeal to set eyes again upon the earthly paradise, he balked at taking the money for a space."

"Clavijo—Ruy de Gonzales Clavijo—goes verily to the Grand Cham!" Michael sat down on the bed and rocked with laughter. "'Twould make the devil laugh. And who else goes?"

"A certain young count of the Mocenigo family—a rare gallant. Soranzi—I heard the thrifty merchant consulted his astrologer and found that his horoscope foretold rare things of him in Tatary. *Verbum sat sapienti*—a word to the wise is enough."

"Soranzi! Who else?"

"Nearly the whole of Venice has begged for the chance. Nevertheless, the wise council knows that the company must be limited to a few; five gentlemen and the men-at-arms."

"Perhaps the Cham would give him the freedom of the city—of Cathay, in the desert—the sandy desert!" Michael remarked seriously.

Bembo gaped and retreated to a corner of the room, fearing that his master might be afflicted with madness, until the reassuring thought came to him that Michael Bearn was only drunk.

"Aye, sir," he grinned amiably, "there is sand i' the desert—"

"Clavijo vouches for it, wise Bembo, and for the saltiness of the sea."

"The salt—verily, sir—ha-ho!"

"Bembo." Michael shook his dark head gravely. "Hark me, man; never will you behold such a voyager as Ruy Clavijo again. We will look no further, wait no longer. The wind is up, my fool, and we will sail with the tide. No quest could be more suited to our hearts than this."

He caught up his cloak, hat, and sword and bowed ceremoniously to the jester.

"Behold, the new master mariner of Messer Clavijo and his party. I go to the council, or, better, to Contarini, for my commission."

Hereupon Bembo scratched his head and cast a tentative glance at the water jar. He had been eager to inform his master that Rudolfo was in the expedition, hoping to turn Michael from thought of meddling with Contarini's plans, and now Michael had said he would join the party.

"Let me bathe your head, master, before you go."

Michael laughed.

"Water, upon such a night as this! Nay, we will drink to our commission and to the Grand Cham. Come, most wise oracle, a toast!"

"To the Grand Cham." Bembo filled a cup reluctantly.

"To the Grand Sham!" Michael emptied the cup.

It was late that night when he returned, but the jester was sitting up, wrapped in his tattered mantle, solemnly eyeing the diminishing candle on the table. He looked up fearfully when Michael pushed in the door, for Bembo had entertained grave apprehensions as to the reception of his slightly intoxicated master—for such he considered Michael—by the members of the council.

To his surprise Michael's step was regular and his glance steady.

"'Tis done, Bembo," he smiled. "Rudolfo being luckily absent, Contarini passed readily upon the merits of our claim. We sail the day after the morrow."

Michael flung himself into his chair and clapped Bembo on the knee.

"'Twas not wine that stirred my brain, Bembo. Knowing Clavijo, I had a grave fear that he would lead his expedition anywhere but to the terra incognita. Knowing Rudolfo, I am assured that the venture will verily seek spoil. And since our worthy friends would fain despoil the Cham, why, you and I must go with them. Because, forsooth, the Cham is of all men the man I most desire to clap eyes upon."

Taking some gold coins from a new pouch at his girdle, he bade Bembo settle their score at the Sign of the Sturgeon on the morrow. The pouch itself he detached and handed to Bembo, who was scratching his head, deeply puzzled by his master's speech.

"What is that, master?"

"For you. I drew an advance upon my pay. We part when the ship sails. This voyage is not for you, Bembo."

The jester pushed the money away and the corners of his lips drew down.

"Wherefore, master? Am I not your man?"

But Michael, glancing at the low partition that separated their room from the other chambers of the inn, shook his head thoughtfully.

"I have good reason for bidding you stay here. This voyage is not like other voyages."

Bembo pricked up his ears and protested, but Michael would say no more. Long after the sea captain had retired to his cloak and bed of boards, the jester remained awake, watching the candle flame moodily and glancing from time to time angrily at the purse.

He was hurt and his curiosity was stirred—two strong emotions with the hunchback. As the candle spluttered and subsided into grease, Bembo reached out a claw-like hand and pouched the money.

In the annals of the Maritime Council, in the pages devoted to the voyages into terra incognita, it is recorded that of Messer Clavijo and his company only one man returned to Venice.

Chapter VII
The Castle without Doors

Clavijo, in choosing the *Nauplia*, had selected the most comfortable means of travel to be had in those days. The pilgrim galliot was broad of beam and fitted with extra cabins in the stern castle. A dozen great sweeps aided the lateen sail. The sides of the vessel were high, and sloped well inboard—affording good protection against the waves.

The pilgrim galleys were designed to provide some ease for passengers. Live fowls were carried. The master of the ship could not remain at any given port for purposes of trade more than three days. He was also obliged to put in at any port they might fancy.

Clavijo, Mocenigo, and Rudolfo had all quartered themselves aft; Soranzi had made shift with sleeping-space below decks. But Bearn, who had discovered for himself the unattractiveness of quarters under the deck where the passengers camped all over each other, appropriated space for his mantle and bundle on the main deck under the overhang of the bow.

He was somewhat surprised to see that the ship's captain was hugging the shore, keeping a course well within sight of land. "Coasting" it was called in those days. Since this was the popular route, favored by the passengers, it was more liable to attack by Moslem pirates than the more direct course out into the Aegean.

Pirate galleys frequented the sea lanes to the East, off Greece, and Michael had observed at a glance that the *Nauplia* was poorly equipped for defense. Moreover he wondered that Clavijo was not afraid of encountering thieves. The Spaniard had been entrusted with a treasure of some fifteen thousand Venetian ducats and valuable goods.

It was the second night out and a full moon hung in a clear sky; the man at the steering oar guided the *Nauplia* within sight of the shadows of land.

Near Michael groups of Armenian and Muscovite traders slept, men and women together, heedless of the clamor of voyagers at dice and wine, or the quarreling and singing below decks, where torches of pine-pitch made sleep difficult, if not perilous.

Michael found that he missed Bembo's light tongue and deeper philosophy. The jester would have been in his element on such a night. But Bembo had left him without farewell the day before the galliot sailed.

The tumult and lights of the pilgrim ship formed a great contrast to the silence and speed of a smaller galley that swept out of an inlet with oars plying on either side and spray flashing in the moonlight.

For a second Michael studied it, then took up his sword and ran aft to where the captain slept by the helmsman.

"Look at yonder craft," observed the Breton, shaking the slumbering seaman, "and then dream if you can."

The Venetian stumbled to his feet, gazed, and swore roundly.

"Saint Anthony of Padua! I like it not."

He strode to the break of the stern castle.

"Ho, there! Cressets! Women into the stern! Out with your swords, messers. There be pirates at hand or I am a blind man!"

The gamesters sprang up. Men of the crew ran to fix torches in place at the ship's side; fagots contained in steel baskets were kindled at bow and stern. The women, wailing and crying, were driven below decks.

"Captain," suggested Michael, "it would be well to man the sweeps and get the galliot well under weigh. Your sloping sides are comfortably devised for boarders. Our safety lies in ramming the galley with our wooden beak, such as it is."

The Venetian, experienced in such matters, saw the wisdom of this and was giving orders for the rowers to push out the great oars, when a tall figure appeared on the balcony below the steering-platform and silenced him.

"Nay. No time for that. Summon up your oarsmen to fight on deck."

Michael, leaning down, saw that it was Rudolfo who spoke. The *condottiere* had drawn his sword and was giving swift instructions to his own men who tumbled up, pulling mail hoods about their heads and stringing their bows.

"You hear me, fool!" Rudolfo cried at the Venetian. "I am in command of the armed forces of this cursed galliot. By the rood—"

The captain shrugged, glanced at the oncoming galley—now not a dozen ships' lengths away—and complied. The crew hurried to the danger point at the ship's side, shepherded by Rudolfo, while the *Nauplia* barely moved through the water, for the wind was light.

Young Mocenigo reeled upon deck, more than a little the worse for wine. Michael saw Soranzi peer from a cabin and straightway vanish.

The brazen sound of the ship's bell voiced a warning to all who still slept. From the dark huddle of Muscovites and Armenians emerged men with bows—oriental traders, well able to fight in a crisis. On the waist of the *Nauplia* tumult reigned.

Glancing up at the sail, the Venetian skipper whispered to Michael: "Let the gallants do as they please. By Saint Anthony, I'll keep our bow against the other craft."

Michael took his stand beside Rudolfo. The *condottiere* was a brilliant figure in the ruddy light of the torches, his silver-inlaid helmet glittering, his crimson mantle flung back from his mailed chest. He ceased his directions to his men long enough to look swiftly at the Breton and his teeth shone at his beard.

"By the rood, messer, you stand behind me? I see you love not the front line of battle."

Now Michael wore no armor under his jerkin and mere prudence had dictated that he shelter himself behind the high rail as long as possible to escape the first arrow flights of the pirates, until they should board.

"As you wish, signor."

He pulled himself up into one of the platforms fashioned for archers to stand on. Rudolfo moved slightly away and Michael smiled at the inbred suspicion that took the *condottiere* beyond his reach.

But the arrows from the galley rattled high against the mast and tore through the great square of the sail that bellied and flapped as the Venetian skipper came about to present his bow to the pirate craft.

Rudolfo's half-dozen archers plied their long bows with disciplined precision.

"Saint Mark and Rudolfo!" Their shout went over the water to the galley. Answering cries identified the attackers as Turks and Greeks.

"Dogs!" snarled young Mocenigo. "The Lion of Saint Mark! Ha—do you like his claws?"

He seized one of the cressets by its supports and cast it out upon the deck of the galley as that craft moved past—the maneuver of the Venetian skipper having kept the galley from striking the side of the pilgrim ship with its bow.

For a moment there was a pandemonium of shouts, cries of anger and pain, and the flicker of javelins and arrows. The archers of Rudolfo, bearing long leather shields in front of them on their left arms, escaped injury, but Michael saw a pilgrim or two fall writhing to the deck.

Then the galley was past its prey and turning slowly—one bank of oars plying.

"*Pando!*" called the *Nauplia*'s skipper. "About!" He pushed the two steering sweeps over and the galliot swung slowly into the offshore tack on which it had been when the pirates were sighted.

Only one more attempt the galley made to close, and the motley defenders of the pilgrim ship were lining the other rail when something whizzed past Michael from behind and stuck into the wooden planking between him and Rudolfo.

The Breton glanced around and saw only the confusion of undisciplined men taking up new positions. Then he drew the knife from the rail.

"A pretty present," laughed the *condottiere*. "For you or me?"

The knife was a long, heavy blade, its bronze hilt richly inlaid with silver. Michael thrust it into his belt and observed that the galley was drawing off, followed by the taunting shouts of the Venetians.

"They have small stomach for a fight," he muttered.

"Thanks to God and our good friend Pietro Rudolfo." Clavijo's bull voice filled the ship. "Come, Master Bearn, I do not see that you were any too forward in the affray. Doubtless your skin is tender and you hang back lest it be pricked."

Now Michael had not seen Clavijo at all along the embattled rail of the galliot and he strongly suspected that the man had remained in his cabin until the pirates had drawn off. Then a stronger suspicion assailed him, and he touched the knife in his girdle.

"Aye," he assented seriously, "the skin is very tender—upon my back, and this poniard is both heavy and sharp. It was cast at me from behind."

He held it up by the point before the eyes of the Spaniard, who blinked and pulled at his long beard. Rudolfo took it, glanced it over, looked searchingly at Clavijo from under his thick brows, and tossed it over the side of the vessel.

"Some sailor's blade," he shrugged, "and doubtless meant for my kidneys. I am not over popular with the seamen of the *Nauplia*, because, verily, I enforce discipline upon occasion."

It was a long speech for the taciturn *condottiere* to make. Michael would have chosen to keep the dagger, in hopes of learning who its owner was. Yet, as Rudolfo said, it might well have been intended for him.

"Hark ye, Messer Clavijo." The Breton folded his arms. "Neither master of this vessel nor leader of your men-at-arms am I. The Maritime Council engaged me to aid you to navigate unknown waters if need be, and to arrange transport upon land. This will I do, so well as I may. Methinks the time may come when you will have need of my services."

He was looking at Clavijo, but Rudolfo spoke.

"As a slave, Master Bearn? It is said that you sleep alone in your cloak, so that no other may see the marks of a whip upon your shoulders."

So saying, he stepped back, laying hand lightly on the hilt of his sword. Michael Bearn drew a long breath, but his left hand—that Rudolfo, having learned his lesson once, was watching—reached up to the clasp of his mantle instead of to his weapon.

The cloak fell to the deck, and Michael's muscular fingers ripped open the collar of his jerkin, drawing it down over his bare shoulder. Both Clavijo and Rudolfo saw the deep red welt of scars.

"Aye," nodded Michael, "there be the marks of a Turkish scourge."

At this Clavijo started and a curiously intent frown passed over his smooth brow. He eyed the Breton's square, hard face and wiry, gray-black hair as if seeing him for the first time.

"Moreover," went on Michael tranquilly, "signori, you will note that my right arm hangs useless. It was broken by those same servants of the sultan. Perhaps this is why I have no longer any love for fighting when there is no need—"

"But surely, Master Bearn," smiled Clavijo ironically, "there was need to repel these pirates, who would have made short matter of us otherwise."

Michael laughed. The attack by the small galley had had in it more bark than bite, and once it was clear to their enemies that the pilgrim ship was not to be surprised, the Turks and Greeks seemed to lose heart. Such an affair bore little resemblance to the grim struggles Michael Bearn had shared in, along the frontier of the Orient.

"You laugh, signor?" Rudolfo's voice was heavy with insult. "Perhaps you would relish another scourging?"

The dark blood flooded into the young Breton's face. Around the three a circle of Rudolfo's men and sailors had gathered, scenting a quarrel. The gleam of torches lighted the scene. He wondered if the others had expected the *condottiere* to challenge him.

Rudolfo was not the man to be forced into a fight that he had not anticipated beforehand.

And then Michael heard an exclamation from one of the seamen. A strange whirring filled the air. Shrill squawking resounded on all sides.

One of the torches was knocked to the deck by a fluttering, animated ball that leaped and bounded among the men. The deck of the *Nauplia* in a moment was full of poultry. Hens, roosters, ducks and guinea fowl dashed about underfoot and overhead.

"Ten thousand devils!" Rudolfo struck viciously at a fat pullet that collided with his face. The spectators, the tensity of the quarrel broken in a flash, started running about, clutching at the flying meat.

It was each man for himself and the best dinner to the quickest. The torches were soon darting into every quarter of the deck, leaving Michael in semidarkness. Clavijo was leading the angry Rudolfo away.

A grotesque figure rose from the deck at Michael's elbow—a misshapen, stained, and grimacing form clad in striped raiment.

"Master," cried Bembo, "the field is mine. My light cavalry, released by a purloined key from their storage prison, have scattered our foes. Come, good master, let us make good our retreat!"

In the shadows of the bow Michael sat down on his bundle and laughed, more than a little provoked.

"A fair night, cousin mine," chattered the jester, taking this as a good omen. "Give me thanks for carrying you bodily away from the demons o' the sea. Black Rudolfo would ha' cast you overside as easily as I could suck an egg. Marry—the sight of eggs turns my belly for I lived upon them, hidden in the hold with the fowls for three days and two nights. Then, not an hour since I was awakened by a shouting as of the foul fiend, whereupon the roosters crowed, thinking it was day. Master, a soldier crawled into my castle, in the dark, and I thought the pirates held the ship and I was to be ripped open without the services of a confessor. *Pompa mortis!* Oh, the trappings of death!"

Bembo shivered and looked around anxiously at the tranquil moonlit sea.

"But, forsooth, the big soldier thrust his thatch through the window of the hold and bawled to the other vessel to stand off, that the plan had been changed, and it was useless to attack the galliot. A brave lad, thought I, to bid the pirates mend their ways and be gone. Verily he was a potent bully, for the miscreants gave back and left us in peace. So I—being sorely athirst from fear and hen's feathers and bad eggs—I climbed to the roof o' this house and saw Rudolfo about to spit you, whereupon I ran back for my winged allies."

"Was the man you saw in armor?"

"Armor, quoth'a, verily so. When his face was i' the window I saw a steel cap as big as a bucket. Master, chide me not for coming. Nay, no voyage that was ever brewed could make me leave the good man who shared his wine and meat wi' me; nor would my curiosity leave me in peace until I learned wherein this voyage differed from other voyages, as you said."

Michael arranged his pack for a pillow and laid his sword close to his left hand. The jester blinked at him from shrewd little eyes, the great head turned to one side, like a dog's, questioningly.

"A ship, Bembo," murmured the Breton, his eyes closed, "a harmless pilgrim galliot, beats off an attack by well-armed raiders because—a soldier calls secretly to the foe from below decks. One of Rudolfo's men. A dagger is thrown from behind the mast. Feed your curiosity with that and let me sleep."

It was a leaner and dirtier throng that lined the rail of the *Nauplia* when that good galliot entered the dark waters of the Golden Horn and anchored off the crowded shore of Constantinople after the storms of the Aegean that followed the attack by the pirates.

And when Clavijo and his party re-embarked for Pera and the Black Sea in a small Venetian trading galley, Mocenigo was no longer with them. The young count, Clavijo explained to Bearn, had found paradise enough in the Hippodrome and palaces of the emperor, and women to his liking. The departure of the others had been hurried by the insults of Moslem warriors who thronged the waterfront.

Michael said nothing but sought out Bembo, who was sitting on a chest on the jetty, eyeing the preparations for departure.

"The first of us has fallen by the wayside, Bembo," he observed gravely. He had been apprehensive about the jester since Bembo bobbed up as a stowaway, but had not reproved him. "Will you not follow his example and remain here?"

"I would see the Grand Cham."

Michael looked at him and laughed.

"You will never see the Grand Cham."

"Well—" Bembo was surprised—"you must know, master, for you have traveled near Cathay. I would see the city and the gold palaces—"

"There is no city."

"Master? You have heard Clav—"

"Clavijo—" Michael's smile broadened into a wide grin—"Messer Ruy de Gonzales Clavijo is the greatest liar in Christendom."

Bembo gaped and glanced from the ship to the stores on the jetty and at the Breton as if doubting his senses.

"Clavijo, my good Bembo, is a man with one talent. Aye—a tongue. The sun never shone upon a greater liar. What he did not pick up at the waterfront of Genoa and Venice he heard related of the traveling monks. When that failed him he had his tongue, and wit to match. It made his fortune in Venice. Until the council took him at his own value, forsooth, and sent him to find the city that is a lie."

Michael chuckled at the memory. "When Clavijo by his own testimony was in Cathay I saw him among a throng of camp followers, fleeing along the Danube."

At this Bembo scratched his head vigorously. Then his eyes lighted and he leaped from the chest.

"Aye, master. Well, then, since this is a quest of folly, who should be the leader but a fool?"

When the galley cleared the Horn, Bembo stood beside the helmsman, a wooden sword stuck in his ragged girdle, his twisted legs planted wide, and his bearing as important as that of an admiral of the Venetian fleet.

And when, a month later, the party of explorers rode inland from Trebizond, Bembo took his place at the head of the column, mounted on a caparisoned mule.

"On, into terra incognita!" he cried, waving his wooden sword valiantly.

In fact Trebizond was the boundary of what we now call Europe. It was the eastern door of the fading Byzantine Empire, the last trade port of the Serene Republic of Venice, which had its *bailio* stationed in an arsenal on shore. The walled city, rising on rocks from this shore, was the home of Manuel the Second, almost the last of the Comneni-line emperors of Trebizond for generations.

Now they were bound, as Bembo had stated, into unknown territory—into blank spaces on Venetian maps. No one in Trebizond had been anxious to accompany them for it was known that the mountains to the south and east as far as the Salt Sea were occupied by tribes who paid tribute to a monarch of Tatary.

Soranzi and others of the party had taken this information as a good augury and were in high spirits. So also was Bembo.

"Come, my flock!" He jangled the bells on his hood. "Follow your bellwether. Ply your spurs, sound the timbrels! A fool is your leader, and folly your guide. Ride, my cousins in folly, and —— take him who first draws rein!"

Journeying to the southeast, they entered bare brown plains and passes that wound among stunted, rocky hills where the valleys were yet snow-coated and the air was chill. For the first time the voyagers were alone in a strange land. And stranger than the aspect of the country where isolated shepherds ran away at their approach and the inns were no more than walled spaces, where the animals could be picketed and fires lighted—stranger than this was the castle without doors.

The highway they had been following was no more than a trail from valley to valley. The castle overlooked this path from a barren cliffside up which wound a well-defined way cut in the rock.

Halfway up the ramp, as the travelers termed the road, they were halted by a ragged man on a shaggy pony who called to them harshly. Clavijo appeared to meditate on the meaning of the horseman's words, then shook his head. Michael, however, interpreted.

"The man is an Armenian. He says we are in the land of his lord and must pay the customary tribute. It would be best to do so."

Soranzi, who handled the expenditures of the expedition, demurred, and the rider retired, bidding them stay where they were. Presently a thin man clad in leathers and furs appeared in the roadway, followed by thirty or more even more ragged horsemen armed with bows.

At this Rudolfo swore and began to muster his mailed men-at-arms to the front of the column, when Michael checked him.

"This rider declares that he is lord of the castle, although he does not dare occupy it owing to the attacks of the Turks who are in the habit of raiding the country from the sultanate to the south. He says that he is very poor and a Christian—which, forsooth, is but half true—and needs money to carry on his fighting. What will you give him, Messer Soranzi?"

The merchant scowled, for besides the presents destined for the Grand Cham the only other goods in the caravan were his own large stock in trade from which he expected a profit of several hundred percent at the least.

"Tell the Moor," he commanded, "that we be merchants seeking the court of the Grand Cham. Travelers do not pay tribute at castles of the Grand Cham."

Michael grinned and spoke with the Armenian chief, who frowned in turn and responded testily.

"He says," announced the Breton, "that he knows naught of any Grand Cham or khan except himself and the Turkish sultans and that if we are to travel in his land we must make him a present."

Clavijo and Soranzi argued the matter hotly and finally produced a piece of scarlet cloth and a silver cup. These the Armenian refused angrily, saying that he must have more.

Darkness was falling and a thin rain pierced the garments of the travelers uncomfortably. Soranzi shook his thin fists and chewed at his beard.

"And this dog calls himself a Christian! Well, give him a roll of Phrygian purple velvet from the lot we carry for the great Cham—"

"And a handful of gold from your own fat pouch, Messer Merchant," snarled Rudolfo, who was both cold and hungry. "A pox on your bartering!"

This brought a wail from Soranzi, but mollified the Armenian, who withdrew up the hillside with his motley army and his spoils. But the Venetians found that the horsemen had not remained at the castle. It was quite empty; moreover every door had been removed from its hinges.

When the beasts had been quartered in the courtyard and Michael with some of the soldiers had succeeded in lighting a fire in the great hall—not without difficulty—and after they had dined on cold mutton, cold bread-cakes, and wine, Clavijo, who had been very thoughtful for some time, spoke up—

"My friends, look yonder."

Rudolfo started nervously and they all stared at a sign on the stone wall of the hall, a cross, obscured by smoke, chiseled into the granite.

"That is a potent symbol of the Cathayans," nodded Clavijo, "one of the talismans of their alchemists. Aye, this castle bears evidence of their magic. Why is there no castellan? Where be the doors?"

As the men were silent, the snarling cry of a jackal came to their ears from the darkness and rain outside and Soranzi paled.

"Where vanished the knavish riders that we met?" continued Clavijo.

"To their tents, elsewhere," broke in Michael. "As for the cross, it is Christian in sooth. The doors were doubtless removed by the Turks who, the Armenian said, recently sacked the place and left orders that it was not to be defended again."

Clavijo shrugged, with a dubious smile. Since learning that Bearn had been a captive of the Moors, as he chose to call them, he had been careful to avoid discussion with the Breton.

"As you wish. But soon we will come upon the piles of human skulls. I suppose you would say there is no danger there." He shook his head in gentle reproof. "Now, sirs, I have a plan. Messer Soranzi seeks to avoid robbery. Methinks you all would fain live longer. So be it. I, who have mastered the dangers of the mountains and the sands and the Cathayans, I will go ahead from here alone."

Michael glanced at him searchingly and was silent.

"You will be safe here, sirs," continued the Spaniard, "under the potent protection of Rudolfo and his men. I have no fear. What I have done once can be accomplished again. Even though I may never return, I would prefer to press on from here alone. A score of swords and halberds will avail us little against the Cathayans. Better one should die than all."

"If I am not back by the first of winter, sirs, you can retrace your steps easily to Trebizond. By tying the mules, head to tail, in a fashion I wot well of, I can make shift to bear with me the gifts for the Grand Cham, placed in packs upon the mules."

Rudolfo, however, voiced a blunt negative.

"By the rood, sir, we have made a bond between us. We will go in a body or not at all."

This view was shared by Soranzi, who, despite privations and plundering, had hugged to his bosom the dream of fabulous profits promised him by his astrologer in Venice.

"Aye," put in Bembo seriously; "we will go in our bodies or not at all."

"I would fain see the bull-stag that you say is to be met with in Cathay," insisted Michael.

"A most curious beast, Master Bearn," observed Clavijo mechanically. "It has more hairs on its tail than a lion in its mane.* The pagans in Cathay entrap the beast by setting a snare artfully between two trees so that when the taurus—which is the name bestowed upon it by Herodotus—passes between the trees, its tail is caught fast. So tender is the beast of its fine tail that it remains passive lest a hair be pulled out, when the Cathayans may easily make it prisoner."

"Yet, signor," added Michael, "they must take care in freeing it, for if they should sever the tail from the body by stroke of sword, the bull-stag would perceive that its valued member was lost beyond repair and would no longer feel constrained to quietude. I fear that many imprudent Cathayans have died unshriven because they cut off the tail of a taurus."

Clavijo pulled at his beard—a habit when he was dubious.

"Most true, Master Bearn. Only one such as I who have knowledge of the wiles of the Cathayan beasts may cope with them. I remember a

---

*Clavijo had heard of the Central Asian yak.

mighty serpent that I set out to slay. I found the serpent engaged in a monstrous struggle with a dragon before its cave."

"Saint Bacchus preserve us!" Bembo glanced fearfully at the shadows in the corners of the damp, leaf-strewn hall. Several of the men-at-arms who were listening from their fire drew nearer and gaped.

"The dragon is the mightiest monster of Cathay," resumed Clavijo more readily. "It has a lance at the end of its armored tail that can strike through the stoutest mail. Signori, I carefully avoided the sweep of the deadly tail and waited. As God willed, the dragon seized the serpent by the head. Both pulled mightily, and when their necks were taut I stepped nearer and smote with my sword, severing the Medusa-like head of the dragon from its shoulders."

"Well struck!" approved Michael. "And the serpent?"

"Alas, that was a most fearsome beast. For days I awaited an opportunity to slay it. Before long it transpired that the foul beast came from its lair to attack a passing lion. Verily, signori, it twined about the king of beasts and swallowed its victim hindquarters first. Forsooth, that was my chance. Rushing forward, I swung my sword upon its neck as it lay sluggish. When the head of the serpent fell to earth the head of the lion fell off with that of its conqueror, and I rode back with double booty to the city of the Cham."

Michael was rolling himself in his cloak on a table for the night when Bembo approached.

"Master," whispered the jester, "verily just now I looked without the castle and saw two spirits."

"Bah! Your own fears you saw."

"Nay, they had two great heads. Gian, the big lieutenant of Rudolfo, was with me and we both said a paternoster. Then Gian, being a braver man than I and somewhat the better for wine, crept closer and cast his knife at one of the two. Whereupon they disappeared."

This incident Michael did not permit to disturb his slumbers. He, as well as Clavijo, had noticed that the Armenians—the chief of Cabasica, the castle without doors—had left riders to spy upon them. The turbans of the watchers had served, doubtless, to make Bembo exaggerate the size of their heads.

He was well aware that the Spaniard was caught between two fires. Beheading was the penalty that the Maritime Council would inflict on

Clavijo if his deceit were discovered and Venetian officials should lay
hand on him. So, Michael reasoned, Clavijo, possibly through Rudolfo's
agency, had arranged for the mock attack by the pirates on the *Nauplia*,
hoping to be taken prisoner and robbed by friendly hands.

But the galliot, owing to Michael's warning and the skill of the Venetian captain, had been able to offer unexpected resistance. Clavijo, if he
had thought to have himself and his companions captured by a conve-
nient foe, had been disappointed.

Mocenigo, a well-known Venetian and hence dangerous to Clavijo, had
been persuaded, not with great difficulty, to fall behind at Constantinople. And the life of Michael—another dangerous member—had been attempted during the sham attack on the galliot. This puzzled the Breton
more than a little, because he did not think that Clavijo was the type to
turn so quickly to assassination.

Thinking over the situation drowsily, Michael remembered that Bembo
had just said something about a man who cast a knife. What knife? Rudolfo
had thrown the silver-chased weapon into the sea! Rudolfo—a knife . . .

Hereupon Michael slumbered fitfully, dreaming that Clavijo had taken
the form of a dragon with a man's head and that flames and smoke were
spouting from his nostrils. He imagined that he was bound and helpless
and the monster that was Clavijo came nearer until the flames touched
his face . . .

At this point Michael jerked into wakefulness and perceived that Bembo
had heaped fresh brush on the fire which had blazed up nearby. Soranzi,
his cloak wrapped closely about him, sat hunched by the flames, shivering and grunting in his sleep, looking for all the world like an old and
dingy vulture with an overlarge belly and bald head.

Rudolfo and Gian were standing, fully clad, in a corner of the hall and
both were looking at him.

Sleep had refreshed Michael's brain. It struck him that Gian had been
the man who cast the knife at him.

For the remainder of the night Michael kept awake.

Chapter VIII
The Sitting-Down Beast

Messer Ruy de Gonzales Clavijo was a man of many cares. His expedition made slow and weary progress among the mountain passes, guides
could not be hired, food was scanty, hardships many. Yet they advanced
to the south all too quickly for him.

For he could not turn back. Soranzi and Rudolfo and Michael Bearn would not hear of it. Nor could he confess that he did not know where he was going.

Once he tried losing his way. But Michael promptly rode ahead through the rain and found a fresh trail of many horses going in their direction. This new route took them out of the rocky hillocks down into more fertile fields.

"A fairer country," announced Michael, as the rain cleared, "with vineyards and date groves. On, to the Grand Cham!"

Looking back, Clavijo beheld a majestic summit, snow-crowned, with bare slopes rising to the height of the Alps.

"The Holy Mount Ararat," he said bravely, and crossed himself. "Forward, signori—if you have heart to face the dangers that beset that other mountain of skulls."

Their followers were not overeager. Some of the few servants were sick. Rudolfo's men-at-arms, accustomed to the machine-like wars of Italy, where an army marched but a league a day and where every hillside had its village and food and women, and the peasants had to bear the burden of both armies—Rudolfo's men muttered and sulked, except the lieutenant Gian.

Some whispered that the party was followed, that the spirits of the castle kept at their heels. Others pointed to distant bands of horsemen on the plain, bands that Clavijo declared were Moors and pagans and Michael asserted to be Turks.

One night Gian and several men stole away, to rifle houses in a village. They returned with poor spoil but many tales. Bembo, who had slipped off to accompany them, stoutly asserted that he had beheld a monster walking among the houses of the Moors or Saracens or whatever the heathens might be.

He thought at first the animal had been sitting down, until it had moved off at the approach of the men.

"Signori," he protested, "it was still sitting down, yet it ran. It had the body of a horse, spotted like a snake, the legs of a deer and the head of a stag. And its neck! Beshrew me, signori, may I never eat pudding again if its neck did not rise up from its body like Gian's spear when he lances an apple from a peasant's tree. Nay, it was as tall as the mast of a ship, for the monster stopped and smelled of fruit over a garden wall that was too high for us to climb."

Bembo had seen a giraffe.

This interested Michael, for he had never heard of such animals in Asia Minor.

After this inroad upon the inhabitants, the Venetians were shunned more than ever. A hot sun beat upon their heavy garments. The road they followed was no more than a track of deep mud.

Clavijo was very unhappy. For, in spite of his brave tale, he had never before been farther east than Constantinople. And the last thing he wished was to return, a prisoner, into the Venetian power that stretched even to Trebizond.

And then came the night when, encamped at a short distance from the road, they were awakened during the last hour of darkness by the rushing sound of horses' hoofs passing by along the road.

They saw nothing of the riders, only heard the horses sweeping past with incredible speed. Clavijo wondered fearfully what kind of men could ride at that pace in the darkness.

Dawn revealed the bodies of three of his servants, their throats cut, lying by the ashes of the campfire.

"It was the spirits of the waste!" cried Soranzi. "We must hasten; we are near the city in the sands."

The merchant pointed to thin traces of sand in the earth. But when they looked for footprints of the assassins approaching their camp they found nothing. Nothing, that is, except the hoof-marks that were quite fresh in the road nearby. Michael, however, knew that Gian's excursion into the village had brought the pursuers upon their tracks.

Clavijo was more than a little superstitious. He fancied that the phantoms he had summoned up by his words had pursued their steps. The spirits that he had invoked had taken form. In his tale he had said that his servants met death.

"Hasten!" he cried. "Away from here!"

The three bodies were buried in a shallow grave. There were now only eight attendants—Bembo, a sick servant of Clavijo who was carried in a litter, Gian and his four men, and Soranzi's servant.

When the pack animals were loaded and trudging forward, Michael reined his horse in beside the Spaniard.

"Signor Clavijo," he said softly. "You have left the path that we were following. By the sun, unless I am blind, you are taking us in a circle. Wherefore?"

The Spaniard pointed toward the site of the distant camp.

"Death is upon us. We are in the land of Gog and Magog, where *djins* pursue Christian travelers. Oh, it is an evil day!"

"Do *djins* cast a dagger, a heavy poniard, with bronze hilt overlaid in silver, at a Christian's back? On shipboard?"

The black eyes of Clavijo widened.

"Nay, forsooth! You describe the dagger once owned by Gian. I have not seen it since—"

"Rudolfo, your friend, threw it into the sea. Come, signor, here is need of truth."

"As God is my witness, I have spoken the truth."

"About Cathay? And the Grand Cham?"

Clavijo was silent, sullen almost.

"Signor, the death of your men ends all buffoonery. You were their master—"

"*Por dios!*" Clavijo's full face went livid. "Do you suspect me of that? I did not do it. Nor do I know aught of the dagger cast at you."

Michael glanced at him thoughtfully. "Then confess to me, signor, that you never saw the court of the Grand Cham."

"Master Bearn—" Clavijo started, and drew a long breath. "You heard what I told the council. Have you not believed?

"Have you not seen the holy Mount Ararat and heard Bembo relate the aspect of the strange beast of—" he lifted his head stubbornly— "Cathay?"

Michael laughed shortly. "Faith, signor, it would take a magician of Cathay himself to tell what is true and what is false." He checked the other's exclamation. "Nay, listen. I have sounded the bottom of your tale. You were in Constantinople, not Cathay. Your wonders were garbled stories of travelers picked up on the jetties and in the markets. Your city—an illusion of the sands that some call by a strange name—a mirage. Your tower of skulls—a heap of stones."

"The Grand Cham—"

"Of him will we soon learn."

Clavijo shrugged.

"You heard the emperor at Trebizond speak of a great Tatar king."

At this Michael smiled.

"Man, you are wonderful. You pulled wool over the sharp eyes of the Signory, and beguiled two emperors. It has been a rare jest, this voyage.

I could love you for that. Nay, I cannot think that you wished to stick me in the back, or to slay those poor fools."

He nodded thoughtfully.

"If a man's child could tell when you lied and when not, I would be your friend, Gonzales. This much I will do for you. You cannot turn back. Soranzi's greed is fired by the strange sights he has seen and yearns for his promised profits. Rudolfo will not give in to you, unless he is in your confidence—"

"God forbid!"

"That had the ring of truth. Well, by my reckoning we are near the Tatar tribes. Now that death dogs our steps we cannot push on blindly. We are followed, without doubt. I shall strike back along our track and seek to take captive one of the riders, whether Armenian or *djin*, and make him tell us where we are and what is in store for us and why we are followed. Do you, call a halt to rest the beasts and await my coming. Do you agree?"

Clavijo chewed his beard, and flushed.

"As you will, Master Bearn. We will wait."

It is more than possible if Michael Bearn could have had his way that Clavijo and those with him, who were yet alive and well, might have returned in safety to Trebizond.

The Breton was barely gone, however, when events took another turn. Rudolfo had been more silent than his wont that morning and now he dismounted, nodded to Gian, and strode to Clavijo's side.

"Signor, your sword and dagger."

The Spaniard drew back, surprised. Whereupon Rudolfo reached out and secured the weapons for himself without trouble. Gian and another soldier took spear and poniard from Soranzi's servant. Seeing this, Rudolfo turned to the merchant, who was armed only with a knife.

"Messer Soranzi, an unpleasant duty has fallen upon me. Since leaving Venice I have suspected this Spaniard of deceit. By the rood, it is plain that he knows not the way he follows. Just now he has doubled on his tracks. I think his tale was but a pretext to get money from the honorable council."

Soranzi's little eyes narrowed and his thin face darkened. He cast a venomous look at the unhappy Spaniard.

"Witness, Messer Soranzi," continued the *condottiere*, "that this deceiver cannot speak the language of the country he claims to have traveled. He would have left us at Cabasica and taken the Cham's presents with him."

Conviction leaped into the twisted face of the merchant and he shook with rage.

"The man's face declares you have the right of it," he hissed. "What can we do?"

"This. I am the leader of the men-at-arms. I take command, forsooth! Every man except the five troopers and myself must give up arms. You, Soranzi, assume charge of the money, articles of trade, and gifts. Take an inventory of the goods, and keep it. The —— himself knows in what quarter this liar has led us. We will strike back to Trebizond and consult further—Ha, dog! Would you do that?"

The roving eye of the *condottiere* had fallen upon Bembo as the hunchback was stealing away quietly in the direction Michael had taken along the back track. Rudolfo spurred after him and struck the jester into the mud with his mailed fist, leaning down from the saddle to glare at him.

Bembo rose, drew his wooden sword from his girdle with a flourish and handed it to Rudolfo.

"You have overcome me, *vi et armis*. Take my sword."

Rudolfo's answer was to cast the thing away contemptuously; nevertheless he kept a wary glance on the jester.

"We will wait for Master Bearn," he said shortly. "When he returns he must answer on the spot for the death of the three varlets."

Now Bembo would have given a leg to be able to run off and acquaint his friend with what had happened. The fool, like most unfortunates who are crippled in body, was sensitive to impressions.

He was afraid of Rudolfo, and more afraid of Gian. He looked upon Michael as his sole protector and Michael would presently walk back, armed only with a sword, to where his enemy waited with a half-dozen men-at-arms.

These same men were alert and eager, pleased at the chance of reaching Trebizond again. Bembo noticed that they did not seem surprised at the turn in affairs, and that Gian was a-grin.

"Saint Bacchus aid me and keep good Cousin Michael away," he prayed. "Or our guts are in the saucepan!"

They had not long to wait. Michael stepped from between two trees against which the men-at-arms were sitting at the road's edge. He had come through the dense thorn thicket without a sound.

Rudolfo and Soranzi were not a little disturbed by this sudden apparition in their midst of the man for whom they were looking down the road. The captain of mercenaries glanced at the thicket and saw that half-hidden within it was a queer kind of native shrine—a mere heap of stones with rags stuck upon sticks hanging over it.

Soranzi tried to read the Breton's harsh face—a task that was no longer easy. Michael's brown eyes were half-closed and the merchant noted that he worked the fingers of his right hand slowly as if testing long unused muscles.

"Signor," said Michael to Rudolfo, "I heard, while I was coming through yonder thicket, some words of yours. You made bold, methinks, to say that I slew the three varlets. Is it not so?"

Michael glanced around the ring of faces that had gathered close to him. The men-at-arms were gaping, fingering their weapons, intent on Rudolfo. It was significant of the natures of the leaders that Michael seemed, for the moment at least, to enjoy the mastery of the situation.

His dark face was lighted by a kind of inward amusement, while Rudolfo was pulling at his mustache with lowered eyes. The watching attendants ignored Soranzi and Clavijo, knowing that the test of leadership lay between the Breton and their own captain.

"And reason enow!" said the latter curtly. "Fore ——, masters, here have we a lowborn churl who stinks of the sea and who bears the scars of slavery on his wrists and back. Since our landing he has held intercourse with the pagans of the countryside. Aye, did he not interfere on behalf of the knavish robbers of Cabasica? And warn my good Gian from his excursion into the native village some time since? What more of reason would you have?"

This arraignment, although it satisfied the servitors, raised grave doubts in the keen mind of Soranzi—doubts which were heightened when Michael responded gravely that he had slept in a tent with Clavijo the night before and that the Spaniard could testify that he had not left the tent until aroused by the others.

"Yet," growled Rudolfo, who was gaining confidence, "you can walk out of a wood without a sound. Why can you not move even more silently in the hours of darkness when the evil powers are strong? There is black magic in the air, by the rood! How else could riders gallop like the wind—as those we heard anon—when an honest Christian cannot see where to put his foot to earth?"

"Master Bearn speaks the truth," broke in Clavijo bluntly, "and—my head on it—he is an honest Christian."

"You are not lacking in lies," growled Rudolfo. "We may no longer believe you. Moreover, by the mouth of his friend Bembo, the Breton stands accused."

Michael glanced at the hunchback keenly. He would have staked his life on the fool's faith. The tie between the two had been strengthened by the hardships of the journey.

In fact it was pity for the hunchback that had impelled Michael to join the party again. He had been approaching them through the thicket, moving silently as was his custom, when Rudolfo's loudly spoken threats arrested him.

Understanding that the *condottiere* had taken the leadership of the party from Clavijo, and that the Italian's first blow would be against himself, Michael had been strongly inclined to part company with the others and strike for the Tatar country that he knew could not be far from here.

Thus far the course of the voyagers had fitted in with the plans of Michael, who was anxious to appear before the khan as an accredited representative of a European power, with the gifts that experience had taught him were needful in gaining the friendship of an Oriental monarch.

More than once he had steered Clavijo to the west, away from the south where bands of Turkish irregulars were thick. Michael had no desire to be brought a second time before Bayezid as a captive.

Now Rudolfo had seized the reins, and while Michael could not know precisely what intrigue the *condottiere* had in view, he knew that Rudolfo had penetrated as far into terra incognita as he dared to go, and also— after events had shaped themselves to the Italian's satisfaction—he would be most likely to head back to Trebizond as soon as he had the treasure of the expedition in his hands.

It was the sight of the blow Bembo received, and his warm love of the cripple, that brought Michael to face Rudolfo.

"'Tis a lie—" Bembo had started to cry when Rudolfo's cold glance shut him up as a knife-thrust closes a turtle.

"Bembo had gossiped with my men," he said dryly. "The fool hinted that his master was bent hither on revenge. What revenge should he seek save against me with whom he has a feud as good Messer Soranzi knows well? Aye, and against the Signory of Venice that requited him with scant usury for his services."

Bembo hung his head. It was true that he had liked to babble of the Breton's prowess.

The others nodded in owl-like wisdom. In the minds of the servitors Rudolfo had gained the mastery over Michael. Soranzi and Clavijo were puzzled. Michael, who was by no means a slow thinker, sensed the drift away from him.

"I must take measures for our safety," Rudolfo was saying, "for the pagans are close on our heels. Bind me this miscreant."

"Verily—" Michael smiled quickly—"you are a rare leader, signor. Were you not among the captains of Nicopolis? Did not you, Clavijo, see him there? Rudolfo saw you?"

"Aye," admitted the Spaniard.

"Then answer me one question. If you saw Clavijo at Nicopolis, Rudolfo, why then must you have known he lied, even when you embarked with us upon this venture. Why were you fain to wait until now to accuse him?"

The *condottiere* could not repress a scowl at this sudden thrust, but he answered composedly:

"I may have seen him at the battle by the river, but a pox on't! I marked him not. Verily I did not recall his face when he told his tale at Venice."

Rudolfo lied well. Michael, failing to catch him off his guard, turned to Soranzi, who was too shrewd a judge of men and too alert where his own money was at risk to be convinced by Rudolfo's charge against Michael.

"Your lives, signori," the Breton said gravely, "are at stake. Would you know why?"

They were silent at that and the thin mouth of the merchant pinched together as he answered—

"Why?"

"You call it black magic—faith—when horsemen gallop i' the night, signors. Nay, they were Tatars who ride with a loose rein in day or dark. I know because I have this hour caught one who followed in our trail. Some news I had from him. War threatens between the Turk and the Tatar—the sultan and the khan. Signori, these be mighty monarchs and their bands of riders on this borderland are more numerous than the good people of Venice itself."

"Then," Soranzi's logical mind probed for information, "the Tatars slew our men last night?"

Rudolfo and Gian glanced at Michael, who shook his head gravely.

"Nay. The Tatars passed us as the wind passes. Our varlets were slain by Kurds of the village that Gian and his men visited. So said my prisoner. After Bembo left the place, frightened by sight of the sitting-down beast, our brave men-at-arms made themselves free of the women of the village, the Kurdish warriors of the place being absent with the riders of the Turkish army."

Gian and the others were silent at this and uneasy, lacking Rudolfo's calm.

"Two Kurds only reached our camp in the night," went on Michael, "or our throats as well might have been cut. The Moslems do not forget a wrong, Rudolfo. Wherefore, death follows in your track."

"And what manner of man was he you caught?" inquired Soranzi uncomfortably.

"A Tatar who sighted our cavalcade and followed 'till more of his fellows could be summoned and our merchants despoiled. Mark me, Soranzi, the Tatars are grim enow, yet they attack boldly and do not slit throats i' the night. Nay, they would rip your belly with a sword. You would fare better with them."

Soranzi squirmed and the men-at-arms muttered under their breath. All glanced up and down the wooded ravine and at the impassive rock shrine.

Suddenly Gian broke the silence with a great oath and strode to Michael, his dagger flashing in his hand. The point of the weapon he set against the Breton's bare throat. Michael, after a quick glance at the ring of armed men, had not moved.

"Speak the truth, master," he growled, "or your gullet will be slit for the ants to crawl in. What devil's work brought us to this place? Whence lies Trebizond? Speak!"

The man's face was twisted by anger and fear. Michael smiled, for he could read Gian like a book and the man's diction and words had told him three things.

One—Rudolfo had confided in his lieutenant that the Breton was to be made captive or done away with, or Gian would not have dared what he did. Two—Rudolfo, as well as Clavijo, had lost his bearings but did not wish the men to know it. Three—they were all afraid, and so much the more easily handled.

"You have got yourself a new poniard, Gian," he observed, "in place of the one you cast at me and Rudolfo tossed overside. It was a poor cast for such a clever thrower."

He paused interrogatively and the man, angered, caught at the bait before Rudolfo could speak.

"The mast—" he muttered and stopped. "Death and damnation!"

"The mast interfered with your throw? Precisely. Then, after the mock attack of the pirates—I thought them in the hire of Clavijo till your master cast aside his mask just now—had failed to despoil our venture for Rudolfo's profit, your master waited till he was beyond the last *bailio* of Venice. Men will wag their tongues. It was necessary to have us beyond the *bailio* and the trade routes before Rudolfo could seize the gold and riches entrusted to Clavijo by the council. That is why we are here, Gian."

Michael had guessed at this, but he had hit the mark. Gian glanced at his master inquiringly, but Michael spoke first.

"Do not make another mistake, Gian. With my life, your guidance would be lost. If you doubt it, ask Rudolfo whither lies Trebizond."

"You will tell us," said the *condottiere* dryly.

"Tut, signor; have you time to waste? Soranzi—a bargain. My safety and Bembo's pledged on your word, and we guide you to safety? Do you agree?"

It was to the men-at-arms rather than the merchant that Michael directed this shaft. The Venetian was thinking furiously and he nodded.

"Agreed. But stay—what proof that you can bear us hence?"

"The Tatar lies i' the thicket yonder, bound with his own belt. Your addle-pates, Rudolfo, would never find him. But bid them look i' the thorns behind the shrine—"

In a moment Gian and his worthies dragged forth a squat figure, wrapped hand and foot with strips torn from a shawl girdle. His broad head was set close to square shoulders, and while his body was long and muscular, his legs were short, and bowed. His slant eyes glared at his captors, who freed his ankles so that he could stand without difficulty.

The Tatar's sword had been tossed by Michael into the bushes, well out of the prisoner's reach.

"What this man knows he will tell me," explained Michael, "and no man of you save, perchance, Bembo, will understand aught of what he says. I know a word that will conjure us our safety through Tatary."

Hereupon the men-at-arms crossed themselves and muttered under their breath. They were more than ever convinced that Michael had intercourse with the powers of evil and that this native was his familiar.

"The bargain is struck," asserted Soranzi again.

But out of the corner of his eye Michael saw Rudolfo gnawing his thumb and presently, leaning toward Gian, to whisper a quick word. Gian in turn muttered something to his men and took his stand behind the bent form of Bembo. Michael waited alertly.

Rudolfo cried at him suddenly—

"Your sword and dagger, throw them down!"

The words were prompt and so was Michael's answer. He thrust his captive forward against one of the oncoming troopers. Snatching out his sword, he parried the rush of another, beating down the man's blade and sending him to the earth.

Instantly Michael dropped to his knees and the third assailant tripped over him, cursing. The fourth, a short, wiry fellow in pliant mail, thrust at the Breton before he could rise. Michael caught the blade in a fold of his cloak and lashed out as he came erect. The man dropped with a split skull.

Rudolfo had set spurs to his horse, while the others looked on aghast at the swift clash of weapons. Before Michael could step aside, the *condottiere*'s beast struck the sea captain, knocking him a dozen feet. Then came the grinning Gian, who leaped upon Michael's sword where it had fallen and glanced inquiringly at Rudolfo.

"Do not slay," instructed the *condottiere*. "Bind Master Bearn to the Tatar or Turk or whatever breed of devil it may be—"

"And where may the devil be, signor?" inquired Gian, gripping the half-stunned Michael in his great hands.

They looked around at that and beheld the Tatar vanishing into the bushes up the slope by the road. His long turban cloth trailed after him as he leaped with the nimbleness of a goat from rock to rock until he passed from sight before the men-at-arms could draw bow. Nor could a horse follow where he had gone.

"No matter," grunted Rudolfo. "Messer Soranzi, verily you are a greater fool than I took you for. The guile of Master Bearn bewitched you. Not only would you have let him ride free, but you would have followed where he led—to his allies the Tatars or fiends or whatever they be."

He leaned from his saddle to jerk Michael, who was more than a little hurt, to his feet.

"So, my friend," he sneered, "you would hide your knowledge from us and bargain for it! By the Pope's head! Tonight I promise myself we will know all you know. Gian has a rare knack with a dagger's point inserted in a man's ear. There is no time for't now; this is a perilous place—"

Whereupon the men-at-arms set Michael on a horse, binding his wrists together behind him with the wrappings taken from the escaped Tatar. The Breton was badly shaken and bleeding from the mouth, but they handled him in no wise gently.

The minds of the servitors were full of the idea of satanic powers pursuing them. Since Michael showed no fear and had familiar knowledge of the pagan tribes, these men had no doubt that he was in league with the powers of darkness that their superstition conjured up.

Soranzi was torn between fear and greed. The astrologer in Venice had assured him of profits passing through his hands such as he had never seen before.

As for Clavijo, he was burning in the fires of conscience. He had lied. In his story before the Venetians he had repeated that his followers had been slain at the edge of terra incognita, and that the spirits of the wasteland had dogged his footsteps.

And now these two things had happened. He felt as if he were under a spell and found himself looking about for the tower of skulls that he had included in his tale. Only Rudolfo was free from superstition.

Under his quick orders the bulkier and less valuable portions of baggage and stores were abandoned. Sick horses were set loose. When they had mounted, Clavijo saw that no provision had been made for the sick servant or the dying soldier.

"You would not leave them, signor?" he cried.

Rudolfo shrugged.

"They will die anyway—"

When the cavalcade of mounted men and pack-animals moved off, Bembo slipped from the thicket where he had hidden during the hurried departure and ran among the horses, clinging to Soranzi's stirrup. The merchant, reduced to a state of panic by the events of the past hour, drove him off with kicks and blows.

"Leave the fool to his folly," gibed Gian, who noticed Bembo's frantic efforts to keep up.

"To leave him would be to reveal our course to those who pursue us," observed Michael. So Bembo was suffered to hold his friend's stirrup.

Chapter IX
The Ravine

There is a subtle intoxicant of fear in the hurry of many persons to be the first to reach a point of safety. The trot of the horses broke at times into a gallop. Some of the stores fell from the packs. Soranzi alternately cried upon God to witness the loss of valuable goods and prayed for greater haste.

The sun was obscured, a thin mist veiled the pine thickets and the stretches of sandy ground on either hand. The heat wilted their strength. Rudolfo turned many times, apparently thinking to throw pursuers off their track, but the track of a score of horses could not be concealed, Michael knew.

As evening closed in they were threading through gorges that hastened the coming of darkness. Often they looked back in the failing light. No one desired to be last. And then Rudolfo, in the lead, halted abruptly.

Before them in the twilight stood a great mound of human skulls.

"'Tis the Sign o' the Skull," muttered Bembo, "where we will sleep the night."

The jester voiced the fear that had come upon the party with the evening. Clavijo had ordered a huge fire to be lighted near the mound of human bones, and the ruddy glare of the flames shone upon a hundred grinning masks that had been men. Nor was it any chance collection of skeletons piled together on a battlefield. The pyramid of skulls was regular in shape and no body bones were visible.

The lighting of the fire brought night upon them with a rush, down the black bulk of the mountain slopes and the mouths of the rock gullies that opened into the gorge on either side. Instinctively the men kept close to the blaze, and they ate little dinner although they had fasted since morning. Michael sat apart under guard of a sentry and without food. By Rudolfo's orders he had been bound hand and foot and only the unexpected sight of the monument of skulls had delayed the torture that was preparing at Gian's hands.

Sight of the pyramid told Michael something unknown to the others and only guessed by Rudolfo. The *condottiere* had lost his way.

During the panicky run of the afternoon, when the sun was invisible behind clouds, Rudolfo unwittingly had doubled again on his course. Whereas Clavijo had started them north that morning; since then they had been circling blindly to the south and east.

And they had penetrated to the terra incognita—the gateway of the unknown land about which Clavijo had babbled. And to the place that Michael had known as the Gate of Shadows, where the five Christians had been buried.

It was a rare jest, thought Michael. Rudolfo was entering the place he had tried to shun, whither Michael had intended to lead him—and Clavijo, the liar, had beheld reality.

He heard a footfall behind him in the gloom and turned his head cautiously, for it was not the sentry's step. The soldier had moved off a score of paces toward the fire and stood leaning on a spear, his back toward Michael.

A foot from his eyes Michael made out the glimmer of steel in the faint light, and stiffened. A cloaked form took shape behind the dagger—a figure bent and stealthy. The knife was thrust forward even as Michael saw it, and its edge sliced away the bonds at his wrists.

Next, food on a wooden platter was placed in his cramped bands.

"Eat, for love of San Marco," breathed a trembling voice. "Brave Master Bearn, worthy captain, hearken but do not turn your head. I have given to the sentry—a murrain on his greed—a whole purse of good silver dinari, that he be blind and deaf for a short moment."

It was Soranzi, and a terrified Soranzi. Michael, as he munched the meat, reflected that Rudolfo's men were capable of taking a leaf from their master's book in selling their services.

"Pietro Rudolfo has dropped his mask with me," began the Venetian swiftly. "Alack! You spoke the truth this noon. I am ruined—beggared! He holds me captive and will take my goods—aye, every packet and bale. Every *soldi*'s worth."

He wrung his hands and plucked at his thin beard viciously.

"Once in Trebizond again, under the weak rule of the Comneni, Rudolfo claims all my store and the fine presents for the Cham as his, as payment for saving our lives, he said. O body of San Marco, O blessed head of the Pope! He will hold me for ransom—a prince's ransom—" Soranzi sighed, whereat his meager teeth fell to chattering.

"Do you not see the rest, Master Bearn? The varlets, save his *bravi*, are dead or will be. Clavijo cannot impeach him, for dread of the retribution of the council. You he will first try to bribe, believing that you, like himself, are bent on spoil. If you refuse his offer Gian will handle you till you reveal the way by which we may return to Trebizond."

"This is no news," said Michael shortly. "It means merely that Rudolfo knows that he has lost his way and is losing patience."

"But you will never see the walls of Trebizond. You will be left in a grave at Cabasica. Nay, more. Rudolfo, see you, with my goods and person in his hand, will attack and overpower the small Venetian outpost in the city. He will sell his spoils and perchance his sword to Genoa, which will pay a rare price. It was for this he sailed with us. Oh, we are lost! Yet the wise astrologer of my house in Venice predicted sight of extraordinary profits for me on this venture—the like of which I had never handled before."

Soranzi crept closer and clutched Michael's shoulder in a sweating hand.

"Good Master Bearn, you know this country. You are intimate with the pagan Moors and other infidels. I will pay well for a quick hand to aid me. Is it true you can lead us back from this accursed spot?"

Until now the Breton had been surveying the changing shadows on the black mountain walls that seemed to press down toward the fire.

"It is the Gate of Shadows," he said. "The *tengeri darband*. The Turks say that the spirits of a thousand dead, slain by this sword, walk in the valley of nights. It is the site of a massacre a generation ago. They shun it. Aye, it is a pass in the Ectag Mountains, through which Fra Odoric made his way out of the unknown land that lies beyond."

Even in his panic the merchant was struck by his companion's tone.

"You were here before? How may I know it?" Inbred suspicion struggled with his new desire to propitiate Michael.

"Behind the tower of skulls, in the sand of the gorge between two rocks that have the semblance of men's faces, you will find a grave with a cross, Soranzi."

"I have seen it."

"Five men are buried there. They were my mates, Christian slaves taken from a French caravel off the Anatolian shore."

"In the name of ——, why did you return hither?"

Michael stretched his stiff arm and laughed.

"To see the face of the king who did not fear the Turk."

The merchant's fears were thronging upon him.

"Hearken, Master Bearn. I see Rudolfo talking with Gian. You are a man of your word; I never doubted it. If I free your feet with this dagger—the knots be overstrong for fingers—and give you the weapon, will you stab Rudolfo when he comes hither? He will think you bound. The sentry is my man. He and I will set upon Gian, until you can join us. Money and their own fears will deliver the other two soldiers to us—"

"And if I will not?"

"Gian's knife in your ear. You want a larger bounty? Name it."

By now Rudolfo and his lieutenant were moving toward them slowly. Soranzi fairly capered in anxiety, holding the dagger just beyond Michael's reach.

"Swear!" he whispered. "Five hundred gold *byzants*—nay, seven hundred of Venetian weight and measure—"

"A pox on your mouthing," grunted Michael. "Be still!"

He was studying the surrounding darkness with interest. A stone had rolled from the mouth of a nearby gorge. From the plain outside the ravine he could make out the soft click-click where a horse's hoof struck upon rock.

Riders were closing in on the men by the fire. Michael had expected them for some time. Rudolfo, after carelessly letting the Tatar slip away, had left a trail broad enough for a blind man to follow.

Then, as if this were not enough, the Venetians had made a bonfire in the ravine that would indicate the exact position of their camp.

The question in Michael's mind was—were the newcomers Tatars or Turks? Evidently the former, since the Ottoman bands shunned the gorge that they had named the Gate of Shadows.

As he reached this conclusion Michael made out the figure of a horseman at the edge of the circle of firelight. It was a Tatar and the same Tatar that Michael had captured that noon.

One of the men-at-arms beheld the newcomer at the same moment and gave a startled cry. The cry was echoed by Michael's shout.

"Cast down your weapons, fools!"

He knew the danger of resistance if men of the Tatar horde had surrounded them. The dozen Christians, afoot and framed against the fire, would not be a match for half their number of mounted warriors, armed with bows.

Too startled to heed the warning, or believing that Michael meant to betray them to the riders who were emerging out of the shadows, the man-at-arms who had given the alarm cast his spear at the foremost rider.

Michael rose, felt the hindrance of the cords on his ankles, caught the knife from the petrified Soranzi, slashed himself free of bonds and thrust the weapon back into the merchant's hand.

Soranzi was clawing at him.

"Guard me! I will pay what you ask."

A score of horsemen rode into the firelight. The Venetian who had cast the spear was cut down by the Tatar who had dodged the missile easily.

Again Michael shouted to his party:

"Stand back! Sheath your swords if you do not love death. Ah, the cattle—" as the men ran about, seeking their weapons and sending a hasty arrow or two at the riders who swept over them with a quick rush of snorting horses and a red flash of swords in the firelight.

Gian ran close to the fire and wheeled, to cast a javelin at a gnome-like rider. The man went down, but a second Tatar caught the lieutenant's sword-thrust on his small round shield and split Gian's steel cap with a sweep of a heavy curved sword.

With a clash of armor Gian fell prone. The sentry who had been standing by Michael as if paralyzed now turned to flee into the dark, crying:

"The fiends of hell are loose! God have mercy upon our souls."

Michael reflected even as he ran toward the fire, avoiding the rush of a horseman, that men who fled from sword strokes and cried on God for help merited little mercy.

The sentry's shout of fear turned to a moan as the Tatar who had passed Michael overtook him in the outer rocks. Soranzi had fallen to his knees and being patently unarmed—the knife had dropped from his trembling hands—was spared for the moment.

Michael saw that Rudolfo had taken a stand between the fire and the tower of skulls, his sword gleaming, his thin lips writhing.

A rider spurred upon the *condottiere*—Michael noticed that the Tatar horses seemed trained to go anywhere, even near flames—and a squat black body swung from the saddle. The Tatar leader leaped at Rudolfo's head, taking the thrust of the Venetian's sword on his shield.

The weight of the flying body broke the blade like glass and the two men grappled on the ground.

"My left arm for a moment's truce!" thought Michael, turning to face the riders who were trotting up to him. The last of the men-at-arms had been struck down.

"Pax. Oh verily pax! Peace, my gentle dogs. If you are men, bethink you, there has been enough of slaying; if hellions, begone to purgatory, I conjure you—avaunt!"

With the exception of the warrior who was locked in Rudolfo's arms the Tatars reined in and looked up with exclamations of wonder. They saw Bembo.

The grotesquely striped and bedraggled figure of the fool squatted mid-way up the pyramid of skulls. His teeth were chattering and his long arms shot out from his body in frenzied exhortation.

Bembo had seized the first vantage-point to hand. Now he gazed hope-fully and imploringly at Michael. "Conjure the demons, Brother Michael; weave the spell you told us of—"

The half-moment of quiet was what Michael sought. He lifted his empty left hand and shouted one word in Turki.

"Ambassadors!"

One or two of the riders looked at him in surprise. Michael had learned in Bayezid's camp that in the Tatar country envoys to the khans or chiefs were inviolate. Ordinarily merciless, the Tatar war chiefs took pride in the number of emissaries from other lands that came to them with tribute.

And in several instances the Tatars kept faith better than the monarchs of Europe. They respected an envoy and were bitter in their rage against enemies who slew Tatar emissaries.

"Ambassadors are here," repeated Michael. "Are you dogs, to worry the stranger who comes with gifts?"

Those who understood his words repeated them to the others. The leader heard and rose from Rudolfo to stride to Michael.

His men joined him. They were short, brawny warriors, wearing furs and leather over their mail, and with bronze helmets bearing pointed guards that came down over brow and nose. Scarcely less black than their lamb's-wool kaftans were their faces, with slant hard eyes and thin mustaches.

Their short swords were broader at the end than the hilt, and each had a target of bull's hide on his left arm. Michael saw that the empty sad-dles bore quivers and bows.

"Well conjured, Brother Michael," chattered Bembo. "The charm was a mighty charm. I will aid you."

He started to scramble down from his mount when one of the warriors seized his leg and jerked him to earth, staring at him with ox-like curios-ity. Bembo's zeal dwindled.

He skipped away. The Tatar, no taller than the hunchback, made af-ter him with the rolling gait of one better accustomed to a horse's back than the earth.

"I am Gutchluk, a *noyon** of the White Horde," growled the leader to Michael. "I heard your bellow. Whom seek you?"

---

*A rank equivalent to baron.

Michael hesitated, for he did not know the name of the monarch of Tatary.

"The sultan?" queried Gutchluk. "Say so and we will sit you in the fire, for the sultan has made prisoner some of the lords of Tatary and our Horde is angered."

"Nay," said Michael promptly.

"At Cabasica your men said they were merchants."

"I am not a merchant. I seek the khan."

At this Gutchluk's expression changed.

"Tamerlane the Great," he cried. "You go to the Lord of the World?"

"Tamerlane the Great," repeated Michael.

The warriors who had been pawing over the stores now desisted and came over to the fire, bringing with them Rudolfo, who was watchful and alert in spite of his bruises.

Gutchluk stared at his captives for a space, grunting under his breath as an animal does when disturbed.

"So be it," he made decision. "We will take you and your gifts to the Mighty One and you can spit out your speeches to him."

With that the Tatars fell to ransacking the half-empty pots and sacks of food, gorging themselves enormously. Soranzi, who crept from hiding in the rocks, marveled at this and at the callous way in which the men of the Horde stepped on bodies of the slain. He sought Michael and found him talking to Clavijo.

"Now, my lord the liar," the Breton was saying; "here must you serve yourself. Lie roundly and mightily at Tamerlane's court or you are lost."

He withdrew to talk long with Bembo, while Rudolfo slept in company with the Tatars who were not on watch by the fire and where the horses were picketed.

Before an hour had passed Soranzi, who had been intent on binding up his goods again, saw that Bembo sat alone. Michael was not to be seen.

The Breton had seized a moment when the sentries were away from the fire to move back into the darkness of the outer gorge. He had marked the position of the outpost Gutchluk had placed and circled this with care for he had a healthy respect for the keen senses of the Tatar watchers.

Nor did he make the mistake of attempting to take a horse from the pickets. Instead he felt his way patiently out of the ravine at the place where they had entered it. He found the grave he had dug, and its cross. Then he crossed the plateau to the woods on the western side.

The first glimmer of dawn showed him one of the horses belonging to the Venetians that had strayed out to the grass during the fight. This he mounted and rode back along the trail Rudolfo had taken. Once he paused to dismount and search in the thicket for something. He emerged with the sword he had taken from Gutchluk twenty-four hours ago.

Thrusting this through his belt, he continued on to the west.

Michael had not left the camp because he feared retribution by Gutchluk for his attack upon the Tatar leader at this spot. Gutchluk had been following the Venetians, and Michael had surprised him and overcome him fairly. This would raise rather than lower him in the other's esteem.

But Michael was aware that emissaries to a Central Asian monarch were always detained for a long space before given an audience. The more important the ambassadors, the longer the delay. It would be weeks before Clavijo and his companions could hold speech with Tamerlane.

Meanwhile Gutchluk had said that the sultan and the khan were at the point of war. Michael, if he was to have a hand in events, could not afford to be kept idle in the Tatar camp. Moreover the foolish resistance of Rudolfo's men had lowered the status of the Venetians.

If Tamerlane was the man Michael thought him, it would take more than trade goods wrung from the captives to gain his ear. So Michael must bring to Tamerlane more than that.

Gutchluk had said that Bayezid and all his power was at Angora.

Was not this a good omen? Michael smiled, reflecting that he had sworn to the sultan that he would return to his court.

Now as he rode he kept swinging his right arm stiffly at his side. The blood was beginning to run through thinned veins and before long he would be able to use his crippled arm.

Chapter X
The Topaz Ring

It was as if Clavijo and his party had been snatched up by a hurricane. They were swept down from the gorge called the Gate of Shadows, swept out to the south upon the high, rolling steppe of Iran where the receding hills of Mazandaran showed purple against the sky to the north.

Beyond these same hills, farther to the north, stretched the Sea of Sarai—the Caspian—about which Clavijo had permitted his tongue to wag and which he had never seen, although Michael Bearn had bitter knowledge of it.

The Tatars halted for nothing, except a snatch of sleep at the hamlets of sheepherders or the bare walls of a Moslem khan by a caravan track. They, so Gutchluk explained by signs, were anxious to leave the borderland of the Turk behind. Not on their own account, for the men of the sultan were dogs, but to safeguard the precious persons of the ambassadors.

So they passed over the dry grass of Iran, away from the clay valleys and the groves of the land that was called Kuhistan, in Persia, and many interminable lines of clumsy camels they saw passing over the steppe at night, and many ant-like bodies of Tatar warriors mounted on shaggy ponies inimitably swift of foot. And Clavijo and his people marveled. The Tatars had swung to the right and were journeying now toward the setting sun.

But they saw naught of the city with brazen walls or the gold trees or the fountains of wine of the earthly paradise that Clavijo had called Cathay.

"*Hic ignotus sum quia passum,*" quoth Bembo the jester blithely three weeks later. "Here we are the barbarians, and the barbarians are the great lords and signors. Lord Gutchluk quarters us i' this penthouse and furnishes us a live ox, that we, poor Frankish outlanders, may eat in our cage like the hunting leopards I saw dragged past i' their leash this day at time o' mass."

They were, in fact, at a *serai* where a huge fire glowed over which the Tatars roasted the pieces of animals whole. The *serai* was almost the only building in what seemed to the travelers to be the encampment of a limitless army. For two weeks they had been kept waiting, in the midst of this army.

Bembo was like a man born anew. Gutchluk and the other Tatars had treated him respectfully, for he bore himself boldly and had clad his person in new finery from the stores.

"The mummery is on, i' faith," grinned the jester. "Aye, each buffoon of us has his part to play. Behold Signor Dominus, the consul-general Clavijo—the great lord-treasurer, *proveditore*, Soranzi—likewise Rudolfo, the lord-general and master of armies. And most of all, behold Bembo, the wise councilor, the privy coz, the whisperer of kings. Without him, my hearties, the rooks would be emptying your eye sockets back in yonder Inn o' the Skull."

Clavijo frowned.

"Tamerlane will see us this noon," he said. "We have been kept waiting long."

"Aye, verily. The delay measures our importance i' the eyes o' these gentlefolk. Two days agone Lord Gutchluk and a baron who looks like a prince of Eblis took our gifts to the king, along with the camels of a khan of Karabak and the painted giant beasts with a tail where their nose should be—the beasts that are gifts from a lord of Khorassan. Now our turn has come and you must lie cleverly or be fed to the beasts, see you?"

"We can say we are an embassy from Venice."

"Nay, San Marco forbid. Firstly, the council, hearing that we who are mere voyagers have usurped ambassadorial role, would slit our throats. Secondly, there would be no need o' that, for Tamerlane would have us tied to the ground for his giant beasts to walk upon."

Bembo smiled at the consternation written in the Spaniard's face.

"Signor Gutchluk," he explained, "confessed to me not an hour since that recently certain merchants of Venice penetrated so far as Damascus and endeavored to sell nostrums and false sovereign waters i' the fashion o' mountebanks, and to claim exemption from taxes and gifts as is their wont. The Tatars threw them into the river. So, my cousins, we cannot be Venetians for the word rings so ill i' the ears of these barbarians as the Venetian nostrums i' their bellies."

They were silent at that, looking blackly at the man whose tale had brought them—Soranzi, Rudolfo, and the injured Gian—hither.

"I tell you," swore Rudolfo, "that Bearn has betrayed us. Why else is he escaped here hence with a whole skin, leaving us to damnation?"

Michael's departure from the Gate of Shadows had puzzled the Tatar guards as well as Rudolfo. The warriors had searched for him briefly without result and had then pressed on to their army. What mattered it to them if one of the Franks chose to part company with them, so long as the chief ambassadors, as they considered Clavijo and Rudolfo, and the all-important gifts remained?

"He will return to us this night or the morrow," asserted Bembo stoutly. "He pledged it me the night he left us. Who are we that we should know his comings or that which he seeks in this land?"

"'Twere wiser, methinks, to question who he is." Rudolfo strode surlily back and forth in front of the clay platform by the fire on which Bembo squatted.

So pliable is human nature that Clavijo and Soranzi had come to look upon the *condottiere* as a possible protector in their plight. At least they feared the Tatars—who seemed to them like animals—more than they feared Rudolfo, now that Michael had vanished.

"Is he not leagued with these pagan demons?" demanded the Italian. "What will his coming avail us? Nay, we must trust to our wits to cut a way out of this coil. I have heard the Sultan of the Turks, whose power is not far from this camp, is a rich monarch, different from these beasts. Now if we could—"

He broke off as Bembo chuckled.

"So this is Cathay!" grinned the jester. "We must be bewitched, for we saw naught of Clavijo's golden city."

The Spaniard winced.

"Your master swore we would be safe here," he said uneasily. The coming ordeal of the audience with Tamerlane weighed on the three of them. Bembo alone was careless.

Having the gift of tongues, the jester had conversed in broken Greek with Gutchluk and his faith in Michael was strong.

"My master is a true man," he insisted. "He said he would join us at Tamerlane's court at the first of the new moon. He will keep his word."

Here they looked up as Gutchluk entered with another powerful warrior in black armor; the man Bembo had termed a prince of Eblis. The ambassadors were summoned by Tamerlane, who awaited them.

They mounted and rode through the Tatar encampment, seeing on every hand nothing but horses, sleeping warriors, smiths who labored at smoking forges, herders who guided great masses of cattle hither and yon in the dust.

Then a vista of round tents opened before them. Some of these were on massive wagons; some bore standards of fluttering yaks' tails. It was a veritable city of tents.

Hard-faced men glanced at them casually; black slaves made haste to get out of their way. Once a line of elephants passed, hauling sleds on which were wooden machines of war, unknown to them.

It seemed to the cringing Soranzi that they had invaded a city of beasts. He heard a lion roar from the cages where Tamerlane's animals were kept. He saw giraffes brought from Africa penned in a staked enclosure. Yet his merchant's eye noted the barbaric splendor of gold-inlaid armor, jeweled weapons, costly rugs spread within the tents and women's cloaks fashioned of ostrich feathers.

What kind of monarch, he thought, ruled over this hive-like multitude of pagans?

Tamerlane the Great, King of Kings, Lord of the East and West, extended a gnarled hand across the chessboard and touched his opponent's king.

"*Shah rohk*," he said. "The game is mine."

He freed a long ruby from one bent finger and handed it to the man who knelt across the board from him—a silk-clad Chinese general who had come from the edge of the Gobi to pay homage.

Few could match wits even with fair success with the Tatar conqueror, for Timur-i-leng* had fashioned himself a board with many times the usual number of squares and men.

Gathered about the board were princes of Delhi, emirs of Bokhara, and khans of the White and Black Tatars and the powerful Golden Horde that reached to the shores of the Volga. They were standing under a gigantic pavilion stretched upon supports taller than the masts of ships. Over the head of the conqueror hung silk streamers, swaying in the evening breeze, for the sides of the pavilion were open and the men within could look out from the dais on which they stood, over the tents of the army.

"Summon the Frank ambassadors," ordered Tamerlane.

They came through one of the outer porticos of the purple pavilion—Clavijo and Soranzi and Bembo, each with his arms gripped on either side by a Tatar noble. They were worried and anxious, for they had ridden for six hours through the army that never seemed to have an end.

The custom of holding envoys by the arms seemed to them ominous. Clavijo stared at the kneeling Tatar, noting his big, bent shoulders, his massive length of body, his shaggy brows and hard eyes. Tamerlane, nearly seventy years of age, was near-sighted—a peculiarity that made his naturally fierce stare the more difficult to bear.

Soranzi blinked at the low table of solid gold on which the Tatar leaned and muttered under his breath as he tried to estimate the value of a blue diamond in Tamerlane's plain steel helmet.

"From whom do you bear submission and greetings to me?" demanded the monarch. His speech had to be translated into Persian and then Greek, through two interpreters.

---

*Timur the Lame.

Clavijo's broad brow was damp with perspiration. To gain time to think, he said that he did not understand.

"Then take those dogs of interpreters and lead them through the army by a rope thrust into their noses," commanded the Tatar at once. "Bring others who are wiser."

The two unfortunates threw themselves on their knees, and Clavijo paled. Bembo spoke up, kneeling and crossing his hands on his chest.

"Great khan," he observed in Greek, "their words were clear; it was my companion, the dominus, who was dazed by the splendor of your presence."

This, being interpreted by other mouths, satisfied Tamerlane and he motioned to the interpreters to continue.

"Franks," he resumed, "I have taken your gifts. The cloth-of-silver and gold pleased me. From what king do you come, from the other end of the earth?"

Hereupon Soranzi could not restrain a murmur of anguish. The bales of cloth had been his personal stock in trade, now lost beyond repair. Clavijo bowed and at last found an answer.

"From the King of—of Spain," he replied.

"Good! I have heard of him. How is my son, the King of Spain? Is his health good? Has he much cattle and treasure?"

They stared at Clavijo, these Armenians, Tatars and Chinese. The Europeans were quite a curiosity—petty envoys from a tiny kingdom somewhere at the end of the world.

They had come, so reasoned the Tatars, to bask in the magnificence of the Lord of the East and West.

Clavijo was very much afraid. He would have welcomed the sight of Michael Bearn's cheerful face. But he gathered assurance as he began to describe the splendors of Aragon, enlarging upon the great ships and towns of Spain.

At this, however, Tamerlane began to pay more attention to a topaz ring that he turned and twisted upon a sinewy hand.

Fearing that his tale was lacking fire, Clavijo began to exaggerate as was his want, until he was boasting hugely. Tamerlane scowled under bushy brows, first at the speaker, then at the ring. Finally he held up his hand for the Spaniard to see.

"Behold, Frank, a magician's stone," he said gruffly. "The topaz turns purple when anyone lies to me. I always watch it and it has served me well."

Superstitious, as all men of his time and race, Clavijo stared in dismay. Indeed his round face turned a very good shade of purple. His flow of words dwindled as he scanned the topaz and fancied that it changed color.

This might well have been due to the twilight that was falling upon the great pavilion.

"Frank," observed the conqueror, "you come at a good time. My army is mounted for war against the Sultan Bayezid. He has preyed upon my subjects in lesser Armenia, and I have offered him terms by which he may save his head. We will hear what he will reply."

To hear the sultan who was the scourge of Christendom mentioned as Tamerlane might speak of a slave added fuel to Clavijo's active imagination.

"If there is a battle, you will see a goodly sight," repeated the old conqueror. "Does my son the King of Spain fight battles or is he a dog of a merchant like the Venetians?"

Clavijo essayed a reply, glanced at the topaz ring which seemed to him to be now a deep purple indeed, and the last of his courage oozed from him. Breaking from the Tatar warriors who held his arms, he fell on his knees.

"Mercy, great lord," he bellowed. "Oh, mercy. Grant me royal clemency if I have offended. Make me a captive, but spare my life!"

This being interpreted, Tamerlane smiled. "Verily," he said shortly, "the Frank is frightened by my face. Nay, Timur the Tatar has harmed no ambassador. Fear not, but join in our feast."

He signed to the men who held the visitors. Soranzi, a-tremble with anxiety, took this to be a signal for their destruction. Without waiting for the speech to be translated, he flung himself at the Tatar's feet, embracing his slippers.

"O King of Kings," he cried, "my companion has lied, even as your wisdom has suspected. He is naught but a seeker after gold, disguised as an envoy. The gifts that pleased you were mine. I will pay more. Do not believe this traitor when he says that I am a merchant, for he is a liar—"

Surprised by this outburst, Tamerlane turned to the interpreters with a scowl.

"Now the fat is in the fire," sighed Bembo.

Tamerlane pulled at his thin mustache, his small black eyes darting from one to the other. He surveyed his topaz ring and grunted. There was something wolfish now in the stare of the Mongol warriors.

Rudolfo swore under his breath and Soranzi did not cease to moan his fear. Since the attack by the riders at the Gate of Shadows his dread had grown upon him. That afternoon he had seen captives of the khan hauled through the camp in cages, like beasts.

"The gifts were mine," he repeated over and over, holding fast to the Tatar's slipper.

"Then you are not ambassadors sent to Tamerlane?"

"Nay." Clavijo and Soranzi were answering in one breath when Gutchluk knelt and addressed his lord, saying that the Franks had purported to be merchants before their capture.

Tamerlane was a man who never minced words and hated deceit. He was about to speak when there was a bustle in the outer porticos. A man flung himself from an exhausted horse, crying—

"A courier for the khan!"

Those who had crowded about Clavijo and his party gave back at this, opening a lane between Tamerlane and the newcomer, barely visible in the half-light of evening, who bowed thrice and knelt before the dais.

"O King of Kings," the horseman cried in Arabic, "I have beheld the answer of the sultan. He has struck off the heads of the Tatars' envoys and placed them at the gate of Angora. Thus Bayezid has made answer to you."

The old Tatar's face grew dark and veins stood out on his forehead. He caught his sword from its sheath and swung it over the head of the unfortunate messenger who remained quietly kneeling.

Then the khan checked the sweep of his blade midway and stood staring out into the dusk, his face a mask of anger. Yet when he spoke, his words were measured and deep.

"Aye, there will be a battle." He looked down at the courier. "You are a brave man. Take twenty horses and go, that your face will not remind me of the deed you bespoke."

Replacing his sword, Tamerlane ordered that the army be ready to march on the morrow. For the first time Clavijo noted the great bulk of the Tatar and the fact that he was lame. In his youth, during an affray with the Seljuk Turks, Tamerlane had been beaten from his horse and cast to earth with three ribs broken and a mangled side.

Turning back to his chessboard, he observed the Europeans who still remained held by their guards.

"Come with my court, liars and merchants," he said grimly. "Instead of jugglers and musicians, you will amuse me, for I will pass judgment upon you then."

Chapter XI
The Thunderbolt

Two weeks before Tamerlane's audience with the Christians, the stars traced the outline of the river Khabur in Anatolia, two hundred miles west of Tamerlane's camp. Down the river toward the flat roofs of the town of Angora drifted a small skiff, only half-visible in the glittering light from the stars, which seemed intensified by the heat of the windless July night.

But the stars were eclipsed by the myriad torches and lanterns of Angora and the illumination of ten thousand tents clustered about the Turkish town.

Bayezid, his court, and his army held festival. Angora, an unfortified trading town, yet served admirably for mobilizing the army of the Ottomans and Seljuks. Galleys had come from Greece, where the Crescent ruled, to land their loads of Moslems on the Anatolian shore across from Constantinople; the mamelukes had sent their splendid cavalry hither from Alexandria; the veteran main army of the sultan had been withdrawn temporarily from the conquest of Constantinople.

So Angora was filled with the warriors of a dozen kingdoms. Forbidden wine flowed freely and revelry held the courtyards and roofs. The sultan knew how to hold the loyalty of his men by pleasure and by generous pay, which reinforced the natural fanaticism of the Moslems and the devotion of the janissaries—that formidable mass of soldiery recruited from Christian child slaves raised by Moslem teachers.

The skiff drifted with the current of the river to the jetties of the town, already crowded with native craft. Michael Bearn raised himself cautiously, clutched the side of a fishing-boat, and climbed to the jetty.

"Who comes?"

A sharp challenge rang from a pair of spearmen standing at the shore end of the dock. Michael stiffened, then advanced carelessly.

"A sailor," he made answer in his good Arabic, "from the Byzantine coast. I have heard that the great sultan is here and I have come to look upon his face."

A lantern was brought from an adjoining hut and the two spearmen looked him over casually. Michael's skin was burned a deep brown by the sun and he had secured a short cloak that concealed the outlines of his stalwart body. His leather tunic and bare knees bore out the identity he claimed.

"Does a son of a dog think to look upon the favored of Allah?" gibed one of the Moslems. "Stay—you have been a slave on the galleys."

The soldier's sharp glance had noted the scars on Michael's wrists where the irons had pressed.

"Aye," assented the Breton; "a galley slave." He tapped his stiffened arm. "But useless, my lord warrior. I have been freed in a battle."

His pulse quickened, for he knew the strict discipline of Bayezid's army—despite the appearance of revelry—and was aware that every precaution was being taken, now that the battle with Tamerlane was impending.

"You are no true follower of the prophet," said the sentry sharply. Michael's curls, escaping from under his loose cap, revealed that he was not one of the orthodox Moslem peoples.

"Your wisdom is fine as a rare gem," acknowledged he. "I am a Christian who has not seen his own country for many years. My lord warrior, I pray you let me pass into the town where there is wine to be given away and sweets made of grapes and flour and butter. I have not eaten for two days."

This was strictly true. Michael's tone was that of the hopeless slave addressing his guards. The sentry sneered and ran his hand under Michael's cloak to make sure that he held no weapon, and then fell to cursing his own fate that kept him from the feasting. Michael made off.

At the river gate of the town he was confronted by the head of a Mongol—one of the envoys from Tamerlane—caked with dried blood, stuck upright upon a spear. The crowd of soldiery and townspeople surging through the gate paused to spit at the wax-like features and to heap insults on the Tatars.

Michael was carried in with the throng, but now his eyes held a new light and his lips were hard with purpose. He knew for the first time the certainty of conflict between the sultan and the khan.

At the river's edge, upstream, he had bought his new cloak with a few silver pieces and the cap to match. He had cast away his sword to carry out his character of freed galley slave.

Now Michael was among the alleys of Angora over which the crescent standard hung. He glanced indifferently at the lighted balconies where costly rugs were hung and at the magic lantern pictures that Arabs were displaying in darkened corners. He heard the distant chant of fanatical imams, exhorting the Moslems in the mosques.

Asking his way from a drunken *sipahi*, he approached the walled gardens where Bayezid and his court held feast.

The heat grew instead of lessening that night. The glimmer of heat lightning more than once darkened the gleam of the stars. This the imams, crying from balcony and courtyard, announced as a good omen.

"The Thunderbolt will strike!" they said. "The world trembles."

The heat impelled Bayezid and his divan—the councilors who feasted with him—to leave the torrid rooms of the house, where they were guarded by a double line of Ottoman infantry, and to seek the gardens where an artificial lake shaded by cypresses offered moderate comfort.

On this lake was a floating kiosk of teakwood inlaid with mother-of-pearl, its roof fragrant with flowers, with curtains drawn back to allow free passage to the air.

Bayezid, flushed with the stimulus of bhang and opium, lay back on his cushions, idly watching the play of torchlight reflected in the lake. The grandees were intent on a spectacle of women and boys who danced in iridescent garments of moghrebin and chrysoliths at the edge of the garden by the kiosk.

These feasts had been ordered by Bayezid, who felt himself at the summit of his power. Now he surveyed the splendor around him through half-closed eyes.

"We will make a welcome," he murmured, "for the Tatar boor. News has come to me that he advances with his power upon the Khabur."

They nodded assent—sheik, malik, and caliph.

"When he comes to the Khabur," went on Bayezid, "I will have a hunt declared. My troops will aid me in the pursuit of game. That will show the Tatar how much we esteem him."

Some of the councilors looked more than a little startled. It was no light thing to hunt game in the presence of Tamerlane's army. And Bayezid had ordered the Mongol envoys slain, wantonly, as it seemed.

The man who was called the Thunderbolt turned sleepy eyes to the dark face of the Sheik of Rum, in whose country they were encamped.

"Give orders for ten thousand beaters to be mustered from the town. It is my will."

The official prostrated himself and muttered:

"Tamerlane has forty thousand infantry and twice that number of riders, O Guardian of the Faith. Will you pursue the beasts of the field when such a host stands across the river?" He plucked up courage from the sultan's silence. "Bethink you, Star of the East, there is but one cloud upon the face of your sky—Tamerlane. You have gained the Danube; Constantinople will be yours as Greece is now—then the rest of Frankistan. And, when Tamerlane falls, Iran, Tatary, and India—"

"Sheik," Bayezid smiled, "have you forgotten my spies in the Tatar camp?"

In this manner was it ordained by the sultan that they should mock Tamerlane. Festival was to be held in the town, even when the Tatar horsemen occupied the opposite bank of the Khabur. The bulk of the Seljuk knights—the pick of the host—was to be kept in its tents by the town.

The councilors, hearing this, wondered whether ceaseless conquests had not affected the mind of Bayezid. But the leaders of the mamelukes and janissaries smiled, saying that they were invincible and—some beasts to be slain must be first trapped.

Michael Bearn, sitting among the cypresses on the farther bank of the lake where there were no guards, watched the feast of Bayezid until dawn reddened the sky across the river and the call of the muezzin floated over the roofs of Angora.

He was studying again the brilliant assemblage of grandees that he had seen at times from a distance during his captivity. He noticed the councilors start up from their cushions. By the fading light of the torches he could see them staring up at the sky.

Almost at the same time he heard a sound—a shrill cry that was more like a scream. It rose from one side of the miniature lake, swelled, and dwindled swiftly.

Michael knew the cry of herons and waterfowl. This was different. It was more like the scream of a horse in pain. Yet it had sounded a hundred feet above the kiosk. A shout reached his ears from the kiosk, a bowshot away.

"The warning of Tamerlane!"

Guards were running here and there about the lake. Torches advanced along the shore toward him from the palace. It was no time to sit wondering about the source of the queer sound in the air. Broad daylight would be upon him in a moment.

Cautiously Michael began to crawl through the willow thickets of the lakeside, toward a gully by which he had gained his point of vantage. The light was strong enough for him to see his way.

He stumbled over something projecting from the ground and found that it was an arrow. With some difficulty he pulled it out, for his curiosity had been aroused by its weight.

Instead of a point, the shaft terminated in a hollow steel cylinder, perforated in the sides. Michael weighed it in his hand and chuckled. Such an arrow as this, sent from a powerful bow, would emit a loud whistling sound when passing through the air. In fact it had been the passage of this shaft that he had just heard.

The arrow was plainly of Tatar make and Michael guessed that some man of Tamerlane's, hidden in the rushes across the lake, had sent it as a warning to Bayezid. He thrust the shaft under his cloak, and, hearing footsteps approaching, made his way down the gully.

For several days thereafter Michael was very busy. He frequented the bazaar, heard the news of the preparation for the sultan's hunt, and out on the plain of Angora behind the town saw regiments of janissaries drilling constantly.

And he noticed another head on the Angora gate-posts—an old Tatar fisherman who had been seen more than once dragging his nets in the river. Under the head a large bow had been placed.

Michael guessed that the man who had fired the whistling arrow would not report his feat to Tamerlane.

He heard great emirs say openly in the town that Bayezid was drunk with power and with wine. Litters of Moslem women and captives from Georgia and Greece were passing constantly through the streets.

The finest cavalry of the sultan was encamped a league behind the town, apart from the rest of the army. Angora was continually a-throng with merrymakers, as if the fast of Ramadan had just been broken.

Knowing the inexorable discipline of the Ottoman army and the merciless cunning of Bayezid, Michael doubted the evidence of his senses. This was no idle laxity or sport such as the Thunderbolt was accustomed to use in pleasuring his men.

Even when Tatar horsemen were seen, swooping about the plain across the river, there was no sign of any preparation made to meet Tamerlane.

But when Michael made his way down to the riverbank one cloudy night, he found the boats that were drawn up on shore filled with men, and out in the center of the Khabur he could discern the black bulk of guard ships moving back and forth.

"Bayezid waits!" He laughed silently. "Aye, and thus he waited at Nicopolis! I begin to see the answer to the riddle. And now, for a visit to the sentry post that welcomed me at the jetty. Grant the same two janissaries be on watch; the hour is the same."

Dawn revealed two unexpected things to the officers of the janissaries who commanded the guard at the riverfront.

On a small dock two spearmen lay bound and gagged beside an extinguished lantern. The white woolen turban, the kaftan, and bow of one were gone.

And one of the guard boats reported that its steersman was missing. A janissary, the men of the galley said, had come on board when they were putting out from the shore—a warrior who declared that he knew the river and was skilled in managing a galley. He had carried a bow.

Before an hour had passed, so the tale was repeated, this helmsman had disappeared from the craft, taking with him the steering oar. They had not heard him fall overboard. But at the end of the hour they heard a whistling arrow, shot into the air from the other side.

Michael's penetration of the Ottoman lines had been comparatively simple because the Turk guards—not yet drawn up in battle order—had not looked for a foe from within.

One of the sentries he had found at a distance from the lantern and had stunned with a blow on the forehead. The other, running toward the slight noise, had been easily overcome by the powerful Breton.

Michael exulted in the fact that his right arm was once more serviceable after a fashion. Stripping one of the guards of tunic, cloak, and cap, he had gained access to a galley.

Not trusting as yet to his right arm, he had taken the steering oar with him when he dropped over the stern of the galley to swim to the farther shore.

Here, to disturb further his late companions and to test his arm, he had let fly the cylinder-headed arrow over the river.

Now he began to run up from the bank of the Khabur, casting aside his cloak as he went and unwinding the cumbersome turban. It would not be very long, he knew, before he would encounter Tatar patrols and he did not wish to be cut down as a janissary.

Michael had gained what he had come for. He had guessed the riddle of Bayezid's inaction and the revelry in Angora. An ambush was being prepared for Tamerlane.

The Tatars were to be beguiled into an attack and a trap was to be set for them on the river.

Michael studied the stars overhead and shaped his course by them, shaking his head as he made out a crescent moon on the horizon. He would be late for his rendezvous with Bembo.

Chapter XII
Tamerlane Decides

It was the night set for the Tatar attack. The Lame Conqueror had been riding slowly among his host, listening as was his wont to the talk of the warriors about the campfires. Tamerlane, what with his age and the pain of his old injuries, seldom slept.

When the middle watch had ended and quiet had fallen in some degree on the Mongol army, he retired to his small tent and lay down on the plain mattress that served him for a bed. He read slowly, because of his poor sight, the annals of his ancestors and the tales of past battles written down by the chroniclers.

The plan of attack for the coming day had been decided upon, and every *khatun* had his orders, which in turn were transmitted to the *tumani*—the commanders of a thousand and to the khans of the hundreds. Tamerlane, however, was restless. News had reached him from the fisherfolk of the river that the Turkish grandees were at revelry, and Bayezid himself had ordered a hunt, even within sight of the Tatar array.

This puzzled the Conqueror.

Impatiently he ordered his ivory and ebony chessboard set before him, then brushed it aside, for there was no one in attendance who could play the mimic game of warfare as Tamerlane desired. He lifted his broad head and signed to a Mongol archer at the tent's entrance.

"Bring hither the Franks. I will pass judgment upon them."

It would amuse him, perhaps until dawn, to probe the souls of the Christians from the end of the world who had tried to throw dust in the eyes of the Conqueror of the World.

He surveyed them grimly as they knelt before him, their finery rumpled by the confinement of the past few days. Fear was plainly to be read in their white faces—save that of Bembo. The jester was a philosopher.

Bembo was thinking that Clavijo's Grand Cham had proved to be a
strange sort of monarch indeed. Steel and wool that clad Tamerlane's
long body were hardly the silks and chrysoliths about which the Spaniard had boasted.

The brazen city of Cathay had become a city of tents. The gold house
of the khan was constructed, so Bembo perceived, of bull's hide. And instead of winning wealth, joined with perpetual life, they had been deprived of their own goods—or rather Soranzi had—and bade fair to earn
a swift death.

The others had not failed to remind Bembo that Michael Bearn had not
appeared as he had promised. To this the jester returned only a wink.

He had recognized Michael in the courier who had come in native attire from Angora. He knew that Michael was in the camp and would seek
him out.

The moon was already five days old.

"Does this Frank," Tamerlane observed to the interpreters, indicating
Soranzi, "confess that he is a merchant and a thief?"

At this Soranzi, reading Tamerlane's harsh countenance, broke forth
into feverish words, which the interpreters explained to their lord.

"Aye, sire. O Great Khan. Splendor of the World! O monument of mercy
and essence of forgiveness! O Conqueror of Asia. Grant but one small iota
of mercy to your slave."

Tamerlane nodded, unsmiling.

"I will. See yonder weapons?"

"Aye my lord." Soranzi's eyes widened at sight of jewel-inlaid scimitars and gold-chased helmets and silver camails hung upon the walls of
the tent.

"They were taken from my enemies, merchant-thief. It will now be
the duty of your life to furnish and cleanse the spoil that I shall take.
Dog, do you understand? You may smell of the riches you may not taste.
Pocket but one *zecchin* of this store and your bowels shall be let out with
a knife. Go, to your work."

Soranzi trembled and could not refrain from a frantic plea.

"But my goods?"

"Begin by writing down an account of them—for me."

The Tatar was not lacking in a rough sense of humor. He was naturally
merciless, yet he had no love of torture. A man without a god, a man fash-

ioned for dealing destruction, he could still tolerate another man's faith
in God, and he admired courage.

"You say that you are a warrior." He addressed Rudolfo, who was watching him in sullen dread. "Good. You have seen my ranks and the camp of
my foe the sultan. Tell me how your Frankish would plan the battle."

Rudolfo licked his lips and tried to speak out clearly, but his voice quivered. He described the order of battle of the Italian mercenaries—skirmishing by irregulars, the entrenchment of pikemen behind abatis, the feints and
countermarches that produced the bloodless battles of his knowledge.

This recital Tamerlane ended with a grunt of anger.

"I did not ask you how your children played. I will have you placed
with the Tatar boys and girls tomorrow by the river, where you may see
a battle."

Glancing contemptuously over Clavijo, he stared at Bembo's sad face
and gay attire.

"What kind of man is this?"

The jester rose and bowed ceremoniously.

"I am your cousin, O King," he stated cheerily.

Tamerlane frowned, puzzled.

"Because," pointed out the jester, "I am maimed for the fight, whereas
you are lame for the flight."

"If you are maimed, you are useless and need not live."

"So be it," agreed Bembo. "I am not afraid. Nevertheless, I would fain
set eyes upon my other cousin who is only maimed in the arm."

"Who is that?" asked the matter-of-fact khan.

"A wiser man, Messer Tamerlane, than all of us put together."

Tamerlane looked around as if to mark this other Frank. He noticed a
helmeted emir who salaamed within the entrance of the tent.

"The other Frank," announced the newcomer, as Tamerlane signed
for him to speak, "seeks admittance to the presence of the Lord of the
East and West."

Two archers of the guard held Michael Bearn by the arms. Bembo and
Rudolfo—Soranzi and the Spaniard had been dismissed—stared at him
in surprise.

He had grown leaner, his face blackened by the sun. Around his shoulders was a rich fur kaftan and silk trousers covered the tattered bindings
of his legs.

The emir who had announced him bowed again before Tamerlane.

"O Kha Khan, we know not this man. Yet, because of his claim, we could not refuse him admittance." The officer glanced at the silent khan and pointed to Michael. "He claims that he is to play with you at chess—as you play it."

In contrast to the flowery etiquette of Bayezid's court, Tamerlane, who was impatient of ceremony, always encouraged direct speech. Now he frowned at Michael as if trying to recall something that escaped his mind.

"I have come to play," assented Michael gravely, "the game that the great khan plays. It is known to me."

Tamerlane's brow cleared. Michael had spoken in his good Arabic, and with this the Tatar, who liked to read the Moslem annals, was familiar. The Lame Conqueror made a practice of treating well all scholars, astronomers, and men of learning whom he took prisoner.

"You are a bold man," he said. "Three days ago when you came to me as a courier from Angora I ordered that you should not let me see your face again. I gave you horses. Why did not you ride hence?"

Bembo had known that Michael was the horseman who had reached the purple tent in the plain three days before. As Michael had not greeted him at that time Bembo had kept silent, trusting that what his friend did was for the best.

The jester did not know what a desperate game his friend was playing nor that Michael, having heard that evening of Bembo's plight, had resolved to stake their lives on a single throw.

"Because, O Kha Khan," the Breton rejoined, "it came to my ears that you lacked a man to play at *shahk** in the manner of Tamerlane, which is not that of other men of feebler minds."

The khan weighed this in silence, then motioned for the emir, the captives, and interpreters to withdraw to the farther side of the tent, in the shadow. He signed for the two archers to kneel at either side of the chessboard which lay in front of him under the flickering candles.

"So be it," he assented grimly. "Frank, set up the men. Your daring earns you the chance. If you have deceived me, and cannot play as you profess, these two dogs of mine will cut you in two. Your countrymen, Frank, have deceived Tamerlane. Beware lest you do likewise."

---

*Chess.

It was a long speech for the blunt Tatar to make. He was interested. His small black eyes gleamed as he watched Michael squat on his heels before the board. Only the Persian, the Grand Mufti, Nuruddeen Abderrahman Esferaini, who had come to Tamerlane from Baghdad, and the Chinese general of Khoten had been able to cope with the Conqueror on the enlarged board and with the double number of pieces.

Now Tamerlane set up his men swiftly on his side of the board and motioned for Michael to do likewise.

Bembo, whose ready wit had grasped much of what was happening, knew that his friend could not play even the simpler game of chess as brought to Venice by the crusaders of the century before. So the jester grimaced and bit his thumb, invoking the lion of Saint Mark to Michael's aid.

The Breton fingered the array of miniature gold warriors, fashioned in the likeness of tiny horsemen, archers, elephants and *rohks*—castles—and with a single large effigy of a king. He knew neither the pieces nor their moves.

"Break off the head of one of your arrows," he ordered an archer.

The warrior hesitated, glancing at his chief, and then obeyed. Michael laid the wooden shaft carefully across the board midway between him and Tamerlane.

Then, smiling, he set up the pawns along his side of the arrow's shaft, and behind them the knights. Taking the thin gold chain given him by Contarini from his throat, he placed it near his end of the board, and within its circle the castles and the towering figure of the king.

In the clear space behind the gold circlet he stood up the jeweled castles. Tamerlane surveyed him fixedly, evidently growing angry. The Tatar's pieces had been set up in the orthodox fashion, very different from the queer array of the European's men.

"Explain!" he barked.

Michael touched the arrow. "The Khabur river." His finger rested on the tiny pawns. "Ships and archers." He pointed to the gold circlet. "Angora and its troops. Bayezid, the king who is the prize of the game." Last he indicated the castles. "The sultan's heavy cavalry on the plain of Angora."

Leaning forward, he ran his finger along the gold pieces—his own were silver. "The army of Timur the Lame, Conqueror of India, and the Caliphate." He looked at the impassive Tatar. "This is the game that you play, O Kha Khan. And there is no other in the world today who can play it with you—save Bayezid the Sultan. His pieces will I play as he has planned. It is for you to make the first move."

The lines in Tamerlane's withered face deepened and his black eyes snapped.

"You are a spy!"

"Perhaps. You may call me so." Michael's thin nostrils quivered, and the smile left his face. "I have been in Angora. I heard the whistling arrow fall. Before that for three years I marched with Bayezid."

Tamerlane did not shift his gaze. "Proof!"

Thrusting his hand under his kaftan, Michael drew forth the long folds of a janissary's turban, spotted in places with blood. He pointed to the scars on his wrists.

"A slave, O Kha Khan." He touched again the gold chain. "A gift for service rendered at Nicopolis where the host of Frankistan was broken by the craft of the sultan. Ten thousand Christians were slain there, after they had been taken captive."

To this Tamerlane seemed indifferent. One religion, to him, was the same as another. He was trying to judge Michael's purpose. His interest in the strange maneuver of the Christian upon the chessboard still held him passive.

Bembo plucked at the arm of the watchful *condottiere*.

"See you, Rudolfo, Cousin Michael holds the Chain in leash, but methinks 'tis a thin, silken leash whereby our lives hang—"

Decision had come to Tamerlane.

"You are an enemy of the Ottoman."

"Slavery under the Ottoman crippled me." Michael's gray eyes lighted. He had risked much to lead Tamerlane to make the statement that, spoken first by Michael, must be received with natural suspicion. "His men slew my brothers-in-arms. I have waited six years to strike a blow against him who is the greatest foe of my faith. I have heard in the Angora palace Bayezid boast that he will set your head, O Kha Khan, upon a spear before the Gate of Paradise at Damascus. Yet you alone can humble Bayezid. Will you let me serve you?"

"How?" It was typical of Tamerlane that he did not ask what reward the other might expect. Those who aided the Lame Conqueror received kingdoms; those who failed, death; unless flight saved them, which was seldom.

"It is for the Kha Khan to move." Michael smiled again and motioned at the chessboard. "The sultan's men have caught a flying pigeon that bore one of your messages to Tatary saying that you would force the passage of the Khabur at Angora and drive Bayezid before you."

"True. The dog hunts. Aye, after he has seen my army. Disaster will come upon him for that effrontery, and the slaughter of my envoys." Tamerlane's eyes glowed fiercely. "Our Tatar hearts are mountains, our swords the whirlwind. We count as naught the numbers of our foes. The greater numbers, the greater glory for our chroniclers to write. Aye thus will Tamerlane move, at dawn—"

His gaunt, callused hand swept Michael's array of chessmen off the board in a single motion. Michael still smiled. He had won his throw.

"So," the Breton said, "did the Christian host at Nicopolis attack. Tamerlane has grown blind, and his wisdom is dust before the storm of the Thunderbolt."

The dark blood flooded into the forehead of the Kha Khan. Veins stood out on his forehead and the yellow around the black pupils of his eyes grew red.

"Think ye, slave, Christian cur—" his deep voice cracked. "Think ye, sucking child, the horsemen of Turan and Iran are like to the mongrels of Frankistan?"

His great hand clenched and writhed in front of the eyes of the younger man who drew back before the vehemence of the Tatar's wrath. The two watchful archers gripped Michael's arms, and Bembo sighed mournfully.

"Is it thus," said Michael swiftly, "that Tamerlane plays at *shahk*? You have made your move. I have not made mine. And Bayezid will make such a move. Do not doubt it, my khan."

The cold rebuke of the Christian wrought upon Tamerlane's anger and he became silent—as motionless as a snake coiled to strike.

"Aye," snarled Michael, twisting in the grasp of the archers, "your horsemen will sweep across the Khabur, my khan. They will carry the line of boats Bayezid has drawn up along the farther bank and filled with archers, hidden from your sight. Aye, my lord khan. Your warriors of Turan and Iran and the Horde will not be stayed by the trap that Bayezid has set for them in the tents on the shore. Within the tents is an entrenchment of lances sunk into the ground. It will not check your myrmidons."

He laughed in the face of the old Conqueror.

"And then, verily, your Tatars will carry the town. By midday they will have beaten back the *sipahis* stationed on the crest of the Angora plateau. Aye, Timur. But then what? Your ranks will be faced by forty thousand fresh cavalry—the janissaries. Aye, and by the mamelukes, hidden in the valleys beyond—the pick of Bayezid's army."

The black eyes of Tamerlane were riveted on Michael's face.

"More than that," cried Michael, "the line of boats will be ablaze, my Conqueror. Casks of naphtha are hidden within them, to be set alight. Your men will find no water to drink upon the plain of Angora; the river is foul. Your back will be to the river. Bayezid will turn aside from his hunt, which is meant but to cast dust in your eyes, and set his heavy cavalry against your tired and thirsty followers. By nightfall the riders of Turan will be slain or in the river. Aye, there are war galleys awaiting you, around the upper bend of the Khabur. Your men have never fought against the Turkish ships."

At this Tamerlane brushed his hand across his nearsighted eyes, and a hissing breath escaped his hard lips.

"Bayezid revels—to make you the blinder," concluded Michael bitterly. "He ordered your emissaries slain, to anger you to attack. In this manner, not otherwise, will he make of your name a mockery, O Kha Khan, and of your empire—dust."

For the space of several moments there was complete silence, while a dozen men hung upon the next word of the old Conqueror.

Instead of speaking, Tamerlane rose and limped to the tent entrance, while the guards fell back with lowered heads. He glanced at the stars, marking the hour, and at the dark masses of men assembling under the wan gleam of the new moon, low on the horizon.

"Take the captives hence," he said at last to his attendants, "save the Frank in the kaftan. Summon Mirza Rustem, my grandson, Mahmoud Khan, and the *noyons*. Take through the camp the new command of Tamerlane; my men are to sleep. The order of battle is to be changed."

Alone with Michael and a single servant in his tent, Tamerlane signed to his cup-bearer to fill two bowls with wine.

Obeying the request which was virtually a command, Michael bent one knee, touched the cup to his chest and forehead and put it briefly to his lips. The Tatar emptied his with a single gulp.

"Have you a thought," he asked bluntly, "how this sultan who has set a trap may be caught in his own deceit?"

Michael looked at the old Tatar thoughtfully, and smiled, reading the purpose under the other's words.

"Does a sparrow," he countered, "give counsel to a falcon—when the hood is removed from the eyes of the falcon?"

If he had made a suggestion, it would in all probability have been futile and would have opened him to the suspicion of being, after all, a secret agent of Bayezid, who had many such.

"Aye, if Tamerlane commands!"

"Then send a hundred of your horsemen to cut out a river galley, to learn whether the boats be not manned and equipped as I said. Dispatch another hundred up the Khabur, to locate the war galleys that I have seen."

Tamerlane tossed the empty bowl from him and poured Michael's scarcely tasted wine upon the rugs of the tent. It was an unpardonable offense to fail to empty a bowl bestowed by the khan; but Tamerlane dealt with such things in his own way.

"Those men have already been sent," he grunted. "I bade you spit out your thought how Bayezid may be attacked. He is too shrewd to force the crossing of the Khabur, and by the sun of heaven, my Tatars would throw dirt in my face if I sit here in my tents like a woman with child."

Thoughtfully Michael traced out the imaginary line of the river upon the chessboard.

"The sultan has shaped his strength to meet an attack," he responded slowly.

"It is true that he is too wise to cross the river. It is written, O Kha Khan, in the memoir of the Ottoman that he who trusts too greatly in his wisdom shall stumble and eat dirt. Bayezid's strength would be more like weakness were he forced to attack—"

"Speak a plain thought!"

"Pretend to fall into the sultan's trap. And meanwhile get the pick of your army above or below Angora and across the river—"

"How?"

Michael smiled.

"If Tamerlane wills, a sparrow may become a falcon. I have taken the hood from the eyes of the falcon."

For a space the Tatar considered this, while one after the other the councilors and leaders of his army stepped into the tent—lean-faced men in armor—the few who had been selected by the Lame Conqueror from the warriors of mid-Asia.

"What reward claim you for this?" demanded the old man abruptly.

"I would ride with your horsemen to see the downfall of Bayezid."

Tamerlane grunted and glanced at the scattered miniature warriors of the chessboard.

"So, Frank," he growled, "you cannot play chess!"

Michael shook his head.

"That is a pity," said Tamerlane regretfully. "You would make a rare player."

Dawn had broken over the river and the Tatar standards before the tents were outlined against the streaks of sunrise when Michael walked alone from the council of Tamerlane and sought Bembo.

He found the fool huddled beside a cage of the khan's beasts, guarded by a black Kallmark.

"San Marco heard my prayer, Cousin Michael," cried the hunchback joyously. "I prayed right lustily and bravely while yonder giant of Magog was washing his hands i' the air and bobbing his head i' the wind and talking with the sun."

Bembo had been interested in the dawn prayer of the Muhammadan Tatar. He skipped to Michael's side and grimaced at the warrior.

"Now make what magic ye will, son of Eblis," he chanted, "and the devil take ye, as he will, for his own. Cousin Michael, did the mad Cham outroar you, or are we saved? What's to do?"

"Where are the others?"

Bembo could not forbear a chuckle. "Rest you, good cousin. The master-merchant Soranzi is counting a myriad gold coins for the Tatar *wazirs*, as the pagans name their money-tenders; Rudolfo is departed with good grace and Gian to be escorted by Tatar children to the river."

"And Clavijo?"

Bembo nodded toward the cage. "With the apes, who love him like a brother. This black giant was to cut off my head—"

"You will be safe with me. Come." Michael smiled. "The Cham, as you call him, has given us some good sport. We will fly pigeons and when that is done, sleep. Then this night will you see a rare jest, my Bembo."

"So said Rudolfo to Gian when they went off. Gian has been grinning like a dog that scents a bone. Two days agone did I ask them what was i' the wind. That was before they knew that you were with us in pagan garb. Rudolfo cursed me, but his henchman, forsooth, muttered that my master was not the only man who could devise a plan."

Michael frowned, but could learn nothing more from the jester, except that Rudolfo had talked at times with a certain *wazir* who was open-handed with his gold and knew many tongues.

He could not waste time to search into a possible new intrigue on the part of the Italian, for Tamerlane had ordered him to assist in preparing messages to be sent up with carrier pigeons—messages intended to fall into the hands of Bayezid.

In the annals of the Ottoman dynasty it is written that during the space of that day Bayezid, surnamed the Thunderbolt, hunted with falcon and dogs upon the plain of Angora, having in his heart naught but contempt for the Tatars.

With his grandees and picked cavalry the sultan rode from sunrise to sunset, his beaters spread across the steppe, without thought of water or bodily comfort. His men stood under arms all that time. His ships in the river remained at their moorings. His spies reported that Tamerlane was taking more time to muster the Tatar horsemen to cross the river.

But Bayezid had burned and broken down the few bridges on the Khabur, and knew well that, save at Angora, there was no ford. This gave him assurance that Tamerlane could not cross except at the point where the sultan awaited him.

Further assurance came with a carrier pigeon, struck down by one of Bayezid's hawks. From the bird was taken a message addressed to the court of Samarkand, saying that Tamerlane would that night cross the Khabur and crush the Ottoman army.

Whereupon Bayezid retired to the palace by the lake at Angora, hearing fresh news at sunset that the Tatars were assembling in their ranks.

So Bayezid feasted and received praise from the leaders of the Moslem world.

"The beast," he said, "may see the trap; yet, being a beast, he has no wit to do aught but charge upon the bait."

"Nay," amended his advisers, "where else could the Tatar cross the river, having no bridges or boats?"

Well into the night a tumult arose on the shore opposite Angora. Many lights were to be seen in the camp of Tamerlane, and the neighing of horses could be heard clearly across the river. Soon came the ring of weapons and the shout of the Mongols. A line of fire grew along the waiting galleys. Flights of arrows sped into the masses that were moving toward the ford. Bayezid laughed, well content.

Rumors reached him from fishermen that Mongols had been seen far down the river, but Bayezid could see and hear the conflict that was beginning at the ships. Moreover the torches of the Tatar camp were plainly to be seen.

It is written likewise in his annals that at this time a Christian captive, escaping from Tamerlane's camp, swam the river.

This man, who was attended by another Frank of powerful build, was taken captive by guards at the Khabur shore and carried up into the town where the officers of the janissaries had assembled near Bayezid.

The two were Rudolfo and Gian, who had discarded their mail and broken loose from the half-grown Tatars, slaying one with their hands—so stoutly had the boys pestered them with miniature weapons.

Once safely in the town, they made signs that they would be taken to the sultan and offered as proof of the urgency of their mission a ring that bore the signet of a Turkish *wazir*.

When the litter of the sultan passed, attended by torches and mounted grandees, Rudolfo and Gian knelt. Bayezid halted. He examined the ring and his brows went up. It was the signet of one of his spies.

"Where is the *wazir*?" he demanded of the Greeks in his retinue who could converse with Rudolfo. The *wazir* who was the sultan's man had not been able to leave his post in the Horde without discovery and he had sent the ring by Rudolfo, who was prepared to seek reward from Bayezid for information given.

"'Tis small gain I seek from the Thunderbolt," he assured the Greeks. "Some gold and goods of mine taken from me by Tamerlane, who is a foul fiend. Lists have been prepared of the stuff and when the sultan overwhelms the camp of the Horde I will point it out. For this small gear I have tidings for the ear of the sultan."

Meanwhile up from the riverfront came the clash of steel and the shouting of men. Bayezid, never impatient, scanned Rudolfo's face and observed that the man did not meet his eye. "More like," he whispered to the Sheik of Rum, "that this Frank has had the slaying of my spy and has come to beguile me with words of Tamerlane's. Promise him his gold and get his news."

Rudolfo's message caused a stir throughout the grandees.

Tamerlane, he said, had left the camp across the river at dusk with the bulk of his cavalry, which meant the bulk of his army. The demonstration at the ford was being made by old men and boys—slaves and horseherders. The array of fires that winked at Angora from the other shore had been lighted to deceive the sultan into thinking that the mass of the Horde was still there.

As he spoke the tumult seemed to dwindle, and for a second, doubt was written on the hard face of the Thunderbolt.

"If the Tatar has tricked me—" He thought of his preparations to defend Angora on the river side and the men he had thrown into ships and trenches on the shore.

"But there are no bridges and no fords," his councilors pointed out. "Where else could Tamerlane cross the Khabur? Perhaps he was fleeing with his army."

Bayezid had never met defeat. Astrologers had assured him that the greatest event of his destiny was to come to pass. He felt sure of his plan and of himself. Had not his hunters' falcons struck down a carrier pigeon that day with news of Tamerlane's purpose to attack?

So Bayezid laughed and questioned Rudolfo lightly as to which way the Tatar riders had passed from the camp. When Rudolfo replied that they had headed down the river, the sultan gave orders that a detachment of mamelukes should ride down the Angora side of the Khabur and report if they sighted any Tatars. Meanwhile the two Franks were to be kept in attendance on him, for they would be useful.

The scouts never returned. Quiet settled upon the Khabur.

Some hours after dawn a Turkish war galley was sent down the river to reconnoiter. So it was after midday that the vessel arrived at a point a dozen miles down the river and learned that here during the night the Horde had crossed the Khabur to the Angora side—the Tatars swimming their horses and the foot soldiers holding to the beasts' tails.

Tamerlane, in fact, was now drawn up on the Angora plain with all his strength.

Chapter XIII
The Conqueror

Bembo had secured for himself one of those animals of the Kallmark Tatars, a beast that was neither horse nor mule nor ass. This steed he had caparisoned gaily. Thus mounted, he trotted at Michael's side, discoursing cheerfully.

"A fair day, my cousin, and a goodly steed between my knees—albeit it savors not of bull-stag or cameleopard. Alack, my wooden sword is broken; yet I have got me another weapon which is a favorite among these barbarians."

Michael, clad in a mail shirt with a Tatar helmet on his head and mace and sword at his belt, glanced down inquiringly. He did not see that Bembo carried any weapon.

"Nay, it is invisible, good my cousin," chattered the jester. "I learned its use in the Venetian fields and it likes me well because it avails best at a distance from my foe—ha! Are devils loosed on the plain yonder?"

A distant clamor of horns and drums came to their ears. Michael had taken his position among a regiment of Chatagai horse commanded by Mirza Rurtem, the grandson of Tamerlane—a strong-bodied youth in rich armor. Directly behind them the standard of the Genghis family was raised, the yak-tail standard of the Mongols.

"The Ottoman attacks," explained Michael, rising in his short stirrups. "Bayezid has been maneuvering throughout the morning, and now his front ranks advance upon the Horde."

The plateau of Angora was nearly flat. The field favored neither Tatar nor Turk, except that Tamerlane had his left flank upon the river. Michael could see the masses of Moslem spearmen that had acted as beaters the day before, and other brilliant groups of irregulars—archers on either flank. Behind these, almost concealed in the dust that floated up from the hard clay, were mamelukes, closely packed, and beside them the glint of lances of the *sipahis*.

Bayezid, taken in flank by the swift move of the Tatar Horde, had been compelled to realign his troops that morning and draw out of Angora, away from his galleys and trenches, to give battle. He had no other course open to him except to retire since Tamerlane refused to advance from the river.

There was no outcry from the Tatars. They waited as they stood. They flooded the yellow plain like bees clustered upon a board. And like an army of locusts was the advancing host of the sultan, fatigued by continuous marching, and tormented by thirst, but high-spirited and conscious of a hundred victories.

Michael's dark face was grave as he scanned their ranks—a hundred thousand souls, hitherto invincible, moving forward in the shape of a half-moon to the sound of their horns, Seljuk shouting to Ottoman, Turko-

man to mameluke. He knew the fighting ability of these veterans and
was more than a little surprised at the calm alertness of the Tatars, not
knowing that every Mongol shared the reckless spirit of Tamerlane and
would rather fight than eat.

"A thirsty sight," murmured Bembo, quaffing heartily of one of his
skins of water. The day before, Tamerlane had ordered that each man be
supplied with two such skins of water.

Emptying the goat's hide, Bembo dismounted to pluck stones from the
ground, surveying each with care and throwing away all that were not
round and of a certain size.

Michael looked up as arrows began to fly in dense clouds from the sultan's skirmishers. The front ranks of the Tatars took this punishment
without cry or movement. By now the Turkish regiments of mailed horsemen could be plainly seen, moving forward at a trot.

Then the sun glinted on ten thousand arrows loosed at the same moment by the Mongol archers who shot three times while one shaft was
in the air. The clamor among the Turks shrilled with shouts of pain and
anger. Horses broke from the front lines, and the curtain of dust swelled
so that it covered the scene of the battle from view from the rear where
Michael and the Chatagais stood with picked regiments of Iran and the
Tatar steppe.

The roar of voices merged with a pandemonium of clashing steel and
thud of horses' hoofs. The tumult swelled until they could no longer hear
their own voices.

Stationary at first, the brunt of the battle began to move onward toward
the waiting masses of Tamerlane's horse, under Mahmoud Khan and the
Lame Conqueror himself—the center of the army that was between the
foot soldiers and the cavalry in reserve, where Michael was.

"Bayezid's mongrel skirmishers have been killed off," he mused, "and
his *sipahis* are at work."

Even Bembo looked a trifle downcast. He glanced at the glittering figure of Mirza Rustem seated on a black stallion near them. The grandson
of Tamerlane was chewing dates.

Plucking up his spirits at this sight, the jester took some fruit from his
girdle and tried to follow the mirza's example. But he gagged and coughed up
the food, thereby raising a laugh from Michael and the nearest Tatars.

A hot wind tossed the dust clouds high overhead and the glare of the
sun pierced sullenly through the murk.

"Hai-Allah-hai!" the deep shout of the janissaries came to them.

Mirza Rustem finished his dates and began to eat dried meat that he pulled from under his saddle where the heat and the chafing of the leather had softened the stiffened meat. Bembo, watching in fascination, found the sight too much for his stomach and turned to look at the masses of Tatars before them.

Tamerlane, his standard, and Mahmoud Khan were no longer to be seen.

The red ball of the sun, high overhead when the conflict began, was lowering to the west.

A leaping, furtive form passed the jester's vision, like an incarnation of evil. One of Tamerlane's hunting leopards had escaped from its cage. No one paid heed to it.

Bembo began to tremble, and found that the perspiration that soaked his garments was cold. The hideous din in front of him had dwindled for a space and now swelled again until it seemed to embrace the horizon.

He looked for captives to be led back, but none came. Surely, he thought, there would be wounded Tatars running from the front, and others not wounded who had escaped the eye of their leaders. That had been a familiar sight in the orderly battles of Europe.

"The Mongols fight each man for himself," grunted Michael impatiently. "They do not keep lines as we do; that is why Bayezid has not broken their center yet. Tamerlane's cavalry met the charge of the janissaries—"

He rose in his stirrups, looking eagerly over the field. He could make out that the two armies were engaged from wing to wing. The Turkish half-moon was no longer clearly drawn and the bodies of reserve cavalry behind the half-moon had been brought up into the line of battle.

Unconsciously Michael had edged his horse up abreast of the stocky pony of Mirza Rustem. Now he felt an iron hand seize his bridle and draw it back.

Looking into the eyes of Tamerlane's grandson, he found them cold and spiritless. The Breton was flushed and impatient as a hunting dog held in leash. But there was no fire in the glance of Mirza Rustem who gazed upon the death of thirty thousand men with utter indifference.

"Do you fight for your God?" asked the Tatar.

"As you for your khan."

Mirza Rustem turned to glance fleetingly at where he could make out the yak-tail standard in the black mass of the Tatar center.

"Aye," he said slowly, "yet your God is gold, no more. A *wazir* spy of the sultan confessed before we beheaded him this day that a Christian had gone over to the enemy for gold. That is the word that is ever in the mouths of your breed."

Michael stiffened, knowing that Rudolfo must have tried to betray the plans of Tamerlane. He thought, too, of the mercenary Comneni, of the grasping emperor, and the Venetians who had been sent to plunder the khan.

Then there came to his mind the vision of the chivalry of France who had thrown away their lives with reckless bravery in the crusade against Bayezid. And he thought of the Christian graves that marked the cities of Palestine where the knights of the Cross had struggled vainly with the conquering Saracen.

This he did not try to explain to the Tatar, knowing that it was useless.

"See," said the young Tatar again; "the standard advances. The wolf has shaken the dogs from his flanks."

Michael saw that the masses of Tatars that had been stationary were moving forward now. It was almost imperceptible at first, this hive-like movement of men waiting grimly to slay.

Tamerlane's center had stood fast for three hours. Bayezid's last attack had been broken.

What the chivalry of Europe could not do, the Lame Conqueror and his Horde had done. To Michael this was a strange thing. Where was then the power of God?

Hunger and the nervous suspense of the last hours had made his mind clear and unnaturally alert. He found that he was dwelling upon some words of a woman who had taught him wisdom before he became a man.

"The ways of God are past our knowing," his mother had said.

He wondered if she were reading from the Book wherein she had found these words, and smiling as she did, alone in her room in the tower of the seacoast. She had smiled like that when his father's ships brought in word of new conquests of the Moslems on the borders of Europe.

It did not seem to Michael to be a strange thing that the strongest faith should be in the hearts of women, who knew nothing of warfare.

This had passed through his thoughts almost subconsciously while he watched the battle. Now the dust curtain thickened, cutting off his view. There was a pounding of hoofs and shapes that looked like birds crossed in front of Mirza Rustem and a man shouted something. Then they were gone, wheeling toward the Mongol right. Michael spoke to a Tatar squatted upon the ground sharpening his sword.

"Beduins—our men," he announced to Bembo, a new note of eagerness in his voice. "Be of good cheer, cousin esquire. Five regiments of *sipahis* have been surrounded and are doomed in yonder melee. The janissaries are reforming. Presently will we, God willing, bear our hand to the fray."

"I am well content here," rejoined Bembo sincerely. "San Marco—"

Almost at his ear a hideous clamor of kettledrums and cymbals broke out. The jester clapped his hands to his head, only to see the standard of Mirza Rustem raised and the masses of Tatar horsemen move forward at a walk.

Michael touched spurs to his pony and Bembo sighed deeply. He looked longingly toward the rear where the leopard had fled, only to see lines of broad grim faces advancing and shaggy horses swarming together like bees.

The sound of the Tatar *nacárs* throbbed over the plain of Angora, summoning the Mongols to attack.

Whereupon every warrior of Tamerlane who could hold himself upon his feet ran or galloped forward. Some, who could not stand unaided, grasped the stirrups of the riders and struck out with their free arms.

And it was upon the checked and disheartened array of the janissaries, ordered to charge a second time, that the Horde advanced. Defeated on both flanks, half his men slaughtered, and half of the rest staggering from wounds or thirst, the Thunderbolt ordered the flower of his veteran host to drive again at Tamerlane's center—only to be met by the picked horsemen of the Mongols, held in reserve until then under Mirza Rustem.

The janissaries, shouting their war cry, met the oncoming tide, wavered and broke up into scattered squares that melted away into mounds of dying and dead.

Michael, fighting beside the Chatagais, glimpsed the body of Gutchluk outstretched on the earth beside a mangled horse. The long hair of the Tatar was matted with blood and his black eyes stared up blindly at the passing riders.

Then through the dust Michael made out the *noyon* who had been called a prince of Eblis by Bembo. The armor of the noble was cut and hacked away and one hand held together his nearly severed abdomen. He was seated on a heap of sprawling *sipahis*, and he was smiling. The dead lay thick about him, for the Sheik of Rum had penetrated here into the center of Tamerlane's host.

The Chatagais were galloping now, enveloping and sweeping over detachments of white-capped janissaries. The remnants of a regiment of Turkomans, kin to the Tatars, threw down their arms and were spared.

"Bayezid is in flight to Angora with his grandees," cried Mirza Rustem. "We must not return without him."

The grandson of Tamerlane staggered in his saddle as an arrow embedded itself in his mailed chest. He dropped his shield to break off the end of the shaft. Michael slew the archer who had sent the arrow, and presently found himself riding alone through the dust clouds.

There he turned aside to follow a horseman who had entered a rocky defile at a headlong pace. The aspect of the man was familiar.

"Rudolfo!" he cried.

He had known some hours before that the *condottiere* had escaped from the guard of Tatar boys, slaying one in his flight to the river. But Michael had not thought until informed by Mirza Rustem that Rudolfo had sought protection and reward from the sultan.

Rudolfo, in fact, had been kept beside the retinue of Bayezid until there were no longer any to guard him. Then with Gian he had circled the remnants of the Turkish regiments to seek safety in flight.

He knew that his life was forfeited to the Tatars. It seemed incomprehensible to him that Bayezid should be routed. It was part of the ill fortune that had dogged him since the Gate of Shadows.

So panic—the panic that had seized him at Nicopolis—claimed him, and he turned into the first ravine that offered shelter.

Michael's shout caused him to glance back swiftly.

He saw that the Breton rode alone. In the fear that beset him, Rudolfo felt that his only chance of life lay in slaying Michael. The issue between the two had been long in coming to a head. Now, Rudolfo thought, it was at hand.

The *condottiere* checked his horse and flung his javelin deftly. The spear missed the Breton but struck his mount, causing the beast to rear and plunge. Michael jumped to earth and hurled his mace.

It crashed against Rudolfo's round shield of rhinoceros hide, and the man winced as he dropped the crushed target from an injured arm.

He reached for his sword, but Michael was on him, had grasped him about the waist and hauled him from his saddle.

"Now may we settle the issue of our duel," muttered Michael, stepping back and drawing his weapon.

They had, in fact, strange weapons. Both had been deprived of the swords they had brought from Venice. The curved scimitars felt strange in their hands. Rudolfo hung back, shaking the sweat from his eyes and gazing sidelong at the rocky defile in which they stood.

"Gian!" he cried. "To me!"

Michael waited for no more but leaped forward, slashing at the other's head. Rudolfo parried skillfully, calling again for his follower.

Out of the corner of his eye Michael saw the tall figure of the man-at-arms on a panting horse. Gian had been following them.

At this Michael set his back to a rock, warding off the counterthrust of Rudolfo, who pressed the attack, certain now of the presence of his ally. Gian plucked forth a long knife and held it by the tip, reining his horse nearer for an opportunity to cast his favorite weapon.

Michael heard rapid hoofbeats approaching down the ravine. He caught the flash of the dagger as it flew toward him, only to rattle harmlessly off the rock at his back.

Gian grunted and flung up both arms, reeled in the saddle and tumbled to the ground. But Michael had not seen the thing that struck him down.

"*Habet!*" a shrill voice chanted. "Goliath is dead! Stand aside, Cousin Michael, and let the other devil have his due."

By now Michael was aware of Bembo on his mule-ass, waving something about his head.

"Nay," the Breton growled, "this is my affair."

The fall of Gian had brought a scowl to Rudolfo's olive face. He pressed Michael desperately, cursing under his breath. The two scimitars clashed and the helmet was struck from the Breton's head. Rudolfo, panting, exerted every effort to follow up his success and reach his enemy's bare skull. Michael was taunting him softly.

As Rudolfo's blow fell, Michael sprang forward, dropping his sword. The other's scimitar passed over his shoulder and Michael's powerful left hand caught the other's wrist, pinning it to his side.

At this the Italian grinned maliciously, for, with his enemy's left hand occupied, he fancied that Michael was defenseless. So Rudolfo gripped Michael's throat, bending his head back viciously with his free hand.

Somewhat he wondered at Michael's passivity, not knowing that the Breton's right hand, useful once more, thanks to long and patient practice, was feeling in his own girdle for the dagger Rudolfo carried.

Michael's searching fingers freed the dagger and plunged it into the other's throat, over the mail.

Sword in hand, Rudolfo swayed on his feet, choked, and wheeled about as if to run. His knees sank under him and he blundered against a rock, falling heavily upon his back. Both his hands gripped the hilt of the dagger, strained at it and were still.

Bembo, having dismounted, bent over the *condottiere* and ripped off the bulging pouch that was tied to the dead man's waist. Michael saw for the first time that the jester held a long sling, made of thin strips of leather, a stone ready in the pocket. Catching his glance, the jester laughed.

"My weapon," he said proudly. "Gian's thick head was cracked like a hen's egg. Gian's thick purse was full of gold trinkets plundered, methinks, from the slain. So I would fain crack open his master's nest-egg—"

From Rudolfo's pouch a stream of Turkish gold *byzants* poured forth.

"*Consummatum est,*" murmured Bembo. "It is finished. Gian's spoil will pay me for saving your life, coz. These belong to you."

As Michael shook his head, the jester, nothing loath, poured the coins into his goatskin, after emptying out the remaining stones.

Breathing deeply from his effort, Michael gazed around at the shadows of the ravine and listened in vain for the war cry of the Tatars.

"You will not hear it, coz," remarked Bembo. "What is left of the grandees is flying toward Angora with worthy Mirza Rustem in hot pursuit. The victory is ours, as I prayed San Marco it should be."

He tied up the sack and surveyed Rudolfo philosophically.

"Cousin Michael," he declared thoughtfully, "you are a wise man. In Venice did you assert that a man follows his bent. And here is Rudolfo, a noble seller of himself, a *condottiere* to the king's taste. He sold himself to Genoa, then Venice, then back to himself again. Last night he traded him to the sultan, and now methinks he has gone to purgatory to sell his soul to the devil."

Out on the plain of Angora the sun had set over the red mist and the red dust where the bodies of fifty thousand men lay motionless.

It was night when Michael and his follower sought Mirza Rustem and Tamerlane in the town of Angora. They knew that where the khan was, the sultan would be. Men had told them that Bayezid had been taken before he could leave the field and that a hundred of his grandees had died around him before he could be taken.

Torches borne by the Tatars and the glare of building tents revealed to Michael a strange sight. Tamerlane sat his horse at the entrance to the pleasure lake of the palace. Mirza Rustem in bloodied armor and the scarred, dust-coated *noyons* attended him.

Huddled groups of women and slaves stared in a kind of fascination at what stood before the old Tatar. Pushing past the onlookers to the side of Mirza Rustem, Michael saw the great bulk of Bayezid kneeling in front of Tamerlane's horse.

The sultan wore his embroidered cap with the blood-colored ruby, and his tunic of cloth-of-gold. His head swayed on his shoulders and his eyes were half closed. His glance went from one to another of the *noyons* and finally rested on Michael.

The black eyes of the defeated monarch widened as he recognized the Christian who had been his slave. His lips twisted as he half-made a gesture of appeal, and then drew back before the passionless scrutiny of the Tatars.

Michael folded his arms and waited, to hear Tamerlane's word that would speak the fate of the man who was called the Thunderbolt.

"Live—if you can," said the old Conqueror gruffly.

He signed to a group of his followers who brought out a cage that had held one of Tamerlane's leopards.

In this cage Bayezid was placed and the door locked. He could no longer look into the eyes of the watchers as he was picked up, with his prison, and carried through the flame-ridden streets of Angora.

Somewhere in the huddle of captives a woman screamed and the other Moslems took up the wail of lament.

News of what had come to pass in Asia spread to the world of Christendom. The wave of Ottoman invasion had been broken. In his marble palace standing over the dark waters of the Golden Gate, the Byzantine emperor held revelry to celebrate the delivery of Constantinople.

The crusaders of Saint John took new heart; the pilgrim galleys that sailed from Venice were filled with new voyagers to the Holy Land. *Te Deum* was sung in the cathedrals of France. But no mention reached France of the share in the victory of Angora that belonged to an obscure voyager of Brittany. Nor did the mother of Michael Bearn hear the name of her son in the mouths of pilgrims.

The Maritime Council of Venice planned new inroads into the field of Oriental trade, and wrote off the moneys advanced to Signor Clavijo and his party as a total loss. In fact it was recorded in the annals of the council that Clavijo and all those with him were lost.

This, however, was not the case. Clavijo lived—outside the knowledge of the council that he dreaded—in Spain and wrote a book of his travels that was filled with most marvelous tales.

And Tamerlane rewarded Michael Bearn. The Tatar monarch bestowed on him a khanate in northern Persia—Fars, with its palace and riches.

But Michael did not accept it for himself, giving it, instead, to a friend. He turned his back on the East to seek a galley bound for the Brittany he had not seen for ten years and the castle where his mother waited.

So it happened that the *bailios* of Contarini and the Maritime Council of the Signory of Venice reported a curious thing.

In the heart of Tatary, they said, sometimes called the land of Gog and Magog, not far from the Salt Sea, there was a fine palace in fair groves of date and cypress trees.

The ruler of this palace of Fars was a weird man, with emerald rings on his toes and cloth-of-gold on his broken body. He called himself sometimes the Grand Cham or Khan and sometimes Bembo the First.

The Black Road

When he saw the first stars over mountains, Mark pulled in his racing horse and laughed. It was dark and he was safe. "Faith," he said to the roan mare, "we are still alive in our skins." But he spoke between his teeth; he made little sound.

Even though he now felt himself to be safe from the danger that followed his heels, he kept moving along the path. Mark, late Sieur de Kerak, believed in taking no chances. He reined his horse to the side of the roadway where he could not be seen under the pines. His long body was covered with mesh, darkened so that it did not gleam and oiled so that it did not grate when he moved. Over this he pulled the black mantle that he had picked up when he began his long ride, months before. No ponderous helm of steel showed the outline of his head; he wore only a round steel cap. No long unwieldy sword clanked at his hip. Mark had left the family swords behind him.

Instead he carried, loosely thrust into his belt, the most deadly and efficient of weapons, a morning star. This morning star had a two-foot shaft of wood, strengthened by iron, with three slender chains hanging from it and, at the ends of the chains, three spiked metal balls. A swinging blow from this morning star—as Mark's arm swung it—could crush in the armor or the head of a man.

Mark knew weapons as well as he knew war. His hard body had scars in it that ached when he felt the night's cold. Only a sure instinct had kept him alive, and Mark trusted his instinct more than any talisman or prayer.

Now that instinct told him to keep on going. Behind him, witless people were dying each day by the thousand under the hoofs of that strange horde emerging from the steppes of Asia. It was like a whirlwind, that tide of horsemen.

Mark listened, as he rode, to the heaving breaths of his horse and the stir of the wind in the forest mesh. He put his hand into the small sack of barley tied carefully to the saddle horn. Beneath the barley, his fingers touched objects like sharp stones; only these were precious stones, carefully selected—pigeonblood rubies, emeralds of Ind, and glorious amethysts, a treasure of them, enough to ransom a king.

His father, the first lord of Kerak, had voyaged out of England with the heedless Richard the Lionheart, and his father had left his bones in Kerak overlooking the barren ridges beyond the Dead Sea. Mark, born in that waste borderland, had wrested wealth from it and he meant to return to England with that wealth; to make the acquaintance of the homeland he had never seen. He had grown very tired of his castle above the greenish-blue of the Dead Sea, and its sour wine and olive trees.

"The crusades," he told himself, "are running out, like the sands of an hourglass. Aye, they are done!"

Suddenly he checked his horse. A gleam of light showed above the trees. So high up, it must come from a tower. A tower, by the same token, meant a good large seigniory, and that meant food. He ached with hunger, and the mare would be the better for an hour's rest.

Seeking along the edge of the trees he found the break that marked a road going up, and up this he made his way, alert for a challenge. It came when he saw the loom of a wall and the light overhead.

"Sloy!"

"Slava bohu!" he shouted. "Glory to God!"

A torch flickered in a doorway, and three bearded men looked him over, jabbering a speech he did not know. The one with the torch took him by the hand and led him into the hall, where logs blazed in a huge fire hearth. Mark took in the place with a glance—the heads of stag and buffalo fastened to the walls, the flax hanging from the rafters, the crude swords and huge embroidered coats of the score of armed men who filled the benches by a long table, the yellow-haired maids carrying wine jugs, the spinning wheels stowed away in the corners. "The hall of a small nobleman," he thought, "who likes hunting. But where is he and what is he?"

There was a high seat, empty, at the table near the fire. There were gold dishes and a white cloth at that place; behind it, a shield of arms bearing something like a dragon, obscured by smoke.

It surprised him that these people seemed to be getting ready to dine, rather than flee the place. One of the men bowed to Mark and pointed behind him. Mark did not turn around. He preferred to face these strangers and he chose to keep the sack of barley slung over his arm.

"Panna Marya!" growled the bearded man.

"I hear you, brother," said Mark to himself, "but the devil himself couldn't make me turn my back to twenty swords."

Then he heard a woman laugh softly behind him and he swung around quickly enough.

She had not meant to pose there. Only she looked like a painting, like the stiff dragon on the shield. For pearl strings lay heavy on her young shoulders, and silver tissue made a crown on her dark hair. Such things did not fit her because her lips were quivering with laughter, and her eyes merry and knowing. She was holding a silver tray and on that tray, a dish of salt and a piece of broken bread.

"*Chlieb sol,*" she said, curtsying. She chattered at him, the words meaning nothing to Mark. He had not seen a maid like this in his life's time, because he was newly come out of the East. "*Eheu, hospes,*" she cried at him. "Oh, guest, speak, can't you?"

She was speaking Latin then, and Mark had once been taught that language by a wandering friar. Only this youthful Marya rattled it out like a bird singing: "I greet you, sir. And the bread and salt of my house I offer you."

A side of mutton was what Mark craved. Swearing silently, he took a morsel of bread, dipped it in the salt and chewed it. Then the girl Marya in her queenly garb fetched him a gold cup of spiced wine.

It felt heavy in his hand, and he guessed the gold to be solid and old. As he drank, he thought that this cup, slipped into his bag, would pay his way to Venice. "A kiss with the cup is good," he grinned, remembering a verse that the friar had not taught him.

For a second, Panna Marya's eyes searched his. Then they widened, fastening upon something on his shoulder. "A kiss, truly," she whispered, slipping up to him, taking his hand. She still looked into his eyes when his lips touched hers and his arm pressed hard against her slim back.

"Nay, you will spill the wine." She smiled. "I did not know that you were crucifer. An honor it is, so to greet a cross-bearer."

No more had Mark known that he was a crusader. The black mantle he wore had a cross sewn on the shoulder because it had belonged to his father.

But Panna Marya acted as if Michael the Archangel had dismounted in her hall. She clapped her hands, she cried out, the towheaded maids scurried around like hens when grain is scattered, old men climbed into the gallery among the stag heads and began to make music. The men-at-arms clanked around Mark, jabbering, and Marya skipped back to interpret.

The giant Kmita, captain of the men-at-arms, pulled off his iron cap and swept his beard below his belt in a bow.

"My people say it is a good omen that you should come at this hour," cried the girl. "And I say so, too."

She led him to the high seat by the fire and made him sit where the gold service gleamed on the boards, while a flustered maid offered him a silver basin of water to rinse his hands before eating.

Kmita drove the maids back to the hearth and brought the platters of smoking pigeon and pork and venison to Mark himself, bowing each time. It was the custom of her people, Marya explained—the Polish people. Didn't he know? He shook his head, eating fast.

When he got up, taking his bag on his arm, Marya looked at him, dismayed.

"But it is night. You must sleep and rest and break your fast with us, Mark!"

He did not think he had heard aright. "You mean to stay?"

"I? Yes."

"Here, in this castle?"

The girl Marya seemed to be troubled because he did not understand. She had been visiting Krakow, she said, for the Easter festival when she had heard the country was invaded. So she had hurried back to the Dragon—as she called the castle.

"You think you can defend this place?" Mark asked. "With what?"

Hesitating, she pointed at Kmita and the henchmen, chewing tranquilly at their meat.

Mark shook his head impatiently. "Lady, the horsemen who follow after me have laid Cathay in waste. Men say that they cracked open Kiev like a melon, and now they may be venturing into these mountains of yours—"

"True—we know. But I had hope"—her gray eyes appealed to him—"that you, a war wager, might abide with us."

How her eyes held him! He could feel the touch of her lips and he did not want to leave her behind.

"Listen"—he was glad the henchmen could not understand him—"it is too late now to evacuate the folks here. But we can drive our horses tonight and with luck get others at Krakow. Change your dress." He glanced at the old-fashioned strings of pearls. "Take your jewels in a bag. Have a fast horse saddled, but hurry!"

The girl Marya gripped tight the carved arms of her chair. "To go away, with you? Only we two?"

"It's a chance, a good chance. What did you say about an omen?" Mark was thinking of the road ahead, full of refugees. "In a month we can be in Venice. And if Venice is not safe, then, there is the sea and England."

"Eng-land?" She did not seem to understand. She said something—about her father the castellan, and her grandfather, and the way they had built the castle, and something else about a dragon that watched over it, protecting it.

"Dragons are not what they were," Mark laughed. It was so like the girl to think of a legend at a time like this. "Not in these days."

"But this one is!" She brushed the mass of dark hair from her cheeks and smiled at him. "Come! I want you to see!"

Slinging the bag on his arm, he followed her out of the hall through the massive doorway of the donjon. "Now, look," she said, holding to the door.

Bedlam resounded outside. Torches flared in the courtyard where wild figures pushed through the outer gate—huntsmen with game on their shoulders, peasants pushing long wagons creaking under loads of kegs and sacks of food. Women with babies lashed in shawls behind their backs, and older children herding in steers and sheep.

Mark recognized these people as refugees he had passed on the road.

"My father said the castle was of ours in time of peace, and it is for them in time of war. They have no other place to go."

"By the eyes of God," Mark muttered, "are you coming?"

"I—they would not know what to do without me."

Her fingers caught at his and then let go. Why had he sat here gossiping like a midwife for two hours?

He jumped down the steps, pushing toward his horse. "Close the gate and knock out those torches!" he shouted, his skin cold with the feel of danger here. Swinging into the saddle of the roan mare, he rode through the gate without looking back.

At the main road he stopped, listening. Evidently the Poles were all inside the castle, because he could hear nothing. But down the road the way he had come, a gray patch blacked out and then reappeared. Something was moving there without making any noise.

Wheeling the roan mare he trotted up the road. Drawing the morning star from his belt he held it where the chains would not jangle. He did not see the riders ahead of him until he was close to them.

There were three of them, waiting, silent. Mark dug in his spurs, bent his head and swung up the battle mace. A bow snapped and something jarred against the steel mail above his belt.

He took the middle rider on his right hand and lashed out with the morning star. The spiked balls smashed into metal and flesh, and that man fell from the saddle. Mark spurred through between the others.

He did not see the rope that caught him over the head and shoulder. Since he was bending forward, it tore him from the saddle when it tightened. Hours later he saw that one of the Mongols had a pole tipped with a long rope ending in a noose. If Mark had seen it cast—

But he felt the dirt of the road in his fingers and the soft run of blood in his mouth, and in a moment he felt the sharp wrench of a twisted arm. The rope held him tight, helpless as a trussed pig, with his horse vanished into the night. Leather creaked above him—he caught the stench of wet hides. A figure picked up something from the road, and he heard the clank of the morning-star chains.

The man standing over him groped for Mark's head. "*Adam tzee!*" this one demanded. "What man?"

"Farang," Mark said. A Frank of the West, he was.

The Mongols seemed amazed that he could speak a language some of them knew. One said, "This one truly has a voice. It will be of use to us."

They pulled him to his feet by the rope, to see if he could stand. For a moment, curious as children, they examined the morning-star they had taken from him, passing the weapon from hand to hand. Then one of them noticed the light in the tower above the pine trees. At once they covered the blue, painted lantern, and a low command was repeated back through the ranks of the pagan riders.

Turning off the road into the pines they began to climb toward the castle, taking Mark with them . . .

At sunrise, Arslan Khan, the Mongol officer, called Mark up to him. "Our bows are strong, our horses swift, our hearts hard as the mountain rock," he said, smiling. "Do you understand my words, Farang?"

Mark nodded. It was easy enough to understand the words of Arslan Khan, but not so easy to guess what his meaning might be.

With an effort Mark drew closer, dragging the leg on his injured side and holding his wrenched arm carefully.

"Then tell me," demanded Arslan Khan, "why the white-faced men in that stone house do not come out?"

They had climbed to a knoll opposite the massive, iron-studded gate of the castle, over which floated a banner bearing a white eagle. The gate was closed. The round towers, nicely spaced for cross fire, appeared stronger than the Englishman had thought in the night. But along the battlements no heads showed. This silence puzzled the Mongol.

"How would I know?" Mark said thoughtfully, "Ask them."

Instead, Arslan Khan sat down on his leopard skin tranquilly. He leaned back against a stone slab on which the outline of a dragon showed. This slab, Mark thought, was the entrance to a tomb overgrown with ivy, set into the knoll. At least, it bore Marya's family crest.

"Nay, you will ask them, Farang, with these words."

Carefully Arslan Khan placed Mark's morning star by his knee. Two other gnome-like horsemen sat impassively behind the prisoner, apparently paying him no attention. Down by the road, a half-dozen Mongol troopers let their horses graze. No others were visible, although Mark felt certain that three or four hundred had come up the road that night. They want those Poles to sally out, Mark reasoned. So far, the Poles were lying low.

"Tell them," the Mongol went on, "we are servants of the great Khan who holds the world between his hands. We have no bad hearts toward the Christians. Tell them to throw their weapons over that wall and open that gate. Then if they give up to us what treasure they have hidden away we will take it with the weapons and go. The living people and their cattle we will not take." His eyes shifted to the silent Englishman. "Make your voice clear. We have no mind to kill those Christians."

"And if I will not?"

"I myself will kill you."

Mark shrugged. "I will do as you wish. Only give me a horse. I am too lame to move."

The Mongol glanced at him impatiently. "A wounded bird has no need of wings," he grunted.

That, Mark reflected, was true enough. Arslan Khan was much too experienced to give his prisoner a chance to ride for it. So Mark began dragging himself painfully down the rise toward the silent gate, a long bowshot away. Close behind him the two guards followed, not troubling to draw their swords.

Midway to the wall he stopped, noticing a movement within the embrasures over the gate. "Panna Marya!" he called.

After a moment her voice answered.

"Listen," he said clearly. "These Mongols who hold me offer you a fair surrender if you open that gate."

"Yes, Sir Mark." Her voice came down to him, muffled.

"Don't do it. Don't hear to their promise. Belike, they will try other tricks. Keep lights going at night and watch, or you are all dead."

"We hear, O Knight of the Cross," the voice quavered as if laughing, "and we bow to thy wisdom! It must have served thee well." Then the voice changed: "Only, listen to me now. Kmita hath a plan to reach thee. Aye, to go out—"

"Devil take Kmita! Keep him behind the gate."

"But he will not—"

"If he follows his feet a spearcast outside he will be dead before you can say orisons for him. Let be!"

For a moment the Polish girl kept silent. "What will you do?" she asked.

Mark hesitated. "What can I do? Nay, I go with these pagans and I will keep my hide whole."

Her foolish valor angered him. At least, he thought, now these Poles would trouble no more about him. Being angry, he almost forgot to drag his leg as he turned away with the two Mongols.

Painfully he dragged himself up to Arslan Khan's observation point. "Those Christians," he said bluntly, "will surrender. They ask only for the time until the sun is highest in the sky, to consult together and dig up their treasures."

Arslan Khan's eyes narrowed. "*Kai*—the voice that spoke for them was a woman's voice."

"*Ay-a tak.* Aye, so. Their commander is a woman, a princess."

Still the Mongol pondered. "What precious things have they? What treasure?"

"Cups of gold and strings of pearls. Enough to fill the arms of one man." For an instant, Mark remembered his own lost jewels.

The Mongol's eyes glowed green and he struck his hands together. "Now I will go over those walls and rip those Christians open like melons."

He shouted an order.

Mark heard, at first, only a stirring and trampling along the ground. Then he knew it to be a rush of hundreds of horses.

The charge came headlong out of the pines, along the road. Lashing their horses, the riders spread to each side. Sharply the speeding mass divided, half of it reining in almost under the shadow of the wall, the riders snatching arrows out of the sheaths at their hips and sending a flight of shafts upward at the summit of the wall. They kept their horses in motion, yelling, *"Kiari-ghar!"*

The first half of the riders did not rein in until their horses wheeled against the stones of the curtain and a tower. Those pressed against the wall stood up in their saddles, grasping at one another and the rough surface of the stones. Above them lances were thrust up against the wall, and men scrambled up on the shoulders of the first, hauling themselves higher on the locked lances, clutching at the crenels at the top.

In less than a minute they were at the parapet, climbing like monkeys, screaming their *"Ghar—ghar!"* Somewhere kettledrums pounded in cadence with the voices.

Mark knew the attack had been blinding in speed, the racket meant to confuse the garrison until the first Mongols could get their footing on the wall itself.

That wall, however, came alive. Men rose between the crenels, and battle-axes smashed down on the climbers. Giant Poles swung flails down as if threshing wheat. Two of them heaved a heavy beam over the parapet. Kmita's swordsmen, running up from the gate, began to slash with their blades, and the leather-clad Mongols were smashed down like fruit from a shaken tree.

For the moment, Arslan Khan was paying no attention to his prisoner. Swaying on his haunches, he was staring at the wall but not at the spot where his riders still struggled to climb on the bloodstained lances. He was watching another face of the wall, in deep shadow.

Here a half company of his men had slipped up to the foot of the wall. They had no horses and they wore gray felt capes that made them look like giant moles crawling up. And the first of them carried pole lariats that they cast up at the parapet. Metal hooks on the ends caught over the stones. Men hauled themselves up the ropes bracing their feet against the stones.

Mark swore silently. The racket by the gate drowned out the noise made by the climbers.

Then he saw figures running on the summit of the wall—figures of Polish women. They began to chop at the ropes with axes and to throw blankets over the climbers while they worked at the ropes. Panna Marya was among them. In a minute the ropes were cut. The Mongols below, enraged, could only loose arrows at the women.

Arslan Khan shouted an order, and Mongols began to run back clumsily toward the knoll.

From the wall, crossbow bolts flickered. The archers covering them circled desperately to avoid the iron bolts that smashed among them. They will not try that again, Mark thought.

Moving his head slowly, he saw that the two men behind him were intent on the road below. Arslan Khan sat rigid as a statue before the tomb, his breath hissing from his body. For the moment he was not thinking of the prisoner who had deceived him.

Without hurrying, Mark got to his feet, crouching. The leg that had seemed helpless was firm beneath him as he jumped at the Mongol. And Arslan Khan moved with the swiftness of an animal. One hand snatched the long knife from his girdle, stabbing at Mark's throat.

Mark swung down his head, feeling his shoulder strike under the Mongol's arm. They rolled over on the ground. But Mark gripped hard the shaft of the morning star for which he had made his leap. He rolled over in the dust, gathering his feet under him, knowing that the Mongol was quicker than he. "*Ghar!*" he heard at his back.

He gave himself no second to stand. Crouching, he whirled, lashing behind him. One of the spiked balls of the morning star caught the Mongol's leg and he staggered, off balance. Swinging up the steel flail, Mark brought it down on the Mongol's light helmet; and Arslan Khan whirled to the ground, his skull crushed—even as his dagger arm struck at Mark.

Reaching down to pick up the dead man's shield, Mark thrust his injured arm into it and stepped forward to meet the rush of the two guards, who had drawn their swords.

He took a blow on the shield and struck with the morning star. But the agile Mongols sprang back, having seen how death flashed from the flying spikes.

Facing them Mark backed toward the stone slab of the tomb. Other Mongols were running up from the road with bows. He could not reach a horse now and he tried to put the tomb at his back, to face them, as an arrow whirred by him.

He heard a grinding and a crash beside him. He saw the stone slab fall into the dust and a giant figure raced from the tomb. *"Slava bohu!"* it roared. And with flailing sword, it crashed into the nearest Mongol.

It was Kmita, mad with excitement. Behind him the dragon tomb spewed forth clumsy men in mail racing one another toward the leading Mongols. They struck with heavy battle-axes and they threw long spears.

Those Mongols, startled by the apparition of men pouring out of the hilltop, turned and ran down the hill dodging among the pines for their horses. Behind them labored the Polish men-at-arms arms, calling to them to halt and fight.

Mark looked once into the tomb, seeing no grave, but an open passage leading down, crowded with the garrison of the castle pushing out after Kmita. He went with them.

To the Mongols it seemed as if an army, hidden in the ground, had been lying in wait until now. They hurried away with their horses and wounded, down to the road through the mountains . . .

"It was," said Panna Marya, "a thought of my father, who was castellan of these mountains. He said we should have two gates here—one seen and one unseen. We called it the dragon's lair."

Reflectively, Mark rubbed his lame arm, sitting on the doorstep of the hall beside this girl.

"Now it is clear to me, lady," he said, "that you have met pagan fighters before."

"We have so," she nodded, "for a hundred years." She looked at him, pleased.

Sitting there in her gleaming gown, she thrust the dark hair back from her slender throat. The scent of the hair was in his nostrils, and the light of her in his eyes. She will never be afraid, he thought.

"They come over the road because it is the road through these mountains," she said. "The black road, we call it." And she hesitated, turning her face from him. "You will not be taking to the road now, Sir Mark?" she asked.

He thought about that. Through the courtyard he saw Kmita pushing by the cattle and carts, past the peasant women who were milking cows and piling hay for the wounded to lie on. Through all this bedlam of a farmyard with its folk, Kmita was carrying a cloak which Mark recognized as his own.

When Kmita reached the steps he held it out in his great paw. Bowing to the belt he shouted angrily, his eyes gleaming.

"He is saying," Panna Marya explained, "how he wanted to go out and rescue you when the pagans made their surprise attack. He is saying that if harm had come to a Knight of the Cross at our gate, it would have been a shame to us forever."

Mark took back the cloak which the Polish captain of men-at-arms had found along the road and he thanked Kmita. He smiled and Kmita grinned.

Here he was, with the cross again, with his wealth gone galloping off. Here he was, not in a palazzo of Venice but shut up in a frontier castle with hordes of pagans roving the countryside.

Panna Marya looked up at him, troubled, trying to read his mind. "Last night," she whispered, "when you rode away, I was frightened."

"You?"

"Yes, of the night and being left alone. I—I wanted so to go away with you to Venice and to live."

Mark, late lord of Kerak, swore silently at himself, understanding now for the first time how frightened this girl was and how she had made a feast of supper, the evening before, thinking it might be her last. He shoved away a bawling calf, put his good arm around her, and laughed.

"Panna Marya, the devil take Venice! This is where we belong, both of us!"

Knights with Wings

That morning began when the sun came through the mist. It was the warm sun of early spring, and when it struck through the pines and into the ferns of the forest it warmed the heart of the Pole named Szary, and the girl lying beside him—close beside him for warmth.

They were lying there shivering, and they heard the melting ice trickling into the hollows of this Baltic forest. They were looking out between the ferns, across the ribbon of river toward the black castle, secure on that far bank.

"It looks," she whispered, "like a buffalo lying down, very comfortably."

"No, it doesn't," Szary objected. "A buffalo gets up after a while, and goes to some place, to fill his belly with grass or with water or with whatever a buffalo likes. This stronghold of Vorberg will not move itself away. No, it has bedded itself down to stay there by the river."

She smiled, while her teeth chattered from cold and excitement. "Vorberg hath no need to go away, Szary" she objected, "to fill its belly. Nay, it sits there atop the river, and it eats our countryside."

"Hush you, chatter bird," he growled. He thought he heard a hunting horn. And he moved his hand stiffly toward the damp, broken branches, putting them on the steaming embers of last night's fire. She did not try to help him, knowing that she might hurt him by that. For this chattering girl, this Yadvi of Krakow, knew Szary's mind, and she wondered often how she might ease that black temper of his until it would not hurt him.

White smoke swirled up from the wet pine branches, making, Yadvi thought, a new white giant's plume in the forest. She knew that Szary wanted this. Careful had he been to make an eye of light by night where the watchers on Vorberg's keep could see it—and now a heavy smoke for the huntsmen to observe.

"They ride this way," said Szary, his head close to the ground. Here, in the ravine, sounds carried far, and he thought that stones rattled down below them.

And Yadvi's head, with its disordered, straw-like hair, pressed close beside his. The devilkin of a girl was lying on her back, her gray eyes half closed. She was hiding the chill and the fear that tore at her; but she could not hide the pulse throbbing in her throat. And she begged something of him, quickly, while the telltale smoke rose over the two of them like a tent. "Szary, do not be angry again. When you feel hot rage, say to yourself it doesn't matter. I want you to think of me, and say that to yourself. Do it."

Her gray eyes, close to his, held him as if her bare arms were around his neck. He looked over her, through the ferns, without seeing anything.

"Do it!"

"Certainly," he grunted.

"Swear it!"

"Yea—by Our Lady."

But his eyes were questing among the ferns for sight of the riders. "Yadvi—you are like a burr under the saddle—you are always sticking close where I have to feel you. Now, please, get on that pony, and get you gone—"

"Swear," her eyes never blinked, "by the *bratsva Polskiego.* Or I will not go because you will need me to watch after you like a footless child—"

He could hear brush crackling below him, and the echo of a man's shout, and quick anger ran like fire through his blood. "By the hide and horns of the Lord of—"

"Hush, Szary!"

He slapped her face and thrust her away, toward the tethered horses.

Years before this, Szary had been able to ride with the *bratsva Pol-skiego*—the winged knights of Poland. Then he could toss the twelve-foot lance in one hand, or slide himself under the neck of a running horse. Now he lived with a stiff right shoulder, and the bones of his hip so knit that he could not grip a horse with his knees again. He could still ride, but not in the rank of the armored fighters that were the best of Poland. And at times black anger made him drunk as with wine. It did not seem to matter to this madcap girl, who laughed at him, and said that now she must be wise for both of them, so that both should live. She wanted to bear the children that would one day climb over his knees.

"Now I think you will remember," she said, as he stared at her. "And that will be well." Then tears gleamed in the gray eyes. "Oh, Szary, I have seen you die once, foolish and headstrong. Now are you something else because you are part of me, so be wary as a wolf—be careful, and live. Here!"

She threw her arms around his neck and her lips touched his mouth. Then because he had to move so slowly—she seized the bundle by him, and shook out his bright blue-and-white cloak, clasping it over his shoulders, which had already begun to grow thin. She lowered his battle sword of gray steel into the sheath at his belt. Then she ran to her shaggy pony, and waved to him, before trotting away through the trees.

"Keep out of sight," he called to her: "Stay with the regiment until tomorrow's night hath passed."

She did not call back to him. He waited until he could see the huntsmen in their green tunics coming up the ravine as if after boar before he hurried toward his mare tied by the fire. He moved slowly, because he limped. He reached the gray mare, set his foot in the stirrup, and hoisted himself into the saddle. He slapped the mare with the end of the reins and turned her up the bank, among the wet ferns. He heard a shout close behind him, and he looked back to see that the huntsmen had spears, and not crossbows. For he did not want to be hit by a crossbow bolt. They were spreading out through the ferns behind him. By now, Yadvi would be clear away.

Szary forced the mare up the slope, but unseen by the huntsmen he pulled hard on the rein. The mare labored and slipped back.

So Szary was caught by the half ring of riders. A dozen of them closed around him, while he turned the mare on her haunches to face them. When he drew his sword and slashed awkwardly to one side, the boar spears of the huntsmen thrust at him. He saved his body from the points, but he could not get through the ring of riders.

The mare staggered from the shock of a heavier charger, and Szary thought his fight was about over. He saw a man over him, massive as a bear—a spear's point held in check.

"Yield you," this rider grunted.

"Tell me your name," cried Szary.

"Arnold of Prauen, Komtur of Vorberg."

Szary let fall his sword and sat back in the saddle, rubbing his side where a steel edge had hacked along his ribs. The fight, he thought, had been just long enough.

Von Prauen motioned for one of his men to pick up the sword, and his blue eyes gleamed with satisfaction as he surveyed it. A gold cross shone on the hilt, and he could make out letters in the worn steel. *Pro patria ad mortem.*

"We have caught," he said to his men, "what is better than a boar. Bind up his side; take the mare's rein."

"To go where?" Szary asked quickly.

"To Vorberg's gate, where no Pole has been before you." Von Prauen smiled. "Does that please you, my Pole?"

Szary hid his gladness. He would get inside Vorberg's gate. "Faith," he lied, "I have heard that the Lord Devil who was accustomed to dwell within Vorberg's halls now seats himself in the nether regions because he finds it pleasanter. I shall see for myself if this be true."

At the hour of nones the chimes sounded in Vorberg's chapel.

To the workers in the fields the castle looked like a dark mountain rising from the plain. A man-made mountain of stone, overlooking the river and the highway to the Baltic. The easternmost castle of the Deutsche Ritter, the Teutonic Knights, who had come up from the south of the German empire to build a chain of such castles into the eastern lands among the pagans of the Baltic. The Knights had built a citadel of their Order at Prague, among the mountain highways, and at the port of free Danzig where the traffic of the Vistula met the sea.

These castles, stretching eastward, had the center of their chain at Marienberg, where dwelt the Meister of the Order. For long, they had been advancing step by step through the forests of the pagan Prussians. With their swords the Knights had overthrown these stubborn pagans, and had baptized the survivors. And now, toward the end of the fifteenth century of grace, they had taken another step toward the East, and Vorberg had risen within the Pole, on the plain itself.

At noon this day as always, von Prauen made his rounds. But this time he took Szary, his prisoner, with him. It suited him that Szary should see the strength of Vorberg.

"What have you equal to this?" he asked curiously, when they climbed to the summit of the keep, where two men-at-arms paced, watching the distant signal towers on the highroad.

Squinting down an arrow slot, Szary shrugged his good shoulder. "Nothing so high," he said, "nothing so big. We have, however, some good horses and women."

Horses, thought the komtur, were desirable to carry the weight of armored men to battle, women to breed sons to bear arms. The sounds from the courtyard below made an orderly hum, each particle of which carried its message to him—like the instrument of an orchestra. A clank sang of a smith's hammer on anvil; a heavy rustling, of hay being thrown out in the stables for the horses of the afternoon patrol. A curious thudding meant that the armigers were rounding out the stone cannonballs. The dry voice of the drillmaster echoed faintly: "Cut . . . cut!"

"Yes, my sir," von Prauen admitted, "you warfarers of the plain have good horses; and you can ride like centaurs. But you cannot ride your chargers through these walls, nor leap over them."

"As to that," Szary objected, "I am not so sure. I am thinking, brother Knight, I can ride with my war band into your gate before the morrow's nightfall."

"Why not to the moon also?" von Prauen asked.

"Some other day for that." Szary looked amused and kept a rein on his temper. "But I say truly, my lord brother. Yea, now I can see a way into this stronghold of yours, and I must say that you are kind and well disposed to bring me hither to this eyrie that I might see it plain."

Von Prauen smiled. And anger stirred in him slowly, for he thought the Pole was mocking the strength of Vorberg. With his eye he measured for the thousandth time the distance between the double walls below him—the nicely calculated flight of a crossbow bolt down, so that the defenders could always command the outer works. He checked over the flame-pourers on the battlements, the stone curtains over the two gates. The walls themselves had been built too massive to be shattered by siege engines, even if the Poles had engines. And their height had been calculated to exceed the length of ladders that could be raised by human strength.

As to mining—the barrier of the river and the moat prevented that. No, the keen intelligence of the experts in the Order, versed in the arts of fortification and siege, had built Vorberg's walls to be impregnable; von Prauen knew that so long as a garrison of any skill held Vorberg's walls, the castle could not be taken.

"That was a senseless boast," he said coldly.

"Nay," Szary laughed, "I have the gift of foresight. I am seeing what is to be, on tomorrow's night."

The smoldering anger flamed up in the German.

"Remember," said Szary, watching him, "I speak as a prisoner, not as a guest. I ask you to surrender Vorberg, to save men's lives."

"To you?"

"While there is time."

Then, even while the hot blood surged into his brain, the komtur saw something below him out of the usual. He heard the chime of a woman's laugh. A girl with unbraided hair had edged herself through the men-at-arms loitering in the water gate. With a basket on her arm, she was chaffing a leather-clad armorer.

"Remain here," the German told Szary. As he turned to descend the stair, he noticed that his prisoner was watching the gate intently.

Her name, she explained to the Germans, was Yadvi and she had come to sell cherries, the first picking of the trees. The Swabian questioned her before von Prauen. The Swabian, who could talk to a mule, understood the chattering Polish tongue.

"The little Yadvi knows it is forbidden to set foot inside our monastic military burg," he said. "But she wanted some coppers, and we have pence—"

"Ask her how she came over the river."

Von Prauen could remember no cherry orchards on this side of the river, and he thought that Yadvi had come far for her pence. A fisher's boat, it seemed, had brought her.

Were many such boats along the far shore?

Yadvi, thoughtfully, admitted seeing only the one.

Had she seen any Poles riding toward the river?

Her gray eyes met von Prauen's stare, and words tumbled out of her, laughing and indignant.

"She says no." The Swabian stretched his long body, enjoying himself. A white scar ran from his brow to chin, and his clipped hair gleamed gray. "She says, what are we getting at? There were Zmud charcoal burners and hunters in the *wald*. Not a wight with arms. She says, what next?"

"Hold her. Let her wait in the stable yard with the Polish prisoner."

The yard was close to the water gate. Von Prauen watched the girl, while the Swabian translated, and he thought the arrest did not frighten her. She grew quiet, and when he motioned her away under guard, she curtsied to the two Knights.

"A sweet mouthful," the Swabian sighed, when she was gone. "Why not let her go without harm?"

Von Prauen shook his head impatiently, and the Swabian drank wine from the cup in his fist, grumbling, "Faith, she is no witch."

"I think I know," the komtur reflected, "what she is."

"Cross yourself and spit thrice, Brother Arnold, when you think you understand a woman. I never could."

His great body rigid, hardened by the weight of armor, von Prauen kept his temper with an effort. The demon of anger still irked him, and he felt the need of a cool head. Wine he never touched, nor had he looked twice at any woman since he took the vows of the Order. But this Swabian, who led Vorberg's spearmen and had fought from Toledo to Danzig, had a wild manner of jesting. Nay, in that moment von Prauen felt that this other brother was more like the dreaming Szary than a servant of the Order.

Before he took the vows, this Swabian, Friedrich, had been a baron. It was whispered in the halls of Marienberg that Friedrich alone had spoken against the Polish war, asking what was the use of it, when the minds of the leaders had understood the need of a new war clearly. For the Deutsche Ritter had come into being as an order of knighthood to rescue that holy place Jerusalem from the pagans; and now that the crusades had ended long since, how was the Order to continue its growth, unless it made itself necessary to the new Germany by involving the Baltic in war. Without war, the military order would have no just claim to exist longer. Even the Hansa merchants, sitting in the council at Marienberg, had understood the necessity for a major war. Brother Friedrich alone had spoken against it, saying that now the pagan Prussians had all been put to the sword or converted to Christ, and the savage Lithuaniani had turned Christian overnight, baptizing themselves in a mass, and the Poles certainly were worshipers of this same Cross the Knights carried—what reason had the Knights to bring a new war to the Baltic?

"Friedrich!" he said abruptly. "What devil of doubt plagues you?"

The Swabian twisted the cup in his heavy fingers. "No devil, Komtur. I have felt too many of my bones break apart." Suddenly he looked up. "No, not that. That was a lie. Only, sometimes I think of those two other men, you and I, who might have been."

"We have Vorberg in our charge!"

"Admitted!" The Swabian smiled. "I was thinking how that other Friedrich could walk in his cherry orchard with his sons. I will never know who my children are—"

"Discipline!"

Von Prauen knew how to jerk the Swabian out of such a black mood. "Two riddles now we have to solve. Item: This Szary, speaking good German, permits himself to be caught like a blind dog and led into Vorberg. Yea, a belted knight yields his sword after a child's scuffle. Item: A Polish girl who is no peasant's wench strays into our gate two hours later. The answer?"

"Both spies of course."

"Granted. They will be watched. Yet can we find a truer answer."

Friedrich nodded. "The little Yadvi lied. My huntsmen have sighted armed bands in the forest moving toward the river. And on the water the Zmud fisherfolk all seem to be casting their lines just out of sight of our towers."

"Boats."

"Sufficient to ferry a regiment across the river. And yesternoon when I rode after boar beyond the forest I saw the regiment. Polish lances, of armored riders. The sun gleamed on the metal. All this, Komtur, you know well."

"It sums up to this: An attack by the forest folk and Poles."

"A surprise onset—"

"And so, to be expected after dark."

"But where?"

The komtur smiled. "Our two Poles, I think, will tell us that."

"The fools!"

"So we will use them." The demon of anger, stiffed by Szary's boasting, gnawed at von Prauen. "Perhaps that wood is the weak point in our defense—when it is leveled and my cannon are in place—I shall have no more to fear. But now we shall first teach the Poles a lesson. It is necessary."

And he explained what he intended to do. The Swabian, surprised, listened intently. Von Prauen felt reassured. Once the action began, he knew that he could depend on the wayward Friedrich.

Long after the vesper bell, the stars came out in a clear sky. Left to themselves in the courtyard, Szary and the girl watched the posting of the night guard, the closing of the water gate. And Szary whispered his anger while she pulled the cloak around his injured side:

"Why can't you stay where you belong, devilkin?"

"Because it's disgusting to be left, and lonely." Yadvi, in the shadow, pressed close to his good side.

While she could touch him, she felt comforted. Her hands had nursed the lance wounds in his frail body, until he could rise and limp around again, miraculously surviving death in that first battle with the terrible Knights. Her voice came softly to his ear: "Now you can't send me away, Szary. You can't."

He took her chin in his hand, so he could see into her eyes, and he felt her tremble. "Yadvi, if you love me, go to the chapel. Keep away from here."

And he hauled himself up to limp along the stones toward the water gate. The stars were clear now, and he expected to hear the bell any second. Keeping away from the fire, where three men idling on watch inside the gate warmed themselves, he edged himself forward. Across the courtyard a torch flared by the stables where serving brothers moved. He looked up, but could not tell how many eyes might be watching from the dark roofs, behind the inner battlements that commanded the courtyard. And he had a feeling of failure in him—he was taking so slight a chance to open up this dominion of armed power.

Then he heard Yadvi's voice, singing softly: "Kyrie eleison—Kyrie eleison." The three men by the fire looked that way with interest.

In the glare of the torch, her basket swinging on her arm, the girl was moving toward the chapel's steps. The light glinted on her hair as she sang. Small wonder that these men-at-arms feasted their eyes on her.

Once the bell sounded and began to toll for evening prayer over the chapel, and Yadvi sang louder, gaily, Szary drew himself in the shadow to where he could reach the bar that had been slid into the socket back of the gate. It was heavy, but he could move the end by straining. He shoved it along until the end barely rested in the socket. The guards were still watching Yadvi. He thought he heard a man shout.

Then, leaning close to the gate, he heard a boat grind against the stone step outside. An oar thumped and feet pattered.

"Ho—the watch!" a voice bellowed.

Szary pushed against the end of the bar, and it fell. The three pikemen at the fire turned to stare. And the gate swung open, toward them. Szary thought that the men on the river had been prompt to come at the bell's tolling. They were pushing now at the iron-studded gate.

"*Vitsi bratsva!*" he called. "Up with the weapon, brothers!"

They came running and leaping through the gate, fur-covered men of the forest, swinging up axes and flails, going for the Germans nimbly. Szary pushed through them, out the gate. Other fishing craft were thrusting out of the darkness, after the first, to the landing beside the big, empty barges of the Germans.

Out of them climbed wild Zmuds and river men, yelling. They ran into the gate.

Up on the chapel steps, Yadvi, shivering with excitement, watched these weapon bearers rush into the courtyard. And it seemed to her that all the inner space of Vorberg came alive at once. Out of the barrack by the gate, giant pikemen advanced to aid the three fighting by the fire. Torches flashed from the inner battlements, where Genoese crossbowmen began to snap their pieces at the onset. The bolts tore through the running men, sending them sprawling. Out of the Knights' hall ran mailclad armigers and, after them, groups of heavy men in steel caps, their white surcoats with the black crosses filling the courtyard, the Knights.

Then Yadvi understood that Vorberg had been waiting for this attack. She could not see Szary in the rush of men. Crowds of Prussians surged past her steps, moving into the gate. The few men swarming up from the river were knocked down and swept back like straw shapes in the wind. Voices barked commands: "Ropes along the barges! Follow with the boards."

The komtur, with the Swabian beside him, walked out to take command. At the gate, von Prauen saw the fishing smacks pulling away, with the remnants of the attackers. Across the river fires glowed, and bands of the forest men crowded restlessly. By the stone steps, carrying out the orders he had given, his men-at-arms were poling the heavy, empty barges into place. Above his head the crossbowmen were following the retreating smacks with their bolts. The attack had been broken in less time than it took the cresset lights to burn bright. Every detail of it had been foreseen by von Prauen's experience.

Across the gleaming water the bands from the forest bayed their anger. The trained men of Vorberg worked in silence. They laid barge against barge, roping them together, out from the steps, driving poles down between them to hold them against the current. Servants laid down a flooring of heavy boards across the barges. With miraculous speed a bridge thrust across the narrow river toward the attackers.

Crossbowmen on the outermost barge kept up a covering fire, against the seemingly masterless crowd on the far bank. The Prussian infantry began to press over, to the other shore.

Then the mailed Knights, who had mounted their chargers at the stables, moved out at a foot pace over the boards. The Swabian took the lead of the first company. "We'll hunt the boars out of their cover," he cried.

When he had gone off, von Prauen called for his own banner and charger. He climbed into the saddle, still feeling that dull anger against the mob that had challenged his stronghold—Szary's boast still rankled. He called to the master armorer to hold the bridge in place with his castle reserve until the return of the Knights. "So we will not wet our feet at our homecoming."

These men of the forest, he thought, had need of a lesson.

And the Knights cleared the far shore without ceremony. The shaggy Zmuds melted away from the fires into the murk of the fens and the trees while the Knights broke up into small companies to follow. The squads of pikemen kept close to the stirrups of the riders, as they pushed through the forest trails, following the dark bands that slipped through the ferns, pausing to fire their bows among the trees before fleeing on. Only on clear ground could the Knights charge, to scatter the bands. They followed torches dancing like St. Elmo's fire through the trees.

"Faith," said the Swabian, "they light the way to the hunt."

Slowly the disciplined array of Vorberg drove the pack, their halberds thrusting through the light flails of the forest men, their mail proof against the flying arrows. Few men fell.

Before them the lights danced away, and the chill of the forest closed in on them. Von Prauen would not turn back. "In the open, we will drive them, and make an end of them."

When he emerged from the trees into the plain with its dark oak clumps he waited until the other formations came through on either flank. Then for the first time, he noticed that the lights of the fugitives had been put out. He had to guide himself by the faint starlight.

Then he noticed how the stars had dimmed overhead. A damp breath from the wet plain chilled his hot head. And a pale lantern, low over the plain, flooded silvery into his eyes. An old moon had risen.

And it showed him that a dark mass which he had taken for an oak grove was moving toward him. He looked at it under his hand, and shouted suddenly: "Halt, the riders! Stand, the pikemen!"

The darkness on the plain moved swiftly now, and it howled as it came. Cold exultation touched the komtur. These, coming at him, were riders in shaggy furs, on nimble ponies. Some of their heads glinted with buffalo horns. Dogs snarled in the rush.

"*Par dex*," he breathed, "what are these animals?"

The voice of the Swabian answered at his shoulder: "Riders of the swamps, Mazovi hunters, Lithuanian bands, boar hounds." And he stood up in his stirrups. "*Gott mit uns!*"

The war shout of the Knights sounded down the line as they met the rush of the wild horsemen, who howled and struck at the long line of the Germans with javelin and sword blade. Their great hounds leaped at the German chargers, and the line swayed here and there. Von Prauen reined back to a rise to watch and the Swabian kept at his side.

"Faith, Arnold," he grumbled, "your hunt is a long hunt. These were waiting for us. They knew well we would come here."

"They save us the trouble of running after them." Von Prauen's eye ran along the steady line of the Germans. Their pikes and swords held easily against the scramble of such wayward fighters. Some wounded dragged themselves back from the line. Then he thought the savage mob gave back a little. He waited to see if it would drift away.

"Now," said Friedrich "they are lighting candles for us."

Off on either flank stacks of old hay blazed up, glowing red in the thin ground mist. Yes, the Lithuanians were drawing back, punished. Von Prauen waited for the moment when he could launch his horsemen across clear ground, to scatter them and make an end of the night's hunt. Already he was thinking it had been a good sally, giving his Prussian infantry a valuable lesson in night work.

And then he saw the movement on the ground, out from the oak grove off to his flank. The Swabian also looked that way, intent and silent. A disciplined body advanced there at a trot, horsemen who kept an even front. Lances raised—lances longer than any von Prauen had seen before. Strange wings bobbed at the riders' backs, and armor gleamed on them.

Polish knights, von Prauen thought. Szary's brothers. He could make out the red banner of Krakow, and the white eagle standard. So, they had been held back in ambush!

"Get the riders moving!" the Swabian grunted suddenly. "Hide of the devil, are you moonstruck, man? Get into motion!"

"Go, you!" von Prauen shouted. "The first company to the left! The second to follow! Wheel them into column—"

But the Swabian had already left his side, riding fast. The Knights on the left had seen the new attack and were turning. Then von Prauen saw the Poles launch into a gallop. Their horses kept close ranks at incredible speed. He thought: "Those men are riders."

The long lances came down with a clash, leveling just as the Polish charge struck his flank. Bright sparks flew where the steel struck, and a rending roar drowned the komtur's voice. He motioned to the trumpeters behind him, and they blew for a wheel to the left.

"Pikemen form on me," von Prauen shouted, raising his helmet on his sword tip. Only the nearest men heard him, because the smashing of wood and metal on the flank drowned his voice. The blare of his trumpets cut through the tumult. And the disciplined Germans began their wheel by companies.

Through the shrilling of the horns, he heard a new sound, an undertone of voices, rising and falling. It sounded familiar, this slow cadence of prayer. He caught a few words: *"Ave Maria gratia plena"*—and it seemed strange to him that the voices of the Poles as they prayed should reach his ears. He did not believe at first that they could be so close. Their long swords slashed before their eagles' wings. They were shearing through his moving men, their great horses racing. They picked openings and came through with swinging swords. They were almost at his mound.

The uproar of that charge beat at his ears. Beyond it the red flames leaped in the mist, and von Prauen felt cold sweat on his skin. He had been shouting and no one had heard him. Why, all this was not to be believed. Hay burning and dogs howling, and mad men praying and weeping through the shriek of steel pounding and breaking. Riders speeding like stone balls from his cannon, and horses overthrown like stacks of wheat—

He was watching a nightmare, under the witchery of that lantern in the sky. He was trying to drive away the nightmare by his voice. And all the while his brain reasoned clearly. Item: The long lances of the Poles had overreached the German weapons. Item: The momentum of the Poles had thrown them like stones through his first and second companies. Because, by sheer carelessness he had allowed his Knights to be caught at a foot pace, in the beginning of a wheel, by an unforeseen charge on the flank.

So, the answer of course was to hold the mound with his Prussian pikes. The disciplined Knights would form on the company leaders and fight their way to a new line at the forest, where they must rally on him.

A Knight without a helmet broke from a knot of wheeling horses. Von Prauen saw, for that instant, the face of the Swabian turned toward him. A Polish rider struck him at an angle, and the Swabian's tired horse went over. The Pole swung down with his sword as he passed.

A hand pulled at von Prauen's rein. The white face of his trumpeter peered up at him. The man's voice quavered: "Sir Komtur, what is the order?"

Von Prauen's mind repeated the order clearly: To draw back to the forest. *They must cut their way back to Vorberg.* Then he heard a man laughing. It was such a jest, this nightmare on the plain, where the damp mist hid his straining, panting men and the white cross of the Poles moved toward him like the wind. His trumpeter tugged, groaning at his rein. And von Prauen knew that he himself was laughing, because no one, now, could hear him give an order.

His clear, orderly mind had betrayed him, and he felt only hot anger. His knees gripped the tired horse under him. His fingers gripped his sword hilt, and he rode down from the mound into that tossing sea of steel.

A blow he took on his shield. His sword smashed out at the buffalo horns on a head, and the head became dark with blood, cracked like a dried melon by the good sword. Something ground into the iron links binding his chest, and he lowered his head. His dry mouth felt damp and sweet, and the red fire before his eyes grew dim. He felt the bones cracking in his chest.

And he looked through half-closed eyes at a clear morning sun. Wet grass cooled his neck, and his empty fingers felt dirt when he moved them.

The heads of two men, unhelmed, looked down at him. Szary's dark face shone with sweat; his eyes blinked wearily. Szary, von Prauen thought, was hurt again, but Szary was alive. Yes, he could smile.

"Sir Komtur," said Szary, "do you hear what I say?"

"Of course."

"Can you ride?"

Von Prauen nodded, and set his teeth against the pain of broken bones grating. The other man spoke. They were waiting for him, if he could sit a horse, to surrender Vorberg to them. By now those of his men who had been fighting their way back through the forest without a leader had yielded themselves in surrender. They had been surrounded in the forest.

"You see," said Szary wearily, "you cannot defend even such a castle as Vorberg without men."

All this, von Prauen thought, could not be so. Even when he rode across the bridge of boats, still intact over the river, that noon, and saw the water gate of Vorberg standing open, with the people of the countryside thronging through, staring at the deserted battlements, he did not believe his eyes. The courtyard of Vorberg was silent, and empty except for that fool-ish girl perched on the chapel steps, waving her head veil at Szary as if such an absurd action could have some meaning.

"It is impossible, this surrender!" von Prauen shouted.

"Perhaps," Szary said. "But it sometimes happens, when a castle is built on a land that will not endure it."

The Making of the Morning Star

Chapter I

*From the Roof of the World we led out our steeds, to follow
the wind for a little play.*

*Where the banners of Islam were unfurled on the ram-
parts of Sarai.*

*Not for wall or door did we draw our reins, till the last
of the banners were laid away,*

*And the shout of "Allah" was heard no more on the ram-
parts of Sarai.*

—The Minstrel's Song

It was a year of many omens. Lightning made the sign of the cross in the
sky, and meteors fell along the road to Jerusalem. When the dry season
began, locusts came and destroyed the vineyards.

In that year, early in the thirteenth century of our Lord, the mailed
host of the crusaders was idle. There was a truce between it and the Saracens who had reconquered Jerusalem and all of the cities of Palestine except the seacoast and the rich province of Antioch.

Before the truce the crusaders had suffered heavily in an attempt to
take the port of Egypt, Damietta, and its triple wall. And the retreat over
the desert to Ascalon had taken its further toll of the lives of peers and
men-at-arms alike. Meanwhile, on three sides of the strip of seacoast, the
Moslems gathered their power for the blow that would send the Croises
back into the sea from which they had come.

So the omens were interpreted as a warning.

The veriest springald of a squire of dames, new come from Venice or
Byzantium and gay with curled ringlets and striped hose, knew that the

truce would not last. The older men-at-arms who had fought under the banner of Richard of England, a generation ago, shook their heads and spent their days in the taverns.

Why not? The omens were evil—so the monks said. And the truce had been arranged by the paynim Saracen—an interval before the storm. The monks also said, it is true, that the locusts had eaten the vineyards but had spared the corn, and that this was a warning to drunkards. But the older warriors preferred to drown thought in their wine cups.

In the great northern province of Antioch, the nobles took refuge from the heat of the dry season. Led by Hugo, Marquis of Montserrat and lord of Antioch, they crossed the long valley of the Orontes and made their way to a castle on the western March, a stronghold in the hills where they might hunt and listen to the tales of minstrel and troubadour.

Robert, castellan of Antioch, made his way out of a labyrinth of clay gullies and gave his bay charger the rein. A glance to right and left revealed no human being astir on the yellow desolation of sand over which he was passing to gain the thicket of reeds ahead.

These withered rushes, he knew, bordered the Orontes River, now low in its bed. The horse lengthened its stride as it scented the water, and Sir Robert urged it on with knee and voice. The bay was dark with sweat, for the knight had pushed on at a round pace since sunup, when they left the last mud hovels of Port St. Simeon and lost sight of the sea.

But they had still far to go before nightfall, and the valley of the Orontes was an ill place to linger—without a strong following of spears. And Sir Robert rode alone.

He had landed the day before at St. Simeon with his horse and little else. Two years ago he had been wounded in the Egyptian campaign and had been made prisoner by the mamelukes at the wall of Damietta. It had taken many a month to arrange for his release, for among his enemies Sir Robert bore a name that set him apart from his fellows. By reason of the great sword he carried—a straight, tapering blade, a full four feet of blue steel—they called him Longsword.

And so did the minstrels name him when they made a song about him thereafter.

As he entered the rushes he drew rein sharply and turned in the saddle to stare down at a fresh trail that ran athwart the path he was following. Many a man would have passed it by with a casual glance. But the castellan had been born in the hills that towered over Antioch, and he knew the sandy wastes of the Orontes as his father before him had known the courtyard of an earl's hold in England.

The trail was a narrow one, yet possibly a hundred horses had passed over it. The tracks were made by unshod hoofs, so the riders must have come in from the desert. And they had kept to the rushes instead of the main path, higher up where the clay was firmer.

They had wished to hide their tracks as far as possible, yet they had chosen a route in the open where they would be easily observed, unless—the castellan fancied they had traveled at night.

He would have liked to follow the trail. But a sound from the heights he had just left caused him to glance up quickly. The faint drumming of hoofs was unmistakable. An arrow's flight distant, he noticed dust rising above the red clay ridges that lined the gullies.

Waiting long enough to be sure that only one rider was coming after him, he put the bay at the ford and crossed over the river, restraining the horse from stopping to drink. Nor did he look back as he rode slowly up the far bank.

Entering a dense growth of gray tamarisk, higher than the crest of his helm, Robert halted and wheeled his horse to face the back trail where it turned sharply. Pulling the long, triangular shield from its loop over his shoulder, he slid his left arm through its bands and took his sword in his right.

Sir Robert smiled, and his gray eyes, under the steel of the helm, lighted with pleasure. The day's ride, that had been dull and hot until now, promised entertainment.

When he heard hoofs thudding over the sand he pricked the flanks of the bay with his spurs and the two horses met shoulder to shoulder at the edge of the tamarisks. And the castellan, learning forward, thrust the top of his shield over the stranger's sword hilt, gripping the weapon in the fingers of his left hand.

The other rider was not slow to act. A twist of the reins, and his horse lunged aside. But the weapon, held by Sir Robert under the shield, slipped from its scabbard and remained in the hands of the knight.

"*Ma kaharani!*" said the stranger under his breath. "And what now?"

He was a man gray-haired and massive of limb, clad in splendor of embroidered vest and kaftan, and his brown eyes were shrewd. A Moslem by his garments and turban, yet a Moslem who did not sit in the saddle like a Turk or Arab.

Slung over his shoulder, instead of a shield, was a lute. Behind his saddle, a prayer rug. Sir Robert thought him to be a wandering minstrel.

"Your name!" he demanded, for he ever liked plain words.

Arabic came easily to his tongue, as he had been raised among his father's slaves.

"I am Abdullah ibn Khar, the teller of tales, the cup-companion of an emperor."

The castellan considered him and saw that he was not afraid, though disarmed. The horse Abdullah bestrode was a remarkably fine one, a black Kabuli stallion.

"When does a minstrel of Islam follow the shadow of a Nazarene?" Sir Robert asked curtly.

The white teeth of the stranger flashed through the black tangle of his beard.

"*Wallah!* You ride with a loose rein. Surely a penned tiger is kin to the young warrior who is freed from camp. Not otherwise was I, in another day. To a woman or a battle, a man should ride boldly."

"And you?"

"I followed to see your face."

He studied the dark features of the Norman, the thin, down-curving nose and the powerful neck. Sir Robert had his mother's hair of tawny gold that fell to the mail coif on his shoulders. The hot temper of his race was his, yet the quiet, as well, of those who have great physical strength.

"Aye, a woman could summon you across the Orontes," nodded the minstrel, "if you chose to come. A battle is another thing. Are you the paladin of the Franks—the Longsword?"

"Aye, so."

"In the village by the sea a saddlemaker pointed you out and said that you were he, although many thought you dead. So I found my horse and sought you, for company on the road. There is a truce between our peoples."

"So that your spies may enter our walls."

"And your great lords may hawk and dice at leisure. Many things have I seen—your men-at-arms picking their noses, having no better thing to do—your king holding court on an island, because his foes cannot ride over the paths of the sea. Yet I have not seen a leopard change his skin, nor a spy look otherwise than faithless. *Allah kerim!* Do I look like a pryer?"

Sir Robert thought that the man was bold enough. The horse under his hand might have been the gift of an emir.

"You do not look like a minstrel," he laughed.

The man's words rang unpleasantly true. The Christian barons spent their days in bickering with each other. They were a weaker breed than the first crusaders who had fought their way over the desert to Jerusalem and left their bones in the land they conquered. Venetians, Genoese, Bavarians, and French—the new lords were more apt at gleaning profit from trade than at defending the fiefs they held.

In the last years the men who had been the heroes of Sir Robert's childhood had passed elsewhere, some stricken by the plague, some thrust into the torture chambers of the neighboring Saracens. Others had sailed back to the courts of Europe.

Now the galleys brought to Palestine disorderly throngs of pilgrims who were more than willing to pay a fee to the Saracens to visit the Sepulcher and bear away a palm.

This troubled Sir Robert, who had known no other land, and no fellowship other than that of the Croises.

While he mused, Abdullah had been studying his face. Now the minstrel leaned down swiftly and caught up a fistful of sand.

"My lord," he said, "I can read what passes in your mind. Who can change a book that is written, if that book be fate? No one among the Franks can keep Palestine for long, and your people will go again upon the sea whence they came. And their empire will pass—so!"

He loosed his fingers, letting fall the sand, and the castellan started.

"In the Fiend's name, mummer, did you ride from the sea to tell me this?"

"Nay, am I a fool?" Abdullah's thick chest rumbled with laughter. "I sought the Longsword, and I found a youngling," he added. "Did you, in truth, hold the wall of Antioch against Nasr-ud-deen and his spears?"

"Now that you have found me, seek another with your tricks. I have no largess to give."

Abdullah glanced reflectively at the castellan's faded surcoat and weather-stained shield from which the armorial device had long since been battered out.

"Largess, my lord, awaits me in the hall of Montserrat, whither I think you draw your reins—unless," he added gravely, "you fear to have Abdullah for *refik*—companion on the road."

Robert frowned and tossed the Moslem his scimitar.

"Go where you will, knave!"

Turning the bay aside, he passed by the minstrel and let his horse go down to the river to drink. Meanwhile his glance swept the Orontes and the bare, red hills that pressed down upon it, for signs of other riders who might have followed Abdullah and lain concealed during the talk.

But the far side of the river, shimmering through the heat haze, was empty of life.

Abdullah had followed his example, and when the stallion had lifted its fine head to let the water run out between its teeth, he turned in the saddle.

"Will the lord grant one boon to his servant? Your word that I shall not be harmed by the Nazarenes at Montserrat?"

Robert shook his head. He had been taught by his father never to break his word, whether given to a Moslem or one of his own peers. Abdullah, however, seemed satisfied with this response, and rode ahead up the trail of his own accord.

They had no more than entered the tamarisks again when both reined to a halt, and the horses fidgeted. From up the hill loud voices drew nearer, with a clattering of iron, a yapping of dogs, a braying of asses, and a creaking of wheels that made a small bedlam of the quiet of the valley.

From between the gray bushes emerged a gaunt man, stumbling under the weight of a tall banner of soiled samite upon which was embroidered a crimson cross. On his heels tramped a throng ragged and filthy, living scarecrows with feverish eyes.

Drawing aside from the trail, Robert watched the company pass. Some carried bundles slung to pike or staff-bundles that jingled and clanked, spoil beyond a doubt snatched from some native village. Many lay sick in the lumbering oxcarts, and a leper walked alone at a cart tail, his bell clinking when he stumbled.

In another *araba* lay a woman, suckling a child scarcely a month old. A lad whose only garment was a torn shirt peered up through the dust at the knight and the minstrel.

"Good my lord, is't far to Jerusalem?"

"Too far for a springald such as you," Robert responded gruffly. "What company is this?"

The boy pointed proudly to the red cross sewn on his shirt.

"Messire," he piped, "I am from Provence, like the demoiselle herself. We heard the blessed de Courcon preach, and we are come to deliver the city of Christ out of paynim duress."

He trotted on, and an English yeoman in green jerkin and feathered hood stopped to scowl blackly at Abdullah, and spit.

"A murrain upon yon infidel! When we set forth we e'en had forty thousand such as that—" nodding after the boy—"and now, by the shadow of ——, we have but two. Aye, he and the lass."

"——'s wounds!" cried Robert. "Was this a crusade of the children?"

"Ah, that it was, tall my lord! Verily the mob did betake itself to divers paths from Byzantium, some adventuring upon the sea—and St. Giles and St. Dunstan ha' mercy on them—some upon the coast, where they did fall to quarreling and warring with the Armenians, and are no better this day than crow's meat, drying i' the wind. Our company was five hundred strong when we left Byzantium behind. And now—" He leaned on his staff and jerked a thumb at the rear of the party. The pilgrims numbered no more than five score.

"A black malison on the infidels, say I."

Robert wondered who the lass of this array might be, but just then some dozen men began to crowd around Abdullah, cursing him and fingering the axes at their belts. Someone flung a stone that made the black horse rear, the minstrel keeping his seat in the saddle with easy grace.

"Salvation awaits him who sheds the blood of a Saracen!" cried a giant with a pocked face.

"Seize his horse for Father Evagrius!" suggested another.

"Send him to pare the ——'s hoofs!"

Taking up his reins, Robert urged the bay between the angry throng and his companion. Whatever the mission upon which Abdullah of Khar had been sent, the man was of gentle blood, and the nobles of Palestine had sworn a truce with the Moslems, giving hand and glove upon it. This oath Robert felt to be binding unless the enemy broke the truce.

"Back, ribalds," he commanded. "Pass on. This is a minstrel who rides with me."

The mob seemed made up of villains, of commoners, and the knight did not feel called upon to voice reasons for his action to them. As some men in rusty haburgeons drew their swords, he rose in his stirrups to peer through the dust.

"Ho, the leader of this pack! The chief of these rogues, I say—call hence your varlets or it will be the worse for them."

At this the throng parted, and an old priest rode up on a white donkey led by a young girl. Flinging back the hood of her gown, she looked up angrily at Robert.

"Messire! Unsay what you have said, and that without ado."

She took the charger's rein in a gloved hand, and stamped a slender foot angrily and a little awkwardly, for it was clad in an Armenian red leather boot several sizes too large. Robert glimpsed a white face pinched by hunger and eyes shadowed by ripples of hair dark as a raven's wing.

"This is our patriarch, Sir Lout," went on the maid in a clear voice, "and Father Evagrius is blind. Climb down from your big horse and kneel and ask his pardon and blessing."

"Nay, Ellen," put in the patriarch, "it is not seemly that a stranger and a man-at-arms should kneel—"

"I say he shall! Nay, he is no sergeant-at-arms but a spurred lordling. His companion is a black-browed Moslem, and surely that is not seemly."

Against the crowd of grease- and vermin-ridden men the slight figure of the maid stood out in bold relief. The pulse throbbed in her delicate throat, and the circles darkened under her eyes that blazed with the tensity of long suffering. Abdullah glanced from her to Robert with some amusement.

"Father Evagrius," observed the knight, "if you are verily the leader of this company you do ill to turn your back on the castle of Montserrat. The river is scarce a safe abiding-place."

"Messire," responded the maid Ellen quickly, "the lord of Montserrat hath seen fit to order us away from his hold to the river."

"How? His Grace, the marquis—"

"—doth lack of courtesy, even as you. Perchance he feared lest the ribalds trample his coverts or disturb the sleep of his hunting hounds."

"Demoiselle," explained Robert calmly, "I am the vassal of Hugo of Montserrat, and even now I seek his hold, above in the border mountain chain. And I do maintain that he would not send a Christian company into hazard of their lives."

"Sir Stiff-and-Stuffy, I do maintain that your Hugo hath turned us off."

While Robert stared at her perplexed, yet finding an unexpected pleasure in meeting the glance of a girl of his own race after years spent without sight of a woman, he heard the gentle voice of the priest.

"The good marquis hath given his word that he will protect us against all foes upon his marches. And the Orontes, where we will pass the night, doth lie within his border."

"Then are you safe," nodded Robert. "Montserrat, having given his pledge, will keep it."

"And now, Sir Vassal," added the girl, Ellen, "do you kneel to the patriarch. Ah, he is a very saint, and his spirit dwells near to the throne of God—whom you miscalled a moment ago."

Robert, looking down upon her youthful rage—the maid scarce numbered more than fifteen years—tried in vain to stifle a hearty laugh. At this she flushed from throat to eyes and slipped off the hawking gauntlet upon her hand. Standing on her toes, she struck him swiftly across the lips.

The force of the blow knocked the glove from her grasp. Robert swung down from his stirrup and picked it up. When he stepped toward her she did not draw back, but clenched thin hands and stood her ground. Her followers, who had time to take in Robert's spread of shoulder and the length of his sword, made no move to molest him—though he paid no heed to them.

"I give you back your glove, demoiselle," he said, smiling at her boldness. "And I would that you and the good father would turn back with me to Montserrat."

"You mock us! Never—we would never go with you."

"By the saints! I meant no ill to you or the blind priest," denied the knight gravely.

"Come, Ellen," said Evagrius, "you have delayed our march, and I feel that the sun is sinking near the earth. A week from this hour we shall bathe in the Jordan, and you shall see the Mount of Olives."

His lined face was lighted by inward rejoicing as he felt for the donkey's halter. But the girl bent her head, and Robert heard her sob as she moved away. Frowning, he watched them pass into the dust cloud.

Why, he wondered, had the maid wept? Surely there was pride in her, and gentleness, for she tended the helpless Evagrius.

"*Yah refik*," observed Abdullah, "You know little of a woman's spirit. That was a comely child and—I had fancied, lord, that you rode in such haste to meet with a woman."

"There are none in the castle we seek."

"*Wallah!* Can it be?"

He looked more than a little skeptical, yet the other's response appeared to give him satisfaction. As they passed up into the rocky gorges of the foothills Abdullah swung his lute around to his saddle peak and began to sweep his fingers across the strings, chanting in his fine voice.

He sang of the joy of racing the stag over the hills, and of watching the falcon stoop, and of wandering under the dome of the stars. Robert, hearkening despite himself, felt the magic of the other's gift of song. In his mind's vision he went back to boyhood, riding with his father over the desert floor, calling to staghounds. He knew again the thrill of loosing a hawk against the midday sky, and the cheer of the fire when the hunt was done and the wine cup made the rounds.

Abdullah sang on, and Robert's memory changed to the days of stark hunger when a Moslem city was beleaguered; he watched the men fashioning great mangonels and massive siege towers—for he had been taught the arts of the siege engines when most boys were playing at jousting.

Lean years thronged into his mind. Years spent in the saddle with the nucleus of the mailed host that had struggled to keep the banner of the Croises upon the walls of Jerusalem. Days of hideous din, when streets under the eyes of the lad had run with blood until the very bodies were washed into the gutters.

As the minstrel sang on, he felt a restlessness in his veins. A craving to wander, as he had often done with his comrades, beyond the border and try his strength against foes.

"Faith!" he cried, spurring on the big bay. "We loiter apace."

Abdullah put aside his lute and brought up the black stallion, bridle to bridle.

"Aforetime," he observed, "I made that song for my master, who is master of all men."

Robert did not ask him who this might be, because at that moment they heard rising from the depths behind and below them a hum of human voices.

"*Te Deum laudamus.* We praise Thee, O Lord—we praise and magnify Thee forever."

It was the chant of the pilgrims, who were visible only as a thin line of dust moving into the maw of the Orontes, where the network of gorges was shadowed by the early sunset in royal purple, the pinnacles crowned with red and gold. The two men paused to look back.

"See, how Allah hath hung in the sky the crimson banners of death," remarked Abdullah. "And we—who knows what days are before us?"

Chapter II
A Year and a Day

The glory of the sunset had dwindled when the two riders halted without the barbican gate of the castle of Montserrat. In the western sky the afterglow ran the length of the horizon, forming the semblance of a dull-red river flowing above the earth.

Light glimmered from the upper embrasures of the black donjon. The wall behind the moat shut out the courtyard from the travelers' sight; but they heard voices and the clinking of bowls on wooden tables and a snatch of song.

Robert, who was mightily hungry, struck the bars of the peephole with his mailed fist. In the hall of the main keel he knew that Hugo, his liege lord, Marquis of Montserrat and master of Antioch, sat at table with a goodly company. And the castellan was eager to greet his peers, who thought him dead after an absence of two years in Egypt, and to satisfy his hunger.

"Ho, the gate!" he shouted. "Open in the name of Montserrat."

But the face of the warder that peered through the barred opening in the portal did not withdraw.

"Thy name! And thy companion's name! Small thanks would be ours, I trow, if we unbarred to a Saracen after sundown."

"Sir Robert, castellan of Antioch, am I—Longu'-espée, Longsword, forsooth. And he with me is a paynim minstrel with a song for the marquis. What now?"

Robert's mustache twitched in a grin of amusement as he heard an exclamation, followed by whispered voices. Other faces pressed to the bars to scrutinize him in the dim light.

"Out upon thee for a lying wight," growled one. "Sir Robert was racked, carted, and buried by the accursed mamelukes."

Behind the gate was heard the grinding clink of a crossbow, wound up to speed a shaft. Robert turned to Abdullah.

"Minstrel, are you resolved to enter this hold? Methinks they give but an ill welcome to wayfarers—though Hugo loves well a good tale and a tuneful voice. Forget not that I stand in no way your protector, and what befalls is e'en your hazard."

"So be it."

"——'s death!" Robert kicked the gate impatiently. "Set wide the gate and make an end of words. Fetch a cresset, varlets, or I'll set the pack of you aswim in the moat."

Someone remarked that this sounded rarely like the Longsword, and a torch was brought while they examined the visitors. Then the bars were let down slowly, and Robert pushed inside, followed by Abdullah.

A bearded captain of the warders crossed himself with a muttered—"Mary preserve us—'tis he!"

The men who were lowering the drawbridge glanced at each other and whispered behind their hands, and it was several moments before the castellan and his companion dismounted in the courtyard and were greeted by a staring squire.

Word of their arrival had passed to the main hall before them. A slim *poursuivant* who bowed low at the door seemed to share the general hesitation in announcing them, and Robert was fain to chuckle again at the bewilderment of those who greeted him. At the end of the lofty hall candles gleamed on the table set on a dais for the master of the castle and his guests, and here a man stood up to peer over the candles as the knight strode forward between the long tables of the henchmen and commoners.

"Madre a dios!"

His broad, olive face paled, and he grasped the arm of his chair.

"If ye be a spirit, why—why, know then that I have mourned you right hardily, having given to the shave-pates a ten shekels, aye, and thirty *soldi* for clank of bell and patter of prayer for this your soul. If ye be Sir Robert, lad, i' the flesh, why—"

"That am I, and sharp-set with hunger into the bargain."

"Ha, that would be the Longu'-espée. Why —— boil me, lad, but we heard that you were cut down at the gate of Damietta. Aye, a Templar saw you carried within, and shortly thereafter your bare body hung out on the wall headless, to despite your comrades."

Hugo shook his head doubtfully—a craggy head, yet covered with curled ringlets, oiled after the fashion of his native Italy. His broad, stooped body was clad in silk, covered with a damask mantle, fur-trimmed, that fell below the toes of his velvet shoes, which were turned up in the latest style and held by silver chains running from his girdle. His nearsighted eyes blinked at Abdullah, and Robert made known the minstrel.

"A fair greeting have we," quoth the marquis, fingering his chin, "for *trouvère* and *déchanteur*, for makers and tellers of tales. But a noose and a fire beneath for spies. Bid him to the lower board."

He turned to his companions.

"Messires, give greeting to this Englishman who is well come, having cheated the Saracens yet another time—though I vow to St. Bacchus my spleen rose to my gullet when he fronted us."

After removing his *bascinet* and handing his shield to a squire-at-arms, Robert hooked his sword over a chair and seated himself to wash his hands in a silver bowl offered by a serving knave. Hugo divided his attention between his footgear and his guest impatiently until Robert had stayed his hunger.

"*Olá*, knaves—wine of Cyprus for our guests. Come, lad, the tale! Messer Guiblo—" he nodded at a thin, handsome Venetian whose rich velvets were the envy of the poorer liegemen—"made search for you in the camp of the king, and all reports had you dead."

He bent forward to lean on the table addressing the other guests.

"Know, messers, that Sir Robert, called Longu'-espée, did once save for us our city of Antioch, being rarely skilled at the making of stone-casters and fire-throwers, aye, at counterwalls and curtains, *chat-castels* and all the engines of siege."

Besides the Venetian, Guiblo, a young Provençal, sat at the side of the marquis. Hugo spoke of him as the Sieur de la Marra, a Hospitaler. On the far side of the knight of the Marra was a dark-faced Lombard whom Robert knew as Hugo's seneschal. Other warriors and a scattering of Venetian merchants he did not know. No other Englishmen sat at the table. But Robert had noticed a woman who had the chair on the right of the marquis.

"The Madonna del Bengli —" Hugo followed his glance—"honors our poor dwelling of Montserrat for sake of the hunting and hawking in the hills."

Robert rose and bowed courteously, wondering why such a woman should come over the valley of the Orontes for the sake of a little sport. She was a Venetian undoubtedly, and, he learned later, the cousin of the man Guiblo. Certainly she was beautiful and aware of it, for her bronze-red hair was scented and coiled skillfully on her bare shoulders; her white skin gave no evidence of the sun's touch.

"Equally honored are we," she added lightly, "in such a visitor and his grace of Montserrat in such a vassal."

Her curving lips accented the word vassal, and she turned to stare at Robert out of clear blue eyes. Guiblo leaned back to pick his teeth and exchange a word with the seneschal. Robert was little skilled in the manners of a court, or in play of words, yet it struck him that his welcome at Montserrat lacked of heartiness.

"By Venus, her girdle," lisped the young knight of the Hospital, whose cheeks were warmed by wine, "would we had a Provençal to make song out of Longu'-espée's tale. Nay, his name is already known from Antioch to Ascalon. Didst bind the infidel jailers with their own fetters, Sir Robert—or win the heart and abetment of some fair Saracen maid, as the fashion is?"

"Not so," made answer Robert bluntly. "Your Grace, I bring but two words. One a warning, one a request."

Hugo set down his cup.

"Then let us have the warning."

"A hundred Saracens armed and mounted for war passed through your border within the day."

"Now by the slipper of our fair madonna, that could not be. Our watchers on the borderland have seen no foray pass. Nay—"

"I saw the tracks, across the river."

The marquis pursed his lips and shook his head, then signed for a servant to fill the Longsword's cup.

"I pray you, Messer Englishman," put in Guiblo incredulously, "how could you discern from tracks in the sand what manner of men passed over?"

"How? The hoofs were small—blooded Arabs or Turkomans. They were unshod and so from the desert. To my thinking no pack-animals were among them, and so each horse had its rider."

Mistress Bengli raised slim fingers in polite surprise, and by so doing displayed gleaming sapphire and turquoise rings, rarely fashioned.

"Truly we have a magician with us. Do they not say that the Egyptians are masters of the black arts?"

"Some band of villagers," scoffed Hugo, "chanced to wander along the river. And now your boon. Hawk or horse, or—a fair maid of Circassia for your beguilement; 'tis granted ere asked."

"My life it is," Robert smiled, "I seek at your hand."

"Misericardé—how?"

"At the Damietta wall I was struck down by a mameluke's mace. It is true they pulled my body within the gates; but the hurt mended, and in time I could mount a horse. Being captive, they held me for ransom, yet could no letter be sent in the turmoil until truce was made between Saracens and Croises. Then did the paynim emirs grant me a year and a day to journey to my overlord and raise the payment for the freedom of my body."

Some of the Venetians looked skeptical, for seldom did the enemy put trust in the crusaders to this extent. Yet they were aware that the Longsword had before this kept his promises to the Moslems.

"Well," observed Hugo, "you are here, and you are free. The Cairenes cannot lay hand on you now. On my life, I was not aware that you had a tongue to trick those unshriven dogs."

"I gave my word to return to their camp if the ransom is not in their hands within a year and a day."

"Oho, a prayer and a gold candlestick to the cathedral at Antioch will eke shrive you of a pledge to infidels. So say the monks."

Robert shook his head gravely. "My word was passed."

"But, fool, the mamelukes would tie you to horses and split you. You have emptied too many of their saddles and wrought them woe too often for them to forego the pleasure of torturing you."

He glanced sidewise at the set face of the youth and emptied his goblet, then laid his hand on the shoulder of the woman.

"Do you, make shift to alter the mind of our stubborn vassal; perchance he will listen to reason from other lips than ours—"

Seeing that Robert frowned, he thought for a moment. "What then is the sum of your ransom?"

"Two thousand broad pieces of gold."

"Horns of the fiend! 'Tis the release of a baron of the realm."

A smile touched the lips of the knight.

"My lord, having fought against Longsword, it chances that the Saracens do hold me to be greater than I am."

The demand of the vassal was a just one. By the feudal laws Robert was bound to serve in the wars of Montserrat, and to come mounted and fully armed at the summons of his lord. For this service, instead of a fief and lands, Hugo had appointed him castellan of Antioch, granting him the payment and perquisites of his office—for though the Englishman was young for such responsibility he had shown his ability to handle the defense of a stronghold against siege. If Hugo had been taken captive, Robert would have been obliged to raise his share of the marquis' ransom. So he had sworn when he placed his hands between the knees of Hugo, and his lord was equally bound.

The marquis flung himself back in his chair with an oath, and Mistress Bengli studied the jewels on her fingers, a slight frown creasing her smooth forehead.

"Two thousand *byzants!*" he muttered. "It passes reason—to raise such a sum for a mere punctilio, a splitting of hairs. *Mort de ma vie!* Shall we mortgage our souls to swell the wallets of filthy unbelievers. Eh?"

The woman close to his ear spoke softly, and the Italian shrugged.

"You went to Egypt on no mission of mine, Longsword; and, now I think of it, you are cursed with wandering. Let the matter stand for the nonce, and we will talk of it at a better time."

"Not so, Lord," objected Robert at once. "If you cannot advance to me the entire sum, I must make shift to find a share of it, and perchance sell my office of castellan."

"Pardon, messire," put in the Venetian, Guiblo, "you are no longer castellan, for the king hath appointed another."

"Who?"

"Aye, now it comes to my mind," laughed the marquis, "our new monarch out of France hath brought with him a vassal who hath rendered loyal service to the State. Believing you dead, he did appoint Messer Guiblo here castellan."

The thin Venetian bowed.

"I regret the mischance suffered by the youth, and I would that he had seen fit to endeavor to advise his liege of his situation while in Egypt."

"I give you thanks for your courtesy," responded Robert, frowning; and Guiblo's eyes narrowed.

The Englishman had not kept his disappointment out of his voice. True, he could not quarrel with the turn matters had taken. The king whose standard he had followed, Baldwin, had died in the last years when Jerusalem had been lost, and the baron who had been chosen to succeed him was a favorite of the French king. But now, unless the marquis aided him, as he was bound to do, Robert would have no means of raising his ransom in Palestine. And not a man present at the table doubted that the

Englishman would keep his promise to return to Damietta and his captors if the sum were not raised.

"My lord," he asked, "what is your answer—yea or nay?"

Hugo curled an oiled ringlet around his forefinger and sucked in his
lips. Silence fell on the company, and Mistress Bengli exchanged a quick
glance with Guiblo.

"Alas," she sighed audibly, "our table doth lack of gaiety since the coming
of Sir Robert. Will your Grace permit me to answer the Englishman?"

"Aye," quoth Hugo, pleased. "Let us hear the judgment of Diana. *Pardi*,
Sir Robert, it would have availed you more to urge your suit more gal-
lantly. Then the madonna might have smiled upon you—for you are comely
enough to win favor with the fair."

"The fairest face in Palestine," murmured the Hospitaler a little
vaguely.

"And now," she added, "having heard the plea of the vassal, we must
take counsel of the learned. How now, O seneschal and merchants—are
not we in the hands of the moneylenders? Hath his Grace of Montserrat
such a sum where it can be called in and rendered into gold?"

Piculph, the Lombard seneschal, had gauged the pleasure of the marquis and made answer accordingly.

"Nay, *domna*, the very jewels of the rings you wear are paying usury
to the Jews."

"Then must we pawn our very lives, that this dour Englishman—"

A chuckle from Hugo interrupted her, and she wrinkled her brows in
pretended displeasure. The marquis lolled in his chair, delighted with the
wordplay of his favorite, while he stroked the feathers of a favorite hawk
perched beside him.

"—be safe," she concluded, "unless he dare seek his ransom with his
sword from the hands of those Moslems about whom he doth prate so
roundly."

It became clear to Robert that they were mocking him, for the marquis was lord of wide lands and great treasure. Guiblo disliked him, realizing that the former castellan of Antioch might urge his claim upon the
king. Hugo, indifferent to everything that did not minister to his pleasure, had little desire to grant a small store of gold to the knight for what
he held to be merely a quirk of conscience.

"And so," said Mistress Bengli, smiling full upon Robert, "it is our
pleasure that you should seek to gain your treasure from the castles of
the paynims—a worthy quest for the Longu'-espée—"

"Aye, let the wild boar root i' the thicket," shouted Piculph.

"—for a year and a day," cried the woman shrilly above the maudlin merriment of the feasters, "and that is the sentence of the court of his peers."

"Is it yours, my lord?" Robert leaned forward to address his host.

"It is so," responded Hugo without looking up.

But up from the table rose the Sieur de la Marra unsteadily, yet with a purpose in his bleared eyes.

"By the throne of Antichrist, by the palladium of the Horned One, 'tis a foul wrong so to mischief a warrior of the Cross. Has your Grace forgotten that he kept your wall of Antioch against the Saracen spears when the waters of the moat were red with blood?"

Alone of those present the knight of the Marra was not bound to the fortunes of Montserrat by ties of ambition, and Guiblo frowned at his words. The recent truce had altered the situation in Palestine and the mastery of the rich coast cities was passing into the hands of the Lombards and Venetians who had no wish to see the barons of England or France return to the court. Knowing that Hugo wished to be rid of the Longsword, Guiblo made answer accordingly:

"Hast wooed the cup too long this night, Sir Hospitaler. Art a fool to give belief to the tale of this wanderer. If my lord of Montserrat had not deemed his tale a lie, he would have granted the Longu'-espée his boon. But two thousand pieces of gold for a vassal's ransom passes belief—when the asker rides with a Moslem."

"Now by Venus, her girdle," cried the Sieur de la Marra, reaching a quivering hand for his sword, "that touches upon mine honor—"

"I give you thanks, Sir Hospitaler," broke in Robert, "for your abetment, but no man's aid seek I."

The red lips of Mistress Bengli curled, for here was a quarrel brewing, and she loved well to see men put themselves to the hazard of drawn steel. She did not fear for Guiblo, knowing that her cousin was well able to make shift for himself, and as for Hugo—a vassal might not strike or miscall his lord. But she was more than a little puzzled when Robert signed for his cup to be filled and waited until Hugo had done likewise.

"My lord," he said slowly, "I greet you with this, my stirrup cup. In this hour I ride from Montserrat, and my allegiance is at an end. No vassal am I, but my own man henceforth, by your will. With Messer Guiblo and the seneschal I shall have other speech."

He emptied his goblet and Hugo did the same. Then the Englishman beckoned to Abdullah at the lower table, and in the silence that had fallen upon the company his summons was clearly heard.

"O minstrel, a song for the people of the castle. We have had our dinner, it seems, and the wine thereof, and in this place a man must pay a reckoning for all that is bestowed upon him. Sing, O Abdullah, of gold and gear and treasure, that they may be pleasured, for my entertainment was but indifferent and dull."

At this the marquis flushed, while his followers fingered the poniards in their belts; but Mistress Bengli laughed musically, for the Englishman promised to be entertaining after all. Abdullah rose without comment and salaamed to the marquis and the woman. Advancing to the edge of the dais, he lifted his lute and plucked softly at the strings.

"In the name of Allah, the All-Compassionate, the All-Wise," he began in liquid Arabic, "will the illustrious lords hearken to the tale of a poor wayfarer?"

His powerful hand swept over the lute, and he chanted, deep-voiced:

"With Allah are the keys of the unseen, and who is bold enough to take in hand the keys? Doth lack of gold, O king, or jewels for the hilts of swords, or horses fleeter than the desert storm, or garments softer than the petals of flowers? Then hearken to my tale of Khar, the Land of the Throne of Gold."

Those of the listeners who understood Arabic, and they were many, glanced up in some surprise. The legend of Khar had come to their ears before this, but never in the same guise.

They had heard that beyond the eastern mountain wall was a wide desert and beyond this a sea of salt water. Far to the east lay the greatest of the Moslem kingdoms, so it was said. This was known as Khar, or Khorassan,* and many were the tales of its wealth.

Like Cathay or the land of Prester John, the myth was voiced by wandering minstrels, and no man knew the truth of it, and no warrior of the Croises had penetrated farther to the east than the city of Damascus.

"Know, O auspicious lord," chanted Abdullah, "that it hath been my lot to follow the path of a wayfarer. From the Roof of the World I have looked down upon a land fairer than moonlight on a mountain lake; I

---

*Khar, or Kharesmia, is now known as Persia. The old name is to be found on maps as late as the end of the eighteenth century. (In the present day it is known as Iran.—HAJ)

have walked through gardens where roses were wrought of rubies, with emeralds for leaves; I have sat in a marble tower and beheld the passing of a monarch who hath more riders to his command than the Sultan of Damascus hath stones in his highways. Verily, as grains of sand is the number of warriors in this land. They walk in silvered mail with the plumes of birds upon their heads; their weapons are of blue steel, and the power of their host is such that the mamelukes of Egypt would bow down to them, even as grass before a rising wind."

Some of the guests smiled, and the Venetians, who were the wisest of the assemblage, sneered openly as at a palpable lie.

"*Yah maulaya*, O my lord, this is truth. The very trees of the palace gardens in this place are silver; and the monarch thereof hath a lake within his city—a lake built by the hands of his slaves. Within the courtyard of his castle stands a fountain, casting forth water perfumed with musk and aloes."

Hugo of Montserrat sighed and curled the lock of hair upon his forehead.

"In this land the lords are carried about by their slaves; save to mount a horse they do not set foot to earth. When the king drinks *nakars* and trumpets sound; when he walks in his chambers, rolls of silk are spread before him. He dwells in a city so great that the eye cannot measure it from one place. The women of his court are the fairest in the world, for they are brought from every land that his riders can adventure to.

"Verily," said the teller of tales slowly, "this king is the lord of life and death, for men seeking the joys of his court oft-times perish in the journey thither. But, having come, their joys are the fullest that life can measure out."

Chapter III
The Riders from Khar

"With Allah are the keys of the unseen." Abdullah ceased his say and took his hand from his lute. "But who will seek them out?" he added.

The listeners glanced at each other, and Mistress Bengli, chin on hand, smiled and watched the gleaming jewels on her fingers. Many had come to Palestine believing that it held the lure of the fabulous Khar and had found it otherwise.

"I have not heard the tale related so," observed Hugo. "Ha, minstrel, you are skilled in your craft—for you make us think you have dwelt in Khar."

"Sire, I have."

Guiblo shook his head.

"Then, rogue, you must have crossed the great desert and passed through the Iron Gates of which your folk prate."

Abdullah bowed assent.

"The road is no easy one. Nay, a full three moons must a man sit in the saddle, and the horse should be of good blood. In an elder day one of the heroes of the Franks led his host over the desert and saw the salt sea that lies in the desert."

"His name?"

"Iskander."

From the end of the table a monk who had not spoken until now looked up with a gleam of interest.

"By your leave, my lord, that should be Alexander, King of Macedon. Aye, the misguided scholasticists do relate in their profane books the deeds of the Macedonian."

"And how did Alexander pass the Iron Gates?"

"With his sword," Abdullah said calmly. "And yet—did he live to set foot in his own land again? Nay; the Iron Gates take their toll."

"What manner of thing are they?"

"In the books of the cosmographers Strabo and Herodotus, Messer Guiblo," explained the monk, "there is a mark on the road to the East inscribed with the words 'Caspiae Pylae,' or Gates of the Caspian. Their nature is unknown, for since the day of the caesars no Christian hath ventured there."

"Riddles," scoffed Hugo in his own speech. "'Tis a myth that holds no profit for us."

Abdullah appeared to grasp his meaning.

"O king," he observed gravely, "riders have come out of Khar on a foray, and the traces of their horses can be seen within your borders."

"My watchers beheld them not."

"Who can behold the stars in broad day, or the djinn folk who ride upon the winds at night? Does the lord of the castle wish to see a *talsmin*—a token that his servant's word is true?"

Thrusting his hand into his girdle, the minstrel drew forth something that flashed in the flickering candlelight—a neck chain of rubies cut into the semblance of roses, strung on a cord of finely wrought gold.

"Such jewels as these the women of Khar wear upon their throats."

Mistress Bengli caught up the chain in her white fingers, and the others crowded close to stare from the gleaming rubies to Abdullah, who seemed inwardly amused by the excitement he had caused.

Now, considering him narrowly, Longsword thought that no playing of the lute could fashion such muscular hands, and no warbling of nights could give such note of command to a voice. Abdullah bore himself more like an *atabeg*—a leader of a host—than a minstrel.

"Here is a strange rogue forsooth," muttered the seneschal, Piculph, "with a baron's ransom in his belly band."

Robert frowned, for he wished no ill to the teller of tales, and Abdullah might as well have cast his valuable chain into the Orontes as to have shown it to the woman of the Montserrat. Hugo would cheerfully slit open a hundred natives on the chance that one had swallowed a single ruby like these. But Abdullah seemed no whit fearful of the fate he had called down on himself, for he had ceased to watch Mistress Bengli and was eyeing the great tapestries that shook and bellied upon the walls as the gusts of a rising wind buffeted the castle walls and whined through the cracks. The man, heedless of the company at the table, was listening to the sounds of the night beyond the walls.

At that moment there was heard a mutter of voices at the entrance to the hall, the clank of a long scabbard on the stone flagging of the floor, and the captain of the warders stood within the curtain with uplifted hand.

"Pardon, good my lord, I bear tidings. On the river road we have seen an array of Moslems. At midnight I went forth beyond the hamlet to overlook the valley, and in the lower gorge armed men do assemble in ranks. Wilt give command to man the walls, or sally forth?"

"Ha—so!"

Hugo stroked his heavy chin and glanced at his companions. "Sir Robert had the right of it, methinks—and the watchers upon the hill towers shall taste of the strappado. What is your counsel, messires?"

The young Sieur de la Marra struck the table with his fist and set the flagons dancing.

"By the Cross, messires, the paynims do challenge us. My men and I fare forth to seek them."

Hugo exchanged a low word with Messer Guiblo, and the Hospitaler caught the mention of Longu'-espée's name.

"Let it be so. Ho, armiger—my helm and shield. Without there, sound the oliphant to muster our followers."

Mistress Bengli put her hand to her throat to stifle a scream, and the chain of rubies fell to the table and slid down upon the rushes, whence Abdullah picked them up without being observed. This done, the minstrel made his way quietly to the wind-whipped tapestries in a dim corner.

An ivory horn sounded a mellow note in the courtyard, and the clatter of horses, led from the stables, made answer. When Hugo's helm was laced on by a squire-at-arms, he summoned the captain of the guard and peered around the hall.

"In the fiends' name, where went the infidel? Seek him out—you, and you—and retrieve me his chain, or Piculph shall strip and flag you. He stood here but a moment agone—"

"The knave hath a rare trick of foretelling the mind of your Grace," muttered Guiblo. "And his crony the English boar hath forsaken us as well. Methinks he bears you ill intent."

"Nay, the youth is a wildling no more. You dared much when you miscalled him. The man's courage is proof, and he will seek you out ere he parts from us."

With a smile the Venetian pulled on his mailed gloves and tightened his belt.

"Grant me leave to deal with him—else will hie him to the court and brew trouble for our quaffing. Hearken, lord—there be too many eyes and tongues in this hall. Once in the gullies by the river, ere the search for the infidels is ended, my men will attend the Englishman. A blow from an ax, and he will lack his right hand. Thereafter will he bray less loudly of his wrongs."

The marquis shrugged.

"I'll hear no more. Yet must I ride forth lest the cursed Hospitaler suspect something amiss."

Pausing at the donjon gate to tell off a score of men-at-arms to remain and secure Abdullah, he strode to his horse and signed for the clarion to sound the march. Flaring cressets on the walls cast a smoky light over the courtyard and the lance streamers of the knights. Behind these, dark masses of pikemen and archers were forming under Piculph's orders.

Under the lifted portcullis the Hospitaler and the Longsword sat their powerful chargers impatiently, having put aside their private grievances in the presence of the common foe.

Hugo glanced around and saw that Abdullah could not have left the donjon without being seen; nor was he visible in the courtyard. Satisfied of this, the master of the castle called for his standard to be lifted, and the first line of riders lowered their lances to pass under the portcullis, following the Sieur de la Marra over the drawbridge.

The great hall was being ransacked by servants and men-at-arms, who turned over tables and peered into chests, clustering upon the stairs that led to the chambers above, while Mistress Bengli cried to her serving women to lead the search for the Moslem and his jewels into the kitchen and cellars. Eagerly she urged on the men and ran to one of the doorways to listen to the tumult above-stairs.

Standing there in the shadow, a powerful hand closed over her mouth, holding firm her chin.

"O lady," whispered the voice of the minstrel, "would you live to greet the king, your lover, this night? *Ai-a*, life is sweet, is it not? Nay, do not lift your hands, but walk between me and the light—so—and seek the way that leads to the kitchen—so!"

Rigid with fright, Mistress Bengli stumbled along the swaying arras and turned into an archway that brought them to a narrow hall. From the corners of her eyes she saw that Abdullah had his scimitar in his left hand, and the gleam of bare steel sent a chill into her veins.

"It is not fitting, lady," went on the minstrel, "that a man of Khar should loiter in the hall of the feasters, when a battle is joined. So, pray that no man of yours shall meet with us, and lead me to the stables—nay, not into the light!"

While she grasped little of his speech, his intention was clear and Mistress Bengli breathed a sigh of relief when they stood in the shadow of the horse sheds. Abdullah whistled softly, and somewhere a charger neighed. Drawing the woman with him, he found and saddled his horse, taking his time; for the sheds were deserted after the departure of the riders. He had noticed a small gate in the outer wall, and toward this he walked the black stallion and tapped the bars with his sword.

Trembling, she lifted the bars and set them aside, then turned the key and tugged open the gate. Abdullah glanced out and saw that the moat did not extend to this angle. Mistress Bengli stepped back, only half be-lieving she was to suffer no hurt from the wayfarer.

"Say to your lord," he laughed, "that Abdullah ibn Khar rode to Montser-rat upon a mission. Aye, to find one among the Franks who was worthy to adventure to the Throne of Gold. Say that he found not such a man within Montserrat, and so—the peace!"

At the edge of the wooded land the Montserrat archers who were the advance of the marquis's array halted and studied the open valley below them. The remnant of a moon hung over the hills to the south, lighting the expanse of rolling sand that extended to the riverbed. In a hollow by the water glowed the embers of a half-dozen campfires.

A raven croaked from the shadows, and the screaming snarl of a panther made response. Listening, the archers heard stealthy rustling in the dry brush on either side. They had come upon no sign of the Moslems in the march of a full league, down from the castle. And they saw nothing amiss in the camp of the pilgrims below them.

So they reported to Longsword and the Hospitaler who rode up presently, followed by the main body. After scanning the valley carefully, Sir Robert surprised his companion by putting spurs suddenly to the bay and galloping out upon the sand.

He rode into the camp unchallenged and halted by the oxcarts that were ranged near the fire. The Sieur de la Marra paused to look down at the pilgrims who lay in scattered groups in the hollows, and to swear under his breath.

"——! Montserrat feared an ambushment, yet methinks naught lies in wait here save Death."

At the coming of the crusaders jackals and snarling four-footed things slipped out of the camp into the shadows. Even the oxen had been cut down, and one man still gripping an ax was prone in the ashes of the fire, his head half burned away.

Torches were kindled by the archers while the riders quieted their horses, made restless by the penetrating smell of blood. Some stared at the carts where a score of bodies lay about the woman who still held the baby in her arms—all pierced by arrows. In the shallows of the rivers the standard-bearer sprawled, the shaft of the banner floating beside his head. In all quarters the sand was trampled by horses' hoofs, yet the pilgrims had had no horses. The Hospitaler dismounted to examine one of the arrows and announced that it was a kind he had not seen before—a short shaft, unbarbed but with long feathering.

"It smacks of an Arab bow. Ha, messires, I wot well the minstrel spoke the truth! The riders who did this pretty business came from the desert, and mayhap from Khar."

Whoever they were, the raiders had taken the camp by surprise and had wrought fearful havoc with small loss to themselves. No bodies of Saracens were to be seen, and if any had been slain they were borne off by their comrades. The attack—judging by the numbers of beasts that gathered about the scene—had taken place some hours before, so the Montserrat watchers must have beheld the foray riding back from the river to one of the trails that led through the mountains.

Pursuit was not to be thought of. The Croises had learned after bitter experiences that their heavily armed warriors and sturdy chargers could not deal with the swift-moving Saracens in broken country.

"A fair riddance, messires," mouthed Hugo, turning over the body of a ragged lad with his lance point. "We need no longer feed the rabble, though we must e'en bury it—Fra Anselmo will see to't. Come, who is for the castle?"

The archers and pikemen who had been combing over the scattered packs of the pilgrims, already pillaged by the raiders, began to move toward their officers, while Guiblo and his following with Piculph the Lombard and Hugo's squire drew closer about the three.

But the young Hospitaler stooped to the stained sand and held up a slender gauntlet embroidered with silk initials.

"E. de I.—*requiescat in pace*, whosoever ye be—a woman's hawking-gauntlet, or I'm a turn-spit. What—how now?"

Robert had taken the glove from him and turned to face the marquis.

"Messire," said he, "it lingers in my memory that you did give your knightly word to the rabble that you would defend them against all foes upon this, your land." As Hugo was silent in surprise, he added—"Those who utter what they will not defend with their bodies, I do hold arrant cowards, recreant to their vows."

Whipping out his sword, he placed the glove near its point and, leaning forward, tossed it deftly on Hugo's saddle peak.

"By this do I challenge Your Grace, Hugo Amardis of Montserrat, to try by combat in this hour which of us be true and which be false."

Now at this the liegemen of Montserrat stared and muttered and drew closer, so that a ring of armed men was formed about the group, and there fell a silence in which the snuffling breathing of the horses was clearly heard. Passion darkened the swarthy face of the marquis, but before he could frame an answer Robert spoke again.

"My lord, the laws of Palestine do not permit one who hath been a vassal to summon his liege into the combat of justice. So, will Your Grace name from among your vassals a champion to take your place?"

Hugo knew well that he could not have withstood the Englishman's sword, but his anger flared the higher with the thought. Snatching up the gauntlet and casting it down on the sand, he shouted hoarsely:

"Piculph—Guiblo—Sir Curthose, to me! Wilt suffer this upstart to badger me? A thousand —— , I say—to me!"

"Nay, one will suffice, your Grace," laughed the Hospitaler, who had recovered from his surprise at Robert's plain speaking after his self-control in the castle hall. "It were a foul wrong, meseems, to set three devils on one Englishman."

Two retainers of the Venetian who had been hovering close to the Longsword's flank drew back when spectators thronged about them. Messer Guiblo urged his horse close to the powerful form of the Lombard and whispered to him swiftly. Piculph gnawed his lip, then nodded assent.

"I'll cut his comb, my lord," he said aloud, "then he'll crow less loud, I ween."

"Good!" cried Robert. "'Twas my wish to bid you farewell in this fashion."

Hugo reined back his horse to glance questioningly at Messer Guiblo, who nodded reassuringly and slipped back among his men. The Sieur de la Marra also retreated to leave the ring clear for the fighters.

In the half-light of the low moon it was easily seen that the two were a match in bigness of bone and height, though the Englishman had the better horse. Piculph glanced about him once and swung down from his stirrup, choosing to fight on foot.

It was in the code of the law that in the lists of justice the two combatants should be armed equally in all particulars. Robert dismounted without hesitation, trying the firmness of the sand with a mailed foot and letting fall his shield—as the Lombard carried none.

But when Piculph drew his sword a grim laugh went up from the Montserrat liegemen. The Lombard's weapon was no longer than his adversary's yet it tapered hardly at all, being blunt at the tip and heavier by half than the Longsword's brand. It was a sword to be wielded by two hands, and so Piculph had no need of a shield.

The watchers pressed closer, jostling one another and muttering between set teeth. The hollow where the camp lay was in a natural amphitheater that held the heat of the day, and they sweated under the weight of armor, their veins warmed by the late drinking. Many stood on the huddle of the slain to see the better.

Piculph was no loiterer. Striding forward, he swung the two-handed blade in circles, his muscular arms cracking.

"A purse of gold that he slays the Longsword or makes him cry mercy," offered Sir Curthose of Var to the young Sieur de la Marra.

But the Hospitaler gnawed his lip in silence as he watched Robert, who stood erect in his tracks, his sword held close to his chest, the point upraised.

With a grunt Piculph struck down and sidewise at his foe's throat, and steel sang against steel. The Lombard's sword flashed in a circle that ended high above his own head. Robert, by moving his arms quickly, had deflected the heavy blade so that it passed harmlessly over his helmet.

Piculph recovered and smote again, straight down at the Englishman's head. Robert planted his feet and whirled up his blade, turning the other's aside and into the sand.

"Thy purse likes me well, Sir Curthose," cried the Hospitaler. "Ha—treachery!"

Near at hand his quick eye had distinguished one of the Lombards kneeling with a short battle mace drawn back to throw. In that elusive light the iron club might have been cast unseen, and at such short range it could not fail to reach the Longsword. Drawing his sword, the young knight ran at the front of the circle of men-at-arms; midway in a stride he faltered and flung up his arm.

A dagger, wielded by one he had passed, had struck fair into the side of his throat, and gasping, he sank on his knees, choking out his life. The quick movement had caught the eye of Robert, who cried out and sprang aside from Piculph.

"A deed most foul!" he grated through set teeth. "Montserrat—"

Picking out the man who had stabbed the knight and who was trying to work back into the throng, he slashed him full between neck and shoulder and used his point on the henchman who still balanced the mace.

"——, Montserrat, since when have you plied the trade of cutthroat? Ah, Piculph!"

Whirling to meet a fresh onset from the seneschal, Robert gave back the Lombard blow for blow, until the clashing of steel drowned the shouts of the aroused liegemen. Sweat gleamed on the Lombard's broad cheeks, and his breath labored as he exerted all his strength, fearing now for his life. Robert whipped his sword over the other's guard, and the edge of the blade thudded against Piculph's neck under the ear.

It struck upon the fold of the mail coif and glanced up, biting through the chain mail, and stripped the end of the jaw-bone and the ear from the side of the man's head. The Lombard plunged down upon the sand, and Robert ran to his horse. The bay, trained to stand where he had been left, was in motion before the warrior had settled in the saddle.

An arrow whistled through the air, and Robert put his horse to a trot, making the round of the circle once, seeking Guiblo, the Venetian. But Guiblo had withdrawn far into the ranks of his men, and Sir Curthose and many of the older liegemen stood their ground, unwilling to draw weapon against the man who had once been castellan of Antioch.

"What, my lord," Robert gibed, "do you lack of murderers? Then summon up your hunters and the hounds and so—fare well!"

He had reached one end of the irregular cleared space; now he wheeled the bay and raked its flanks with rowels. The charger leaped forward, gained pace, and the throng gave way in haste before horse and rider, permitting Longsword to pass through. He headed for the nearest gully amid the foothills, and the voice of the marquis roared after him.

"After him! A cap full of gold to the wight who brings him down."

The bay charger, wise and swift of foot, swung clear of the running men and gained the shadows of the rocks before the riders could draw near him. Guiblo, his swarthy cheeks pallid, stared down at the lifeless eyes of the young knight whose white cross was slowly obscured by a dark tide. Beside him was the hawking gauntlet.

"A good plan," murmured the Venetian. "Aye—but three lie slain and a fourth maimed and another hunted by the liegemen, for so slight a thing as a ribald's glove."

Chapter IV

A fat hound does not hunt well.

—Chinese Proverb

Robert had hunted a fleeing foeman too often not to know that a fugitive who rides blindly is soon overtaken or cut off. So he galloped up the twisting gully, scanning the ground on either hand, and when he was barely within the shadow of the hills turned sharply to the left.

The bay pricked up its ears, braced its forefeet and half slid on its haunches down into the rocky bed of a dry watercourse. Here a stand of gnarled cedars hid them from view, and Robert was out of the saddle and holding the horse's muzzle before the last pebbles had stopped rolling.

His forehead was bleeding and his head was ringing from a glancing blow of the two-handed sword that had ripped off his helmet. And black bitterness clouded his thoughts. To be baited like a buffoon at table, to be hunted over the glens like a runagate cutpurse! To be tricked by the man who no longer had use for his services!

True, he could endeavor to make his way to Cyprus, where the new king held court—Jerusalem being in the hands of the Saracens. There, however, the influence of the Montserrats and the Venetians would be at work against him, and a poniard in the back in some tavern or alley would make an end of him. As for raising his ransom in Palestine under the shadow of Hugo's enmity—that was out of the question.

If he escaped pursuit—and the people of Montserrat would spare no pains to silence the voice that might be raised against them in accusation of the murder of the Hospitaler—he must seek the road that led to the eastern mountain wall and there make shift as best he could in the hills until the hue and cry had died away.

"And look ye, Sir Charger," he observed under his breath, "we do lack the services of squire and valeret, likewise of shield and helm and purse—which last is a sad matter, for we stand bound to garner us a many broad pieces of gold before the year is told. Yet hath the year still many moons, and we have been in a worse strait than this—*Olá*, softly, softly!"

Gripping the nostrils of the horse, he looked up as a rider plunged off the trail overhead, plowing recklessly through the sand until he reined to a sudden halt amid the cedars. And then came a new thudding of hoofs along the ridge and a clanking of steel. Men shouted back and forth and passed on, unseen. Neither Robert nor the stranger moved until the detachment had galloped out of hearing, and they were certain that no others followed.

"By Allah, do the Franks of this country never sleep? The gullies are aswarm with them, and I have all but broken my leg on these rocks. *Bi al-taubah*—they do me too much honor."

"Abdullah!"

Robert walked over to the minstrel.

"How came you from the castle?"

"The red-haired woman unbarred a gate for me. When you would enter a dwelling seek out for companion a man with a sword; when you would leave unseen, ask a woman. But honor is due first to Allah and then to you. I watched from the height and saw you cut down those who came against you. Before that I observed you in the hall of the feasters, when the wine went the rounds and a woman would have smiled upon you. *Ohai*, my heart was cheered and I said to myself—'There is one who hath the bearing of a *bahator*, a prince of warriors.'"

"Nay, these Franks do not search for you. They ride to seek me out."

"Wherefore?"

"To bind me and make an end of my doings."

Abdullah laughed, running his fingers through his beard.

"What is written is written, and who shall say otherwise? For I was sent hither to find among other things a Frank who was indeed a warrior and to bring him back with me to my king."

"What lord is that?"

"The master of all men."

"His name and place?"

"Nay, in time you will know that as well as other things. We will ride to Khar, for I have come from there. Have you heart to cross the desert and scale the Iron Gates?"

Abdullah was silent a moment. "The path is one of peril," he went on. "If you live to reach Khar you will never come back—to this. Whosoever ventures to Khar abides there. But this I can promise you; before the summer is past you will behold a mighty warring of peoples, and a treasure uncovered. Of this you shall claim a share that will suffice to build a castle like yonder hold and fill it with a thousand slaves and as many steeds—"

Robert smote the stallion's saddle softly with his fist.

"Words—words!"

The breath of the minstrel hissed through his lips.

"I read you not aright if you are one to seek *talsmins* and surety for a venture such as this. Yet if you fear, turn aside now. I have seen the Iron Gates crush a trembler—"

"Faith!"

The knight gripped Abdullah's shoulder. "Wherever you dare set foot, I would go beyond you."

"Oh-o-ho!"

Abdullah rocked with inward mirth, as at a huge joke.

"The young cub growls—the fledgling lifts its beak. *Ohai-hai!*"

"Mount then and show the path. For I will adventure with you into paynimry."

"Aye, *bunnayi*, little son. The young warrior would level his spear at an elephant! O most darling fool; had I a son he would be like you, yet wiser. Think ye, Nazarene, I will not betray you at the first Moslem village beyond the hills?"

"Nay, for you are no Moslem."

In the deep gloom under the trees Abdullah leaned closer to peer into his companion's eyes.

"How? What words are these?"

"And you were not always a minstrel. Though you carry a prayer rug, Abdullah, you have no use for it. I have not seen you pray the *namaz gar*, and in the castle you shared forbidden wine and meat."

Abdullah was silent for a full minute, pondering this.

"Then you think I am *atabeg* of the Kharesmian raiders?"

"Not so. For you warned the baron of their approach, and you did not seek them when you won free of the castle."

"True, O father of ravens. Had I led the raiders I would have stormed the Nazarene hold, for there was a woman more to be desired than the white-faced maid of the pilgrims—and a lord to be held for ransom."

The minstrel paused to take the saddle from the stallion and let him roll in the sand, though it meant risk for himself.

"Many things, have I seen, O youth, but not this thing—that a babbler of secrets lived to be white of hair. Remember that I am Abdullah, the teller of tales, no more."

"Then we ride alone—we twain?"

"Not alone."

Abdullah laughed softly.

"Upon our road we shall have a brave company. Your Iskander and the hero Rustam—aye, and one of the caesars of Rome—will be our road companions. They who died, seeking the treasure of the Throne of Gold, which we may seize and keep."

Leaning on his sword, Longsword listened in silence. The minstrel could have said nothing better suited to his mood. Robert never hesitated over a decision, and when he felt that he could trust Abdullah he thought no more about it.

Meanwhile the minstrel was busied about his saddlebags.

"And if we die," he muttered into his beard, "we will spread such a
carpet of slain about us that men will not forget our names. O Nazarene,
you may not venture beyond the hills without a name and garments to fit.
Hai, you are dark enough in the skin to pass for an Egyptian, being lighter
than the Arabs. You speak the language easily—yet not like an Arab. So
you must be a Lion of Egypt: Alp Arslan, the sword slayer, the cloud-
scattering, the diamond sheen of all warriors—the Emir Alp Arslan. And
remember to pray the *namaz gar*," he added under his breath.

Presently Robert stood in changed garments. Abdullah had cast away the
knight's surcoat and mailed thigh-pieces, sleeves, and mittens. From his
pack he had produced a loin cloth, baggy cotton trousers and slippers. Over
the youth's mail he had slipped a flowing *khalat* of silk and bound it in
at the waist with a shawl, working skillfully in the dark. Lastly he gave
Robert a light Saracen steel headgear with peak and nasal, and mailed
drop that hung about ears and shoulders.

"The horse and saddle may pass for spoil taken from the Nazarenes,"
he pronounced, "likewise the long sword. In the first village we will seek
out a barber, and when he has shaved your head and mouth we will cut
him open lest he talk too much. What now?"

Robert stooped and found his gold spurs on the ground. Feeling about
for a large boulder in the gully, he put forth his strength and rolled it
aside. Then, dropping the spurs in the hollow, he thrust back the stone
upon them.

"So that no other may wear them," he said calmly. "For here doth Sir
Robert, castellan of Antioch, end his days; and from here doth Robert the
Wayfarer step forth."

Taking advantage of the dawn mists, they worked out of the foothills into
a cattle path known to Robert, and sunrise found them well away from
the castle. Avoiding the main road to the east, they climbed steadily until they were past the line of the Montserrat watch towers, Abdullah re-
marking grimly that the warders of the marquis would pay little attention to two Moslem riders when they were seeking a fugitive of their own
race upon whose head a reward had been placed.

Here they turned back into the trail that had been taken by the raiders, as they judged from the hoof marks. Abdullah started to give the stal-

lion his head when he swerved in the saddle and reined in sharply. An arrow whistled between them, and another shaft grazed Robert's ear as he urged his horse forward.

Crashing into the underbrush, he drew his sword and slashed at a tamarisk bush behind which a man was crouched. The archer turned to flee, but caught his foot and fell headlong. Robert swung from his stirrups and stood over him, surprised to see that it was the lanky bowman who had marched with the pilgrims. The man snarled up at him, unarmed—for his bow had fallen from his hand.

Robert sheathed the long sword and signed to Abdullah to do the man no hurt. The bowman must have thought them stragglers of the raiders, and Robert had no desire to make himself known, until he noticed a handsome pony with a Moslem saddle tethered to a nearby tree.

"Which way went the raiders from Khar?" he asked in English, for Abdullah desired to avoid the path taken by the foray. "You have one of their horses, methinks."

The bowman sat up, his close-set eyes agleam with hatred and suspicion.

"Aye, that have I, Saracen. And no aid wilt thou have from me to find the unshriven dogs, thy companions. Ha, by token of that long sword and high horse thou hast slain a Christian knight that did bespeak me a day agone upon the road to Jordan."

He spat on the ground in front of Robert and sprang to his feet, palpably astonished that he should have been left alive so long.

His tousled red hair stood up from his freckled skin, and the shagreen hood upon his bony shoulders was rent by thorns, so it barely concealed the greasy leather jerkin beneath. His thin face was defiant.

"Heave up thy hacker, Moslem, and make an end—for Will Bunsley o' Northumberland will ask no mercy from a blackaviséd knave. Had I my good long bow I'd spit me the twain of ye. Ah, that I would. This lewd Moslem bow, seest thou, carries wide o' the mark."

He kicked contemptuously at the short Moslem bow with its looping arch and silk cord that lay near at hand. In some way he had lost his own weapon and had found him another, less satisfactory. And his failure to bring down the two riders seemed to irk him deeply.

"Nay," Robert smiled, "the feathers of your shaft tickled my ear. And that is close enough."

"Close, quotha!" the bowman sneered. "Why, lookee, my rogue—with my yew bow I'd split thee thy forehead fair and featly at fifty paces."

His jaw dropped, and he fell back a pace. "St. Dunstan be my aid! Thou art the knight himself in paynim garb. Aye, that yellow hair—"

He scratched his head, looking from Robert to Abdullah suspiciously.

"And I would have slain thee in quittance of my revenge."

"Your revenge, bowman?"

"Ah. Three lives I seek of the Saracens that fell upon our company, to wit: One for the blind priest, good Father Evagrius, that they carried off to torture; another for the maid Ellen that they seized and bound upon a horse—may they sup in purgatory, may their tongues rot out and the kites beak their eyes!"

"And the third?"

"I vowed to St. Dunstan to feather me a shaft in the losel that smote me a dour ding upon the sconce."

Will Bunsley rubbed a lump on his skull ruefully.

"Aye, a knavish clout it were on this my mazzard."

"Tell me the story of the affray."

Robert sheathed his sword slowly. He had thought all the pilgrims slain, but here was news of two taken captive.

"Affray, quotha!"

The archer shook his head.

"Nay, 'twas a shambles and we the sheep."

The surprise, he explained, had been complete, for the pilgrims thought themselves safe on the Montserrat lands. The raiders must have been concealed in the gullies near the river, and they rode into the camp plying their bows on all sides. Those who stood up to them were shot down before sword or pike could be used, and Bunsley had barely time to string his bow before he saw the patriarch and the girl snatched up and placed on one of the horses.

He sent a shaft into one of the riders and ran after the captives, who were led away at once. Before he reached them he had been struck down by a club or mace from behind, and when he came to his senses the slaughter was over. After washing his head in the river he was able to catch a riderless pony that was circling the camp.

Without delaying Bunsley had set forth on the trail taken by the raiders. This was before the coming of the Montserrat men, and he pushed up into the mountains, becoming weary and confused on the descent, until he dismounted and sought some sleep, being awakened by the tread of Abdullah's horse. The Moslem bow he had picked up when he left the camp.

"And if thou be'st true man, thou wilt seek out the infidel dogs and prevail upon them to release the maid and priest. If not, then for love of the Cross thou didst wear, bear me company until we come up with them."

"You would not go far, bowman."

Robert liked the stubborn courage of the yeoman, yet knew that Bunsley would not live to see the sun set if he kept on as he planned.

"Turn back and seek service with the Montserrat, who hath an eye for a man who pulls a good bow."

"Nay, I'll seek no service with him. Ah, he is too glib with promises and too sparing of deeds. 'Tis a good lass and loves me well."

Bunsley heaved a deep sigh.

"What says the redbeard?" asked Abdullah.

Robert explained, and the minstrel studied the archer curiously.

"Take me with thee, lord," Bunsley begged doggedly, "and, God willing, I'll cry a greeting to the lass and strike a blow for her ere she be lost to Christian folk."

The girl, he added eagerly, was no more than a child when, a year and more ago, she had listened to the preaching of the monk de Courcon in Blois, where Bunsley happened to be stationed. She was Ellen d'Ibelin, daughter of a knight, and she had had schooling with the nuns.

At Blois she took the Cross with many youths and children, for the monk declared that Jerusalem might be delivered by the children. Will Bunsley fell under the spell of the crusade preacher—also he confessed to a mighty fondness for the girl—and adventured with the pilgrims through many barren and hostile lands to Byzantium.

"And 'tis gold I seek," cried Robert. "Nor will I turn me aside for any maid, captive though she be."

It irked him that the men from Khar should have borne off prisoners from the lands of the Croises, and he spoke bitterly, for his warning to Hugo and to the pilgrims had gone unheeded. Having formed a purpose, he would not swerve from it. Moreover the red archer was the last man he wished to take with him on his venture. It was impossible to disguise that rawboned figure and stentorian voice; yet to leave Will Bunsley to follow the trail alone—

"I'll tend the horses, good my lord," insisted the yeoman, "and draw thee wine at every inn, aye, and keep watch o'nights for slit-throats—"

"Ho!" Robert chuckled. "Fare with us then, an' you will. If my companion—"

But Abdullah gave his assent without ado. The redbeard, he said, could go as he was, and they would claim that he was Robert's captive. So should the Emir Arslan have more honor. Bunsley's appearance would be enough to make the Arab, through whose country they must pass, think him a simpleton, afflicted by Allah.

Clearly Robert explained to the yeoman the hardships they would face, first in the desert, then in the heart of Moslem power. But Will Bunsley merely grinned—although he grimaced when told he must cast aside his weapons to play the part of captive.

"Ha, for the land of gold—and the fair damsels of paynimry. How sayeth the song?"

He chanted in a tuneful roar—

> *Though I have a man i-slaw*
> *And forfeited the king's law,*
> *I shall guiden a man of law,*
> *Will take my penny and let me go!*

Robert hearkened with relish to an English voice, yet felt grave misgiving at taking the archer, thinking that the man could not survive for many days. Before long, however, Will Bunsley of Northumberland proved to be a man of many surprises.

Although Abdullah pushed forward at a furious pace, the archer kept up with his nag, grumbling and groaning, but never allowing the two wanderers out of sight. The heat and the scanty fare stretched the skin taut on his bones, and he came to look like a scarlet skeleton, so that when they stopped at a village, the men of the desert thronged to stare at the red Frank captive in astonishment.

Robert noticed that the minstrel rode in a strange fashion with a longer stirrup than the Arabs and with his weight eased well forward. He picked his course by the stars—for they covered most of their way at night. Robert had a habit of watching the constellations and judged by the position of the Great Bear that they were working steadily east. The Milky Way—which Abdullah called the Path of the Wild Geese—was directly overhead as they dropped down into a country of baked clay, where the tents of the desert tribes were no longer to be seen.

Here when the moon waned they crossed by swimming a sluggish, reed-bordered river that Abdullah called the Frat and Robert thought was the Euphrates. It was well for the knight that long years in the saddle had hardened him for such a journey. Abdullah seemed to be made of iron, and Will Bunsley, ever on the lookout for traces of the raiders whom they followed, moaned and cursed with the weariness of the saddle and the plaguing of midges and huge flies.

Abdullah had bartered in a Kurd village another pony for the archer and Bunsley changed saddle from one to the other, complaining bitterly that it was a sin to ask one man to do the work of two nags. Yet the hope of coming up with the men from Khar kept him from falling behind. Once they passed around a hamlet of merchants on the river that had been sacked and burned by the raiders, and Robert waxed thoughtful at seeing that the riders from Khar took spoil from Moslem and Christian alike. But in those days upon the desert floor he gave little heed to aught but the necessity for keeping pace with the minstrel, who rode recklessly through the night, and while the two Nazarenes slept, utterly wearied in the midday hours, played softly upon his lute and sang in a guttural speech that Robert had never heard before.

And this flight across a strange and barren land did much to ease the bitterness that had been in Robert. They hunted where they could and avoided the villages, and daily covered stretches that the crusader would not have thought possible. So the three rode from Palestine, one seeking the price of his life, another searching for a captive girl, and the third intent on keeping a rendezvous with his master, whose name he would not reveal.

Unexpectedly, late one afternoon, they came to a muddy stream swift running between low, sandy banks—the boundary line of Khar, Abdullah said; and, pointing to clusters of skin tents on the far bank where some hundred horses were turned loose to graze, he added—

"The riders from Khar."

Chapter V
The Redbeard

It was too late to go back out of sight, for watchers on the other bank had seen them, and their horses were too weary to escape pursuit. Hesitation would have been fatal, and Robert urged his horse into the river, to be followed promptly by the minstrel.

Once they had climbed out on the sand drifts they were surrounded by dark-skinned warriors in silvered helmets—lean, slow-moving men who swaggered in crimson and white kaftans and polished hauberks, who took in every detail of the newcomers' steeds and trappings at a single glance and bared their teeth at Bunsley—who returned their scowls with interest.

"Kankalis, these," whispered Abdullah meaningly, "hillmen, Turkomans, and the best of the light cavalry of the master of Khar—our companions on the road to the Iron Gates, O Arslan. Be wily in talk, O Egyptian, and think before each word. Do not try to aid the redbeard if they seek him out for sport for their long knives."

Two mounted warriors who had been posted at the river pushed in between the strangers and the crowd, heedless of the insults hurled at them by those who were jostled by the ponies. Commanding Robert to follow, they conducted the three to a large tent where sat the leader of the band—an old man with a beak of a nose, his sword girdled high on his middle. He knelt on a silk carpet, casting knuckle-bones idly, and though he appeared scarcely to notice the strangers he looked them over carefully.

Abdullah related the tale agreed upon, that he, a minstrel wandering from Khar, had fallen in with an emir out of Cairo who journeyed to the court of the Throne of Gold, and with him one Nazarene, a captive taken in the valley of the Orontes. Inalzig Khan, as the leader of the Kankalis was called, did not see fit to ask them to sit as yet, although they had dismounted.

"Where are your followers, O valiant lion," he demanded of Robert ironically.

"Ask the kites and the wolves. They were slain in affrays with the Nazarenes and the Bedawans."

"Allah, can it be so? What do you seek of me?"

"Guidance and protection through the Iron Gates."

The khan bared long teeth in a mocking smile.

"Nay, you know not the Gates. Who can protect a stranger who lacks the right to enter?"

Knowing that a display of temper was expected of him, at this, Robert touched his sword-hilt.

"By the ninety and nine holy names, does a son of the Seljuks and a great-grandson of a caliph take grass between his teeth to bespeak a gate-keeper?"

Months of dwelling with the nobles of Cairo enabled him to imitate the mincing temper of a high-born Egyptian; with his mustache and head shaven and his bare feet blackened by the sun of the plains, he had little to fear. Yet Inalzig was not satisfied, although his tone became more courteous.

"Upon what mission do you ride to the shah, O Cairene?"

Abdullah threw in carelessly, as if explaining to a friend—"None leave the Sialak, the Gates, or enter to the great city except they go or come upon an order of Muhammad Shah on whom be peace—the Emperor of Khar and the shield of Islam."

"Does the jackal ask of the wolf, 'Why are ye here?'" Robert took his cue. "I will speak of my mission to the governor of the great city, and to you, Inalzig Khan, I say—" he thought swiftly—"that the Sultans of Cairo and Damietta have withstood the Nazarenes and send word of their deeds to Muhammad Shah."

The Kankali nodded without emotion, and made room for the twain on the carpet.

"*Hamaian*—contentment be upon you, O emir. I care naught for such matters, being sent on a foray to fetch a quota of maidens and spoil from the accursed Nazarenes and the desert tribes. If you can pass the Gates you will have fair greeting in Bokhara, the city of which I spoke. For the shah draws his sword and mounts for war."

"With whom?" demanded Abdullah with sudden interest.

"*Ma'shallah*—have I been within the walls of Bokhara this last year, that I should know? Some tribe of unbelievers from the north dares to withstand the emperor."

Will Bunsley had been staring about eagerly at the piles of wicker baskets holding the fruits of the foray, and certain tents set apart for the captives, without seeing any sign of the girl or the priest.

"It is my wish," remarked the chief of the Kankalis, leaning back on his cushions, "that the infidel be stripped and bound and stretched out for some of my men to try the edge of their scimitars. Is it not written that he who causes the death of an unbeliever will not fail of paradise?"

A glance from Abdullah warned Robert that this request was not to be lightly refused. The khan had halted his men for a day's rest, and a curious throng had gathered about the archer, who had forgotten to mumble and gape as usual.

"It would bring ill fortune upon us to slay him, O captain of many," objected Robert, heedless of the minstrel's concern.

"How?"

"He is djinn-infested. The devil of madness is in him."

Inalzig signed for a slave to bring wine cups and shook his head indifferently.

"I am no servant of the priests and herder of the afflicted of Allah. The Frank could not pass the Gates, so why weary two horses in bearing him thither?"

"Do you see the color of his hair and skin?"

"Aye, red as heart of fire."

"When a man is blind, what is the color of his eyes?"

"White."*

"True. Allah hath set his seal on the eyes. Now when the devil entered this man, his skin turned red. Verily, it is a strange devil. The infidel, being mad, believes that he can overthrow any warrior with all weapons. *Yah ahmak*, the simpleton will bring mirth to your heart."

"Allah!"

The Kankali smiled and sipped at his cup.

"Let us see what he does. Nay, do not give him a bow—" as Robert reached for one in a corner of the tent—"for the —— might send the shaft this way. Let him try his skill with a spear, a stabbing-spear."

Robert glanced at Bunsley and risked speaking to the archer.

"Canst withstand one of these fellows with a quarterstaff?"

"Aye, by all the saints, that can I, lord brother."

The yeoman grinned cheerfully.

"Last Martinmas I won a silver shilling for a bout—"

"The Moslem will have a long stabbing spear, and he will not stop at the first blood. You stand in dire peril, Master Will, and it will go hard if you do not prevail."

The archer declared that he would hold his own with anything on two legs at brawling or dicing and desired nothing better than to crack the skulls of his tormentors.

"The fool," Robert explained to the Kankali, "will think that a stout stick is a spear, so let him have one. Yet if he is victor, will you permit him to ride with me unharmed?"

"Verily," laughed the warrior, who was studying Robert curiously. "Have you also a devil that you speak the language of the infidel?"

---

*Owing to the almost inevitable cataract.

"He dwelt at their court for a year and more," put in Abdullah quickly, "and learned much of their ways. For this was he chosen to ride to the shah with his story."

Saying that it was all one to him and that he fancied there were three fools instead of one at his tent, Inalzig called for one of his men to stand forth with a spear. A thin warrior with a huge, knotted turban stepped into the cleared space, carrying a five-foot weapon. Will Bunsley cast about until he found a spare tent pole of teak as long as he was tall and as large around as his two thumbs joined together.

Tossing up the staff, he caught it in the fingers of one hand and twirled it around his head. Then, setting his long legs, he gripped the quarterstaff with both hands widely separated, well in front of him. To the onlookers this seemed the merest bombast, and the eyes of the Kankali glittered as he advanced on the archer and thrust at Bunsley's ribs, meaning to wound the red man a few times before killing him. Instead the yeoman warded the blow by lowering one end of his pole. Again the Kankali thrust with no better result.

Angered by the gibes of his companions, the spearman shortened his grasp and feinted, minded to end the matter out of hand. But Will halted him abruptly by bringing up one arm and jabbing wickedly at the throat. Choking, the Kankali staggered back and the yeoman smote him on either ear so quickly that the two thuds sounded as one.

Blood flowed down the warrior's jaw, and he rocked dizzily, then crumpled down on the sand.

"The fool is strong in the arm," observed Inalzig. "Now we will try his skill."

He barked an order, and a stocky warrior sprang out from the growing throng of watchers. The khan tossed him a javelin—a throwing-spear no more than a yard long with a small, barbed point.

"Send him to *jehannum* or taste a hundred lashes."

Robert, who had watched English yeomen practicing with the quarterstaff in Antioch, had known that Will could make a long spear look ridiculous, but a javelin was not to be warded so easily. Nor could he come to the archer's aid, for such a move would mean drawn weapons and a swift end for them both.

But Will, watching his adversary keenly, yelped cheerfully.

"So-ho, here be a dog with sharp teeth, so give heed, Master Robert, to some pretty work."

Leaping about in front of the Kankali, he whirled the quarterstaff in the man's eyes until the warrior decided that the Frank was not going to attack, and launched the javelin. Will, having waited for just this, dodged alertly, and the short spear did no more than glance from one shoulder, cutting it to the bone.

The warrior snarled and drew a curved dagger. Rushing in, he slashed at the archer's ribs, only to drop like a log and lie where he had fallen. Will had stepped aside and slid one hand down to the other, swinging lustily with the full weight of the staff upon the Kankali's skull.

"Now, St. Dunstan send that he be the one that cracked my pate in the battle," he remarked.

To the Moslems his skill with the staff savored of the marvelous, for they were men who used none but edged weapons. Even the khan was stirred to interest and asked if the red man could do tricks with anything but a stick.

"Put a bow into his hands and set the best of your archers against him," suggested Robert.

After some hesitation Inalzig agreed and had one of the short Turkish bows brought out for Will, who took it with misgivings, saying that it might do to use from a horse's back but was no thing to tickle the fancy of a Northumberland lad. He selected his arrows with care, choosing the longest he could find.

Thus equipped he outdid the best of the Kankalis, who withdrew from the contest with as much dignity as they could muster, explaining loudly that the Frank was surely djinn-infested. Indeed Will was strutting about with a lop-sided grin, for he had more than his share of vanity. Inalzig had fallen into a rage and nursed his wine-cup sullenly until Abdullah, who had followed the archery with mild interest, arose and declared that he had come from a country where men used bows otherwise.

"Then put the fool to shame, O minstrel," grunted the chief.

"Nay," responded the minstrel, "I lack his skill, yet have I learned a trick that your men know not."

Taking a small turban cloth, he walked to the nearest tree. Rolling the cotton strip tightly, he wrapped it around the bole of the tree so that a strip some two fingers in breadth showed white against the dark trunk.

Then, calling for a saddled pony, he chose a short, powerful bow and a quiver with six arrows. Mounting and riding off, he wheeled the pony some two hundred paces from his mark and set it to a gallop. One after the other he loosed three shafts rapidly as he rode, gripping the ends of the arrows between thumb and forefinger.

Abreast the tree Abdullah swiftly unstrung the bow and used the flying cord on his pony as a whip. Then, stringing it taut again, he emptied his quiver as he drew away from the mark. It was no easy feat to loose the shafts over the pony's rump, and the Kankalis raised a shout of gratification when it was seen that all but one of Abdullah's arrows had struck the bole of the tree, and three were within the cotton band.

"Such nimble finger work is not our way," remarked Will, studying the hits made by the minstrel, "for we pull a long bow and draw each shaft to the head. Yet no man can say Will Bunsley gave ground to him in honest yeoman sport."

The warriors crowded closer when they saw that the Frank would attempt to equal the minstrel's feat. They had been weaned from boyhood with bows in their hands, but like Abdullah were accustomed to shoot from the saddle.

Will signed for the bow Abdullah used to be brought him, and again selected a half dozen arrows. Instead of standing, he knelt this time about a hundred yards from the trees and stuck the heads of the arrows lightly in the sand in a half-circle under his right hand. After testing the pull of the new bow, he thumbed the silk string and fitted an arrow, holding it in place between his first and second fingers which gripped the string. He let it fly and caught up another deftly. His long arms worked smoothly, and he set his jaw stubbornly.

It seemed to Robert that two arrows were in the air at once as his eye followed the first to the mark before looking for the second. When the last shaft was sped he shouted approval. Although Will had not tried his skill from a saddle, he had bettered Abdullah's hits. All the arrows were in the tree and four in the white band.

"Good!" grunted Inalzig. "The fool may live if he can; and it will be your turn, O emir, to think of a trick when we stand at the Gates."

Chapter VI
The Word on the Rocks

Robert frequently pondered the warning of the khan as they made their way at a rapid pace through the wooded uplands that lay beyond the river. And he had other things to think about.

To Will's chagrin there was no sign of the maid or the priest in the raiding party; nor would Abdullah give them any word of the fate of the cap-

tives. The minstrel fell into a moody silence, broken only by his harsh
songs sometimes at evening when they lay at ease in the tent openings
and listened to the gambling and gossip of the Kankalis.

Abdullah became impatient at any delay—though these were few, because each day brought Inalzig fresh tidings of impending warfare and
the chief was anxious to reach his destination, Bokhara, as quickly as
possible.

"The maid and the monk live yet," he assured Robert, "and it may fortune that you will see them again. But who can foretell what the turn
in the road will bring? By the host of the dead! Only fools prophesy before the event!"

He studied the face of the young warrior as a wise man might read a
book, sheet by sheet. And the finely wrought lips and candid gray eyes
made him shake his head.

"Nay, you pray as a Moslem, and you walk as one—a little slowly—and
you sit the saddle like a Seljuk and an emir, but your eyes and mouth say
otherwise. Why, by the white horse of Kaidu, do your thoughts dwell on
a Christian child, scarce a woman?"

Robert merely nodded at Will Bunsley, who jogged ahead on his nag,
heedless of the inevitable dust cloud and the midges that swarmed about
his eyes

"Ha, the redbeard!" Abdullah smiled. "A skilled bowman and a man
without fear. Yet he rides on a vain quest with room in his skull for no more
than the idea that brought him forth. Allah, do we draw rein again?"

He shaded his eyes to gaze where Inalzig had halted the head of the column to let a string of camels pass. They were racing Bactrians, and the
riders jeered at the weary ponies of the Kankalis. Robert, who had an eye
for weapons and the men who bore them, observed that the camel riders wore splendid, silvered mail under black *khalats,* that their targets
were bossed with gold and their voluminous turbans crested with peacock feathers.

"Warriors of the Caliphs of Baghdad," muttered Abdullah under his
mustache. "Mark the white camel of the leader. Ha, it will be a great war
if the caliphs are sending men to the shah. Verily the Moslems are gathering their might, like a leopard crouching to spring."

On other days they sighted detachments of furtive hillmen, who kept
well away from Inalzig's standard, and horsemen mounted on splendid
Arabs, who raised the shrill ululation of the Saracens at sight of friends.

These were heading through the villages, tending in the same direction as Inalzig, which was toward a line of blue summits that rose each day a little higher upon the horizon, with one great peak bearing a snowcap standing upon the travelers' right hand.*

"To the Iron Gates," Abdullah nodded. "All who ride to Khar from the West must pass the Gates and give surety to the warders of their purpose. These arrays are no more than the outlying detachments, bound for the main armies at the great cities."

"I had thought them a mighty force," observed Robert.

Abdullah smiled.

"The puppy thought the jackal was a wolf! Nay, the master of the Throne of Gold hath five times a hundred thousand riders to his command."

This, Robert fancied a jest, for such numbers were incredible. In Palestine the host of the crusaders amounted to no more than fifteen thousand.

"If the red archer," quoth Abdullah, his eyes gleaming, "would see vengeance at work, he has come in good time. Aye, he shall see what will fill his eyes. And you, O young warrior, will taste the mead of a man." With that he urged his horse up close to the heels of a pair of Kankalis until the dust nearly choked them and hid the rest of the detachment somewhat from view. Thrusting out his hand suddenly, the minstrel gripped Robert's fingers and when he drew away something hard and cold was in the knight's hand. Realizing that he was not to attract attention to himself, Robert did not look down for a moment. When he did so, he recognized within his fingers the chain of rubies that Abdullah had carried, carved in the semblance of roses.

"Place it within thy girdle," whispered the minstrel, "and show it only at the Sialak. The *talsmin* will pass you through."

He glanced about and reined closer.

"You will have need of all your wit if you live to reach Bokhara. Remember that no Kharesmian has proof against you, and you are fairly safe

---

*The route taken by the crusader and his companions was not known to Europeans in that age. From the few landmarks observed, they must have crossed the Euphrates near Aleppo and the Tigris a little south of what is now Mosul, entering modern Persia within the next few days by the highlands of Kurdistan. The snow mountains must have been Demavend, some two days' ride northeast of Teheran. The Sialak Pass is today just as it was then—or as it was in Alexander's day, for that matter.

if you do not betray yourself—so beware of tricks. Remember, too, that it
is ever best to face forward and to shun no risk. The Moslems are a folk
of many tribes and quarrels—and that is their bane. If a man mocks you,
cut him down; if a spy is sent, laugh at him. By all the gods, I have not
brought you so far, to find you a weakling!"

Robert reflected that a good Moslem does not swear by more than one
god.

"And you?" he asked.

"Whatever happens, I will seek you out in Bokhara. *Yah bunnayi*—O
little son, tomorrow we climb the Sialak."

In the minstrel's dark eyes was something like concern for the youth
who, towering half a head above him, he addressed as his little son. Yet
when these words had passed he withdrew into his cloak of silence and
sat for hours on his saddlecloth without turning hand to his lute or lifting his voice in song. And that night the heat of the plains was tempered
just a bit by a long breeze from the north.

Robert sniffed it as he lay outstretched on his cloak, studying the canopy of stars, and though he thought surely it must be fancy, the breeze
seemed to bear with it the tang of the salt sea and wet rocks.

They made a long stretch the next day and Bunsley complained that
the Moslems hemmed him in as if he were part of the treasure of loot they
were guarding. Other caravans made way for Inalzig's standard, and all
through the day they drew nearer to a line of peaks that had lifted from
the skyline two sunrises before.

The wind whipped and buffeted them as they ate their rice and dates
and mutton that evening in the very shadow of bare slopes that flung back
the red glory of the sunset. Robert had studied the line of mountains carefully, to pick out the pass that might let them through; he had seen cavalcades of hurrying riders sweep up to one point in the foothills and immediately pass from view.

When the last shaft of red light vanished from the tallest of the peaks—
the one streaked with tiny spots of something that gave back the glitter
of the sun—darkness settled like a cloak upon the *serais* where the caravans had halted for the night. The smoke of the dung fires was not to be
seen, and the glow of the flames spread upon bearded faces and lines of
picketed beasts.

This was the signal for Inalzig to order his men to saddle again, and
four of them came and grinned at the two Franks before ranging them-

selves on either side. They went forward at a trot until a line of camels, grunting protest at the night march, slowed them to a hand pace.

So strong was the illusion of darkness that Robert felt that they were entering the breast of the hills. High rock walls closed in on them presently. By the echo of the hoofs on stones he judged that the cliffs were sheer and immense. When torches appeared ahead of him, he found that he could not begin to see the top of the canyon walls.

At places great boulders encroached on the narrow pass, leaving no more than a bridle way. The muffled voices and the uproar of the camels ahead sent the echoes leaping from side to side, to diminish to whispers drowned by the gusts of wind.

"Master Robert," quoth Will, "did the minstrel say that we would fall in with a company of dead lords, and ride with King Caesar and roguish Alexander—ha, St. Dunstan aid us!"

The echoes caught up his words and shouted them to the sky—

"Alexander—Alexander—aid us—aid!"

"Methinks this is the place."

Will lowered his voice to a whisper. And—

"Methinks this is—the place—the place!"

The windborne whisper passed overhead. Will fell to pattering what prayers he could muster on the moment, mixed with lusty curses on the paynims who had led him into such a stronghold of demons. The cliffs repeated back his mutterings and garbled the curses with the prayers so that presently he fell into a gloomy silence. The way twisted interminably, and they had to edge past the camels, which had been halted at one side while their riders, apparently, went forward. The ponies shied at the smell of the gaunt beasts, and presently the word came back to dismount.

As he pressed after the torches that flared and smoked in the gusts of air, Robert noticed that he was splashing through cold water. Reaching down one hand, he discovered that a cut on his forefinger smarted keenly; and, tasting the water, he found it salt.

Will merely shook his head when this was called to his attention.

"Aye, tall brother," he pointed out, "where water is salt, there a sea must be. What sea lies within the desert—save the Styx? Nay, we will sup wi' Satan and bed down wi' the ghosts this night. Seest thou yonder writing? How reads it?"

Glancing where the yeoman's finger pointed, Robert noticed first the portion of a ruined wall stretching athwart the pass, then a row of charac-

ters carved in the side of the cliff some distance over his head. The words
were not Latin or Arabic, and he could make nothing of them; but a stalwart Kankali at his heels noticed his interest and enlightened him.

"'Tis but one word, O Cairene, and that is—

"'Victory.'"

"How old is the word?"

"Am I a prophet, that I should know? Some say it was carved so by the
men of the hero Iskander, in the elder days, when news came to him of the
death of his foe the lord of Parthia.* But now leave your horse and climb,
for these are the Gates."

Robert looked ahead and found that Will was already scrambling up
what seemed to be a solid wall of rock, in reality a mass of boulders, up
which the Kankalis were swarming. Whether the rocks had been piled
there or had fallen from above, Robert cared little. So steep was the ascent
that he was forced to use hands and knees, and water trickled down on
his shoulders as he pulled himself up to where a line of men were standing with torches.

This proved to be the crest of the natural rampart, and the knight
saw that a score of bowmen placed here could hold back an army. The
wind smote him full force and staggered him. A spearman reached out
an arm and steadied him, thrusting him beside Will, facing the leader of
the guards.

On the other side the boulders fell away to the dark surface of water,
and Robert suspected that the stream flowing down the gorge had been
penned back by the wall of rocks, forming a pool on the upper side. He was
surprised to observe a number of women ranged beside the defenders of
the pass—veiled women, variously garbed, but all slender and long-haired,
unmistakably youthful. He noticed, too, that the Kankalis had passed on
save for Inalzig, who stood beside the captain of the warders.

Abdullah was not to be seen, although Will stared about hopefully.

"Would I had a good yew staff at hand!" the archer sighed. "Aye, to
make the sign of the cross, and so—ha, look below!"

Near the surface of the water they saw a white face surrounded by a
mesh of dark hair, and—in the glow of the torches—the silk-clad limbs
of a woman moving gently with the currents of the pool. A moment more
and she sank out of sight, but Will stared wide-eyed at the spot.

---

*Darius.

"You are from Egypt?" a courteous voice questioned the knight. "And alone—yet sent by the lords of Cairo? Verily, riders are coming from the far ends of the earth to the Throne of Gold. A strange sword!"

The speaker was a handsome Moslem, who made a respectful salaam and studied Robert with unwilling admiration.

"I had it from an unbeliever—who died," responded the knight quietly.

"And from the lords who sent you, O emir—have you a token or a written word?"

"The word is—victory. The swords of the faithful have scattered the host of the Franks, and the day of the unbeliever in Jerusalem is at an end."

"*Ma'shallah!* So, too, will the Protector of the Faith, the King of the Age, of Time and the Tide, smite the other infidels who dared to mount for war upon the northern border. And your token, O captain of men?"

Robert drew the chain of rubies from his girdle, and the chief of the guards glanced at Inalzig curiously. Others craned their heads to look at the miniature roses threaded on gold.

"Where had you that?" Demanded the Kankali, frowning.

"From one who brooks no questioning of his messengers, and who has a whip for a churlish slave," hazarded the knight, aware that this was a reasonably good characterization of any Moslem noble.

"Upon whom be peace," assented the officer. "Well do I know the ruby chain that is a token given by the King of kings, the Shah of shahs, the favored of Allah, the sword arm of the faithful, Alai ud-deen Mohammad, master of Khar. Aye, this token he gives to the *anis-al-jalis*, the favorites, the cup companions of his hours of pleasure."

He bowed profoundly.

"And the ruby chain admits whoever bears it to the Gates, but no more than one. Yet it is passing strange, O favored of the shah, that you, who have not passed this way going from Bokhara, should have the chain when you enter the inner country of Khar."

Robert glanced at the chain with some interest and returned it to his girdle. Then he turned suddenly on the Moslem.

"O brother to a parrot, O pack-saddle of an ass—"

He had learned a fair flood of forcible insults during his captivity, and he called upon his memory for a full minute while the spearmen gaped, and the officer began to look doubtful.

"Another question," he ended, "and I will open thy breast to see if water or blood be in thy veins."

So indeed might a noble of Cairo have spoken to one who stood in his way, and it was clear to the warders that the Emir Arslan would like nothing better than to make good his words with sword-strokes. Inalzig's eyes blazed, and unseen by Robert he made a sign to men who stood back by the cliff.

"If the Caliphs themselves rode out of Baghdad to join the shah," he snarled, "the keeper of the Gate would cast them into the pool if they gave not a good account of themselves as Moslems. Look yonder!"

Robert did not turn, but Will Bunsley yelped like a hound viewing its quarry.

"Now praise be to all the saints and martyrs! Here be the demoiselle of Ibelin and Father Evagrius!"

Running to the ledge of rock that served as a pathway back from the buttress on which they stood, he tried to cast himself on his knees and seize the edge of the girl's robe to kiss. A spear-butt planted in his ribs by an alert guard sent him sprawling.

Ellen d'Ibelin stood between two warriors with drawn swords. Her torn hood and bedraggled smock had been replaced with rich silks and white cotton, bound about her waist by a velvet vest. A circlet of silver held in her black locks above the ears, and a transparent veil covered her face below the eyes. But eyes and hair and the poise of her young head were unmistakable.

Her glance showed that she knew Robert, but she did not break silence to make an appeal for help. Evidently she and the priest had been among the riders of the camels, and she must have seen all that passed on the edge of the pool.

"Aid, tall brother, for the maid!" cried Will hoarsely. "Draw and smite— bows and bills! See, the dogs would cast her into the water."

Then Robert realized that Ellen's arms were chained and her ankles bound together with a girdle. With the priest and the two Moslems she stood on the brink of the ledge, swaying in the wind. The other women who had screened the captives until then had been herded ahead along the narrow path. This path, no more than two paces wide, ran between the wall of the cliff and the dark space of the abyss.

As he watched, Inalzig made another sign, and one of the guards seized the girl's long tresses, twisting them tight in his grasp. Her eyes widened in horror as the warrior, grinning, forced her to the very edge of the rock.

"Yonder maid," observed the keeper of the Gate reflectively, "was taken from among the Franks. We have other women, from Armenia and the Bedawan villages, and they are kept for the pleasure of the shah. Such is the custom of the forays beyond the border—yet, O emir, the redbeard may have touched her, and the touch of a dog of an unbeliever is defilement. So—thrust her over," he ordered the warrior who held her fast.

And Inalzig's white teeth flashed under his thin mustache.

"Ha! Would a Cairene act thus?"

Robert had leaped the space between the dam and the ledge. The warrior who stood over the girl released his prey and lifted shield and scimitar as he strode to meet the knight.

"Ah no, my lord!" Ellen cried, raising her chained arms eagerly. "Keep to your guise and your own purpose. No man's aid will serve to abate our misfortune, and you would be lost!"

She covered her eyes.

"The sweet Mother in Heaven give strength!"

The Moslem who opposed Robert took time for a swift glance at the two chiefs, who shouted an order at him, and the knight drew his sword. The guard's lips lifted in a snarl as he braced his legs for a leap forward. Then he flung up his shield.

In a gleaming arc the heavy blade of the crusader flashed, and the Moslem's scimitar was knocked down. His shield of hide and wood crumpled, and the blade hewed through his left arm, deep into his side. The man was swept over the ledge, and Robert freed his blade with a jerk as the body dropped out of sight.

"Well struck, O Nazarene!" applauded Inalzig. "Said I not you would be put to a test at the Gates? Ha, no guise will veil your heart hereafter. Like your follower, I had a devil from the first day, and the devil was doubt."

The second guard rushed low at Robert, to be met with the point of the sword and slain in his tracks. Will Bunsley scrambled to his feet, wrenching the scimitar from the hand of the falling slave.

"Let us show them our heels, brother," he muttered excitedly. "Do thou take up the maid and run along the path."

Robert, however, knew that this was just what the Moslems must desire him to do. Moreover the blind priest could not run, and there was no time to release the girl's bonds. He had been tricked and well tricked.

And fierce exultation warmed his heart. No need, now, of racking his brain for the words of deceit. He had jumped to aid the maid instinctively, and even now he might have explained his cutting down of the guards—if Inalzig and the captain of the warders would listen. But he had no desire to try them and for their part they prepared readily to make an end of him. There was the gleam of steel, red in the torchlight, before him and the feel of his sword-haft in his fists.

"Stand clear," he growled at the archer, and stepped to meet the first two spearmen who crossed from the dam to the pathway.

Ellen had slipped to her knees and was moving toward Father Evagrius, who was trying to draw her back to the cliff, his face upturned in the patient questioning of those who cannot see what goes on about them.

As Will pushed forward stubbornly beside him Robert swept him back with his left arm and slashed at the nearest spearhead. The steel point flew humming through the air, and the crusader dodged the thrust of the second. The Moslems crouched and reached for their long knives. They had not yet learned that the round targets of bull's hide were no protection against the long weapon of their foe. Robert cut through one shield and the skull of the man behind it.

The other warrior shouted and leaped, and Robert missed catching his dagger arm as it came down. But he stepped forward, and the man's knife snapped on the chain mail of his back.

Robert caught hold with his free hand on the man's shoulder blade and—sensing Will's presence behind—jerked him back, to be dealt with by the yeoman's sword. A snarling grunt that changed to a scream sounded from the path, and presently a splash in the water below.

"Sa-ha!" chanted Will. "Another knave a-swim in the Styx. Guard thee, tall brother—so! Pretty work—yeomanly struck."

A third Moslem had followed close upon the other two and raised his scimitar. Robert, caught with his blade down, jammed the heavy hilt into the man's beard and took the scimitar stroke on his helmet. The blow sent flames flying before his eyes, and the light steel cap spun from his head. But the Moslem was down, choking, and the knight took another pace forward, leaving Will to dispose of the injured warrior.

A spear splintered against the mail on his chest, and he reeled, coughing, for the point had lodged in his breastbone. The man who had flung it shouted and whirled up his scimitar. The knight parried one cut that would have hacked a knee in half and staggered again, when another spear tore into his left shoulder. The guard—a big-boned Turk—pressed forward too hastily and was dashed down when his legs were cut out from under him by a slash of the long blade.

"By the ninety and nine holy names!" swore Inalzig, who had followed the fighting with glittering eyes. "Here is one who should be brought alive to Bokhara, for he is not as common men. See, he strides forward again."

"Then, do you, take him alive, O khan," snarled the captain.

Will was feverish with exultation. Only three men beside the two chiefs stood on the dam, and these held the torches. Behind them the Kankalis had vanished from sight and hearing. If the strength of the knight could crush these five as well as the six who had died, they would be free, for the moment, in the gorge. But he did not mark how the two wounds had bitten into the thews of his companion.

Inalzig Khan rushed as a falcon stoops—warily, quick of eye, and with his long cloak sweeping about him. His scimitar glittered above his shield. Someone behind him hurled a torch at the knight.

Bending low, Robert moved to meet the Moslem, and the two swords grated. The scimitar bent nearly double and whipped clear—whipped down on the crusader's sword arm, cutting to the bone. Robert stumbled forward, threw himself against Inalzig and felt for the Moslem's knife hilt, while Inalzig felt for his throat and found it.

Jerking the curved dagger free, Robert thrust with failing strength at his foe's thighs under the mail. Inalzig's eyes glared into his, blood-seared and protruding. The knife-blade slipped upward on the Moslem's thigh-bone, and the curved point caught within his ribs.

His grip on Robert's throat fell away, and the knight gasped for air and felt himself drop through space. Instantly the torchlight faded, and he crashed into water, still locked with his adversary. Blackness grew denser, and then red flames shot up before his eyes and his nostrils stung. Blood flooded his throat.

He coughed—found that he could gulp in air—and moved his limbs feebly to keep afloat. For what seemed an interminable time he swam in a gigantic chasm, conscious of lights above him and—once—of Abdullah, the minstrel, looking down at him calmly. Then water splashed over his face, and the blackness was complete.

Chapter VII
Osman the Wazir

Many things appeared to Robert to take place very rapidly. He felt delightfully at ease, although aware that his body was being jolted, the creaking of leather and the jolting made him think he was riding again, though how he could ride lying down he knew not. Then the sun smote full into his eyes, and somebody shaded them. Robert peered out between two curtains and saw the green expanse of a wide sea with a sail drifting along the horizon. A salty wind caused him to shiver violently, and, still shivering, he dropped back into the inertia.

Again he found himself studying the stars, looking for the Great Bear and recalling that Abdullah had called it *jitti karatchi,* the Seven Robbers. He could not make out the robbers, and told himself that this was a strange sky as well as a strange sea.

Once he lay on his elbow, looking down at the earth. It was whitish gray. Taking up some in his fingers, he put his tongue to it and found it to be salt. A strange earth. He was bathed in sweat, and a woman came and wiped his face and hands with a cool, moist cloth.

He began talking to the woman, telling her about the changed earth and the remarkable sea that was so cold and so hot. By and by he noticed that the woman was weeping and that she was the Demoiselle d'Ibelin. Henceforth events happened less swiftly and Robert grew irritable with pain, but more often he felt the girl's touch and drank things from her hand.

"Where is that rogue, Abdullah?" he asked, his voice ringing clear.

"He is not here, my lord. Nay, I have not see him since the night in the mountains when he talked with the infidels, and—but, hush, please you, Sir Robert."

"Demoiselle," he remarked with dignity. "I am not Sir Robert of Antioch. I am Robert the Wayfarer; and as every man's hand is against me, so is mine against every man. Where is the lout, Will?"

"The archer is chained—nay, do not miscall him, for he jumped into the gorge and saved you your life many days ago."

"Now that is verily a lie," Robert responded angrily, "for this is but the morrow of that night."

With that he slept, to awaken master of his senses again.

They were in a boat—he and the maid and the priest, and a score of strange warriors. He lay upon a cloak stretched on rushes, with a woven screen over his head.

His first thought was for his sword. It was gone, and he reflected that his horse, also, was lost to him. Then he fumbled about for the chain of rubies and found it not. The mail shirt had been removed, and he was clad in loose cotton, with a light *khalat* wrapped over him.

When he moved, one shoulder irked him with its stiffness. Further investigation revealed a stubby beard and mustache and a growth of hair on his skull that had been shaven. After considering this he asked Father Evagrius, who sat quietly beside his couch, how long he had lain ill, and how he came to be brought alive through the Gates.

"For ten days the fever was heavy upon you, my son. The maid prayed that you would regain your wit and strength, and her prayers were heard. I could not see what befell in the mountain pass, yet meseems Abdullah did persuade the guards to send you living to the lord of this land."

"Did we pass the border of a sea?"

"Aye, Sir Robert. A week agone I heard the wash of the waves for the last time. Since then we have been placed on camels, and yesterday within this long skiff."

Robert thought this over. They must then have left the Caspian behind them, and by now should be near to the main cities of Khar. So Abdullah had outlined the journey to him. He asked Father Evagrius to call for Ellen, and the priest shook his head, saying that the maid was kept within the after part of the boat, guarded by Ethiopians. The Kankalis, the priest explained, had permitted her to nurse him during the height of his fever, while he was being carried in a horse litter; but now the Moslems took care to keep her apart. Of Will Bunsley he knew little, save that the archer had survived the gorge of the Sialak and his voice had been heard at times thereafter, complaining bitterly of his chains and a diet of rice and sour wine.

Unable to sit or stand, Robert was fain to be content with this. He could not see over the side wall of the boat, nor could Evagrius see anything at all, and neither of them might speak with Ellen.

So for days the knight was constrained to lie gazing at the roofed-in afterdeck where the slender form of the maid of Ibelin sometimes appeared, heavily veiled. At such moments her eyes would seek him out, and she stood where he was visible until one of the guards signed for her to enter the hangings that separated her from the men.

Father Evagrius spent his time in contemplation, eating slowly when food was brought and fingering the cross that hung from a cord about his lean throat. Robert, waxing more irritable with the confinement and the odors of the boat, marveled at the grave quietude of the priest who was preparing himself to meet death at the hands of the Moslem tormentors.

There came an evening when he could stand and look out from the boat, as the Moslems were at the evening prayer.

The river proved to be broad, and thronged with other craft. Gardens, divided off by lines of flowering trees, lined the bank, and Robert observed at once two marble pillars downstream. These rose from the dark mass of a wall, and until they drifted through the water gate he would not believe that he had judged truly the height of the wall.

Within it he saw the glimmer of lighted pavilions close to the water, and black spires rearing against sunset over domes that gleamed purple and crimson. Straight down upon their boat rowed a barge, draped in black silk and driven by a score of slaves.

On the raised platform behind the rowers a half-dozen men, turbaned and robed in many-colored silks, leaned on brocade cushions and stared down at the smaller craft and its crew.

"Ho, Moslems!" A tall man in the bow of the barge challenged them. "Who enters the water gate after nightfall?"

Robert could not understand the reply of his captors, but presently a command issued from the barge and the sailing skiff was brought alongside, the rowers lifting their oars. The same speaker, who seemed to be overseer of the slaves, ordered the warriors to send up their prisoners and the woman of the Franks. When Robert's guards argued, a mellow voice called out from the stern in liquid Arabic.

"Surety? Am I not Osman the Hadji, Wazir of the Throne and master of Bokhara? I will be surety to the shah, and that will suffice thee. Jackals—sons of jackals and sires of dissension! Yield up the Franks and seek thy pay in the appointed day and place! Am I a hireling to be affronted by slaves in the hour that Allah decreed for pleasuring?"

To a man the soldiers in the boat cast themselves on their knees and beat their foreheads against the planks. Yet Robert heard one murmur to another that the wazir had kept in his own purse the pay that had been promised them. The negroes ushered Ellen forward, through the waist of the boat, and in the deep shadow under the side of the barge she stumbled.

"Abdullah's word to you, my lord!" she whispered quickly. "Hide it!"

He heard the rustle of paper sliding over the reeds of the deck, and leaned forward.

"And what of you, demoiselle?"

"Father Evagrius hath prayed. Tend him—let no injury be done to him."

One of the negroes thrust Robert back, and steel gleamed in the shadow. The girl was lifted to the barge, and he took advantage of the respite to search for and find a narrow roll of parchment that lay near his feet. Putting this in his girdle, he helped the patriarch out of the boat and followed, rendered dizzy by the sudden movement but finding his limbs steadier than he had thought.

"So this is the champion of the Franks," observed one of the Moslems about Osman, "who named himself the Lion and clawed Inalzig, the *bahator*, to death with a score of warriors at the Gates. Shall we match the lion with a man-eating tiger?"

"Nay, 'twould take an elephant to crush his bones," responded another lightly. "He is greater in bulk than the tallest of the Ethiopians."

"You are both wrong, my cup-companions," put in a third. "The Frank, like the maid, is to be kept alive against the coming of the shah."

Osman, who had been staring at the girl, frowned at this, and a slender boy with insolent eyes ceased tuning a lute long enough to murmur:

"*Allah la yebarak fili!* May Allah not prosper *his* coming!"

"What words are these words, O Hassan?" reproved the wazir. "Am I not the slave of Muhammad, and was not he—"

"A slave himself, O most generous of lords," quoth Hassan, bending ear to lute again, "when he was my age and caught the eye of a woman."

Somebody mouthed a gibe about the eyes of women, and the assemblage laughed. Osman struck upon a silver gong that hung by his side; and the overseer of the slaves bellowed to the rowers, who brought the barge about and headed down the river into the heart of the lighted city.

Robert, utterly unnoticed, studied Osman curiously. It was the first time he had seen a Kharesmian of the higher classes, and it was difficult to believe that this was not the shah himself. Osman had pallid, weak-muscled cheeks, surrounded by a narrow beard, and his jeweled turban would have bought a castle in Palestine. His dark lips curved like a girl's, and his fine brown eyes had the blank stare of a dreamer or a user of drugs. From the instant that the demoiselle of Ibelin was seated at his side he did not cease to pay her attention.

"Let my counsel be as earrings in thy pretty ears, O damsel. Incline to me, and I will robe thee in samite and cloth of gold, and scent thy eyebrows with attar of rose—so that the shah himself shall fall bewildered by thy beauty."

He seemed loath to believe that the captive did not understand his praise, but when it was clear that she knew no Arabic the courtiers launched remarks that made the knight turn away so that they could not observe his eyes. It was wiser that they should not be aware that he could follow what was said.

"To the seller of perfume," smiled the boy with the lute, "what remains save the dust of the rose petal? How long, O treasurer, wilt thou labor to keep safe the treasure of the slave who claims to be thy master?"

Osman glanced at him warningly, yet seemed to find food for thought in the idle words. He lifted a drinking cup of pure jade, and from the waist of the barge cymbals and drums resounded as he drank.

"Nay, Osman," called out a stout man in purple silk who was being fanned by a Nubian slave girl. "Am I not crowned king of the hour of pleasure? What royal honors are accorded me when I lift my cup?"

"The dogs bay."

Hassan displayed white teeth.

"And spent hags pluck thy purse away—"

"Out upon thee. Pfagh—you are rank of the dunghill that bred thee. Who but I bore to our master, this excellent fellow Osman, the news of the taking of Otrar by the barbarians?"

"The tidings that sent Muhammad to the northern border," nodded one who had something of the warrior about him. "It was three moons ago that the Manslayer took Otrar into his maw and sent the head of its governor to the shah. Allah, he was angered!"

"And I made a song about it," quoth Hassan.

"The imams and *kadis* wagged their beards and fouled the carpet of counsel with the spittle of quarrels," nodded the wine-bibber unsteadily.

"And I made a song about that, too."

"Yet the news was good for us because it gave the reins of government in Bokhara to our lord, Osman."

"O sharp-of-wit, canst thou truly see an anthill when the ants bite thy toes?"

"The chief of the Kankalis who was leader of the garrison could not," put in the warrior, signing for a slave to fill his cup again. "At least he drank too much opium by mistake—"

"Thy tongue wags!" whispered one of the courtiers.

"Nay, he was a fine sight in his shroud. By Allah, it came to my ears that his favorite singing-girl slew herself with a dagger—"

"And that was not so fine a sight," broke in Hassan, "because a shroud was an ill garment for so fair a wench."

He glanced from under kohl-darkened lashes at the Nazarene maid and swept delicate fingers over the strings of his lute, singing under his breath:

> Wilt to Bokhara! Oh, fool for thy pains!
> To come from the desert to Bokhara's chains!

The river became narrower and darker where high walls of palaces and mosques lined the banks, but Osman's barge kept to midcurrent, and Robert noticed that the other craft got out of its way hastily and other pleasure-seekers knelt as the wazir passed. But Osman had eyes only for the Nazarene maid, and Hassan, perceiving the mood of his master, sang of love and the beauties of women in a voice that was softer than a silver flute. A brazier, burning in the prow, cast a scent of aloes and musk incense into the air, and at command of the leader of the revels, different powders were put into the wine cups by slaves—hashish, opium, and bhang. Robert, feigning exhausted sleep, heard other references to the Manslayer, to Otrar, and the treasure of Muhammad Shah, as the tongues of the drinkers were loosened.

He made out that Osman was the keeper of the shah's treasure, which was kept in Bokhara, where no Moslem band dare venture theft. And that Muhammad knew to a dinar's worth the value of the treasure. Otrar, he suspected, was the northernmost fortress of Khar, and its capture by the new foe from the mountains to the north had impelled Muhammad to collect his army and march thither some months ago.

The chief of the barbarian tribes who had entered Khar was spoken of as the Manslayer.

On a landing-stair of carved marble a throng of Nubian slaves awaited Osman's party with sedan chairs. Link-bearers attended them, and the girl was put into a closed palanquin, Osman riding in a chair close behind. Robert, taking the arm of the blind priest, walked in the center of the company.

From the shadows of the alley ragged shapes emerged like lame crows hopping to a meal. They croaked for alms, and the slaves thrust them back with their long wands, shouting against the outcry of the beggars for a way to be opened for the wazir.

One of the ragged men stumbled against Hassan's chair, and a flood of obscenity welled from the lips of the singer. The beggar crouched, whining, and Robert saw that his cheeks were blotched, the flesh eaten away to the bone.

"A bow!" Hassan commanded one of his followers and snatched the weapon, ready strung.

The leper lifted swollen hands, and Hassan, smiling, ordered two of the slaves to hold him. Shivering, the Nubians sprang to obey. The bow twanged and the arrow shaft plunged into the creature's stomach.

The knight, who had seen many men die, was sickened, and fought down rising nausea.

"Have we come to the prison, my son?" the gentle voice of Evagrius asked.

"Nay, we are within the streets of a great city."

"The sound of it is evil," nodded the priest. "And the smell is foul, both of dirt and incense. So must Babylon have been ere it was cast down."

In spite of the fact that Osman seemed anxious to take dark and unfrequented ways to his destination, Robert was amazed by the size of the walled-in dwellings, the stone towers and marble pools that were glimpsed as they passed. Loitering crowds sighted them and stared at the two Franks, spitting and clenching their hands on perceiving the dark robe of the priest. Robert thought that surely Babylon could not have been a greater place than this.

At a bronze gateway Osman's escort halted, and the master of revelry hastened to his side. The man had sobered perceptibly.

"Lord and hadji," he muttered earnestly, "do not stumble with the foot of recklessness upon the pit of misfortune. The maid was to be sent to the palace of the shah with the other women captives. Will you dare take her within your dwelling?"

"O small-of-wit," responded the wazir slowly, "if harm came to the Nazarene, who would face the blame?"

"You."

"Most true. And so shall I keep her safe, under my eye, until Muhammad returns. Who else is to be trusted with a pearl such as this, beyond price?"

"It would be better," objected the courtier, "to take under your hand the throne treasure, for safekeeping. That would buy allegiance of a host of chiefs, whereas a fair woman will—"

"Please the eye of Muhammad more than countless swords."

Osman signed for the palanquin bearing the captive girl to be taken to one of the buildings about the central garden, and gave over the knight and the priest to some guards, who led them to a postern door and up a

winding stair for so great a distance that Robert knew they must be ascending a tower.

Upon a landing of the stair a narrow door was unbarred, and they were
pushed into darkness. Robert bade the priest stand still while he investigated, and discovered that they were in a small, semicircular chamber
furnished only with a rug and mattresses to sleep upon. An oval window,
barely large enough to admit his head through, enabled him to look out
over the garden, and he heard a voice like a nightingale's where lights
glowed under the trees beneath the tower—

Wilt to Bokhara? O fool for thy pains!

Osman's tower proved to be the highest of the many minarets and cu-
polas of Bokhara—higher even than the emperor's palace, as Robert observed the next morning. Moreover in the open square and marketplaces
near the tower were the tents of several thousand Kankalis—easily distinguished by their black cloaks and trappings.

Beyond the mosques and academies were the tents and picket lines of
a host of mounted warriors. Where the caravan roads led into the gates
of Bokhara's wall other pavilions were pitched. Although the distance
was too great for the knight to be sure of the numbers, he estimated forty
thousand men under arms within his range of vision and guessed at as
many more elsewhere.

Hourly long lines of camels threaded through the gates and pushed
into the already crowded marketplaces. Passing along the alleys beneath
him, he made out throngs of mullahs, followed by their disciples, jostled
by swaggering Turkomans and pushed aside by the riders that were continually entering and leaving Osman's palace.

And four times a day there floated out over the humming confusion of
alley and bazaar the musical call of the summoner to prayer.

"*Allah akbar!* God is great . . . There is no God but God . . . Pray ye!
Prayer is good, and the hour of prayer is at hand!"

The gigantic concourse, the uproar of voices, the smells—that rose
even to the tower—wrought upon the senses of the watcher even as Osman's music and incense had failed to do and brought home to him the
power of the stronghold of Islam. It was during the first dawn prayer,
when the light was strong enough to read by, that he took out Abdullah's
scroll and scanned it in the window niche where the guards in the outer
corridor could not see him through the aperture in the door that served

to pass in food and enable them to spy upon the prisoners. The letter began abruptly.

> Salaam, yah ahmak—greeting, O fool! I have brought you to Bokhara,
> in spite of your folly which nearly made the Gate the end of the
> road.
>
> Have you never learned that one rider can pass where four may
> not go abreast? Why then strive to befriend three others, and two of
> them weaklings?
>
> But what is done is done, and what will be, will be. I have claimed
> on your behalf that you are the greatest of all the Franks, and it is
> well that the name of Longsword has penetrated even to the borders
> of Khar. The shah will desire to see you, and until his arrival you are
> safe, for I swore on the Koran that your disguise was needed to take
> you through the desert tribes.
>
> I also swore that you had been cast out by your peers of Palestine
> and sought the service of Muhammad, for that also was necessary to
> keep you from being put into a shroud by the followers of Inalzig.
>
> Your sword is more eloquent than your tongue; keep silence and
> listen, for Bokhara breeds more gossip than a dunghill vermin. Take
> these matters to heart, chiefly: Osman is only lip-loyal to the shah.
> The treasurer is the companion of Muhammad's mother, Turkhan
> khatun, who holds the allegiance of the Kankalis, who in turn are
> the backbone of the Kharesmian host. Osman secretly poisoned the
> emir who commanded the garrison of Bokhara, and would do away
> with the council of the imams, who are the Moslem elders. The shah
> fears him, the imams hate him. If he could lay hand on the throne
> treasure he would be master of Khar.
>
> Ponder these matters and gather your strength again, for you will
> have need of wit and daring when I seek you. Bahator, a new path
> will be opened up by the next moon, and we will ride again.

Three times Robert pored through the delicate Arabic scroll writing
and then thrust it into a crack between the bricks outside the window,
wondering more than a little what manner of man might be Abdullah,
who seemed to go freely wherever he willed and to judge any situation
with a clear mind. The crusader was beholden to him for his life, and yet
could not be sure Abdullah was his friend.

For days he paced the chamber, or slept heavily as they sleep who are
casting off the inertia of sickness. And though he often pondered Abdullah's message, he could make little of it. He had come among men who
learned to plot before they were weaned, who built mosques that out-
rivaled the Temple of Solomon, who could fashion weapons that made
the clumsy arms of the crusaders look like flails and scythes. Without a

weapon in his hand and a horse between his knees, he was restless; and often he found himself thinking of the girl who had come with the pilgrims to seek the Holy Sepulcher and had been led to Bokhara. Father Evagrius talked of her after his fashion, blaming no one for her fate.

"When all is told," the knight observed thoughtfully, "is not her state better here than on the roads of Palestine?"

"Is yours?"

"Nay, my case is different."

"You, my lord, have achieved much against the paynims. Will you swear to me that you will strive to speak again with Ellen d'Ibelin and ransom her from this infidel king?"

Robert frowned, chin on hand.

"Nay, that will I not. What ransom would suffice him who sits on the Throne of Gold? What have I?"

"My son, in this life we serve not ourselves. Not long ago the good yeoman leaped into the pool of the gorge and saved you from drowning, and thereafter the maiden tended you when the fever ran in your veins. What will you do for them?"

Glancing from the embrasure, Robert shook his head.

"Could you see the vast city and its wall, twice the height of Jerusalem's—aye, and the array of Moslems passing in and out upon the roads, you would not talk of hope. We have been brought hither like beasts for the eyes of the emperor to scan. Nay, Evagrius, 'twere folly to deceive ourselves. If the maid and the yeoman were free, and I, and we had horses—could we ride over these walls? And, even so, could we achieve a passage through five hundred leagues of Moslem lands?"

He laughed without merriment.

"Nay, Abdullah spoke truth to Montserrat. Whosoever enters Khar returns not."

The priest smiled.

"My blind eyes have seen more than that. The Red Sea dividing its waters, so that the Christian host passed through. Aye, and water issuing from a rock in the desert."

Evagrius nodded gently and sank into one of his long musing spells. Robert leaned back against the door, where he could listen to the talk of the guards in the corridor, and presently both were aware of a change in the sounds that drifted up from the alleys and gardens below.

The hum of talk had died away, although it was past the hour of evening prayer for the Moslems. In the water garden of the palace the companions of the wazir were sitting about their cups, and Hassan's clear voice rose in mockery above their laughter. Somewhere a woman began wailing, and slippered feet pattered along a corridor. A horse galloped furiously along the palace wall, and presently the hum of talk arose again in the alleys.

"What do the warriors, our warders, argue?" asked Evagrius, for the voices were louder than usual outside the door.

"They are disputing about the war. Otrar, one of the cities of Khar, fifty leagues from here, has fallen into the hands of the barbarians. There has been a battle between the host of the shah and the barbarian chief who is called the Manslayer."

Robert listened with rising interest.

"They say that Otrar was taken in a week, and ten thousand Moslems slain. A short siege, forsooth. Before that there was a battle in the northern mountains. One man claims that the shah overthrew his foes; another that he lost half his warriors—a hundred thousand."

"Who is this foe?"

"They name him now the Great Khan, which is to say Genghis Khan, and his tribe are called Mongols."

Chapter VIII

Not by the robe of honor on his shoulders, not by the sword on his hip, not by the words on his lips is a man to be judged.
When a friend calls for aid—then is the warrior weighed in the balance. And by his deeds, not by his promises, is the bahator judged.

The next morning the talk of the warders was that Muhammad was approaching Bokhara with his army and there was rejoicing in the bazaars. Carpets were hung out on the balconies overlooking the wide street that led from the Otrar gate through the *righistan*—the central square on which the great Jumma mosque was situated—past the two palaces of the shah and Osman, over the bridge that spanned the canal, to the western gate.

All this Robert observed, for his embrasure faced the east and north; but he saw too that while the Bokharians prepared a triumphal entry for the shah, many caravans came out of the east and passed by the city while none went the other way. He reflected that if the shah had overthrown his foes, merchants would not be bearing away their goods.

While he was watching, visitors came to his door, and he beheld bearded faces topped by huge turbans peering in at him. A low-voiced argument between the owners of the turbans and Osman's guards followed, until the door was flung open for the first time since his entry and a stout man with worried, sunken eyes walked in.

"This is the mullah," announced one of the spearmen, "who has in his keeping the Jumma mosque, and Allah alone knows why he is bearing you hence for a day, O dog of an unbeliever," he grumbled.

The mullah drew up the skirts of his silk robe as he passed Father Evagrius, and stared for a full moment at Robert.

"Are you verily the infidel *bahator* who withstood Nasr-ud-deen at Antioch and broached the wall of Damietta?" he asked in scholarly Arabic.

Robert bent his head to conceal his surprise, but the Bokharian guessed his thought.

"We of Khar are conversant with the events of the borderland of Islam, for this is the heart of Islam. The heart would not beat as high if a vein in one finger were opened. Speak, O *caphar*, for Abdullah sang your praises and made known to us that you are acquainted with our speech."

"True, O hadji."

For the mullah wore the green turban cloth that showed he had performed the pilgrimage to Mecca.

With another scornful glance at the impassive blind man the mullah signed for Robert to follow and led the way down the tower stair. In the street they were joined by a half-dozen dignitaries of the town, imams and *kadis*—hawk-faced Turkomans and stalwart Uzbeks, all looking more than a little troubled and all armed. They took the shortest way—as Robert knew from his study of the streets—to the canal and the wall beyond the bridge.

Once he set foot on the walk that ran on the summit of the wall, Robert strode to the crenellated parapet and stared down. The nobles watched him silently as men might eye a horse that was going through its paces.

"Abdullah," observed one presently, "who is a cup-companion of the shah—upon whom be peace—said in our hearing that the Saracens of Syria set the price of a king's ransom on your head because you were master of the art of siege."

Robert kept silence, inwardly cheered by the knowledge that the various Moslem races were more often than not tearing at each other's throats and that the Kharesmians apparently were not allied to the Saracens whom he had fought. So he waited for the speaker to explain himself.

"In the mulberry grove below," the man went on, "is the *mazar* of a venerable sheikh who dared to prophesy. Aye, he foretold to Muhammad that a day would come when the walls of Bokhara would be one with the plain, and cattle would graze where its mosques had been."

The mullah pushed forward to add his word.

"By command of Muhammad, the shadow of God upon earth, this man was cast into the pit of vermin, having first been blinded. Thus his death was slow, yet because of his sanctity, the *mazar* was erected. Muhammad did not act wisely."

Seeing that they sought something from him, Robert continued to gaze indifferently down at the grove and its shrine.

"How long, O *caphar*," demanded the mullah at last impatiently, "could Bokhara withstand a siege?"

"With how many men for garrison?"

"You have seen them, and you have seen the wall."

Robert shook his head, smiling.

"Will one claw show the size of a tiger—or its teeth?"

After consulting together they led him a league or so around the summit of the wall until they were winded, and the knight waxed exultant with his first hour out in the sun. The guards at each tower and stair looked at him until he was out of sight. The sentries that squatted by each ballista to cast arrow sheaves and each mangonel for the casting of naphtha jars forgot to scratch themselves and salaam to the mullah.

Robert, standing half a head taller than the Bokharians, with his tawny beard uncombed and his yellow hair falling on his square shoulders, strode in the lead, for his interest was aroused; and his gray eyes gleamed as he studied the engines of defense, which differed little from those in Palestine. The murmurs of the warriors gathered around stew pot and dicing reached his ears, but he gave them little heed—though the *kadis* were more attentive.

The men were saying to one another that here was another Iskander from the land of the Franks. The mullah knew better, but one of the *kadis* twitched his sleeve and held up a row of coins that served to ornament his sword belt. They were old coins, dug out of the cellars of the city, and one bore the head of Alexander.

"Nay, he is no Iskander," they decided. "But the poise of the head, and the brow and the hair—aye, and the chin are the same. He must be of the race of Macedon."

They seemed to take comfort from this, although the knight could have told them otherwise. In the memory of the councilors, old men had told stories of the rule of the Bactrian-Greek generals who governed Bokhara until a Chinese horde came out of the east—to be driven away in turn by the Arabs, who were succeeded by the Khar dynasty, the emperors before Muhammad.

"How long could the wall be held?" they asked all together when the mullah halted at the Otrar gate, which, being the chief gate of the city, was used as the site for exposing the heads of men slain by order of the shah— being ornamented by wizened shapes of skin, and hovering birds.

"Forever," answered Robert briefly. "If two things happen not."

He was amazed at the labor that had gone into the fortification. The blocks of sun-dried brick were hard as stone, and the wall was solid, a full eight spears' lengths in height and three in width. Moreover, except where the river flowed, the country outside was a wind-whipped, sandy waste. A besieging army would need to drag timber for engines and food from a distance. There was plenty of water within the city and ample forces to man the wall. No ordinary stone-casters could make a breach wide enough to do harm.

"What two things?" demanded the Moslems in unison.

"Treachery, or poor leadership."

The councilors stared at him with hard, covetous eyes and fingered their beards.

"*Inshallah!* That is a truth. Cannot the wall be made stronger?"

Robert nodded.

"Dig a ditch at its foot—a wide ditch. Or the foe would start tunnels to run under and collapse the towers."

"And what else?"

"Nay," the knight smiled, "am I also a prophet, to tell of what is to be? What I know, I know, and words are easily twisted. I have answered your question."

They drew apart to talk again; and when they began to argue, he suspected that the Bokharians had no one who could put the city in a condition for defense. The leader of the garrison being dead, and Osman occupied with his own affairs, the forces in the city lacked a head.

"You have told us no more than we understood before!" exclaimed a *kadi* with a narrow skull and a wisp of a beard. "Surely you have greater knowledge than that, and we have means to make you speak. The vermin pit is an ill dwelling place."

"Lies are easily had," assented the knight, "and in Bokhara I have heard much lying and little truth."

"We will make a bargain with you, O Nazarene. If you will advise our captains how to prepare the city for defense we will speak a word on your behalf to the shah."

"And if I tell them what to do, who is to see it done?"

After much argument the Moslems offered to let the crusader come to the wall each day, to watch the progress of the work, and to give advice to the various chiefs who would command the slaves who would do the work. Muhammad was expected in three days. Robert stipulated that the mullah and the judges were to give him a signed promise that no harm would come to Father Evagrius during this time.

At sunrise, the next three days, he was on the wall, attended by guards of Osman's household, and the nobles, who at first listened contemptuously to the plans of an infidel, began to stroke their beards and to ask for fresh suggestions. A multitude of slaves were turned loose outside the wall to dig the ditch.

Across the canal at both entrances a chain was stretched, and a bridge of barges set in place inside the chain. Wooden parapets were erected on the barges and detachments of archers told off to practice shooting in triple ranks; the engines were greased with sheep's fat, and new timbers shaped by craftsmen where the old were decayed.

The chiefs of the Kankalis and Turkomans were better skilled in leading their men on forays than in preparing for a siege, and the headmen of the city saw the worth of what Robert advised. The knight himself, glad of something to do at last, went among the soldiers showing them by example what he wanted done. Meanwhile the councilors did not neglect to seize the cattle of the countryside and to fill up the granaries of the city.

By the third evening the slaves had been joined by throngs of merchants and idlers, for it was known at last that the Moslem host under Muhammad had suffered at the hands of the barbarians, and that the shah was actually in flight before the Mongols. He had with him a formidable army, and with Bokhara prepared for siege and the shah to lead the defense the Moslems of the city had no fear of the outcome.

That night Robert found a scroll from Abdullah awaiting him on the silver platter that bore his evening meal, in the tower room. The missive ran:

> O little son you have done well, and I have not been idle. Gold, in Bokhara, is the key to all gates save that of the treasure, which is hidden. Your warders have pouched gold from my hand. On the morrow demand to be taken to the street, to stand in the crowd when Muhammad passes. Speak boldly when the time comes, for the devil had his paw on a timid man.

With the first streak of sunrise the knight confided to Father Evagrius that Abdullah had appointed a meetingplace, for what purpose he did not know. He had been content to follow the hints given out by the minstrel, who seemed to wish to make known the worth of the man he had brought to Khar.

He found that the three men who were on guard in the corridor were quite prepared to take him down to the street. They wanted to watch the spectacle themselves, and Robert had been allowed to go out before this. But the knight suspected they had been bribed.

From the window he saw that the flat housetops were lined with throngs of watchers and that carpets had been laid in the street through which Muhammad must pass to go to his palace; and before the guard had been changed, he perceived dust rising in a long line out on the plain.

When the first horsemen entered the Otrar gate under the sightless eyes of the heads exposed there by order of the shah, Robert was taken down to the garden and thence to the street where Osman's followers were jammed against the wall. His guards, anxious for a better view, elbowed their way forward with the knight, claiming that the wazir had ordered Robert to be displayed as his prisoner.

Room was made for him in the outer line, and for hours he watched the passing of bodies of horsemen. These were strange to his sight—darkskinned warriors, well mounted, who cursed the crowd when the way was obstructed. The ponies were sweat-streaked, and many of the riders bore wounds. Robert noticed that they had no spare mounts and no baggage. They looked like men who had been in the saddle throughout the night.

The tumult in the street was echoed from the housetops when it was seen that the van of the cavalry did not halt at the river. Instead they crossed the bridge and passed out of the southern gate. The Bokharians mocked them for cowards who did not dare make a stand in the city, and the shah's men answered in kind.

Other riders followed—Persian mailed archers, with high lambskin hats and bronze shields. One of the guards at Robert's elbow shouted a question, which was answered by a blow from a scabbard. But rumors were buzzing in the crowd.

"To Samarkand—the army goes to Samarkand! Nay, to Herat, for I heard—Allah, they lost their tents, and all but—to the mountains, I say—they draw their reins to Khorassan."

Behind Robert the press grew greater. A gaunt Turkoman *beg*, smelling of sheepskins, bared yellow teeth and roared in his ear:

"Pillage! The door is open to plunder! Death to the Franks!"

They were thrust forward into the dust cloud as the slaves of Osman issued from the palace gate and beat a path for their master, who sat in a palanquin. Catching sight of Robert, he signed for the guards to bring the captive after him and ordered his bearers to run toward the *righistan*.

"Where is Muhammad Shah?" bellowed the Turkoman, running with them. "Where are the emirs?"

Osman lay back on his pillows, closing the curtains against the dust. They passed an array of spearmen mounted on camels and—thanks to the wands of the Nubians—emerged into the great square at the same moment that some score of elephants came swaying up the street on the other side. Before and behind the elephants galloped horsemen, white with dust, drawn scimitars in hand. Abreast the pillars of the Jumma mosque the leading elephant—a towering beast painted green and red, with steel blades lashed to its tusks—slowed its ambling gait and threw up its trunk. The lines of Bokharians near Robert cast themselves on their knees, pressing their foreheads to earth. So he was able to see the mullah of the mosque standing on the steps of the edifice.

And, when the elephant came to a halt, the man who sat alone in the glittering howdah stared first at Osman and then at Robert, who remained standing.

"Hail to Muhammad Shah, the mighty, the victorious!" roared the crowd.

Robert saw a face under a turban that glittered with jewels—a puffy face with restless eyes. Osman climbed from his litter and salaamed.

"O monarch of the world, make thine elephant kneel. Thy palace is in readiness."

He spoke boldly, and under the words was a shadow of mockery. The shah leaned forward.

"Upon thee the peace, O hadji!" he greeted the mullah first. "Necessity has changed my plans. I ride to Herat, there to gather together the new forces from the south."

The dark eyes of the wazir glittered, although he did not seem surprised.

"And what of Bokhara? What is thy command?"

"To defend it against the Mongols," replied the man in the howdah slowly. "In council the emirs of the kingdom have given decision to retire to the walled cities. Against these the foe will spend his strength, while a fresh army gathers under my standard."

"And is this thy decision also, O king?" asked Osman loudly.

"It is my command."

The minister bent his head.

"To hear is to obey. Give to thy servants the boon of the Presence, if it be only for one night, that our hearts may be strengthened."

Muhammad hesitated, and Robert thought then that this man was not of a race of leaders, if he knew not his own mind. Instead of answering he signed for Osman and the mullah to approach closer, and they talked for several moments in low voices. Then deliberately the wazir made a response loud enough for Robert and the nearest horsemen to hear.

"Lord of the Age, Companion of the Warriors of Islam, Mirror of the Glory of Allah—give to thy poorest servant, Osman, the wazir, thy signet ring and the command of Bokhara's garrison, that his back may be straightened and his courage heightened and thine enemies confounded."

Again Muhammad hesitated while Osman waited at ease. It occurred to Robert that if Osman was powerful enough to speak insolently to the emperor, a successful defense of the city would strengthen the wazir's hand. Osman already had under his influence an army as great as the shah's; a considerable victory would win him new followers.

"Nay," said the man in the howdah, firmly this time, "the care of the treasure is thine—and the mullah's. Is not that enough care?"

Other officials now approached the elephant, and there was a brief conference. Osman dissembled his disappointment and listened attentively. Presently Robert recognized Abdullah's voice and saw the minstrel close to the howdah, laughing as at some excellent jest.

Muhammad glanced at the mullah.

"Is it true, O hadji, that the imams have asked for a new leader?"

"Protector of the Faith, it is true."

"Then I name the emir of the Franks, the conqueror of the Saracens, commander of the garrison of Bokhara."

A murmur went up at this, and men pushed closer to study the face of Muhammad. Until the shah signed to him Robert did not realize that he was the man in question. Osman for once looked utterly astonished, but the mullah seemed satisfied. When he stood under the elephant Robert saw that the lines of fatigue and worry were strongly marked in Muhammad's broad face, and that he was too restless to keep still for long.

"Will you swear, O Nazarene," the mullah asked, "to serve the shah in this thing and to give your utmost to the defense of the city?"

The knight looked up silently at the man in the howdah, who turned impatiently on the officers below.

"What is this? We have escorted this warrior from Syria, and you have failed to give him sword or armor or horse. A robe of honor for his shoulders, and do you, choose a horse from the best."

Several of the imams hurried off to obey, and Robert saw Abdullah smile. Osman was chewing at a strand of his mustache, his brow unruffled but his eyes dark with anger that heightened when Muhammad loosened the signet ring on his finger and tossed it down to one of the mounted emirs, who pressed it to his forehead and extended it to the knight.

"Do you swear allegiance, Nazarene?" cried the mullah again.

"Tell me first," Robert answered slowly, "what authority goes with the ring?"

The keeper of the mosque opened wide his eyes; and Muhammad, listening, started as if he had set his hand on a scorpion.

"Power of life and death! Bokhara is in the hands of its garrison, and you are the leader of the garrison. My favor is accorded you."

The knight faced Muhammad, and perhaps he was the calmest man of them all because he was skeptical.

"O king, I have heard. What then of Osman? Can there be two moons in the same night? Is my word to be obeyed over his?"

"Boldly have you spoken, O emir."

Muhammad did not seem displeased this time, and he gave the knight the Moslem title.

"*Yah khawand*, the men of the garrison will obey your commands; a *firman*, a decree, shall be written for their leaders to see. The good wazir has authority in matters of the treasury."

He glanced restlessly at the tall crusader.

"It has been dinned into my ears by my councilors that you are the one man who can defend the wall of Bokhara. Give me your pledge that you will do so!"

"Speak, fool," whispered Abdullah, reining his horse nearer Robert.

"First," observed the knight, "do you, pledge me safety from harm for three persons."

"Allah, what are they?"

"The Nazarene damsel carried from Palestine by Inalzig Khan and her companion the archer, and—" Robert turned to the mullah—"the priest Evagrius."

"They are yours."

Robert bent his head.

"O king, there be many witnesses to that promise. And to mine. I swear that I will do my utmost to hold Bokhara for you against your foes."

"You have my leave to withdraw."

The man in the howdah turned to speak to the mullah, when a rider passed forward from the rear and rose in his stirrups to exchange a quick word with Muhammad—a word of warning, Robert thought. The shah uttered a sharp command, the mahout tugged at the elephant's neck with his hook and the great beast swayed into a walk, then broke into a long shamble, followed by the others.

The Bokharians were forced to scramble aside, out of the way, and a disorderly horde of infantry flooded the square, pushing after the elephants. The throng on the housetops and about the mosque knew by now—for tidings travel swiftly in a Moslem crowd—that the shah was minded to leave the city with the troops that attended his person, and that he had appointed a captive, an infidel, to take command of the garrison. Even now the crowd, fatalists without the power of acting on their own initiative, made no protest at the departure of their shah. As the glittering elephant swept by, the throngs prostrated themselves; and something like silence settled on the square, where a dozen officers stood about Robert, who was staring at the ring in his palm.

Osman was the first to move forward.

"*Salaam, yah khawand*. We have heard the word of the lord of Khar, and there is naught but obedience in our hearts. Command, and my men obey."

The mullah came next, followed by the nobles, who bore a shirt of silvered chain mail, a crested helmet and a cloak of black silk. They took off Robert's old *khalat* and fitted on the mail, slipping the cloak over it and winding his waist with a girdle of cloth of gold. A scimitar of blue steel with a hilt set with glittering gems was offered to the knight, and he took it. Still doubtful of the reality of the honor, he gathered up the reins of a white Arab pony with the mane and head of a king's charger. When he swung into the saddle he flushed with sheer pleasure.

"*Salaam, bahator*," his companions saluted him.

Robert raised his sword and took up his rein.

Abdullah came to his side. "A slave's greetings to Iskander," he cried. "May the road of your namesake be open before you."

Chapter IX
Will Finds a Bow

With some ten thousand staring at him, the new Emir of Bokhara issued his first commands and watched without seeming to do so to see if each were acknowledged—Abdullah finding great amusement thereby.

Robert appointed a conference for the chiefs of the various tribes in the courtyard of the shah's palace two hours hence. He called the several *atabegs* within view to him, and sent one to take immediate charge at every gate of the city. The imams he requested to draw up lists of the amount of food in the granaries and the total of the weapons stored in the armories.

From the crowd he picked out the Turkoman *beg* who had talked about killing him, and the man knelt with quivering cheeks, evidently expecting that he would be given over to torture. Instead he was bade to select a hundred riders and set out to the east to establish an advanced post beyond sight of the city. Other detachments were ordered off, to patrol the river and caravan tracks beyond the walls.

His commands were received with the deepest respect and executed at once. Robert, aware of the mullah at his elbow, turned in his saddle.

"O hadji, is it fitting that the leader of your warriors should stretch his cloak in an alley and have the sky for a roof?"

The keeper of the temple started, eyed the knight keenly a moment and nodded gravely.

"True. A house shall be made ready in the garden quarter by the river, and slaves—"

"To this house," Robert suggested to Osman, "the blind priest and the archer can be sent before the hour is ended."

The wazir bowed in silence.

"And the Nazarene maid."

Their eyes met, and the minister of the shah twisted his fingers in the pearls that hung from his throat.

"*Yah khawand!* What words are these? In this place? To name a woman before listeners is to shame a follower of the Prophet!"

"Yet, O wazir, I am a Nazarene and a man of my word. If the maid is not placed in this dwelling, unharmed, before the sands have run from the hour-glass I shall open your gate with a thousand spears."

Osman exchanged glances with the mullah and extended both hands open before him.

"Who am I but the slave of him who has honored you? It shall be as you have said."

Robert watched him out of sight, well aware that he had made at least one bitter enemy. Turning the long ring on his finger, he studied the massive sapphire, cut in the form of a seal, in the gold setting. Then he raised his head and smiled.

"Here is a riddle, and I would know the answer in true words."

"Command me," suggested Abdullah promptly, but Robert shook his head.

"Hadji," he asked of the mullah, "have you in your house a *hamman,* a bath where the bathmen are discreet? Then may I be your guest for one-half of the hour?"

Surprised, the mullah signed for him to ride to the rear of the mosque, and Abdullah stared after the two thoughtfully. The boy Hassan approached his horse and peered up mockingly.

"Lick thy palm, O teller of tales. The cup-companion is the favorite of a day and then—the dust of the rose petal remains to the seller of perfume."

Having launched this shaft the boy darted away and overtook Osman's palanquin at the gate of the wazir's palace, hearkening with interest to the low-voiced exclamations of his patron.

"O dog of a mongrel pack! O eater of filth! To claim with a loud tongue what was mine! Son of dishonor and father foulness! To speak of the maid that would have been mine—aye, before a multitude! O fool and madman—Nazarene, prince of unbelievers—thy grave will be dug by jackals, and dogs will tear it loose again. May the bones of thy mother and thy father's father suffer a like fate."

Perceiving Hassan awaiting him, Osman mastered his rage somewhat and ordered the singer to run to the dwelling that was being prepared for the Frank, and stint not gold among the slaves selected by the imams for his service. Having confidently expected this command, Hassan made off blithely, for here was a matter dear to his heart, and a quarrel out of which a song might be made to quiet his master in another, more fortunate hour.

Robert understood the Turkish character well enough to be quite sure that the shah's ring and the imperial decree would not serve to keep him his command if he failed to enforce his authority by his personality. He did not wish to appear before the chiefs in council until he had learned something about them and the situation in general. To talk with Abdullah would be a mistake, because the Bokharians would conclude that he relied greatly on the minstrel.

Nur-Anim, the mullah, was a man wise beyond his years and a shrewd schemer, with the fire of fanaticism behind his close-set eyes. Robert had reasoned that he was the second most influential leader of the Bokharians; and he wished to question the mullah before Osman could talk with him, knowing well that he would be answered with half-truths and lies, out of which he might put together some guess as to why the sword and the ring had been bestowed upon him.

"Little time have we, Nur-Anim," he observed, refusing the offer of sweetmeats and fruit and a seat on the mullah's carpet, "to sit on the carpet of counsel. Is it not true that Muhammad was overthrown in the battle at the Takh-i-suleiman and lost half his men? And that his foes the Mongols are pursuing him apace? Nay, they are not fifty leagues behind."

He had reasoned this out in the bath, judging that no one not harassed by pursuit would appoint a commander in the great city of Bokhara in such haste. Nur-Anim inclined his head.

"The Mongols are horsemen and ride swiftly," went on Robert, who had remembered what his guards gossiped, but chose to let Nur-Anim think he was well informed. "And they number full as many as the warriors within Bokhara."

"Nay, the sum of their strength—may Allah not prosper it—is somewhat greater than one hundred thousand."

The mullah considered.

"We have twenty thousand more under your orders, and the slaves besides."

"Who are the most experienced *atabegs*?"

"Kutchluk Khan, the Uzbek."

The mullah pronounced the name with distaste.

"Leader of the horsemen of Turan—a one-eyed wolf who can scent plunder farther than a vulture can see a dead horse. And next to him Jahan Khan, chief of the Kankalis, who can cut a sheep in halves with a scimitar stroke. Sixty thousand follow them, and their pay takes the revenues of one-tenth Bokhara's trade."

There were others—the captain of the Persian mailed archers, and only one a noble of Khar. Robert began to see light. These leaders of the tribes were hired retainers. Gold was the tie that bound them—for the most part—to Muhammad, who had much gold. Their homes were elsewhere, and they lost little chance to quarrel and plot against each other.

If Muhammad had chosen one of them for emir the jealousy of the others would have flared up, and the leader would have had his hands full with the pack. Whereas, led by a stranger, they might fight well; at least until the fighting around Bokhara was at an end, and Robert was glad to learn that he had such men among the garrison.

When he asked about the Mongols and the Manslayer, Nur-Anim could say only that the foes of Khar were wild tribesmen, infidels, who had emerged from the Himalayas, coming down from the Roof of the World like a black storm. Ignorant of the strength of Bokhara, and lacking siege engines, they would be crippled under the wall and cut up by Muhammad when the shah raised a fresh army in the south.

"Where does Osman keep the treasure of the throne?" Robert asked suddenly.

He knew that the treasure was in the city, and that the shah had not taken it away.

Nur-Anim started and suppressed a smile.

"Would Muhammad entrust the treasure of Khar to a wazir whose palace was surrounded by wolves like Kutchluk Khan?"

"Yet Osman knows the place of its hiding—as you do!"

"Am I a servant of the shah—that I should keep the keys? Nay, I serve the mosque."

He glanced contemptuously at the Nazarene who could be foolish enough to ask such questions.

"What if the Mongols take the city? The wealth of Khar would fall into their hands."

"They would not find it. Not if they tore down the dungeons and let the water out of the tanks."

This explained somewhat the readiness with which Muhammad left his personal hoard of riches behind. And Robert fancied that if he had tried to bear off the treasure the *atabegs* and the garrison would have made trouble. Pretending disbelief, he asked if a guard should not be set about the place where the treasure was kept.

Nur-Anim turned aside to take up some sugared fruit.

"There be watchers that stand over the Throne of Gold. For a hundred moons they have watched, and not Osman himself would dare draw sword against them."

"With Allah are the keys of—the unseen."

Robert took his leave and went out, the mullah staring after him a long time and wondering whether the new emir was really as simple as he seemed, for Nur-Anim was shrewder than others. The knight circled the precincts of the mosque, within which he was forbidden to set foot. He found an escort of a score of Kankalis and its many lean Turkomans awaiting him.

"*Yah khawand,*" greeted a Kankali *beg* in a sleeved cloak of red satin, "by order of Jahan Khan do we, thy slaves, attend thee."

"O emir!" growled a bearded Turani. "We also be here! Command us!"

They held his stirrup, then raced to their horses, and Robert rode off musing upon the power of an emperor that could raise an unknown warrior to such dignity. From his talk with the mullah he suspected that Nur-Anim was well acquainted with the hiding-place of the treasure—if he was not actually its keeper.

If Muhammad remained away from Bokhara and the city should be besieged for a long time, the possession of the treasure would mean power to the holder. Robert did not intend to let Osman put his hand on it. One thing puzzled him; if Osman knew where it was hidden, what had kept the wazir from seizing the treasure? And who was the Manslayer, that men who had never set eyes upon him should fear him?

This question was answered for him sooner than he expected.

It was sunset before he left the *atabegs* after issuing his orders and finding out that they knew less than he did about the Mongols. In the courtyard a familiar voice hailed him.

"Now by the shank-bone of the blessed St. Dunstan, here be Master Robert!"

Will Bunsley sprang forward and grasped the knight's hand in both fists, grinning hugely. His hood and hose were somewhat the worse for wear, but he looked fat and hale; in fact a strong odor of wine of Shiraz hung about him.

"Praise be to St. Bacchus—who was a fair trencherman if he lacked of sainthood—that I ha' found thee. Abdullah brought me hither with tidings—"

"How left you Ellen and the blind priest?"

"Safe as an arrow in quiver, and chattering like magpies, God wot! Has Gabriel sounded his trump, lordling, or is the day of miracles at hand again?"

"*Yah khawand,*" spoke up Abdullah impatiently, "the Mongols are within the gate."

"How?" The knight's eyes narrowed. "Where?"

"An envoy came to the Otrar gate to have speech with the ruler of the city."

"Ha—and no word from our outposts?"

The minstrel snapped his fingers significantly and pointed to where in the gathering darkness red glows were visible in the distance—the reflection of fire upon rising columns of smoke. Bunsley followed his gesture with an appraising eye and explained cheerily.

"Abdullah doth fret because the light horsemen sent out from this citadel be somewhat heavy this night. Methinks they are, in a manner of speaking, dead, my lord, and divers paynim villages aflare on the horizon; by which token are we beset, and the goodly walls of this town invested, and I lack a bow, Master Robert. A fair long bow, seest thou, is a goodly thing when a siege is toward, and I pray thee—"

But the knight waited not to hear how Bunsley had managed to gather his tidings. Putting his horse to a gallop, followed by his escort and the minstrel and archer, he made for the eastern gate. Riding with loose rein, he glanced about him and saw that in the bazaar the merchants were hurrying to gather the goods from their stalls and that men ran about shouting aimlessly. As when the shah passed through, crowds of slaves and women lined the housetops to stare at the fires on the skyline. Torches were lighted by the Otrar gate, and here a body of Kankalis stood beyond spear-throw of three men.

At first sight of the three Robert thought that Abdullah and Will had jested.

They were mounted on shaggy ponies not much larger than donkeys. They were clad in coarse wool and leather, loosened over their bare chests for coolness in the windless evening. Only one, the most powerful of the three, wore mail of sorts—a haburgeon of iron plates knotted together with leather thongs.

The face of this rider was dark as burnished bronze and clean-cut as iron. His bare right arm was heavy with corded sinews, and the sword at his thigh was broad as an English battle-ax. He spoke in explosive gutturals, barely moving his lips, and one of the Moslems interpreted.

"The Mongol says he is Chatagai, a commander of a hundred. He says Genghis Khan offers the people of the city their lives."

The envoy glanced once at the crusader and his horse and spoke again.

"You are to bring the people from the walls to the plain," explained the Kankali, "with food and forage for a hundred thousand men and double that number of horses. He has gifts—a bow and an arrow. Look upon them; such bows are strong, such arrows shoot far."

Robert took the weapons in his hand and found the bow to be massive indeed, as heavy as a spear and as long as the English bows. The arrow was of cloth-yard length, its solid silver head pierced with holes.

"He says you cannot cope with such weapons. If the gates are opened to Genghis Khan he will slay no man; if the gates are shut no man will live."

Curiously Robert studied the Mongol, the first of that race he had seen. The warrior was strongly built, and horse and man remained as tranquil as if the rider had never known any other seat than the saddle. Chatagai stared for a long time at a dried and wrinkled head stuck upon a spear by the gate, seeming to take especial interest in this one grim remnant among the many skulls about the gate.

"Can you bend this bow?" Robert asked the archer.

"That can I," assented Will, who had been circling around the weapon like a dog that had sighted a side of venison.

He dismounted, examined the double stringing of twisted gut, and, exerting his strength in knee and arm, strung it swiftly.

"The bow is an honest longbow, but the arrow hath a lewd hammer head. Natheless if yonder churl can loose it, loose it I will—"

Planting his feet he gripped the feathered tip between fore and middle finger upon the string and drew it to his ear. The arrow flashed up into the night with a shrill, tuneful whistling that dwindled and passed beyond hearing. Chatagai grunted in approval.

"Now that is a pretty conceit!" observed the archer in surprise. "The holes i' the silver made a fair flute—sa ha! Master Robert, grant me the bow for mine own, an' it please thee."

The knight nodded, wishing that he could find a weapon to fit his own hand as easily, and turned to the Mongol.

"Tell him we can handle his weapons. Bid him say to his king that I hold Bokhara for Muhammad Shah, and the gates are closed to him."

Chatagai pointed at the head on the spear and spoke vehemently.

"*Yah khawand*," explained the Kankali, "this barbarian reminds you that the man whose head stands there was an envoy sent by Genghis Khan to Otrar. He dares to titter the warning that the person of an envoy was sacred before the time of Muhammad the Slave; he says God alone knows what will be the issue of this. *Ai-a*, shall we cut him down?"

"He goes free!" growled Robert.

The Mongol glanced briefly at the tall crusader and at Abdullah. Then, lifting his hand to his forehead and lips, he jerked the pony about in its tracks and swept through the gate with his men after him.

In an instant they had vanished into the dust and the night.

"That was ill done, my Frank," quoth the minstrel. "Until now you have walked forward through peril with a sure step, but now you have stumbled. Would you know the reason? Then dismiss your men beyond earshot, and we will talk—you and I alone—of the fate of an empire and the souls of a million men."

Chapter X

*In the temples sit the priests, seeing all things, for they are slaves of
the gods. Aye, the wisdom of the gods is one with Fate. Yet the lips
of the priests are locked.*

*In the palace are the rose-faced women. Their hair is fragrant as
a garden at dusk, and their fingers are like silver, for they are the
slaves of a king. They have covered their lips with perfume and their
hearts with secrecy.*

*One key only will unlock the hearts of the slaves, and that is
Fear.*

—Persian proverb

Robert ordered his followers to remain where they were and reined his
horse through the gate after Abdullah until they were a stone's throw beyond the wall but still within the glow of the torches. The minstrel bore
himself like a new man. Lute and pack were gone, and the good nature
had faded from his broad face; he sat restlessly in the high-peaked saddle,
peering into the maw of the dark plain as if watching the retreating Mongols and eager to be after them.

"My quest is ended, O companion of the road. I have found you and
brought you hither with honor enough for us both."

The crusader nodded and laughed.

"Verily you are something of a wizard, Abdullah. You led me hither
to serve—as you said—the master of all men. And I serve Muhammad in
a high place."

"My master—" Abdullah glanced on all sides—"is not Muhammad,
who is a slave, served by slaves. I follow the Manslayer."

"Genghis Khan?"

"Aye."

Robert's eyes narrowed. Here was a riddle, and he waited for the minstrel to explain it. And after perceiving that his friend would not speak,
Abdullah went on.

"Hear then, lord companion, one last tale from the teller of tales. Before your mother bore you, there lived a tribal chief in the Gobi Desert,
which is beyond the Roof of the World. This man came to be called Genghis
Khan later, but at that time he herded sheep and cattle and fought with
the other tribes. One day there came to him a youth who could sing the
hero songs of the tribes, whose tongue was quick to boast, yet who drew

back from no man's sword. This was Chepe Noyon, and they called him the Tiger.

"Again there came one who had the strength of a buffalo, who quaffed a cask of wine before setting it down, and Genghis Khan named him Sub-otai, or the Buffalo. When the other chiefs of the Mongols were in tatters and saw their herds thinned and their women carried off by their foes, they hung their heads and rode away to another place; then Genghis Khan said to these two, the Tiger and the Buffalo, that they should be his chief men, and they kept at his side to spy out the way in front of him and to guard his back against arrows. Sometimes when they were stiff with wounds they fled to the mountains; they tasted the dregs of treachery, which was worse than the *buran*—the black wind-storm that sweeps the high desert and freezes men in the saddle."

The minstrel folded his arms and thought for a moment. "When the dust rose from the plain or the mist descended from the sky these three did not lose the path they followed. In time came reward. The other tribes were trampled down. So they joined the Mongol standard, and Genghis Khan became leader of the Horde—the riders of the Gobi. They counted their herds by the hundred, and friends came to them from the white world of the north* and from the west and the south.

"When Cathay sent its bannermen against them they rode over the Great Wall, which was stronger than this."

The minstrel nodded at the wall of the city.

"So in time they humbled Cathay and rode their horses into the palaces of Yen-king, which is as great as three Bokharas. The wise men of Cathay served them, and they sat at table with Prester John of Asia. But Genghis Khan always kept the Tiger and the Buffalo near him and gave them honor. They were three brothers who would give up their horses, one to the other, in a battle.

"Then the Gur-khan, who was lord of the Roof of the World,† mustered his warriors, and Genghis Khan mounted his horse and went up against him. The Horde did not sit again upon the carpets of ease until they took the tents of the Gur-khan.

"I am Chepe Noyon, the *orkhon*, leader of the right wing of the Horde, and brother-in-arms to Genghis Khan."

---

*The Arctic Circle.
†The Himalayas.

The minstrel drawled his name, and his eyes twinkled.

"From the Uighurs, who are Turks and scholars, I learned Arabic and heard of Khar; and the desire came upon me to ride down and look upon this shah who was himself a slave.

"And I came because at the table of Prester John my master had heard of a race of Franks who had landed on the Moslem shores and made havoc with their swords. Hearing of their deeds, Genghis Khan laid a command on me. And the command was to fetch to him one of the Christian Franks who had a strong arm and a stout heart. This was because Genghis Khan wished to see for himself one of these warriors who had come over the seas, to overthrow all of the Moslems as he had struck the Cathayans. And I went, for a command is a command, even from a brother.

"Aye, the *orkhon* became a minstrel, and good sport was his. Muhammad, the shah, after seeing him ride and shoot an arrow and empty a flagon of wine without setting it down, took him into favor—not knowing his name or race. Abdullah became the cup-companion of an emperor's revels—and bethought him of his mission. So he asked the way to the strongholds of the Franks, and Muhammad gave him a chain of jewels."

The Mongol—Robert still thought of him as Abdullah—laughed heartily at the jest, probably aware of what kind of a chain Muhammad would have set upon him if his true name had been known.

"Why," asked Robert, frowning, "did you bring me with you? There were greater knights in Syria."

"Of the very few who could have made the journey and lived, none except you had the heart to set forth. Oh, I have watched you and tested you, and my choice was good."

Chepe Noyon nodded reflectively and continued:

"When we drew our reins to the Sialak I first heard of the war between Muhammad and Genghis Khan, and many lies were told me. But while you were a captive here I rode to Otrar and there learned the truth, and this is it:

"The Moslems, being traders and traffickers by nature, sent caravans to the Mongol empire to sell their wares. And so Genghis Khan sent an embassy to Muhammad to greet him. The governor of Otrar was a fool, and he mistook the envoys for common men."

Robert thought of his first impression of Chatagai, and judged that this might easily happen.

"First the governor of Otrar cut off their beards and then their heads," went on Chepe Noyon carelessly, "and kept their goods, to win Muhammad's favor. The head that hangs by this gate—" he pointed to the wall behind them—"was the brother of Chatagai. Genghis Khan will let no man of the Horde suffer injury unavenged. Aye, in our land a young woman might carry a sack of gold in her hand from Bishbalik to Kambalu, and she and the gold would be untouched. Nay, can there be two suns in the sky? War between the shah and the khan was certain, and now it has come to pass. Muhammad thought he was dealing with a nomad—a herdsman. So he was. But he thinks otherwise."

Throwing back his head, he laughed, white teeth flashing through his beard.

"By the white horse Kotwan, by the sky dancers, that was a ride we made, from your gate to this gate! These men of Khar be liars! Aye, the men of Khar have tasted fear, and the day is at hand when they will eat shame! Bokhara's wall will be level with the plain and herds will graze where the palaces stood."

Thinking of the prophecy of the dead sheikh, Robert held his peace.

"In Bokhara," resumed Chepe Noyon with relish, "I sang your praises, so that the shah would hear, and demand to see you; then Osman would not dare put you to the torture as he planned. *Hai*—it happens oftentimes that a pit is dug for a tiger and an ox is trapped. Behold what happened. The imams and the mullah besought Muhammad to make you emir of the city, to lead its defense. And now you may surrender to Genghis Khan, winning honor thereby. If Bokhara resists it will fare no better than Otrar."

Robert held up his hand.

"Is a promise made at sunrise to be broken at sundown?"

"Not the promise of a true man."

"Then I will defend Bokhara. My word is passed, and I will not unsay it."

For a full moment Chepe Noyon gazed up at the vault of the sky and sniffed into his nostrils the odor of the warm sand.

"Tell me this, O companion of the road. Can one man cast himself into the water and so stem the rush of a river in flood?"

The crusader was silent, having no answer, and Chepe Noyon did not seem ill pleased.

"The men of Khar are foxes, apt at stealing and flying to cover. I have lived among foxes on the steppe. You know not the depth of treachery in these Moslems as I do, who have sung my songs in *diwan* and *riwan*—in council and feast. Each one lusts for the treasure of Khar."

"Is the throne of gold in Bokhara?"

"Aye, well hidden. It lies below ground—so much a drunken priest babbled. The wazir knows the way to it, but priests stand guard over it, and Osman cannot hew them down because his foes would cry sacrilege and muster enough Moslems to cut him and his men to pieces."

He laughed again shortly.

"O fool—to think they gave you honor in good faith! I overheard the talk between Muhammad and his advisors in the *righistan* where his elephant took stand. He would have waited to bear off the treasure, but Osman's men declared that he must leave the gold as surety that Bokhara would be relieved by him. He fears Osman and his own mother."

The Mongol looked long at Robert.

"Your eyes would be opened in time, but then it would be too late," he added. "The shah left you behind as a figurehead, to deprive Osman of honor. The mullah took your part because he has a dread of the Kankalis—without someone to hold them in check. Osman is shrewd; you cannot deal with him. Bokhara is doomed. We are clear of the gate. Ride then with me. I go to Genghis Khan and the fellowship of true men."

"Go!" said Robert briefly. "I will keep to my place."

"By the eyes of ——!" cried the Mongol. "Bold words, but what deeds will follow? Summon your men—or they will question you about me. *Hai*—I will lead them a chase."

He gathered up his reins, and the horse, sensing the purpose of its rider, reared impatiently.

"Nay, there is peace between us, for you saved my life."

"The debt is even, since you shielded me in Palestine. Now the sword is between us."

He lifted his muscular hand to his forehead and lips.

"Ahatou koke Mongku-hai!"

Although Robert did not know it, Chepe Noyon had given him the salute of the royal Mongols.

He listened awhile to the drumming of hoofs on the baked clay of the road and then turned back to the gate reflectively. Abdullah, or Chepe Noyon, had been a wayward kind of friend, but Robert found that he missed the minstrel now that the Mongol was gone for good.

The next day the men on the walls of Bokhara watched columns of Mongols move up from the east and spread out over the plain. All day the dust hung in clouds over masses of riders and herds of horses. The sun gleamed on the horns of cattle and the spears of the guards that shepherded thousands of captives from Otrar.

Robert, studying the array, saw that the Mongol warriors were all mounted, and all looked the same. He could not pick out the leaders. All wore the dust-stained leather and skins, and crude, rusted armor was on a few; here and there above the masses of the Horde moved immense standards—the horns of a stag or buffalo, trimmed with streaming tails, on long poles.

When the dust settled, lines of gray tents, built over a wooden framework, stood in place; back of these the captives and the cattle were herded on the open plain, with the heavy carts of the Horde forming fences around them. Robert bade Will try to count the warriors, and the yeoman estimated a trifle over a hundred thousand, the knight somewhat less.

"By the foul fiend, his cloven hoof!" muttered the archer. "Here is woundy work, i' faith. Our foes be quartered already, and the day is not yet done. A besieger now in Christendom would set about the work in seemly wise. Aye, he would first fashion him out of beam from his baggage-train a fair array of battering engines—mangonels and trebuchets. Aye, stone-casters and rams-chats and foxes and eke towers of assault. Then in another week he would cut and fit together storming-ladders, and we would harry him with a-many cloth-yard shafts and cast back his ladders on his poll—"

"The Mongols lack siege engines to my thinking, Master Will."

"Then do they lack sense, Master Robert. Rede me this riddle: How may men ride horses up a wall? Or tear down the wall with their hands? 'Tis a thing impossible."

He rubbed his long chin and scowled.

"This paynim wizarder hath the right o' the matter. My lord, as he says, we should sally out and fall upon the foe, pikes and bills—sa ha!"

Osman had suggested a sortie of the garrison, arguing that the Bokharians outnumbered the Mongols. But Robert would not give assent to the plan. The Horde puzzled him, and he wished to see what they were about before trusting the Moslem soldiery against them on open ground.

Meanwhile the besiegers established mounted patrols that cut off all communication with the world outside, and this pleased the knight. The shah had given him authority within Bokhara, and now no message could reach the city gainsaying this authority, and he meant to hold the command until the Mongols were beaten off. Beyond that he had made no plans.

By noon of the second day he noticed work in progress within the Mongol lines. Ox-sleds dragged up loads of earth, which was dumped along a front of a hundred yards, facing a portion of the wall where no towers stood. The captives labored at this spot, thousands of them, and the earth mound grew in height as it neared the wall.

"A causeway," he explained to Will. "And a great one. They will push it nearer until it reaches the rampart of our wall."

Whereupon he set to work to place on platforms built behind the menaced point, machines for casting sheaves of arrows and stones.

Throughout the night the Mongols kept at their labor, and the creaking of the carts sounded nearer. The defenders kindled cressets on the rampart and contented themselves with shouted insults and laughter, while Robert slept in a tent under the wall and the archer dozed at the tent entrance. An hour before dawn the knight roused and went to the battlement.

The causeway had crept forward and mounted higher. Now it reared against the stars about a hundred feet back from the edge of the ditch. Robert sent a warrior for Jahan Khan, the leader of the Kankalis, and the *atabeg* came, rubbing the sleep from his eyes and cursing under his breath. He was a slender man, glittering from knee to throat in gilded mail. Pearls were sewn into his turban, and a heron's plume marked him apart from his men. The right sleeve of his *khalat* was turned back on a supple shoulder and held by a diamond chain—this marking him for a notable swordsman—yet his eyes were heavy with the after-sleep of opium as he made his salaam.

"Take twice a hundred of your bowmen to the rampart," ordered Robert without salutation, "and scatter the workers upon the mole."

"*Ma'shallah!*" The *atabeg* smiled. "Am I a captain of bowmen? Bid me sally forth from the gates, and I will bring you the head of the Mongol chief on a spear."

"You are a *bahator*, chief of thirty thousand. Can you check the advance of the causeway?"

Robert permitted the torchlight to flash on the signet ring he wore, and after a moment it was clear to the Kankali that the Nazarene meant to be obeyed. Robert dismissed him and ordered food to be brought to the

tent. He broke his fast with keen relish, after instructing Will to mount
to the wall and mark the progress made by the defenders.

The archer came back indignant. The Mongols had brought up to the head
of the mound wooden frames, upon which raw hides had been stretched.
These frames were triangular in shape at the front and while they covered
the besiegers, permitted earth and stones to be dumped down into the angle and the causeway moved forward as steadily as before. The Moslem
archers with their short weapons were doing no damage at all.

"Bid the khan," Robert ordered one of his followers, "set the engines
to work."

Response came back promptly that Jahan Khan declared the handling
of stone-casters was not in the order given him.

"Then say to the khan that he is to come to my tent for a new order."

The knight was finishing the last of his rice and fruit and washing his
hands when Jahan Khan approached and made as if to sit beside him.

"Stand," said Robert quietly, and while a hundred pairs of eyes watched
intently he commanded two bowmen who came with the chief to chain
Jahan Khan's arms and lead him away to his tent, there to guard him until relieved.

"What shame is this?" yelled the startled khan. "Am I dirt—I, Jahan
Khan, the *bahator*?"

He gripped his scimitar hilt convulsively, and a great sigh went up from
the crowd that had gathered about them.

It was the first real test Robert had made of the power given him, and
he sat on his carpet without stirring or looking up at the raging chief. If
he had started to explain his action, Jahan Khan might have pushed the
quarrel to blows; if the crusader put hand to weapon, the man would strike
first and claim afterward that he had done so in defense of his life. In the
shadows at his back he heard Will Bunsley slip an arrow from quiver.

After awhile he motioned toward one of the younger *begs*, the tallest
of the officers present. This sign among Moslems was as if Robert had
beckoned, and after a second's hesitation the warrior strode forward, the
crusader waiting until he saw fit to make a salaam.

"Ho, Moslems," snarled Jahan Khan, "this Nazarene takes upon his
shoulders the mantle of the shah, and that is a shame upon us all."

It was just too late to appeal to the religious zeal of the Kankalis, because
now they had grown curious as to what Robert wanted of the younger *beg*.

They pressed closer to stare, and after a little reflection Jahan Khan took his hand from his weapon, choosing to make the conflict one of words.

"Do you," Robert remarked to the attentive younger warrior, "take the leadership of the Kankalis, and fight as a man should. And you—" he turned to the doubtful bowmen—"confine this *atabeg* until he has slept off the opium in his tent. You have leave to go!"

With that he turned his back and no more words were spoken. Jahan Khan was too surprised to argue, and one or two laughed as he went off. Robert had made good his authority against the most troublesome adherent of the wazir, and he knew that the account of the quarrel would be in every quarter of the city by dawn. It was well worth the risk he had taken.

To help the new leader, he sent Will Bunsley to the wall to show the Moslem archers how to loose their arrows in a high arc, to fall behind the protecting shield. The tumult above grew louder, and the grind and thud of catapult and mangonel sounded above the whistling of the arrows as the sun rose. Although the Mongols suffered from the fire, they pressed the work. The remnants of the captives were sent to the rear, and lines of armed men bore sacks of earth and stones up the causeway. The shields were wrecked, and, for a time the bodies of men fell over the head of the causeway as thickly as the sacks.

Then arrows began to fly from the Mongol lines and sweep the battlement.

"Ha, lord," muttered Will, "mark how yonder shafts cleave the paynim shields! They be stoutly sped, with a true eye. Would I had fourscore Lincolnshire lads here upon the rampart!"

He sighed and presently uttered an exclamation of astonishment.

Under cover of the arrow-flights the Mongols began a new building-up of the causeway, which had ceased to move forward. The ox-carts were driven out of the camp by hundreds and steered up the incline.

Men with torches herded the bellowing animals up the causeway, and once the mass started forward, the oxen kept on, goaded by spears and the smoking torches. The first carts reached the brink of the embankment and rolled over and the rest came after in a steady stream of frantic beasts and splintering wagons. The arrows of the Moslems fell fruitlessly among them, and Robert saw that the carts were loaded with sand and stone. Men, caught in the rush of surging animals, stood up and shouted defiance at the wall. One powerful warrior in a tigerskin hurled his torch at the Kankalis and leaped out from the cart, to fall into the ditch and be crushed by the carts that came after him.

When the causeway stood upon the edge of the ditch, as high as the wall and some twenty feet from it, the Mongols withdrew and quiet settled down. Robert left the Kankalis in charge opposite the causeway and rode to seek out Kutchluk Khan, who was camped across the city with his Turkomans.

The one-eyed chief came forward on foot, and the crusader did not dismount, for he was entitled to speak to the old warrior from the saddle.

"Take half your men—ten thousand of the best armed—and clear away the stalls and sheds of the *suk*. Quarter yourselves in the marketplace which is in the center of the city. When a wide space is cleared, assemble your men and report to me. Can you reach any point in the wall, riding four abreast from the *suk*?"

"Allah pity any who stand in my way," boasted the Turkoman, grinning. "Are we to sally forth by the river? The Mongols have no more than a few riders on watch on the banks of the Syr."

"Who spoke first to you of a sally, O *atabeg*?"

Kutchluk Khan thought for a moment.

"'Twas Osman, or one of the cup companions."

"You have seen many battles."

"By the ninety and nine holy names, I have seen rivers run with blood and the dust of the fighting hide the sun, O emir."

"Have you ever given your men an order to ride whither your foes wished them to go?"

"Nay! Am I a smooth-faced boy, to listen to false talk?"

"Then why incline your heart to a sally? The Mongols fight best in the saddle, and on the open plain they would be at home."

The Turkoman grunted and fingered his beard, not too well pleased at the rebuke.

"Likewise," went on Robert bluntly, "tell me if Osman holds me in honor or not?"

"By the sword-hand of —— he doth not. *Yah khawand*," Kutchluk laughed, baring yellow teeth, "he would be content to pour molten lead in your ears and make of your skull a drinking-cup. He has sworn he will."

"Sworn to whom?"

"To me and others, having gone among us with whispered talk. Slay him while the hour is propitious; it is all one to me, and my men would stand aside. I know not why the shah chose you to be over me, but Osman is an adder that strikes from a hole in the wall."

Kutchluk became good-humored again as he watched the crusader ride away. To his men he observed that the dog of a Nazarene was good steel shining from a dunghill.

"He knows well the worth of a mounted reserve of warriors such as we be. He hath given command for us to clear the bazaars—aye, and a way through every quarter of the city, so that we can mount and ride to his aid when he summons us. Allah send the wazir slay him not, for a feud comes to a head between them."

"*Inshallah*—then the door of looting is opened!"

The Turkomans, who had become quarrelsome from long idleness, waxed supremely content and prepared to go and plunder the stalls of the merchants. And by the time they were in saddle the words of the new emir had been repeated so often that to a man they were ready to swear they had been ordered to loot.

Chapter XI
Two Men and a Plan

The sun was a brazen ball hanging in a shroud of dust; and even the dogs of Bokhara had got up, panting, and left the alleys when Robert sought the dwelling where Ellen d'Ibelin and the blind priest were quartered. He found the narrow street filled with men who squatted where there was shade, and sweating horses. Pushing through, heedless of the scowls and imprecations that followed, he led his horse into the door of the garden that, behind a high clay wall, separated the house from the street.

It was a rose garden, bordered with jasmine and thyme. A fountain splashed where the shade was coolest, and about the fountain sat Osman and Hassan and several other followers of the wazir. Robert glanced toward the entrance of the house and saw Will Bunsley seated on the threshold with half a dozen weapons—the archer had a way of acquiring whatever dagger or sword struck his fancy without bothering to pay the owner—spread out on the stones beside him. Father Evagrius and the girl were not to be seen.

Osman had entered and brought in his men unknown to the knight, and Robert waited for an explanation of his presence. The wazir rose leisurely and called the crusader by a dozen complimentary names—Lord of the Planets, Perfection of Chivalry, a second Iskander.

"I bear thee tidings, O emir—good tidings. Because the heat in the alley without was a curse upon us, we made bold to enter thy garden."

His eye quested over the barred embrasures of the dwelling for a glimpse of the girl.

"And Hassan of the ready tongue hath made a song for thy mistress."

Robert gave his charger to Will to lead back to the stable and walked over to the Kharesmian.

"This house belongs to the damsel," he said slowly, "and I have not come here save to ask of her welfare. Send your buffoons from the garden and say your say in few words."

Osman hid his anger behind a smile, and Hassan laughed. When the cup-companions had departed the wazir motioned Robert to the carpet and sat beside him.

"You are not wise to tarnish the mirror of friendship with me, O Nazarene. Our paths in Bokhara lie together, and we seek the same end of the road—"

"Your tidings?"

"Are that the Mongols have food and fodder for their horses sufficient for only three days. At the end of the three days they must enter Bokhara or strike their tents and go elsewhere."

"How had you this?"

"From my spies, who traffic with the barbarians under guise of shepherds and wood-carriers."

"No men have come into the city in two days."

"True. My followers send messages over the wall. They took from Bokhara pigeons that fly back when they are loosed, and the messages are written and bound to the claws of the pigeons."

He looked amused at the ignorance of the knight who had never heard of carrier pigeons or water clocks or naphtha.

"Lo," went on Osman agreeably, "the seal of fate is on the foreheads of the accursed Mongols. They cannot complete their causeway, and their horses cannot leap the wall elsewhere. Your skill will save Bokhara, for the three days will soon be at an end. And then—" he hesitated—"what reward will be yours?"

Robert merely glanced at him inquiringly, carelessly at first, then attentively. Osman's hand shook and the pupils of his eyes were dark; a muscle twitched in his sallow cheek. In Cairo the crusader had seen Moslems who had taken an overdose of bhang or hashish, and they had looked like this.

"I will take," he observed suddenly, "two thousand pieces of gold."

"Two thousand! Thy palm would scarce be covered. Ask for more and it shall be thine! But not from the hand of Muhammad."

"How then?"

"I can show thee the treasure of Khar."

"Ha!"

Osman chuckled with secretive satisfaction.

"Aye, the throne of gold that an elephant scarce may bear on its back! *Miskals* of gold piled in caskets and the caskets as many as the stones of this garden. Jade scattered upon the floor, and an ivory table—"

"Nay, it is hidden."

"Beneath a mosque. A hundred men might search every mosque in Bokhara for a twelvemonth and find naught. They could dig until they wearied their loins. Only one way leads to it."

Osman's thin arms clutched his stomach in uncontrollable excitement.

"*Ai-a*, there are blue sapphires and chains of rose pearls! Diamonds that could put to shame the light of the sun lie there in darkness—for how long?"

"Have you seen it?" Robert's lean face was attentive.

"May Allah grant me joy for the pain! Aye, I have seen each thing that was sent down, under the eyes of the priests. And Muhammad the Slave fears to bring his riches to the light. Were I the shah I would keep it within my hand."

His thick lips drew back in a sneer. Taking Robert's silence for a reflection of his own greed, the wazir explained how tribute had been levied on the caliphs of Baghdad to get some of the finest of the jewels, and how Herat and Balkh had been searched to add to the treasure of Khar.

"And now you have a plan," nodded Robert.

Remembering the heat of the day and the quivering nerves of the man beside him, he wondered how much the drug had affected Osman. Certainly the man was telling the truth.

Osman's plan was a bold one. The wazir dared not draw upon himself the rage of the Moslems by violating a mosque. He offered to tell Robert how to reach the entrance to the treasure vault. With some of the lawless

Turkomans the crusader could beat off the priests and hold the mosque above the vault long enough to make away with the jewels and the bulk of the gold. Meanwhile Osman would assemble the Kankalis and would protect the Nazarene and his men from pursuit. Robert could take a part of the gold, leaving the rest with the wazir in his palace.

They would not make the attempt until the Mongols had been driven from the city. Robert could escape to the gates with his portion of the gold; his escort of hillmen would be sufficient to force a way through the pass. The Turkomans would like nothing better than such a venture; Khar was torn by strife, and Osman, with the treasure in hand and the city held by his men, would be able to raise his standard against Muhammad. The victory over the Mongols would heighten his influence

"And if the Turkomans turn against me?"

"That is thy affair and risk. Thou art winning honor among them, O emir, and they love a bold leader."

Robert remembered that Osman had said nothing of the maid of Ibelin. Probably the wazir would prove treacherous. Yet with some of the treasure in his grasp and a horse under him and the road from the city clear—with a few of the wild tribesmen to follow him!

"If thou canst win a victory over the foe, Muhammad will soon put thee in thy shroud," whispered the Kharesmian. "That is ever his way."

This was probable. Osman's plan offered a desperate chance, but it stirred Robert's pulse. Nothing could have been said more to his liking. To ride through paynimry into Palestine with an emperor's ransom—to hew out a way of escape at the sword's point for Master Will and the priest and the maid Ellen!

He looked at Osman. The man was dreaming, his cheeks flushed, his eyes dull.

Surely the wazir would lose nothing by making the attempt, and—by a stroke of fortune Robert might find himself at the head of an army, lord of Bokhara in truth. Weighed in the balance, Osman would be found wanting if the ownership of the treasure stirred up fighting.

"Seek me out when the Mongols have been scattered," Osman whispered. "Our paths lie together—and the end of the road is in sight."

Robert nodded and rose as a warrior entered the garden.

"*Yah khawand,*" the newcomer salaamed, "there is brawling between the men of Kutchluk Khan and the merchants of the *suk*. The Turkomans are riding down the stalls and snatching plunder."

Osman rolled over on an elbow, secretly pleased at the trouble in store for the crusader, when he should attempt to interfere in the dispute.

"Are the riders clearing the marketplace?" Robert asked the messenger.

"Allah—as kites clear bones."

"Good!" Robert nodded to the surprised wazir. "Go you and adjust the troubles of the merchants. They are in your charge."

Left alone, he stood by the fountain, his lips set in a harsh line. In his journey from Egypt to Bokhara he had met nothing but treachery and plotting. Even Abdullah had proved to be otherwise than he seemed—and Robert found that he missed Abdullah. Were there no men who kept faith? And why should a man keep faith?

Chapter XII
Concerning a Maid and a Surcoat

"Nay, Messire Long-Face, you may not shun our company this time as heretofore. For I have made ready a pudding of dates against your coming, and Master Will hath fetched some rare wine and, what is more, hath saved some of it."

So saying, Ellen took Robert's sword belt and shield and pushed a chair forward to the table where supper was spread.

"Aye," growled the archer. "Wash, wipe, sit, eat, drink, wipe, and depart. ——'s blood, tall brother, dost never loosen thy belt and stretch thy legs under table like a Christian?"

He noticed that the girl's fingers trembled when she placed food and wine before the knight and saw the ominous breaks made in the steel rings where arrows had struck his haburgeon. Ellen had sent away the slaves who had been placed in the house, for she wished none but herself to tend Father Evagrius. And the priest lay on a mattress in another room. The heat of the day had wearied him, and he had declined to join them.

Robert watched her trip back and forth to clear the table and minister to the priest, and the lines of weariness fell away from his eyes. In truth had he longed for this sight of the maid of Ibelin, and several times had turned aside from his riding in Bokhara to pass through the street and listen for sound of her voice lifted in song.

And now he racked his brain for words, wishful that he had been raised in the court where apt speeches were to be learned. He looked expectantly at Will Bunsley, but the glib tongue of the yeoman was still, for a marvel. Meanwhile Ellen settled down on a cushion under a great candle and began to embroider a pattern on a fair sheet of linen stretched upon a small frame.

Her dark head was bent over her task.

In this way had she whiled away the long hours of loneliness. Not once did she raise her eyes to the knight.

"Demoiselle."

Robert blushed and lowered his voice, for he had spoken as if addressing a squadron of men-at-arms.

"Prithee—my thanks for—the supper."

The long locks hid Ellen's face as she made answer quickly.

"Messire, my thanks for—saving my life."

"How? In sooth—"

"Indeed Master Will hath told me how you won us from the hands of the wazir."

"Nay—"

"And Father Evagrius did relate how you took his part in the tower dungeon."

"And sent the wizarder a-packing from the courtyard before vespers," observed the archer with a nod.

"And so," went on the girl, "my lord, you have repaid me in most courteous wise for—the despite I put upon you. Once, my lord, I struck you. They tell me you are ever minded to pay a debt and to hold good your word. So do we render you—thanks!"

Suddenly Robert smiled, and when he smiled the tight, down curving lips grew merry.

"I cry quittance, demoiselle. 'Twas a fair good buffet you dealt me at our meeting, and a just one. Nay, child, hast forgotten our second meeting, beyond the Gates, by the desert sea? Your hand was gentle then—to a churl."

Ellen bent over her embroidery, and her fingers tangled in the thread. For when Robert had lain ill with fever she had often taken his head upon her knee and stroked his forehead until he slept. She wondered how much he remembered, and, observing with a swift, sidelong glance that he still smiled, she waxed haughty.

"My lord, I am no child. Next Martinmas I will be seventeen."

"My lady," Robert laughed, "I am no lord. Nay, you have spoiled the pattern. What is it?"

She untangled the thread and went to work anew, and he saw that she was embroidering a crimson cross upon a white background.

"Father Evagrius did ask it of me."

"A surcoat? Then the patriarch grows stronger?"

"He doth not mend."

She glanced anxiously toward the door of the other room.

"It was his wish that I make it for you."

Robert thought there was slight chance of his donning the garments of a knight again—or of leaving Bokhara alive. And what chance had the girl?

"See—'tis nearly finished."

She tilted the frame and surveyed it critically.

"The one you wore was sadly stained."

"'Tis a fair gift," he said, surprised that the girl should remember details of this meeting six months ago.

And he listened while she talked lightly of the strange slaves of Bokhara, the pretty garden and the music that she heard upon the river near at hand. Will, she said, had seldom been absent from the house; servants of the priests had brought her all she could wish of fruits and sweetmeats.

"And Will must not leave this place to seek the wall again," responded Robert gravely. "I give you in his charge."

"Nay, tall brother," put in the archer, "'twas she that sent me hence, saying—'Hie thee to my lord, and stand at his back; for he hath many foes, and if harm came to him—'"

"Why, our case would e'en be a hard one," interrupted Ellen swiftly.

Will shook his head doggedly. "By all the saints, thy words were otherwise. I mind—"

"Be still!" The girl's eyes flashed, and the work on the embroidery ceased altogether. "I sent you for tidings of the siege. Will the wall withstand assault, Sir Robert?"

"We will hold it. And the foe must withdraw in three days."

Will Bunsley scratched his head. "Now verily, and by thy leave, lord brother, thou didst hold forth contrariwise upon the rampart. Thou didst swear in good broad words that the Sooltan's men were overconfident, and the Mungals—or howsomever they be called—were brewing trickery for our quaffing—"

Robert reached out his foot under the table and, finding the yeoman's understanding too dense to heed a kick, frowned warningly. "You have quaffed too many cups of Bokharian brewing to remember aught aright, Master Will."

"Nay, by St. Dunstan—"

"Curb thy tongue, rogue, and cool thy head in the garden for awhile."

The archer went out, muttering under his breath, and Ellen laughed merrily.

"You would make light of our peril, Sir Robert. But you cannot silence your eyes, and they were troubled."

She looked at him frankly. "Will hath described the barbarians, and it would seem they fight best upon their horses. If I were leader of the besiegers I would take your wall upon the flank. I have seen a point where horsemen could enter a score abreast without dismounting or unbarring a gate."

Robert did not smile.

"If so—but where?"

"Where you and I entered Bokhara—" she paused to stitch the last thread in the cross—"the foe could swim their horses upon the river through the water gate."

"A chain hath been stretched across and a barrier made against boats, yet the thought is a good one. How came you to hit upon it?"

"When I was a child, messire, my father held command in the stronghold of Carcassonne for the queen, and I remember a siege and seeing the foemen swim their chargers across the moat."

She glanced at his hand where the great sapphire of the shah's ring gleamed. "Is that the talisman bestowed by the paynim king?"

"Lightly given." Robert turned it on his finger, and lifted his head with sudden purpose. "We have shared peril, you and I, and you have a heart for true words. Our chance of winning free from Bokhara with our lives is slight."

The brown eyes searched his without a trace of fear. "Ah, let the archer attend you, messire. If—if harm befall you he should seek me out, for I would then have need of one arrow from his bow."

"You would have need of it." Robert forced himself to speak coldly. Beholding her pride and her trust in him, he clenched his hands and strode the length of the chamber, to pause beside her.

"Nay, I am a wildling and worthless—as the peers of Palestine did maintain," he went on. "Hither came I to loot gold and gear and raise myself to a high place, and this day I plotted how to profit by the treachery of the wazir to his master. When I cast aside my spurs I put aside my vows and I have mocked the prayers of good Evagrius—thinking to drown memory of the past in a sea of blood. And this thing is true."

She began to loosen the long surcoat from the embroidery frame so that he could not see her face, and she made answer softly. "Among the peers of Palestine—aye and France—who hath done the deeds of the Longsword? Is life, forsooth, such a little thing that we must spend our years in kitchen and hall, making love to some and quarreling with others?"

Robert frowned down at her, wondering, for this was a maid of many surprises.

"In my father's castle, messire, were many who painted their shields brightly and made a song of each slight dent won in the pleasant jousts. Faith, they tested their skill at romaunts and gestes in the banquet-hall, and they were bold in the hunt—and the war of words."

She smiled wistfully. "My father was otherwise, and many a time did he tell me of the brave days of Richard of England. When he died I took the Cross, being heavy with grief, and now am I in a paynim hold, long leagues from Jerusalem."

She stood up, tossing back her dark hair. "I would not have it otherwise. For now, messire, perchance, I share the last hours of a brave knight and true."

"O maid," Robert replied gruffly, being stirred by her bold words, "this is no fit place for a child of d'Ibelin to end her days."

"Then forsooth and verily," she cried, her mood changing lightly, "let us adventure forth and win us honor. Nay, the troubadours shall yet make a tale of us, and we will yet see Jerusalem. Master Will hath planned a plan for me whereby I may go forth when the time comes. 'Tis but a make-shift of a plan, and yet—"

Ellen turned and disappeared into her sleeping-chamber and emerged with her arms full of garments.

"—and yet 'twill make a man of a maid."

Her dark tresses were hidden by a light helmet of silvered steel, and a cotton drop that fell to her boyish shoulders. "Well for me," she said gravely, "the Moslems of this quarter are slender men, for Will hath looted shamefully."

She held out a finely wrought haburgeon of delicate chain mail with a silk girdle, and wide damask pantaloons with embroidered slippers, and—smiling merrily—a long *khalat* of the richest purple.

"Ha, Master Robert," quoth the bowman, who had come in when he heard his name called, "she hath the bearing of a likely esquire-at-arms and a temper to boot. I have found for her a small shield and a bow suitable for her hand—"

"*Yah khawand,*" interrupted Ellen blithely, "wilt take me for a companion upon your road—your road of peril?"

"Aye, verily," smiled the knight. "Yet no *khawand* am I, for that is 'lord and master.'"

"Lord and master," she whispered; and there was no mockery in her eager eyes.

"Hearken," said Robert suddenly.

A sound as of a multitude of bees came through the open embrasures. The two men glanced at each other. To their trained ears the distant hum resolved itself into the mutter of kettle-drums and the clashing of cymbals mingled with the uproar of human voices. Robert picked up his sword belt and helm.

"That would be a bruit upon the wall."

Swiftly he girdled on the long scimitar he had chosen for lack of a better weapon of the size and weight to which he was accustomed. Ellen dropped her belongings and caught up the white surcoat.

"Wear this, my lord, for the sake of—of Evagrius, who hath blessed it."

Skillfully she slipped off the *khalat* that covered his mail and thrust the mantle over his shoulders, fastening his belt upon the outside. As he strode toward the garden he gripped her hand, and she skipped beside him to the outer gate.

"Fare you well—the good angels fight at your side!"

"Brave heart!" cried the knight. "Keep hidden until I return."

The alley door flew open, and a bearded Kankali peered within and saluted Robert as Will ran up with the saddled charger.

"Will the lord grant his servant permission—"

"Speak!"

"The barbarians have bridged the gap between the wall and the causeway. Aye, they have launched a storm, and Allah hath caused a battle to be."

Heedless of Robert's last advice, Ellen watched him ride away from the gate and waved farewell as he reached the turn in the alley.

"A fine mark hath thy mantle made of him," grumbled the archer, who was disappointed at being left behind. "Ah, for the shafts of the foe—Why, lass—why, as St. Dunstan hears me, thou art weeping!"

Chapter XIII
The Storm

As they trotted out of the alley Robert signed to the messenger to come up with him, and sent the man to command Kutchluk Khan to saddle his ponies and hold his men ready to ride. He pressed forward alone, seeking the shortest way to the wall. Here the alleys, odorous with fish and wool and stagnant water, twisted and turned, and his horse was forced to pick a way among heaps of refuse. White walls loomed out of the darkness and voices flung hearty curses after him in many languages.

He turned aside into a quarter where the wooden barrier was let down, and lights gleamed from lattices and the scent of incense and aloes was in the air. In gateways under great lanterns the tinted faces of women peered at him, and from a roof nearly over his head came the high-pitched song of a Circassian girl with the monotonous accompaniment of a lute. In the labyrinth of the alleys the dwellers of Bokhara had come forth after the heat of the day and Robert wondered whether in truth there could be fighting on the wall.

A woman's form, veiled and sinuous, moved toward him in the swaying walk of the Bokharian slave. Her henna-tinted hands drew back the veil, and he looked down into a face thin yet beautiful, and saw in the half-light of the stars eyes, darkened with kohl, wise with the unhallowed wisdom of Egypt.

Anklets tinkled as other girls fled with ripples of laughter from his horse. In his path a handsome boy caressed a lute, singing with a full throat, his head thrown back to the stars.

"Time passes and no man may stay it. This hour alone is thine. Turn not from the rose and its fairness, for thorns lie thick on the pathway!"

Robert reined in his horse and gripped the singer's shoulder.

"Where lies the wall?"

"I am Hassan," the boy responded with the gravity of the intoxicated. "Lo, the wall is not here, for this is the street of delightful hours."

He laughed at the set face of the crusader, and Robert loosed him, setting spurs to the charger. The spring of the horse sent the boy rolling in the dust that eddied up from the plunging hoofs.

Hassan sat up, muttering, and a veiled woman ran to his side from the deep shadow of a wall.

"The moon hath come down from the sky," cried the boy. "Ah—"

A thin length of steel darted into his side and was withdrawn. The woman's hand felt for his purse, which had jingled when he fell, and slipped it from his girdle. Then she merged again into the shadow.

Rising to his knees, Hassan felt about in the dust as if for something he had lost. Suddenly he screamed, and the song of the Circassian on the roof above ceased for a moment.

Robert rode over the bridge that spanned the river, and glanced to either side. Although the tumult on the wall was nearer, pleasure barges drifted along the banks, and Bokharian nobles made wagers as to the length of the fighting. Passing through the gardens at a gallop, he began to hear the ululation of the Kankalis and the clashing of weapons. Dismounting among the tents behind the wall, he climbed a stairway to a tower and found the *beg* he had left in charge.

"*Yah khawand*," the man greeted him, "you are in good time. Watch."

The causeway was crowded with packed masses of Mongols, and more were moving up on foot from the lines of the camp where the drums and *nakars* kept up their clamor. At the head of the earth mound, beams had been thrust across the gap by the besiegers and hastily covered with spears, planks, and hides. Over this bridge warriors were rushing the rampart, climbing upon the bodies of the slain.

They were half-naked, and those who had shields hurled them at the Moslems. Then they ran forward, stooping and smiting with axes and heavy, curved swords. Most of them fell under the arrows of the Kankalis, who shot from the wall and the nearest towers. The survivors were hurled back by spears and maces in the hands of the mailed defenders.

"Twice have we hewn down their bridge!" exclaimed the captain. "See where our stone-casters thin the numbers in the rear! Allah send victory!"

"But, do you, send for reinforcements from the palace," retorted Robert, watching two human tides beat against each other and a sprinkling of dark bodies, outflung from the press, drop into the beds of jasmine and roses underneath.

After awhile he picked up his shield and ran down the stairs toward the wall. Greater weight of metal and steadiness of foot was needed here.

Thrusting through the struggling Moslems, he whipped out his sword, hewing his way well in among the Mongols without waiting to see if any of his own men followed. A mace crashed against his helmet, blurring

his sight; a spear clanged on his shield. All around him there was a tearing, sobbing sound of tired men striving to rend each other, a snapping of
wood and the moaning of the wounded underfoot, Moslems for the most
part. The short, grim men who surged at him fought in silence.

Robert thrust the hilt of his sword into a snarling face, swept clear the
space before him with his blade, and felt himself caught about the legs.
Stumbling, he dropped his sword, and his mailed mitten grasped a short
battle-ax on the stone surface of the wall. With this he smashed free of
those who grappled him and gained his feet—a thing that few did who
went down.

Now as he stood his ground he felt that shafts flew past him. A giant
who rushed at him with open hands was transfixed by a long arrow and
fell upon his feet. Another was pierced through the throat, so that the
blow he aimed at Robert fell feebly against the steel casque. He could see,
through the eyeslits of his visor, the black mantles of the Kankalis on either hand, and the flash of their scimitars. So in time he rested against
the broken rampart and the bodies that lay upon it, panting, while the
Mongol tide receded down the mole.

Still, however, was heard the summons of the drum and cymbal from
the Mongol camp.

"*Yah khawand!*" the voice of the *beg* spoke at his side. "Evil tidings have
come. The Mongols have struck in another place along the river. They stole
up and smashed the chain with sledges and swam their horses between
the towers of the river gate. They are slaying the men in the barges—"

"Send to Kutchluk Khan. Bid him ride with all his men to the river.
Half his division should cross the bridge to this side. Then order five
thousand Persian archers to the house-tops along the river to support the
Turkomans! Haste!"

While he waited anxiously for news of the fight at the river he saw
torches assembling in the Mongol camp. Fresh warriors walked to the
lower end of the causeway and began to mount silently.

Under the flaming cressets of the wall he could make out that these
were powerful men with the horns of beasts upon their fur caps. Those
in front carried beams; behind these came ranks of swordsmen in rude
iron armor, followed by masses of archers.

Robert realized that the Mongols had launched their main attack at the
river under cover of the assault on the causeway. The fresh effort might
mean that they had been checked by Kutchluk, or that they had been vic-

torious behind him and meant to press home the attack. As yet he heard
no fighting on the river nearby, and he breathed a prayer that the one-eyed
Turkoman had driven home his charge.

Again the Mongols thrust forward their beams and swarmed to the
assault. An arrow struck the Kankali *beg* in the throat, and his body fell
under the feet of his men.

"Are ye dogs?" Robert cried at the Moslems. "Come with me!"

He climbed the rampart, followed by all on the wall. The Mongols
stood their ground, shouting and wreaking havoc with their heavy weapons. With his long ax Robert cleared a space around him and planted his
feet, dizzy with the blows that smashed in the steel of his helmet. Warm
blood trickled down his ribs, and hot air seared his lungs.

Until his arms were wearied he stood his ground, until the ax broke
in his hands, when he fell to rallying the Moslems, who gave back on either side. The weariness crept into his brain, and he fancied he was standing at the head of a great stair up which writhed grimacing dwarfs with
hands outstretched to drag him down into darkness.

A moment's pause enabled him to wipe the sweat from his eyes, and he
saw Chepe Noyon clearly. The Mongol chief was halfway down the causeway beside a thickset warrior. This man leaned on a spear, staring up at
the fight without expression. His massive arms were bound at the biceps
with gold rings, and he wore the long horns of a buffalo on his helmet.

When his glance fell on the knight the powerful Mongol tossed down
his spear and strode up the causeway, thrusting friends and foes from his
path as a man might push aside cornstalks.

"Subotai—Subotai!" the nearest Mongols howled exultantly.

Robert fought for breath and looked about vainly for a weapon suited
to his strength. Measuring the man with the buffalo horns and his own
weariness, he felt that he would not be upon his feet for long.

"Yield thyself," Chepe Noyon's voice reached him through the uproar,
"to the paladin, Subotai, and no shame is thine!"

"I yield to no man!" Robert cried and stepped forward.

A fresh onrush of Moslems from the wall swept between them as reinforcements came up at last from the Persian camp at the palace. Subotai
crushed in the head of a warrior with his sword and leaped to one side,
knocking two others from their feet. Then other Mongols sprang to the
aid of their leader, who was drawn back, snarling angrily, as the besiegers
were thrust back by weight of numbers, and the incline cleared.

Robert watched until the fight on the causeway was over. For the first time he noticed that a broad streak of light ran along the horizon. The struggle had lasted through the night.

"O captain of thousands and companion of heroes," a glittering Persian addressed him respectfully, "the barbarians have been scattered at the river gate. They have left the waters thick with their dead, and Kutchluk Khan hath passed to the mercy of God with more than the half of his men."

When the sun rose the sound of the drums ceased. The crusader sought his horse and climbed stiffly into the saddle, while throngs of Bokharians clustered about him and cried praises on the infidel emir. Men fought for the privilege of taking the reins of his horse and leading him into the thick of the shouting mob, while women tossed roses from the housetops.

"The barbarians are withdrawing their tents from the river!" A warrior stood up in his stirrups to call out. "*Hai*—they are scattered! The favor of Allah is with the faithful! The triumph is with Bokhara!"

Robert was aware that the rejoicing was ill-timed. Yet was he too weary with his hurts to think of the future. He had held the wall and had made good his word to Muhammad. So might Alexander in other days have ridden through the streets of the ancient city and received the salutes of his warriors.

The tumult died down when he reached the square where some Persian mounted archers were drawn up by the mosque. At their head was Jahan Khan, relieved of his chains, sitting his horse beside the litter of Osman. On the steps of the mosque stood the mullah, Nur-Anim, with a paper in his hand and an array of priests behind him. The Moslem who had been leading his horse withdrew, and the crusader halted before the steps of the Jumma.

"Greeting, O prince of warriors and paladin of swordsmen," Nur-Anim said in his high voice. "Upon thee—the Salute! And now hear the word of Muhammad, Shah of shahs. This *firman*, this decree, he left with me to be read when victory had fallen to our arms."

Robert glanced at Jahan Khan, who had been released without his order, and saw that the Kankali was staring at him curiously. A thousand eyes were on him as he sat his charger without helm or sword, with armor and surcoat hacked and stained.

> It is the will of Muhammad Shah that Osman the wazir shall watch
> closely the deeds of the infidel leader of the garrison. If the Frank pre-

sumes to set foot in a mosque or to contrive aught against the trea-
sure of Khar or raise his hand against a true believer he is to be put in
chains and held captive until my return. If he resists this command
he must be slain with a sword. The Peace upon my servants.

Robert's lips drew into a hard line, and he lifted his head angrily. Yet, thinking of the three who looked for his coming in the house of the fountain, he waited until he could speak calmly.

"Have I kept my word to Muhammad?"

"Aye," assented Nur-Anim, rolling up the decree. "It was written that victory should be, and you have served fate."

"Then will the shah make good his word to me?"

The mullah glanced at Osman, who raised himself on his elbow to speak; but the knight was before him.

"O Moslems, it is also written that he who breaks an oath is without honor. I have been guilty of none of these things. Who is to be my judge?"

"The wazir and I."

Robert rallied his wits and tried to shake off his weariness. His head pained him, and loss of blood made it hard to sit erect in the saddle. His eyes went from one face to another and read in them only exultant mockery—save for two or three of the officers who had served him on the wall.

"And who speaks against me?"

"I!" cried Osman loudly. "Give heed, O Moslems, to the ill deeds of this Frank. He schemed in his garden to steal the treasure of Khar from the mosque. I made a test of him, and witnesses without the wall heard."

A murmur of astonishment and anger came from the lips of those who listened.

"He cast dirt upon the beard of Jahan Khan," went on the wazir. "And the boy Hassan he slew in the night for no cause. Women saw it done and will testify."

Seeing clearly that Osman had determined to get rid of him, Robert held up his hand silently, and after awhile—such was the prestige of the man who had defended the city against the Mongols—the murmurs quieted down.

"These be words, and lying words!" he cried. "Do ye believe, ye who have beheld my deeds?"

Some of the warriors looked about restlessly, and all eyes sought Nur-Anim. The mullah could have cast his influence for either man, and he chose to favor the wazir.

"Ye have heard the word of the shah!"

He lifted the rolled parchment.

"I obey the word."

Robert tightened his rein and urged his horse slowly along the line of the Bokharians, glancing into each face. And now he beheld only sullen fanaticism and hatred. He had been tricked and cast aside when they believed his work was done. The anger that he held in check swept over him.

"O fools! I could have let the Mongols into the city. Who will lead you when I am gone?"

He ripped the signet ring from his finger and hurled it at Nur-Anim.

"Greet Muhammad with this, and do you, find honor in it if you can."

"Take the dog of a Nazarene!"

Robert wheeled his horse and headed for the Persians who closed in on him. One man he threw from the saddle, and his charger shouldered another out of the way. Vainly he sought to win through the press to reach the three who awaited him in the house of the fountain. A warrior struck him on the head with a mace, and he fell, under his rearing horse. A red mist gathered before his eyes, and powerful hands forced him to his feet. His wrists were bound behind him, and a cord was slipped over his head. The cord tightened, and he stumbled forward.

When his sight cleared he saw that he was being led out of the *righistan* beside Osman's litter, and the wazir was leaning on his elbow the better to feast his eyes on his prisoner.

"Is thy memory so short, O Nazarene? Not three days ago you put yourself before me. You took from me the treasure, the diamond sheen, the houri out of paradise. Didst thou believe I had forgotten? Nay, I will take again the treasure that is more than gold—my eyes will take delight in the face that is fairer than diamonds. Ha, you will live to see that—dog of an unbeliever."

At the gate of his palace he paused to stare a moment longer at his captive.

"Put upon him the chain that may not be loosened and the weight that may not be set down."

In the courtyard Robert was seized by slaves who riveted upon his wrists fetters to which chains were attached. These chains in turn supported a round ball of iron half as heavy as a man—a spiked ball, stained with dried blood.

"This is the morning star, Nazarene," Osman smiled, "for when you awake from sleep it lies near you, and when you would go forth it stirs not. Many who have looked upon it long have cursed the sun and prayed for death."

The slaves urged him toward a postern door of the tower. To obey, he was forced to pick up the weight and carry it, for the chains were too short to allow him to stand upright. He went forward, and the door closed on him, leaving him in darkness. But for a moment before the door was shut, he heard the distant mutter of great drums and the clash of the Mongol cymbals.

Chapter XIV

For those who watch the highway and for those who sit by the carpet of sickness, the sands run slowly from the hourglass, and the water lingers in the wheel of the water clock.

That day the *muezzin* did not call from the minarets at the noon hour. Will Bunsley and Ellen had grown accustomed to hearing the cry to prayer when the sun was at its highest point, and they looked up at the white spires without seeing turbaned figures in the tiny platforms that stood against the blue of the sky.

It was a cloudless day, and no wind stirred the spray of the fountain in the garden. Ellen hung about the path, making pretense of gathering flowers, but really listening with all her ears to the sounds in the street beyond the wall, to be ready to unbar the door the moment she heard Robert's ringing—

"Gate ho!"

She noticed that the noises of the street had changed. There was a steady mutter of voices and a shuffling of feet. The cries of children and the quarreling of loiterers were lacking. And no word came of Robert.

"Lady," quoth Will Bunsley, arranging his collection of arrows in sundry quivers, "the foe doth make a bruit with drum and horn, so methinks Sir Robert is yet upon the wall."

"But there is no fighting now."

Will scratched his head and looked up at the sky dubiously. "Fighting? Nay, I think so. Armed bands do pass a-nigh us; so perchance Sir Robert hath driven the foe out upon the plain."

"Master Will! You know as well as I that my lord would permit of no sally!"

Squinting down an arrow, the archer paused to cut back the feathering a trifle. Every day of their stay in the garden he had come in with news of Robert's deeds and his health, and he was well aware that the maid loved the knight with an enduring love.

"Hum. Why then, being weary, my lord doth sleep. For, look ye, a night of swordstrokes doth weary a wight somewhat. Even I—"

Ellen smiled at him. "You are a brave liar and a hardy rogue, Will Bunsley. Think you Sir Robert would sleep when the clarions were sounding? Oh, for one word—"

She broke off to listen to the murmur outside the gate, her brown eyes dark with anxiety, for Ellen herself had not slept while the clarions were heard upon the wall.

"Why, lass, he will be here anon," nodded the archer confidently. "Aye, he sought you out i' the mountain pass and in the wizarder's palace. So go thou within and change to thy warrior dress to greet him."

The girl knew that Will was hiding his misgivings and wished her to be clad as a man because he thought danger was at hand. So she went to her chamber and donned the light mail and steel cap, thrusting her hair beneath the cotton drop. Casting the silk *khalat* over her shoulders, she hurried forth to the garden. For a moment her glance quested in search of Will, who had disappeared. Then she heard his voice, loud with amazement.

"Lass—lass! The good father sees—he sees! A miracle hath come to pass!"

Ellen caught her breath, and, realizing better than the yeoman what his words portended, ran swiftly to the room of Father Evagrius. The patriarch was sitting up, one hand clasping his thin chest, the other outstretched in the air; his emaciated face was flushed, and his lips quivered. Will Bunsley stood agape in a far corner.

"Monseigneur!" cried the girl.

The eyes of the priest held a new light; no longer did they wander or lift viewlessly to the sky. They were fixed on the white wall, where the sunlight struck through a latticed embrasure.

"The mercy of God!"

Evagrius framed the words with difficulty, and then his voice grew clearer.

"I see the light of the sun! O blessed and fortunate! Nay, this is no abode of paynims!"

He glanced into the shadows, and Ellen sank on her knees beside him, supporting his shoulders with her arm. The hand of the patriarch felt her mailed throat and the steel head-piece.

"Who attends me? I cannot see you, but surely you must be one of the warriors of the Sepulcher. Behold—" his finger darted at the wall—"the tomb! Aye, the sun is bright on the Via Dolorosa and the walls of the blessed city. I can see the ensign of the Cross—there."

His eyes closed, and Ellen felt under her hand the heat of the fever that had made him delirious. Yet his lips twitched in a ceaseless smile.

"Happy are those who have taken up the Cross!" he cried again, stretching out his thin arms. "They are at home in Jerusalem, and the weary lie here at rest. O warrior, will you come with me to the tomb—yonder, a little way?"

"Aye, father," said Ellen, bowing her head.

"And bring the good knight Robert. For the Lord hath called to him the mighty men, and they come from the far places."

"Aye, father."

She eased the patriarch back to his couch and looked steadily into his face. After a moment she bent forward to close the blind man's eyes and to cross his hands on his breast.

"Evagrius hath died," she said to the archer, who had drawn nearer uncertainly.

"Nay," objected Will. "A moment agone he could see. 'Here is a miracle,' said I, and a miracle it was."

"Perchance it was, Master Will," assented the girl. "Now, do you, leave me, for a prayer must be said and candles placed fittingly. And then—what can we do?"

Will sought the garden and halted in his tracks. A dull crashing resounded from the alley, and the outer door quivered back against its bars. The wood splintered, and the head of an ax showed through. Catching up his bow, the archer strung it swiftly. Kneeling in the threshold of the house, he emptied a quiver at his foot and stuck the heads of a score of arrows in the earth in front of him.

"So-ho!" he muttered. "No friend knocks in that fashion."

The door fell into fragments, and the bars were cast aside by a tall Kankali who strode into the garden with drawn scimitar. The light of the afternoon sun was full in the man's eyes, and he saw nothing of the archer until Will's bow snapped and a shaft struck the warrior's throat, knocking him down.

Two others leaped over the dying man and started across the garden. Will sent a shaft fairly between the eyes of the first. The other reached the fountain, where an arrow clanged into the mail above his girdle, and he plunged into the water. An angry shout from the alley showed that the fall of the three had been observed, and the door remained vacant for a moment. Will heard Ellen's step behind him and called over his shoulder.

"We are beset by the paynims. Go thou to the roof with thy bow, but keep below the parapet. Watch lest they climb the wall in the rear."

"Who are they?"

"What matter—ha!"

The yeoman drew a shaft to his ear and paused alertly. Two shields had been thrust across the opening on the alley side, and behind this protection two warriors knelt hastily, bow in hand. They could not see Will, and he waited until they had sped their shafts hurriedly and without harm to him.

The attempt was repeated, more boldly this time, and an arrow thudded into the empty quiver at his foot. Evidently the assailants hoped that they had wounded the archer, because a Kankali ran into the garden, keeping his head down prudently so that the steel helmet protected his face. His round shield he held in front of his body.

Will rose to his feet and loosed an arrow that ripped through the tough hide target and pierced deep into the warrior's chest. The man stumbled and lay where he fell.

"They will eke be wiser now," he muttered, fearful that the Moslems would scatter around the wall and climb it out of his range of vision. "What tidings, my lady?" he called cheerily.

"I can see naught beyond the wall. What happened in the garden?"

"A fat man hath gone to pare the ——'s! hoofs! His comrades hang back. Nay, I think they are brewing mischief."

He heard feet running in the alley, and a loud outcry. Then a couple of Kankalis swept past as if the fiend Will had invoked were after them. Ellen appeared at his side, fearful that he had been hurt, and they ventured a few steps into the garden.

Horses trotted up from somewhere and halted outside the wall. Through the door stepped a man who was not a Kankali—a warrior whose long beard swept his bare chest, whose iron helm bore the upper portion of a tiger's head by way of a crest and whose wide shoulders were wrapped in the tigerskin. Will fingered his bow, planting himself before the girl. But Ellen caught his arm with a cry of amazement.

"'Tis Abdullah, the minstrel!"

Abdullah, or Chepe Noyon, the Tiger Lord, glanced at them and laughed. Then, while a dozen squat Mongols crowded after him, he began to turn over the bodies in the garden to look into the faces, evidently seeking to identify one of them.

When he reached the last of the Kankalis, who had been smitten through the shield, he bent over and uttered an exclamation of satisfaction. The dead man was Osman, the wazir.

Chepe Noyon signed to one of his followers, who promptly struck off the head of the Moslem minister. Then the Mongols crowded around the two Christians to stare and finger Will's tattered garments. The archer faced them defiantly, while Chepe Noyon studied Ellen curiously. Resistance was useless, and the girl was the first to throw down her weapons.

Chapter XV
The Throne of Gold

Robert had been without sleep for a day and a night and the part of another day, so he had not been an hour in his dungeon before his head sank to the rushes and he fell into a dreamless stupor.

The opening of the door brought him back to consciousness, but his wounds ached and his limbs were stiff. He heard guttural voices that dwindled and left him to sit and to wonder first why he was in the dungeon and then—as the events of the last morning flashed back into his mind—why the door had been opened. The men who had come to his cell had merely glanced in and passed on.

He tried to get up and cursed the massive weight that cramped his arms. Picking up the spiked ball with an effort, he went to the door and thrust it wide.

The sun was setting, and the minarets of Bokhara were touched with the last crimson of the western sky. For awhile he gazed at the courtyard and listened, suspecting some new trick of the wazir's making. Every detail of the place was familiar to him, and yet everything was different. It was the hour of evening prayer, but no call of the muezzin was to be heard; no lights hung in the palace gardens, and no men moved about the courtyard. The gate stood open.

Robert picked up the morning star and walked out into the street, and his eyes puckered thoughtfully. The street was deserted. Opposite him was a potter's bench with a half-formed jar on the stone wheel and water in the bowl beside it. A dog trotted across the alley and entered the door of a shop. Bokhara was wrapped in silence. Although he listened, Robert could not hear even the whine of a beggar or the grunting of a camel. He surveyed the alley reactively, wondering if his senses had not failed him. Then he set out to walk painfully toward the house where he had left Ellen and Will.

At the first crossing, near the *righistan*, he heard horses approach, and blinked at the glare of torches. Three riders came up and reined in when they saw him—slant-eyed, squat warriors with spears slung at their backs. They wore wolfskin cloaks and rode small, long-haired ponies, and Robert saw that they were Mongols. They exchanged a few words, and one started to draw his sword, when another uttered an exclamation and pointed to the knight's surcoat on which the red cross was still to be made out. Robert caught the word "noyon"—chief—and guessed that the warrior had recognized him as the leader of the garrison.

They stared indifferently at his chains and the iron ball, and motioned him to accompany them, slowing their ponies to a walk to keep about him.

Entering the *righistan*, they joined other mounted patrols and headed for the Jumma mosque. At the steps two of the warriors took Robert by the arms and rode their ponies up the stair into the pillared transept. Here they dismounted and led him within the mosque itself, where torches glittered on white marble and gold and the great tiles of the flooring. Gathered near the entrance he found groups of the chief imams and *khadis*. They were holding the bridles of several Mongol ponies. Beside the noblemen were ranged scores of the shah's singing-girls, guarded by armed Mongols. Robert asked the nearest Moslem what had taken place in the city. The man only seized his beard in both hands and bowed his head.

"Hush!" whispered another. "The wrath of God stands near us."

"Where are the people of Bokhara?"

"Where is the snow of last year? Wo! Wo! All were ordered out on the plain save the grandees, and we—we must tend the conqueror's horses, aye, feed them with hay from the Koran boxes. *Ai-a—ai-a!*"

"How did the Mongols enter the city?"

The *khadi* glanced fearfully toward the rear of the mosque and tore at his beard. His plump cheeks glistened with sweat.

"How? Allah be compassionate to his servants! They rode in through the gates before sunset, for the keys of Bokhara were rendered up to them."

"Why?"

Now the man looked at Robert and knew him.

"It happened thus, O captain of many. Osman and Jahan Khan decided on a sortie of the garrison, for the Mongols seemed to be withdrawing in confusion. Nay, it was a trick. When the warriors of Islam rode forth they were cut to pieces as a hare is torn by dogs. The plain is covered with the bodies of the Kankalis and Persians, and Jahan Khan fled toward Herat like a leaf before the wind. Then we within the city gave up the keys on promise of our lives."

Robert started and gripped the man's shoulder.

"What of the other Franks?"

The *khadi* moaned.

"What of one bird in a storm? Ask of him if you dare!"

A solitary rider sat in the saddle of a white horse under the colored dome of the mosque, apart from the captives. He wore no armor or insignia of rank. In the shadows at the rear of the edifice he might have been a statue cast out of iron. Even the white horse was motionless on the black marble flooring.

"Who is he?" Robert asked.

"He is the scourge that has come out of the desert. Aye, the Great Khan, Genghis Khan."

The crusader glanced with quick interest at the conqueror, measuring the spread of the high shoulders and the sinews of wrist and forearm. Only the keen black eyes of the Mongol moved, and Robert fancied they glinted with amusement when they lingered on the grandees holding the horses.

A touch on his arm made him turn, and he saw Chepe Noyon standing beside him; but a Chepe Noyon that no longer resembled Abdullah, the teller of tales. The chieftain had cast back upon his shoulders the tiger muzzle, and Robert noticed that the hair on his head had been shaved except for a long scalp-lock that fell from his skull to the tigerskin.

"Where are the Nazarene maid and the archer?" Robert asked him.

Chepe Noyon chewed his lip reflectively, glancing from Genghis Khan to the imams who were tending the ponies. Throughout the mosque there was only to be heard the snapping of the torches and the munching of the horses that were feeding from the Koran boxes.

"From that high place Nur-Anim was accustomed to read the book of the Moslems."

Chepe Noyon nodded at a miniature tower, some dozen feet in height, that rose behind Genghis Khan. It was shaped like a minaret with a platform and cupola in which rested on a sandalwood stand a massive Koran.

"There is the book that no one but Nur-Anim might touch."

He looked at Robert reflectively.

"Your archer slew Osman, which was a good deed. I have him and the maid in man's attire, in my tent. I came upon them when I followed the wazir. But Nur-Anim I have not yet unearthed. In all Bokhara there is no trace of his passing, yet he must have fled from the city."

He snarled in sudden anger.

"What avails the capture of the city without Nur-Anim?"

"The mullah? Nay, he is harmless—"

"As the fangs of an adder! You were slow to see the evil in these servants of the shah. Osman was no more than a cup-shot fool, and he died like one, striving to put his hand on a woman. Nur-Anim used him for a moment, no more. The mullah was the true master of Bokhara, for he had the treasure in his hands."

Chepe Noyon laughed grimly. "The mullah persuaded the shah to leave the treasure in the hands of their god, Allah. I have spoken with one or two of his priests with a dagger in my hand, and I know that Nur-Anim wanted you to be emir because he feared Kutchluk Khan, who was a wolf. Then he overthrew you and whispered to Osman and Jahan Khan to lead forth the army, and they knew no better."

He made a gesture as of gathering up sand in his fist and casting it into the air.

"A little trick served to break their formation, and then the Horde rode them down."

"But why did Nur-Anim—"

"O little son, you held the wall like a man and a *noyon*. But you know not the ways of snakes. Muhammad is already shaken, and his power grows less; Bokhara will be razed to the plain, yet the treasure is hidden beneath it, and Nur-Anim knows the hiding place. When we have passed on he will come out and dig it up again. A hundred thousand have died that he might do this thing."

A warrior spoke to the chief, who took Robert's arm.

"Genghis Khan summons you."

Robert took up his shackles and stepped forward at once, Chepe Noyon walking at his side.

"I cannot aid you now. Speak boldly!"

A sigh of relief went up from the Moslems as Robert was singled out to face the man on the white horse, but he himself was too weary to feel either excitement or fear. For several moments he waited by the muzzle of the Khan's pony, while the eyes of Genghis rested on him. Chepe Noyon, after making his salutation, stood to one side to act as interpreter.

"The khan asks," he said briefly, "if you are one of the heroes of the Franks who came over the sea?"

"I am a Frank."

"Are you he who held the wall against our assault?"

"Aye."

The gray eyes of the knight sought the broad, lined face that looked down at him, utterly without expression.

"And if treachery had not put these chains upon me, I would have kept the wall."

Chepe Noyon interpreted, and the old conqueror glanced at the iron weight that hung from Robert's wrists. He spoke slowly in his deep gutturals and raised his hand.

"He says—" the Tiger Lord drew Robert aside—"that no man has stood so long before the rush of the Horde. The chains are to be taken off, and you are to eat and sleep. On the morrow you will be matched against a man as great in strength as you. The khan will watch. If you slay the other, you are free to go where you will."

As Robert turned to go back to his guards, Chepe Noyon signed for him to remain. The white horse of Genghis Khan had grown restive and was pawing the marble flooring. As if the mood of the horse had aroused the chieftain, Genghis turned in the saddle and pointed at the Moslem grandees, his dark eyes snapping with anger.

"O ye imams and *khadis*," cried Chepe Noyon, translating the words, "the Khan bids you to reveal the riches that are hidden in the ground. What is aboveground his men will care for. Who among you knows the hiding place of the treasure of Khar?"

The nobles answered with many voices that they knew nothing of the hiding place. Some cast themselves on their knees, and the echoes of their cries were flung back by the dome in the roof.

"We have fire and steel that will wring the truth from you," pointed out Chepe Noyon dispassionately.

Several began to relate how their personal hoards might be discovered, but all insisted that Nur-Anim alone could lead the Mongols to the treasure of Muhammad. Chepe Noyon turned to Robert.

"The throne of gold and the jewels must be near to a mosque," he observed. "Have you come upon the way to Nur-Anim's secret?"

"I think it lies beneath the grounds of this mosque. Osman disclosed as much."

Robert, in fact, cared little what became of the hoard. It had passed out of his reach, and his only wish was that Muhammad and the Moslems would not regain it, possibly to use it against the crusaders in later years.

Chepe Noyon spoke briefly with Genghis Khan.

"The floor at this place rings strangely when the horse stamps. Is there a space beneath?"

Echoes sprang to life as some of the priests of the mosque made answer that there was no chamber beneath.

"I would believe them more readily if some had said they did not know," muttered the Tiger Lord, frowning. "Why do you think it is near to us, O little son?"

"Because Nur-Anim must have kept it where he could watch, and his own dwelling is small and scanty. The garden of the mosque would not be safe. Besides, Muhammad came hither when he entered Bokhara."

He paused to watch Genghis Khan who, without touching the reins, was kneeing his pony back and forth over the square of black marble. And it did seem to Robert that the tread of the horse echoed differently when it passed under the reader's stand. Genghis Khan dismounted and moved to the tower, as clumsy on foot as he was graceful in the saddle.

He climbed the tiled steps to the cupola, while Chepe Noyon issued a command to the Mongol warriors about the door. A score of them went out, to return quickly with heavy blacksmith sledges.

Meanwhile Genghis Khan had caught up the great Koran, which must have weighed as much as Robert's shackles and ball, and poised it over his head. Then he flung it out, over the edge of the stand, and it crashed down on the marble beneath.

"He said," muttered Chepe Noyon to the knight, "that if the Kharesmi-ans had spent their gold for walls along the river and if they had fed the army of the beggars and the sick in the city they would not be captives now."

Once more the echoes of the vast interior started up as the Mongols began to smash at the marble—some kneeling upon the flooring, from which the white horse drew back at once, others standing about the walls, pounding down the gold plaques with the Arabic inscriptions.

The Moslems, who had quivered and crouched as the great Koran was flung down, fell on their faces beating with their fists against the tiles. The women huddled together in a corner, and the night wind whisk-ing in through the wide-flung portals moaned an undernote to the hid-eous clamor of the echoes; but no thunderbolt came down from the sky to crush the man who had thrown under the legs of his horse the sacred Koran of the Jumma.

Robert thought of the Gates in the Mountains that had barred the way to Khar for a thousand years. Now the bars were falling. Whole segments of mosaic crumpled up and rained down from the walls, and the gold plates toppled out and down.

In spite of his weariness and his hunger Robert drew closer to the men with the hammers. He was seeing the empire of Islam cracked asun-der—something that the crusaders had striven in vain to bring to pass for a hundred years; and his pulse leaped. The thin marble blocks were split into fragments on the floor and tossed aside, revealing an under-sur-face of brick. Once more the hammers went to work, and more torches were brought.

Two of the sledges smashed through the brick at the same time, and the Mongols leaped back. The square that they had uncovered sagged and dis-appeared in a cloud of dust, leaving a hole wider than a man could leap.

Chepe Noyon flung back his head and roared with laughter. Robert peered down, dazzled by the reflection of the torches on a hundred glit-tering surfaces. As the dust eddied and settled, he beheld a chamber of considerable size below the floor of the mosque. Near the opening stood a long ivory table, covered with silver, bronze, and jade caskets.

He was looking at the riches of Islam, the spoil of Baghdad and Ni-neveh—the plunder of Balkh and India. It shone from the hilts of weap-ons hung upon the walls of the vault—it sparkled from the piles of jars and incense holders, of necklaces and anklets upon the floor. And almost under the opening gleamed the throne of gold.

Who had fashioned it and how long ago, the knight could not know. Assuredly it was older than the wall of Bokhara, for in the massy metal of it were inscribed arrows and darts and emblems of another age. Perhaps Alexander and perhaps Darius had sat upon it. But just then—and Chepe Noyon had been the first to perceive him—Nur-Anim crouched against it, staring up with writhing lips, a dagger gripped in his hand.

"Ho, the snake is in its hole!" cried the Tiger Lord.

Some food and a water-sack and several candles showed that the mullah had planned to lie hidden for some time. Robert noticed steps running up into a corridor near the priest, and judged that they led to a door concealed somewhere in the reader's stand.

Chepe Noyon drew his sword at a sign from Genghis Khan. Turning to Robert, he explained swiftly that the knight was to go to a tent in the Mongol camp with the warriors who had brought him to the mosque.

"What of the maid? I must see her," Robert demanded.

"You will see her on the morrow."

With that the chieftain leaped bodily into the chamber below, and Robert saw Nur-Anim spring into the dark corridor. He heard Chepe Noyon laugh again, and as he moved away to join his guards, the Moslem grandees moaned and gripped their beards. From the opening in the floor arose a scream that swelled and dwindled to a hoarse babble.

Chapter XVI
The Road and Its End

It was late when Robert was led into a small woolen tent pitched near the horse lines of the Mongol camp, and the rivets of his fetters were struck off by a smith. But he did not go to sleep at once.

The warriors had sought out one who knew a smattering of Arabic, and of him the knight requested water and rice and mutton, and ate until the Mongols smiled approval, believing it a sign of a strong heart that a man should eat mightily before going forth to fight for his life. They asked what weapon he would select, and brought him a varied collection of Moslem mail and swords.

From these the knight selected a strong haburgeon, and tossed away his own, that had many broken links. He refused all the scimitars, and the Mongols inquired if he wanted one of their shorter swords.

Robert, however, had determined to fashion a weapon which would not break in the combat on the morrow—as his scimitar and ax had broken on the wall—and which would decide the issue swiftly. Hope had forsaken him, and he longed only for two things—the strength to stand against the champion selected by the Mongols, and a sight of Ellen.

He called for a stout staff of hard, seasoned wood as thick as his wrist, and the smith brought him one reinforced with iron—the broken handle of a great mace.

Then Robert took up the spiked knob and the chains from which his wrists had been freed and set to work grimly to fit the fetters at the ends of the chains upon the staff.

The Mongols watched the making of this unwonted weapon with attentive interest. They had orders to deny the champion of the Franks no request, and the smith helped find bolts that would fit the holes in the shackles.

When the work was finished, Robert had the mace-handle attached to the two chains, each about a foot long. From these chains swung the spiked knob of iron that had been his gift from Osman. The warriors took turns trying to swing it around their heads, and only a few could do so, with an effort.

"What is this thing?" they asked of the interpreter.

Robert smiled.

"It is the morning star."

"How is that?"

He thrust the handle in the water cask so that the wood would swell and grip tighter the iron bands.

"When it falls a man dies."

The guards squatted down to watch while he slept on a pile of skins. And in whispers, not to disturb him, the Mongols discussed his stature and mighty muscles, the lines in his dark face that were deep even in slumber. They pointed to the tawny mane of yellow hair and shook their heads, for they had never seen a man like this. With equal interest they watched the morning star soaking in the water cask, certain that this was some kind of magic.

When the sun scattered the mists on the sandy plain, throngs of Mongol warriors moved toward the standard of Genghis Khan. They squatted down, keeping clear a space some hundred yards square in front of the pole that bore the horns and the yak-tails. A little later the chieftains of the Horde walked over from their tents, and all raised their arms as the Khan appeared in the entrance of his pavilion and mounted a pony.

It was ever his custom, bred of a life of constant warfare, to be in the saddle, and he was never known to walk when a horse was at hand.

After he had taken his place at the edge of the cleared ground and received the greetings of the paladins, Chepe Noyon rode up and dismounted. Two warriors with drawn swords forced a way through the ranks of watchers at one end of the square and halted. Robert, clad in mail from knee to throat, walked between them, bearing the new mace in his hand, and a thousand pairs of eyes fastened on it curiously.

The knight swept a quick glance at the lines of silent warriors, who sat or stood where they willed, each with a spear or sword at hand—at the savage standard and the deserted wall of the city that loomed above the round tents of the Horde, and the pall of smoke that rose behind the walls and overspread the sky. He stood, erect, smiling a little.

For here was no fair list, fashioned for jousting, with heralds and poursuivants to tend the combatants and enforce the rules of the tournament—no minstrels to make memorable the names of the men who bore themselves well. He rested the spiked knob on the earth and turned to where a commotion at the other end of the square announced the coming of the antagonist whom he was ordered to overthrow if he would live longer.

He saw a tall figure, glistening in the finest of Damascus mail, and a crested helm. The man left his guards and moved toward the knight, who noticed that he carried only a battle-ax, a heavy blade with a long haft.

"Will Bunsley!" cried Robert, taking a pace forward.

It was the archer, and he was pale to the lips as he moved closer. Within easy speaking distance he paused to wipe his forehead and to lean on his ax.

"Aye, Sir Robert, 'tis Will Bunsley, who will ne'er pull a bow or buss a lass again. Harkee, time lacks for parley, and so do thou listen while I gabble—as is my way.

"The demoiselle d'Ibelin rests within Abdullah's tent. Some words the minstrel did contrive to make clear to her, as follows: *Item*, thou and I, my lord, must e'en stand and smite each other till one is done to death; *item*, the maid doth pray for us both, but her heart aches for thee; *item*, these Mokals be dour fighters—as witness yonder fair city taken in despite of sword and bow and wall—and they will be an-angered if thou dost quibble or draw back."

He glanced with widening eyes at Robert's new-made mace, and with a muttered, "St. Dunstan abet me!" went on. "*Item* four, and last, Sir Robert, by no means might I prevail against thee in combat, so do thou, hew me down—would thou hadst chosen another weapon—and fail not. To make sport for these our captors I will rap thy ribs a time or two and e'en deal thee a buffet on the sconce."

Drawing a deep breath, he tightened his grasp on his ax. "And so—fare thee well, my lord."

It was a changed Will Bunsley that faced Robert, the merriment vanished from his blue eyes, his jaw set stubbornly. Whether Genghis Khan or Chepe Noyon had selected the archer to oppose him, Robert did not know. Probably they had singled out the two Franks for the duel, aware that Robert was more than a match for any man of Khar. And Robert, knowing that Will Bunsley was no match for him, took a step forward.

"A true man are you," he said, smiling, for he saw his way clear before him now.

Will heaved up his ax hurriedly.

"Nay, Master Robert, get thee to the work. One of us must fall upon the ling, and—what would it avail me to strive with thee? Come, lad, a few good blows—"

"Aye," cried Robert and, striding forward, thrust aside the other's weapon and gripped his shoulder hard. "We will show them how two Englishmen can bear arms. Shoulder to shoulder, bowman—"

"What would ye, master? Ah, the good Christ aid us!"

For Robert had turned and was walking toward the nearest Mongols, swinging his mace in widening circles.

"'Tis madness for both to die. Bethink ye of the maid Ellen—"

"—who would hold me a caitiff and recreant, to strike you down!"

Robert sprang into the Mongols, who rose to meet him, growling and catching up their weapons. Steel ground against steel, and the great morning star swept clear a space about the knight.

Will Bunsley thrust a quivering hand across his eyes, then leaped after his comrade. His ax smashed down on the iron armor of the scattering Mongols and rose red, to flash down again until he gained Robert's side.

The warriors, who had started back in astonishment as the captives turned on them, closed in swiftly, making a circle about them. But Robert kept moving onward, and ever the iron flail kept clear a space before him, crunching into the heads and breasts of the men who leaped at him.

The knight was making his last stand, and all the power of his long arms went into every sweep of the mace. The ring shifted and changed to a black knot that writhed and twisted and finally came to a halt near the standard, where Will went down voicelessly and disappeared under the stamping feet. A man's spine snapped like a bent branch, and someone cried out:

"Subotai! Way for the Buffalo!"

The knot about Robert fell away as the warriors drew back, glaring and snarling at their victim—as dogs might leave the sight of a stag half pulled to earth. On his pony Genghis Khan had not stirred, although the beast snorted and stamped, a spear's length from the struggle. Only the eyes of the old Mongol followed every move of the men below him.

Robert reeled and steadied himself on his feet against Subotai's rush. His breath was whistling from his lungs; both hands were slashed to the bone, and blood streamed from his forehead into his open mouth. Recognizing the warrior of the buffalo horns as the one who had sought him on the causeway, he swung up the morning star as the giant leaped forward.

Instead of plunging on, Subotai halted, digging his heels into the earth. But Robert did not strike as he had expected, thus leaving himself open to a slash of the massive curved sword of the Mongol. The other warriors stood back to watch the two champions.

This time Subotai rushed in earnest, head up and shield down, his lips snarling and his sword arm swinging at his side. Both struck at once. The knight's mace smashed the Mongol's iron shield, and the sword swept the helm from Robert's head, sending him back, staggering.

"*Hai!*" Subotai grunted and leaped in, slashing low.

Robert could not parry the blow; instead of trying to do so he stepped forward, into the sweep of the sword. It bit into the mail on his side and thigh, snapping the steel links, and glanced down to the earth.

The spiked knob smashed down on the Mongol's chest, ripping off the iron plates and drawing blood in streams. Before Subotai could leap clear Robert dropped the mace and gripped him about the knees. Gasping with the effort, he put forth all the strength of sinews and back muscles, raising the struggling body of the chieftain to his shoulder, shifting his grasp in a second to throat and belt of his foe, holding Subotai at the full reach of stiffened arms.

No one among the watchers moved to intercept him, and, filling his laboring lungs, he hurled Subotai to the ground. The warrior, striking on head and shoulder, rolled over and was still.

Robert stood looking down at him, swaying the while on his feet from utter weariness. He heard Chepe Noyon call out, and the deep voice of the khan bark a command, and he tried to step toward the place where his mace had fallen, but had no longer strength to move foot or arm. He saw Chepe Noyon running toward him, felt the iron embrace of the Mongol's arms about his bruised ribs and looked up as a shout roared forth from ten thousand throats—

"Ahatou koke Mongku, ho!"

"O little son," cried the Tiger Lord, "you overthrew the Buffalo! You lifted him in your hands and tossed him down! *Hai!* I chose well—by the white horse of Kaidu, by the eyes of all the gods—I picked a man!"

He drew back to look into Robert's scarred features.

"Did you hear the salute of the Horde? No man hath overthrown Subotai before. Nay, you know not the words of the Horde. 'Ho, brother, warrior of the Mongols, ho!'"

Genghis Khan spoke again, first to Chepe Noyon, then to a group of swordsmen who ran to the fallen Subotai and stood over him. The Buffalo had opened his eyes; now he shook his head savagely and sprang up. Instantly a score of powerful hands gripped him and held him, while the red glare faded from his eyes and he looked at Robert curiously.

"The command was given," explained Chepe Noyon to the knight, "to stay the Buffalo until his anger passed. You and he must pour water on your swords. The Khan is not minded to lose either of you."

Robert lifted his head with a wry smile.

"What mockery is this? I fought against you and slew many. Make an end!"

"Then will I tell you the judgment of the Khan. He said—

"*'The two Nazarenes kept faith with each other, and so will they keep faith with all men.'*

"If you will ride with us, you will sit in a high place at the feasts and ride the best of the horses and have a great tent. Little son, this battle was a test, even as my offer to you to surrender Bokhara was a test, and in each thing you have stood your ground and held to your faith. We have honor for such a hero, as you will see."

The knight was silent, finding this hard to believe. Yet the warriors he had wounded came to look at him closely and examine the morning star, utterly indifferent to their hurts. Subotai after awhile walked over and took up the mace, whirling it about his head like a sling.

He grunted something, and Chepe Noyon interpreted:

"He says that you are to make him such a weapon and he will go against you or any other three warriors."

Now Robert laughed a little unsteadily.

"Well for me he did not have the mace awhile ago. Nay, spare me another such test."

He remembered Will Bunsley and sought him out, to learn from Chepe Noyon that the Mongols had refrained from slaying the archer and had had him borne away to a tent to mend his wounds. As they talked, Genghis Khan wheeled his horse and made off, a lane opening for him through the Mongol ranks. Robert saw that smoke was rising in dense plumes over the wall of Bokhara, and flames, fanned by a stiffening wind, were leaping through the smoke over the mosques.

"'Tis the end of Bokhara," nodded Chepe Noyon, following his glance. "But the treasure is safe. Come, I have put aside a tent for you, and your share of the treasure awaits you."

As the windstorm lashed the plain and the horse herds of the camp turned their backs to the eddies of dust, the flames raged in Bokhara, and the plumes of smoke grew into great clouds that hid the sun and swirled down on the quivering tents. Robert and Chepe Noyon wrapped their mantles over their arms, and the knight shielded his torn face as best he could from the smarting dust. Coming to the closed flap of a round woolen tent, the Mongol raised it and signed for the crusader to enter.

Still holding his mace, Robert stooped under the pole that served as a lintel and the next instant he was fighting for his life. A scimitar smote his chest, and he warded a blow at his head with the handle of the mace. In the semidarkness of the heavy tent he could make out the figure of a Moslem in armor—a flying cloak and a curved sword that sought vainly for his head.

The figure leaped at him fiercely, and he brushed aside the steel blade with surprising ease and caught his antagonist fast within both arms. As he felt for the Moslem's sword wrist his right hand closed on the warrior's throat, and he was aware of a pulse that throbbed frantically under his fingers. The helm of his adversary fell off, and Robert released his grip.

But only to tighten his arm about the dark tresses that fell about the slender shoulders of Ellen, who stared bewildered into his eyes.

"By the Cross, demoiselle," he laughed out of a full heart, "hast still a mind to war?"

Her hands caught his cheeks and held him with rigid strength, while her warm breath beat against his throat. And he saw that she was pale as the white silk *khalat*.

"Ellen!" he cried. "Dost not know me—Robert?"

At this her eyes glowed, and she pressed her lips against his, running trembling fingers through his clotted hair, her throat quivering with sounds that made no words. Robert kissed her closed eyes and felt the weariness pass from him. Both flaps of the tent were ripped back, and Chepe Noyon strode in, hand on his sword hilt, looking greatly surprised.

"What—ha! No need to lead thee to the treasure, O Nazarene."

Ellen looked up as the light flooded in and brushed a hand across her eyes.

"My lord—I thought you slain when you came—I deemed you a Mongol, and I did not want to be—parted, again. Oh, what have I done?"

Her eyes widened, and she swayed back against his arm.

"What?" Robert smiled.

"Your face—and your armor hacked!" Tears started to the girl's eyes. "And see, your hand is slashed. Nay, I sought only to die, and now I have hurt you sore."

Robert stared for a moment in astonishment and then rocked with laughter.

"Little warrior, these few wounds were dealt me by the men of the Horde. Nay, Ellen, methinks you make a better maid than man-at-arms."

For many an hour they sat upon the rugs of the tent and talked, hand in hand, recounting all that had befallen them; and Chepe Noyon, leaning against the pole of the pavilion, took up a lute—for he was well content—and sang again for them the song with which he first greeted Robert. Until Ellen fell silent, her glance ever on the man who sat, chin on hand, looking through the entrance at the swirling sand and the riders that came and went.

"In another day, brave heart," he said, "Bokhara will be no more, and the road will be before us again. Chepe Noyon hath made clear to me the

Mongol plans. I told him we would ride with them no-wither save to Palestine. For there is my place—and you did promise the good Father Evagrius
to seek Jerusalem."

"Then will we go together, and you shall take Jerusalem," she nodded decidedly.

"Am I an emperor with a host?"

"Aye, so."

"Nay, I think not. Fair heart, our king lies at the island of Cyprus, and
there we will seek him if we reach the end of the road. Yet none before us
hath returned alive from Khar. These barbarians set out upon a way of
peril, for they seek out Muhammad to overthrow his power and will follow him even beyond the Gates, to Baghdad or Byzantium. They would
have me strive to aid them at siege and assault upon the great cities. Will
you come with me?"

"Aye, so." She bent her head. "If you will have me."

"Then is your promise given." He sprang up, and Chepe Noyon rose.
"And I will hold it binding. Aye." He looked at the Mongol, who held up
his hand for silence.

From the center of the camp came the mutter of drums and the brazen note of a great gong. Chepe Noyon spoke, and the knight nodded understanding.

"The summons to saddle hath been given," Robert said, and his eyes
gleamed with swift joy. "Never a queen shall have her coming heralded
as yours, and never a maid shall put such a song upon the lips of the troubadours of Christendom."

Afterword

Six months passed; and John of Brienne, thirteenth King of Jerusalem,
and his court rested at Tyre, upon the seacoast, where the barons of the
northern provinces had gathered in general council to discuss means of
holding their ground against fresh inroads of the Saracens.

The Moslem power had grown during the long truce, and the Croises
knew themselves to be unable to stand in battle against the armies of the
caliphs and the Sultan of Damascus if these hosts should be launched toward the seacoast.

At this council were gathered the lords of Ascalon and Acre, and the
Marquis of Antioch, with their peers, and the leaders of the Genoese and
Venetians. And the council came to naught because the young king lacked
the personality to hold men united in a cause, and each baron thought

for the most part of his own fief. Yet one curious and notable happening marked the assembly of the peers. A caravan entered the east gate of Tyre and passed through the wall coming from the valley of the Orontes.

The leader of this caravan was a strange figure. Garbed in the finest of Persian silks and the brightest of nankeen and cloth-of-gold, he rode a horse with trappings of silvered cloth. He was attended by a score of savage men armed with spears and bows, whose like had never been beheld in Palestine.

He bore with him a certain store of gold which he guarded carefully and was at pains to dispatch by agents of the chief Venetian merchants to Egypt, there to be paid to the Moslem masters of Damietta. This gold amounted to two thousand broad pieces, and the bearer explained that it was the ransom of a knight, one Robert Longsword, so called, who had been thought slain on the border.

As to the messenger himself, when his mission was done he called for the best wine of the taverns and the most skillful of the musicians and held revelry from the Tower of the Sea to the Sign of the Broken Sword in the French quarter. When he drank, his tongue was loosened, and it was learned that he, who had been esteemed a wealthy lord, was merely Will Bunsley, a wandering yeoman.

And when his gold and silver was spent he took service among the archers of the king and in time went from Tyre on a galley to Rhodes and thence to France. Those who had listened at first, drawn by the gold he had in his purse, began to laugh at his tale and call him a lying knave. Some, however, remembered the strange riders who had escorted him to the gate of Tyre.

But these had turned back at once, and few men believed the story of Will Bunsley, of Khar and its treasure, and an emperor of Islam who fled before an unknown conqueror.

Yet in time his narrative returned to the minds of the barons who had been at the council, and chiefly one Hugo of Montserrat, who had held his peace when mention was made of Khar.

This was when tidings came over the border of defeats suffered by the Moslems. Of Herat stormed by a new race of conquerors called the Mongols, and Balkh lost to Islam, and finally Baghdad itself fallen. So it happened that the power of the Saracens was not turned against the crusaders.

And when the fear of invasion had passed, the court of the king waxed merry. The minstrels and troubadours had a new song, made from the talk of the caravans that came over the border, and they sang of a crusader who adventured into paynimry itself and waged war upon the great cities. This they called the "Romaunt of the Longsword," and many a time in hall and woman's garden they related it for the pleasuring of the people of the castle who had ever an ear for something new.

This romaunt came to be known even in the courts of Europe, and some of the minstrels sang of a maid who rode in armor beside the knight.

It is the song of a man of high honor, though no more than a youth in years, who kept faith in all things. And now this tale, from which the song came to be, has been told.

The Bells of the Mountains

Rorik the Yngling tried to catch up with the bell. It was the only thing he could hear moving around him, but he couldn't find it.

He had taken the wrong path; he was lost, and unless he worked his legs fast he was going to be late for the battle.

It would never do if Rorik the Yngling missed the battle, for then he would have no gold—neither pay nor plunder, or the chance of finding a girl somewhere about afterward.

Shouldering his long two-handed sword, he hurried his lanky legs after the clank-clong of the elusive bell. Being a Dane, Rorik was not accustomed to mountains. Up through the pines a black shoulder of rock showed, and far above that a white summit of snow, but no sign of a road or the camp he was looking for.

The Good Lord, thought Rorik the Yngling, had made the farming land down in the valleys, and up here the devil must have piled everything evil. Up here in these Swiss mountains. No, Rorik wouldn't be surprised if he found a forest troll ringing that bell to fool him.

Running up the path he found a cow standing there alone, with a heavy brass clapper bell hanging on its neck. The bell grated when the cow looked at him, but it didn't clatter as before. Someone had been driving the cow—someone who couldn't be seen. Rorik listened and dropped suddenly to a knee.

A rock swished over his head, and he jumped into the laurel bushes by the path, sliding the sheath from the five-foot blade of his sword.

"Pfut!" he said. He reached out and caught the arm of a girl who was trying to slip out of the bushes. She tried to bite his wrist. He felt beads around her bare throat.

"Kitten," said Rorik, "you can keep the cow. I am too much in haste to drive it off, now. Where is the camp?"

She shook her head, listening.

"The soldiers, the army, the *verlorene Haufen*—where are they, girl?"

Getting no answer he pulled her up to him, rubbing his head against her hair, feeling the gasping of her throat, kissing her. She tried to twist away from him.

"Listen, flaxhead," he whispered in her ear, "I am a Yngling of Jonsson's dale—of pastureland and homestead. No man has gentler blood than I have, child. And no weapon man can stand against me, foot to foot. In truth," said Rorik modestly, "I am a champion."

In spite of this assurance, the girl pulled away, silently.

"I like you well enough," he told her, "and you can tell me your name."

"Maera," she gasped.

That was a strange name and her tongue had a strange, slow twang to it, unlike Danish.

"Why do you stay here where a battle will be with only a cow?"

Maera looked up from the tangle of her hair, and stopped pulling suddenly. Taking his hand, she drew him along the path. "Look," she said quickly, "I have all the cows to milk."

Before he could think about that, she had reached a turn in the path where a hut perched on the mountain slope with cattle and pigs pressing against the pens.

"This is the homestead," she said, catching him from the corners of her eyes, while she tried to keep her arms from trembling. Often, while she peered down through the pines at the lower valley, Maera had wondered what the enemy would look like—those men-at-arms of the emperor, riding over the crops—if she met one face to face.

Now here she was with this giant of a man looking not at all like a soldier, his head thin and brown, his hands hard and curved as if from the grip of a mattock. She had been frightened when she felt his strength.

Rorik wanted to pick her up and carry her into the hut. Such a foolish thing as she was, to stay here alone. The place was certainly empty except for her—with faggots for the fire stacked along its bare planks, and shirts and hose washed clean hanging among the apple trees where a terrace had been scraped from the mountain and walled up with stone.

"Your hide isn't safe here," he said. "Where have your menfolk gone?"

"I won't tell you!"

To Maera it seemed certain now that this prowler was a spy, spying and peering to find out where the Swiss fighting men were gathering, in these Bernese uplands. "You are no champion," she cried at him. "No—a dunderhead, trying to talk like a soldier. You are as full of lies as a hive is of honey, Sir Nobody!"

Now Rorik of Yngling had broad shoulders and a small head. Perhaps he did not think things out easily in that head; but when he did have an idea he was sure of it. Up on the mountain he had expected to meet devils and Swiss pikemen. Instead, he had found the little Maera. And he began to think she was mocking him.

"Sir No—" he stared at her.

"Nobody of Nowhere."

There she stood, with fire in her blue eyes—so thin and young he could have broken her back with his fist. No longer afraid of him.

She had touched the pride of Rorik the Yngling. "I will show you," he said. "Pfut! I will let you see that I am first among all those soldiers." Then he remembered that he had lost his way. "But first tell me where the German camp has moved to."

Maera laughed. Such a clumsy lie!

"The dog would know where his kennel is. Go down past the waterfall, my fine soldier. Take the forest path to your left. And stay away there, or it will be the worse for you."

"No. I will come back. And you, girl—you will wait here?"

Maera looked up at him curiously. "I will be here. But you will never come up again."

As he jumped the stone wall, sliding down by the mountain stream, it seemed to Rorik the Yngling that this girl with her blue eyes and her cowbells had managed to put a spell upon him. There might, after all, be a power of magic in these mountains . . .

Maera, running back from her lookout, flitting through the timber where no path ran, hurried to take her message to the pikemen of the Bern canton assembling at the stone church where the tolling bell summoned them from their land. Her father, waiting among the captains, the blue steel of his pike by his head, breathed deep at sight of her safe.

"Still they stay down in the valley," Maera cried. "Only one dunder-head of a spy came peering up into the *wald*."

"Yes," said her father, "yes, they are careful. If their scouts have not gone up into the forest, they will come along the valley, this way, to the head of the pass. Now that the sun is down, they will not venture where their scouts have not explored."

As Maera made her way back to watch the cattle, she passed the bands of Swiss moving along the mountain trails where they could not be seen in the darkness, to where the church bell tolled.

The echo of the bell comforted Maera. In that gray church atop the pass she had been christened, to drive out the devil in her. There, some-time, she would walk in her bride's veil. She felt that the voice of the bell was speaking to her, telling her she was not alone on the mountain. She prayed that it would drive Rorik and all his fellows away.

"Mark ye well," said the Genoese, "he is a noble Yngling." And he nudged Weiphart, who was turning the spit at the fire.

"Ach so," muttered Weiphart, blinking into the smoke. "From the land of Jonsson's dale. Like a baron he is, indeed. Will his nobility have white wine with the fowl?"

"It is not like beer," said Rorik the Yngling, "but I will have it."

He chewed the flesh from a chicken's back, tossed away the shell of bones, and wiped his hands politely on the straw where he sat before tak-ing the wine jug.

Rorik had followed his nose among the fires of the *gewaltige Haufen*, the main guard, to the smell of fat fowls sizzling by this fire. A good camp, Rorik thought, where the sentries challenged sharp, and the horse lines were quiet. Never had he seen so many great horses together, fit for draw-ing the heaviest plows. And here the men had good steel shirts, well oiled and cared for. How kindly they greeted him!

"Almost you were too late, Rorik, my sir," said Weiphart, pouring wine into his own steel cap. "Before daylight we advance up. Yes, already have the high sirs given orders."

"Good," nodded Rorik the Yngling. "Good! Then you will have me with you in the battle."

Weiphart and the Genoese breathed hard over their meat. "You will win this battle for us?" asked the Italian crossbowman anxiously.

"I do not say that," replied Rorik modestly, "but no man could stand foot to foot with me in Jonsson's dale."

Conrad the Schwarzreiter looked up at him. "Have you ever," he snarled, "stood in the line of a battle?"

Rorik shook his head. "The messenger of the emperor said in Jonsson's dale that his majesty called, for men broad of shoulder and long of leg. To me he gave a silver thaler. I walked to Cologne, where they said the army was up the river. Pfut, at the river they said it was here, in the mountains of the Swiss. Eight gold florins they will pay me for a battle."

"Eight—gold!" grunted Weiphart.

Rorik the Yngling nodded. He remembered the amount very well. And he had calculated what he could buy with the gold. "Eight they said, and eight it is."

"Dane gold," said Conrad.

Conrad thought that he had never seen a recruit with such broad shoulders and so little wit. "This one," he nodded at Weiphart, "is *doppelsoldner*—frontline-pay man. For an open attack he gets one gold piece and for an assault on fortification, one and a half pieces."

They were all veterans of long campaigns from Spain to Bohemia—the Genoese being in a high-paid class, with the best of the new steel crossbows. They had horses and body armor, while Rorik seemed to have lugged along only the heavy two-handed sword.

"Eight it will be," he said, "for me."

"For using that woodchopper?" Weiphart reached over and gripped the handle of the Dane's long sword.

"Yes," said Rorik.

With a grin Weiphart tried to raise the point off the ground. Using one arm, by straining he could raise it; taking both hands he swung it once in the air, and it sagged down.

"Great Lord of heaven," grunted the *doppelsoldner*, "no one can cut with it."

It seemed to Rorik that this German was disparaging his sword. He took the handle himself, gripping with both hands. He planted his feet and the muscles of his long body tensed. His arms shot up, and the five-foot blade slashed the air over the soldiers' heads, whistling.

At the edge of the firelight two men stopped to look. One wore a cloak with an eagle embroidered on the shoulder, and a silver chain shone under the other's beard. Conrad, who noticed everything, sprang up when he saw them.

"If you have not found one, my sirs," his clipped words came, "I offer, with gladness, Conrad, captain in the Thuringen riders."

"We have not decided," the cloaked man said, watching Rorik. "Who is your Hercules?"

The two were staring at Rorik the Yngling as if at a new breed of war horse, marking his stand and his points, as he sheathed the two-handed sword.

"My sirs," said Conrad, stiff, "it is a Dane from the farmlands who fancies himself the best of us."

"He's the tallest, certainly," observed the officer with the armiger's chain. "Too tall, eh, Strube?"

"A lighthouse has its uses. It can easily be seen at all times."

"But he has as much wit, my sir," Conrad grated, "as your Livonian mare. Less."

"That also has its use." The official of the eagle walked around Rorik, studying him. Suddenly he looked up into his eyes. "So you are a mighty man-at-arms, Dane?"

"True enough," agreed Rorik.

"Would you like to be given armor fit for a noble. Or even—an emperor? From helm to spurs, eh?"

"Well enough," Rorik smiled, pleased, "if it is for the battle."

"It is for the battle."

He of the eagle glanced once at the armiger, who nodded. Then between them they conducted Rorik the Yngling away from the fire, through the lines of the Black Riders to a pavilion that glowed with candles. Young squires who were oiling saddles and cleaning leather sprang up at sight of them. And here, where swords and armor were stacked, the armiger took charge of Rorik.

Not once did he look him in the face. First he tried a hauberk of fine linked steel on the giant Dane. It gleamed as with silver. The boys fitted mail to his legs and tried low boots on his feet until a pair was found to fit. They fastened shoulder pieces etched with gold up against his neck—they clasped a cloak over his shoulders. They even combed out his long hair while he admired his gleaming limbs. The steel mesh, being too small for him, gripped his muscles tight.

"With the padding out, it will do," decided the armiger, and the one named Strube nodded.

They studied the effect and seemed satisfied. Strube hung a gold chain around Rorik's neck, while the armorer fetched a shield with two eagles, black, painted on it, and a half-helm with tiny silver figures and an eagle spreading its wings for a crest. "My sir," said the armorer carefully, "I will bear your shield, of course, but you must take the war helm on your arm. So."

With pleasure Rorik contemplated it. The boys were fastening a belt over his hips.

"You understand," pointed out the one called Strube, "that this is the armor of majesty." He gestured at the pavilion. "You wear now the insignia of empire."

Rorik nodded, hardly understanding, but well content at this kindness.

They laid out some swords for him to look over, asking him to take the one he fancied. Suddenly Rorik stopped, shaking his head. If it was a question of swords, he wanted none but his own. For the first time the two officers looked ill-pleased. Strube said it would never do to carry such a thing—the armorer could not hang it over a horse's side. Rorik explained that he shouldered it.

"Oh, strap it on his back," cried Strube, "and take him along. God's thunder—we have no more time to waste."

When they hung the two-handed sword along his back, the armorer signed to him to hurry and went before him to a pavilion entrance where a knight stood with drawn sword by the standard pole. Within the pavilion, voices hummed with long words—the night advance to surprise the Swiss—the Schwarzreiter maneuver—flanks refused—holding back the charge—

Making nothing of this, Rorik watched the sentry who moved only his eyes. A voice rose over the others: "Have they the mock king?"

Heinrich barked, "Here at command."

Then Heinrich pulled Rorik down to a knee, whispering "Altesse." A tall man, muffled in a robe, stepped out, yawning. And Rorik knew that this was the emperor, who slipped a ring from his finger and pressed it into Rorik's hand.

"Faith," said a drowsy voice, "you have found one as tall as the standard itself, Heinrich."

"At command!"

And the emperor went back to his officers.

Ring in hand, Rorik walked away with the armorer. Beyond the stir of the men-at-arms, the calling of orders by the horse lines, he heard the echo of a distant bell. When the wind blew, the chime came clearly, and he thought of that cowbell. But this was a great, chiming bell. Restlessly, Rorik stirred. "Heinrich, I would like a horse."

"In two hours, my sir—when we advance."

"No, not in two hours—now, Heinrich."

"Why now?"

"To see the girl—the little Maera."

Heinrich grunted. This was not the time, he pointed out, to think about a girl. She would keep well enough, until afterward—when Rorik could do what he pleased. Didn't Rorik understand that now he wore the arms of majesty? He would carry them into the battle, wouldn't he? He would get his eight florins, wouldn't he? Wasn't he content?

And Rorik had to say he was content.

When the armorer hurried off to his duties, he suggested that Rorik drink some wine and stay within sight of the great pavilions. He told off an esquire-at-arms to follow the Dane and see that he did not stray.

When Rorik thought of wine, he thought of his companions at the fire, and he walked over to show himself to them. When men passed him, carrying a torch, they stared at the immense figure holding the crested helm, and they saluted.

Only Conrad sat awake by the embers, still drinking. He lowered the jug when the Dane stepped into the embers' glow, with the small squire behind him. The hilt and wide handguard of the huge sword seemed like a cross behind his bare head.

"Eyes of God," breathed Conrad. "They have done it."

Pleased by the effect on Conrad, Rorik sat down in the straw, examining the gold ring. The ring had a flat jewel that shone, and on the jewel were traced letters that meant nothing to him because he could not read. But when Conrad inspected the ring, he interpreted the letters. Gloria.

"Is that a sign?" asked Rorik, curiously.

"A kind of sign," said Conrad, pondering, "to many men. Do you know what they have made of you?"

Rorik shook his head. Truly, something in this puzzled him.

"They have made you the mock king."

"How, the mock king?"

The words sounded both pleasant and ominous to the Dane. Giving him the jug, Conrad explained, low-voiced. In an hour Rorik would be mounted on a high horse and placed at the head of the *gewaltige Haufen*. With the half-helm on his head, he would appear to be the emperor himself to all those who were not close to him, or in on the secret. During the fighting, the enemy would drive at the one who seemed to be emperor, to kill him. Probably they would reach him and kill him. But the real emperor, in plain dress, would be directing the battle elsewhere, unharmed.

"Seven to one," said Conrad softly, "you will turn up your toes this morning."

Rorik thought about that.

The eyes of the Schwarzreiter searched beyond the fire glow, where the squire, seeing Rorik seated, loitered carelessly. Groups of men were in motion already, toward the head of the valley, although they carried no torches and no trumpets had sounded. He knew the step of the Italian mercenaries. He listened to the movement at his own horse lines, where the sergeants called and cursed. The Black Riders would go up with the advance, with the Genoese covering them. His troop mates would be calling for him in a few minutes.

"Don't let them make a fool of you, Sir Rorik," he whispered, straining his ears. "What's the sense of becoming chopped meat—with your face bashed in, belike?"

"Mine?"

"Yours. Look—I know the horses of our troop. We can edge over to the lines now, and get two of the best. We can rein down the valley. Before full light we can be four leagues away. Safe enough. We can pass this ring and stuff to the usurers, and live like lords. We can pick over the girls, Rorik."

"Where?"

"Take our choice—Basle, Munich, Paris—"

Reaching out, Rorik took back his ring, while Conrad still breathed words. Rorik had no wish to go to Paris. He wanted to stay here in the valley. Conrad changed his tone:

"Rorik my sir, you've never felt your bones broken in as I have. The Swiss poleaxes can cut the head from a horse—"

He checked at a quick step near him. A voice called, "Thuringen troop in the saddle, Conrad."

The Black Rider got up, with his gun. "At once!" The step went on. "Quick, Rorik—we can get away."

Rorik shook his head. For an instant Conrad stared at him, then swung off toward the horses. Steel clanked as men swung themselves into the saddle; troop commanders called as they led off their men. Rorik did not want to run off from this. They had made him like a king. He would be the first in the battle. And if he left them, where would he get his eight florins? Conrad, with all his cleverness, had not thought of that.

With the sun full on the valley, Rorik the Yngling was riding up in majesty, with the battle standard swaying in the wind behind him, and Heinrich carrying his shield beside him and the squire leading another horse. Rorik was riding on a great bay charger, his sword strapped fast to him, and the helm on his head agleam with silver.

Ranks of men-at-arms paced beside him, their spears rising like a forest of young, slender trees. Thousands of riders moved up the valley, toward the pass where they could see the spire of a church.

It seemed to Rorik that these marching ranks were fine, and surely he was the first of them. He could see nothing of the real emperor, although he heard the fanfare of trumpets blowing commands. Heinrich, he noticed, listened closely to the notes of the trumpets, but watched the narrowing fringe of pines on either side.

"Tell us, Heinrich," he said, "what to do."

"Nothing," muttered the armorer, "but what you are doing—sit in the saddle."

This suited Rorik, but he had another question to ask: "Heinrich, why do we go up this valley?"

"By command."

Rorik nodded. "But for what?"

"To break the infantry of the Swiss cantons."

The armorer answered with half his mind, because the other half was listening to a faint popping and crackling somewhere ahead. So, the Swiss were making their stand in front of the pass.

For a while Rorik thought about it. "But why is there war with the Swiss?"

In the mountains, Heinrich explained, the Swiss refused to accept the sovereignty of the new Reich. They were, he said, commoners having no king. They had no generals. They had only infantry. They called themselves free men of the cantons. They were stubborn, meeting together like a mob, refusing allegiance to the German emperor whose sovereignty in this new plan of the Holy Roman Empire would dominate from Frankfurt over the continent, from sea to sea.

"They rolled down rocks on Maximilian's array of knights," Heinrich grunted. "They broke back the lancers of His Grace of Burgundy, when those dismounted to fight on foot. But no infantry can stand against the cavalry of the Reich."

Rorik was looking up the mountainside, where a rock summit jutted beneath a snow peak. Barely he could make out the patch of Maera's potato field.

"Is that the battle," he asked, lifting his steel headgear to let the air cool his skull, "going on ahead of us, where the noise is?"

Laughing, Heinrich explained that was only their advance, skirmishing with the Swiss, to bring the Swiss into action. Undoubtedly the Swiss would charge with their main onset from the screen of pines here, on one flank. So thought the sir commanders of the Reich's army. And then the Swiss would be charged by all the horse of the *gewaltige Haufen*, held back in readiness for just such a maneuver—

"But still, Heinrich, I do not see any fighting."

It was noon and Rorik was tired, before he saw it, while the hot sun made him sweat in his steel mesh and the apple orchards around him smelled fragrant with the heat. Stone walls hemmed in the peasants' fields here, and the heavy German chargers labored over plowed land.

Through these trees Rorik could watch a line of Swiss pikemen pressing down the valley with the sun flickering on the steel of their pikeheads. Behind them another brown line carried long axes, coming on slowly, keeping step without trumpets, climbing over the stones. Those lines seemed small in the face of the German regiments now crowding into the narrowing valley.

"Why," muttered Heinrich, "why, they come here—they make no maneuver."

In front of the brown ranks, the Schwarzreiter wheeled in troops, snapping off their pistols when they were close to the Swiss. Bands of Italian crossbowmen sifted back through the trees, fast.

"Bad ground," Heinrich observed. "But now comes our charge—ah, so!"

Suddenly—hearing a call from the trumpets—he caught the rein of Rorik's horse, leading it to a knoll where the figure of the mock king could be seen above the apple trees. Past that knoll the German cavalry surged, with lances down, sweeping up the disordered Italians, forcing the Black Riders off to the flanks.

Through the orchards the packed ranks of horsemen edged around the trees, plunging over the low stone fences. The horses, tired and heavily weighted, slowed in the plowed land.

The Swiss did not stop. The Swiss came to meet the cavalry, closing together. Against those steel pikes, longer than their lances, the German horses piled up, rearing, the first ranks forced into a mass by pressure from the rear. Into the crush of riders the Swiss poleaxes beat like flails. Steel clanged and roared as if a thousand hammers were beating forges.

"Good Lord!" breathed Heinrich.

He heard the trumpets calling to the horsemen to re-form and charge.

Crowded regiments tried to get clear of the press. The steel of the Swiss flashed at their heels. The Swiss were shouting now, digging their feet into the plowed ground, slashing down everything in front of them. They were coming up the knoll where the mock king waited by the standard.

Rorik heard the armorer calling, "Go back—"

"No," said Rorik the Yngling, "now we can fight."

Swinging down from his charger, he pulled clear the two-handed sword. He stepped out toward the Swiss who shifted their pikes lower. He planted his feet, and his heavy sword drove down the pikes. Heinrich held the great shield in front of Rorik, and he elbowed the shield away for arm room. He felt swordsmen pressing against his right shoulder then the steel pike-heads pushed them back.

Rorik did not feel tired now. His arms threshed, swinging the two-handed sword at the bearded men stepping closer. Foot to foot. Something clanged against his headgear and it flew off. He could see better to strike now.

A splintered pike shaft jammed into his shoulder, and he leaned to one side to free himself. A two-foot ax blade ripped the steel rings down his arm. "Ho," he roared, "a good one, that."

Never had he seen so many honest bearded faces in front of his sword. His heavy sword smashed them back, and Heinrich flung up the shield to catch the swing of a poleax. Another blade came down, and Heinrich fell on the stone wall.

Steel struck at Rorik from the side, and he stepped back against the stones of a well. Turning, his long arms threshing, he kept a space clear about him. "Stand up to them, mates!" he shouted, his feet gripping the earth. But he was alone now on the knoll.

The broken cavalry troops, reining back past the knoll, saw this figure in imperial armor fighting on foot. They went on back, knowing that this was a mock king, meant to draw the enemy's attack.

Conrad, getting clear of the orchards at last, stopped to watch and nurse a broken arm bone. He saw the Swiss close in around Rorik, while the tall figure climbed up higher on the stones. The standard was gone and Rorik was alone.

"What if he had been the king?" Conrad wondered, watching until the man on the stones went down, and the Swiss came on over the mound.

And Conrad turned his horse's head. He had kept within sight of a group of officers around a man in plain armor, with four trumpets behind them. They were riding now down the valley, in silence, away from the mountains.

Hard cobbles pressed against Rorik's neck, and a church bell clanged above him. His shoulders ached and a bone's end grated in his hip. Faces of women and bearded men looked down at him and passed on. Blood caked the fingers of a hand when he looked at it, and Rorik thought he was lying here like a calf in the marketplace for the Swiss to stare at. Then one woman did not go away, and he recognized Maera.

Now, he thought, she sees nothing good in me. His steel mesh was ripped, his cloak a rag around one arm, and he could not move.

"Well," he said, "I tried to come back to the hut to show you, but I could not."

She shook her head, staring at him, trying to wipe the blood from his hand. Then Rorik remembered. He pulled the ring from his little finger and gave it to her. She held back from taking it, her eyes startled.

"Girl," said Rorik the Yngling, "even if I am not a soldier, and cannot hold my ground, I can make you a gift. Somehow," he went on, shamed, "I like you."

He could feel her hair brush against his face, and it was pleasant to have her bending over him, "What does it say?" she whispered, looking at the letters inscribed on the jewel. Gloria.

"That I do not know," said Rorik, who could not read. "That is for you to tell me."

Tight she gripped the gold ring, closing her eyes.

"My father says," she whispered, "there was no one like you, in the valley. So I am proud, and I will take your ring and be your wife."

Rorik looked up at the bell tower, to think about this. He had wanted to be first in the battle, to get his gold, and perhaps a girl. Maera had arranged matters in a way of her own, and he found that he liked it.

"They can ring their bells," he agreed. "For Rorik the Yngling will stay in these mountains."

The Faring Forth

The army of Jerusalem was retreating. For a month it had been fighting, without luck. It was a small army, and there was no other to defend Jerusalem against the advances of the Mohammedan powers in this Year of the Lord 1107.

Horses wearied by a forced march of twelve miles past the hills of Bethlehem, the column moved through a stifling defile of red rock, in a haze of dust. The men rode in sullen silence, aching under the weight of their chain armor—six thousand of them. Somewhere, back in the gorge, the caliph's host, thirty thousand strong, followed in pursuit.

Few lances rose through the dust. Most of them had been broken or thrown away, with the saddlebags and shields. The great banner of Baldwin, the king, was furled and carried between two Knights of the Hospital, and Baldwin himself lay gaunt and fever-wracked in a horse litter with a cloak hanging over him to keep the sun from his head. Only the gilt cross of the patriarch was still uplifted.

> *O give him a high, swift horse—*
> *God grant that he ride well!*

A hoarse voice chanted the words, and men turned their heads to stare or curse. Sweat-soaked saddles creaked, and the dull clank-clonk of sword sheath against iron shield kept time to the thudding trot of the heavy chargers.

> *Belt him, and give him a sword to wear,*
> *And call him a cavalier!*

Ahead of them—two leagues more of the dust and sun glare—stood the lofty wall and the great towers of Jerusalem. There they could dismount and throw themselves down in the shade and sleep. And some of them could forget their wounds. Two leagues more.

They had left their dead behind them, and the wounded who could not ride. They were thin and patient—these men of arms who had come overseas to defend the Sepulcher of Christ. They were the foreign legion, the host of Outre-mer. Tall Normans with a restless eye for plunder; red-bearded Rhinelanders; heavy, drowsy Saxons; placid fighters from the clay marshes of Flanders; wanderers from England; and Vikings of the dragon ships, who followed the wars as gulls follow sails at sea. Slender youths in the once-white surcoats of the Hospital, who had once gazed longingly at the pennants of the older knights; gray-headed swordsmen who had managed somehow to live through the First Crusade. Iron men, they were called.

Then the rock walls opened out. The hills on either side sank to low swales. The head of the crusaders' column came out into a shallow valley and halted. Staring into a blinding sun, the leaders shouted hoarsely.

"Come up, ye men of the Cross!"

A low ridge on the left, a rambling mud village and orchard, was held by a mass of Moslems—fresh warriors they had not met before. They could not see clearly through sweat-smarting eyes, but the roar that came from the ridge was like the thunder of a long wave.

"*Allah-akbar*—Allah is greatest."

Now, the column had expected to dismount within Jerusalem's walls before sunset, and it was weary. Crowded in the gut of the defile, it began to be afraid—not of blows and the hurt of dying, but of being cut off. The men could not see what was happening, but whispered tidings ran back from the head of the column—whispers that ten thousand Arabs had come over from Damascus and cut them off. That a trap had been set for them and baited, and the army of the caliph was hastening after them to close the trap.

A Norman duke in the advance looked along the empty road through the quivering air of the valley bed, thought of the column taken in flank by the onset of these new, uncounted foes, reflected that the crusaders, themselves, could not form for a charge in the defile—and led the way at a gallop to the ridge on the right, opposite the Arabs, who shouted insults but made no attempt to charge.

Some of the desert swordsmen, splendidly mounted, galloped down to the road and taunted the crusaders to come down to single combat. But

the six thousand had no heart for that. They dismounted and stood by
their spent horses and looked around them. They saw a network of gullies
behind them—rock ridges overgrown thinly with thorn and gray tamarisk. No way to get through there. They would have to go back to the road.
They were out of the defile but not out of the trap, and they were weary
men standing by spent horses.

"Look, ye men of Outre-mer," laughed the redheaded duke who had
led them hither. "Here is the jousting ground and yonder are the lads who
will break a few swords with us." And he whispered to himself, "By the
life of God, the way out of the lists is narrow."

At the far end of the valley the road entered a gully again. To gain the
road to Jerusalem, they would have to deal first with the mass of horsemen opposite, only a quarter-mile away. Evidently the Arabs were waiting for the pursuing host of the caliph to come up through the defile the
crusaders had just left and close the trap.

Baldwin, the king, looked around him and slid from his litter, getting
to his feet with an effort, for his right hip was stiff with dried blood.

"We will go together, messires!" He coughed, and then his voice rang
out clear. "By God's aid we will mount and charge yonder men and drive
them and so—fare forward again."

He staggered, as fresh blood rushed from the wound in his groin; his
knees bent and his knights caught him and laid him back in the litter,
unconscious. Baldwin had said the thing that must be done—to drive the
Arabs away before the caliph's men came up. But Baldwin could not lead
a charge.

The princes and captains gathered together where the standard had
been lifted and argued in curt whispers. They could not rouse the men,
who had seen Baldwin fall and felt sure that this was an omen of evil.

The red duke went to the bearded patriarch, who had girded a sword
over his bishop's robe.

"Spur them on, my lord," quoth he, "or these, thy sheep, will be fanged
by yonder wolves."

"Let them rest," the man of the church responded, "for they are weary,
methinks. And I will pray that aid may be given us."

So he knelt by the uplifted cross, and the barons perforce knelt with
him, while the sun dropped lower and the raucous shouting of the Arabs
dinned into their ears. But the men in the ranks knew that no aid could
reach them, and time was passing.

And then a miracle happened.

The summons to the crusade had not reached the far Northland, because no tidings came to that snowy country where the fire of the furnace of the gods filled the winter sky of nights. Beyond the Russian land it was, and beyond the last bishop's house of Finland. And this was the roving place of Skol, the pagan.

A manslayer and a troublemaker he was. Six feet and half a foot he stood, his heavy shoulders sagging forward. He had the corded arms of the forest dweller, and the broad and quiet face of a child. His blue eyes, half closed, seemed asleep when he was not fighting. Red was his skin from long ale drinking, and yellow as bright gold his curling beard and plaited hair.

On his skis he wandered from one lord's hall to another, in his leg wrappings of sable fur, and deerskin shirt studded thick with round iron knobs, and over that his white reindeer cloak. He carried a bundle slung to his ax.

Skol had one weapon and one skill. His battle-ax was four feet long, with a ball of iron at the butt of the shaft, to keep his hand from slipping when blood ran down it. The head of the ax had two parts to it: an iron hammer like a blacksmith's hammer, at the back, to smash armor, and a curving blade to hew through bone and flesh. In Skol's long arm, the sweep of that ax head could slice a man's body through. That was his skill, and he lived by it—by this power of manslaying.

His fathers had been Vikings, men of the dragon ships, but Skol followed the wars of the Northmen on land. Many were the gold arm rings given him by earls and princes, whom he had served as liege man. And no man said of him that he was a rear ranker, because he would take his stand where the blows fell hardest, his ax shearing a circle about him. When he passed his word, he held to his word.

But the women had ill to say of him, for his long ax had sent many a husbandman to the stone cairns, and he had left many a house with a burning roof. Skol the Manslayer, they called him. A rover, a wrongdoer. And they said that he would not find his own death.

Because he had no friends except the ale drinkers of a night—most men shunned him otherwise—and because he was alone in his wandering without talk to pass the hours, Skol brooded at times about one thing. He had no rightful liege lord of his own. No one who would sit by him and summon the neighbors to a high tide, if he should happen to be dying.

That was the one hour when a man ought not to be alone. To lie in darkness, without bright torches, or the chant of minstrels, or fellows to sit by with their ale and listen to what words he might care to say. True, Skol was no talker. But in the long silences of his wanderings, he fancied that he would like some little conversation in the hour of his faring forth from life. A bit of celebration that the ancient men and the minstrels would remember him by. That was his hankering, until the morning when he met Daimen the Finn on the forest path—a little man, a minstrel, with his fiddle in a sealskin bag on one shoulder and a broad scarlet cross upon the other.

Skol had never seen a cross worn like that before, and when he had stopped the Finn he asked what sign it was.

"'Tis the sign and seal of an oath I have taken," said the minstrel. "And by reason of it I am faring forth to a new land, by a long road."

And Skol would have passed on, had not Daimen been afraid of the great axman.

"Hail, ax clasher," he said again. "Has the word come to you that there is a truce here in this land, and an end of quarreling?"

"That would be a strange thing," Skol remarked.

"Well, they are making the truce, and the weapon men are going out to take the Cross."

Skol put down his bundle in the snow and leaned on the pommel of his ax. So, here were tidings.

"What cross?" he asked.

"This—"

Daimen pointed to his shoulder, and when Skol remained silent, he explained how everywhere the priests were summoning men to join together in one army and to march to a place called Jerusalem, where was the Sepulcher of the Son of God, and to free this from the enemies of God who had taken possession of it. Followers of Mahound and Anti-Christ these enemies were. The quarrel was a good quarrel, Daimen said, and a man would be well rewarded. Past all counting, the priests had said. So he had taken the oath to go and they had given him that fine red cross—velvet, sewn with silver thread.

"Who is the leader of this host—he who will hire the liege men, and pay what is owing at the end of their service?"

"Well, ax clasher, every lord will look after his own followers, and as to pay, I suppose it will be as it always is. But they do say that this new

host will be led by One who is invisible, and *he* will see that every jack-
man gets a just share of the spoilings and sackings."

All this bewildered the manslayer, who could think of only one thing at
a time; but it stirred his curiosity, and he turned back to go with Daimen
to the next hamlet on the road. And after an hour he asked if it were true
that the weapon men were faring forth to this new war.

Daimen said it was indeed true. For months and years they had been
taking to their weapons, in Flanders and Northman-land. Nay, even new
married women were going, and old wives packing the carts to take to the
long road; priests were arming, and children begging to go.

"Jerusalem," Skol mused, fingering his beard. "That would be far off,
like."

Daimen thought it was farther, even, than Russia; but he had a good
pair of skis, and he had been told to keep due south, to find it.

When they stuck their skis in the snow by the tavern and tramped
through the stable yard to eat supper, Skol gripped the minstrel's arm
with iron fingers.

"Do you think, belike, these priests would make me a cross if I took
the oath to serve this new god of battles?" He thrust his hands in his belt
and nodded slowly. "I would like well to see this weapon drawing."

The priests of the hamlet made no objection. But they made Skol kneel before them and place his hands together and swear that he would journey
on to Jerusalem, and not turn back for any reason whatever until he had
reached his destination. They were glad then, because Skol had caused
many deaths in the land, and the women rejoiced to be rid of him. Only
Daimen was doubtful at first, about his new companion of the road.

"See you, ax clasher," he remarked, "there is another agreement to be
kept. Until you have purged yourself of sin in the blood of the paynim,
you are not to lift weapon or hand against a fellow Christian—like myself? Is that also agreed?"

Skol's drowsy blue eyes looked down on the little minstrel.

"It has never happened," he said slowly, "that I raised hand against a
comrade."

So they set out together with their skis upon the forest road that ran
south.

They did not find Jerusalem that winter, or that spring. Nor did they find
the roads filled with marching men. They did get out of the forests, and

summer overtook and passed them in cleared land where the log churches
had devils painted on their doors and the women stacking hay stared at
the bright ox horns on Skol's helmet. Skol could not speak the language
of these people, but the Finn had a way with his tongue, especially when
he talked to women, and he explained to Skol that they could not go on.

"South of here is the open steppe, where the pagan hordes wander,
aye, and Satan grazes his horses. They have never heard of Jerusalem in
this place."

"Did she tell you how we can go around the steppes," the manslayer
asked, "this black-browed chit who walks with you after vespers?"

Daimen looked uncomfortable. It was becoming clear to him that they
would have trouble in finding a road that led to Jerusalem. And it was
pleasant to be with this Russian girl who had round arms and strong, full
lips that smiled at him in the twilight.

"I will ask," he assented. "But it will take time and great skill with
words to find out all we must know."

So Skol waited at a crossroads ale shop, sometimes selling a gold arm-
band to pay for his ale and sometimes helping to get the grain in from the
fields. Daimen was his voice, and he could not go on without the minstrel, even if he had wanted to leave him. But after the snow came again
Daimen appeared suddenly at the tavern—the woman's tongue had grown
too sharp for him—with tidings.

"A merchant's sledge train is setting out with furs, to go to the west,"
he said. "And they will take you for a weapon man in the guard. We must
make haste, because there in the west we will find out more about Jerusalem."

But it was a year before they could leave the service of the merchants,
and the people who met them on the roads scowled at them, not understanding their questions. All they could learn was that at the edge of the
sea to the south was the great city, toward which all travelers went. And
thither they begged and fought their way, having no more gold left, through
endless hills. Daimen's blue cloak was stained and faded, and he no longer tried to tune up his fiddle at night. The men here had dark faces and
went barefoot or in saddles, except the nobles, who galloped past or stood
in chariots. The crowds became greater on the road as the two crusaders
went farther south.

The sun blazed overhead, and brown-robed pilgrims went swinging
by. Of them Daimen asked one word, "Jerusalem?" And they turned and

pointed to the south. Until the wanderers saw from the summit of a hill
a mighty white wall with square towers, and beyond the wall the gleam
of sunlight on gilded domes. White walls and green trees, and the deep
blue of the sea beyond.

"Well, the priests did not lie!" cried Daimen.

They found it a rich city indeed, with strings of laden mules passing
through the gate, under the eyes of strange guards in gilded breastplates
and shining silver helmets. Skol stopped to stare at them, but Daimen
pulled him on, and they wandered through alleys, past the stairs of marble churches, and a column of carved marble with a rearing horse atop it,
and a bearded king on the horse. But it seemed to Skol strange that the
king had nothing on him but a kind of long shirt, and no saddle beneath
him. Daimen pulled him along until they sniffed the damp reek of wine,
up from a cellar shop.

"Come," cried the little minstrel, "it hath been a long road, this, and
they will not grudge a tankard of wine to crusaders, although we have no
coins or gear to pay for it."

They sat on stools in the cool gloom of the shop, and pointed at an open
cask, and a fat man with an oiled beard bowed to them and hastened to
bring two jugs. They drank more, and Daimen said it was well they had
come to Jerusalem at last. When the tavern keeper held out his hand, the
minstrel pointed to the cross on his shoulder, and the oiled beard spat out
harsh words. The tavern keeper waddled out of the shop and came back
with a tall and glittering figure following him—a weapon man wearing
over one shoulder a red cloak, and carrying in his free hand a short ivory
baton. Daimen had never seen such a splendid man, even a prince, before;
but Skol looked up frowning.

The stranger spoke words they knew.

"Hail, ye far-faring fellows! This Greek is saying ye have robbed
him."

And the prince sat down between them and looked into the jugs. They
were empty.

"What is this?" said he.

Daimen's tongue was loosened, now that someone listened who understood his words, and he told the tale of his crusade, until the stranger, a man
of mild manner, motioned to the tavern keeper to bring more wine.

"Have done," he cried. "Have done, little man. 'Tis a whine and a plaint
I have heard overmuch. Sure it is that Jerusalem was beset and captured

by the crusaders years ago. And now that the weapon smiting is at an end,
every spindle shanks weaned of woman is marching on Jerusalem. When
the fighting was ahead, they were all for being pilgrims, too holy to fight;
and now, by Thor's thunder, they are all cross-bearers, ready to eat and
drink their way to the holy city."

"Well, we're here," said Daimen after awhile.

The stranger paid the Greek and spread his long legs before him, his
hand on his hip.

"And where," he asked, "is that?"

"Jerusalem, and a fair—"

"Some call this Byzantium, and some call it Constantinople, which is
to say the city of Constantine; but it was never Jerusalem, for that is in
the country of the Turks, far to the south."

Daimen stared.

"But this is what we looked to find—a queen of a city, with gold in its
walls and jewels to be picked up—"

"'Tis so, little man. I am from Dane-mark, and I have served the Emperor of Byzantium eight years, and every month now eight gold *byzants*
are paid into my hand, with a largesse for hazardous fighting, and tribute from the shopkeepers like this dog-sired Greek, and a gift now and
then from the slavers. The women are the finest of the world, and when
my service is done I'll be given land in Asia, with slaves to till it, and the
rank of centurion of the mercenaries."

Then Skol spoke.

"'Tis not Jerusalem."

"Better for thee, ax wielder." The strange officer smote his hip. "Six
thousand Northmen are in the emperor's pay, and we have a place—in
my company—for a man of weapons, who can wield steel, shoot a shaft,
and back a horse."

Skol considered all this. It was his skill, to do this.

And he stayed. Six months later Daimen had a new cloak, and he had learned
the names of the wines and the places where the heaven-descended emperor held weekly games and beast slayings for the multitudes; he knew
the luckiest chariot racers and the best horses of the hippodrome. But then
he went home one evening to Skol's barracks and found the manslayer
clad again in his old leather and dull steel cap.

"Have the mercenaries disbanded?" he asked. "Are you dismissed from the service?"

"Nay," said Skol. "I have enough silver money now to buy passage in a galley. We will sail to the Holy Land this night, and the ship will not lose its way as we did."

"Are you mad, ax clasher?" cried the minstrel. "Such a fine figure as you were, a decurion of the ax bearers! Jerusalem was captured long since—are there not pagans enough in Byzantium to give drink to your thirsty steel?"

Skol shook his head, thinking of one thing at a time.

"There is an oath between us," he responded, "that we should fare forth and not turn back from Jerusalem."

"An oath!" But the minstrel looked long at his comrade, for by now he had come to know Skol's moods. "Is your mind settled upon that?"

"Aye."

Daimen sat down, fingering his new red cape. Long he brooded, and began to rock back and forth upon the stool. At times he had the foresight upon him, and this was such a time.

"That will not be good! That will be a road to sorrow, and a breaking of shields, and a sating of wolves upon the bodies of men."

But he went, after awhile, to look for the stained blue cloak with the crusader's cross.

When the afternoon sun beat down upon them, they stopped to sit in the shadow of a broken wall where weeds grew among great stones. They were passing through a half-ruined place in the foothills. Sweat stung their eyes and the heat was like a blanket that could not be pushed off.

They slaked their throats with wine from Daimen's stone jug and chewed at pieces of the bread and shreds of garlic that they had brought from the seacoast, and they listened to the clanging of bells. Sheep jostled past them in the dust. Through the dust women hastened with covered heads. Skol's drowsy eyes noticed the dome of an old church made of square stones, and beyond it a height of black rock. Beyond, he saw only bare ridges and green patches of olive groves.

He was sleeping when a voice roused him.

"I would relish some of the garlic, my sons."

A pockmarked priest, a little father of the Russian land, had stopped in front of them. A man, Skol observed, with lean, starved flesh and a dirty robe. Daimen handed up some of the garlic stalks.

"'Tis a long day since we have heard a word we knew," he said. "What is this ringing of bells here?"

"More sorrow!" The yellow teeth of the bearded Russian bit into the garlic greedily. "They are praying for the armed host."

"For what?" Skol asked, sitting up.

"For the army of Jerusalem."

The priest swallowed and would have gone on, but the manslayer rose, and laid hand upon his shoulder.

"Where will we find these armed men?"

The priest pointed behind him, along the street.

"Go through that gate and follow the road for two or three leagues. God knows if you will find them." And he padded off hastily.

Skol leaned on his ax and reflected.

"I am thinking that the weapon men of Jerusalem have fared forth, and it may well be that they are coming hither to raid this place. However it may be, we are near, and we will join them."

The minstrel followed and grumbled because Skol had had a nap and he had not slept at all. He grumbled more when the heat of the clay valley rose into their faces, and he pointed out that not even the cattle herds were astir in that hour. The doors of the hamlets were deserted, and so was the road that wound through the rocky swales.

The road led them out into the barrens, where the pastures and the villages ended, and they walked in silence through narrow gullies until they plodded up a rise and stopped to look at what lay before them.

An open valley, the slopes rising on either hand like an amphitheater. The empty road running through the pit of this amphitheater to the shadowy entrance of another defile at the far end. Daimen thought it was like the great stadium of Byzantium where the emperor held his games. Only the heights of this valley were full of armed men. To his left he saw lines of men in dull armor standing by horses, some of them kneeling around a high, gilt cross—Christians, they must be.

To his right, among thickets and huts, were massed horsemen he had never seen before—bearded men in cloaks of all colors, wearing turbans and glittering helmets. He tried to count them and gave it up, because he could not count over twenty and there were hundreds of twenties yonder. The faint roar of their restlessness was like the surging of surf against a shore. Skol put down his bundle between two rocks and stood up to tighten his belt and swing the long ax once around his head.

"Well," Daimen said then, "we have come in time for a battle."

Skol began to walk down the road into the valley. He was going to join the men under the cross, up yonder; but the slope near him was covered with brush and it would be easier to climb from the bed of the valley. So he went down the road. He strode along swiftly, because he knew that once those horsemen were in motion a man on foot would have trouble getting to where he could strike a blow. But the men up there made no move toward their horses, although several Moslem riders were down on the midway point of the road, jeering at them.

Then the jeering stopped. The three Arabs had seen Skol and Daimen, and in a moment one of them urged his horse toward the wanderers. He could make out the crosses on their mantles, and he thirsted for the honor that came to a follower of Allah who slew the first infidel in a battle. Moreover the fall of the tall Christian with the horned helmet would be an omen—a sign of victory for the banners of Islam and doom for the crusaders.

"Come into the brush!" cried Daimen, who had already leaped nimbly up the bank from the road.

But Skol's blue eyes, no longer drowsy, gleamed with fierce exultation.

"By Thor's thunder!" he growled. "I have not walked for two years to turn my rump to the first foeman. Stay there, little man, for this road is no place for the like of you."

While he spoke he lifted high the iron shield on his left arm, and his right hand gripped the long ax shaft halfway to the head. The oncoming rider had challenged him, and never had the manslayer held back from a challenge. Daimen shivered, and the Arab came on at a gallop, his scimitar swinging by his right knee, his small round shield well out on his rein arm.

Once the Moslem shouted, kneed his horse to the left and leaned over to slash down with his scimitar. Beneath the flashing arc of steel, Skol flung up both arms.

The scimitar clanged against his iron shield. But the long point of the great ax came up inside the Arab's shield and caught the man beneath the beard. He rose in his stirrups as a stricken deer starts up, and the giant Northman staggered, holding to the ax shaft with both hands.

The horse ran on with an empty saddle, and the quivering body of the Arab dangled from the ax point that had pierced to the bones of his head. Before Skol laid it down, all life had left the body.

"Ha!" roared the Northman, drawing free his weapon carefully and wiping each hand in turn on his hip.

Daimen cried a warning, but the manslayer was watching the other two Moslems who reined toward him, scattering dust and stones in the haste of desert clansmen to avenge a death. They came together, steel swirling over their hooded heads, as merciless as striking wolves, and no single man could have stood his ground in the road before them.

Skol did not. He swung his ax slowly about his head from left to right, his knees bent until he could have struck the foam-flecked muzzle of a horse. Then he leaped to the bank at the left of the road. But as he leaped he whirled and struck, the ax extended in his long arms.

The hammer head brushed aside the sword of the nearer horseman, crushed in the light leather shield, and crashed into the man's face. And the Arab rolled over the horse's tail with his skull shattered.

"Allah!" cried the other, reining in and wheeling his horse swiftly. And swiftly he slashed with his scimitar.

Yet the manslayer was watching the blow. Skol's blue eyes were cold, his breathing unhurried as the sweep of his great arms when he stepped down into the road again. This was his skill, this weapon play. He caught the stroke of the scimitar upon the curved ax head, and the thin steel blade snapped with a sound like the breaking of ice.

The Moslem flung himself to the side of his saddle and pulled his horse away, but the ax reached after him with a twisting motion. The watchers on the hillsides—and thousands were watching now—saw him ride back a little way, apparently unhurt, while Skol looked after him. Then the rider wavered and slid to the ground, with one side of his groin torn out.

A cry rose from the Moslem ranks, and was echoed by a deep-throated shout from across the valley. Three horsemen had gone down under three blows.

"Come back," cried Daimen. "Is it mad ye are?"

Skol was not mad, but the mist of fighting was upon him. His own song was in his ears, and *that* was a song of the breaking of sword blades and the clashing of shields. No more foemen remained on the road, but others sat their horses up the hill. Skol shouldered his ax and went up to them, singing. Daimen stumbled after him.

For a moment the valley was silent except for the chanting of the giant. Then a score of Arabs rode at him. And the six thousand crusaders climbed into their saddles. The cross of the patriarch was lifted. No horns

blared and no leaders cried them on; in silence they broke from a trot into
a gallop, gripping sword and spear. They had seen one man with the cross
on his shoulder marching against an armed host. They had been desperate before, but now they were ashamed.

The charge rolled across the valley and roared as it came.

"Christ and the Sepulcher!"

Eleven thousand Moslems flung themselves against that charge. And
they were beaten back by the long swords of the crusaders. The cross wavered, and then went up to the crest of the Arabs' hill; then the mailed
host wheeled and charged back again, and broke up into fiercely smiting
groups that sheared through the throngs of the desert men. Still the crusaders pressed on, and the Moslems scattered and rode off, their green
banners merging into the sunset.

Daimen, watching from the nest of rocks where he had taken refuge,
had been able to see Skol for a time, when the twenty horsemen first closed
around the giant Northman; he saw Skol's ax rise and fall, and come up
red in a new place, as the manslayer leaped, twisting himself among his
foes. A horse reared there, and a hooded head flew from its body. Then the
rush of the Arab charge swept over the spot.

And Daimen was running toward it, through the last ruck of the fighting, when he heard horns blaring. The crusaders were trotting into ranks
on the hillside about him. But they did not wait for the ranks to be formed.
Down in the twilight of the defile they had left that afternoon resounded
a clamor of cymbals and kettledrums. And in the valley road appeared
the first groups of the caliph's army that had pursued them hither and had
hastened forward, hearing the tumult of battle.

The men of Outre-mer looked, and put spurs to their jaded horses. It
was a mad kind of charge that slid and stumbled and plunged down upon
the head of the caliph's column. The bewildered Moslems were caught
standing, and were crushed by the flailing swords—driven back upon their
fellows in the ravine, lashed into headlong flight. Then darkness, lighted
by torches where the crusaders sought for their wounded.

The red duke caught Daimen by the shoulder and blew the blood clots
from his bearded lips.

"By God's grace, find me that mate of thine—he who showed the way
to us this day."

Bells tolled and chimed, ringing out a lament for the fallen and exultation in the victory; light streamed from the doors of the churches, al-

though the hour was near dawn. The voices of men chanted a *Te Deum*, "We praise Thee, O Lord—"

The long hall of the hospital of Jerusalem was filled with laymen and warriors bearing candles and lanterns among the dead. On the bed by the fireplace lay Skol, his leather and iron cut off his body, and the great slashes bandaged. A white linen sheet was thrown over his body, and his sweat-matted head was propped on a soft velvet pillow.

"Skol," cried Daimen, "this is Jerusalem that we passed through without knowing it."

The blue eyes turned toward the minstrel, and Skol made a sign that he understood. A dozen knights—he knew them by the little shields in their belts and by their spurs—were sitting around the bed, drinking wine. They looked at Skol when they spoke, and one of them lifted a tankard. The same Russian priest who had spoken to him that afternoon was coming toward the bed slowly, and his brown robe was covered by cloth of silver and gold. More priests followed him with lighted candles, bearing something covered with a white cloth. They said things in Latin, and the knights stood up.

The priests even gave Skol a little wine from a silver cup and a small piece of bread. When they went away, Skol turned his head. Two tall candles had been placed a little behind his head, one on each side.

He looked at them, and at the men sitting by him. He listened to the distant chiming of bells and chanting, and his clotted beard wrinkled in a smile.

"'Tis a good place," he whispered, "a good place, and a fine sitting-by for my dying. A man cannot ask more than that."

Secret of Victory

He'd been listening to us quietly, there across the aisle in the ancient restaurant car of the Paris express. I figured him to be a strictly average retired Frenchman, with the usual red ribbon on the lapel of his neat black coat, and his white hair parted dead center, listening in on two foreign officers grousing about their jobs with NATO, which called for setting up military installations in a country like France that didn't seem to want them.

This was almost two years ago—June of '51—when General Eisenhower was beginning to build a defense around and about, setting up skeleton divisions against a swarm of armies. Regiments against hordes. What, if it came to the pitch, was there in Western Europe to stop the manpower of the East? You know how we gripe.

The Frenchman looked up as if he were going to put in a word, but he sipped his coffee instead.

"We have our civilization, Bob," grinned Noel, digging into his brandied cherries. Being a member of His Britannic Majesty's Forces, Squadron Leader Noel laps up French cooking like a hungry pup.

"Do we?" I asked him. We'd all been reading how our Western civilization is on the downcurve, and how this world is whirling into an era of power politics, with armed manpower coming out on top. In other words, with the rule of the Eurasian, or Soviet, state on top. "Then where do we keep it?" I asked. "It doesn't seem to be around here."

Our obsolescent wagon restaurant was creaking through a gray twilight, because in order to save juice, no one had switched on the lights. Outside the window I perceived exactly one human being, the color of dirt, steering a plow behind a horse.

"It's in Paris, Bob," Noel told me cheerfully, spooning up the brandy, "'specially the opera house—the Masked Ball for us tomorrow night. It's also across the Seine, where the youngsters make love under the stars."

How can you argue with a guy like that? Noel reads ancient poetry and works out those double acrostics, while I like to keep my facts separate from such fancies. "That's fine," I conceded. "So we have our civilization in Paris. Where's your army to defend it? Are you going to mobilize an Allied army of one commanding general and those youngsters playing along the Seine, and these"—I pointed out the window—"farmhands? It could happen that you'd have to defend a line somewhere against the combined armies of Asia."

Our French neighbor leaned over. "It did happen," he said in good enough English. "Yes, *monsieur le capitaine*, in the battle of long ago."

Evidently he knew insignia of rank when he saw it. A network of wrinkles around his dark eyes showed that life had not been all operas and brandied cherries for him, but he grinned like a kid as he explained that his name was Vesny. His red ribbon of the Legion of Honor might mean that he was either an ex-professor or an ex-soldier.

"In what battle?" I wondered.

"In the one of which monsieur speaks. Of the combined forces of the West against the East."

Noel and I looked at each other. What was happening now couldn't have happened a long time ago—"You mean, Monsieur Vesny," Noel ventured, "that history is repeating itself? Like a clock striking the same hour?"

"But certainly." The little guy flourished two fingers across his flowing mustache. "You are of course officers of the newer army, and no doubt you are greatly occupied with the radars and the swept wings. Yet human beings were the same fifteen hundred years ago." He peered eagerly out of our window. "Even this place is the same, although it was called the plain of Mauriac then."

Outside, the flat farmlands stretched to the hazy horizon. A few windmills turned lazily, and one bare hill stood up. Except that we'd left Châlons and crossed the river Marne, I had no idea where we were. However, I had a queer feeling, because everything outside our car looked as if it had been there for dark ages. "In the Dark Ages?" I asked, wondering if professors could be shell-shock cases, like dogfaces.

"Exactly! The age when the civilization of our ancestors was near its death in the West. The month, also, was June."

Suddenly Noel, who had been figuring to himself, smacked the table. "Fifteen hundred years ago! June four-five-one! Attila and the Huns!"

The Huns were from the steppes of Asia (assented M. Vesny—I can't give his twist to words in my GI lingo). They had crossed the Danube and they were here in this plain of Mauriac. It was this same hour of sunset—of vespers, you understand, although no church bells rang in Gaul, as they called France, because doom hung over the land.

My ancestor really began the battle, because he was leading the first combat patrol up the road there by the windmills, coming from Troyes. He had orders from the commander of the Christian allies to drive in the enemy patrols and feel out the enemy line of resistance, but not to let himself be drawn into close combat. Well, my ancestor, whose name was Meroving—the Son of the Sea, you understand—was a big blond, very brave, and accordingly foolish. He rode by an empty bathhouse and a burned church without seeing a living soul, because the civilians had all fled to the coast or been gathered up by the invisible Huns.

So when big Meroving sighted something moving in the shadows ahead, he and his Franks ran up and let fly with the heavy axes they carried. These Merovingian Franks were the true barbarians of the allies, being without armor—or sense, according to some others. But they got their fighting blood warmed up quickly, and they cleared the road beyond the ruined church by using their hacking knives after they threw the two-bladed axes. And, just as quickly, Meroving forgot his orders.

He ran on, over hill and dale, with his comrades, calling to the foemen to stand and be killed. Yes, he was a fool at fighting; he dismounted to share the hard blows with his comrades, and to give his poet, Oud the Voice, some brave deeds to sing out. By starlight Meroving was going on strongly, attacking bivouacs, and Oud the Voice was singing about slaying a host of pagans, when horsemen came galloping from a side road. Meroving and the comrades accordingly made ready to throw their axes again.

But the riders were armored and shielded Visigoths—the West Germans—with their prince Torismund, and he was hot with anger.

"Fathead Franks," young Torismund hailed without proper courtesy, "do you think you are boar hunting? Get back where you were ordered to be!"

Now, my ancestor hated the guts of the West Germans because of their conceit and because they had taken the best river lands of Gaul to farm, and most of all he hated the hard-riding Torismund, who dangled a fine jeweled long sword at his hip. Yet for this campaign of the Christian allies, my ancestor was oathbound to raise no weapon against his rival.

So he responded politely, "Son of Theodoric the Visigoth, dismount your fine carcass, take your toy sword, and stand your ground if you can against Meroving, chieftain of the Franks, and no fathead."

Willingly enough, young Torismund swung back his gold-crusted cloak; then he checked himself, saying, "I might well have known, although I did not, that Meroving was here, by the stink and uproar around me. Since we are oathbound to exchange no blow, I cannot draw my sword against that wood hewer you carry."

At that, Meroving's fighting blood boiled up—"We do not think, Torismund, that we drive boars this night. No," he said politely, "we are driving the horde of Huns while the noble Visigoths sit at the cook pots."

"Where falls Frankish foot," Oud the Voice chanted, "there lies meat for wolves and blood for the sating of ravens."

"Bats in the belfry!" swore Torismund. "If you think you drive the Hunnic horde before you, you are greatly mistaken. Those yonder are Gepid tribesmen who screen the Hun horsemen." Anxiously he bent down to the Frank, his rival. "Have you seen no sign at all of Attila?"

"Not yet," quoth Meroving, more angry than ever at the prideful West German. Although baptized Christians, those Germans always put on their gold rings and brocade cloaks for a battle, in order, if they were killed, to take their place honorably clad at the banquet table of Valhalla. "Now look," he added, "if you are so reluctant to draw that fine sword, will you condescend to use it on our enemies? I challenge you, Torismund, to see which of us twain goes farthest into the enemy, when this affray is done."

"Fathead," quoth the German, angry in his turn, "I will take that challenge! Wherever you go, you will find me there before you!"

And he galloped off, while Oud the Voice leaped and cracked his heels for joy at hearing such a brave challenge.

Ah, they were young and headstrong. The night fell dark, and in the darkness the Flail of God lay waiting, mocking them. Trotting forward with his comrades, Torismund no longer heeded his own orders. Until he came to the dead watchers.

They sat their horses in a line, set up on stakes, with lances tied to their hands. Torismund reined his plunging horse up to the dead riders and identified them as deserters who had gone over to the Huns. "I see well," he told his men, "that Attila has been here. Column, guide on me."

There was a blackness rising ahead against the stars; there was the smell of cattle dung and the sound of creaking wagons. By those signs Torismund knew the Huns themselves to be near. He led his column up the height against the stars, and found himself on the bare summit of a hill with no living foeman near. He could smell the pagan horde and hear it, but he could not see it. So he halted there on his hill . . .

Meroving was racing on, fearing that Torismund would outspeed him. Leading his Franks with their short axes hewing and flying, he raised such a hue and cry that it seemed as if an army were rushing away before him, but he could see nothing at all. Then from the blackness of a wood he came out into the grayness of an open plain where campfires smoldered in a ring, and within their circle uprose a strange pavilion, like a dome, and all deserted.

A musty smell came from this silent tent. For a moment Meroving hung back, thinking it was fey and ill-omened for him. It stank of the nomad Huns, but they were not there.

Lighting torches from the embers of the fires, he led his Franks into the dome tent. They all shouted and snatched at plunder, for furs and gold bowls lay strewn about on horsehides. And hanging on the tent pole Meroving beheld the sword.

In the torchlight it gleamed with the fire of rubies, its tapering blade unlike any short Roman blade—a long sword, worthy of a king.

Craving a noble weapon like Torismund's, Meroving thrust aside his comrades to seize it himself. When he gripped the hilt, it felt light in his hand. A prisoner, a wolf-like Gepid, cried out that it was Attila's sword.

"If this sword is his," cried Meroving, staring through the smoke of the torches, "then this tent is his that we have taken!"

Oud the Voice leaped to his full height and cracked his heels twice for joy. And Meroving, exulting, sent a fast runner to report to the allied commander that he had captured the tent of Attila, supreme khan of the Huns.

So swiftly did the Frank runner find his way back that the Roman legions—the mainstay of the infantry—were barely digging in for the night, when he dropped at the feet of Aëtius, the general commanding, yelling, "Victory!"

Aëtius was munching a biscuit soaked in wine, and after the runner reported all of the great victory, he asked one question, "Where?"

When the runner pointed out the glow of the fires, far ahead in the dark plain of Mauriac, the Roman commander threw away his biscuit and sent a legate to warn Theodoric, king of the West Germans, that the situation had gone from bad to worst, because the Franks had fallen into the trap of the Huns.

Sitting on a log and quieting his nerves with strong Rhine wine, Aëtius the patrician, the last of the Roman commanders, reviewed the situation before him in the fourth hour of that June night, to see if any hope remained.

He had no support behind him. His boy emperor played striptease with girls at the Ravenna seaside resort, and chariots still raced in the Roman circus, but Rome itself was dying. The only surviving army was here, digging a defensive ditch by torchlight—sixty thousand barbarians drilled in the equipment of Roman legionaries. And the unreliable Franks and the suspicious West Germans—

Behind a staked ditch, he thought, *they may stand against the charge of the Huns, because of their farms and families back of them. It's the one chance.*

How much of a chance? Somewhere in the darkness the horde of the Huns was moving, with the conscript armies of the satellite peoples, the Slavs and Gepids, the mountain Alans and Ostrogoths—the East Germans—and the tribes of the Don and Volga—two hundred or four hundred thousand in all. Aëtius could not know their numbers.

That was bad. But Aëtius dared not hope that the sagacious Kagan of Asia would make a frontal attack on his skeleton legions. For Attila wisely held back his own army; his spies announced through the west that the Kagan was bringing only peace and liberating all oppressed people from Roman imperial rule and taxation. Then, if a town in Gaul resisted, Attila would set his Gepids against the Franks, holding back the terror of his Huns. Until he had ended resistance and could ride to the Channel of Britain, and rule from Africa to the Great Wall of China.

Aëtius believed that Attila would win. For he had studied the victorious Hun, going up in the guise of a hostage to the nine-times-guarded Ring, the wooden fortress of the Huns on the blue Danube, where converted Romans like Orestes and the Italian banker Constant served Attila and enjoyed their freedom, paying no taxes. Or so they said. They feasted well in the Ring, with toasts before every course—poking fun at the Roman ambassadors while Attila jested about how the Romans paid out gold for peace, and demanded of the ambassadors whether they wanted peace or war. Attila, jesting, set the price of peace higher each year—up to two thousand pounds of gold a year, along with the return by the Romans of all deserters from the Hun frontier. Until the Roman senate paid out all available gold. Until the senators cried to Mitius to put these last legions in the field. And Attila crossed the Danube to invade the West.

I was a fool not to take his offer, the Roman soldier thought, *of an estate on the Danube and command of an army of Asia. For until now he has won what he needed most without war, and if there is a battle he can easily win that also.*

Then the giant Theodoric came with the legate, taking off his horned helmet to sit on the log and ask, "What is the worst?"

Theodoric, king of the West Germans, used few words because he had many troubles. Attila had sent to urge him to become an ally against his old enemy, the Roman Empire, but Theodoric had chosen to make a stand with the soldier Aëtius, and now he worried about that.

Aëtius knew his mind. Aëtius had to hold the West German cavalry fast. "The Franks are lost," he said, wearily and truthfully. "We have to decide—to try to reach them tonight or hold our line here."

Every word the bearded Theodoric weighed carefully. "How are they lost?" he demanded.

"When we gained contact with the Huns at Orléans, you remember how they retreated from the siege of the city. Why? They are nomads, dangerous with bows and lances. Their strategy is to simulate hurried retreat, to draw pursuit straggling after them. When they reach a level plain like their own steppes, they turn and attack like a whirlwind. Now, on the Mauriac, they have reached such a plain." Aëtius nodded at the darkness ahead of them. "No civilians will be left alive to inform us of their position." He poured wine for the German. "The Merovingian Franks are out there; they report they have forced Attila to retreat and have captured his tent and sword."

"Umpf." Theodoric pulled aside his mustache to drink, while he pondered.

"I have heard, general, that he has a sword of power."

"So? Do you think he would leave it behind unless he wanted it to be found?" Aëtius shrugged. "Noble Visigoth, he wants to draw us on. What do you say?"

After thinking, Theodoric said, "Let God decide."

For the moment, Aëtius had forgotten that the Visigoth, being newly converted, believed in the unseen Almighty God. He did not know how to answer.

"Listen," muttered Theodoric, putting down his cup.

Out on the plain there was a murmur of sound. After calling for silence in the trench details, the Roman commander identified the sound as hand combat in advance of his right flank. "Now, what—" he muttered.

Theodoric straightened with pride. "That is my son, Torismund, searching for the Huns with the finest horsemen."

Aëtius struggled with a spasm of fury. Both his flanking forces had wandered forward after Attila's lures.

"All right, that does it," he gave in. "Theodoric, God Almighty never meant us to wait, split up into three parts, for sunrise. . . . Legate, sound the trumpet for advance with all equipment, including trench stakes. The advance will be to the new line of the flank parties. The time of the advance is now."

So it happened that Aëtius, the veteran commander, led badly tired legions forward in the last hours of darkness in the face of rested, alerted cavalry, position unknown. It seemed to him that he was being drawn forward to his doom by Fate itself.

"Look," said old Theodoric, riding at his side.

The bearded face and helmet of the Visigoth showed more clearly in a dim light that came from no true dawn. Abruptly the Roman turned in the saddle, staring into the east. There was no gleam of the sun along the dark horizon.

"Mist," said Theodoric. "The Lord hides us from the eyes of our enemy."

And the Huns, Aëtius thought mechanically, *can be on top of us before we see them. But he did not say it.*

Attila the Kagan waited for the sun to burn away the mist. Although it was late in the morning, only a pale light showed above him, as if a lantern had been hung there in the sky.

Patiently the Kagan waited, kneeling on the white horsehide, his handsome gray head bent in thought, his robe of the finest silk clinging to his small, stooped body.

A *teghin*, a commander of a thousand, came before him. "Nephew of Roua, the Christians hold to the hill, making a wall of their shields."

Attila's eyes probed the mist. Below him the *teghins* moved restlessly, awaiting his commands. The mist hid the great encampment that was his moving empire. Over the grass-grown ruin of an old Roman camp, his massed wagons walled in the horse herds, the cattle and myriad captives, the round yurtas that held the treasure of Europe. He could barely make out the silent group of subjected chieftains—the Slavs, Alans, Gepids, with the khans of farther Asia, and even the Chinese observers, his allies in name, who had come with gifts, to decide his real strength. The watchful Chinese observers from the Eight Banners of the Liu.

"Let Ardaric, the chief, and his Alans," he ordered, "go against the hill."

He would not send his horsemen of Asia through the curtain of mist against a height. Better for the Christian swordsman of the east to kill those of the west.

Hissing submissively, the *teghin* bent close to him. "Master of the encampment, we have heard the Romans digging in the mist. Attack them now—strike like an eagle, unseen."

When Attila closed his eyes, his lined face became a mask, revealing nothing. For a second he was tempted to do as the officer wished.

But the strange darkness of the mist troubled him. He felt the watchful eyes of the Chinese on him. He remembered how other, little things had led him to change his plans. How he had started to lead his army from the Danube in the guise of a maker of peace, without conflict. Yet when food was taken from the fields, men in the farms began to resist, villagers gathered to defend their stone churches. He had changed then, swiftly from deception to terror, burning the villagers in their churches, making a road of terror from Metz to Reims to Orléans—where he had been amazed to hear the trumpets of a Roman army coming up, an army gathered from the peoples who had been quarreling among themselves. It was led by the one man Attila respected, Aëtius.

No, he would not change his plan again because the sun did not shine in the eyes of his enemy. Moving his fingers as if casting something away, he said, "Does an eagle strike with hooded head? Does a commander of a thousand think his wisdom to be greater than the Kagan's?"

Crossing his arms before his belt, the officer withdrew. Fear of Attila lay upon him and all the encampment.

Yet they were all troubled, waiting restlessly around him, by the littlest thing of all. By the loss of the sword. That sword, found in a Scythian grave and brought to Attila by a sheepherder of the Don, had been different from other weapons, and his ignorant people took it for an omen that the sword had come from the earth to Attila; his soothsayers prophesied, "Who holds the sword of power may never be defeated in battle." And his people believed that his conquests came from the iron of the sword.

Attila did not believe that. His sagacity had led the stubborn Aëtius after him to the center of this plain, whence the Romans could not escape. He had tricked the Christians by leaving his tent standing last night, as if he fled; then his idiot body slaves had left the strange sword behind in the tent. All those slaves had been killed at once, but his bodyguards noticed the absence of the sword. His sword bearer, empty-handed, rocked on his heels, mourning as if power had departed from the Kagan. Attila felt anger rising in him at the stupidity of the man.

Attila forced himself to wait, impassive, until early afternoon, when the sun burned away the last of the mist. There lay the new Roman line, completed. A brown furrow in the green grass, topped by pointed stakes, stretching as he had expected from the solitary hill to the far-off swamps, with the Roman standards glittering above it.

Faintly then he heard the blast of their trumpets, challenging him. The Chinese came closer to stare at him, and blood pounded in his brain. The Romans were calling him to attack.

Yet he knew that he must wait. His hour would come when they would be forced to leave their lines to seek food, and his massed horsemen would sweep down on them; then Orléans and Rome would yield to terror, and his will would be supreme to the sea.

Behind him he heard a grieving voice, "The power is gone from the Kagan. A Christian Frank holds it in his hand."

Anger gripped him like a fever. Instinctively he reached back for a weapon to slay the speaker. His fingers caught at the air.

Springing up, he screamed, "Ride and slay! The entire camp against the Roman line!"

Saddle drums beat. Horns blasted the signal. Past Attila's seat, massed riders moved at a trot, with lances and lariats. They swept down into the plain like dark rivers in flood.

The racing horses made a sound of myriad stones beating the earth. Over it came the howling of human throats. The first flight of arrows seethed up through the dust toward the gleam of the Roman standards . . .

An hour before sunset, the Huns still drifted in open order through the dust; they were still stopped by something where the Roman eagles marked the line of the ditch and parapet. And the mounds of bodies of animals and men.

The man who held the sword—Meroving—shook his head to clear it of the roaring sound. He felt the chill of water on his legs where he stood in the swamp, where few of the Huns had attacked. But not even Meroving had ventured forward out of the swamp to the plain where no one could live on foot.

"Oud!" he shouted. His poet crouched on a boulder, arms over his head. "Oud," said Meroving, who felt awe in him, "where is your voice, that you do not sing of this mighty thing?"

Swaying his head, Oud chanted, "Now I have no voice in me to sing this thing. It is the Flail of God we are seeing."

Out of the dust behind them came a mounted legate, calling for the chieftain of the Franks, and when Meroving answered, the legate reined in. "If you can come," he called, glancing down the tangle of the swamp, "come to Aëtius behind the front line. Now."

So Meroving splashed out of the swamp water, with Oud and all the Franks following, for they knew no more than to follow their chieftain in battle. So he ran fast behind the lines, leaping over the wounded Celts of Brittany who dragged themselves forward to take the place of the dead.

Where the catapult machines thudded against the thunder of the battle line, he found the heavy infantry of the front line. With thrusting spears and short swords, the men held a one-man line at the stakes where had been a three-man line. Meroving looked around him and sighted Aëtius's cloak spread over a body on the ground.

When he bent down to inspect the body, a hand caught his arm. Whirling around, he faced Aëtius, who had got rid of his plumed helmet as well as his cloak, while sweat and blood dripped from his shorn head.

"Let be, Meroving, lord of Frankland," said Aëtius, in measured, polite words. "That body is Theodoric's, who was king of the Visigoths and the bravest of men. His death must not be known or the Visigoths will lose spirit. Now, in this lull between onsets, you must find Torismund. Do you understand that much?"

"I understand well enough," grunted Meroving, "but if this is a lull, may I—"

"Find Torismund," went on Aëtius; "tell him to take over for Theodoric. Torismund must take over."

It was strange to Meroving as he ran on—the rattle of the machines, the calls of the centurions to brace shields against the stakes—the strange ways of disciplined legions. Then he remembered that Torismund, who had a horse, would be far ahead of him in this battle and would accordingly win his challenge. So he raced through the horse lines and leaped the mounds of the dead, until he learned that Torismund was on the hill.

Then he raced with his Franks up the hill to where the young prince stood in the shield wall of his comrades, beating off assault waves.

Torismund looked from his head to his feet and said, "Fathead, I see that you have lingered long behind my back to wash your feet."

Meroving's fighting blood warmed at that. "It is true," he admitted politely, "that I come up from behind you. But now my feet will go before you." Then he took Torismund three paces to the rear. "Theodoric is gone," he whispered, "Aëtius says you must take over or the Visigoths will lose heart."

At the word of his father's death, tears came into Torismund's eyes. Then he cried out in anger, "You will see if the Visigoths lose heart in battle!"

Below them came the sound of the Huns beating again at the thin Roman line. "Shields away!" shouted Torismund, running to his horse. "Pass the word! All to follow me!"

So the Visigoths got to horse. But when Torismund reined forward, Meroving grabbed the mane of his horse to race beside him. All those Franks did like their chieftain; they held to manes or tails or the ankles of the Visigoths, hewing and throwing their axes. So the charge came down on the Huns, down the hill and around the hill . . .

Attila rose to his feet when he saw it at sunset—the madmen racing and riding, and throwing weapons before them. He saw his Huns broken, who had never given ground to horsemen until then.

And he knew he had failed. The Master of the World had used his army and had been beaten back. The legend of the invincible Attila, like the legend of the sword, was no more . . .

After dark, Aëtius found them by forcing his way through their comrades. Meroving had dropped his sword and was hewing into the Hun wagons at a corner with an ax, while Torismund covered him with a shield. Aëtius swore that he found them where neither was a foot in advance of the other, and so he pulled them away.

That night the two armies lay apart, licking their wounds. The next day Attila was gone with his wagons, on the road back to the Danube.

In our restaurant car the lights had been turned on. It gave me a comfortable feeling to be sitting at ease like that, speeding toward the Paris we knew. I wondered what we would be doing if things had broken differently on that dark plain of Mauriac. Squadron Leader Noel put down his cognac glass thoughtfully.

"But it was a drawn battle, Monsieur Vesny," he observed. "At least, history says so. Attila still had his army and his empire."

The little Frenchman shook his head, smiling. "Ah, but no, monsieur. There was no empire but Attila's will. So long as people believed him to be infallible, it existed. The battle ended it."

"You'd find that," I put in, "hard to prove."

"On the contrary. Consider what happened afterward. In two years he died and those conquered people revolted—the Gepids and East Germans gathered in Yugoslavia and drove the surviving Huns out of the West, into their steppes of Asia."

He thanked me for listening with courtesy to an old soldier. He wished us a pleasant leave in Paris, and added something in French to Noel. Then, with a bow, he left the car.

"He may be right, at that," I admitted. "What was that he said?"

"An old French saying, Bob. 'The more things change, the more they are the same.'"

The Village of the Ghost

I

"Yes, sahib, it is undoubtedly true. There is a devil in the castle, and that is why no one else will sleep there."

Jaswat Das, *khitmatgar*—butler—inclined his head gravely, and Sir A. Cunningham did not smile. Years of service in the Honorable East India Company and as Resident of the Jumna district of Upper India had made Cunningham very well acquainted with the demonology of India. Moreover he knew that Jaswat Das, his butler, was relating the common talk of the countryside.

It was the Year of Our Lord 1802 and the two white men sat under the *chenars* by the Jumna River bank just outside the walls of Agra. Squatting on the ground in front of them, the butler looked from his master to the stranger.

"How do you know, Jaswat Das, that there is a demon in the castle if you have not seen him?" inquired Cunningham.

The other white man asked no questions, contenting himself with listening closely to what the native said.

"Because, sahib, the men of the village have seen him. Sometimes the demon takes the form of a snake and sometimes that of a deadly sickness. When he is in his own body he looks like an old man with long hair and a face the color of old ivory; he wears a black *khalat* that covers his human body down to the ankles so that no one can tell what his form is really like. He has lived in the castle for a hundred years and it is said he once inhabited the form of the daughter of the *potail** of the village."

---

*Proprietor.

"Then why," pursued the Resident, "did the demon slay the two sahibs who went to Bhir when he has never molested the villagers?"

"The two *farangi* died because they slept in the castle of Bhir that was the demon's home."

"Aye, Jaswat Das, that is true. But natives—even the *potail*—have slept in the castle at various times and have come to no harm."

The *khitmatgar* nodded understandingly.

"True, sahib. Yet you do not remember that the folk of the village when they wanted to sleep in the castle always made holes in the walls first. Then they lighted fires within and rushed about, firing their weapons and making great outcry. In this way they made a spell and the demon did not hurt them."

"Yet if the people of Bhir did not make offerings to the ghost, it would attack them?"

"Assuredly, sahib—either in the form of a snake or a sickness. Their womenfolk would be childless and their cattle would die."

"Very well, Jaswat Das. Still, in spite of their fear of the ghost of Bhir castle, the villagers and the merchants endure the demon, you say?"

Patiently Jaswat Das explained, knowing the wisdom of his master and suspecting rightly that his story was for the benefit of the strange sahib who sat in uniform and with a sword at his belt beside the Resident.

"Aye, sahib, it is so. For Bhir has waxed prosperous since the coming of the ghost who takes much wealth, but gives more. The merchants have rugs and store of gold in their houses—and fair wives."

Cunningham frowned thoughtfully at this. The district of Bhir, beside the great river Jumna, had long been a thorn in his side.

"For how much silver," he asked the butler, "would you take up your abode in the castle of Bhir?"

The dark eyes of Jaswat Das widened and he salaamed.

"*Ai*, my lord—I am but a poor *khitmatgar*. In my sahib's command are many soldiers who are paid to be killed. Give them the silver and a piece of gold for their families and let them die. Has not the demon of Bhir castle slain travelers who came within the district? Have not strangers dropped out of sight overnight, without a trace of the manner of their going?"

"Enough, Jaswat Das. You have my permission to depart."

When the two Englishmen were alone Cunningham turned to his companion with a smile that was not altogether merry.

"There, Malcolm, you have the native side of the mystery of Bhir. Let me add a few words of my own to show how heavily it weighs upon the success of our affairs in the district."

Punctuating his remarks by prodding his cane into the dust at his feet, the Resident explained that following upon the signing of peace between the English and the Nawab of Oudh, the Northern Provinces had been established along the Jumna. Rajputana was on friendly terms with its white allies. Everything had gone well except in the district of Bhir—a fertile district, eagerly exploited by Portuguese traders a hundred years ago.

In that quarter a malignant force had been at work against the *farangis*. This power for evil had been located in the ruins of the castle of Bhir—a citadel built by a long-dead raja and deserted for three generations.

"It began with the death by sickness of Mr. Powell, a commissioner of the company, three years ago. He was robbed of his revenues after he had established himself in the castle. The fortress, you know, overlooks the countryside, the highway, and the river, and seemed to him the most suitable and honorable quarters.

"And then, last year a worthy gentleman who was my friend took over the office of magistrate and collector of Bhir. He also availed himself of the castle. Certain hostile manifestations of an uncanny nature alarmed him—so I am informed by his native cook who fled the place before him—and he was hastening back to me when he disappeared. He literally vanished, horse, revenues, servant, and all, on the highroad."

Cunningham sighed.

"Added to the untimely death of these two kindly and respected gentlemen is the loss of several couriers sent by them to me—both English and native troopers. We were never able to trace them after they started forth on the high road. Nor were we ever able to learn how they died."

With that the Resident rose and began to pace back and forth, his ruddy face palpably worried. His young companion gazed reflectively at the river.

"Bhir," mused Cunningham aloud, "is attracting miscreants and malcontents who believe that we fear to send a magistrate there. They think the proprietor-ghost is friendly to them, and hostile to us *kafirs*—unbelievers, you know. The mystery is still unsolved, and unless we can occupy the castle, Bhir may become the keystone in an arch reared against our rule in northern India.

"Anticipating your natural questions, Captain Malcolm," he resumed, "I will add that none of the neighboring rajas is unfriendly to us. Nor have the people of Bhir displayed untoward feelings openly. The ghost alone stands revealed as our enemy.

"And now, my dear Captain Malcolm," he concluded, "what do you make of the tale of Jaswat Das?"

John Malcolm, who had not spoken until then, shrugged square shoulders. Two years before he had led the first embassy from the company into Persia; and at that time he was known as a veteran of Seringapatam.

He had been in the Indian service since childhood and possessed a familiarity rare in those days with the native languages and manners. Malcolm's homely face was expressionless; his uniform and accoutrements were more than a little travel stained. Cunningham, a stickler for the niceties, fancied that the new officer sent to him from Calcutta seemed dull, even indifferent.

"Nothing very palpable, sir," responded Malcolm. A Scot by birth, he was reticent and slow to express an opinion.

"But, zounds! My dear fellow, your experience with the natives must have taught you something. I am informed that you can do wonders."

"I regret, sir, that you have been misinformed." Malcolm surveyed his muddy boots gravely, noticing that the Resident was glancing at them with some choler. Cunningham was brave in finery of lace and red coat, London cut. "What is your own opinion of the deaths, sir?"

"Ha—you do not know?" The Resident chose to forget that Malcolm had dismounted only that morning from a week's ride to Agra. "I judge that the story of the ghost has been devised to frighten us away from Bhir. Within Bhir are a number of wealthy Muhammadan merchants, who have bribed the lawless elements of the ghost's village to kill our officials. Poor Powell, for instance, did not die until a month after leaving the castle. He was poisoned, because, Captain Malcolm, no physician could diagnose his illness."

"He died here, at Agra?"

"Yes. But my other friend vanished on the way hither—a victim to some of the same cursed native witchery—" Cunningham checked himself—"trickery, I should say. Do you not think I am correct in this?"

Malcolm considered his dusty boot through a half-closed eye.

"And you say that strange natives, travelers on the highway, were killed on this road?"

"Yes."

"Then you, sir, cannot have the right answer to this. Because the men died, not in the ghost-village of Bhir, but *after* they had left Bhir."

The Resident, chagrined, coughed and took snuff without offering it to his companion.

"Moreover," pointed out the Scot mildly, "it—the mystery of the ghost—can hardly be merely an attempt to frighten us, sir. Not if other *natives* were killed by the same agency."

"Hum." Cunningham smoothed the lace at his throat moodily. "I repeat, sir, it is all part and parcel of the same damnable plot against me—against us."

A quick smile rendered the Scot's hard face agreeable.

"Sir, you will permit me to appeal to your own knowledge of native superstitions. Ghosts, to a Moslem, are nothing supernatural; and to a Hindu they form part of his religion. A native is seized with an epileptic fit; his family pay tribute to the suspected ghost; the man, perhaps, recovers and all is well—if he dies the ghost was not sufficiently propitiated. Haunts, distemper, and demon-ridding are all part of their scheme of existence."

"Well, sir?"

"It would never occur to the Bhiris to frighten away sahibs by a tale of what is to them perfectly natural phenomena."

"Ah." There was respect in the Resident's ejaculation. But it was with a dry smile that he drew a folded yellow sheet from the pocket of his coat. "Here, Malcolm, is evidence to support my view. Powell brought it back with him, having found it in the possession of one of the Bhir landholders."

Malcolm studied the sheet and saw that it was a lease deed, made out in the ordinary form, dated about a hundred and twenty years ago. The lessee was a Moslem of Bhir and the deed was made out on behalf of the ghost of Bhir.

"Sheer hocus-pocus," shrugged Cunningham. "Powell related that even up to three years ago all deeds in Bhir village were made out with the ghost as proprietor."

"And so, because Powell and the other usurped the place of the ghost, they died."

Cunningham laughed uncertainly.

"You believe that? Really, I am surprised! Why, the name of the ghost-proprietor appears—"

"As Dom Gion. A curious name."

"More fiddlededee! It is not even the name of a native."

"Well, sir." Malcolm looked up seriously. "Jaswat Das assured us that the familiar spirit of Bhir wore a full-length black cloak—which is not a native garment. In fact it smacks of the, ah—demoniac. The deed is not a forgery. You have asked for my opinion—"

"I have sent for you, to that end."

"There is a ghost in Bhir, somewhat old, of the name of Dom Gion."

"Ridiculous."

"Or a demon, if you prefer."

"Absurd!"

"But unfortunately true. This deed relates that a stated tax is paid the ghost by Bhir. Powell and the other displaced the proprietor-spirit, and cut off its perquisites. Consequently they suffered."

Cunningham looked helplessly at the deep blue expanse of the river and the jungle mesh on the other side beyond which lay Bhir.

"Yet the travelers on the high road—the natives, you know—did not trespass so," he muttered.

"Their fate was the product of sheer malignancy. Sir, you know the existence of a cult in northern India that worships Kali, the All-Destroyer. I think we find a center of the cult in Bhir and that our friend the ghost plays his part therein."

"Zounds!" Cunningham's handsome face was utterly serious. He, too, had heard of Kali. "We must not let Bhir go. No matter how many sentries are killed off, a sentry post must be maintained, sir—at all costs." He took snuff vigorously. "Now, Captain Malcolm, what precautions does your experience suggest on behalf of the next officer I detail to the post?"

Malcolm considered.

"I'll go," he said.

"Eh, what?" The Resident stared at his young companion. "You, sir? My dear Captain Malcolm, I could not call upon you, when my own men have vanished in Bhir and poor Powell—the only one to leave alive—died of an unknown disease."

"If you will be so good, sir, as to appoint me magistrate and collector of the district of Bhir for a time sufficient for me to investigate this matter? The ghost, you know, must be laid."

Cunningham was troubled. He had sent for the young captain of Sepoys to get his advice, which the Resident valued; now Malcolm had volunteered for the dangerous post. The peace of the Northern Provinces demanded a white man should remain in Bhir.

"Confound me—I'm cursed if I don't accept," he acknowledged frankly. "Provided you will keep in touch with me. How many men shall I detail to go with you?"

"None."

"Will you have your camp established near the river? It is safer than the village."

"I think," smiled Malcolm, "I'll camp in the castle of Bhir. It won't do to give up our chosen post, you know."

Cunningham laughed.

"Man, you are stark mad, but I'm blest if I don't like you for it. Do you take snuff, Captain Malcolm?"

II

It was a few days later that Rawul Singh, a Rajput veteran, returned to his home in the Bhir valley after a long absence in the wars.

Since the truce with the English the Nawab of Oudh had dismissed a great part of his soldiery without pay; the great chief Ranjeet Singh had sheathed the sword, and Rawul Singh would not serve under a Mussulman leader. So, having played his part in the recent battles with the English, Rawul Singh was glad to see the roof-tree of his hut near the Jumna road. He yearned to see his daughter, who was just reaching womanhood, and his son of ten years who would presently run forth to welcome him.

Rawul Singh brushed up his truculent white mustache and swaggered in his saddle as he touched spurs to his tired horse. The silver ornaments on his harness were few; the purse at his girdle was empty.

He was one of those good-hearted, utterly brave men who cannot prosper, who are a prey to the merchant and moneylender, and who are born to be led, not to lead. Over his shoulder was a shawl, bought for Tala, his daughter. In one hand he held a small bow and arrows for the boy.

In order to purchase these he had fasted on his journey.

"*Hai*, Tala! *Hai*, little lion—it is thy father who calls. Fear not!"

Smiling, he leaped from his horse and strode into the hut. It was in neat order, but empty. So also was the cattle pen beside it. Rawul Singh laid down his presents and frowned. It was evening and his children should have been in the house, and the cattle penned, for there were jackals about.

Convinced that the girl and boy must be in the village in spite of the late hour—because the aspect of the house revealed that they had been there not later than noon, as the ashes of the fire were still warm and water in the jars still fresh—Rawul Singh remounted and rode on to the outskirts of Bhir, no more than a gunshot away.

Overhead towered the crumbling walls of the castle outlined by ruddy shafts of sunset. As the Rajput passed, hurrying to escape a storm that was overcasting the sky behind him, an eye of light winked out from the battlements of Bhir castle. Rawul Singh noticed it as he did everything within his field of vision.

A moment later his keen glance picked out a white blotch in the dull glimmer of the road. It was his daughter's shawl, worn threadbare.

The Rajput looked quickly about, marking the place where the shawl had lain.

Within the village men turned away from Rawul Singh, and yet stared after him when his broad back was toward them. No one could tell him anything of his children until a water carrier in a dark corner of the bazaar muttered that the boy and girl had been in the village that afternoon, to ask after Rawul Singh. The boy had stood guard over the cattle outside the wall while Tala made her inquiries. They had started back a good hour before twilight.

"Didst thou see, *bheestie*," asked Rawul Singh, "this shawl upon the girl?"

"Aye." The carrier of water bent over his goatskin. "Her face is like the moon, good sir. She smiled at me and her eyes were like dark stars. Perhaps another looked upon her beauty. Beware of the man of Bhir castle who wears a cloak."

With a hiss of rage the soldier clutched at the beggar to learn more. But the *bheestie* and his goatskin had vanished into the shadows of an alley. Rawul Singh remembered that more than once he had given silver to the man.

At the house of the *potail*—village chief—a servant looked long into the Rajput's dark face and shivered.

"*Ai*, Rawul Singh," he whispered, "the heart of the honorable *potail* has turned to water at news of thy grief. He cannot give aid, and knows naught of the fate of thy children—except this. There is a *farangi* in the castle who has seen the face of thy daughter and lusted after her. When the sun had changed* this day, he waited for her and the boy outside the village gate—"

"And the boy?" interrupted Rawul Singh, speaking very slowly and distinctly.

"He defended her, and he was killed by the *farangi*."

"Who buried him? Where?"

But the servant, looking into the stricken face that was thrust near his eyes, turned and fled.

Rawul Singh loosened the folds of his turban and drew them down over his brow so that no prying eyes should behold his grief. Sitting very erect in the saddle, he rode back to his home, pausing only once when he came to the place where he had sighted the scarf, to glance up at the ray of candlelight that winked from the castle.

He could make out a break in the jungle mesh where a path ran from the road in the direction of Bhir castle. A hot wind was blowing the dust of the road into his face and the treetops were threshing under the approach of a storm.

"By Ram and Vishnu, by the sun-born gods and Siva," breathed the Rajput, "may I be avenged for this day!"

Dismounting before his home, he took the shawl of Tala and wrapped within it the two gifts he had brought for his children. The bundle he laid at his feet and squatted on the earth floor.

He was praying that the gods would bring the body of his enemy within reach of his sword. On the morrow he would seek out the body of his boy and show it to the murderer.

Outside the hut lightning flashed and a rush of rain swept over the jungle. With the rain came the sound of horses' hoofs. A man pushed open the closed door of the hut and entered.

Apparently he had not perceived the occupant of the place, for he busied himself with a lantern, striking steel on flint until he had it lighted. Captain Malcolm faced Rawul Singh.

"I am the sahib from the castle," said the Scot. "The storm has driven me under thy roof. What is thy name, Rajput?"

He spoke Hindustani fluently. Rawul Singh did not rise as Malcolm expected. Instead he sat on his heels, his black eyes boring into the gray eyes of the visitor. The Rajput had fasted for two days, except for the stim-

---

*In the afternoon.

ulant of bhang that he had chewed as he rode. The influence of the drug had left his nerves frayed.

"Thou art welcome," he said quietly. "I will tell thee my name."

Silently he watched Malcolm tether his horse under the eaves of the hut, beside the Rajput's steed.

"Sahib," observed Rawul Singh between his teeth, "the gods have brought thee hither, out of the castle in the storm. It is as I prayed."

"Nay," answered Malcolm carelessly. "I was riding by the river on my way to the castle when the storm made the path impossible."

"Hast thou many servants, my sahib?"

"Not one."

"Then hast thou lied. For a light was in the towers a short space ago. No one dwells there except thee, Malcolm sahib. Where is Tala?" He rose lightly. "Thou dost not know that I am Rawul Singh whose home thou hast made a desolate place. Verily, the gods brought Malcolm sahib to my door."

The Scot's searching glance sought the wild features of the native, and his feverish eyes.

"Drunk or mad," he reflected, "and armed to boot." Not otherwise would a native have interrupted an Englishman or threatened him. Aloud he said—

"Stand back!"

But Rawul Singh leaped, his short sword flashing out as he did so. Crazed by his grief and his mind inflamed by the drug, Rawul Singh struck at the white man. A Ghurka or Maharatta would have knifed Malcolm from behind.

The Scot had barely time to draw his sword, a sturdy weapon of the hanger type. The two blades clashed, parried, and clashed again. Rawul Singh was the better swordsman but was handicapped by his blind rage.

Repeatedly he threw himself upon the Scot, his breath hissing between his teeth. Once his blade slit Malcolm's coat. The white man retreated slowly around the lantern that rested on the earth beside them. He had no chance to speak, or to do anything but keep the flashing curve of the other's weapon from his throat. And then Rawul Singh dashed out the light with a kick of his heel.

"——!" said Malcolm heartily.

He heard the Rajput laugh and the laugh came nearer. Quite easily Malcolm might have thrust his sword into the reckless native, but he shrank from doing that and stepped aside softly. The swish of a steel blade sounded at the spot where he had stood.

"Aha, my sahib, thou dost not stand thy ground—as a man should. Yet thou didst slay my son who was the light of my eyes and the meat of my liver—"

Rawul Singh fell silent, listening, and the Scot tried to stifle his panting breath. The native was between him and the door.

A second time Rawul Singh leaped, as noiselessly as a cat leaps. At the same instant a flicker of lightning revealed him to Malcolm, against the opening of the door.

The white man dropped to his knees, let slip his sword, and clutched his foe by the waist. The impetus of the Rajput's rush carried both to the earth where they rolled, crashing against the table.

Malcolm felt the sweat of the other's body strike his face as he gripped the snake-like sword arm. The greater weight and muscle of the white man told on the other and in another moment they lay quiet, Rawul Singh pinioned in the Scot's arms.

Catching a fold of the native's turban in his teeth, Malcolm shook it loose, and taking care not to relax his hold, with one hand bound the man's wrists and ankles behind him. It was well for the white man that Rawul Singh was exhausted by his efforts.

Then the Scot lighted the lantern and sat down on the low table to recover his breath. To the average English officer Rawul Singh would have appeared merely insane; but Malcolm was puzzled.

"I'm thinking," he muttered, wiping the sweat from his hands, "that there's a method in his madness." Aloud he added: "Tell me the story of thy grievance, Rawul Singh. I am the new *kotwal** of Bhir."

"*Pani sara kyun?**" snarled the other.

But fearlessly, as was his nature, he unfolded the nature of his wrong, believing that whatever happened he would die.

Malcolm listened to the grieving story as stonily as Rawul Singh spoke.

"A forked arrow, Rajput," he said at length, "can strike down two birds at one cast, and a forked tongue is a serpent's tongue."

---

*Magistrate.

†"Why does pure water wax putrid?"

"Nevertheless, the *bheestie* spoke truly; my heart told me he did not lie."

Malcolm nodded impatiently.

"He said naught of me, Rajput; he said to beware of the man of Bhir castle who wears a black cloak. Nay, Rawul Singh, where is thy wisdom? Many men must have made away with thy children and cattle, if they were not to be seen when thou didst ride to the village. Alone, I could not have driven away so many head of cattle in so short a space of time. Also would I have come thus, like a blind pig to thy house? Nay, throughout this afternoon I was engaged in marking the boundaries of the fields beyond the village. A score of men will tell thee so."

Rawul Singh looked at the white man and was silent. Hotheaded as he was, he could understand when a man was speaking the truth.

"Why did this evil come upon me?" he muttered. "Lo, it was to tend the grave of my wife who died upon the journey that I remained in this accursed nest of Mussulmans. They are not my people nor my caste—"

"And because, Rawul Singh," mused Malcolm, "there were evildoers in this village, they wished to be rid of thee, even as they desired to slay me. They learned the hour of thy return; they took the cattle, Tala, and thy son. Then the servant of the *potail* lied, and thou didst believe." He frowned thoughtfully. "And you saw a light in the castle?" he muttered in English.

"Yes, sahib," agreed Rawul Singh, who understood.

Malcolm wondered if the invisible foemen who had struck their first blow at him that night through Rawul Singh had actually taken Tala to the ruins. He thought not. But then who had made the light?

"Rawul Singh," he said abruptly. "If I were the murderer of thy son, would I let thee live, to be revenged upon me?"

"Nay."

"Yet I will do thus. I trust the faith of a Rajput chief."

So saying, he undid the knots in the man's turban cloth and picked up his own sword, sheathing it. Rawul Singh expressed no pleasure.

"Why should I live?" he said. "My son who was the blood in my veins is no more and my daughter has come to shame. My beard is dishonored and my name is no better than a dog's. Let the jackals tear open the grave of my wife that I and those two have tended and watered the young willows by it. *Ai*—it matters not."

Malcolm turned away from the grief of the old man, to hide his own sympathy. There was no way to console Rawul Singh nor would the Rajput have thanked the Scot for attempting it.

The rain was still beating down and Malcolm decided to remain the night where he was. Under the circumstances he judged the hut safer than the darkened castle where the other men might be waiting for him in the storm. He slept fitfully on the low divan that had been built for Rawul Singh's children.

Waking, he found the sun well up and the Rajput squatted beside him. There was a new light in the eyes of the old man.

"Sahib," he said at once, "your servant sought the road before dawn and the place where the scarf had been. Listening, he heard jackals snarling and found them scratching at loose stones. The stones were piled upon a new grave. Sahib, I have looked upon the dead face of my son, who was strangled to death and his belly slit with a knife."

Malcolm rose and checked an exclamation of pity.

"And thy daughter, Tala?"

"Her body I did not find. The slayers of my son have taken her alive with them. It is my thought that she is kept in this neighborhood, because the slayers could not sell her, knowing what she does of their crime. Likewise, in Bhir are many hiding places on the hill slopes near the castle where they would be safe."

The Rajput seemed to be on the point of saying more. The sight of his son's body had stirred him to tense excitement. But, looking at Malcolm, he was silent.

Making a mental note that the old man knew more than he was admitting, the officer asked another question.

"Knowest thou the slayers?"

"If that were so, I would not be standing here, wasting words," Rawul Singh grunted. "Sahib, natives have done this thing. Not one but many, of a powerful band. They cast dust in my eyes, so that, almost, I slew thee. That was for a purpose. So also are they keeping Tala for some other purpose."

It was a long speech for the Rajput to make, and Malcolm knew that his anger was aroused to fever pitch.

"Sahib," he concluded, "before I met thee, I made a vow. Suffer me to be thy servant for a space; then may I come upon my enemies, for the wisdom of the sahib can find them."

Thoughtfully Malcolm considered the matter. He had brought no attendants from Cunningham's establishment because he had not wished to have any strange natives about him—although his dignity in Bhir suffered accordingly.

He knew, however, the hereditary loyalty of Rawul Singh's race and realized the value of a trained fighter who knew the terrain. It would be a happy stroke to ride into Bhir village attended by the man who had been almost tricked into murdering him.

"Very well," he agreed.

Gravely the Rajput took his hand and placed it against his forehead. Then, stepping back, he said impassively:

"The sahib's horse is groomed and fed. Will the sahib mount now or partake of food?"

Under his arm Rawul Singh clutched a bundle done up in a shawl that contained the bow and arrows he had meant for his son.

In the small stone chamber opening into the main hall of the castle—the quarters Malcolm had appropriated for himself—he found his saddlebags, desk, and portmanteau as he had left them.

But upon the bags were several drops of a glazed white substance.

"Candle wax," decided Malcolm, examining it.

Inasmuch as the Scot used lanterns in preference to candles, and as he had noticed no wax there before, he judged that a visit had been paid to his quarters during the night.

"The ghost, it was, my faith! I'm thinking 'tis not a proper spirit if it must light its way. Well, it would find little worth among my papers."

Malcolm's outfit was purposely meager and the more important papers, money, and reports he always carried on his person.

The boldness of the visitor of last evening could have only one explanation; whoever had searched his belongings had known that Malcolm was away from the village and that the Scot might be detained by Rawul Singh.

When he first came to the spot Malcolm had made a careful examination of the castle. It was solidly built of finely shaded sandstone, much corroded; its deep moss-coated cellars were basalt, as was the great hall, where decaying vegetation covered the floor.

All around, the undergrowth was thick—junipers and thorn bushes pressing against the crumbling walls and lush grass growing thick on the *dahlan*, the front terrace.

The cellars were half-filled with foul water at their lowest level; openings in the thick stone walls were few, and sunlight penetrated only feebly into the chambers of the dead raja. Malcolm judged that it had been unoccupied for three generations at least. Perhaps because of this, a strong odor filled the place.

Yet he was certain that the terrace and the slender, square tower had been visited frequently. The soft ground had been trampled by feet whose outline he could not make out; moss had been broken from the tower top and the damp slime on its steps was scored in more than one place.

"The demon," thought Malcolm, "does not quarter himself in the castle but comes here from a nearby haunt. Very well, we will watch for him."

They saw nothing out of the ordinary, however, for several days. Thick mango groves covered the *nullahs* below the rise where the castle stood. Often jackals and leopards passed by, but the village cattle were kept at a distance by the herders and no human being approached them.

Malcolm, going about the routine duties of his office, was struck by this isolation of the castle. He had observed that the signs pointed to its having been occupied before he came.

This led to the conclusion that the person who had lived in or near the castle before Malcolm arrived had vacated the premises in his favor; also, that the villagers who had been in the habit of coming to the castle now made a point of avoiding it.

"It looks," he thought, "as if my neighbor demon had had friends in the village. If—as the series of murders indicates—our distinguished ghost is a servant of Kali, a goddess to whom murder is an acceptable ritual offering, his friends might well be the slayers of Rawul Singh's son. And I think the Rajput knows they are Kali worshipers, although for some reason he will not admit it to me."

When he was not in attendance on Malcolm, the Scot noticed that his follower spent hours in casting about through the jungle around the village, and that whenever Malcolm went to survey the boundary lines, Rawul Singh made a thorough search of the hillsides.

Furthermore the Rajput reported that he had tried to find in the village the servant of the *potail* who had lied to him about the fate of his daughter. But the man was not to be found. And the lips of the *bheestie* who had warned Rawul Singh were sealed by fear.

So no trace was found of Tala, although Rawul Singh was convinced that the girl could not have been conveyed from the district of Bhir without his knowing it.

Taking all this into consideration, Malcolm believed that the man who called himself or was called the ghost had Tala in his keeping, and that both were very cleverly hidden in one spot that all Malcolm's surveying and Rawul Singh's search could not locate.

This spot might well be a rendezvous of the worshipers of Kali, who, having enjoyed unlimited power in the rich district of Bhir, now sought the extermination of the English magistrates.

Before many days had passed Malcolm fell sick.

The Scot had grown pale and his eyes were heavy. He was listless at times, although he never ceased his work. His orders were to assume the duties of magistrate, and he went about the work of measuring the boundaries, taking the census, and holding a criminal court.

Malcolm's condition puzzled himself. He had no fever; the water and air were good; Rawul Singh, who feared poison, gathered their food in the village, taking pains to select his own rice and flour and to kill his meat by hunting.

One day the Rajput absented himself and returned with a lean, dirty native, naked except for a loincloth and turban. It was an old man, watery of eye, who trembled in the presence of the English officer.

"This is Cheetoo, the *bheestie*," explained Rawul Singh. "And he will eat of the food we share and sleep without thy door. Thus if thou hast a plague, we will know of it, because either he will catch it or he will confess what is the evil that attacks thee. If he refuses I shall cut out his liver."

Cheetoo's trembling increased and he looked around fearfully.

"O Sun of Benevolence," he cried, "do not make me sleep within the castle."

"There is nothing here to harm thee," said Malcolm impatiently. He was irritated by his own indisposition.

Cheetoo glanced at the ruins and renewed his pleading.

"Peace!" muttered the Rajput, aside. "Twenty silver rupees wilt thou have, son of a pig, if the sahib gets well. If he dies, thy liver will be fed to the jackals as I promised. Do not think to escape, for thou knowest I will hunt thee down—"

In this manner Malcolm's party increased to three. The *bheestie*, torn between fear of the castle and dread of Rawul Singh—coveting the unexampled wealth of silver rupees and tormented by visions of what might happen to his own organs—Cheetoo went so far as to urge Malcolm to pitch his tent outside the walls and to shun the interior of the ruins.

The Scot took this as an attempt to get him to give up his quarters in the home of the rajas and lose dignity thereby. Rawul Singh whetted his sword and looked meaningly at the native's bare limbs.

"In the village bazaar," chattered the *bheestie* mournfully, "it is said that the sahib's breath is in his nostrils. He will soon be dead."

Malcolm had noticed how the natives stared at him and whispered behind his back. He had expected resistance when he collected the revenues from the landholders and the wealthier merchants; no one in this hostile province withstood him, but the eyes that looked into his were covertly mocking.

It got on his nerves—which few things did. He had expected to find an antagonist in the castle; he found no one. In the first week of his stay he had nearly been slain by a clever trick of his invisible foes. And now the sickness was gaining on him. His head throbbed and his sight was blurred. It was harder than ever to sleep.

III

One night he wakened at a slight sound near his head. Sleeping lightly as he did, he was fully conscious on the instant. Soft, regular breathing mingled with a rasping snore from the open doorway of his chamber assured him that Rawul Singh and Cheetoo were dreaming away as usual, just outside.

Malcolm reached for a pistol quietly and lay passive. The only other opening in the walls of his room was the broken aperture of a round window from which many stones had fallen away. Through this he could see clearly the panoply of stars over the blur of the jungle. On this opening he focused his attention, for the sound had come from that quarter.

Several of the stars were blotted out. Malcolm sat up silently and raised his pistol. He waited, scarcely breathing, for what seemed many moments; and then the faint light from the round window was darkened further.

Malcolm was puzzled. He had expected that the object, whatever it might be, that had come into the opening would continue its progress within his room. Instead, another object had appeared in the window.

Resolved to investigate, the Scot slipped from his bed and moved to the door in his stocking feet. At once Rawul Singh's heavy breathing ceased and the white man was aware of the Rajput standing beside him in the dark.

"Someone is outside," whispered Malcolm. "Come."

He felt that the Rajput accompanied him along the hall, to the gate of the castle—the way being familiar to both. Stepping cautiously out on the terrace, they examined the wall without result until Rawul Singh drew a quick breath and grasped the arm of the white man.

"Above, sahib," he breathed; "look at the tower."

Twenty feet overhead a figure stood on the summit of the square tower, outlined against the stars in the faint light of a new moon. Malcolm saw arms raised to the sky and the arms were knitted to the body like those of a bat. The head appeared very small compared to the grotesque body.

Malcolm shivered, believing for the moment that he was looking at a man in the form of a bat. Tales of werewolves that he had heard in his youth in Scotland flitted into his mind; he thought of the Witches' Sabbath and the night when evil spirits cast themselves into the air from a great height.

"A bat," he whispered.

Checking the momentary play of imagination, due to his weakened condition, he ordered Rawul Singh to stand watch on the terrace while he went into the tower. It was built, as was generally the case in fifteenth-century structures in Rajputana, against the corner of the castle, and a postern door opened into it from within the front passage of the main building.

There was but the one door and through a window Malcolm could see the tall form of Rawul Singh watching from the terrace below. Up the stairs he went, pistol in hand, his heart beating heavily.

The circular stairs were narrow and Malcolm was sure no one could have passed him. Yet when he stood on the tower summit it was vacant and there was no sign of the visitor of the night.

"If it was a bat," growled Rawul Singh, "it flew away, sahib, as you climbed up. It vanished into the air."

Disturbed, the Scot did not sleep again that night, and with the first light of dawn he inspected the tower anew. He was convinced that nothing could have got by him on the steep stairs, nor was there any opening in the wall by which the apparition might have leaped to the terrace un-heard—if that had been possible—by the Rajput.

One thing attracted his attention, and that was a portion of vine dis-placed from its hold on the stone upon the side of the tower away from where Rawul Singh had stood—the side of the tower that had been in deep shadow the night before.

The Rajput tested the strength of the vines and found that they broke under his light weight.

"It was not thus, sahib," he shook his head, "that the demon came down."

"Yet he must have come down," pointed out Malcolm irritably. "How long had he been gone from the tower top before I reached it?"

Rawul Singh considered.

"The space of time that a man might hold his breath without pain. That I know well, for I held mine until I saw thee. Nevertheless the time would not suffice for the bat"—so the old man chose to think of the visitor of the night before—"to escape out of the tower through the door within the castle before thy coming."

"So, you saw me look out of the window halfway up the stair?"

"Nay, how could I see through the shadow that was like a cloak?"

The explanation of the Rajput worked logically enough in its own bent. Since the bird-like visitor of the night had been seen at the tower top and had not been seen on the ground below, it must have vanished between tower and earth, and hence its appearance had partaken of the supernatural.

But Malcolm, frowning, reasoned that since the bat-man had not come down the stairs and had not climbed down the vines, he must have done, logically, just one thing.

He had run down the stairs, on seeing Rawul Singh appear on the terrace, as far as the window. Hearing Malcolm coming up from below, the man had climbed through the window, working down into the vines which had broken under his grasp, and had thus fallen to the terrace beside Rawul Singh.

If this were true—and Malcolm could not believe otherwise—Rawul Singh had held back information again, just as before when he had failed to admit that he knew the slayers of the highway to be servants of Kali.

Cheetoo gave it as his opinion that the ghost of the castle had been on the tower and had flown away on the back of a *ghil*—an invisible spirit of the air.

But Malcolm, inspecting the window that opened into his chamber, was certain that two large stones had been added to the ruins of the wall within the opening. It had been these stones, he reasoned, that he noticed against the starlight. Someone had pushed them into the window as noiselessly as possible.

Taking pen and paper, the Scot wrote to Cunningham as follows:

> *To the Honourable Sir A. Cunningham, Resident of Jumna:*
> SIR:
>
> *As regards the occupant of the Castle, formerly alluded to by your-self as the Ghost, I have to report that he has visited the tower wear-ing his long cloak which creates a resemblance to a bat.*
> *This personage has means of entering and leaving the aforesaid Castle unseen. He is endeavouring to wall me up in the Castle, or at least to close the openings of our quarters so far as possible without being perceived. That is a curious matter. Owing to a distemper that has attacked me, I beg that you will send at once a detail of soldiers to convey the revenues to Agra in safety, as I am bedridden.*
>
> *Yr. most obed't. servant,*
> MALCOLM.

This message Rawul Singh sent off by a chit bearer.

"Dog and son of a dog," said Rawul Singh to Cheetoo, "soon thou wilt dig thy grave, for the illness of the sahib gains upon him."

In spite of the Rajput's care and his own fight against the poison that was entering his system, Malcolm had been forced to take to his cot.

At this Cheetoo moaned and tore at his scrawny beard. Conflicting fears reflected themselves in his emaciated face, and the fear of the Raj-put's steel overmastered his dread of the Scot's enemies.

"*Ai,*" he whispered shrilly, "the poison that is killing the *farangi* is in the air of the castle. Know you not, O blind buffalo, that a man cannot live where fire will not burn?"

Rawul Singh was perplexed by this. Air, to him, was the same every-where, and the idea that their enemies might have poisoned it was absurd. As for fire, it was true that they did their cooking on the terrace, yet they carried their lanterns about the castle.

He went to Malcolm with the message, and the Scot pondered it. They had both noticed the dank, vitiated odor of the place but had accepted it as natural.

"Light one of the lanterns, Rawul Singh," ordered the officer. "Bear it first out upon the *dahlan,* then into this chamber, then down to the low-est cellars. Observe carefully whether the flame diminishes or not."

The soldier obeyed and came back more puzzled than before.

"Sahib," he reported, "this is a strange thing. On the *dahlan* the flame was big and strong. Here, it is not so strong. In the lowest prisons it dies down to a hair."

Malcolm stared from the lantern to his friend and whistled reflectively. He had not observed this peculiarity of the light as he had not visited the prison. He remembered that Cunningham's servant had said that passing natives forced by chance to quarter in the castle overnight always made openings in the walls. And this circumstance joined itself in his mind with the fact that the bat-like visitor had been trying to close the opening in his chamber.

Moreover the natives lighted fires and rushed about, clamoring and waving their weapons to scare off the deadly spirits of the place. This would be a very effectual way of displacing the vitiated air—the dank, curious-smelling element of the place.

Displacing the air—that would only be necessary in case it was heavier than ordinary air.

"Carbonic acid gas!" he exclaimed. "Comes from the stagnant water and decayed vegetation and the general decomposition of this old ruin. It hangs low of course and it's little better than rank poison.*

"My friend the demon," thought Malcolm, "was not satisfied with the rate of my demise; he wanted me to get the full benefit of the bad air by walling me in. Especially as he wanted the revenues, which would have gone to his own lease deeds. No wonder the doctors couldn't find out what was the matter with poor Powell."

Whereupon he ordered Rawul Singh to pitch on the terrace against the castle wall the tent he had brought with him to use in hunting expeditions. Then, aided by Cheetoo, he took up his new quarters. That night and the next he slept well for the first time in weeks. Rawul Singh kept watch on the terrace.

On the third evening the Rajput, well pleased, went to where Cheetoo was lying at the other end of the terrace by the fire.

"The sahib gains strength," he growled. "He will live. So, thou also wilt live."

Cheetoo did not answer and Rawul Singh, looking a second time, saw that he was dead, a cloth girdle wrapped around his twisted throat and his belly slit open by two slashes in the shape of a cross.

---

*Several hundred English soldiers died after leaving their quarters in ruined Indian castles, before the carbonic acid gas was discovered and the men forbidden to occupy the ruins. Rawul Singh had escaped the effect of the gas for the reason that the Rajput had slept in the great hall of the castle where the air was better, and had never come into the castle except to sleep.

Unwinding the girdle, the Rajput brought it to Malcolm, who observed that it was such a thing as was used by a Moslem for a waist sash.

"God receive his soul," he said moodily. Fingering the stout sash, he observed to himself:

"A *rumal*, or strangling cord, of the slayers who are thugs—worshipers of Kali. Did Cheetoo die because he warned me, or was his death to be a warning?"

They buried the *bheestie* without delay at the edge of the jungle, and as Malcolm helped Rawul Singh roll the stones on the grave—he could do little more, being still weak—he turned to his companion thoughtfully.

"Are the two slashes of a knife across the stomach of the *bheestie* similar to the mark of a knife that thou sawest upon the body of thy son?"

"Aye."

"Dost thou know, Rawul Singh, that when a certain band of murderers calling themselves thugs slay a victim they slash open the body in this manner before burial? They do this so that the gas contained within the human body will not swell the corpse, thus disclosing the place to jackals or dogs that might dig up the body and so reveal the traces of the crime."

Rawul Singh hesitated.

"Aye," he admitted, "that was known to me."

"And didst not reveal to me thy knowledge that we were dealing with thugs? Is this thy loyalty to thy master?"

The Rajput folded his arms and bent his head, his lean features working under strong emotion.

"Perhaps thou didst think," Malcolm accused, "that if I knew there were thugs in Bhir I would have fled and deprived thee of my aid in seeking revenge?"

"Nay." The other's head jerked up quickly. "I have watched thee, sahib, and I know thee for—a brave man."

"Words." As Rawul Singh was stubbornly silent, the officer hazarded another guess. "Thy daughter—the thugs hold her and have threatened her with harm if thou didst disclose their secret?"

"Nay. That may well be, yet no word of it has come to me."

"What, then?" The Scot was frankly puzzled by the demeanor of his follower.

There was no doubting the menace of Bhir, if there was—as he believed—a *thuggi* band in the village. Throughout the central provinces

of India it was becoming known to the English officials that these slayers, who at first were supposed to be merely dacoits, infested the main
villages and highways. The native officials were often bribed and more
often powerless to interfere with them.

The thugs formed a fraternity made up of every caste and profession.
By day they appeared as reputable merchants or craftsmen; by night they
assembled in bands to seek out victims carefully selected, and—as they
believed—foreordained to their hands. The cult was handed down from
father to son, and its existence was just becoming known to the English
officials.

So much Malcolm knew. Cunningham's story had led him to suspect
there were thugs in Bhir. What puzzled him was that, until now, the native slayers had not ventured to number an Englishman among their victims.

Moreover there was the peculiar individual known as the ghost to be
accounted for.

"What, then?" he repeated grimly.

The reply of the Rajput came like a flood when a dam is loosed. Malcolm's accusation had stirred his sense of honor, which was very high
indeed.

"Sahib, it is true that thou couldst aid me in my revenge, and that
these words—if they are overheard—may mean the death of Tala. I have
sworn to serve thee. Judge whether I am faithful to my oath. Two sahibs that were here before thee were slain. Thou art a brave man. Thou
wouldst not go from this place until the revenues were collected. As it
is, the thugs seek only to drive thee away, or to harm thee secretly. Once
they suspect that thou knowest their secret, thy fate is sealed. Thou wilt
lie beside my son."

He pointed quietly to the grave of Cheetoo.

"Thus! But there is still a chance for thee to escape. I say—go.

"Sahib, thou art well enough to travel. Mount, then, this night for Agra
and ride fast. If there are thugs in Bhir, they have marked thee for slaying.
Know, sahib, that secrecy is the veil that shields the servants of Kali; my
son they buried, but Cheetoo they left under our eyes. That means that
they have determined thou shalt not leave Bhir, to report their presence.
Otherwise they would have dragged away the body before slashing it and
we would have thought that a tiger had struck him down."

"Yes," acknowledged Malcolm, "I thought of thugs when I first heard the tale of the servant of Cunningham sahib. But what of the man who visits the castle and who is my enemy?"

"I know not. But consider this." Rawul Singh pointed at the fresh mound of stones. "*They* know now that thou wilt not die by the poisoned air, nor by my sword. So they may attack thee at once."

"Yes," said the Scot dryly.

"I will stay, sahib, and search for Tala alone. But you must go at once."

"No."

That night two men watched on the terrace where the moonlight threw a jagged shadow from the walls of the ruins. Under the tower where his outline blended with the wall, Rawul Singh squatted, his drawn sword across his knees.

Lying on his cot in the tent, Malcolm watched, pistol in hand, the play of light and shadow over the cotton roof. He was wondering whether Rawul Singh was not an ally of the man in the cloak—who took upon himself the resemblance of a demon—Rawul Singh, who might have slain the unfortunate Cheetoo, and who was now urging him to fly from Bhir, which was the thing his enemies wished.

Tossing on his cot in the hot hours of early night, Malcolm could hear the sounds of the nearby jungle, a buffalo crashing down to water somewhere at the edge of the rice fields—an owl hooting—the slipping passage of a leopard—the snarl of a jackal.

Wearied by his sickness, his senses sharpened by edged nerves, Malcolm felt that hostile forces were gathering around him. He knew that he was cut off from his kind—the chit bearer who had been gone ten days had not returned. Worst of all, he wondered whether he could feel certain of Rawul Singh.

Through the opening in his tent he could see the moonlight on the roofs of Bhir village, could glimpse a torch passing down the bazaar front or a turbaned group of men moving quietly across the central square.

These groups merged together, and lights danced across his eyes that persisted in closing with the lengthening of the night. It seemed to him as if the beasts of the jungle had halted in their tracks and were crouching, their eyes shining in the darkness as they looked toward him.

A cold wind blew into his face and he seemed to be lifted into the starlit air. A high voice shrilled down the wind, and laughter sounded in mocking words of a tongue he did not know.

It was strange, he thought dully, that the voice in the night air should laugh. It was very cold among the stars and their light hurt his eyes . . .

Malcolm awoke to find himself stiff from the chill of dawn and a gray light filling the tent.

Rawul Singh was standing beside him, looking curiously at the pistol still grasped in his master's cramped hand.

"Sahib," he said, "while thou didst sleep I heard someone call from the tower. I know not what it was, for the words were neither Hindustani nor Turki nor English. So, as thou didst, I ran into the castle to the tower stairs. Yet when I came to the window that looks out on the terrace I bethought me that this might be a trick to separate us, and I stayed at the window, watching and listening.

"Sahib, it was only a moment before I heard a man breathing very near. It was not behind me but in front of me. So I looked out, very carefully. And my face was within a foot of the face of the demon, who crouched below the window with his feet on the vines and his fingers on the stone ledge of the opening. I struck quickly with my sword, but he was more swift and dropped to the terrace. The window was too small for me to climb through, and by the time I reached the terrace by way of the castle door he was gone. Verily is he a thing of the night."

Malcolm read in the man's eyes that he was telling the truth. He saw now how the visitor had eluded them on the previous night, waiting probably crouched against the tower wall in the shadow until they had left the terrace, when he had slid down easily, breaking the vine in the process.

"So," he thought, "my friend the demon is very small in body, is quite fearless, has a sense of humor, and—speaks Portuguese."

"Sahib," concluded Rawul Singh gravely, "from this hour thou and I must keep together and one of us must always watch. I am afraid that the demon overheard our speech of the thugs."

IV

Ali Khan was as heavy as a buffalo and as light on his feet as a panther. He was of Afghan blood and his father had been a *rokurrea*—a professional carrier of money. His grandfather had been a Said, so good Moslem blood ran in the veins of Ali Khan.

A square jet-black beard was his pride, with a brace of silver-chased Turkish pistols and a Persian sword that curved nearly to his heels. Ali Khan was a bold man and boastful, likewise crafty.

It was for these reasons that Rawul Singh had picked the Afghan, ten days before they heard the voice in the jungle, for the chit bearer, to go to Cunningham sahib. Being an Afghan, the soldier was not one of the men of Bhir; being son of a hereditary messenger, Ali Khan was reasonably faithful to a trust—when he swore on the Koran, as he had done in the rear of a wine shop in the Bhir bazaar before Rawul Singh.

"Send a child, Rajput," the Afghan had gibed. "The task is not worthy of me."

"Thou wilt not think so when I tell thee there will be thugs behind thee and perhaps before. "

"Ho!" Ali Khan had fingered his beard. "Aho-ho-o. Well, I will go, and to Jehanum with all thugs, dacoits, and slayers."

"Hss!" Rawul Singh's sibilant warning had cut him short. "There be thugs about us now. Do not join company with any on the road; travel by day, and if thou dost esteem thy bull-neck dismount not from thy horse on the road; sleep in the jungle at night and then only after crossing the river—"

So had Rawul Singh spoken, as quietly as he might, but sharp ears had heard the boast of Ali Khan, and before the big Afghan flung his weight upon his horse a rider had slipped out of the bazaar and passed up the Jumna highway toward Agra.

Obedient to his instructions, Ali Khan rode swiftly until dusk the first day; then he swam his horse across the river, picketed it in a mango grove, and snored peacefully until dawn.

Regaining the highway, he pressed on, the letter of Captain Malcolm concealed in a fold of his turban. Passage through the jungle bypaths from village to village was more dangerous than the main road where merchant caravans, parties of soldiers, and peasants were usually within sight. A group of a dozen poverty-stricken Hindus besought the protection of the Afghan on their journey.

Ali Khan grinned and bade them be off, saying that the smell of a Hindu irked him.

Toward evening that day when he was hot and thirsty a party of Moslem cloth traders bound for Agra overtook him and invited him to camp with them that night and share their fire.

"Bismillah!" Ali Khan eyed them sharply; they seemed wealthy and peaceable; there was nothing about them to suggest assassins. "I would like to, but it is forbidden. Allah be with you. I go my own way."

They persisted in urging him to dismount and pressed around him. The Afghan's beard bristled and he touched spurs to his tired horse. When he had gone on a way he looked back and found the merchant cavalcade staring after him.

"*Yah Allah!*" muttered the khan. "They were thugs."

He shared the knowledge, common among natives of India, of the secret slayers of the highway. He knew that they followed their trade only when unwatched; that they slew only when the omens vouchsafed by Kali were propitious, and that they killed by strangling.

Very rarely did they use other weapons; moreover they were accustomed to choose certain spots for the assassination and travel with the victim until the appointed place was reached, where they could bury their victims at once.

More than one courier from Bhir, he knew, lay under the grass by the Jumna highway, and he suspected that the body of a sahib-magistrate of Bhir had been cast into the Jumna after the Englishman had imprudently joined company with a party of mild-appearing merchants.

So that evening Ali Khan said his prayers devoutly, alone. The next day brought no signs of thugs and he knew that he was no longer followed. Throughout the night he rode, resting his horse at intervals.

Dawn brought the sight of Agra's towers, and relief to the heart of the chit bearer. A few hours more would bring him to the cantonment of Cunningham sahib, where he could sleep, eat, and boast his fill.

"*Yah Allah,*" he muttered, satisfied. "I am out of the snake's nest. At the dawn prayer I will give thanks—"

He reined in beside a group of mournful-looking Moslem soldiers who were burying one of their companions in a grave by the road. The body was cleanly robed in white cloth, but the survivors stood disconsolately by, a Koran in their hands.

Seeing Ali Khan dismount and wash at a brook by the grave and prepare his carpet for prayer, one of them approached him and asked if he could read from the Koran.

"May I strangle if I can't read like a mullah," responded the Afghan.

He understood that they could not read, nor repeat the burial formula over the body of their mate. They asked him if he would do so.

"I would be a dog if I did not, and my beard would be defamed," acknowledged the big warrior frankly. "Besides, I owe such a kindness, for my life has been miraculously spared."

He cleansed his hands anew, took the Koran, and knelt on the cloth by the body and the grave. As custom prescribed he laid aside his weapons, and two of the party knelt beside him.

In a sonorous voice Ali Khan began to repeat the burial service. In a moment a sash was passed about his neck from behind, the two men at his side grasped his arms and he was strangled silently.

Then his big body was tumbled into the grave; the man who had taken the part of the dead Moslem rose. A caravan of traders came into sight from Agra at that instant and the thugs, perceiving it, began to complete the burial service over Ali Khan.

Before the last camel of the caravan had passed the erstwhile soldiers had filled in the grave, and Malcolm's messenger had passed from the sight of men. Only when the thugs took a folded paper from his turban did the act excite interest on the part of the passers-by on the caravan.

"Why do you take aught from the dead?" someone on the caravan asked.

"It is a message to his people—his last message," explained the young thug who had impersonated the body and who possessed a sense of humor.

The thug who had secured the chit stripped Ali Khan's horse of its silver saddle-trappings and mounted, forcing the nearly exhausted beast to gallop back along the Jumna trail. His companions remained behind, to light a fire—now that the caravan was out of the way—on the grave, thus obliterating the traces of a burial. The weapons of Ali Khan they divided among themselves.

It was nightfall of the second day when the thug messenger—Hossein by name, a *bhutote*—strangler—of the Bhundulkhand clan of Jumna—arrived at the outskirts of Bhir. Instead of entering the village, Hossein slowed down to a walk and took a cattle path away from the highway.

After following this a short distance up in the direction of the castle, he dismounted, tethered his horse, and slipped into the jungle mesh. Passing silently through a bamboo thicket—no easy feat—he parted a dense mass of junipers and stepped out into a cleared space that seemed to have for its center a square black hole.

Here Hossein was very careful to give the cry of an owl, repeating it after an interval of silence. Advancing with more assurance, he stepped out upon what appeared to be the square cavity. Here a flight of steps led down and Hossein disappeared from view.

The hole was, in fact, an empty tank, or well, built after the fashion of Hindustan with stone platforms a little way down and recesses opening into the platforms. Here the wives and daughters and servants of a raja aforetime had cooled themselves during the stress of a hot season. But the sandstone walls of the tank were now dry and overgrown with weeds. A snake crawled away unseen by the boy.

Coming upon the lower platform, he turned into a recess. Here a ray of light flashed into his face and a man peered at him. Hossein passed the sentinel and advanced along a stone corridor into a small chamber lighted by a single lantern set with red and green bull's-eyes of glass.

"Tala," he whispered almost noiselessly.

"Peace be with thee, Hossein," a low voice answered.

The youth stooped to peer at the form of a girl upon a divan against the wall. Costly Persian rugs and silk brocade covered the stone floor under the divan. A taboret containing fruit and fresh water stood by it.

The lantern hanging from the ceiling was so arranged as to cast its glow on the passageway rather than the curtained recess where the woman rested. But Hossein's sharp glance distinguished a pallid brow, circled by heavy, black hair, and black eyes that returned his stare dully.

There was something languid and indolent in the aspect of Tala stretched on the silks of the divan; there was indifference and lack of purpose in the slow movements of her eyes.

Her face, under the kohl and crimson stain, was lax. Yet it was young and wistful.

"Allah be good to thee," whispered the youth fervently, glancing anxiously over his shoulder as he spoke. "Thy beauty is like the moon and thy lips are flower petals. Happy the man who owns them!"

Tala stirred, as if trying to arouse herself to consciousness of something forgotten.

"Why am I kept waiting? When will I go forth from here, Hossein?"

"Soon, soon."

"Sometimes I walk on the bottom of the tank and see the stars, Hossein."

"Thine eyes outshine the stars, Tala, little flower-delight of my life."

She put out her thin hand and touched his tunic, and the heart of the thug swelled within his chest.

"Once, Hossein, I thought I heard my father speak—far above. He was crying pardon to Nag for killing a snake that had come out of the tank.

Why are there snakes here, and why does not my father, Rawul Singh, come down? He is a brave man."

Hossein moved uneasily, dragging his eyes from the girl's face.

"No one comes where the snakes are, Tala. Soon, *inshallah*, you will go up to your father. But do not talk of that to him—" Hossein motioned along the passage—"who is yonder."

Lightly he touched the girl's hand and was gone. But at the curtain at the end of the passage his swagger left him and he hesitated, feeling the chit that he grasped in his hand.

"Enter, Hossein," came a voice from behind the curtain.

The youth stepped into a poorly lighted chamber in which the air was very stale and cool. This was of more recent construction than the tank or the recess that was Tala's abode. Sun-dried brick formed the walls, which were bare. A pallet and table occupied one corner and by the table squatted a hunched figure of a man who smoked a hookah.

Into the mobile, handsome face of Hossein came a look of great respect. The man on the rug lifted a hairless face the color of old ivory. His mouth was a slit, and his eyes were very large and prominent.

He held out his hand. Hossein placed in it the letter that had been written by Malcolm.

Although the light from the single candle was dim, the man on the rug seemed to have no difficulty in reading the message. His face did not change as he laid it aside.

"You had no trouble?" he asked in Turki.

"No, *jemadar*, not at all. Warning reached us from Bhir of the approach of the big buffalo with the message. So we went out from Agra to meet him and persuaded him to read the Koran to us. That was because I played the part of a dead man, and I—"

"Enough of yourself." The man on the rug had a very shrill voice. "What are they doing in Agra?"

"They are talking together and holding council like a lot of old wives at a *dewan*, *jemadar*. They have sent couriers to Bhir—the thugs in the village cared for them, of course—and they are worried at the sahib's silence. Cunningham sahib is getting together a detachment of red-coated *farangi*—"

"When will he come?"

Hossein smiled.

"In a week. Master, your servant took care to learn all that before we left Agra to intercept the messenger from Bhir. Aye, we of the Bhundulkhand band accompanied the *khitmatgar* of Cunningham sahib into the native bazaar by the Jumna bank. We buried him in the mud. But first we put a sack of hot ashes over his head and beat it until his throat was seared and his lungs were half full—"

"Enough of your deviltries! I care not to hear of them."

"Cunningham sahib comes in a week—as soon as the passage of the rains and the decline of the river make the road fit for his *farangi* devils. We promised the *khitmatgar* that we would leave him in peace if he told us. And so we did leave him—under the mud of the river."

"How many soldiers will come?"

"Tenscore of sepoys—may their beards be defiled—and twoscore *farangi* troopers. Is it true, *jemadar*, that they breathe fire when they are angry and put a charm on their bullets?"

"Peace, parakeet!" The yellow man rose and Hossein saw that his dingy black cloak hung down to his ankles. The man was very lean, and his bones were small as a child's. Yet the wrinkles in his skin proclaimed him old. "You are very shrewd, Hossein, but you have not yet killed a dozen men and you know naught of the English. When they come they must find the castle of Bhir empty, without a trace of the sahib and his Rajput."

"Is the sahib-magistrate still alive?" Hossein was surprised.

"Ah." The man in the cloak smiled wryly. "It is strange that he is. He survived his first encounter with the idiot of a Rajput who was meant to slay him, and he was warned of the poison in the air of the castle."

"So, the sahib who took your place was not to be frightened away?"

The yellow man frowned, as if he could not understand that fact, and in his frown was something wild and vacant. A gleam of supreme cunning flashed into his dark eyes.

"It is better so. The higher powers, the wisdom of Kali Bhwani, has ordained that the *farangi* usurper will not die until the revenues he has collected from the district and the countryside beyond Bhir—until all that store of silver and gold is at the castle. Thus will we be rewarded for slaying the man."

Hossein bowed. He was thinking that it would be good booty.

"Within four days will Malcolm sahib have completed the toll and gathered the revenues together," he assented. Then, in an altered voice, "But what of Tala?"

"She will have her part to play when we strike against the sahib."

The man had answered with complete indifference, and Hossein's eyes widened.

"Tala, the Rajput flower, must not be placed in peril! Dom Gion, I will give—"

The breath of the yellow man hissed in the face of the boy. His thin hands clutched at the other's throat and fear leaped into the eyes of Hossein.

"That name!" Dom Gion's voice trembled with rage. "You dare to speak it? Have I not said to you that I am *jemadar* of the Jumna thugs, and master of Bhir—no more?"

The boy's sturdy strength easily pried loose the lean fingers of his assailant, and at this evidence of his own power Hossein's fear was displaced by a veiled cunning. He watched the old man as a dog will eye a snake about to strike.

"To no one else have I said your name," he responded smoothly. "Am I not your servant?"

Under the mask of complaisance he was measuring the old man's intelligence and craft as a strong young wolf of the pack will study the strength of the old leader. Dom Gion was *jemadar*—chief—of the Jumna band of half a thousand thugs; Hossein was the most youthful of the *bhutotes*—stranglers.

Dom Gion held the mastery of Bhir in his hand; he took toll of the wealth of its merchants, yet he gave wealth of merchandise to them—merchandise that was the spoil of the thugs' bands upon the highway.

And the countryside held him in fear as being a demon incarnate. This was because Dom Gion, who took pains not to let them see him face to face, talked to himself in a tongue that they did not know, and because the snakes of the ruins were friendly to him. Likewise his wisdom was more than theirs.

"Come, come," snarled the old man. "Indeed you are my servant and the bonds of *thuggi* hold you. The vengeance of Kali would blast you and bar you from paradise did you lift hand against me, or the thugs, your comrades. Go, and bring report to me when the revenues are complete. Think not of Tala. She is not for you."

Hossein departed, outwardly humble, yet as he went he cast a sidelong glance at the form of the girl sleeping upon the divan.

And, sleepless himself, he paced the jungle paths for many hours that night, his desire hot in his veins and his brain in a tumult. Hossein had taken from life what he coveted, and now he longed to possess Tala, who was ordained for other things by the master of the thugs.

While Hossein walked the jungle Dom Gion retired to his closet behind his bed. There, it was said by the thugs who waited on him, he prayed to his image of Kali, and after praying he often came forth in the form of a snake to glide among their feet and listen to what they said. And as proof of this they pointed out that Dom Gion, the *jemadar*, had no fear of snakes, nor had the cobras any dread of him.

But there was no image in the closet. Layer upon layer were placed squares of gold bullion and boxes of silver. Jade statuettes—spoil from itinerant Chinese caravans in Kashmir—jeweled rings and gems taken from inlaid weapons—for Dom Gion wore no weapon himself—strings of pearl that had been on the throats of women of Rajasthan before they were strangled to death—all in all the treasure of Dom Gion was a goodly store. And with the treasure were many dusty lease deeds made out on his behalf.

He knew every item of it. Although the closet in the rock was almost dark, he lifted necklaces of pearls and touched the shimmering balls gently with his fingertips. For Dom Gion was a miser.

Long residence in the half-light of underground had accustomed his eyes to the dark. In large measure he had the ability of animals of the cat family to see in the night.

Because of this, and knowing the plan of the castle as he did, it was possible for him to stalk the two occupants, Malcolm and Rawul Singh, without being cornered.

Dom Gion had not slain them with his own hands because there were two of them and he feared both and they were always together.

On the wall of the closet was a painting done by an Indian artist of a harsh-featured Portuguese merchant. It was clad in the fashion of a century ago. It was, in fact, the grandfather of Dom Gion, who had taken the daughter of the village *potail* to wife.

And in one of the chests was a *firman*, or deed, made out to his grandfather to trade in the district of Bhir. Dom Gion—as he was called, after his father—glanced at the parchment and smiled.

V

"Thou seest, Rawul Singh," said John Malcolm, "that all signs point to our friend the demon being a half-caste. I think he is more native than white even though he wears a cloak that has the seeming of a priest's garb."

"The gods know."

"A man of mixed blood always bears in his heart a grievance against the white man. And in the tale of the *khitmatgar* of Cunningham sahib it was related that the demon of Bhir was kin to the daughter of the village *potail*. In Agra I made inquiries among the traders of the bazaar and they knew of a Portuguese who owned the district of Bhir during the last war with the English, three generations ago. So this man of Bhir, knowing that his authority over the district is not lawful and nursing his own enmity against my countrymen—he is the one we have to deal with. And I believe that the thugs serve him."

Malcolm frowned into the fire. It was full moonlight without the castle and the wind was damp with the passing of a heavy rain. The two sat close to the embers, muskets at their sides. The collection of the revenues had been completed that day and Malcolm had hidden the money in the wall not three feet away, having removed a stone on the inside to make a niche for it.

It was a sorry treasury, he reflected, and, harassed and spied upon, he was a sorry figure of a king's magistrate. Nevertheless the money was there, the surveys and census completed, and—he and Rawul Singh still held the castle.

"It is the part of wisdom to study thy enemy, Rawul Singh," he nodded, puffing at his long clay pipe. "Now," he went on in English, "I'm not liking this quiet. We are watched. I don't think my chit bearer got through."

"Sahib," observed the Rajput suddenly, "it is in my mind that Tala is near us. Last night my ears heard her song, not so far away. Yet her voice was altered and I could not be sure—fearing a trick I dared not leave thee."

The Scot's eyes grew moody.

"That's a score we must settle," he thought. "This poor chap is waiting for me to give his daughter back to him and I'm blessed if I can see any way to it. We've learned that she is not in the village, nor in the farming districts. God grant she isn't dead."

"If it was a trick," the Rajput pursued the tenor of his thoughts, "it means that our enemies are girding themselves for fight. Aye, it was a warning, perchance. They will only attack us openly when all other ways are proved useless. Aye, they fear that the noise of our muskets and the sight of fighting in the castle—which can be seen plainly from across the Jumna—would bring down retribution from the *farangis* on their heads."

Malcolm nodded.

"So," he added, "they will try to get rid of us secretly. Aye, we will not be fools enough to leave our fortress. We have food and we will wait until they come, or Cunningham sahib comes."

"As the gods will—it may be that Tala will come, for she is near."

Rawul Singh glanced at the jungle. Malcolm sahib, he thought, might have escaped weeks ago from Bhir. But the *farangi* was a man without fear. Now it was too late; the net had closed around them, the wiles of the demon of Bhir would be loosed on them secretly so that no word would spread around the countryside that the men of Bhir had slain a sahib. It would be done inevitably as Powell sahib had been disposed of, and the other.

And now, leaning forward the better to listen to the noises of the night, he touched Malcolm on the arm.

"Danger is at hand," he whispered, "for men are coming up the path from the village.

Soon Malcolm noticed what Rawul Singh had observed—a muffled clamor on the highway beneath them. And presently he made out torches advancing up the trail to the castle. The patter of naked feet sounded in the jungle.

He leaned forward to light his pipe with an ember from the fire.

VI

That night the chief of the village had announced that there would be a *tamasha* at Bhir castle.

Word had been passed about the bazaar and the outlying districts by the chief's servants that the *tamasha* would be a very fine one—in celebration of the good harvest that had been gathered in. The leading men of the village, the visitors in Bhir, and the merchants would see a delightful buffoonery.

There would be fiddles and comedy-men and—the devout Muhammadans said it under their breath—a beautiful *katchani*, a dancing-girl.

All this would be for the pleasure of Malcolm sahib. So said the servants of the village chief. Yet he sent no word to Malcolm. Above all he was insistent that none of his friends should carry weapons, except perhaps knives that could not be seen.

Whereupon the men of Bhir began to gather in the bazaar and with them were the visitor traders, many of them acquaintances, it seemed, of Hossein, for they spoke with him in the alleys and nodded understandingly.

Another order of the chief was that none of their women should accompany them. This, in a Moslem community, was deemed quite fitting. When the slaves and the merchants of Bhir were in motion toward the castle Hossein vanished from the cavalcade.

The young thug slipped aside into a cattle path and ran swiftly up the slope to the castle, picking his way easily in the bright moonlight. Avoiding the bulk of the castle, he threaded the jungle to the side of the old tank that peered up at him from its malevolent shadow.

Here Hossein went more cautiously, keeping an eye out for the giant cobras that lived in the ruin. He did not meet any, however, nor did a sentinel of Dom Gion challenge him. Somewhat surprised, he felt his way into the corridor, calling softly:

"Tala, Tala! It is I, Hossein. I am come as I promised."

Finding that only silence answered him, he knelt, striking steel upon flint and kindling tinder taken from his girdle. Lighting a candle, he surveyed the chamber that had been the prison of the Rajput girl for the past two months.

It was empty.

Hossein muttered under his breath and ran into the quarters of the Portuguese half-caste. He knew that if Tala was absent, Dom Gion must be gone from his room. The *jemadar* had not loved Tala as Hossein loved her. Rather, Dom Gion had cherished her as he might a favorite snake, as if he were keeping her for some object other than his own desire. Hossein had made sure of this by jealous watching.

Moreover, that afternoon he had found opportunity to whisper to the girl that while the thugs and the men of Bhir were at the castle and the *tamasha* was in progress he would take her away, on his horse, from Bhir to Agra where she would have comfortable quarters and jewels and rich silk garments.

It was a risk, but the thug did not weigh that against possession of Tala.

Hossein had mustered up courage to do this. Had he not strangled the boy that had been Tala's brother with his own hand by order of Dom Gion, unknown to her? Had his men not driven away the cattle and sold them in another village? And slain Cheetoo?

This, according to the strict laws of the thugs, gave him a claim upon the woman that Dom Gion had taken for himself. Desire to possess the girl had decided him at last to risk flight from Bhir. Was he not strong and young? True, it was only when under the influence of the bhang that Dom Gion plied her with, that Tala spoke kindly to Hossein. But he fancied that the use of the drug had dulled her memory of her father, and that if he took her from Bhir, she would turn to him.

As for the Rajput, Hossein had no apprehension. Dom Gion would take care of Rawul Singh and Malcolm sahib as well.

But now the nest was empty and the bird had flown. Hossein's dark face twisted with the hot anger of the young Moslem whose desires are his fulfillment of life and whose enmities are his religion. He strode into the chamber of Dom Gion, peering about vindictively, and fearing that the half-caste had harmed the girl.

But the room with the cot was empty. Hossein's eye fell on the curtain that veiled the closet and temptation surged into his breast. No one other than the *jemadar* knew what was within there. He would look within and see the god to which Dom Gion prayed—a god that was all-powerful, since its servant was all-powerful in Bhir.

Very cautiously he parted the curtain, fearing the snakes that Dom Gion said were there. He saw no snake nor any image of Kali. Instead, Hossein glimpsed vast loot. He had not known that his master, who assumed the aspect of poverty, had treasured so much of the spoils of *thuggi*.

It did not occur to Hossein to rob his master as he might easily have done. It is one of the ethics of *thuggi* that the spoils of each member of the clan are inviolate.

But Hossein's heart swelled at the knowledge that Dom Gion had no god. There was no divinity that gave him power, not Kali the deity of the thugs—and Hossein was a devout servant of the woman-god.

"*Ohai,*" he muttered. "So, my master sought to keep the eyes of men from his treasure by fear. Well, I fear him no longer."

The thought of Tala returned swiftly to his agitated mind and the boy turned to run out of the chamber in the rock and up into the jungle. Dom Gion, he knew, had gone to the castle and where he was the Rajput girl must be.

Slipping noiselessly from the undergrowth, Hossein climbed the debris of the crumbling rampart until he could see upon the terrace where a score of torches flickered in the hot wind of the night, adding their glow to the pallid radiance of the moon.

In a serried half-circle sat the men of Bhir, with the visiting merchants. They passed the hookah stem from one to another. Behind them stood their young male children, gazing wide-eyed at three or four buffoons who, dressed as women and native dignitaries, danced about and sang to the sound of fiddle and drum.

The little boys laughed, with a great show of white teeth, for the *by-ropees*, the comic actors of the village, were very funny. They had painted their faces grotesquely and their antics as they imitated their superior lords were clever indeed.

Isolated from the gathering, Hossein could see Malcolm sahib and Rawul Singh sitting against the wall of the castle beside an open niche. The Scot was smiling, but the Rajput's lean face was grim.

Having carried out his orders from Dom Gion in bringing the assemblage from the village to the castle, Hossein was free for the moment and he squirmed nearer until he lay in the deep shadow of the tower.

The thug was trying to discover Dom Gion and Tala. Neither was visible; yet he knew both must be within sight of the *tamasha*.

He paid no attention to the shrill-voiced *byropees*, because he knew that a sterner drama, a conflict in reality, was impending. He knew that blood would be shed and the lives of the two men sitting by the wall would be attempted, yet in such a manner as to leave no suspicion of murder in the minds of the visiting merchants or the children.

On their part Malcolm and Rawul Singh were alert and watchful, although the Scot puffed at his clay pipe tranquilly and the warrior played with the fire.

Malcolm had received the gathering from Bhir calmly and expressed his pleasure at the *tamasha*. He noticed that no one bore arms—at least weapons that could be seen—and that the young boys were with the Bhir men. This might well be meant to drive away suspicion.

Yet he could not understand why the men of Dom Gion, who he expected were present, would attempt violence before the *bula admees*—the respectable persons—among the visitors who were with them.

Only one inkling did Malcolm have of what was in store for him. A big trader made a low, mocking salaam.

"Sahib," the man said, "it is written that he who takes usury from others shall suffer."

Rawul Singh would have responded at once and insolently—the idea of a bazaar moneychanger invoking the term usury had in it something of the farcical—but Malcolm checked him.

"The revenues of the government," the Scot said crisply, "are not a tax but a payment between friends. For what we take, we give value. Are your harvests gathered in?"

"Aye."

"Then, for this season they have not been destroyed by native raiders from other states. And tell me this: have you been forced to pay tax on lease deeds to him who calls himself Dom Gion and master of Bhir—since my coming?"

The man was silent, and Rawul Singh noted that he glanced covertly at the shadows on the right, the shadows cast by the tower.

"The man who made himself, illegally, master of Bhir," went on Malcolm with assurance, "will no longer tax you. He has slain wrongly and his reward will be that of a murderer—hanging, if we take him alive, but in any event, death."

Malcolm had been thinking of the fate of his predecessors when he spoke, but the Bhir men fancied that he referred to Dom Gion's connection with the thugs and deep silence fell for a moment.

They watched Malcolm with shifting, avid eyes. Before their eyes a contest was being waged between the *farangi* and the master of the thugs who did not permit himself to be seen. In fact, much of Dom Gion's prestige lay in his concealment within the confines of the castle. Judged by his acts, he was a man of immense power.

It was a strange thing, thought the men of Bhir, that this sahib should show no fear of his enemy. Dom Gion had assured them through Hossein that the sahib would, in the midst of the music and shouting of the *tamasha*, fall to earth shrieking with fear.

So they watched eagerly, to miss no detail of what would come.

And it came so swiftly that Malcolm and Rawul Singh were unprepared. A cloak fell away from a figure squatting beside the musicians and a woman stepped through the ranks of men. In her hand was a bare scimitar.

She walked forward slowly. On her dark hair was the silver tinsel cap of a Persian dancer, and she was dressed for the sword dance. Yet she swayed uncertainly, and her glazed eyes barely moved in their sockets.

Under the rouge the woman was very pale and by this and the dark rings under her eyes the watching Moslems knew that she had been given the heavy stimulus of drugs—probably bhang and opium mixed.

"Tala!"

The girl looked at her father when he cried out, but her face did not change. She had been set on her feet to do the dance that she had often given before Dom Gion. Yet, so were her faculties numbed, she could barely lift the sword or step forward. Still, she looked long at Rawul Singh.

Hossein rose from the ground, his hand on the hilt of his sword. He had not imagined that Dom Gion would allow Rawul Singh to see his daughter; the appearance of Tala, he knew, must foreshadow the blow that Dom Gion would strike. The young thug saw Tala snatched from his arms, and blood rushed to his head. For he fancied that he heard the shrill laugh of Dom Gion near him.

The Rajput girl had stepped forward among the actors, until she was only a few feet from Rawul Singh, at whom she was still gazing in a bewildered fashion.

Sight of his daughter painted and garbed for dancing, in the possession of his enemies, was like a blow in the face to the Rajput. Her indifference to him was a lash to his fierce spirit.

"By Siva and Vishnu—by the many-armed gods!" His sword came into his hand swiftly. "Woe to you who have done this thing!"

He took a step forward, his weapon raised. The actors looked at each other and their hands went under their loose robes. Malcolm caught the glitter of knife blades, and saw the trap that had been laid for Rawul Singh. In a broil the Rajput would be slain, and everyone present would swear that it was merely a quarrel over a woman.

"The girl is mine," observed the *potail* of the village uncertainly, drawing back as he did so.

Malcolm's hand checked the Rajput before another step was taken.

"Wait," he said. "It is my command."

Loyalty to his officer and fierce resentment struggled for mastery in Rawul Singh, so that he stood transfixed beside Malcolm. And then every head in the assembly became still.

The hookah stems were withdrawn from bearded lips; the clamor of the music ceased. A long sigh escaped the lips of the watchers.

"It is a trick," whispered Malcolm, "to make you attack them and to separate us."

Although they must have understood, none of the watchers moved or spoke. Their eyes were fastened on a spot a little to the right of Malcolm. Tala alone gave a low cry as if perception had pierced the numbness of her mind.

A yard from Malcolm's elbow, the head of a large cobra weaved from side to side. The hood, fully inflated, showed the brilliant spectacle mark. The light hissing of the snake was barely to be heard under the murmur of the wind in the vines of the ruined tower.

Rawul Singh, however, marked the sound and looked down, Malcolm following the direction of his eyes.

"Sahib," uttered the Rajput under his breath, "do not stir. The snake has been angered."

Malcolm could not take his eyes from the reptile, whose long length coiled near his foot, the tip of the snake's tail still within the aperture of the wall—the niche near which they had been sitting.

He reflected quite coolly that if he had moved—if Rawul Singh had continued his advance to his daughter—the snake would have struck. It had appeared quite by chance—yet Malcolm had made certain in the first day of his stay in the castle that there were no snakes in the ruins.

And, as if by chance, a twig fell from the air to the earth near the cobra, which seemed to swell the more thereat.

"Dom Gion is devilishly clever, after all," thought Malcolm.

Rawul Singh was powerless to aid his officer, who stood between him and Tala and the snake. He was certain that no one in the assemblage would risk his life by slipping behind the snake and striking at it—the only chance of preventing it from striking.

And the bite of the snake, Rawul Singh knew, would bring death to Malcolm sahib. The *farangi* might cauterize and bind the wound, but—deprived of the protection of the Rajput, other poison would be injected into him secretly—and a hundred persons would swear it was the snake that had caused his death.

He heard his daughter's cry, and his sharpened senses caught the slight sound of silk slippers on grass. Then there was a flash of steel in the shadow behind the snake.

The cobra darted its head at Malcolm, but the head writhed on the ground and there were two coils instead of one. Tala stared down at the stain on her scimitar, her eyes dark with the fear that comes to one who is wakened from sleep by an evil dream.

Rawul Singh jerked Malcolm away from the thrashing coils and the spectacled head that was still menacing. He snatched Tala back and peered into her face.

"Dost know me—thy father?" he said harshly.

"The snake frightened me. It was near thee." Her voice was dull and low but the glaze had passed from her eyes.

"Well for our honor that it was so and thou didst slay it."

A slight movement near them caused Rawul Singh to wheel and Malcolm to look around. His head bent in salutation, Hossein emerged from the shadow of the brush pile where he had been standing.

"*Ma'shallah*, sahib," he smiled. "God be praised that you escaped the snake. Now that it is slain you should be safe." His words were low-pitched and held a double significance. "It is a pity that this fine *tamasha* be interrupted. Sahib, favor your servant by commanding that it proceed."

Politely he saluted Rawul Singh and as he did so, the torchlight flashed on rich pearls in his turban. Hossein was quite composed, for he saw his chance to play a part and to strike where he knew Dom Gion had failed.

"Tala, thy daughter," he added to the Rajput, "has long been under my humble protection. Misfortune, perhaps the fate of her brother, had unsettled her mind and she could not recall the name of her father. *Inshallah*—what is fated, will come to pass. I did not know that she would appear this night as a dancer."

Familiarly he stepped to the girl's side and looked into her face. As he did so, his dark cheeks flushed for Tala was very fair to look upon. A new excitement had added its luster to her eyes.

"Is it not true," he asked her softly, "that I, unworthy Hossein, have spoken of love to you? Have I not been gentle to you?"

Malcolm, who had been staring up at the sky whence the stick had fallen near the snake, turned and looked quizzically at the girl. She half put out her hand to the thug, then frowned as if uncertain of her feelings.

Rawul Singh surveyed the placid Moslem youth fiercely, and glanced jealously at his daughter.

"I have been sick," she repeated slowly in Turki as if seeking for words. "Sometimes I liked you, Hossein. But you promised—you would take me away where I would find my father. Now Dom Gion has done that, although I do not quite know how—"

"She knows not what she is saying," broke in Hossein. "Too much opium has been given her, Rawul Singh, yet not by me."

Assuring himself that Malcolm was giving orders to the perturbed *potail* for the actors to proceed, Hossein bent close to the Rajput and whispered—

"Rajput, would you look upon the man who slew your son?"

"Point him out, and name your reward."

"Come, then, but quietly. He hides within the castle, waiting to set hands on the revenue of the *farangi*. Say naught to the sahib, for you know that he would but arrest the man and place him in a *farangi* prison."

"It must wait."

There was perhaps no other inducement that would have appealed to Rawul Singh so strongly. But he would not leave his master.

As for Hossein, he shrugged, then cast a significant look at the thugs in the circle of spectators and loosened the long sash that was bound tightly around his waist. In the shadow of the castle wall he might have a chance to set upon the Rajput.

The Moslem youth was a skilled strangler, yet he desired the sound of music to stifle any possible outcry, for Rawul Singh was a big man and would not die quickly even if set upon from behind in the darkness.

It would be a notable achievement, thought Hossein, and would bring him fame among the thugs—fame and possession of Tala. Dom Gion's craft had failed, Hossein meditated, and Tala had almost betrayed them.

He would risk being seen by the spectators, perhaps. But he was young and anxious to distinguish himself.

His deed would come at a fortunate moment for the thugs, for with Rawul Singh out of the way, Dom Gion might deal with the *farangi* that night.

"You have done your share in entertainment," Malcolm assured the *potail* and the other merchants.

"Now I will take part in the *tamasha*."

"The sahib is kind."

Malcolm looked at the ring of faces around him and smiled. Many of these were his enemies and many were thugs; but he knew that they would not openly molest him—at least until he gave Dom Gion an opportunity to strike again.

And this he did not intend to do.

While the *potail* and his fellows watched, Malcolm told off three or four torch-bearers and placed them around the base of the tower. He then looked for Rawul Singh, and noticed that the Rajput was hanging back, glancing anxiously into the castle hall behind him. He was hoping to set eyes on the slayer of his son.

Then Malcolm called to the *potail* and the leading men of the village.

"Come with me," he commanded, "and bring a torch—there are snakes about, it seems."

The men hung back but Malcolm was imperious, his hard eyes threatening. As they approached he beckoned them into the castle. Choosing his way, the Scot went quickly to the foot of the stair leading to the tower. Rawul Singh followed the group, preferring to watch from the rear where he could see any weapon lifted against his master.

Malcolm took a risk in leaving the Bhir men at his back, but he had selected them with care—fat men and wealthy, consequently timid of their persons. The music outside clamored away as the *potail* had commanded and drowned their footfalls.

Hossein slipped behind Rawul Singh. "It's time we took the offensive," Malcolm thought, "after standing 'em off so long. Better for the morale of all concerned."

With that, nodding to the others to follow, he stepped on the stairs running up swiftly. The final few feet he took in a bound and came out on the terrace top, pistol in hand.

Here he crouched, leveling his weapon.

"Stand up, Dom Gion," he cried to the figure that knelt against the parapet. "Or I fire. Come, come, I saw you watching me, and I'm rarely curious to see you, my friend, after this long time."

The merchants had not presumed to ascend the stairs, but presently they heard footsteps coming down toward them. By the glow of the torch they saw the thin figure of the half-caste, his yellow face pallid and his light eyes darting about him. One pace away was Malcolm, his pistol at the other's head.

"I have brought you," said the Scot to them sternly, "to witness the arrest of an evildoer, by name Dom Gion, who has illegally claimed governorship of the district of Bhir."

The *potail* and the merchants gave back readily; in fact, they made haste out of the castle corridor to the lights of the terrace. Dom Gion had built up an aura of fear about his presence—fear reinforced with threats—and it was perhaps the first time that they had seen him so clearly, face to face.

Moreover, not suspecting as Malcolm had done that the half-caste was in his favorite eyrie of the tower, there was something distinctly unnerving in the way Malcolm had, as it were, plucked his enemy out of the air.

Yet as the Scot and his prisoner moved into the light and the music ceased for the second time, many of the thugs among the spectators moved uneasily and felt for their strangling nooses and knives.

"Stand back!" ordered Malcolm, looking in vain for Rawul Singh.

Dom Gion glanced about eagerly, but the first figure he saw was that of Tala, staring at him hostilely, her eyes bright with anger.

"Is this the man who kept thee captive?" Malcolm asked her.

"Aye sahib."

At that fear came suddenly upon Dom Gion.

"Aid!" he shrieked. "Aid for the *jemadar*. Servants of Kali, strike down this man!"

He flung himself on the ground, crouching away from Malcolm's pistol, hope flashing into his twisted face as he realized that the other hesitated to shoot.

"Fools!" cried the half-caste. "Hossein—Oho, Hossein! It is the *jemadar* who calls—"

And then the watchers saw a strange thing. Rawul Singh stepped from the darkness of the castle. About his neck was bound a thug noose that dangled over his shoulders; his face was purple and blood came from his nostrils down over his beard.

In his arms Rawul Singh carried the limp body of Hossein.

"Sahib," he groaned, throwing the body down, "the thug would have strangled me. Aye—almost he overcame me, until he exulted and cried in my ear that he who had killed the son would strangle the father."

The Rajput straightened, glaring at Dom Gion.

"Sahib, it gave me strength—that word. I ask pardon of thee for not keeping beside thee—it was a trick of our enemies."

Malcolm studied the throng of onlookers and saw that many were slipping away. Those who were not thugs prepared to depart as hastily as possible with dignity. The death of Hossein had taken away any desire that they might have had to fight. The followers of Dom Gion lingered, scowling and muttering.

"And I," said Malcolm quickly, "ask thy pardon, Rawul Singh. I suspected thee. Thou art a brave man—a very brave man." Turning on the thugs, he announced, "Dom Gion will be shot if the castle is not cleared within a moment."

The thugs were not open fighters. They looked at one another, and went away, hoping for another opportunity to strike at the white man.

That opportunity never came, for the next day brought Cunningham and his men.

It was not until after Cunningham and his sepoys had reached Bhir and taken the prisoner, Dom Gion, in charge—pending trial before law for the murders he had caused to be committed—that Tala could be prevailed upon to lead her father and Malcolm to the tank in the jungle where she had been kept captive and where Dom Gion had secreted his riches.

This hoard, Malcolm assured Cunningham, should be returned to those who proved themselves kin to the victims of the thugs.

The lease deeds and other concessions they burned. And Malcolm, after convincing himself that all active thugs had left Bhir, deposed the *potail* on grounds that the man had taken thug money.

This done, he resigned his office and said good-bye to Cunningham, mounting immediately and riding away to his duties. For the ride out of the village, Malcolm was accompanied by Rawul Singh, who leaped from his horse and saluted the Scot standing, looking long and regretfully after the vanishing form of his superior officer.

Not until the dust of Malcolm's passage had settled down did Rawul Singh return to his hut and Tala.

Cunningham had rewarded the Rajput by appointing him *potail.*

Peace was established in Bhir. And for awhile Rawul Singh enjoyed his new prestige and the favor of the sahibs. He asked Cunningham frequently about Malcolm, when making his reports, which were always very brief and concerned mainly with the summary punishment of Mussulmans.

In time, as the district continued law abiding and prosperous, Rawul Singh became very restless, and his reports ceased entirely. He mounted his horse and rode to Agra to seek the Resident in person.

And in the course of time Captain John Malcolm, then quartered in one of the hill stations of Kashmir, received a letter from the Resident which said among other things:

> It is just as well perhaps for the influence of the Government among
> the natives, my dear captain, that the Rajpoot, Rawul Singh has re-

signed his office as potail. *I asked him for the reason that inspired his decision and he responded that Bhir was only fit to be administered by a trader or a woman, now that there was no fighting to be had.*

Rawul Singh then asked for your address, and, although I informed him that he is clearly beyond the age limit for our non-commissioned native officers he insisted that he would ride to Kashmeer and that you would have a place for him near you.

I fancy that almost any day you may see him ride in at your Quarters with his daughter on the horse behind him and his luggage in his saddle-bags. I had not thought that he would leave the grave of his son—you are aware of the persistency of the natives in clinging to such customs—but, upon my word, he seems to have adopted you as his son.

Y'r Ob't & Resp'tf'l Serv't,
A. CUNNINGHAM

The Iron Man Rides

CLING-CLANG! The bronze plate hanging in the summit of the watch-tower sounded its warning. The two men sitting in the shadows of an inner chamber stirred and listened. They did not speak; they never spoke unless words were necessary. Through the round embrasure the red glow of sunset revealed their faces—one hard and masterful, the other plump and patient.

Again the plate clanged, and the two listeners climbed the stairs that wound up to the tower's nest. They came out beside the sentry, who saluted them and pointed in silence between the roof posts at the dark line that was the road across the desert. The Nan Lu they called it, the Great South Road, and it ended here at the desert's edge, at the post station in the red clay barrens where a shrunken river crawled through ridged limestone and a haze of dust overhung the pony corrals and the clay barracks.

It was an important post, this at the end of the Nan Lu, late in the thirteenth century. Behind it a wall of dull brick stretched across the barrens and climbed over distant hills. And behind this wall lay Cathay, the home of Kublai Khan, who was master of half the world.

Along the Great South Road, out of the desert galloped couriers of the khan with a jangling of bells, dismounting at the station to throw themselves on fresh horses; camel and horse caravans halted for the night at the station; visiting ambassadors with their trains filled the barracks at times. In consequence the post commander was a good officer, a Tatar and a veteran—he who had come up out of his quarters below at the summons of the sentry. He was *ming-bashi*—commander of a thousand—and his name was Arslan. He had the broad, weather-beaten face of his people, and he wore with pride his armor of lacquered leather with wide iron shoulder pieces, and the open helmet with a crest of red horsehair.

Looking down the road, into the glare of the setting sun, he saw what the sentry had noticed—tiny dust clouds carried to one side by the wind. He counted twelve riders and two packhorses, and after awhile his keen black eyes identified the horsemen as an officer with a Tatar detachment and—another rider.

Arslan had seen many strange people come along the Great South Road into Cathay to the court of Kublai Khan; pale Russian princes and swaggering Arabs with horses and girls to sell. Once he had written down in the station report the arrival of a man from the Western world, a merchant, Marco Polo by name, of a city called Venice. And now Arslan had quartered in the pavilion of blue felt a woman of rare beauty. Since she was going direct to the court, Arslan had turned over the pavilion to her because it had been erected for high officers and nobility and stood a little apart from the barracks. Arslan had discovered that women going to the court were a source of trouble, and this one had caused him more anxiety than even a caravan of Badawan Arabs, homeward bound.

He went down to inspect the newcomers and, like a shadow, his Chinese secretary trailed at his heels, a solemn and wise scribe, bearded and robed in blue silk, a Chinese who could answer all Arslan's questions and write down anything he said.

In the courtyard under the tower the riders were dismounting, eleven Tatar warriors, one a commander of a hundred. The twelfth horseman puzzled Arslan. He was the biggest man but one that Arslan had ever seen. He sat erect in the saddle of a rangy black charger. He wore no hat, and from chin to toe he was encased in a mesh of steel mail, darkened by exposure to the weather.

From under level brows the stranger glanced calmly about the station as if he had seen many like it. And his eyes were blue, the clear blue of deep water. Upon the shoulder of a faded mantle a red cross had been sewn. So the big man was a Christian.

But what drew Arslan's attention was his sword—a four-foot blade in a leather sheath slung upon his back.

"Whence comes he?" Arslan asked the officer of the detachment. "And how is he named?"

The Chinese scribe at his side drew a paper tablet from his sleeve and wetted a slender brush upon the ink cake in his girdle, in readiness to write down the answers.

"He comes from afar, where the sun sets," responded the officer. "More than that I know not. We call him Timur Eré, aye, the Iron Man."

"Nay," Arslan objected, "he does not wear much iron. The guard corps at Xanadu wear more than that."

"True," nodded the officer. "We did not name him because of the steel shirt. He cannot talk to us, so we do not know his true name. But in the man himself there is unyielding iron. He does not bend under hardships or give way to a blow. *Kai*, I have seen him when others tried to take his sword from him, not knowing."

"Why is a captive allowed to keep his weapon?"

"It was the order that he should keep his arms and bring them to the court of the great khan."

The officer pointed to one of the pack animals burdened with a long triangular shield and a light helmet, and he added calmly—"As the order said, I have done."

Behind them the Chinese murmured persuasively:

"Hast thou forgotten, O Lord of a Thousand Men? Two years ago the order was given by the great khan—" and he bowed three times, his arms folded in his sleeves. "A merchant from the West, perhaps the Venetian, told the great khan of these iron men, invincible in fighting. So it pleased the emperor to give command that an iron man should be captured and brought to him with weapons."

"True," Arslan assented.

"Also," went on the Chinese, "the great khan commanded that a beautiful woman of the Christians in the Western world should be taken and brought to him, for him to see. That also has been done, and for two moons the woman of the Western world has been kept at this station. She is in the imperial pavilion awaiting the arrival of this other Christian so that the two may be sent together to the khan at Xanadu."

Again the bearded scribe bent his head three times before stepping back to write upon his tablet. The Tatar looked past the tower to where the blue dome of a heavy tent rose apart from the buildings of the post, beyond the horse lines. Then Arslan beckoned to the iron man.

Sir John Sheldon, Knight of the Hospital of Jerusalem and special envoy of that high and puissant lord, Edward, King of England, had journeyed far. He had been sent overseas to Jerusalem by his king to make report upon the affairs of the Holy Land. And he had found there only a dismal vista of failure—disheartened crusaders drifting back over the seas, the pilgrim galleys and the hospital in the hands of extortioners and merchants, and the few barons who still held their fiefs in Palestine quarreling among themselves and with the merchants.

And Sir John had little liking for all this. He was, men said, a man of valor in feats of arms. They said, more, that there was no horse he could not back and no weapon he could not swing with either hand. Nor would he turn aside from any venture upon which he had once set his foot. When he had heard talk of the war between the Saracens and the Tatars who had come out of the East, he had gone forth alone to see what the Tatars were like, and he had not returned.

A captive, he had fared for eight months over lands unknown to him, among Easterners who knew no word of his speech.

"Faith," he thought, "this ride is not short, and I am like to see the end of the earth."

Sir John did not think he would ever return over that long road to make report to his king. He had seen in the distance that evening the great wall stretching athwart the plain and mounting upon still more remote hills, as if guarding what lay beyond. And now the Tatars led him to the blue pavilion, unlike any other of the caravansaries where he had been quartered before. Its ropes were twisted silk, and even before he lifted the entrance flap he was aware of the scent of dried flowers and sandal.

When he stepped within, a man rose from the ground and barred his way. A man as tall and great of bone as the crusader. Sir John looked past him, where bright embers glowed. Smoke drifted up toward the hole in the center of the dome. The sides of the pavilion were hung with silk, and the earth was carpeted.

The silence was broken by a woman's voice, a clear young voice, and the giant stepped aside. Sir John saw then that the giant wore a leather tunic and a long cloak of wolfskins, and that his dark head was close clipped, though his curling beard was full upon his chest. When the glow of the fire fell upon the crusader, the woman laughed softly, and the sound was like an elfin chime.

"Well come art thou, O man of the Cross. Long have we waited thee."

Her speech was the lingua franca overseas, good Norman French and some Arabic, with snatches of Latin. Behind the veil of smoke the crusader saw her sitting with her knees crossed on a carpeted divan, a girl whose dark hair lay heavy upon slender shoulders.

And then her eyes widened, amazed.

"Thou art armed! Art thou the captive?"

"Aye, so," the crusader respond gravely. "And thou, my lady?"

Many strange things had he seen in the last months, but he wondered a little at this maid among the Tatars, at the slender figure so unlike the women of his people. She wore soft boots of a red leather, and the long sleeves of her white gown were embroidered with tiny crosses; the clasp of her crimson over-robe bore emeralds cut like a shield.

"They took Sonkor's ax—" she nodded at the bearded giant—"and beat him. He was an axman of my guard. The others they slew out of hand. They came upon us when we were hunting a boar." She looked up at him suddenly. "I am Thamar, daughter of Rusudan, Queen the Georgians."

Sir John had heard of the mountain folk who lived at the threshold of Asia, who were Christians and had always been warriors as stubborn in their faith as their pride. For centuries they had been masters of the Caucasus, between the inland seas.

"Art thou an ambassador?" she asked eagerly.

The crusader explained his mission to the Holy Land, and the mischance that had brought him into the midst of a Tatar force at night.

"They said that an iron man was coming," she answered gravely, "to ride with me to Xanadu, the city of the great khan. And they never harm an ambassador. Hast thou no paper of writing or token of authority?"

"Nay, Princess Thamar."

Chin on hand she gazed up at him, frowning a little. The mass of dark hair penned upon her forehead by a silver fillet set with square turquoise brushed her cheeks, half hiding the fresh curve of her lips and the clear depths of her eyes.

"Then do I fear for thee, my Lord of the Cross, because I know why they have let thee keep thy sword."

Sir John smiled, and her brow knitted the more.

"*Ohai*, thou art a man of might. They chose thee among many. Hast thou no fear?"

"There is no good in that," he said.

"Knowest thou what this place is?"

"A fair hostel after the desert."

"'Tis the gate of Cathay. Thou hast seen the wall? Beyond it thou wilt be a slave of the great khan—no more than a hunting dog or falcon. Magicians will have their sport of thee, and the pagans will stare at thee and

THE IRON MAN RIDES

in the end—" she hesitated, looking up at him steadily—"they will take thee before the emperor of all men. They will make thee draw that long sword and strive against them, until the life is cut out of thee. That is why the great khan made thee captive, to see thee fight."

The ghost of a smile still lingered on the crusader's wide lips, and it seemed strange to the Georgian maid that he was not grieved at her words. Rather, he seemed to be considering her.

"And thou, my lady?" he asked again, gravely.

"Even the Tatars will not harm the daughter of a king. But this is thy last night outside the wall and thou art armed. Take a horse from the lines and ride away into the desert, any whither. What fate could be worse than that ahead of thee?"

While Sir John pondered, for he was a man of measured thought, she added eagerly:

"If Sonkor had such a weapon he could cut down any who stood in his way. If we were mounted on the racing horses we could outride pursuit, and then, perchance, slay a courier, and take his falcon tablet and gain fresh horses by showing it."

The crusader shook his head.

"Better to go forward than to be taken in flight."

Nor would he change his mind when she pleaded anew—until she fell silent and sent Sonkor from the pavilion to fetch the evening meal from the fires of the station. This meal they shared, the crusader and the ax-man sitting together by the embers and Thamar perched upon the edge of the divan that filled all the back of the pavilion. Her moodiness had vanished, and often she smiled and sang brief snatches of Gypsy-like song. Sonkor gazed up at her with the wordless adoration of a dog, and indeed the princess of the mountains was lovely beyond the telling.

"Knowest thou the song?" she asked Sir John. "'Tis the jest of a brave man.

> *Ask for the stars, O Miriam*
> *I will pluck them for thee from the sky . . .*
> *Nay, ask not the moon, for that I have pledged . . .*
> *to Zuleika!*

"What thinkest thou of the Gypsy song?"

"It boasteth overmuch," commented Sir John, rubbing his chin.

"Indeed," she said, "they named thee truly, for thou art a man dull and heavy as iron. I like better the steel that sings and flashes and makes a swift end of misery. And wine. Give me the cup, Sonkor!"

The giant, who seemed to understand their speech, lifted the round bronze goblet filled with rice wine, and Thamar sipped from it.

"O my guest," she said softly, "drink deep, for thou art weary."

Sir John raised the great vessel in both hands. "Hail!" he cried, and passed it in his turn to Sonkor.

"The axman sleeps on the earth," she went on, "but it is not fitting that thou, a man of honor, should do so. I will share the couch with thee, with thy sword between us."

"I thank thee." Sir John bowed.

It was a privilege sometimes offered when women were journeying in strange lands, and quarters were cramped and night alarms were to be feared. And the drawn sword placed between them was the man's pledge that he would not touch the maid.

Sonkor let the fire die, and when Sir John stripped off the steel mesh of his mail and made his way through the near darkness of the pavilion to the couch, the girl seemed to be asleep under her cloak. Quietly he drew from its leather sheath the four-foot sword and laid it beside her, the hilt near her head. Then he stretched out, pulled a saddlecloth over him, and lay with his head on his clasped arms watching the swaying of the dim tapestries under the wind's touch.

He could feel the slight stir of her breathing, and he was aware of the scent of dried flowers that came from her hair, a fragrance that intruded among his thoughts. Tomorrow he would be within the wall. There was no escape. At least he would find his death when he stood weapon in hand before the eyes of this monarch of Cathay. There were worse ends than that. But Thamar? They would be together in the last of the journey, and it would be joyful for him . . . in Cathay . . . the scent of flowers . . .

Sir John woke without a start, and was wide awake on the instant. The pavilion was dark, the air cold; a breath of wind touched his face. Across from him a triangle of faint light disappeared suddenly.

The entrance flap had been lifted, admitting the gust of air that had awakened him, and closed again. He listened, and could hear nothing at all. He stretched out his hand, and then swept it across the couch. Thamar was not there, nor was his sword.

Wasting no thought upon the how or why of it, the crusader got to his feet, felt for the center pole of the pavilion and lurched to the entrance. But when he pushed through the entrance his blood was stirring, sleep gone from his limbs. Kneeling, he looked from side to side along the ground. The light of the stars was clear, and against it he found what he sought, two figures moving away from the pavilion.

On the taller of the two, for an instant, metal glinted—the star glow reflected from polished steel. Sir John was unarmed in his sleeveless leather tunic and leggings; but this did not stay his run and leap upon the taller figure. His arms closed around the waist of a big man, and he threw him heavily.

He heard a woman's gasp beside him and the snarl of an oath beneath him—and the clang of steel upon stones. Bending over, he felt for and found his long sword and rose with it in his hand.

"Bid thy churl keep his distance," Sir John said. "For I have no mind to strike him down."

"Hush—oh, hush!" Thamar's voice whispered.

Sir John heard the stamping of restless horses, saw the dark blur of picketed beasts near at hand, by the black bulk of a shed. Then men came running up from behind the shed, a lantern swinging among them. They were Tatars, evidently the guards of the horse lines, and they stared silently at the three captives, thrusting the lantern close to Sonkor, who was rising from his knees, shaken by the heavy fall on the hard earth.

Thamar's face gleamed white in the lantern light, above the dark folds of her cloak.

"Ill was thy waking!" she cried at the crusader. "Another hour and we would have been riding free."

But Sir John was ill pleased by the taking of his sword.

"A woman's fancy," he responded harshly, "to try to lift horses under eyes like these." And he pointed at the Tatars.

"O churl," she whispered. "Thou art no man, but a dull beast fit to be led to the slaying pit."

And she turned back to the pavilion.

But Sir John sat out the hours of the night by the entrance among the guards who were both puzzled and suspicious.

After the first light Arslan talked it over with the officer of the detachment that had brought Sir John, and it seemed clear to them that the captives had quarreled.

"Before the iron man came," Arslan ruminated, "the woman made no harm."

"A woman," responded the officer reflectively, "is like a magician. Who knows what she will do? Nay, I will keep them apart and not allow them to speak."

So after that morning, armed Tatars rode between Princess Thamar of Georgia and Sir John Sheldon. Only through the tossing horsetail plumes and the shaking lances could the crusader see the hooded head of the girl as they raced along the Great South Road. But when he sat alone of nights over the embers of a fire, he beheld again her dark, lovely head in the whirling smoke, and in his memory he heard again the echo of her song.

The sun struck through the forest of Xanadu where Kublai Khan had built his pleasure palace. Life stirred in the shadows under the blue pines and the tendrils of the willows, for the forest was filled with game. Quail scampered through the lush grass, and deer flitted away in the clearing; waterfowl clamored among the rushes of the lake, and cormorants splashed in the shallows.

The air was heavy with the fragrance of sun-warmed vines and cedars. In a grove of gnarled cedars by the edge of the lake Sir John had been quartered alone, in a gilded kiosk of split bamboos. His Tatar escort had left him at the forest gate, and an Armenian merchant had appeared to guide him to this spot, and to explain that on the morrow he would be led before the great khan. Then the merchant had left him, solitary, to all seeming, but with invisible companions.

Even the little kiosk was full of unexpected things. At first Sir John had seen only a silk-covered pallet and a lacquered table with a low chair beside it. Paper lanterns with long tassels hung from the peak of the roof, and upon the bed lay a light robe of floss silk with long sleeves, very much like a knight's surcoat. This Sir John put on, after doffing his heavy mail and placing it beside his helmet and shield that had been left with him at the bamboo hut.

"Faith," he muttered, "here is comfort enough, but little to eat."

He did not venture out until after sunset, when he heard music over the water; and, going down to the shore, he beheld something that looked like a gold castle moving across the lake. Women's voices reached him faintly, rising and falling in a slow cadence that kept time to the dipping of the oars. The strange pleasure barge merged into the mists, the singing ceased, and the crusader went back to his quarters, pausing on the threshold with a quick-drawn breath.

The lanterns had been lighted in his absence. Some of them were still revolving slowly, and while he had not noticed them before in the obscurity of the pointed roof, he had reason enough to stare now. They glowed in fantastic colors, and leered and grimaced at him. Human faces had been painted within the paper globes. And the table now bore a silver tray filled with sugared fruits and smoking mutton and a bronze pitcher of clear wine.

Sir John looked around and sat him down, drawing out his knife and attacking the meat with good will. He filled a jade cup with wine and lifted it toward the gallery of lanterns.

"Hail!" he laughed, and then sat rigid.

Among the lanterns a human face looked down at him from sightless eyes. The skin of the face was shrunk upon the bone and the lips were drawn back from set teeth.

But the crusader had seen before now the severed head of a man, although not one stuck upon a hook above his own.

"Poor wight," he thought, "his day is o'er. Aye, he has gone before me."

He attacked his dinner again, the head under the roof disturbing him less than the movement and snuffling that went on outside the bamboo walls. Keeping one eye on the door, Sir John listened curiously. The breathing resembled an animal's, but the slight rustling and tread suggested the presence of men.

So he moved his chair to face the door, which stood open, and went on eating in the intervals of quiet. Evidently he was spied upon, and the stealth of the creatures outside was not reassuring. Sir John sipped his wine slowly and waited patiently. The movement ceased, but he still could hear the faint sniffing.

Then he set down the jade cup and frowned. In the square of darkness beyond the door two green eyes glowed. They vanished and appeared again, more clearly, moving toward him.

Sir John's hand closed upon the hilt of his sword and for a moment he sat motionless.

Without a sound a long leopard padded into the room and snarled.

Presently the leopard turned its head, and the crusader saw the mark of a collar on its neck. It wore no collar, but he knew the mark, and the manner of a hunting leopard—a tame animal. When it brushed against his leg he wiped his hands on its fur. The big cat sat down and began to lick itself over, like any domestic tabby. Sir John finished his wine.

Only once more was he disturbed, when a man came to call the leopard away. The crusader saw him outside the door, a bent figure in a short cloak, a dark, seamed face nearly hidden in a mass of hanging hair from which projected the horns of a beast. The figure hissed and the leopard padded out; then man and beast disappeared, and Sir John laughed.

"Faith, they have quartered me among the magicians, and they are the jesters of this court."

Whether he had hit upon the truth, or whether these men of the forest of Xanadu had meant to try his courage, he did not know. He was left in peace until the sun was high the next morning, and then appeared a Tatar clad in shining cloth-of-silver, with a gold baton in his hand. He rode a white pony and led by the rein a bay horse, and he signed for the crusader to put on his mail and helmet. Curiously he watched while Sir John adjusted the loose coif over his shoulders and laced tight the gorget of his steel headpiece, and picked up his shield.

At a foot pace the two rode through the sunlit forest. Other cavalcades going in the same direction drew aside for them, and the crusader saw that all the Tatar nobles were in court robes of stiff silver cloth and gold tissue; some of them carried white gyrfalcons on their wrists, and their saddlecloths were flowered silk or tiger skins. Never had Sir John seen such horses. No one mocked him, although the slant eyes stared at him with grave curiosity. The throng became denser, and Sir John saw that he was passing through a strange gateway.

On either side stood elephants draped in black leather with turbaned men astride their shoulders. First one then another threw up its trunk and the earth reverberated with their trumpeting roar, while the sword blades flashed on their tusks, and the horses danced in terror. But the crusader sat erect in the saddle, his hand firm on the rein, and the Tatars did not guess that he had never seen an elephant before. They signed to him to dismount and led him through a garden of twisted cedars, out upon a stone terrace. And he knew then that he stood before Kublai Khan.

On his right hand rose a marble palace, the crown of a hill that descended at his left, terrace by terrace, to the blue lake. Beyond the lake he saw the dark mesh of the forest and snow peaks rising out of distant mist.

The portico of the palace rested upon gold pillars, each the semblance of a dragon with its head and claws upholding the marble eaves. In front of the portico the crusader beheld a white canopy like a tiny tent against the mass of the palace. But yellow silk covered the marble here, and in the shadow of the canopy a man sat upon a dark jade dais. Around him were grouped the Tatar lords, and on the steps beneath him stood long lines of guards, their black helmets crested with white horsehair.

Toward these guards Sir John was led, up many steps and out upon a second terrace of red tiles. It was an arrow's flight in width and length, and he felt as he strode across it that a thousand eyes took stock of him. Tatar officers came forward to meet him and motioned to him to undo his sword. He did so, and they took it and his shield and carried them up, placing them before the man on the dais.

Two of the officers remained at his side, waiting until they should be summoned to the khan. Meanwhile giant negroes hastened up, tugging at the chains that were the leashes of lean tigers. They led the beasts before the jade slab, falling on their knees and veiling their eyes with their arms. And the tigers, a score of them, lowered their striped heads, swaying from side to side and snarling—making their salutation to the khan. The fierce heads sank to the paws, and then the negro keepers drew their charges away, and a woman was led forth from the guards.

"Princess Thamar!" the crusader cried.

She heard him, glanced at him swiftly, and went on. Her hands had been bound together loosely by silk cords as a sign that she was a captive. Alone she stood before the dais, looking up into the face of the man who sat heavily in a low gold chair, powerful hands resting on his thighs. His head was broad and dark and expressionless; his wide mouth beneath its thin drooping mustache was both cruel and full of power; under a jutting forehead, blue eyes surveyed the beauty of the girl before him.

After a moment Kublai Khan turned his head, spoke a word to the nobles who stood below him, and Princess Thamar was led to one side. So it happened that Sir John came within a spear's length of her when he was ushered forward in his turn. The Tatars on either side caught him by the arms and motioned him to kneel. His sword and shield were brought and laid at the feet of the khan.

Then the crusader was aware of another who knelt at his side, and of a curling beard that brushed the marble step—Sonkor's beard. For a moment the khan upon his golden throne surveyed the two captive men of valor, and not so much as the rustle of a robe broke the silence. The khan spoke, and when he had ceased a peacock on the jade throne stone lifted its wings and spread the glory of its tail; but the wings were gold, and the bird was gold, and the plumes were set with the sheen of pearls and the gleam of yellow diamonds.

"Rise," said a voice in good Norman French.

Sir John found a stranger at his side, a short man in a velvet cloak and somber cap, whose beard was carefully trimmed and whose eyes were keen and patient.

"My master, 'tis an ill word I have to speak thee. The great khan hath commanded me to bid thee arm thyself and fight with this stout fellow." The stranger nodded at Sonkor. "There is no help for it, but whoso slays the other will be spared."

Turning to the Georgian axman he explained again that the two Christians must fight before the Tatars, and the survivor would not be harmed. Sonkor was to choose a shield and a weapon from the guards.

The bearded warrior understood, for he nodded, and suddenly threw himself toward Thamar, drawing his two guards with him as if they had been children tugging at the horns of an ox. On his knees he pressed his lips against the hand of his young mistress, and rose to his feet.

"And what of her, the princess?" Sir John asked the interpreter.

The stranger glanced at the headdresses of the women of the court, as if puzzled, and then at Thamar.

"The captive? Nay, there are a hundred women of royal blood within this place. The khan said that indeed she is beautiful, and will bear strong sons when he gives her as a wife to some brave officer."

A swift rush of blood darkened Thamar's throat and brow.

"No Tatar will boast that he had me in his arms, for if that happens I shall be dead." She bent her head, a faint smile on her dark lips. "Nay, my Lord of the Cross, it is I who must yield up my life, for thou mayest prevail in the weapon play, since Sonkor wears no armor."

Sir John checked the words that quivered in his throat.

"May God keep thee, my lady," he said at last. Grim of face he turned away, for he loved the girl who had mocked him.

He made his way down the steps, through the ranks of the guards that opened to let him pass and closed after him. Not until then was he given his sword and shield, and the one he thrust on his left forearm, the other he gripped and swung about his head until the fine-edged steel hummed in the air. Out upon the red tiled terrace he strode, into the great cleared place where Sonkor awaited him, in the heart of the watching concourse.

Turbaned men and slaves, scarred veterans of Tatary, long-robed savants of Cathay—all watched impassively the two champions of Christendom.

"By the rood," said the crusader, "let us make an end of this, Sonkor."

A glance showed him that the Georgian had chosen a round shield of rhinoceros hide, and a long-handled ax with a heavy head. Bearded jaw outthrust, legs bent, he poised himself against the first blow. Sir John still held his sword tip down; he knew that he could slash that shield into fragments and then cut through the clumsy guard of such an ax.

"Thy death is at hand," he said slowly. "Dost thou understand?"

Sonkor's teeth gleamed through his beard as he growled assent.

"And so is mine," went on Sir John, resting the point of his sword on the tiles. "Never has it been said of me that I sought to gain life by the death of a companion. I will not lift weapon against an unarmed churl, but together we will go against the Tatars. Wilt thou do it, fellow?"

Bewilderment struggled with suspicion in Sonkor's broad face. He knew that he was doomed in any case. But to have a comrade at his side—to go down striving with a multitude—that was good. Fiercely questioning, he peered into the cold blue eyes that looked down at him from under the steel rim of the helmet.

"Aye!" he cried.

"Come," said Sir John quietly, and turned on his heel. "Follow, and keep my back."

Utter silence fell upon the watchers as the two champions strode back toward the steps. The heavy footfall of the axman echoed the clanking tread of the mailed crusader. Nearer they came to the lines of guards. A murmur rose and swelled as a helmeted Tatar went out and motioned them back with his long spear. Sir John stepped forward and slashed off the point of the spear. His long sword swung again, and the guard's head jerked from his body.

Behind the crusader, Sonkor roared his battle shout, and the knight knew that berserk fury had seized the axman. A half-dozen Tatars rushed toward him, and he strode to meet them in silence. He had been brought before this pagan emperor to fight and he meant that this affray should be memorable.

He thrust swiftly over the shield of the nearest guard and the man went down with his throat open. A side slash of the long sword and another fell heavily. Taking the smash of a curved sword on his shield, Sir John sprang back.

Sonkor's ax crushed in the face of the Tatar who had struck the knight. Then, beside himself, the big Georgian smashed out to right and left—flung his shield into the eyes of a foeman, and gripped his ax shaft with both hands. Grimly the Tatars closed in around him, until Sir John, seeing his peril, drove at them with raised shield and lowered point and cleared a little space.

"Back to back!" he shouted, and felt the straining shoulders of the ax-man against his own.

Now they were the center of a ring wherein the clatter and clang of steel sounded louder and swifter. Sir John heard Sonkor groan, and the thudding of steel blades into a human body.

Leaping aside, he swept his sword out and down, turning swiftly on his heels as he did so. Sonkor had vanished as a dog goes down among wolves. He himself was hemmed in, nearly carried from his feet. He felt his peril, and lowered his head behind his shield. Shortening his sword, bracing it against the shield's edge, he thrust suddenly between the men who had rushed in too eagerly to grasp him. Swords smashed in the steel links on his shoulders and thighs, and the glancing blow of an ax stripped the mail from his right arm.

Blood spurting from him, the crusader drove clear of the massed Tatars. Blood was in his mouth, and he felt that his helmet was gone. For an instant he saw the white palace against the deep blue of the sky. Then he turned and hewed at his foes, his battle shout roaring from his straining lungs.

Where the great sword struck, iron shattered and bones splintered. Men ran at him from the side, and he swept them down and sent their bodies sliding and clanking over the tiles.

"For the Cross!" he thundered.

Under the blow of a mace a bone snapped in his thigh and he staggered. The sky was red, all was red, seen through the drip of his own blood. His shield arm dangled, broken from his torn shoulder, and in his ears roared ever louder the cling and the clang, and the *crash*—

It ceased. The Tatars drew back from him, their weapons lowered. Through the red mist he watched them. And then he heard the high note of a horn, again and again. From among the Tatar warriors advanced the stout man in the cloak.

"My master—my master!" Sir John became aware that the interpreter was shouting at him. "Thou art saved. The khan hath spoken."

Reeling, the crusader steadied himself by leaning upon his sword.

"I'll have no mockery! Bid them make an end."

"'Tis ended. Hast thou forgotten? The great khan pledged life to the survivor of ye twain. Little thou knowest of the justice of Kublai Khan. I have seen stranger things—I, Marco Polo, who served him for eight long years—but never before hath a man wielded weapon in Cathay as thou hast done. That is why thou art spared. Put down thy sword!"

"Were thou Michael," Sir John gasped, "the archangel, and were that horn Gabriel's I'd not yield me."

Suddenly his head fell forward on his chest, and the Tatars exclaimed loudly. The crusader had lost consciousness, but a last effort of will had stiffened the muscles of his legs, so that he remained upright, propped against the broad hand guard of the sword, steadied by the weight of the dangling shield, as if indeed his limbs were iron.

And in front of the jade throne stone, below the feet of Kublai Khan, a woman knelt with bound hands, imploring to be heard.

Sir John woke slowly and for a space lay staring upward. Over his head shone a dim silver moon. It seemed strange to him that the moon should be under a peaked roof, until he reflected that it was really a lantern, and the roof was part of the bamboo kiosk where he had once met a leopard. He looked for the head of the dead man, but it was gone.

A gentle wind rustled through the cedars outside and stirred the rushes by the lake's shore. He could smell the water and the night air, and the fragrance of flowers. Bit by bit memory returned to him, but it all seemed unreal—that struggle on the terrace of Kublai Khan. Even the bed was different, and when he listened he caught a faint sound of breathing at his side. After awhile he turned his head to look.

Truly the light was dim, but surely a girl lay on the pallet beside him, wrapped in a gown of white floss silk, her face white under the silver lantern. By the mass of her dark hair and the curve of her parted lips he knew Thamar.

"I' faith," he thought, "I am dreaming two dreams at once, and the magicians of this place have laid a spell upon me."

So thinking, he tried to stretch out his left arm, and grunted with sudden pain. For a man with a broken thigh and arm cannot move without hurt. The girl stirred and sighed and rose from the bed. She went to a low table and drew a wet cloth from a porcelain bowl.

Kneeling beside him, her eyes heavy with sleep, she uttered a crooning sound and pressed the cold cloth against his forehead. Then she withdrew it and saw that he was awake. The cloth fell from her fingers and color flooded her cheeks.

"My lord—the fever hath left thee."

"Fever, or a dream, or witch work!" Sir John muttered. "I know not what. Why art thou here?"

Her head tossed angrily.

"Why? The great khan commanded that I be given thee, for—for a wife." Then her eyes turned aside swiftly, and she whispered. "Nay, thou must sleep."

She rose to her feet and reached up for the tasseled cord that hung from the lantern and pulled down the silver globe. Then the room was in darkness and he could no longer see Thamar. But his ears caught the sound of her breathing, swifter than before. For many moments he lay silent, because he was thinking and that was ever a matter of time with Sir John.

"So the khan gave thee to me," he observed at length.

"Aye—hush! Thou must sleep."

"He did well, for otherwise I would have sought thee in all Cathay—aye, and kept thee. Why dost thou weep?"

"I—I do not know. My Lord of the Cross, when I first saw thee I thought thee a sluggard and a coward. Then when I would have fled from the wall, I hated thee for standing in my way. But when we rode together into Cathay, I saw thee take thy stand at the side of poor Sonkor. And O my lord, never did man so bear himself as thou that day. And I besought the khan to give me to thee." Her voice ceased and then whispered hastily, "Because I did not wish to be a Tatar's slave."

"Yet," Sir John pondered aloud, "I am a captive and a broken man."

She was not crying now, and there crept into her voice the murmur of music.

"And what am I? Nay, my lord, I do not think there is any power of human might that can make thee captive."

He stretched out his right hand, and his fingers fell across the girl's warm throat. She did not draw away and her hand pressed softly upon his. Under his fingers he felt the swift throbbing of her heart's blood.

And so he lay silent, with the scent of flowers near him, and caring nothing for the world, since all was well in Cathay.

"Aye," cried Rob his tongue tripping with eagerness. "You do remember! Ellen, is—is not this one my lord father?"

Coming out to them, the girl helped Rob down from the saddle, and the stranger dismounted. "Nay, Rob," she said gently. "Not this one."

"But, look how tall he is, and his mind is gone from him, so belike he knoweth us not."

"Surely," a smile touched her lips, "I would know my father, who was older than this lord—much older, and dark like myself." Then to the man she added, "I ask pardon, Seigneur, for this whim of my brother, and I bid you welcome. Rob, take the led horse to the shed."

When he had vanished around the hut, the girl spoke to the stranger, low voiced. "Two years ago, my lord, Sir Errant of Dion, my father, died in battle before Jerusalem, beyond the sea. But Rob knoweth not. I have kept it from him, for he hath set his heart upon having his father come home again. Nor do they know it for certain in the village, although they have heard tales."

This girl, the stranger thought, was half wasted with hunger, and yet the lad looked sturdy. She had not stinted him food. In her eyes and lips lay the sign of hurt, yet her voice was clear and she had greeted him, a wayfarer, as if a great house stood behind her; instead, here was a peasant's hutch without serving women, or a man to defend her.

The stranger could not take his eyes from her face. For years he had not talked with a girl of his own race. He knew the long ache of hunger and the empty hours of prison; he knew the dull bite of wounds and the fever that followed. On his body he bore the scars of defeat. Now he had said farewell to the war, and he sought but one thing . . . everything else was a mist of magic. One thing he knew: the very elves of this forest must have woven an invisible thread that bound him to this solitary girl.

"Why are you so fair?" he whispered. "I had not thought a girl could be so fair."

Her dark eyes met his without flinching. "Well do I know that I am grown a forest girl, with a rough skin."

"Then you have but a poor mirror."

"It is a pond," she laughed, "and when I look into it I see the great clouds passing."

"Why, then, are you not at Dion—you the maid of Dion?"

She told him what all the countryside knew. How after Sir Errart had gone forth with the men-at-arms upon the crusade, her mother had died and she at thirteen years of age had been left with the steward to care for the lands and cattle. Sir Trigault had come by with a following of jackmen and had stopped as a guest at the castle. At first he had craved hospitality, then, when more of his men came up, he had told her bluntly that he would abide as protector of the place. Yet he had quarreled with the few retainers of Sir Errart and had slain the steward, and Dion had been his. In these troubled times other lords did not bother about the fate of a crusader's castle and children, and the good king was dead beyond the sea.

"So," the stranger mused, "this Trigault is your Boar, with tusks? I warrant he sought then to wed you, so that Dion should be his in right and law!"

Flushing, the girl tossed her head. "So did he not, for he broke down the door and came in to me at night, and I struck him with a dagger that I had, so that he went away to stanch his bleeding, and Rob and I ran to Father Jehan, who gave us this hut."

"And Sir Boar, did he not follow?"

"Nay, perhaps he fears the curse of Father Jehan, or the arrows of the hunters."

"Seigneur!" Rob came hurrying up to him with a fresh notion. "Even if you are not, belike, my father, will you not abide with us?"

The tall wayfarer looked down at the boy thoughtfully, and Ellen spoke quickly:

"My lord—"

"Black Michael they call me. And I no longer have any man for friend."

Ellen considered him in surprise. This mindless man had riddles about him, for he was light of hair and brown of face, and not at all dark. He spoke harshly, and still his gray eyes seemed not harsh. He did not act as if he had lost his mind. She knew him to be a knight, even if the gold had worn from his spurs, for he had the voice and manner of one accustomed to command. Standing there with the fine war horse, he made the hut seem poor, as it was.

Black Michael brushed his hand across his forehead. "For five long years," he said softly, "I have had no merry Yuletide and there is a longing in me for the spiced wine, and the song and the merry heart of it."

"Good!" Rob leaped up eagerly. "Ellen will make the cake, and we have two candles."

A bleak look came upon the man's face. "This is a sorry hutch. I will find a better place."

He need not have said that, she knew. While Rob stared in dismay, she hid the swift hurt of his words. "There is a tavern in Dion village a short ride on."

"Nay," Michael checked her words, and paced the ground impatiently. "I shall try the castle, where Sir Trigault must have a jolly hall. But I will leave the packhorse in your shed."

"Sir Michael," she said bitterly, "we thank you for yielding the led horse to our poor hospitality."

"More than that, Ellen," he said thoughtfully, "if I come not back again, horse and pack are yours. You will find therein—a mirror and a rare fine dress of velvet."

Again she bowed to him. "I thank you, my lord, for the alms that I would burn before I touch."

"Be not so sure."

For an instant his hand stroked her bent head, and when she cried out angrily she saw that he was walking away hastily with the war horse toward the shed, with Rob following. For a moment she stared after him, and then ran into the hut.

He had spoken harshly to her, and yet her heart beat fiercely in her breast.

"Saw you it?" The boy came running in. "Ellen! He put on fine mail—yea, he took the great shield from its cover, and it was our shield. I saw the lion of Dion."

The girl took him on her knee, and pressed his head against her throat. "Rob, there be many devices of lions, and thou art a child." And as he wriggled rebelliously, she tightened her grip. "Hearken, Rob, 'tis wrong to hide it from thee longer. Thy father died in the war. They told me years ago but I wished not to tell thee, because—he will never come home."

That noon a throng gathered at the great tavern of Dion village to drink their holiday cup, and to gossip and to look at the stranger. For his horse stood saddled by the door, with the gray mantle thrown over him, and Black Michael sat in the high seat by the fire, drinking a bowl of hot spiced wine.

Word had got about that this strange lord had bested three of the Boar's men on the road, yet he said naught of it—in fact, he said no word at all—and

he drank as comfortably as in his own hall. Moreover, at his knee stood
Sir Errart's shield with the Dion lion, and upon the breast of his faded surcoat a ragged crusader's cross was still to be seen.

A little after noon a sallow youth came to the tavern, with a burly axman striding behind him. The youth called for no wine but stood between
Black Michael and the fire while the axman loitered near. The company
of men upon the benches craned their necks to watch, and the tavern-
keeper hung about anxiously, for the youth was a swordsman and lieutenant of the Boar. He stared at the shield until Black Michael turned it
toward him so that he could see the better.

"Know you this?" he asked.

"I know well," the sallow man sneered; "it is the shield of Errart of
Dion, who is carrion in the ground."

Black Michael had noticed that this newcomer had a silver boar's head
on the clasp of his belt.

"Nay," he said equably, "it is mine."

"And who art thou to bear it?"

Black Michael smiled his wry smile. "And have you not heard," he asked,
"how at times the dead walk the earth, bearing their scars home?"

The swordsman stepped back a pace, fingering the hilt of his weapon.
"John o' Ghent am I," he whispered, "and I have stretched out better men
than thou. Tell thy name or taste—of this!"

But as he moved to draw his sword, Michael reached out and caught
his wrist. John o' Ghent wrenched his arm, yet could not pull free. And
before his mate could lift his ax Michael spoke:

"Go you back to the castle and tell the Boar, your master, that I will
visit him when an hour hath gone by."

John o' Ghent considered this in silence, and Michael released his
wrist. After a muttered word together the two visitors withdrew. Michael
watched them from the door and summoned the staring landlord.

"Taverner," quoth he, "I would take my supper with me to the castle.
Roast me the quarters of an ox, Taverner, and roast me some sheep. Fetch
me a keg of Burgundy and a hogshead of ale with it."

"An' it please you, my lord, how—"

"And sleds to carry them up. For, Taverner, I have a whim in me. This
night I shall sup in the castle hall, and my friends shall be with me, yet
my foes shall eat in Satan's cellar."

As Michael stripped the mantle from his charger and mounted, white faces pressed against the windows. He rode off, humming to himself, toward the gray stone tower of the church. Then he turned and trotted up a lane until the cottages fell behind and the wood closed in again.

Two men were following him, cutting through the brush. At a bend in the road he reined in, and walked his horse back upon them.

"Well," he said, "what now?"

They looked like hunters, and one carried a bow unstrung, while the other wiped the sweat from a broad red face. "We come for no ill," quoth he, "nay, master, we would warn 'ee, for all thou be'st mad as a starving wolf. Go not to the castle yonder or—or thou'lt have steel i' thy back."

"Then," quoth Michael, "have I need of one to stand at my back."

"Faith, master," the red-faced hunter shook his head, "an' we did that, the Boar would wring our giblets—eh, Giles?"

Michael glanced at the silent archer. "You are Giles the bowman," he said, "and friend to Sir Errart's children. By that same token, I bid you come with me."

Then he nodded at the red face. "And you run back to the village. Rouse up any weapon men who served Sir Errart. Bid them arm and come to the castle gate in an hour, and wait me there. Fetch Father Jehan with you."

The man scratched his head, then he grinned. "Aye—aye, the lads will come with good will to see thee mauled by Sir Trigault, who will make short work of thy madness. Father Jehan, now he can serve to bury thee."

Whereupon he turned back, running, and Michael leaned upon the saddle horn.

"Giles, I mean to take this castle from Sir Boar. They told me that Sir Trigault hath no more than fourteen men with him. Is it true?"

Giles nodded.

"These fellows would not know Sir Errart if they saw him?"

"Not they."

"Then lead the way."

In a moment they passed a stream, and the wood thinned. A field of untrodden snow appeared on the left, and Giles pointed beyond it with his bow. Michael saw between clumps of pine a steep slope that ended in a height of rock. Upon the rock stood the gray walls of a small castle, and above the walls the red-tiled summit of the donjon tower. A strong place, Michael thought, a friendly place—and he liked it well.

"Go ye up, Giles," he said slowly, "to Sir Trigault. Say this to him—that he hath taken the estate of Dion unlawfully. That is one. He hath cast out the lawful heir, Robert of Dion. And that is two. And he hath laid his unclean hand against the maid Ellen of Dion. Which are three charges. Bid him remember them, one-two-three. I affirm it, and I will support my word with my body. And I will await him here."

Within half an hour Sir Trigault rode from his gate. That morning he had heard of the drubbing given one of his lieutenants, Grigol, on the road; John o' Ghent had told him of this stranger's boast in the tavern. The Boar ruled the countryside by fear, and if one defied him, that one must suffer for it.

Although he knew the challenger waited alone, he took no chance of a trick, and he left six of his men-at-arms at the gate that closed behind him. Most of his men were out in bands on the road, and so he rode down to the field with his two lieutenants and six men.

Trigault reined forward and halted. He wore good chain mail, and carried a shield. The bristling beard that covered his chin had been brushed up at the sides, so that with his small, quick eyes he resembled the boar's-head skin that lay upon his round steel cap.

"They named ye well, Sir Boar," Michael greeted him.

Chin thrust forward, Trigault roared at him. "What name bear ye?"

"I am Sir Errart of Dion."

For an instant silence fell, then John o' Ghent laughed aloud. "By God's mazzard, he lies!"

Michael's voice broke in upon him:

"Sure I have lied, and I am a great boaster in the world, and now I am playing a trick upon all of ye. But true it is that thou art guilty, thrice—one, two, three—and for every guilt a man shall fall to my sword. Trigault, thou art a foul fighter and now thy mind is to egg thy men upon me. Well, I will fight thee and these twain."

He pointed to Ghent and Grigol, who stood by their master. "No mercy," he added, "for now it must be to the death."

"Three against one?" demanded Ghent, incredulous.

"Aye, so," Michael dismounted and passed his rein to Giles the bowman. "Three rogues against one valiant trickster."

It seemed to Trigault then that the crusader was mad beyond doubt. Still, he had challenged him with his lieutenants, and the bowman could bear witness to that. He dismounted and tried the hardness of the snow, which being well packed gave good footing.

"Send back thy pack," the crusader advised him. "Three will I stand against, but not nine."

Trigault ordered his men back a few paces and waved Giles away, so that the four found themselves standing upon clear ground, with Michael a dozen paces from the Boar and his followers.

The watchers saw them draw the long swords—all but Grigol, a heavy man who carried a short ax and knife. Then Trigault whispered a word to his companions and they edged to right and left of him, to take the crusader from the side.

"On with it!" cried Trigault, striding forward.

As he drew near, the Boar shortened his steps and then stopped, to let his men come closer. And the instant he stopped, Michael moved. A step to the side and a leap and another swift stride, and he was before John o' Ghent, who flung up his shield as Michael slashed at his head.

But in the air the crusader's sword swept down, striking the man beneath the shield over the hip. Ghent bent forward convulsively, his shield arm dropping as the sword bit into his side. Michael took one more step to the side and slashed at his head. The steel cap spun off into the snow, and Ghent's body went down like a sack.

"One!" cried Michael, stepping aside as Trigault rushed over to him and cut at him savagely. Michael's shield caught the blade with stunning force, and the Boar barely parried his return stroke.

The crusader's long blade swept in and back so swiftly that Trigault grunted and protected himself with shield and blade, while from the corner of his eye he saw Grigol circling to get behind the crusader.

Michael had kept sight of Grigol, and once more he leaped. Back this time, turning as he did so to face the axman. But he slipped as he struck the hard snow and went down on his knee. Grigol and Trigault rushed in upon him savagely.

Being nearer, Grigol was the first to strike, bending forward and grunting as he swung his short ax down at the crusader's head. Michael flung up his shield, and the ax crashed upon it. Without trying to rise from his knee Michael lunged his body forward. His sword thrust up, past the other's shield, and the point of it caught Grigol under the jaw. The steel went up into the man's brain, and his body hung limp.

Steel crushed upon Michael's side, biting into his mail, snapping a rib
and sending a flash of agony through him. Trigault's blow had fallen upon
his back just as he had lunged against Grigol, and the blade had not struck
fair—the point of the sword raking his ribs.

Setting his teeth, Michael staggered up, throwing his shield around
to meet the Boar's second blow, then wrenched his own sword free of the
dead Grigol.

"Two!" he cried, thrusting the point of his shield at the Boar's snarling face, and slashing beneath the shield. The Boar sprang back, covering
himself again with his weapons, and panting.

"And thou art—the third."

Trigault's blade rang against his steel cap, and it flew off. Michael shook
the drip of blood from his eyes. Bending his knees, he put all his strength
into a sweep of his long sword. His blade fell fair on Trigault's shield, and
the thin steel buckled and cracked.

Michael hewed down at the Boar's broken shield until the bones in the
arm beneath it snapped, and the man whined with fear. Back he stumbled,
cries coming from his open mouth. "Jacques—Le Baux—aid—" And Michael's sword hissed down at him, and down again and struck fair beneath
his jaw. The Boar's body jerked forward and fell upon the snow.

His men, who had come up, stood in their tracks staring down at him—all
but one who ran at Michael's back. An arrow flew and struck this weapon
man, who sank to his knees.

"For Dion!" shouted Giles the bowman, fitting another shaft to his
bow.

"Dion—Dion!" voices echoed. A group of village men who had been
coming along the road and had been drawn to the field by the sound of
weapon play now ran forward. The five surviving Boar's men drew back
toward the castle with no thought but flight.

"My horse, Giles," cried Michael, "Help me up, for these cow herders
of the village have come hither instead of to the castle, and I must—reach
the gate."

Climbing into the saddle, he spurred his horse up the road and vanished
into the wood ahead of the fugitives, as the dozen stout fellows led by the
red-faced hunter and the priest came into the field to stare at the bodies.

"The gate, lads!" Giles cried at them. "The Boar's brood is still at the
gate."

Midway to the castle, the Dion men encountered three of Trigault's band hastening down the road. "How now, my bucks?" demanded Giles, confronting them.

"We seek Sir Trigault," cried one of the three. "A strange lord rode wounded to the gate, and bade us hasten to the tilt field where our master hath need of us—"

"Aye, to bury him!" Giles roared with laughter. "Down with your arms, my bucks!" And when the village men had taken their weapons from the three, binding their wrists behind them and leading them along, Giles chuckled again. "By good Saint Denis, lads, this mad fighting man hath a way with him. Mark ye how he doth hocus and pocus these swine?"

They hastened on, and in a moment came to the outer barbican gate, which had been opened to let out the three men-at-arms. The drawbridge had been lowered and at the far end of it Michael sat his horse, with drawn sword, and shield resting upon his foot.

He did not turn his head, but when he heard Giles and the hunters run shouting upon the bridge, he said to these Boar's men: "Throw down your steel, for your Boar carries his brawn no more, and this castle is mine."

And when they had done so, he turned to the village men. "Take up all weapons, but do these fellows no hurt. Muster them all, let them pack up their gear and foot it away from the Dion lands—every wench and churl of them."

"Yea, master!" cried the red-faced hunter. "We'll see to it—only get thee down and have thy hurt bound up."

Michael's gray eyes fastened upon him. "I will see to it. Whoso sets his foot within these walls obeys me or goes out."

He kept his saddle at the bridge until the last of Trigault's people vanished down the road under escort, and the sledges appeared bearing meat and wine from the tavern. With them came village folk and women who had heard of the taking of the castle. They stood staring in the gate at the crusader in his blood-stained surcoat until Michael summoned them.

"Clean me this donjon hall," said he, "and fetch in wood for fires and torches. Five long years have I passed beyond the sea. My eyes have seen the stars bright over Bethlehem, but never a Yuletide have I had till now. Haul me in a great fair log, and pour out the good mead, and light up—light up!"

He bade the hunters break open the hogshead in the courtyard and help themselves. One brought him the first goblet filled, and he drank slowly.

"Go ye," said he, "to the stable. Saddle the best horse and lead him down to the hut of Sir Errart's children. Ask Father Jehan to go with ye, and ask the maid Ellen and the young cub of Dion to ride hither to this feast we shall have."

Then he went into the hall, leaning on a man's arm, and sat him down in the high seat by the hearth. He bade them take Sir Errart's shield and hang it again upon the chimney piece, where it had been before; but Sir Errart's sword he placed beside him.

Out in the courtyard where the cups passed 'round as the men hauled in the Yule log, Giles great voice was lifted in song:

> *Noel, Noel!*
> *Sir Christmas is here.*

The women at the kitchen fire heard, and their high voices echoed:

> *Noel, Noel!*
> *Come ye all near.*

But Black Michael sat, chin on hand, gazing into the flames. He did not look up when the great log, decked with bright holly, was brought in. When a silence fell upon the hall and the robed figure of Father Jehan appeared, with Ellen beside him, and the burghers of Dion behind them, Michael got to his feet and turned toward them. Taking Rob by the hand, he led the boy to the fire and pointed to the shield.

"Look, Rob," he said slowly, "the shield of Sir Errart hath come back." He picked up the long bare sword that he had cleaned carefully. "And here is the sword that he bore—that he carried as a man should, as I know well. Now have I brought it back to its right place, and it is thine."

The boy's eyes grew round as he looked at the heavy sword. He went closer to the fire and, stretching out his chilled hands, suddenly smiled. "There is a bear i' the courtyard," he cried, "that walks and carries a staff!"

"Aye, so," quoth Michael, and faced the daughter of Sir Errart.

"Ellen," he said, "now am I master of Dion. The Boar and his brood will trouble you no more. This Yule cheer have I made ready for you, if you will share it."

"You are not Sir Errart, my father," she cried, "though you have come hither to his home with his weapons. Nay, these years is he dead."

"I know it well," answered Michael. "For I took his arms after his death."

The girl's dark eyes burned into his. "Then name yourself, my lord—for I will not be the guest of a nameless man."

"I am not nameless, nor am I mindless," Michael smiled. "I am Michael o' Nial, who hath followed the wars for a living. Land other than this have I none, for the good king made me a knight after a deed in battle. Friends have I none, other than those who are here, because my comrades left their bones beyond the sea. I have Dion, and I will hold it."

"That is easily to be seen," cried the girl. "Oh, you are hard of hand and bitter of heart, but did you think I would come as a bidden guest to the hall that should be ours?"

"Not as a guest," Michael said. He went down on one knee before her. "Nay, Ellen, for I am after asking your blessed self to be wife of mine and mistress of Dion. Far wandering and bitter of heart as I am, never have I beheld so fair a maid, and from the moment when I met you, I thought only that I must be asking for you, as I am now. Hasty it must seem to you, but I am not a patient man, and what I want I ever take."

Ellen flushed and held high her head.

"For this I give you thanks, Sir Michael," she said slowly. "Still I think you seek to make a gift of Dion to Rob and to me. Well do I know that only a man like you could hold together castle and lands, and so you have honored me, by asking—"

"Is it my love you doubt, Ellen? Think you I would have gone against death for aught else?"

Father Jehan stepped to the girl's side. "He is sorely hurt, my child," he said.

For an instant longer the girl stared into the clear eyes of the man kneeling before her. Then she clasped his head between her hands. Bending down, half shyly and half fiercely, she kissed his scarred cheek and lips.

Putting his arm about her waist, he turned to the priest. "Ellen o' mine," he whispered, "I have brought hither the wedding gown you would not touch in your house. And now, Father Jehan, you will be wedding us in the chapel here, for I am not a patient man."

Midnight, and they were all asleep within the walls—Giles and the hunters sprawled in the courtyard or watching at the gate. In her old room Ellen slept at last, the gown of velvet hung against a chair; Rob, weary and content, curled beside her, and her hair unbound, spread upon her pillow.

Snow drifted upon the roof, wrapping the walls in silence, and sifting fitfully down the chimney upon the Yule log that still glowed red. On a quilt before the hearth lay Michael, awake and in pain because the priest had only now finished the setting of his broken rib and the dressing of his wound. In the high seat, Father Jehan sat musing upon the pallid face of the master of Dion.

"Some say," the priest murmured, "thou art mad, and others hold thou art a doomsman, sent upon the Boar for his sins . . . But I think not so. In this day, my son, thou hast lied, and taken the lives of three men. And what more? The maid thou hast wed, she loves thee greatly."

"As I do her," Michael said.

"And what more?"

Michael did not answer at once. Aye, the father knew there was something more . . . His mind went back two years, to a dark night within the lines of the Christian army before Bethlehem. The stars bright over the road the Magi had trod, and on Michael's knee the head of a dying man who was his comrade. The words spoken last by Errart, "Michael, will you care for my children? They will be in want." And his answer, "I will do that."

It was finished now, and he had kept his word. To do it he had come to Dion, and taken it.

"Faith," he said to the priest, "there is no more to say."

Appendix

Adventure magazine, where many of the tales in this volume first appeared, maintained a letter column titled "The Camp-Fire." As a descriptor, "letter column" does not quite do this regular feature justice. *Adventure* was published two and sometimes three times a month, and as a result of this frequency and the interchange of ideas it fostered "The Camp-Fire" was really more like an Internet bulletin board than a letter column found in today's quarterly or even monthly magazines. It featured letters from readers, editorial notes, and essays from writers. If a reader had a question or even a quibble with a story, he could write in and the odds were that the letter would not only be printed but that the story's author would draft a response.

Harold Lamb and other contributors frequently wrote lengthy letters that further explained some of the historical details that appeared in their stories. The relevant letter for this volume follows. A second letter comes in response to a query from an *Adventure* reader, also printed here.

As with other Lamb Bison collections, the prefatory comments of *Adventure* editor Arthur Sullivant Hoffman also are printed here, along with occasional additional connecting comments between question and response letters. Extensive additional notes about Lamb's take on crusader history can be found in the appendix to one of this book's companion volumes, *Swords from the Desert*.

The appendix concludes with a short note from a *Collier's* editor about "The Bells of the Mountains."

July 1, 1921

Something from Harold Lamb concerning his story ["The Grand Cham"] in this issue:

Historically this battle—Angora—is pretty much as presented in the story. Likewise the events leading up to it.

Clavijo is an historic liar. See Hakluyt. I have touched up his native ability and advanced the date of his "embassy" a year or so, to get him into the battle. Incidentally, the episode of the ring belonging to Tamerlane is related in Hakluyt. Clavijo, it seems, was much taken aback at hearing that the Tatar's ring was reputed to change color when a falsehood was told. At the moment, Clavijo was telling some pretty tall fibs about the grandeur of Spain, and he shut up when he heard about the ring.

1922

Magic-Lanterns and coyote dogs. But is there any question about dogs crossing with wolves? This letter from our cache dates back a year or more:

Pasadena, California.

I don't know whether this letter is going to be legible, because it is written on a moving train, but it's the only time I can snatch a few minutes to write to you at all.

In Lamb's story "The Grand Cham" is something that I'd like to know more about. Either friend Harold made a slip or he brought up a new bit of information. He speaks of the Arabs using magic-lanterns on the streets of the Turkish capital in the time of the crusades. Is this one time when he nodded or is it just another proof that "there is no new thing under the sun?" Understand, I'm not knocking. Just wanted to find out. I know about Chinese printing and other things but thought the magic-lantern belonged to the last century.

Somebody, I can't remember who, brought up the question of the wolf-dogs of fiction and asked if anybody knew about them. I don't know a thing about wolf-dogs but I do know that wherever you keep dogs in a coyote country away from settlements you get an occasional mixed litter. I've had five such litters come under my observation here in California and Arizona. And if wolf-dogs are anything like coyote-dogs, then certainly the fiction writers haven't overdrawn them, for I never saw a coyote-dog in my life that wasn't a pesky nuisance. You can't teach them a thing except by breaking their spirit, and they fight and steal at every opportunity. As to numbers, I can easily conceive that in a country where they abound and dogs run free, there would be lots of crosses, and if coyotes, why not wolves?

Joseph Gray

The above letter was sent to Mr. Lamb and here is his reply. But why didn't he give us a good long list of "modern" inventions that date back to the Asia of a thousand years ago? Gunpowder, compass, spectacles—these I know date 'way back or are said to, but there my knowledge runs out.

Cresskill, New Jersey

Glad to get Gray's letter. No, speaking of magic-lanterns in "The Grand Cham" was not a case of nodding. Gray, in mentioning the crusades, evidently has associated "The Grand Cham" with an earlier date than 1400, the date of the story.

One of the Arabian story-tellers mentions the magic-lantern; and Sir Henry Howorth alludes to it in Asia Minor, a little before the time of my story, I think. Haven't my notes here, so can't be exact; but as I recall it the magic-lantern was mentioned in a Latin treatise on the miracles of light, published about 1600 by Athanasius Somebody-or-other-not, not Ananias. The Ency. Brit. remarks that it is probably of earlier origin.

What the early instrument was like I confess I don't know. It was used at times by wizards, apparently, to materialize ghosts—also for low comedy. Naturally the use of the phrase "magic-lantern" by the two translators above is not real evidence and if I've turned the clock ahead two centuries or more for the invention, I plead guilty.

However, we don't half guess how many inventions and impulses to the sciences that are trotting around the world today labeled "modern" can trace their parentage back to Asia a thousand years or so ago.

It would be really delightful, to me at all events, to learn for a fact that the newest and most vociferous child of the fine arts—our cinema—had a shabby and forgotten father in the person of an Arabian mountebank; just as our no less vociferous spirit-medium has a prototype in the ancient Mongol shaman with his rattling iron images, his darkened tent, his cultivated frenzies and expert ventriloquism.

"The Bells of the Mountains"

Harold Lamb says this story was suggested by one of the standard tricks of medieval warfare—the use of a stand-in to take the place of the king in battle. He goes on to point out that the Swiss mountaineers he is writing about were poor people. They couldn't afford the elaborate getup of the mailed horsemen who then ruled the battlefields. Armored regiments of horse formed the mainstay of the imperial German armies then as now extending outward in a thrust to dominate the Continent, from the hub at Frankfurt, instead of Berlin.

The Swiss had notions about their personal liberty. They presumed to put up a fight for it—on foot in the narrow valleys. They relied on their quickness; they used a long pike (a spearhead on a heavy staff) and a halberd (a long ax). Such weapons any man could make and own. The Swiss villagers, like the Greek hoplites, made up a fighting citizenry, standing on their own feet, using their own weapons. And they started democracy to functioning in the world again. For the citizens who did the fighting cast the votes. It so happened again at the end of the eighteenth century when the Americans and French fought on foot in the field and cast the votes at home.

About the Author

Harold Lamb (1892–1962) was born in Alpine, New Jersey, the son of Eliza Rollinson and Frederick Lamb, a renowned stained-glass designer, painter, and writer. Lamb later described himself as having been born with damaged eyes, ears, and speech, adding that by adulthood these problems had mostly righted themselves. He was never very comfortable in crowds or cities and found school "a torment." He had two main refuges when growing up—his grandfather's library and the outdoors. Lamb loved tennis and played the game well into his later years.

Lamb attended Columbia, where he first dug into the histories of Eastern civilizations, ever after his lifelong fascination. He served briefly in World War I as an infantryman but saw no action. In 1917 he married Ruth Barbour, and by all accounts their marriage was a long and happy one. They had two children, Frederick and Cary. Arthur Sullivant Hoffman, the chief editor of *Adventure* magazine, recognized Lamb's storytelling skills and encouraged him to write about the subjects he most loved. For the next twenty years or so, historical fiction set in the remote East flowed from Lamb's pen, and he quickly became one of *Adventure*'s most popular writers. Lamb did not stop with fiction, however, and soon began to draft biographies and screenplays. By the time the pulp magazine market dried up, Lamb was an established and recognized historian, and for the rest of his life he produced respected biographies and histories, earning numerous awards, including one from the Persian government for his two-volume history of the Crusades.

Lamb knew many languages: by his own account, French, Latin, ancient Persian, some Arabic, a smattering of Turkish, a bit of Manchu-Tatar, and medieval Ukrainian. He traveled throughout Asia, visiting most of the places he wrote about, and during World War II he was on covert assignment overseas for the U.S. government. He is remembered today both for his scholarly histories and for his swashbuckling tales of daring Cossacks and crusaders. "Life is good, after all," Lamb once wrote, "when a man can go where he wants to, and write about what he likes best."

Source Acknowledgments

The following stories were originally published in *Adventure* magazine: "The Village of the Ghost," May 15, 1921; "The Grand Cham," July 1, 1921; "The Making of the Morning Star," April 10, 1924; "The Iron Man Rides," June 1, 1929; "The Faring Forth," November 15, 1929; "The Tower of the Ravens," December 15, 1929; "The Long Sword," September 1, 1930; "The Golden Horde," May 15, 1933; "Keeper of the Gate," August 1936.

The following stories were originally published in *Collier's* magazine: "The Red Cock Crows," June 9, 1928; "Protection," August 24, 1929; "Knights with Wings," May 10, 1941; "The Bells of the Mountains," September 13, 1941; "The Black Road," January 23, 1943; "Lionheart," March 28, 1949.

"Doom Rides In" was originally published by *Cassell's Magazine*, January 1932.

"Secret of Victory" was originally published in *The Saturday Evening Post*, March 14, 1953.

CPSIA information can be obtained at www.ICGtesting.com
Printed in the USA
BVOW06s1144090916

461645BV00011B/56/P